BROTHER MARIA

Brother Ludovico

1st WORLD
PUBLISHING

Brother Maria

Brother Ludovico

Copyright © 2023 by Brother Ludovico

Published by 1st World Publishing
P.O. Box 2211, Fairfield, Iowa 52556
tel: 641-209-5000 • fax: 866-440-5234
web: www.1stworldpublishing.com

First Edition

ISBN Softcover: 978-1-4218-3541-9

LCCN: Library of Congress Cataloging-in-Publication Data

This material has been written and published for educational purposes to enhance one's well-being. In regard to health issues, the information is not intended as a substitute for appropriate care and advice from health professionals, nor does it equate to the assumption of medical or any other form of liability on the part of the publisher or author. The publisher and author shall have neither liability nor responsibility to any person or entity with respect to loss, damages, or injury claimed to be caused directly or indirectly by any information in this book.

Thou shalt not be afraid for the terrors by night;
Nor for the arrow that flieth by night; nor the
Pestilence that walketh in darkness; nor for the
Destruction that wasteth at noonday; a thousand
Shall fall at thy side, and ten thousand at thy right hand......

Psalm 91
Verses 5-7

For the soul stands forever at her Source,
stands true to the grandeur of her Awakening,
and to her the End itself possesses
the dignity of the Beginning; no song becomes
lost that has ever plucked the strings of
her lyre; and exposed in ever-renewed readiness
she preserves herself through every single tone
in which she has ever resounded.

Hermann Broch,
From 'The Death of Vergil'

Life is a forest; one that is full of the endless
seasons of Its Dream. Man is a hunter who
becomes lost in those seasons and in that Dream;
in a quest, the only Quest, that ever tries to find
the bird that sweetly sings, Forever, in the forest's Heart.

Konrad Bercovici

CONTENTS

Book One: Gypsies, Prayers, Profligacy

Book Two: A Dark Sun

Book Three: A Wrathful God; A Merciful Mother

AN AGE OF......

.......AN AGE of Darkness, and the horrors bred of that Darkness; of ghosts that walked, murderers that plotted, wicked angels that slit the throas of the pious as they prayed.......

.......AN AGE of War: city against city, family against family, brother against brother; of barons, bishops, emperors and popes; the flames of civil strife, the butchery of invading armies; when all were the defenders of a cause; those causes caused by a squinting eye, an itching palm, the baring of a supple knee; when the Earth drank its children's blood like a winebibber slurps his wine, making it drunk with a thirst that could not be slaked.......

.....AN AGE of Famine, when fields grew parched, or rank with weeds, or flooded into sloughs; when the wheat blighted, - the grapes, shriveled, - udders dried of their milk.....when flocks starved, or sick with murrains, fell where they grazed, there to be picked by birds and wild dogs.....when men ate their oxen and their horses.....then dogs, cats, rats, mice.....then crawling on their hands and knees hunted nettles, roots, worms.....in unmanned, shameless wretchedness unearthing graves, eating the brains of the dead.......

....AND this was only the beginning; for in the wake of such a great dearth God would send a greater wrath, a blight of Biblical proportion, an Enemy with a sword none could see, none could flee, none could fend against; as if in His wrath God was bent on destroying that creature He had made in His own likeness, and given that likeness, had disfigured and defiled.......
.......AN AGE of Pestilence, when all who saw the rising sun feared they would not see it set; when no treasure chest of gold, no batting lash or dimpled smile, no prayer to a Saint, or sorcerer's bag of charms proved a defense against a sinister boil.......

.......*THE REAPER'S sickle mowing all in the great swaths of its path: babes in their cradles, priests in their prayers, lovers in love's embraces; those who plowed and gathered, as well as those who stole, tippled, whored..... making the beautiful, hideous, the wealthy, indigent, the scholarly and the pious, lunatic.....burying counts with paupers, virgins with harlots, the saintly with the debauched.......*

.......*AN AGE of Death, when the sun dimmed, and hell heaved its bowels; when the Earth was no longer Earth, but a lower realm; when the end of the world had come, and men were driven to the extremities of what they were.....when Faith, Hope, Trust broke like brittle twigs, and in frothy madness men became the beasts they had ever denied they were..... the righteous becoming thieves,- the meek, bloody killers,- the brave, craven and fearful.....when to be human was to be a blighted fruit rotting on its vine.....when the only ambition was to live another day.......*

......*AN AGE when men were driven to the ends of their nerves, sinews, wits, soul.....when their God had forsaken them, and was no longer their guide, but now their persecutor, sending His destroying Angels upon them.......*

.......*NAKED, forsaken, damned; when men were left clinging to themselves, and the one thing they had left in their keeping.....not God's love, but their own.......*

In Memory of Tom,
First composed in Romania

"*AND you have made a mistress of 'death'. You have lifted her crepe veil, and stolen the kiss all men are afraid of; tasting the honey in her venom.....knowing that She too is shy, even afraid of this strange human thing called 'love'. Unafraid, you have become infatuated with this eternal widow, and the mystery She promises to tell, but will never yield. You have courted 'death', the mistress beneath whose balcony all suitors are afraid to sing, for you know that behind her terrible disguise She is the most beautiful of maidens.*"

From 'Brother Maria'

BROTHER MARIA

BOOK I

GYPSIES, PRAYERS, PROFLIGACY

CHAPTER ONE

THE BAKER GIRL,
AND
THE DREAM OF WILD HORSES

A small Hungarian village: Circa, 1240

IT WAS a thunder so faint and so distant that it had not yet broken on the shore of hearing.....so faint it did not prick the ears of horses, tremble the water in wells, stir sleeping birds on their roosts.....a thunder unheard, unfelt, unknown.....one that did not wake the sleeper as it entered the twilit wilds of his dreams......

.......The dark pandemonium of its tide, like a boiling lava, a gorging flood.....its swiftness as of racing lions with which it swept incredible breadths and reaches.....sloughs, steppes, hills, valleys....deserts and streams, sands and snows.....the like no army could equal, the like no eye had ever seen, the which nothing could withstand, flee, or beg its mercy.....a hundred thousand hoofs pounding the stone drum of the earth, trembling mountains, making flicker the sun...loosed as from the belching gates of hell.......

* * *

HE had been careful not to wake her. She had burrowed and entangled into him, clinging to him like a child, the child she had only recently left behind. He had tenderly taken her arm from his chest, and her leg from where it lay, like a sheaf of silk between his thighs. Removing her head from his shoulder, he had gently laid it on the pillow, as he was placing a bouquet upon an altar. Brushing the muss of hair from her face, he had kissed her, as he could not remember kissing his sleeping wife; first on her cheek, then on her bare shoulder. Still sleeping soundly in the aftermath of the hashish, and the vigorous, nightlong bouts of their love, she had not wakened, and he had risen with a heart happy and serene.

He bound his robe about him, and then lighted the hookah that he had fixed to hang by a chain from the low rafter in the corner. He had taken several long draws, allowing the burning fumes to flood through him, hot and sweet and narcotic, as if rewarding his spent loins and contented heart. He did not need to return today, or for four or five days more; and his darling's husband would be gone for a full week.

He pulled back the dingy, ill-hung curtains, their once bright patterns time-worn and long since faded. It had snowed, and perhaps this, more than any strange dream helped to explain why he had awakened at this early hour. As from a wizard's wand, the stars and a sickle moon had appeared, lending a shimmering light to all, one that now spilled into the small garret where he stood. The peace inside him was one with this snow and these stars. He smiled, and drew again from the hookah, letting its deliciousness slowly delight and burn through the canals of his blood, enlivening memories of the games he had played with his young lover, even when this snow had been silently blanketing streets and rooftops, and the fields and forests beyond.

.....*It was a dream, only a dream, and he would not allow it to disturb this delicious peace he had found.....the snow, the stars, his young lover who gave so freely of her sweet honeys, and in so doing, stilled his needs and comforted his heart......*

.....*or if it was other than a dream, perhaps it was a fantastic fairytale he had heard as a child, buried by the years, only now exhumed in his dreams......horsemen, yes horsemen, hundreds and thousands of horsemen riding as fast as the wind.....riding beneath the stars as they rode beneath the sun, over the snow as they rode through the seas of grasses.....eating and sleeping in their saddles...hunters and herders and gatherers, the followers of stars and seasons, coalescing into a great army....a dream, yes, a dream, a child's dream...a dream of wild horses......*

He had met her a little more than a year ago. An autumn storm had waylaid him, having flooded out a good number of roads and bridges on his intended course. Stranded, he was left to bide his time visiting the village's pawn shops, taverns and hashish houses. It was then he had met her in the small bake shop that sold flatbreads and biscuits. But it had not been her beauty or her shapeliness that had first attracted him. She was young, very young; younger than his daughters. Being a religious man he had never let his eye stray, even disdaining the lechery he had observed in his peers. Besides, she seemed poor and plain, almost wretched, bundled in what appeared to be a hand-me-down, oversized coat, and a ragged headscarf that covered the greater part of her face.

When she had given him his small bag of things, and he had placed his payment in her hand, she had not lifted her face to him when she had whispered, '*thank you sir*'. His heart had winced, and he had been struck with a paternal sense of compassion for her poverty and youth, and he had offered her another copper. Shaking her head in a shy refusal, he had taken her hand in his own, placed the coin in its palm, and then tightly closed her fingers about it. Again she had whispered a '*thank you sir*', this time timidly raising her face to his.

It was then that he was so deeply, unexpectedly moved. Her eyes were the most beautiful eyes he had ever seen; deep brown wells in which a lovely sweetness smiled. But they also contained the sorrows of need and hurt as he had seldom seen before. Yet it was not even these sad beautiful eyes that had stirred him so, but the ugly bruise that her scarf had not succeeded in entirely concealing. It had swollen and discolored a good portion of her face, from her cheekbone to her jaw, and though she tried, she could not hide what was either a broken or a missing tooth.

Both found their selves frozen, as in a spell in this unexpected moment; him, spellbound with her young, injured beauty; her, with the compassion an older, well-dressed man was pausing to give her. But it was a spell that did not last long. The special moment was abruptly interrupted by the shop owner vulgarly calling out from a back room: "*Damn it, wife, come here at once!*"….shattering the brief enchantment, and tragically explaining all.

After returning to his home village, he had not been able to forget her, but he did not know exactly why. Many times he woke in the night with her face, like a wounded angel before him; like the dolorous face of *the Virgin* that must fill the dreams of a Saint. He knew only that he was deeply stirred, but whether with compassion, as for a daughter, or with desire, as for a lover, he was not sure. But once, when in a half-dream, half-waking doze he lay in his bed thinking of her, he imagined removing her coat and scarf, and gathering her young body into his arms. He had felt himself stir, and when imagining her arms and legs about him, had allowed his passion to be freed. Both ashamed and afraid, it was then that he, a widower of more than five years, knew what was happening to him. Several days later he left on another business trip, one that would conveniently take him to the little village.

.....*yes, a kind of fairytale, of horsemen dressed from cap to boot in the pelts of beasts, shooting arrows as they were gods......some with the heads of dogs, elk, wolves.....bearing banners with unusual crosses, not like the crosses on the altars he knelt before, but crosses made of the shoulder blades of sheep, and hung with the tails of goats and cows.....horsemen, yes, a sea of horsemen.....the hooves of their horses filling the bowl of heaven with thunder.......*

He did not know how to go about this courtship, indeed, if it was a courtship at all, or only a silly puppet show conjured by his loneliness to tease and please his senses. After all, she was certainly married, and he was certainly as old, or perhaps older than her father. It was at once against both his religious beliefs and his reason, and besides, he had no idea how to flatter, charm or seduce. His marriage had been arranged by his parents, and he had had no need to know the occult of courtship. He began to feel silly and awkward, like a little boy, and even after arriving in the village at nightfall, and renting a room from an old Jewess, the very room in which he was now standing, he considered dismissing this whim of his adolescent foolishness, and at daybreak departing. Still, lying awake that night, with the opium fumes sluicing through his blood, the face of the beautiful wounded angel came to him with eyes deeper than the summer forests, and he resolved to at least enter the little shop, and if not openly make some introduction, even some initial overture to the young girl, to at least see again the sweetness that was so haunting and tormenting him.

But the next morning, with the gift he had brought her secure beneath his coat, he met disappointment. When he opened the shop door and the little bell rang, he was greeted not by the girl, but by the one he supposed to be her husband, a man not so much younger than himself. He was rough, crapulous, and grossly disheveled, and his bloated face, ruddiness and bloodshot eyes testified of drink and debauch. After he made his small purchase from the man, and he was just about to leave, he caught in the corner of his eye the young girl bringing a towel full of biscuits from the back room oven. Not wanting to seem conspicuous, and not feeling a glance offered from her eyes, he opened the door and left the shop; disheartened, abashed, and confused.

All day he had stayed in his room, smoking, drinking vodka, and playing mindless card games with himself. He often went to the window, the same window before which he was now standing, to look below at the bake shop directly across the street, imagining the young girl bustling about in her heavy coat, and beneath that heavy coat her young breasts, buttocks and thighs. Writhing all night on the rack of infatuation, early the next morning he went to the shop again. This time the young girl waited upon his simple needs. Still, her out-of-sorts husband, mumbling and cursing beneath his breath was very near, and when the purchase was finalized there was no extra copper placed in that young precious palm; no lifting of those dark beautiful eyes; no giving of a gift that was concealed beneath his coat. Upbraiding himself, and feeling like a fool as he had never felt before, he had gone back to his room, packed his things; smoked, drank, and prepared to leave.

But after loading his things into his wagon, he went back to the old landlady, and asking for her solemn word of secrecy, left a silk-fine, apricot scarf in her keeping. Suggesting that she might feign some ache of age, he had asked her to order some biscuits be delivered to her door. Confiding in her that the young bake girl reminded him of his daughter, and that he knew she was very poor, when the young girl brought the biscuits, could she please give this present to her? The old Jewess was agreeable, especially to the gratuity he left her, and although she probably suspected there was more intrigue than compassion in this thing, agreed to carry it out. Without another word he had climbed into his wagon and left the village behind.

A wonderful feeling of wellbeing filled him on his two day journey home, and with it a great relief that he had been spared making a goatish old oaf of himself. He was filled with satisfaction at his charitable act, one that was performed anonymously, and had asked nothing in return. Again and again he smiled when he imagined the young girl's surprise and gratitude with the beautiful scarf that would replace her ragged one, and the candies he had wrapped inside it.

......*in his travels he had spoken with many other merchants, those who had crossed the great river, and traveled into the lands and mountains beyond.....and in reflection he was sure it was this that had sown the seeds of this recurring dream.....children, only two or three years of age lifted by their parents to the backs of these wild horses, horses that like gods grew tame at these children's touch.....so that the man-child grew and melded into a oneness with their swift strength.....so that horse and rider were not two, but one, the ancient wildness in the horses' hearts becoming one with the ancient wildness in their riders' blood.......*

Contented with his charity, and the foolhardiness of his infatuation he had eluded, he had fully intended to put an end to the phantom of this distraction. *Or did he?*

Beyond his will and reason, he continued to think of her, to dwell on her, to dream of her. He had even thought of her when he was receiving the holy *Eucharist*, imagining that he was the priest, and he was tenderly placing the wafer on her tongue. Again and again he imagined the apricot scarf wrapped about this wounded angel's face. Again and again he imagined her young mouth opening to receive a cherry, or a piece of candy from his hand, and the little pink tongue that savored it. Again and again he brought his bearded lips to that dainty mouth, and received its secret sweetness.

It was therefore with great excitement he opened the letter that had been sent to him from the old landlady in the village a week later. In a terse, scrawling, illiterate way the old woman had informed him that indeed the girl had received his gift, and with tears of gratitude held it first to her cheek, and then to her heart. Knowing that the old *Jewess* was insinuating some remuneration for her pains, he immediately sent a gratuity with a note, thanking her and telling her that he would need lodging again next week.

But when the next week arrived and he entered the small bake shop again, the young girl was not to be seen. Entering it the following morning, she was absent once more, the small shop being run only by her surly, scrofulous husband. Leaving another gift with the shrewd old woman, this time a tortoise shell comb, he had left with a heavy heart, one that remained with pain and longing until the following week when again the landlady wrote him, informing him that the bake girl had received his gift, and it had made her delirious with joy. Abruptly dropping his affairs, he had at once made for the small village with the excuse of yet another pressing business errand.

.....he had even imagined he had been one of these young riders on the

backs of these wonderful wild creatures......saddle-less and bridle-less, as he had heard tell they had learned to ride......imagining he was one with the wind and the clouds......the tall bloomy grasses stretching as infinite as a sea in all directions about him......and he, like a lone sailor, his sail a-gallop on that infinite sea......

This time when he entered the small shop he was more fortunate. Her husband was not to be seen, and the girl was alone. At once her downcast, scarf-wrapped face turned, rose, and shot forth darts of grateful, albeit speechless happiness. An awkwardness had ensued; he with his obvious age, and she with her obvious youth and marital predicament; both with great needs begging to be answered, but unsure whether the other understood those needs, or was the one life's mystery had issued to answer them. Tongue-tied and nervous, he had made his purchase, and when again he had placed a copper, and then a second in her palm, wrapping her fingers tenderly about them, he had allowed his much larger hand to rest on hers. To his surprise and ineffable delight she had bent quickly forward and pecked it with her lips, as a pet bird softly pecks the hand that sprinkles crumbs before it.

And this is the way the courtship had begun, the courtship whose players were an aging, graying widower; a young bake girl, the wife of an abusive drunkard; and a crafty old, go-between *Jewess* whose itching palm was being rewarded for her sly, secret shrewdness.

He began to visit the village once each fortnight, making small purchases at the shop, and if fate's dice rolled in his favor, enjoy a moment when he stared into the bake girl's beautiful eyes. When fate was even more propitious, his hands received a lovely little peck from this child's lips, and once even the pressing of her soft cheek. He began to live for these moments. He began to anticipate, even to be consumed by them. Becoming excited, at times even giddy, he began to count the days and hours until he would again visit the village, regardless if the weather was fair or foul. The shame and the absurdity, even the perversity of the thing no longer had a hold on him. He no longer looked at it as a spiritual sin, but as a gift from his prayers. At the end of the day, after he drank his plum wine or sucked the hookah's fumes, her lovely phantom would come to him. She would again give him the sweet fig of her young sweet mouth, and he would again let himself be enfolded in the beautiful wings of her young arms and legs, arms and legs as soft as the cheek that had pressed his hand.

And with the dream of a young lover, the opium also brought this dream of wild horses.

.....this fairytale, this fancy, this dream that did not leave him, not in his sunny journeys, nor in the folds of his slumbers.....the more rumors he garnered, the more his imagination was fed, and the greater these wild creatures grew in fabulous stature in his mind.....he who had been a timid boy, and now a timid middle-aged man, he who had never been a soldier, only a peddler of cloths and trinkets.....now imagined he rode one of these beautiful savage beasts....singing, laughing, shouting, one with sun and storm....one with this new life and love that had come to exhilarate and embolden him......making him the strongest of warriors.....

As the yearlong courtship continued, there were two things that measurably changed. The first was the gifts that he brought the girl. They were increasingly lovely, lavish, and costly. This was a pleasure, not a sacrifice for him. Trading with many from the *Silk Road,* an exotic assortment of treasures was at his disposal: amber, jade, and opal; polished figures of mahogany and cherry; silver jewelries inlaid with bright gems; shawls woven of goat or camel hair; scarves and amices of silk; mirrors with handles of tortoise shell and mother-of-pearl.

But the other thing that changed brought more pain than pleasure. Foolish, lecherous, adulterously wrong and dangerous or not, he grew impatient to complete and vent the ardor that had been kindled inside him. He had long ceased to deny it. He longed to consummate his desires in the girl's embraces. As the opium flooded into him, so he wanted his passion to flood into her. When she raised her face to him from her ragged scarf, he wanted her eyes to tell him that she had received his love in the deepest part of her. He wanted her to be his.

These pent-up passions tormented him. Now when he doused his candle, and the phantom of his wounded angel came to him in the darkness, she brought doubts with her charms, and more times than not he lay awake long into the night, riddled with apprehensions.

Did she know that he wanted her as his paramour, or did she think he was merely a kind old man; a paternal philanthropist? Did she think of him as a daughter thinks of her father? When he left her shop did she laugh at him as he was a senile old fool, a thing for ridicule, even disgust? Was she playing him for all his worth, her lovely little stares and pecks on his hand only baits for more luxurious gifts? Were her occasional bruises and cut lips self-inflicted, only to play on his sympathies? Had she told her husband, or the gossipy old Jewess? Was her husband exploiting her, pawning the things he brought her to support his own debauch? Did half the village know, and he was a laughingstock in their eyes? Was there any chance at all in consummating his hopes, and if there was, what then? How could he marry a young married girl? Adultery was not only an immoral, but a dangerous game. Adultery might lead to desperate acts, even madness; even murder.

.....the dream of wild horses had changed.....it had intermingled incestuously with the fevers that his love for this girl was raging through him..... both were creatures of unruly winds and storms.....both had pounding, untamed hearts......both were as fierce as charging lions, dangerous as rains of sharp arrows......

* * *

AS this strange and awkward courtship reached a year, and he had many times made his out-of-the-way way to this little village through heat, rain and snow, he began to think how futile it was; and what a fool that love, and love's chief-most ally, *loneliness*, had made of him. Still, when his candle was snuffed, and the fumes of the hookah were swimming through his brain, there she was, sweetly promising salvation to the lonely needs of his age. He must know how she felt for him. He must know whether he had been a prince, or the butt of a joke in her eyes.

His doubts at odds with his waked desires, he felt a wildness emerging from his sedentary life; as his heart had found a last passion smoldering beneath his ribs; as his heart was no longer a man's heart, but the heart of a savage brute. *Yes, that was it, he had become a wild racing stallion, obedient to the fingers holding his mane.....the little fingers he had once wrapped about a coin.....urging him, commanding his heart, his loins........*

.....sired in mountain meadows, ridden by children riders since they were little more than colts, over great swaths of steppe-land and the most difficult terrains.....marsh, snow, stone, ice.....into deepest ravines, up steepest hillsides, swimming raging streams...bred and groomed to wake the stamina in their spirits.....a stamina that could race with death itself..... yes, with tender little fingers about his needs, his age.....with the race with death.......

.....the great stallions leading these armies and these hordes as much as the generals that rode them, warming them in winter, guiding them

in storm, fearlessly bearing them into showers of stones and arrows.....
willing to die for they whom they bore.....in the end to be eaten by
their riders' hunger.....in the end to be buried by the love that had
ridden and mastered them.......

Tossing on his bed, he had thought of a way that he might at last
find out her heart. His next gift would be an elegant silk chemise, and
with the chemise, a pair of beaded and brocaded slippers. But to leave
no room for doubt, he would pin red roses on the pink chemise, both
in the places where her breasts would fit, and more daring, where the
flower of her sex would be. A man of few and awkward words, he would
leave a simple note with the erotic gift, one that would convey an unmistakable meaning.

'*I dream of your roses. Antal.*'

If after receiving this gift she gave him no sign of encouragement,
no ardent glance or touch in the shop, no tender message left with the
old landlady, he was resolved to never enter the village again. He would
go to the big city, to the dark narrow streets where the women who
sold their bodies sat in windows with peacock feathers and parrots, and
silver-chained ferrets crawling on their bare shoulders. He would find
a young whore. Paying her generously, he would ask her to wear a pair
of silk slippers like the ones he had given the girl. He would kneel on
the floor before the prostitute, and kissing the slippers, take them off
her feet, and then kiss each of her toes. He would ask her to wrap an
apricot scarf about her face, before he enjoyed her favors; in the darkness
imagining he was giving himself to a young bake girl he had foolishly
given his heart to, as he had not given it before, not even to his wife.

*.....and after he had dared make such a brave overture of his passion
to this young girl, he became impaled on doubts and fears in the interlude
when he waited for her response, knowing that indeed he could lose this
precious thing that had given his age such a wonderful new meaning.......*

*......he began to neglect his business, to become lazy and absent-
minded.....to suck deeper and longer from his hookah in his bed.....the
fumes now bringing dreams that merged with his passions for this child for
whom he had become enslaved......this child whose young sweet body was
riding him, spurring him, in all ways ruling him.......*

*.....the riders of these horses with heads of dogs, lynxes, giant owls......
some whose faces were painted, some scored with ugly scars.....shooting
arrows and swinging great swords as they twisted on their saddles.....their*

cuirasses made of ox-hide, their caps of the furs of fox and monkey......the dream in the hookah's fumes, the dream of the wild horses becoming more and more vivid......riders, savage malicious riders who left the most grisly carnage in their bloody wakes......his need for this young girl becoming one with their rapine......one with the desperate, savage need of his heart..... as her loveliness was not a gift, but a plunder......not to be given, but violated.......

When next the landlady had written him, she indicated in her scrawling way that the girl had indeed received the beautiful gifts that he had left for her, but she had left no note of '*thank you*', or anything else to be passed on to him. For the first time the old woman had inserted an insinuation of her own regarding the situation that had long since been suspicious to her, suggesting the girl was very young, and though her husband was a lout and the village drunkard, he was nevertheless her husband. She was a good Christian girl, and although she was sure she was thankful for the good man's generosity, she perhaps did not want to mislead, or provoke the gentleman in a wrong way. Reading extortion between the lines, and not rectitude, in a drunken furor he had sent the inveigling old spinster more money, and begged her to keep such opinions to herself.

He became very dejected, and a gloom of twisted nerves came over his life. He began to drink and smoke heavily, even to excess. And yet when he closed his eyes on his pillow this wounded angel arose before him, tantalizing him with many promises of playful pleasures. He became sick at heart. He lost his appetite, and all business concerns.

He became temperamental, choleric, and quick to lash out. His opium dreams became more vivid and more violent, and in the middle of nights he would wake in cold sweats with a pounding heart.

......scenes that harrowed him, that would not let him escape to the sanctum of sleep, the wild horses and their barbarous riders leaving blood and death wherever they passed......more than a myth or fable.....more than a dream.......

Against his better judgment he decided to make one last trip to the village, and even if it meant a fistfight with her husband, tell the girl how he was smitten. He would not take a gift, and if the outcome was what he supposed it would be, he would leave the village the next morning, go to the city, and purchase from a whore the gratification that God and his own foolishness had conspired to foment in his mind and heart, only in the end to deny and cheat him of.

When he entered the shop there were other customers inside it, chattering and quibbling as they made their selections. And though the young girl was present with her husband, she was preoccupied, and he received not so much as a glance from her. Making his purchase with her sour and blowsy husband, he had left the shop feeling not only robbed, but cruelly chastised by Heaven; a Heaven that had devilishly held all the cards all the while.

That night he packed his things and prepared for his departure early the next morning. He smoked heavily from his hookah, and lay in his bed thinking of many things; first and foremost his courtship of this young girl whose name he had been too shy to ask, and now would never know. And as he did tears rolled down his bearded face, knowing that he had grown old, and had been a fool many times over. He asked God for forgiveness, and when he did he upbraided himself for the silly wicked overture he had made to a child less than half his age, one that had made brazenly clear his lascivious desires. How stupid he had been. How wretched he had grown with age, hashish, and loneliness. It had been better to go on vainly hoping to possess her than frighten and disgust her, as he had certainly done.

He drew long and deep from the hookah, the fumes blurring his fears with his dreams, his dreams with reality.

......*some called them Mongols, others, Tartars.....others, mad devils sweeping the Russian steppes like a great fire, razing and plundering and destroying cities.....Bulgar and rich Novgorod, Smolensk and Vladimir, Cherven and Kiev.....yes, even Kiev, the great jewel of Russia.....its Byzantine treasures rifled, the bones of its Saints scattered.....its nuns publicly raped and its monks sodomized......its citizens impaled, burned and beheaded......*

It was during these ghastly musings when he thought he heard a creaking stair, then the hallway floor; and then the unlatching and opening of his garret's door. The only light in the room was lent by the faintly-glowing hookah, but there could be no mistake: just as he had conjured her phantom many times from the darkness, the young bake girl now stood at the foot of his bed, bundled in her coat and ragged scarf. Quickly sitting, he had begun to speak out in his surprise, but more quickly, she, kissing her fingertips and pressing them to his lips, sealed them tight.

In one swift moment the pauper metamorphosed to an *Angel,* exchanging her ragged attire to the raiment of a pink chemise she was wearing beneath it. Unbinding her headscarf, she let fall lush vines of dark glossy ringlets down past her breasts.

Holding his bearded face between her two small hands, she brought a kiss to his mouth, a kiss full of youth's fruits and flowers, breathing into his blood the sweetness of her young years. And when she did she whispered in his ear:

"He will be at the tavern late tonight. I am yours, even as I have always wished to be yours. My body quivers and cries for you in the night. I want you to still its quivering. I want you to answer its cries."

And when he lifted the gown over her head and she lay back on the bed, he was given yet another surprise as he bent to smell, kiss and tenderly explore her secret places. Braided in the nest of her treasure, even as they composed a dainty coronet, were petals of roses, *his roses.*

He had been very excited, and his pent-up passion was spent very quickly, and after he lay unspeaking, shy and ashamed of his performance, regretting the impetuosity of his lust. But she had tenderly caressed him, and whispered in his ear that he was the kindest man she had ever known; that he had made her very happy, and that she wanted his love again and again.

He had found the sweetest lover; at once shy and daring, kittenish and tigerish; child-innocent and woman-wise; but always caring, willing, and generously loving. In truth he had felt that he was more her student than her teacher, for although he had been married for over thirty years, and had sired eight children, his lovemaking with his wife had been a numb, passionless act, almost a chore that fell incumbent on him to perform. It had been a tired ritual, its performance signaling sleep and day's end; more times than not, without a word or kiss of goodnight.

His wife had been passive, and seldom thrilled. Her body had been plain and unshapely, owning little allure, even when she was young. Age and childbearing had taken any hint of sensuality away from her, and she had become beefy, flaccid and unlovely. She was a good woman who had been a good mother, and he had often felt guilty when their lovemaking filled him with an obligation that brooked on disgust.

In the sharpest contrast, beneath her raggedness this girl had concealed a sleek and felinely sensuous body. And as their affair continued, each time he lifted the chemise over her head he felt as though he was lifting the gown from off an *Angel*. Each time she was a new garden of fruits and flowers to be explored. Each time he was invited, and accepting those invitations, became lost in that garden anew.

She had been long starved of any show of tenderness by her loutish husband, and sometimes even abused. More than once he had seen evidence that she had been slapped or spanked, and once he had seen welts on her hams where her brutish husband had whipped her. But these cruelties had the effect of making her more grateful, even sensually, compulsively greedy when she learned to trust his gentle care; a care that salved her hurts with kisses like none she had ever known.

She gave herself completely, and in doing so cared for his deepest needs and fires, learning to stir, coax, wait and hold, even as he in turn stirred, wakened and waited for her to yield, give, and flower The love she gave him was selfless, and not avaricious; not wanting to be first or last, weaker or stronger, but one with that one who was so tenderly knowing the deepest part of her. Often he imagined dying when he was inside her, with her little purrs and child-like whimpers singing in his ears.

.....As the riders of his dreams became one with their horses, he increasingly felt a oneness with his young wonderful lover, so that the needs of their two bodies rhymed, joined, and indistinguishably melded, so that the one perfectly answered the other. Made blind with his passion, he had even imagined her young body a beautiful colt he had captured high in the mountains, one that matured into a magnificent mare that had become his alone. Delirious with the races of his passion, she sometimes cried out with things he asked her to do, cries that he imagined a horse's neighs....at other times, as he was her horse, and she his rider, she stirred him more deeply than he had ever been stirred before, his young little rider spurring and commanding him.....and then again, and ever again riding her sleekness beneath the stars.....sometimes imagining he wore the hood of a lynx or wolf, making the earth tremble beneath the passion of their beating hearts.......

......recovering his senses after such lovemaking, he deliriously kissed up and down the length of her exhausted body, as in atonement.....the wild savage horseman now weeping like a little boy...."O Martuska, O my little darling, Martuska, have I hurt you?.....O my precious little angel, you must forgive me.....you see, I did not love my wife as I love you.....and I sometimes have a dream, a childish dream, a dream of wild horses.....I was never a brave man, but you see I so want to be brave and strong for you"......

Her lips and gentle fingers upon him, she would smile and softly giggle..... "*You silly man, you silly, wonderful, lovely man, do you not know that I feel your tenderness in your strong needs? Do you not know that I would do anything, even die for you?*"

He had long decided to marry her. Although it might prove scandalous, it was against no law, secular or religious. And it was certainly not unprecedented. There were barons and other members of the gentry that married young girls in their elder years: milkmaids, scrub girls, the least scullions. He was still vital. He was still young enough to give her children. He owned property, and more than enough wealth to make her happy.

It would be easy to steal her away. The old *Jewess* was the only one who knew where he lived. Besides, she was old and decrepit, and he could easily poison or strangle her to eliminate any chance of her telling his whereabouts, and the illicit affair she knew full well was happening in the garret above her parsimonious head. He knew the small tavern where his lover's husband drank each night. He had imagined a thousand times lying in wait for him as he stumbled his besotted way home, and in a flash cracking his skull open with a stone, or slitting his throat with a knife.

* * *

AGAIN he allowed the hookah's fumes to swim and tunnel through him, and again he looked out the window at the beautiful blanket of snow; its pristine whiteness laving the street and rooftops, cleansing mud, stones and poverty into a royal, alabaster purity; the sky, spangled with stars, like a magnificent candelabrum, God's candelabrum that let fall a shimmering purity upon the world He had made.

Oh, like this snow, love had cleansed him; had washed and baptized him anew; had given him a communion with a higher, purer grace. Someone now loved him, as he had never been loved before, and he would do anything...be a soldier riding into hearts of bloody battles for such love.

"*Antal, Antal my darling, you silly beautiful man, what are you doing standing there in the window, and not in your Martuska's arms? Are you tired of the little girl who makes bread and biscuits? Does she not still taste sweet to you? Come my sweetheart, come to your Martuska. She has many games to play, and many secrets to tell. Come to your little Martuska.*"

17

.....a sweetness too sweet to deny.....her young, fawn-lithe sweetness filling him, dizzying him almost to a faint, to a weakness and surrender, to death itself.....kissing her small white feet, and then up her slender legs, deliriously, like a honey-drunken bee, kissing and sipping each tender part, each honeyed clover of her.....fearing only that he might miss a precious knee, finger, ear, nose........

.....and then, downier than feathers.....exploring her sweetness sweetness yet again.....to die in this secret pleasure cave beneath the little hill of her belly that he alone, of all men in the world had been invited to explore.....her body like the waves and the songs of the sea.....undying with her young sweet fury.....her dainty little cries in his ears.....thrilling him alive like thunder.....like the thunder that the dream of wild horses had once thundered through him....."O Antal, my darling Antal, you are so strong and sweet!".......

.....but then suddenly stopping, as she had never done before, stopping him midst the fury of his brute joy.....breathing in his ear not an endearment, but something more akin to concern....more akin to fear.......

"Antal, do you hear something? I was sure I heard something, as of a distant storm....but I am silly, the stars are shining and there is no storm..... forgive your little bake girl, will you my darling?.....it is only the trembling of my body and its great hungers for you.....come, let us make a prince with your eyes and your hair and your beautiful heart.....I want to make a little prince, 'our' little prince this very night......

.....but, there it is again.....do you not hear?.....a thunder, as of the hooves of many horses.....and see, the old woman's knickknacks on the shelves are trembling, as if dancing.....neighs of horses, shouts and screams.....you must look out the window Antal, and see what it is!.....O please darling, look at once.....I am suddenly very frightened!".......

* * *

HE wanted only to die, but they did not want him to die. Artisans and tacticians of torture, they were practiced in this savage art of leaving their victims to linger on the verge of death, so that in interminable, unbearable anguish they longed for death as a starving beggar longs for bread.

He could feel his viscera spilling down his legs. He knew they had disemboweled him, but to what extent he could not see, and he did not want to know. His wrists, bound, he hung from the rafter where his hookah had hung, the tips of his toes touching the floor, but unable to reach and stand upon it.

They had hung him like a butcher hangs a beef, a noose made with an apricot scarf about his neck; left to slowly bleed to his death. But worse than that death, he had been made to watch them take beastly turns with his beautiful angel, before dragging her from the room to be their slave, or yet another slaughtered victim. He was left alone with the old *Jewess's* head on the bedpost near him, scalped bald of her gray hair, an apple stuffed in her mouth like a suckling pig.

He hung near the window where only a short while ago he had stood, smoked and contentedly mused of his young lover, the stars, and a new-fallen snow; its pristine whiteness now stained with bright blotches and gaudy trails of scarlet blood; and the limbs, torsos and heads of those that had been butchered as they woke in their beds. Across the street, in the bake shop window, the head of the degenerate proprietor was gruesomely propped.

To make the godless irony complete, the sun had brightly risen, making glisten the roofs, gables and chimneys, as in a child's fairytale, a fairytale he had once dreamed of life, of love, of lovely wild horses..... all now wickedly despoiled to this grisly scene of hell.

.....*There was no God, or if there was, the Devil was laughing in His heart. Hope and pleasure had been baits, sugary baits that had been poisonous banes in the end. Meaning, purpose.....stars and snows, innocent bake girls whose thighs opened to be sown by men's wild lonely hungers..... puppets hung to dream and smile, only to be dismembered and burned by the evil children that had made them dance.......*

.....*on the hill that rose above the village he could see three or four horse-pulled wagons, as well as several sleds climbing its snowy flank, making for the dark thick forest.....in the scouring sunlight he could see the brightly colored coats, skirts, scarves and bandannas of those the wagons were bearing, as well as the children running and tumbling in the snow beside them....copper kettles and smithy tools hung from the wagons' sides, sparkling in the sun.....behind them, tethered goats and donkeys.....in a middle wagon were two caged bears, those they had trained to dance, roll barrels and walk over burning embers.......*

.....*the band of the bear tamers, fortunetellers, kettle-menders and basket weavers.....those that played wild music, danced, sang and swallowed fire.....the Tziganes, yes, the Tziganes, those that had been nicknamed 'gypsies'......*

.....they had somehow not been killed, and they were fleeing.....left free to wander and dream life's dreams....the wicked lovely dreams men dream beneath the sun and stars.......

.....Perhaps they would escape into the dark forest.....perhaps the Devil-God would not find them there.....perhaps in the dark forest their bright clothes would change to the bright plumage of birds; their hearts, fill with pretty songs.....perhaps some would become bears, and live in the forest forever.......

....

....

CHAPTER TWO

THE RAPE

Moldavia; The Carpathian foothills; Circa 1300

THE bears had shown the first signs; waddling restlessly back and forth in their cages, standing on their haunches, bawling from their prison bars into the dark forest. They were followed by the horses in the stables of cleverly woven briar and fir bough: thrashing at their tethers and stomping on the blankets that their rearing had shed from their backs; their first soft snorts waxing to nervous whinnies, their whinnies to neighs shrill as trumpets. And with the riled horses the crazing of the dogs, followed by a cacophony of goats, chickens and a braying ass, all climactically joined from the tents and wagons by the wails of squalling babes.

The night had been balmy, full of stars and summery health; sweet with cuckoos and mignonette. The wind was warm and southerly, shivering through the tall pines and beeches with breezes pregnant with the musky bloom of the meadows below; breezes that washed wave upon redolent wave into the hollow that their caravan of wagons had claimed since the sickle moon of May.

Richly perfumed with seduction, the night, like a rebel's whore seemed to spoil with treachery. As they were holding their breaths, the amorous breezes stopped, and then suddenly veered from the voluptuous south to the unsexed north, sweeping down in torrents from the snowcapped mountains that rose high over them.

And as the breezes changed, so were swapped the articles borne in their gusty arms. These were no longer winds laden with spells and spices, but ones that pricked the ears and stung the nostrils of beasts with scents and footfalls of menace. And this was a people that believed in these neighs, barks and bawls. They believed in them as they believed in no priest or prophet. Their cries told them these breezes were no longer friendly; no longer filled with the carefree dreams of dance and song; that in their cold arms were swords.

But their cries had spoken too late.

.....the sudden halting of the sad sweetness of the violin, the strummed lute, the lazy rapping of the tambourine.....the castanets halting their rhythmic clicks in the lifted hands of the frozen dancer who with bright scarves had been dancing about the fire.....the halting of the hammer on the copper kettle, the fingers on the loom, those twisting a rope, a braid of hair.....all halting at the trembling of the earth and wagons, a trembling caused by the hooves of two dozen horses plunging down the steep bluff, and like a lava spilling with boiling savagery into their camp.....the flaxen-haired, Saxon riders shouting, armed with clubs and great-bladed swords.......

She peeked from the beaded curtains of the wagon. Many of the tents, and now some of their wagons had been set ablaze, the flames burning away the night into a coppery noon of brightness. The attackers had loosed both of their bears from their cages, and the one that still bore its bonnet and petticoat was riddled with arrows, while the other had been set afire, and was burning supernaturally bright, like an angel. Both were wildly bellowing, and while the first kept turning in deranged circles, swatting at the arrows as they were stinging hornets, the burning bear had charged into the stables, setting them at once ablaze. As it was a carnival performer loosed from hell, it had leapt on one of the horses, and sinking its claws into its flank and back, bolted forth, beast upon beast, and in a hideous drama of rearing and screaming raced burning into the night. Several of the dogs had been killed and impaled on spears, left to cough blood and deliriously yelp their last. One had been beheaded, its head propped in a fire, lending the illusion that it was laughing midst the flames.

Of their men, only the old had remained behind, the young having gone to beg and thieve in the outskirts of the village. And seeing this, the attackers had seized at will a number of women and young girls, and even some of the boys, and were at once violating and sodomizing them; savagely throwing up the bright skirts of the women, and baring the buttocks of the boys. With knives pressed to their throats, the helpless victims were being made to yield to their barbarous lust.

She had no time to slip into her bright blouse, tasseled skirt and beaded sandals. Bundling them in her arms, and obedient to the screaming shouts of her mother, she broke from the tent into the forest.

She was of that tender age that most tantalized these cruel marauders, and seeing such a prize dressed only in a sleeping smock, with a mane of long dark hair decorated with beads and jewels, three of the horsemen bolted laughing and shouting into the forest after her.

But this was a prey which was as clever as it was lovely. She was as sure and swift-footed as a fox, and she knew these parts of the forest well; its great trees, its thickets, and the marshy places made by the little stream that gurgled through it. With the protection that the dark shadows and thick foliage offered her, she thought her hiding would be secure. She thought that after a little way into the forest the riders would be confounded, and they would abandon their chase of her.

She had been wrong. These were men who had long lived in the womanless wilds. They wanted the pleasures they had seen blossoming upon her young body. She was a milky doe, they, bloodthirsty hounds that would flay her. They would capture her and take their hungry turns with her; sharing her like brothers would share a roasted goat.

The horsemen did not halt the hunt of their light-footed quarry. Although there were times the fleet young gypsy girl managed to scamper through brush where they could not, evading, and at times stymieing them, they seemed to always catch sight of her again, resuming their chase into the deeper and darker shadows of the forest. The advantages she gained with her cunning and swiftness were quickly eaten away by the advantage her pursuers' horses lent them. They would again apprize her in open places, the jewels and bangles in her hair, ears, nose and ankles sparkling like fireflies where the light of their torches reached.

This young gypsy girl was as illusive as any boar or hart they had ever hunted. It was as they were following an enchantress, the sorcery of her loveliness beguiling them into deeper and deeper folds of the forest, deluding them with a fleeing beauty that seemed at once winged, at other times hoofed, and at still other times racing with the bare feet of a scantily clad young gypsy girl.

She was phantom-like; a lovely phantom with a narrow waist, gently curved hips, and apple-round breasts. In the torchlight they glimpsed her fawn-delicate throat, and the sparkle in her dark eyes. And with each of these glimpses they were seized with a greater need to quench the flame that her youth and beauty had excited in them.

She had led them into a region of the forest that she did not know, where she had never gathered roots and berries, or mallows by the stream. Although she was swift and strong, she knew she could not continue to outrace her pursuers, her exhausted body quickly becoming a burden to her frightened spirit. She feared she would soon be captured by her own weariness. She knew that it was a matter of only moments before the savage men would seize her, and she must submit to her terrible fate.

Charged with a sudden terror of what that fate might be, and at the same time so utterly fatigued she could not trust her weakness to carry her on, the young girl resolved to hide from her savage hunters. Swiftly she climbed into the fork of a great tree, and then with the nimbleness of a squirrel, shinnied out upon one of its leafy, camouflaging boughs.

Her hiding proved successful. When the three riders appeared, they scoured the thickets with their torches, only in the end to conclude she had escaped from their clutches. Still mounted, they met together only a little way from her hiding place, the light from their torches spangling the leaves of her leafy shelter. From her perch she could see their un-kemptness and uncouthness; their coarse grizzled beards, their wolf-pelt coats, their spears and swords. They spoke in a strange tongue, one they had brought from the mountains of the north, but she was certain she could understand the purport of their words by their inflections, inflections that were filled with depravity and coarseness.

"*Damn it, we have lost her, and I am sorry for it. She was a pretty little piece. I would have liked to tickle her.*"

"*She was a virgin if I have ever seen a virgin. When we destroyed the Turks' camp I tasted many of her kind. And once having tasted the tenderness of a true virgin, all others are as tough as horse meat; tough as a drunkard's whore. Damn, I'm sorry she slipped us.*"

"*She could not have run far. She was becoming very tired. Perhaps she is hiding.*"

"*Yes, she is hiding. But she is clever. All of the gypsies are clever. They are part animal themselves. We cannot wait until dawn to fuck her.*"

"*When we return we shall only have those the others have had before us. They shall laugh at us when they see us having to settle for their spoils.*"

"*We do not need to tell them that the girl escaped. We shall tell them that we made a merry feast of her.*"

"*Still, I hate to lose her. She was young and pretty, with nice breasts and a nice round bottom. I would have liked to have given her my groan.*"

"*Come, forget her. Let us return before their men return, or we must be satisfied by tupping a sheep or goat.*"

Gruffly laughing, the rough men departed, the young girl waiting with the heart of a frightened rabbit in the tree until their laughter, horses and torches retreated and were swallowed back into the night. Only when the silence of the forest returned, with its lisping leaves, hooting owls and chirping crickets did she stir from her hiding place, and with sloth-like stealth begin to make her way back to the tree's trunk.

But as she reached its trunk, the tree's foliage seemed suddenly to enkindle; be burning. A bolt of terror shot through her heart when she heard a horse's hoofs softly crushing the twigs and leaves below, and then the sudden booming of a man's great laughter. Terrified, she scampered back to her hiding place on the tree's outreaching bough.

From here the gypsy girl looked down through the glowing leaves upon the one who had tarried behind and discovered her trickery. Seated upon his horse, his face was not far from where she sat hunkered midst the tree's foliage, and this nearness, aided by his torch's flame allowed her to see him clearly: his fairness and broad-shouldered brawn, his golden beard and hair that fell like a woman's hair, full of ringlets down his back. He was armed with a long slender bow, and a quiver full of arrows; and the horn of a ram or other animal dangled upon his breast. He sat on a saddle of pelts, behind which was strapped a bundle on his horse's rump.

She could see his blue eyes, sparkling like sapphires. She had never seen such eyes; eyes that possessed their own light, a light that would bring candles to darkness. They were lifted to her, but they shone with more than savagery. They contained laughter, a sympathetic laughter, to see their prey caught in the clever web of its own making.

The bough upon which she sat was a large spreading one, one that was so low that when the savage man stretched forth his torch, its tongue nearly licked its leaves. And holding his torch near his scared, helplessly treed prey, her youth and her loveliness were illumined to her hunter's eyes, her hunter that was now about to take a precious part of her forever.

He could see that she was young, very young, little more than a child, even younger than he had thought as she had fled through the forest. She was scantily clad, shivering with fright, and perhaps the dews of the night; her smock, muddied and torn from her desperate flight. Her hair was long, dark and glossy, and as she crouched on the bough it seemed to hang in dark veils to her feet, as if to help cloak her. The torch's light burnished her nut-brown skin, and made glisten the jewelry that adorned her; strung like sparkling berries through her tresses, and glittering about her nose, ears and eyes, as well as the red flower of her painted lips. But it was her dark eyes, those windows through which the terrified creature of her young soul now stared at him that softened the stone of his heart. They spoke the terror of her soul, and the stark knowledge of what she knew was about to come: an initiation that would be cold and brutal, rather than warm and tender, forced upon her by one she detested, and would rather murder a hundred times over than yield to him her body's treasure.

He stretched the torch even higher, so that it seemed on the verge of setting her cage of leaves on fire; so that her feet, arms and face felt the heat of its flame. And with this the gypsy girl sprang back to the tree's trunk, and with the nimbleness of a goat among stones, or a monkey among vines sprang onto another bough on the tree's opposite side. The man in turn spurred his horse, and illumined her new place of hiding, at which the girl fled to another bough. As she were a brightly feathered bird, and the large tree her cage, she began to flutter from bough to bough, only to be rediscovered by the man's torch and sapphire eyes each time she alighted. The savage man laughed heartily aloud, as if it were a game two children were playing. And as this gypsy bird flew in the mansion of its cage, the savage man began to speak to her, not in her *Romani* tongue, but in his own. Yet like a melody that speaks all tongues to all hearts, she seemed to understand him as he laughed, swigged wine, and spoke to her as she fluttered from bough to bough.

"Be not afraid, my sweet little bird. Come, fly to my arms, for my arms are a beautiful cage, one full of flowers and stars; one that will keep you safe from the night, and all of its prowling jackals.

Come down, pretty bird, I will not hurt you. I will only cherish and protect you from night's hunters. You need only play in my arms as all women play in men's arms. Come, I will not harm you. I will not break your jeweled wings. I will teach you to fly as you do not yet know how to fly;

not with feathered wings, but with the wings of your heart."

The young gypsy girl continued to leap from bough to bough in the tree, even as the savage man continued to laugh, drink his wine, and chirrup like a bird below her. Preoccupied with her continual flight among the branches, she did not see him fit an arrow into his bow, and was startled when a whizzing arrow stuck into a bough upon which she was about to leap, and another into another bough upon which she was about to retreat, convincing her how deadly was his marksmanship, and how futile it was for her to try to elude it. The game was over. Either she climbed back down the tree and submitted to his savagery, or she would die with one of his arrows in her heart. Acknowledging her defeat, the frightened gypsy girl descended, her slender waist met and firmly held by the savage man's large strong hands: her feet never touching the ground they so longed to touch. She found herself instead seated on the horse with the savage man, imprisoned in his savage arms, and spoken to with a gentle, but half mocking tenderness.

"You see, my little bird, it was not so hard to flutter into your new cage, now was it? You will be safe here. You will have no fears. These arms are much stronger than you are, and they will protect you from all dangers. You need only to sweetly sing for me, sweetly as only a lovely little bird like you can sing. Do not try to escape. I will not hurt you. I will be tender. I will teach you to fly as all girls learn to fly and be a woman in a man's arms."

And with this the savage man held the moon of her face between his hands, and then peered into the torment of her frightened eyes. He was twice her size, and thrice her strength; of an age that made her seem his daughter. And yet her loveliness seemed to contain some voluptuous depth and breadth, some mystery, as of the night itself; an immensity that enveloped him, as if he was in *her* arms, and not she in *his*; that he had become a little boy in the garden of her first sweetness.

Her entire body was shivering, as she was standing with bare feet in a drift of snow. He could feel her young breasts trembling against him, taut and firm, and with nipples raised, as they were tiny swords raised in a prideful defense. She was budding, and not yet blossoming, but each of her buds was rich with promise. She was bathed in that most fleeting, yet most timeless moment of all; the moment that marries the girl with the woman, and in that mystic wedlock makes them one; that moment that at once shuns and beckons her male hunter, and is at once frightened and eager in his arms. She was still a child, but one

27

beneath the bridal veil of womanhood, still innocent of that throne she was inheriting; that throne that would lend her both the miracles and lamentations of life's storms.

One of the savage man's hands stroked through her long tresses, while the other caressed her cheek and down her quavering throat, continuing until it found, and gently held one of her breasts. He bent his face to hers, as she with fear lifted her mouth to receive, like a cherry from a mother bird, the fruit he was bringing her. And yet, even this, was a ploy; for as the savage man's beard brushed against her face, the gypsy girl snapped out at him, like the dog of a drover at the heels of a cow, her sharp teeth biting into his wrist, as deeply as they would bite into an apple, so that at once her mouth was filled with the saltiness of his blood. Startled, his strong arms loosened their hold of her, and she had leapt from his horse and again into the forest and the night.

But the darkness afforded her no asylum. In a moment the savage man was on her trail, again cursing and laughing, sometimes lagging to swig from his wineskin, sometimes gaining, sometimes astride and almost trampling her. She was like a wounded animal, and he its hunter, whose heart exulted and lived for such play before its kill.

Here the forest broadly sloped towards some dark, foreboding depth, gently at first, but then more and more steeply. On its slope the large trees thinned, and in their place were tussocks of briar and fern, and now drifts of snarled brushwood. Once her descent had begun, she could but continue, for her tired legs would never carry her back up the slope's steep and difficult pitch. Any such attempt would be surrender to her hunter's ugly whims, he whose brazen laughter rang like a din of thunder in her ears, and whose torch, like a lightning brightened all around her. And as to compound her dilemma the more, the ground beneath her bare feet was becoming damp, and then quickly marshy as she neared the stream whose cold swiftness threaded this deep seam of the forest.

Reaching the stream's bank the gypsy girl found herself at an *impasse*. To try to struggle back up the hill meant her certain capture, and yet it would prove futile to wade or swim the stream to its other side, bounded by the sheer walls of cliffs, cliffs that she would need wings to mount. Nor could she choose to flee along the margin of the stream, made treacherous with bogginess, and with debris of great rocks that the centuries of melting mountain snows had disgorged with their floods. And yet she could not yield to this savage man, and all the savage things he would surely do to her. She feared him and she hated him. She would rather die than surrender to his barbarity. The gypsy girl had but one choice: to wade out into the stream and either drown, or be borne away by its swift and icy current.

The rider dismounted on the bank of the stream, and there let his horse thirstily drink. The moon had begun to rise over the dark escarpment of the cliffs, lending a sudden illumination to the gorge carved by the gleaming, age-old knife of the purling stream. He doused his torch and looked at the young girl who was so desperately fleeing him. In the shimmering moonlight he could plainly see her wade into the stream and begin to let herself be swallowed by the maws of its ever hungry channel, preferring the stream's icy arms to his warm ones. And for a moment the savage man's heart was stung with a poignant remorse it had not felt before, one that he would never admit to another, and perhaps not to himself.

What a mighty spirit this young gypsy girl must surely have, perhaps every bit as strong and daring as his own. She knew that she could certainly drown in the stream's swirling eddies. She knew that she could be dashed and broken against its stones. She knew that she was daring death in her attempt to preserve this little sheaf still intact between her legs, this little sheaf that was no more than a little leaf in the vast forests; attempting to preserve her innocence from all that in the dark forests of life was crouched and ready to ravish it.

Oh, how she must fear him. Oh, how she must hate him!

The savage man mounted his horse, and then urged it into the shallows of the stream. Its waters were at times little more than a babbling brook, and at other times they rushed like the deep dark bowels of a hungry monster, but here its gurgling gullet, though swift and strong, did not reach to his horse's girths. Here the savage man stopped, and looked down the stream now varnished bright with moonlight. And in the moonlight he could see the girl, as she were a broken-winged swan struggling its last: sometimes flailing, sometimes clinging to rocks, sometimes being carried and thrashed by the voracious current, but again and again struggling back to her feet, still holding the bundle of her things…..still dreaming of flight and freedom.

…..How those small feet must be numb from the stream's cold, and bruised and lacerated from the stream's stones. Oh, how the current of the

freezing stream must be stabbing deep and cold each part of her, those little breasts, that warm little cavern between her legs. This young girl would sacrifice her virgin treasure to this wild and icy river before she would yield it to him. She would rather die than yield to him. Oh, how she must fear him. Oh, how she must hate him.......

The savage man urged his horse down the moonlit stream, its hoofs gently splashing in the sandy and stony shallows outside the channel's rage. *Was he brave enough to drown in these cold swift waters, these waters that promised to drown her frightened heart in the fresh innocence of their melted snows. Were there not times that he too wanted to forget and to be no more?*

Upon his horse he easily overtook his prey. In the shallow places, where the stream was little more than a trickling brook, the rider splashed near, and even directly over her. It was then that the savage man's heart winced most to see how utterly spent the child was; a dying thing, and not a living one; an angel felled by the chase and hunt of men, with broken wings floundering to its end.

But even then when he extended his hand to her, the gypsy girl did not succumb. Once when she had fallen, and was struggling to stand back on her feet she heard the savage man speak to her with tones and inflections gentler and less mocking than he had spoken to her before.

"Come, child, my little daughter, give me your hand. I will not harm you. Your pretty bones will be broken on these stones. You do not want to ruin your prettiness, eh? That would be a great pity. This moon shines on no other as beautiful as you, my little flower. Come, lovely one, come and sit with me upon my horse. I have been cruel, and for that I am sorry. I will take care of you. I will not harm you my little gypsy angel."

But his tender words were in vain. It was obvious that the young, half-dead girl would rather die than give him his pleasure.

Here the river reached a bend in which it spilled into a calm, moon-glistening pool. Here also the forest gave way to an open field, with the night's stars sparkling above it. Here the gypsy girl managed to reach the bank, and partly on her hands and knees, partly afoot and limping, make her bedraggled way through the reedy shallows to the spongy, and finally solid ground. Dismounting, and then leading his horse by its reins, the savage man walked beside the proud, half-dead girl. He draped a blanket about her, a gesture she did not refuse. Walking thus side by side, he proceeded to speak to her in tones even gentler than he had used before; as their words owned melody, a lilt of song.

"*You are hurt, my sweetheart, and your feet are bleeding. That I can see. You may have broken some of your bones on the rocks. You are also very wet, my darling, and the night is cool. There is snow in the high mountains, and soon a cold wind will be in the forests. I do not want you to become ill. That would be a great shame. I want you to be well and happy. Let me take care of you. I will be kind to you, and I will make you happy. Life is full of games, games of sorrow and pleasure. We have played the game of sorrow, and now we will play its game of pleasure. Come with me. Come to my shelter and my fire. There I will take care of you. There you will heal. There we shall watch the great mystery of the stars and the parade of the seasons together.*"

With this the savage man placed his hand gently on the gypsy girl's shoulder. But she wanted none of his kindness. To her his hand was a sharp goad; it stung like a tarantula. At his touch she bolted from the drape of the blanket and into the field of breast-high grain that stretched before her.

As she had seemed a wounded swan in the icy stream, so now she seemed a wounded doe in the moonlit wheat, one whose pride and innocence had lent wings to her heart and heels. Exhausted and wounded though she was, there was a dignity, a dignity that was a grace about her. allowing her to race through the waist-high wheat as a swallow glides on the wind.

But she was fleeing him, fleeing him because she hated him. If she had the chance she would certainly murder him. And yet was hate so very different than love? Was not a devil's cape interchangeable with an Angel's gown? Given the chance this young girl would drive a dagger through his heart and twist its blade. But were murder, and its brother of hate so different than love, and its sister of lust? Was the wish to drive a dagger through a heart so very different from a man's wish to thrust his phallus into a woman's womb? Had his lovemaking with other women been driven by love or by hate? Had his blind, often drunken thrusts into his many lovers.....both those he had enjoyed against their will and those that had surrendered to him.....had these thrusts of his loins been fueled with murderousness, a desire to kill his own need and his own loneliness?

He knew that this young girl would not accept any entreaty of his kindness; that she would rather die than yield to him. He also knew that, alone in the night, and made vulnerable with hurt and fatigue, she could easily fall prey to the night's chill, or to wild animals, or even other men who would abuse her tender youth and use her prettiness for their sport.

The savage man unbound the bundle strapped to his horse. It was a hunting net, one that he used when he hunted boars and the large cats of the mountains. He peered out into the field of moonlit wheat, and the young girl limping and bobbing through it, the swollen moon, like a lamp lighting her struggling way. The savage man spurred his horse into the wheat field, his heart burning as he had swallowed fire.

When he reached her, she seemed not wholly alive. Broken and bleeding, she was delirious with fear and fatigue; whimpering, panting, stumbling. Yet when she had managed to lift her head, she at once saw the man spreading the heavy net out in his arms, preparing to cast it upon her as she were an animal of the hunt. And seeing his intentions, a last defiant breath surged through her, once more lending wings to her bleeding feet and failing spirit.

With his horse walking abreast his wounded prey, the savage man gently tossed his net upon her, even like a fisher casting his net from his boat. The heaviness of the cords, and the stakes that were ingeniously bound to them were as heavy chains to the utterly exhausted girl. Like a flower toppled by a scythe, she crumpled under its weight. Once upon her, its web of heavily woven ropes was like a cage of iron bars, a cage against which her wings were too broken and too weak to beat.

Quickly and expertly the savage man leapt from his horse. With lightning quickness he pounded a few of the stakes into the ground, so that in a few instants her body was firmly pinned and incapacitated; her wrists staked above her head, as were her ankles below her. With several swift, brusque motions his hands reached through the net and lifted her wet skirt above her waist, exposing the little tuft that would be his prize. Within instants the terrified gypsy girl lay helplessly imprisoned, prepared for her captor's gratification.

But the savage man did not have his gratification. Instead, he lay on his back beside her in the dewy wheat, and looked up into the sea of stars.

He had spread his net over other girls running before his horse in the fields and woods, ravished them as they lay frightened and trembling, staked beneath this same hunting net. He had raped many, seduced even more, and had even paid for a few that waited outside taverns and stables. Love was a need in the blood, as was the thirst for the kill. It was a hunger to be fed, a game to be played, a battle to be fought. Like wine it brought with it a brief, pleasing, and often foolish drunkenness.

The savage man continued to lay by the girl, bound, denuded and panting beneath the net, staring at the stars that seemed to be weeping compassion on them both. He was filled with an inexplicable sadness, one that he had felt at rare times after felling a magnificently hart, or a majestically winged bird; a rankling guilt, and not a pleasure, as if the creature's dying was nobler than his living, and by killing it he was murdering something in himself. And as he stared into the night sky he imagined the stars were a forest, as his father had once told him they were a forest when he was a small boy, a forest full of magical creatures.

.....*She had seemed at times a thing enchanted.....a swan, a salmon, a milky doe, a nymph of a legend.....as if her loveliness was composed of many mirrors that reflected countless forms and faces, and the more one looked at it the more it would fashion new forms and faces.....her jewels and bangles glittering in the torchlight, as she were a creature never apprized by men.....*

He had looked into the eyes of those animals his arrows had felled, but death had not yet reached: eagles and wildcats, elk and deer and bears. He remembered as a little boy being surprised to find calmness in their eyes, even as death was making its way to their hearts. There was an acceptance that contained a kind of sublimity; a heroic pride, an equanimity that brooked on forgiveness for their slayer. In this gypsy girl's dark eyes shone such a brave pride, one that could not be killed or quenched; one that deserved to be immortalized among these starry gods and dragons of the heavens. No soldier ever fell upon his sword with a nobler valor. Oh, the net beneath which he lay was far heavier than the one she now lay beneath. One was woven of gut, the other of a deep guilt.

He was quickly becoming old beneath these stars. He too was being hunted in a forest, hunted by these sparkling archers.

The savage man turned to the girl, silently awaiting her cruel fate. The moon had climbed high in the east, and in its silver light she seemed a rarest of creatures, one snared by men. Her eyes were closed, as if giving a last protection to her soul, and he could see the tiny jewels that she had sewn into her eyelids, and the rings that sparkled upon her nose. She was very lovely, lovely as nothing he had ever seen.

The savage man began to kiss the gypsy girl through the thick cords of the net; kissing her more tenderly than he could remember kissing

33

another. He pressed his lips softly to her hands bound tightly above her head; then to her cheeks, and then to her closed eyelids, behind which he knew burned a stare of hatred for him. With little nibbles he kissed down the slender arch of her throat; continuing over the bruised tenderness of her body until, reaching her feet, bleeding and caked in mud, he grew faint of heart.

In his large hands they were preciously small. They were decorated, like a bird's gay plumage; with jeweled anklets, brightly painted nails, and silver and copper rings upon their toes; like exotic birds felled by a storm, birds he had taken into his hands, and tenderly kissing and chafing, must try to give back the gift of their flight.

Like a lion upon its kill, he fed upon her loveliness. Possessed of that greatest hunger of them all, loneliness, the savage man proceeded to kiss up and down the gypsy girl's brown body, from the painted tips of her toes to the painted tips of her fingers. And as he did he began to whisper to his victim; his victim that in truth had become his captor.

"Forgive me my little doe, forgive me. I am sorry that I have so wounded and snared you. But I am a man. I have needs. And you my lovely little fawn are a woman with pleasures that can satisfy those needs. Love is a hunt. Love is a dark hunger. Love is a battle waged in our loneliness. We are creatures of the forest with the songs of the first night and the first stars in our hearts.

Oh my little doe, my little bird, the net about my heart is far heavier than the one I have cast about your young beautiful body."

And with this the savage man brought his bearded lips to the tender-most place of her body. In the moonlight he could see its downy tuft, and inside its secret heart, pink against the brown of her body; the rose she had so fiercely and gallantly defended; the rose that by some law or duty he now must pluck.

He felt himself stir, rouse, swell, the sword of his manhood hardening.

.....a hunt, a hunger, a great battle on the field of loneliness.....

He leaned over the small, quivering body, and prepared to make the young girl a woman before she had finished being a girl. But as he did he was pierced with an ache stronger than desire. He paused midst his need; ruled by a greater need than this lesser one.

He began to unbind the gypsy girl from her bondage. Unbinding last her feet he again kissed them, his beard wet with his tears.

"Do not be afraid. I will not harm you. I will take care of you. I will heal the wounds I have given you."

* * *

THEY rode through the dews and songs of the night, the gypsy girl tightly wrapping the savage man's strong body with her arms; his shirt upon her to keep her warm, its rough cloth full of smoke and uncleanness, and the strange smells of the male animal.

They did not return back through the same forest, neither to her camp nor to his companions. They rode in other directions and through other forests, over different streams and across different moonlit fields. The gypsy girl did not know where the savage man was taking her. She no longer had a will to know or care. Her body, riddled with aches and lacerations, and drugged with an overwhelming fatigue, she begged only for sleep, or sleep's mother, *death*. Still, as the gypsy girl pressed her face against the savage man's shoulder, she was vaguely conscious that they had begun to climb on small steep trails, and that the air was becoming cool and resinous. The oak and chestnut trees were thinning to a preponderance of pine and fir, and here and there she saw what appeared to be drifts of snow dappling the purple-dark shadows.

The cold stillness of dawn was upon them when the savage man finally halted his horse. There was a frost on the ground and foliage, and on the cones and needles beneath the great pine trees. The gypsy girl had lapsed into a fever, and only feebly conscious, she had crumpled from the back of the horse into the savage man's arms when he had reached for her. Enfolding her like a new-born lamb, he carried her into a dark place that smelled of hides and burnt tallow. He laid her gently down upon a bed of pelts and blankets. He lighted a candle, and then knelt, wheezed, and built a small fire. He left the gypsy girl to tend to his horse.

The gypsy girl did not know how long she had slept, but waking she woke to find the savage man knelt next to her where she lay. The ceiling above her was stone, and was dancing with a play of shadows cast upon it by a fire. The air was sweet with cooking, and made warm and honey-golden from a fire in a hearth.

The savage man did not look at her. He was swabbing and gently bathing her naked legs, hips and abdomen with a warm wet cloth.

Unsure whether she was dreaming or awake, she saw her torn and soiled gown, now little more than a rag, hung near the fire. As she was trying to fight from a dream, she began to try to recollect and recount what had happened to her, as if looking for the door of her waking; and waking, her escape.

.....*the burning bear riding the crazed horse.....the terrible men violating the boys and women.....the chase through the forest.....the great tree, the icy stream, the moonlit wheat, the heavy hunting net cast over her.....the savage man's beard and kisses and gentle whispers.....the ride into the pine trees and the climb up the mountain.......*

And suddenly the gypsy girl startled awake with the realization that she was naked in her abductor's hands; that he had undressed her, and that he was bathing each part of her nakedness. Terrified, the gypsy girl violently recoiled from her terrible nurse's caring hands.

But those same caring hands were also wonderfully quick and strong. One of them gripped and shackled together her two small ankles, then wrenching them swiftly and surely, turned the gypsy girl flat upon her stomach. Brusquely lifting the tail of her shirt up to the small of her back, he swiftly gave her bare buttocks each a quick sharp spank, so that she cried out from the smarting stings. Turning her back upon her back as she were a sack of flour, and without uttering one word or once looking into her face, the savage man resumed his tender bathing and salving of her wounds.

Again the gypsy girl rebelled from the savage man's touch upon her naked body, and again she was admonished in the same harsh fashion, only this time with a sharper and more authoritative slap; not once, but twice upon the same tender places. This time the gypsy girl cried out more shrilly, and her eyes blurred with tears of both pain and indignation. Again, in the same stolid manner, the savage man turned her over and resumed his gentle nursing of her wounds.

Once more the proud, humiliated girl rebelled, a rebellion that was answered with even sharper swats, swats that made her break into sobs as she lay still, surrendered at last to his cruel domination.

It was then that the savage man branded the gypsy girl, a brand that burned like a glowing iron through her flesh to her soul; a brand that she would not forget for as long as she lived. It was then that the savage man brought his bearded lips to her smarting buttocks, and kissed their hurt with a strange tenderness she had never felt before.

Submitting at last to this strange and cruel tenderness, she allowed him to methodically and meticulously examine, bathe and salve each of her lesions and contusions. But when he had begun to unbutton her shirt, the gypsy girl once more defiantly shrank away, a disobedience that was met with the same stern response. Twisted over and prepared for her punishment, this time the gypsy girl whimpered her defeat. Sitting up, she unbuttoned and removed the shirt with her own hands.

After he had bathed and nursed her, the savage man placed his hand over the tender place between her legs; the nest that seemed tinier, and strangely more secret beneath his large hand. Lifting his blue eyes to her brown ones, he shook his head, as to tell her it had not been violated. There was that in the size and strength in his hand, and the authority in his blue eyes that she believed.

He held a cup of wine to her mouth, bidding her take sips from it. The wine was warm, strong and fruity, and soon a pleasant tiredness came over her. The savage man continued to wash and salve her naked body, and as he did the gypsy girl fell asleep, and was not afraid.

* * *

Only little by little the light of the sun began to break through the gypsy girl's dreams and fevers. Only little by little the gypsy girl came to know that she was in a pleasantly warm, pleasantly furnished cave.

A hearth had been hewn and enlarged from a natural hollow in a stone wall, and in it a gentle fire burned, over which was hung several kettles. From the fire came the smells of pine and apple wood, and from its kettles the aromas of meat and seasoned greens. Before the cave's one entrance, and its sole window to the sun was hung a brightly colored horse blanket. Beside the blanket hung a large goatskin, one that she was sure wrapped a vessel of wine. In her few glimpses outside the blanket, when the wind gusted, or at the coming or going of the savage man, the gypsy girl saw great trunks of trees, trunks that seemed the legs of giants. The cave's floor was earthen, and scattered with reeds, and she could see a table with crude stools as its chairs, as well as plank shelves littered with a miscellany of bowls, mugs and flagons.

Bedridden, the gypsy girl's feverish mind had wandered in the pine bough rafters that had been cleverly contrived and fixed above. She would wake from her fits of sleep to find different game hung from them: partridges, hares, squirrels. On these rafters also hung various pelts and horns, bunches of drying herbs, and sacks that bulged with onions or apples, or perhaps stashes of acorn flour or nuts. They also contained many things for the hunt and the catch: nets and snares and ropes, spears of various lengths, and a giant bow, tall as a man.

But it was the cave's walls that most fascinated and hypnotized the gypsy girl, playing numinous tricks upon her fever-haunted mind. They seemed to glow, like the inside of an oven, painted with the goldenness that the fire cast upon them. Upon these gently glowing walls a world of shadows danced, yawned and contorted; a race of phantoms proportionate to the hour, the fire's strength, and the fevers racing through her blood. Many times they seemed to be the creatures of a fantastic forest through which she was fleeing, the partridges and hares hanging from the rafters magically transforming into a mythology of horned, tusked, and many-headed monsters. Sometimes midst these chases she would hear a sweet music, one that made the phantoms vanish. At these times the gypsy girl imagined she saw the savage man playing a flute by the hearth, as in some way he was dispelling her frightening dreams.

At other times she would wake to find herself again naked, her many wounds being bathed and salved by the savage man. Only once did she attempt to shrink away, but when the savage man had twisted her over, and she prepared for the punishment of his strong hand, she felt instead his beard, now washed soft and silky, and the lips whose kiss stung her more deeply than his strong hand.

At still other times the gypsy girl would wake in the night when the fire had burnt low, and the stones of the wall glowed softly, only to find that she was tightly wrapped in the strong arms of the savage man. At first she was afraid that he had violated her, and he had fallen asleep after he had spent his need. But feeling her secret place, she knew this was not true. Not wanting to stir, or in any way wake him, the gypsy girl lay awake, enfolded in his arms, listening to the cold wind now in the pine boughs, the hooting owls and the screeching lynxes; and sometimes the distant, lonely howls of wolves.

Once, as she lay thus awake, the savage man stirred in his dreams, and stirring, he pressed roughly into her, into the same tender place he had so sharply spanked. And when he did she felt the male creature of his loins rouse from its torpor, pressing and chafing its hunger into her; even as it was a serpent seething with its venom. Frightened, she eventually felt its urgency soften, and gradually ebb and die, as again it retreated into its dark cave.

* * *

WITH the passing of days, the gypsy girl's fever subsided. Her sleep became sound, and her many wounds healed. One morning she woke to find bright sunlight spilling into the cave's mouth from where the blanket had been lifted away. The savage man was not in the cave, but upon the table was a bouquet of pink and yellow flowers, and from one of the hearth's pothooks hung a pot that filled the cave with sweet and savory smells. A fish, smothered in greens and scallops was readied in a skillet by the fire.

Upon a low bench set near her bed the gypsy girl discovered her bundle of things, freshly laundered and folded; the things that she had let fall as she had waded into the river: her tasseled, dark green skirt, her tangerine blouse, and her intricately beaded, doeskin sandals. With the bundle were also a number of things that had fallen in her flight: a bangle from her ear, a wristlet from her wrist, a ring from her belly, and several beads that had been strung through her long hair. There were also a few things that were not hers, but seemed as they were meant for her, including a comb, a woolen shawl, and the treasure of every girl's vanity, a mirror with a tortoise shell handle.

Without a word or further incident, the savage man and the gypsy girl began a simple domestic life in the mountain cave. The savage man hunted, trapped and fished, and cleaned and dressed his game. He brought firewood, tended to the dogs and horse, mended his nets, and whetted and repaired his tools and weapons. In turn the gypsy girl swept, cleaned, and made modest decorations in the cave. She prepared the meals, mended blankets, and hunted for bulbs and nuts in the forest.

The savage man did not often speak to the gypsy girl, and seldom even looked at her, and in those rare times when he did, the gypsy girl saw only icy pools in his blue eyes. The savage man was never brusque with her, and in no way did he mistreat or coerce her. He did not bind or shackle her, and gave her license to roam for long whiles in the forest alone. But for a reason that the gypsy girl did not entirely understand, she did not use this license to make an escape, and always returned to the cave from her errands at the brook, or in a deep part of the forest.

At night the savage man would drink wine he poured from the goatskin that hung by the horse blanket. Sometimes he would strum a few soft chords on his lute by the fire. The gypsy girl would patch and mend, scour a stubborn kettle, or sometimes in the cave's vaguest corner, her back to the fire, comb her luxurious tresses while holding her beautiful mirror before her.

When the savage man heaped a good heap of firewood on the fire, then bent over the candle and snuffed its flame, it signaled the end of their day. They undressed and prepared for sleep, the gypsy girl in the shadows on one side of the cave, and the savage man in the shadows of the other. The gypsy girl would lie down first beneath the thick pelt blanket, and a moment later the savage man would follow. And though she was ever turned from him, rigid and wary with fear, the savage man would always gather her small body into his large body, wrapping her tightly, but always tenderly, and without provocation or menace.

The savage man did not molest the gypsy girl in any way. They would only lay awake with the stillness of the forest all about them. In that stillness, the curious creature in the savage man's loins would sometimes stir, especially after he had drunk much wine. It would emerge from its hiding as it was a creature only of the night, and not the day. But soon it would make its retreat, and the gypsy girl was left watching the shadows dancing on the walls, and listening to the voices of the ever wakeful night. And in this way the fear of the gypsy girl melted into a kind of peace, and she would drift into an easeful sleep.

As the last green days of summer passed into the frosts and bright berried days of autumn, the savage man would sometimes be seized with a great restlessness. He would sometimes leave on his horse before dawn, only to return in the deep of the night. He would bring sacks of flour, dried meats and tallow, and other staples from the mill and the village. But he would sometimes bring pretty things for the gypsy girl as well, and she would find these things before the hearth when he had gone from the cave to inspect his snares and nets in the morning; ribbons, barrettes, earrings. Once when she returned from the brook she found a softly woven sleeping gown, embroidered with roses, spread out upon the bed. It was like the gown of a princess, a gown more womanly fine than any the gypsy girl had ever owned. When the savage man came to her that night, she felt the serpent in his loins chafe, as with a strange anger against her. Still, after a time it once more became soft, tame and docile, and her apprehensions melted away to the phantoms on the walls and the voices in the forest.

Sometimes the savage man would not return until early the next dawn. The gypsy girl would lie awake, alone and afraid through the night, as if expectantly waiting, almost pining for his return; listening for the hoofs of his horse on the stones of the trail. And when he came to her there would be the reek of smoke and wine in his shirt, beard and hair, and even more pungent, the tart perfumes of women. Exhausted, he would sleep the day through.

And there were times when he did not return alone, times when the gypsy girl, buried in pelts, would hear the shrill, drunken laughter of women mingle with his deep, drunken bellows. The gypsy girl grew to learn that the savage man's quietness was flammable, that it ignited into boisterousness when he drank a quantity of wine. She also learned that the savage man was a great favorite among the tavern women, that they were attracted to him like bees to a honeyed flower. She learned that many women desired the savage man, and that he often answered those desires.

And why should they not, asked her heart? The savage man was indeed very handsome. Even she, his captive, conceded that. In certain ways the savage man was as beautiful as a woman. Washed, brushed and combed, the savage man was handsome as no other man with his long, leonine mane of golden-waved hair, his auburn-streaked beard, and his bright, sapphire blue eyes. The gypsy girl had seen the savage man without his shirt in the garden and at the woodpile, and she saw that he was very lean, strong and broad, with a second, secret bloom of red-golden hair upon his chest, the chest she was cradled against every night.

When the taverns closed, women would sometimes accompany the savage man up the steep hillside from the village. By the sound of their shrill voices, she was sure some were little more than whores. The gypsy girl would hear these women begging for his kisses and embraces.

She would hear them beg to come into the cave to sleep with him. Greatly frightened, the gypsy girl would be relieved to hear the savage man's refusals.

Sometimes the gypsy girl would steal from her bed and peek from the horse blanket. She would see the savage man kissing one of these lewd women, and sometimes two of them at once. She would watch him disappear with them into the small byre full of dry hay. Coming to her at the break of dawn, and reeking of wine, and the perfumes of lust, the gypsy girl did not feel the serpent stir from the savage man's loins when he pressed into her. It remained soft and meek; as if its hunger had been sated; its poison, spewed.

The savage man was kind to the gypsy girl, but he seldom spoke to her. She first learned of the secret melodies in his voice when, once gathering nuts and berries, she heard him singing alone in the autumn woods. It was a beautiful voice, deep and sonorous, with a poignancy that seemed to tell the bloom and dying of all things. Sweet as a nightingale, it sometimes sang to her heart in the forest of her dreams.

And this was not all. Made curiously enamored with this beautiful voice, once the gypsy girl had crept closer to the singer. For the first time in many months the gypsy girl felt a smile spread over her lips when she saw the savage man climb into a tree, and there wondrously imitate the songs of a bird singing on a bough.

When the winter snows and cold dark came, the savage man made fewer journeys down the trail to the village. He remained the long nights in the cave, alone with the gypsy girl. There were times a great restlessness came upon him in this confinement. Sometimes, as the gypsy girl plied her domestic chores, the savage man would break the silence and the tedium by strumming softly on a lute, or piping like a shepherd boy on a flute. Sometimes he would leave the cave and walk in the wind and snow for hours, as if indeed he were as much a wild creature as a man; the cave as much a den as a domicile.

But there were times when these diversions were not sufficient to vent the restlessness of his spirit. Sometimes the savage man seemed a beast in a cage, a cage that denied the wild romp of his blood. But the gypsy girl saw that his need to roar was in fact only a need to sing, and his need to hunt was in fact only a need to laugh. The gypsy girl thought that she had discovered a strange secret about the savage man: that his ferocity was not a need to kill, but a ruthless need to love.

Upon these occasions the savage man began to drink much wine, and when he did his fingers became nimbler and bolder upon the lute's strings; his lips bringing sweeter melodies from his flute. He would begin to sing, and his songs would be a roar that vented his pent-up need, one that filled the cave with a wild and lonely loveliness, like a lion waked without its mate, from a burial of forgotten ages.

And as he continued to drink wine into the night, there were times the savage man began to dance before the fire. At first afraid of his wildness, the gypsy girl shrank back into the cave's shadows. But with furtive glances from those shadows she saw that in his drunkenness the savage man was a very good, able dancer. In the soft fire-glow the savage man reminded her of a great golden bear dancing with the wings of a bird.

Grown greatly drunk one night, the savage man pushed the table roughly aside, and without looking at the gypsy girl, vehemently gestured for her to dance with him. Afraid of his drunkenness, the gypsy girl shrank back. But the savage man would not be denied, and with an angry growl marked out the place she should dance, opposite him, on the other side of the hearth. The gypsy girl froze, to which the savage man lifted a stool above his head, and bashed it to pieces against the cave's wall.

Afraid that the savage man was out of his mind with drink, and about to wreak an act of violence upon her, the gypsy girl stepped from the shadows to where the savage man had imperiously ordered her to dance. Afraid that the wine had made him mad, the gypsy girl complied with his wishes, dancing and twirling in place a few simple steps. She then stopped, as if waiting for the savage man to dance his turn, at which to her surprise, he gracefully did.

And so the night proceeded: first one, and then the other dancing, without once looking at the other; the savage man continuing to drink at intervals from the goatskin. Remaining on opposite sides of the fire, the gypsy girl and the savage man began to dance in simultaneity, and with greater and greater abandon; the golden-glowing stones before and above them, now vitally alive with the shadows of their animated forms.

And once the savage man had greatly surprised the gypsy girl by standing upon the table, reaching into the rafters, and bringing forth a splendid tambourine he had purchased on one of his village jaunts. Rapping it sharply and demonstrably with his hand, and then giving it to the gypsy girl, she began to rap and rattle it, and to dance with its jingling as she had done with her people since she was a small child.

So they continued; the savage man blindly drunk, and the gypsy girl shy and afraid, but obedient to the whims of his drunkenness. And as they danced the savage man wrapped the gypsy girl's red scarf sash-wise about her waist, and he bid her loose her long dark tresses, so that they were free to swirl about her. And once, mad with drink, the savage man bid the gypsy girl rattle the tambourine high above her head, even as he clownishly fell to his knees and clapped his hands before her.

When their dancing had ended, the savage man went to the goatskin, lifted it up on his shoulder, and drank great, long gurgling swigs from it. Then, as in a final fit of his ecstasy, he ran laughing out from the cave and into the night. The gypsy girl listened to his laughter, and to his drunken howls, and when she heard them drown in the night's silence, and knew that he had gone into the snowy forest as he was so wont to do, she began to rattle and rap the tambourine on the heel of her hand, elbow and hip. She began to twirl and dance with her shadow on the wall, dancing as she had danced since she was a little girl; unrestrainedly, freely and gaily.

But the savage man had not gone into the forest. He stood behind the horse blanket, smiling; mesmerized with the gypsy girl as she gaily danced and expertly rattled the tambourine before the fire; as in a ritual of youth and beauty; one prepared with cascades of long dark hair, copper bangles, painted toes and carmine-painted lips.

After a short while the savage man stepped into the cave, and when he did, the gypsy girl knew that he had seen her private moment. His eyes burned with bright blue fire, and when he rushed towards her the gypsy girl shrieked and made a dash to elude him, holding out a knife before her. But the savage man only gently laughed. He seized her, knife and all, and lifting her into his arms, ran out from the cave into the cold night, the knife falling like a child's toy from the gypsy girl's hand.

The gypsy girl did not resist this act of the savage man's drunkenness, this act that he would probably not remember tomorrow. She did not resist it with her fists, or her heels, or her heart. She did not resist it because she had learned to trust the savage man. Held in his arms, the gypsy girl felt safe as he waded into the snowy forest. She knew this strong chest and these strong arms. She had slept and dreamed in their shelter for many nights, protected from the cold, marauders and wolves.

In a small clearing among the trees the savage man stood still with the gypsy girl in his arms, his gaze lifted to the stars, as in a primitive genuflection. Holding him tightly, the gypsy girl lifted her eyes also, so that both were frozen in the same wonder, as they had become one.

.....As that first night when they lay in the dew-heavy wheat, she beneath the hunting net, and he, her hunter, gently at her side.....both staring at the same countless candles.....the same forest of stars.......

That night when he gathered her close into the lea of his body, he held her in a way that he had not held her before. And when he did she could feel his need: one that seemed both a fear to die, and a desperate want to live. When the serpent again stirred and pressed into her softness, she felt it possessed with an urgency she had not felt in it before, as it not only needed, but was asking to give its venom that was not venom, but a honey to her.

Yet when again the gypsy girl felt its retreat, its wrath once more tamed, she smiled brightly in the sanctuary of the darkness. She smiled because her fear had been replaced with a strange happiness.

She felt the breaths of the savage man become slow and even, and the tautness of his body relax as sleep began to drug the excited army of his nerves. But the gypsy girl did not want to sleep, because the gypsy girl did not think she could find a happier dream than the one that was dancing on the backs of her eyelids: the dream of a large shadow and a small one dancing on a glowing cave wall.

* * *

AND so the simple, wordless, hermitic life of the gypsy girl and the golden-haired savage man continued in the cave upon the mountain. Winter melted into spring, spring blossomed into summer, and the summer forests were painted once more with the bright leaves and waxy fruits of autumn. The cuckoos and the nightingales had fled, and the naked bushes, shorn of their green gowns, were bejeweled with bright hips and berries. The squirrels made granaries full of nuts high in the trees, and the trout sought the hidden grottoes in the deep pools. Laid siege to by an army of boreal winds, some with flecks of snow and a grit of ice in their gusts, the sun began to abdicate from its throne. In the dreams of wanderers, wolves howled; and in the dreams of the aged, a ragged fellow played a screechy fiddle outside their windows.

It was at this time that the life of the gypsy girl and the savage man changed in a sudden, dramatic, and unexpected way.

The savage man had risen early, and left on his horse before dawn. And when, mid-morning, the gypsy girl heard hoofs upon the rocky trail, she brightened with anticipation. But standing at the cave's mouth she heard more than one horse, and peeking from the blanket she saw three riders, men who had never visited their cave before; men with coldness and hardness in their eyes; men who had shot arrows through their dog.

Like a wild creature flushed from its den, the gypsy girl at once fled from the cave into the forest. But her flight in her bright blouse and bright skirts, as dazzling as a peacock against the autumn's grays and browns was espied by the men, and after a short, galloping pursuit through the trees, the gypsy girl found herself surrounded by three men who leered upon her with a lustful intent.

She had not time or presence of mind to scream out. With iron grips the three men pinned her arms and legs upon the cold ground. Tearing her blouse away, and with it gagging her so that she could not bite or shriek, like scavenging dogs they began to depravedly lick and kiss her face and breasts. Quickly they lifted her skirt, and while two of the men held her arms and spread apart her legs, the third man knelt down and prepared for his base satisfaction.

But it was a satisfaction he would never know, for as he was knelt before the helpless girl, a great hunting knife was stabbed clean through his back, ending his every living need. Spouting blood both from his wound and his mouth, the gypsy girl's assailant collapsed upon her with the wilted embrace of *death*.

His knife lodged in the man's back, the savage man's only weapons were his bare hands and his deft feet, and with these he prepared his defense against the two ruffians that the gypsy girl now recognized. They were those who had ridden with the savage man, chasing her through the woods the night she had fled the raid of their camp. Both had large knives, and both were bent on killing the companion who had deserted them.

Astonished, the gypsy girl watched as the savage man's strength and agility more than compensated for the loss of his knife. She watched as he dodged and darted, and swiftly kicked and landed vicious blows with his fists. She watched this man who gently held her in his arms each night seize one of the ruffians, slit his throat with his own knife, and then in lightning quickness dash the other's brains out on a stone.

And it was then, with murder in his eyes and dripping from his hands that the gypsy girl knew the savage man loved her, and in turn, she loved him.

Possessed of a boiling rage that exulted him, as he were a lion that had fought and killed fellow lions, the savage man stood over his kill;

the two dead men lying limp, dashed and broken at his feet. But his waked rage had not been sated. It was still hungry with a hunger his heart was incapable of confining. One by one the savage man lifted up the dead bodies over his head, including the one that lay slumped upon the gypsy girl, and time and again cast their corpses down upon stones and against the trunks of trees until their bones, skulls and spines were broken to pieces.

He had lifted her trembling in his arms, and she had clung to him tightly, as does a vine the trellis, knowing that she would give her heart to this man as she would never give it to another. Carrying her to the cave he again cared for her as he cared for her that first night, as she now realized he had always cared for her. But this time she was not frightened, and allowed him to bathe and salve her nakedness. Washing her painted and jeweled feet, she felt his bearded lips softly brush over them, as she remembered feeling them that night as she lay snared beneath his hunting net. This time a quiver rose from her feet and shivered through the deepest part of her; a quiver that was not fear.

After dressing her wounds, the savage man left the cave, and did not return until after dark. What he did with the men's horses and their dead bodies the gypsy girl would never know. The gypsy girl could not sleep. She lay awake, waiting for the savage man's shadow to appear on the cave's wall, and when it did she watched as he gulped long and deep from the goatskin, and then began to undress by the fire. Removing his tunic, the gypsy girl saw an ugly gash on his side. In his combat with her attackers, the savage man had incurred a serious wound.

This night when the savage man blew out the candles and came to the gypsy girl the gypsy girl turned to him as she had not turned to him before. She lifted his nightshirt, and with delicate fingers began to examine the wound that he had received for her sake. She rose and re-lit the candle, and proceeded to nurse him in the same fashion he had nursed her; washing away the wound's dry blood, and then cleansing and salving it.

The knife had gashed his side and part of his groin, and only inches away, even at her painted fingertips lay the secret, dangerous serpent fully exposed in its nest; the serpent that had ever swelled and risen when the savage man had gathered her into him. The gypsy girl had never seen a man's genitalia before, and she thought the serpent, limp and sleeping, not ugly or wicked, as she had thought it to be. She thought the serpent and the two large eggs in its nest were beautiful.

The gypsy girl had seen many cobras; cobras that she knew were full of dangerous venom. She had seen her people keep them in baskets full of reeds and wet fig leaves, and when they played flutes the hooded snakes would rise up from their baskets, conjured by the flute's music, and then gracefully sway before their conjurer. The gypsy girl had thought their creature a thing of grace; possessed of a noble strength.

A great yearning woke in the gypsy girl's heart, one that breathed through her like the fury and beauty of a storm. And as it did the cobra before her began to stir from its sleep. Curious of such sweetness, it began to swell, and erectly rise to the flute of such a strange lovely melody in her heart; rising with fullness; with mystery; with miracle.

She who had charmed it forth was unafraid. This was no creature possessed of wicked fangs and venom. Once risen, it seemed neither wicked nor ugly, but endowed with a graceful loveliness. The gypsy girl was as much mesmerized with this cobra as this cobra was with her. Both were transfixed with the other's need. As to break the spell, the gypsy girl leaned gently forward, and as a child kisses a flower, kissed the beautiful creature that had heard the passionate song of her heart.

The gypsy girl lifted her gown with the pink roses up and over her head, her dark silky tresses falling over her brown breasts and hips. She laid down, and like a butterfly sunning on a flower, spread the wings of her young slender legs.

The gypsy girl no longer wanted to be a girl. The gypsy girl wanted to be a woman, initiated into the mysteries of womanhood by this savage man she no longer feared or hated, but had learned to love more than anything she had ever loved before. The gypsy girl wanted the songs and storms in his heart. She wanted the murder she had seen in his eyes. The gypsy girl also wanted to be murdered. She wanted to be murdered by the beautiful cobra that had risen to please her.

* * *

AND as the snows of winter came, the savage man and the gypsy girl lived as lovers in the mountain cave. Although they did not speak, there were often smiles on their lips, and laughter in their eyes, as if their souls, far wiser than their tongues, were speaking a language known to them alone. Sometimes they would sing, and although neither understood the other's song, they heard the music in their voices. They were like different birds in different cages, singing in one sunny window.

The savage man hunted, trapped and fished, and made great heaps of wood for the fire. The gypsy girl kept the cave clean, neat and pretty, and prepared their meals at the hearth. The savage man tended to their horse and their dogs, and went to the mill and village to buy foodstuffs and other supplies. But the savage man no longer returned late from the taverns, and the gypsy girl no longer heard the shrill voices of tavern women, or smelled perfumes in his beard when he returned. The gypsy girl was happy, because she knew the savage man was saving the gifts of his heart and strong body for only her.

When the savage man came to her in the night the gypsy girl opened her arms to him, because she had opened her heart to him. The savage man taught her many exciting and tender things, things that made her quiver with new joys, and cry out in voices she had not known slept inside her. It pleased the gypsy girl to receive the savage man's love, to excite and tame the wild strength of his passion; to fuel and quench his fires. She liked the storms of his love, and the calms that followed in their wake.

One early afternoon when the winter had passed, leaving only the traces of its deepest drifts in the ravines and the places of darkest shadow, the savage man returned to the cave with a strange, agitated urgency. He ordered the gypsy girl to bundle up her few possessions, and with them mount and ride with him upon his horse into the forest.

They rode swiftly and silently through a part of the forest that the gypsy girl did not know. For an hour the horse's hoofs pounded through the giant pine trees until they finally halted on a bluff overlooking a small hollow. From this hollow wafted smells of burning wood and roasting meat, and with these smells a hammer on an anvil, echoes of children's laughter, and what sounded like the lazy lilt of an accordion. The savage man lay down on the half-frozen ground, and motioned for the gypsy girl to lie beside him. From here both peered down at the bright, vivacious scene that had invaded the gray sullenness of the sleeping woods.

At once the gypsy girl's eyes brightened, and a smile beamed upon her face. She at once recognized the wagons, tents and horses of her caravan, the caravan of which her mother and father, and her brother and sister were still a part; the same caravan that she had fled that terrible night nearly two years before. The savage man was granting the gypsy girl her liberty. He was returning her to her people.

But it was a joy that cleft her heart in twain.

How could she leave the savage man whom she had learned to love in both the nights and in the days, as much in the snowy winter as the green-leaved summer? The gypsy girl looked at the savage man standing near his horse, preparing to depart. She knew she must return to her people's wandering, to her dancing and singing in village squares for pennies and bread. She knew this as well as she knew that the savage man must return to his cave, his taverns and the enjoyment of his whores.

The gypsy girl went to the savage man. And when his face turned to her it was full of tears, even as her face was full of tears; and in their eyes both could see the great ache, disguised as joy, that had come to their hearts. The gypsy girl clasped his large strong hand in her two small ones, and pressed it to her heart, then to her breasts.

The gypsy girl led the savage man to a nearby thicket, its ground still covered with splotches of icy snow. There she slipped her skirt to her feet, and stepping from it, laid her nakedness on the dead needles and cold snow. The savage man knelt, and lifting her slender brown legs so that they rested on his broad shoulders, came into her; even as her ankles kissed his ears, and her painted toes mingled with the hips and sloes of the bushes.

She wanted him one last time in her softness, to be sown deeply with his strength. Her nails bit into his back, and with her arms and legs she tightly squeezed his body as she had never squeezed it before; as if trying to squeeze forth the deepest drops of his manhood.

And as the storm of his passion built, and began to sweep like a wave through her, so did it bring the memories that had made her surrender to its violent sweetness.

.......the flight through the forest and her hiding in the great tree, and how she first peeked through the leaves of the tree to see his sapphire eyes that pierced her heart as no swift arrow could.....the cold river, her race through the moonlit wheat, her capture like an animal beneath his heavy hunting net.....his drunkenness, his moodiness, his murderousness.....his bright blue eyes of care.......

And as she felt his love ready to spill into her, the gypsy girl spoke in the ear of the savage man as she had never spoken in it before.

"Give me your laughter, and the beautiful melodies in your throat! Give

me the way you ride your horse over the mountains, and the way you let fly your arrows at the hawk and the deer! Give me your blue eyes, and the golden curls of your hair! Give me your restlessness, your silences, the music of your dreams! Give me your heart....yes darling, give me your beautiful heart!"

The sky was now a bleared and murky gray, and a light snow had begun to swirl and fall. The gypsy girl turned one last time as she began her descent into the camp of tents, wagons and flamboyant skirts and scarves below. She saw the savage man and his horse riding away into the bleak woods, disappearing into them, not in flight or hiding, but like a wolf or a fox, as he was part of them.

The gypsy girl knew that she would never see the savage man again. But she also knew that he had given her the song in his heart.

····

·······

CHAPTER THREE

THE ABBEY ON THE HILL

North-central Italy: Circa, 1325

THE abbey on the hill had been built by Franciscan Brothers, with countless others from the nearby villages, well over a century ago. Indeed, there were none whose fathers could remember its stony emergence from the cypresses and cork oaks on the hill's crest. All accepted that it had been built in some vague dark antiquity, and would monumentalize the hill and the surrounding country-side for ages to come. It was an integral part of the fertile tapestry of their land; a kind of trophy earned by men, and awarded by Providence; a fortress of goodness and holiness whose stones had flowered from forth their prayers, their hearty soil, and the genial warmth of a sun that nourished the hearts of men, even as it nourished their olives and their grapes.

Its existence was far more than felled timbers, and the countless stones that the oxcarts had borne from the distant quarries, like giant snails inching up the hill's steep flank. It became a vital presence, a living *spirit* among them; one whose voice consisted of a clanging bell, and choirs of solemn chants taking wing on the breezes. But more than that, it was an ever open *eye* looking upon them; and looking upon them, it understood them; rebuking their errors, approving their charities, nursing their hardships. It was at once a severe judge and a loving mother; one that kept vigil over them at all hours and through all trials. Its presence spread over them, enfolded them; at times with sharp talons, at other times with caressing wings.

Like the swallows that came and went from the abbey each year, the tolling of the great bell seemed to announce the rites and rituals of their lives that also came and went: *first communions, marriages, baptisms.....* *plow-times, seedtimes, harvest-times.....youth and age, birth and death.....* as these rites were also hours, were also flights in some incalculable schedule of the stars and seasons.....an incalculable schedule that the creature of *Man*, as its subject, must obey.

The image of its high walls, roofs and bell-tower had been impressed upon all whose eyes had ever lifted to it. From childhood to old age, to the day they quit the toils of this world, it lived inside them. From the break of day when it stood gleaming humbly majestic in the rising sun, to the hour when night's shadows climbed its whitewashed walls, it loomed sentinel-wise, even throne-wise over them, as well as inside them. In storms it was a beacon; in war, a bastion; in sickness, a pillar; at death the abbey became a foretelling and promise of the mansions of the Angels.

As the polestar is to the mariner, so the abbey was to those tossed in the tempests of life's dark confusions. As the plumb line is to the carpenter, it lent them a truth by which things could be seen in their rightness or their wrongness. Like a loving mother, it opened its arms alike to the child with a clean heart, and the one whose heart had been soiled.

Like a coin, its image was engraved on their hearts, a symbol, and constant reminder of all that it represented and embodied. It had become the living pulse, the very heartbeat of this people, meting out and measuring the brief, precarious moments between their cradles and their graves; sounding the faint tolls of their passing hours and days on their journey to Eternity.

As the moon is an hourglass, and the stars its sifting grains, so the abbey on the hill was a sundial, patiently telling the shadows of the passing moments of a rising and setting sun. Before it men felt life's littleness, brevity and vainglory. They counted Time's blind, inexorable march. Before it they felt how brief were the toils of their ploughs and their hammers, how vain their jewels, their horses, and the glitter in their coffers. They felt the certainty and the mystery of their death.

.......Oh, but what passions may rage like wicked fires in the knells and prayers, the swooping swallows and circling stars of Time, even as its grains and brief hours sift softly through its glass.....Oh, how the prisoner may rattle his chains in defiance, before he is summoned to the gallows..... the gallows through which the shadows of night and day pass...

* * *

INSIDE the abbey on the hill the *Brothers of Francis* lived a very quiet, orderly and contemplative life. They lived in constant obedience to the bell, and the canonical hours and offices of prayer it continually announced. Their lives were simple, humble and pure, virtues for which they had sworn vows to uphold. Like soldiers swearing to give their lives for a liberating cause, the *Brothers of Francis* had sworn to live and die heroically for God's love.

To complement and encourage these spiritual soldiers, the architecture and grounds behind the abbey's walls reflected the ideals they strove to exemplify. The arches and pillars, arcades, windows, walks and hallways were constructed in simple *Gothic* lines, mirroring the architecture of simplicity and grace they were trying to construct in their souls.

This simplicity was adorned by a carefully groomed and nurtured beauty. There were lovely flowerbeds of roses and lilies, and on window sills there were potted geraniums, violets and nasturtiums; as they were splashes of bright color dabbed by brushes of the Angels. There was a pool where glittering goldfish swam, and cages hung from archways where linnets and wild canaries sang. There were rose trees, and in one corner of their grounds an orchard with apple, fig and cherry trees. In another corner were a piggery and hennery, a buttery, a barn and a stable for their beasts. Sensing its tranquility and safety, a flock of doves had come to live with the brothers, softly cooing on their walks and roofs, and pecking the meals of crumbs the brothers spread for them. About the bell-tower swallows suavely swooped, like tiny acrobats of a circus, blithely exalting in the serene airs.

The brothers lived a very humble and ordered, and in many ways idyllic life, but one that was not immune from human complexities and trials. Beneath the calm, pure veneer of their simple devout lives, the *Brothers of Francis* remained human, and subject to the same foibles, greed and temptations of the flesh as their brothers outside their walls. Despite their prayers, penances and confessions, antipathies and grudges developed among them, and with them favoritisms, jealousies, and the lisping whispers of spite and scorn.

There were also special friendships, friendships that sometimes developed in surprising ways and among unlikely brothers; friendships among the young and old, the weak and strong, the jovial and the solemn. Such was a friendship that had developed between one of the younger brothers with a priest who was significantly older than he; a priest who was of great importance and stature in their holy community.

Father Giovanni was the sub-prior, a studious priest who was acknowledged for his compendious learning and his unwavering adherence to monastic mores and rules. Although there were other scholars among the brotherhood, Father Giovanni had not an equal among them. His Greek and Latin were impeccable. Concerning legal matters, it was his judgment that was most listened to, and it was his opinion that was often responsible for persuading deciding votes in the Chapter House. It was he who was ever elected their representative at the ecclesiastical conferences. In addition, it was commonly presupposed, and consensually agreed upon by the brothers that Father Giovanni would one day succeed their aging abbot as the new abbot of the *Brothers of Il Poverello*.

Father Giovanni was a scholar through and through; solemn, austere, and contemplative. These qualities were reflected in his appearance. He was thin, tall and erect, and though his complexion was pale, it was in no way washed or sickly. His eyes were quiet, dark, and full of muse and serious consideration, and although not warm, yet they were not cold. When he smiled he did not smile fully, but only partially, as with politic restraint; as if obedient to an ascetic discipline that would not permit his will to forego or overstep its bounds.

Though tall, spare and imposing, there was an overall delicacy about his person, one that brooked on effeminacy. His features were finely chiseled, not broadly carved. His lashes were dark and long, and his fingers felinely, maidenly slender. His mouth was sensual, almost as sensual as a woman's mouth, like a ripe fig or cherry, but a sensuality that was slightly pursed, and firmly safe from yielding the secret of its sweetness.

He was considerate, kind and just, but whether due to his excellent gifts, or the post that he was posed to inevitably inherit, he was enveloped by an indefinable, although palpable air of superiority. The embraces he gave and received were light, and not vigorous, as given by the brushing wings of a bird. His laughter was genuine, but not hearty; issuing from his mind, and not his bowels. His words were measured, and never rushed in the cascade of a moment's passion. Despite the respect his qualities deservedly demanded from others, there was about Father Giovanni a cold air of aloofness.

It was for these exact reasons it seemed most improbable that a friendship had developed between Father Giovanni and a younger brother of the Order; Brother Maria.

In the realm of their brotherhood, a more sharply contrasting personality could not be found. Although by no means a slow scholar, the young brother could not begin to compete with Father Giovanni's erudition. Although punctual and disciplined, and a follower of their Rule in every way, Brother Maria lacked the exactness and rigidity of the older priest. Although one was about to inherit the abbacy, the other seemed altogether uncaring whether he became a priest or not.

Among this flock of humble brothers, Brother Maria was indeed singular. While staying well within the parameters of proper humility, prayer and duty, at the same time he seemed to break the mold of a monk's habits and behavior. His beautiful sonorous voice rang out in their hymns, gathering and inspiring the lesser and weaker voices about him. His ebullient laughter brought smiles to faces in all quarters of their holy fortress, even to the glum and the vinegary; even those deep in prayer and worship. He also owned a special gift for dancing, and was light on his feet as none in the brotherhood had ever seen before; dancing and sometimes singing on the walks and in the courtyard. Strong of body, he was a robust worker, and could lift loads that others could not, and continue well after his brothers were flagged. He loved the four-footed creatures in their fields, cotes and stables, and they in turn seemed to love him. Many were the times he was seen feeding them apples and biscuits, and speaking to them, almost conversing with them, as if speaking a secret language, one that only they could understand.

Like Father Giovanni, Brother Maria's appearance reflected the qualities of his personality. Happy and convivial by nature, his face was fair and flushed with florid health; his tonsure, and fledgling beard, a flaxen gold. This, with his bright, sapphire-blue eyes, the pearl white teeth in his smile, and his broad shoulders that tapered into a lithe, muscle-strung body, at once distinguished him apart from the other brothers. Indeed, most of the brothers had never seen a man with a fair complexion; with blue and not umber eyes; with golden hair, and not dark; a thing that quickly earned him the nickname in the brotherhood: 'Brother of Gold'.

As Father Giovanni's physique touched of the effeminate, Brother Maria's was manly, like a hunter or a warrior. And yet, as it was an androgynous illusion, there seemed the lilt and fragrance of a sensuous loveliness about him. Like his name, a name used by both genders, he seemed at once brutal and fragile, roughly made and delicately honed; a creature at once fashioned for the rigors of battle and the poetry of courtship.

It was therefore curious how the austere, scholarly priest and the jocund, eccentric young brother developed such a friendship; one being solitary and aloof, and the other wearing his carefree heart on his sleeve. They somehow seemed enamored and infatuated with the other's differences. It could not have been more unlikely, and yet in the three years since Brother Maria had entered the brotherhood, it had become obvious to all that it was true. Many were the times they were seen walking together, or sitting, talking and feeding the pigeons together on a garden bench. Hearing a bit of news, the vivacious young brother rushed to the studious priest, that he might be the first with whom to share it. When he had a question about his studies, a passage of scripture, or any other matter of monastic life, Brother Maria sought out the austere priest, and the priest would drop any task in hand to listen, consider, and give an explanation or advice. Inaccessible and aloof to the other brothers, Father Giovanni seemed perfectly friendly and open to this younger, unique brother. In those moments unclaimed by prayer or duty, the priest and the young brother were inseparable.

They were like mirrors, reflecting each other's image, images that mesmerized with the costumes of their opposites: that in some odd, inscrutable way made compatible the incompatible, harmony from antipathy; the tall, dark and gaunt one peering at the well-built, fair and lusty one; the scholarly and refined, looking upon a wild-eyed child of the fields and forests; one who had been raised under a father's strict rule, the other who had played on a mother's breast; one who toiled and studied beneath the sun, the other who sang to the stars and moon.

But there was more than these great differences. There was a likeness and a sameness that did not first meet the naked eye, and this, perhaps more than their antithetical features, attracted, united and bound them.

Both were unique, sculpted apart; distinguished from the other brothers. Both seemed to have tapped the deepest well in their souls, drawing from the deepest place that life had given them. Both had great strengths, strengths that were acknowledged by all. Both had weaknesses, weaknesses that were recognized, as well as lent sympathy by the other. Both were endowed with special gifts, gifts that gave them richness, even a mystery that others did not own.

When Brother Maria was troubled, or when he needed explanations, he would seek out Father Giovanni's counsel and higher intellectual understanding. His confusions would disappear with his friend's clear concise words. This teacher-student relationship was often answered commensurately in the theologian's heart by his friend's impetuosity and childish passion, things that his calmer and graver, more solemn nature did not own, but secretly envied and delighted in.

The great differences, and the mysterious attraction the two monks had for each other's company was accentuated by their upbringings, and some felt that herein resided the inscrutable secret.

Both had been orphans; Father Giovanni having been adopted by a scrivener whose wife was barren. An older couple, they had raised their adopted son with great care, providing for his every need. A quiet child, he had retreated into the great forest of learning, becoming a scholar who quickly outshone all about him. Quiet, shy, and bookish, he showed no interest for the opposite sex, and when he announced his interest in the priesthood, his parents were not only not surprised, but eagerly delighted.

On the other hand, Brother Maria's upbringing was shrouded, at least in part, in a mist of vagueness. In some way he had been adopted from an orphanage of the Church, and like Father Giovanni, had been raised by an older, childless couple; a couple not as prosperous as had been Father Giovanni's parents, but nevertheless, good and caring. He too had been quiet, well-mannered, and of a studious nature, and encouraged by his pious parents, had voiced early on a special love of God and a monastic inclination. It was at this time his given name was changed to *Maria*.

This much was known to be true about the young blond brother. But there had been bits and pieces rumored of his childhood years, the years before he had been found among the unwanted and the illegitimate. These rumors varied greatly, but a popular one was that when a boy he had lived with a band of uncouth wanderers, a band with an unsavory reputation. Embellished as rumors often are, some suggested that the band in which he had lived were no more than bandits and cutthroats. Some rumors smacked of the preposterous, proposing this golden brother had lived deep in wild forests, in the haunts of wolves, bears and cougars, and that, suckled and weaned in these wilds, the milk of these untamed creatures still lived in his blood. It was said he spoke another language, one that wild creatures understood. When asked about such outlandish rumors, the boyish brother crimsoned, flashed his blue-eyed smile, and let forth the trumpet of his signature laughter, at once dispelling such nonsense from his questioner.

There was a thing, common to the two orphans and their upbring-ings that at once illustrated their sameness and great differences.

When he was young, Father Giovanni found moments to draw, and when he drew he drew the solemn, austere faces he saw on the walls of churches; the stern faces of the Disciples, the Martyrs and the Saints, as well as the contorted faces of the damned, those who were being tortured and tormented in hell. Sometimes he even drew the terrible faces of hell's monsters and horned devils.

Maria also drew in his secret moments when he was a boy. But he did not copy the statues, or the characters painted on the church walls. Rather he drew pictures of women, naked women; like the women he saw bathing in the river when he was very small. He decorated their breasts with roses, and between their legs he drew nests of birds. Sometimes he drew naked men as well; men from whose genitals grew vines; flowering vines that stretched to the nests between the women's legs.

The friendship between the priest and the young brother was very unusual. It was inexplicable to those that beheld it. The one seemed to fulfill some hidden need in the other, but what that need was, none could begin to tell.

There were even times, unseen by any other, when Brother Maria brought a smile to the theologian's grave stern face. From a window in his office, Father Giovanni would sometimes look down at the courtyard where the young brother was giving singing lessons to some of the senor brothers; as he was their choirmaster, parading and waving his arms grandiosely before them. On other occasions he watched as he gave these tottery old brothers dancing lessons. Some of the brothers were propped by sticks, canes or crutches, things that Brother Maria would take from them, and with a bent back and limping steps clownishly imitate their dotage, dancing before their laughing faces, laughing as Father Giovanni had never seen them laugh before.

Seen in the privacy of his study, these things would crack the pale plaster of the priest's stoic face into a smile, one that broadened as none in the brotherhood had ever seen it broaden; even bringing a gentle laughter from his heart. Sometimes, with this laughter, his eyes blurred with tears.

* * *

BUT there would come to be another who would compete with the stern, ascetic, future abbot for the friendship of this young brother; one who would take his heart right from his grasp.

The abbey was surrounded by high stone walls, walls that were intended as a defense against the evils of the world. But deviltry and sin are not only armed with battery rams and cannons, but with the cunning of thieves; a cunning that may pick the locks of the heart. Vices existed here. Deceits and envy sometimes spread like angry rashes beneath the brothers' holy habits; breaking out into harsh words, or even, in rare cases, fists of brother against brother. There were occasional larcenies of precious vessels and monies. There were rare, but nevertheless real instances of drunkenness, and sexual depravity.

Nor were the abbey walls sufficient to keep out temptation, that spirit that owns countless faces, and countless tricks to tease and flatter the soul. Although the high walls defended against the hostile dragoons and foot soldiers of the world, it offered no defense against the arrows of its archers.

On warm pleasant days the songs of a flute could be heard in the vale below. This was not unusual. The country-side abounded in sheep and goats that were tended by shepherd boys and girls, most of which had wooden flutes upon which they played to while away the long, lazy hours between dawn and dusk. Their ditties were often quite sweet and clever, and struck through with trilling flights of musicality. Like larks greeting the pavilions of day, they lifted on the breezes to the abbey, their wings of sweetness fluttering over the high walls of its fortress, finding and delighting the ears of its holy prisoners.

Again, this in itself was not unusual. The fields were filled with lovely, soporific melodies accompanied by the lazy tinkling of sheep and goat bells. But what made these particular melodies different, as much a distraction as a satisfaction to the brothers in the abbey was *who* and *what* they conjured. For with the notes of the flute came the picture of its player.

The flute's player was a shepherdess, one who lived in a nearby hut or tent, whose exact whereabouts were not known. The fields that her sheep and goats grazed were the meadows at the foot of the hill upon which the abbey sat, and into which the abbey's own grain fields extended. Toiling in these fields the monks on occasion saw this shepherdess, and became acquainted with she who sent such pretty songs over their walls; deep into their hearts and prayers.

She was young, but not so young as to be still a girl, nor so old as to be yet a woman. She stood on the cusp that was a pedestal of her sex, an angel of beauty on which time could cast no net or stake no claim. She was exchanging the smock of childhood for the gown of womanhood, and in the brief moment when she stood unclothed, she bathed in the rare moment of her sublimity. She was at once a frisking colt and a beautiful mare, a colt and a mare that, on a cusp between adolescence and maturity, possessed the might of a mighty stallion.

As a ripe plum exudes sweetness, so the shepherd girl exuded sensuality, one that was not missed by the laboring monks. Kissed by the sun, and frolicked by the breezes, their humble eyes could not help but stray and fix on her budding breasts, slim waist, and plumping buttocks. These things were decorated with dark, luxuriant, waist-long curls, and a pretty face that peeked like a pink rose from their glossy vines. It was this face, and its delicate lips brought to her wooden flute, that brought more than music to the brothers when they heard the flute's silver trills in their prayer stalls.

The soft lilt of the flute's notes teased the starved brute of *desire* from the dark dens of their blood, and consequently, midst the monotonous drone of their offices the brothers were visited by visions of slender arms, lissome legs, and a freshly budding bosom. Like the flower crowning a vine, they saw a flute raised to a pretty face, and then the opening of a soft pink mouth that was the tantalizing rose of a beautiful, albeit forbidden garden.

When they retired after their last prayers, the flute would fill the violet of day's close, granting even more beguiling fantasies of its pretty player. When they knelt, and harshly slapped their bared backs with flogs, they felt feet, lovely as petals raining upon the sting of their hurt. When they lay upon their board beds, they sometimes felt fingers dance caressingly over their tired bodies, as they had seen her fingers dance up and down her flute. They felt the long tresses of her hair brush over them, from head to toe, brushing, and sometimes tickling the dangerous, poisonous flower of their *desire*.

Not in words, but in the wordless language of the sexes the young shepherdess knew the mystique and sway she held over these mendicants whose teams worked in the fields. She could feel their eyes dwelling upon her. Although she ignored their smiles and halloos, she could feel the stir, bristle and hunger of the male animal beneath their robes.

These things were a great amusement to the shepherdess, and in the idleness of her daylong watch over her sheep she played games with these religious men whose vows were no defense against the woman hunger she incited in them. She purposely pastured her sheep near where they engaged in their labors, and when she did she played upon her flute, or let out little giggles to pique them the more. She sometimes adorned her hair with flowers, or ate a ripe fruit before them, opening her mouth wide to an apple, or playing with grapes and cherries with her tongue. She decorated her bare feet by placing berries between her toes, only then to bring those toes to her mouth, licking them like a preening cat. She sometimes feigned a scratch got from a thorn, and lifting her skirt as to inspect it, offered a peek of her knee, sparkling like a diamond in the sun.

But these games, and the great sway of power the young girl held over the starved senses of these monks was to change, and in a most unexpected way. Another monk began to join the teams that issued from the abbey's gates, another monk that held as much interest and allure for the shepherdess, as she with her artful coquetry held over the monks that were drudging in the fields.

The young brother, Brother Maria, began to labor in their midst; his height and broadness, and the goldenness of his complexion distinguishing him at once among the others. But it was more than his youth and his handsomeness that first made the young shepherdess halt her bedeviling games, and step with a curious eye near the laboring brothers; it was the young monk's laughter that cleft the air like the ring of cymbals, The shepherdess saw that this brother was a bit of a jester in the suit of a monk, at times acting as he was a ship's captain, and his brothers were his slaves, and he went among them playfully whipping them with the cord of his habit. He sometimes even directed the solemn ascetics in little songs, as they were sailors singing a chanty.

And when this brother felt the shepherdess's curious eyes upon him, he beamed brightly, and shouted back at his fellow monks, and as he did, he cropped bunches of wildflowers, tossing them wildly in the direction of the shepherdess; flowers that the girl only gathered up as night was falling, and the team of monks had gone.

"*Ah, now I know why my Brothers in Christ are so eager to leave the abbey and work in the fields! They want to see the 'belladonna' herdess of the sheep!*"

Meanwhile the shepherdess was left alone, as if dethroned of her seductive sorcery by this young monk's flashing smile and bright blue eyes; eyes that did not seem afraid or hungry for her at all. She felt a blush burn through all parts of her, a blush with tongues of a flame that licked from her feet to her cheeks, kindling both her bowels and her breast; searing her softness, and leaving her tenderly burning.

It was spring, and the brothers were turning the winter-fallow soil. Each day the team came from the abbey's gates with their oxen, ploughs and spades, and worked until again the bell would ring, at which they would climb back up the hill for their prayers. Anticipating their descent, and the new young monk among them, the shepherdess would graze her sheep very close to where she knew their toils brought them. She would also make sure her hair fell in its richest luster down her back, its curls decorated with pretty flowers. This primping invariably gained the notice of the golden, carefree monk, who was not afraid to shout out his appreciation as he bent with his labors.

"*Brothers, look at the belladonna of the meadows this morning! The flowers in her hair are almost as pretty as the flower of her face!*"

Or......

"*Ah, pinch me brother, I am not sure if I am awake or dreaming! I see an Angel with flowers in her hair and roses on her cheeks! A vision! A vision! Nothing less than a heavenly vision!*"

Or.....

"*Will the angel of the sheep and goats play on her flute today? We know she can play, because we hear her in our prayers. Will you play for us today, sweet angel? Will you play for us, the poor diggers of dirt and luggers of stones? Will you lift our wretched hearts with your sweet songs?*"

Blushing with shyness, she would shake her head and deny his requests; and drifting away, soon drift back again for more flattery and cajolery.

But one day, unseen behind a clump of ilex trees, and not at all far from where the monks were working, she played her flute. She played the sweetest melodies she knew, only to nervously halt when she had elicited no response from the monks, not even from the young jovial one.

But after a goodly pause, a voice rang out, as from one who had been intently listening. Rich with the same melody she had just completed, it sang the words of the well-known peasant song.

"*Oh come to my arms*
When the moon is bright,
Oh bring me your charms,
Your sweetest maiden blisses,
Your blushes and your kisses,
Oh come when the moon is ripe,
And make a beggar a prince tonight!"

Stunned with the loveliness of this voice, and the singer's knowledge of this old song, the shepherdess stayed hidden from view, too shy to show her face, and knowing not what next to do. After a suspenseful pause, she softly played the first strain of the melody again, only to stop when the monk sang the first words of the song's next verse.

"*Oh will you be mine*
When the nightingale sings....."

The singer stopped precisely where her melody had stopped, as if waiting for her to play more, which she in turn could not help but do; only to stop again, as if waiting for the echo of this rich golden voice.

"*Oh will you be mine*
Beneath the tent of stars,
Sharing the glory that you are......"

She again began to play, but this time she was joined by the singer, and they continued, finishing the quaint love song together.

"*Oh will you be mine, maiden with wings,*
Blessing my heart, Angel divine?
In my arms, when the nightingale sings,
With kisses sweet, like honey-hearted wine."

The song completed, she remained behind the trees, her heart beating like a frightened rabbit's. And even as she did the abbey bell began to toll, calling the monks to prayer. Peeking through the leaves she watched as the brothers began to ascend back up the hill, laughing, and with their arms about each other's shoulders.

But a short way up the hill one of the brothers stopped, turned, and ran back down the hill. It was the brother they called *'Brother of Gold'*, the brother who had sung a duet with her flute. Running across the field, he ran directly to her hiding place.

"Ah, here you are! I thought perhaps I was singing with a ghost! But I see the one who plays such lovely melodies from her flute indeed has a face, a very pretty face, a very pretty ghost! You play sweetly, 'signorina'! You must have a very sweet heart to play so sweetly! Perhaps you can play your flute more often. I sometimes tire of our dreary hymns, and I remember many of the old peasant songs......you see my mother would sing many like them in the streets when we brought the bears......"

"Maria! Come on! We'll be late for prayers! If they bolt the gates before we return, we'll have to sleep in the forest, and in the morning be flogged to our bones!"

"And all because of your wild philandering!"

"Yeah, our backs flogged and blistered bloody raw because of you and your pagan songs, Maria!"

The golden brother smiled brightly at the fun-loving calls from his brothers, and with laughter in his voice spoke kindly to the young girl.

"I must catch the others and go sing some dirges, either that or the rack or tannery it seems. God bless you my good sweet sister!"

And with this he bent over her, and picked out a flower from those she had braided in her hair. He brushed it across her cheek, and then dropping it playfully on the top of her head, raced laughing away.

The next day, early afield and quickened with anticipation, the shepherd girl was disappointed when the abbey gates did not open to issue the team of monks. And when a weeklong spate of showers followed, and the muddy fields prohibited any possibility for plow or seed-sack, she fell into a gloom; angry at the sun for not shining, and the clouds for drenching the fields.

But in her gloom the shepherdess did not forget this brother's words and playful gestures. She thought of them again and again: all through the rain-soaked hours of the day as she sat beneath the dripping thatch-work of her shepherd hut; and in the evening as she was falling asleep on her bed. She remembered the music in this brother's voice, the soft silk of his blond beard, and the sky-blue warmth in his bright eyes. She remembered the special thing he had said to her, a thing like no other had ever said to her: *'You must have a very sweet heart to play so sweetly.'*

She remembered how he had brushed a flower over her cheek, a show of tenderness no other man had ever shown her, and then how he had let it playfully fall on her head. She had kept the flower, secreting it away in her blouse. Sometimes she would remove it, even after it had wilted, brushing it over her cheek and down her neck, imagining its petals a tender finger.

She pined to see this brother again, longing to hear his laughter and songs, and to see his erect frame and strong broad shoulders toiling in the fields. She began to yearn for the thrill that had thrilled through her when he had warmly smiled at her. She had even imagined what it would be like to run her fingers through the stubble of his tonsure, and the soft golden wool of his beard. Despite its wrongness, she wanted to bring her lips just once to his, and be wrapped in the beauty of his strong arms.

It was therefore a great joy to her when, a fortnight later she saw the troop of monks descend the hill with their plows and yoked oxen, reentering the fields that the sun had sufficiently dried.

Adorning herself with flowers, she moved her flock as near them as she could, and when she did she began to freely play her flute. At once the heads of the monks turned and lifted from their toils, and a voice rang out clear as a trumpet in their midst.

"Ah, the 'belladonna' of the meadows! Did you miss us, as we missed you when the sun did not shine? Have you come to play again for the drudging sons of Adam? Play, my angel, and ease the yoke of our labors, the curse of our fall! Serenade our labors, even as you serenade our prayers!"

And this time, without shyness, she complied. She began to play, openly, as she did each day the monks came to the fields. Sometimes the golden monk would shout out:

"Yes! Yes! I know that one! I have sung and danced many times to that one!"

At other times.....

"Ah yes, yes, I remember that melody now. The men used to play that one with their fiddles, and the women would dance about the fire clicking castanets in their hands and holding roses in their teeth! Yes, now I remember!"

He would ask her to play these songs over and over, singing the words he remembered, and inventing new ones for those he did not, sometimes even clapping his hands to their rhythms. Once, when very near where she was making her flute sing, he became very excited and rushed to her with his arms outstretched, inviting her to dance with him. And when she blushed and shyly declined, he laughed and danced a little dance before her, by himself. It was then, when he was so near she could touch him, so near she could smell the soot and candle-smoke in his robe, and more, the sweat of his masculine aroma, it was then that she first felt the brute might of the body beneath his robe: its strong arms and chest.....the throb of its mighty heart.....the wild animal she was sure that no prayer could ever tame. It was then she knew she wanted to know his strength and sweetness. It was then she was certain she wanted to hold his golden beauty; to subdue it, and if only for a moment, make it her own.

This play between the shepherdess and Brother Maria continued through the summer, whenever the team of brothers issued from the abbey to do work in their wheat and barley fields. Each morning the shepherdess would make herself pretty with flowers, hoping the abbey's gates would issue forth its gang of holy laborers. When they did, she would graze her flock near the brothers' worksite, playing melodies on her flute, at which the 'Brother of Gold' hallooed her, laughed and shouted how pretty she looked, and often accompanied the melodies of her flute with words sung with his beautiful singing voice.

On those days when the team of brothers did not issue from the abbey's gates, the shepherdess grew very sad.

One day when summer was leaving, and autumn was painting the fields and forests with its first colors; when the wheat beards were heavy, and the orchard fruits, ripening, this capriciousness between the shepherd girl and the handsome monk also matured, and as if one with the changing seasons, was given another complexion. The monks had descended the hill as usual, but after taking up their chores, the *Brother of Gold* separated from their pack. With a pouch slung over his shoulder, he walked away alone; only to disappear in the forest, a part of the forest the shepherdess knew very well.

Her sheep and few goats had found a nice plot of timothy grass. The monks were in the nearby field, and she would hear the barking of her dogs if a predator approached. No one would see her follow the handsome monk into the forest. No one would know. Perhaps she could see why he stepped into the trees alone. Perhaps he might want her to play her flute for him. Perhaps he would say tender things to her, or even brush her cheek with a flower again. Perhaps she might tell him in some way that she thought he was very kind. Perhaps she could show him in some way that she liked him.

Meanwhile Brother Maria had found what he was sent to find; the bank of a brook lush with watercress, and nearby, chamomile, the two herbs the Father Infirmarian had sent him to collect. Such errands were very welcome to Brother Maria, and filled him with a great pleasure. Near the brook he knelt, laid his pouch at his side, and closed his eyes. He inhaled the smell of the hatching earth and the decaying leaves, and listened to the rippling, purling brook. For a moment he imagined he was very small, a leaf or a petal being taken away on the brook's current. This thrilled him very much; to feel so small and so carefree, to be floating away into life's mysterious immensity.

But Brother Maria's meditation was suddenly disturbed, and he opened his eyes and looked about him to find the one who had intruded upon it. He had heard a trill of a flute, the shepherdess's flute; yes, certainly, it was the young girl's flute, even as he had heard her play it so many times in the meadow. But it did not seem to come from the fields that her flock was grazing, but from here in the forest, perhaps only a hundred paces from where he was knelt.

Smiling, Brother Maria began to expertly select and pluck the herbs he had been assigned to collect, only to stop a moment later when he heard another capricious trill. Standing, he surveyed the trees and thick foliage about him, but seeing no trace of the flute's player, he knelt once more to his task; only at once to spring to his feet at the beck of yet another trill.

Brother Maria beamed brightly, recognizing the game being played on him by the shepherd girl. Knowing that he was being seen by one he could not see, he laughed, and made the sound of a warbling thrush. This in turn was answered by a trill of the flute, which in turn was answered by another warble from his mouth. Another trill, answered by another warble, brought laughter and a shout from his mouth:

"Where are you my pretty little bird? From where do you sing your sweet song?"

There came a pause, and then another trill. Leaving his pouch at his feet, he climbed back up the bank, and shouted once more.

"Do you want me to find you, pretty bird? Do you want me to follow the sweet trail of your song?"

As in reply, there came another trill from somewhere beyond the green wall of foliage before him, at which Brother Maria stepped across the brook, and then a few steps in the flute's direction. As with approval, there came another trill from the invisible spy; and after a few more steps by the monk, still another. Delighted with the prospect of the little game, Brother Maria whistled like a thrush again, and forgetting his errand, stepped briskly into the trees to find the one that so teased him.

But when Brother Maria had made his way to the place where he was sure the trills had come, he did not find the one who had played them. As she was indeed a winged bird, the flute's player had flitted away. Brother Maria smiled when he once more heard the flute, this time its invisible player deeper in the forest. Amused and charmed, he brought his hand to his mouth and let forth another warble, even as he remembered doing so many times when he was a boy, and sped away to find this illusive player of songs and games.

And so the game of hide-and-seek continued; the trills of the flute teasing the holy brother to follow, and as he did, to echo the flute's trills with the birdsongs he remembered making when he was a child. Laughing, he would sometimes call out to this phantom somewhere in the green trees before him:

"Do not be afraid, O little bird of such pretty songs! Why must you fly away from me? I will not hurt you. I only want to see your pretty feathers. I only want you to flutter into my hands so that I may cherish you!"

There were times when he caught glimpses of her running before him; her homespun smock, her bare arms and bare throat, the raven mane of her flower-adorned tresses glimpsed like a frightened doe fleeing its hunter through the green and golden foliage. At times he was sure he heard her as from a tree, as indeed she was a magical creature of a fable, whose wings had lifted her to the bough of a tree.

But the flute trills and brief glimpses of the chase were to come to an end, an end punctuated by the deep, emphatic silence of the forest, and a place in that forest where the panting brother had never been before. Laughing at still another twist in their little game, Brother Maria called out:

"Where have you flown, little bird? How may I find you if you do not sing?"

But the only answer to the brother's shouts was a thunder of solemn, un-answering silence; at which, after a pause, he whistled like a bird, and shouted again.

"Do you not want to fly to me, O pretty bird? Do you not want to fly to my breast, where I shall protect you from the owls and the foxes?"

But again the only answer to his words was the muffling silence of the forest. Puzzled, and yet amused, Brother Maria remembered his errand he had left on the brook's bank, an errand he must complete before the bell rang for prayers.

He began his return to the brook, a way he was not now entirely sure of. As he did he felt an indefinable sadness, a disappointment at the game being over; so much that at each few paces he stopped, and let forth a warble, as if asking to play some more. And when he did he felt a strange, lonely longing, one he did not remember feeling before; as he was not a monk, or even a man at all, but a creature of the wild, one that was alone and lonely in the great wilderness of life. Again and again he stopped, and each time he did his little warble bore a greater want, a greater pain; as there had been a yearning waked in his breast, a yearning that he had never known, and never known, never quenched; its pangs somehow a deep part of him, and part of him, part of the forest as well.

As if in answer to this sharp longing, he heard the flute again. But this time it was more than a playful trill. It was a sustained melody, one whose sweet sad longing matched this strange, sweet new pain in his heart. It was not far away. It was not flitting here and there. It was not teasing, but imploring, like a bird singing near its nest, lonely for its mate. With warbles of his own, ones that welled from a deep place in his heart, he began to make his way to this song, one that seemed the sister of his longing.

He stepped into the small clearing from which the flute was playing, and there she was, her youth and sweetness free at last of all hiding. And yet like a forest sylph, she seemed an unworldly vision to his eye; too lovely to be true. She was sitting on a low bough of a great broad tree, her legs and feet dangling down, even as she was the tree's fruitage.

She did not speak; as did not he. And yet their hearts sang to each other: one with little flourishes of a flute, and the other with little warbles of a bird; her heart inviting, and his heart answering at the approach of his small slow steps; steps that were like the fluttering of wings back to their nest.

And reaching those small naked feet, he could not turn away. Like glistening apples, he took one in each hand, and closing his eyes pressed their sweetness to his cheeks, smelling and feeling their firm young ripeness.

Famished with hunger, the hunger that was the longing that had woke in his heart, he did what his blood, singing with that hunger demanded he do. He brought his lips to these apples, and began to nibble their delicious sweetness with small, soft, child-like kisses…..their toes, soles and heels smelling and tasting of the fertile fragrances of the earth…..their filth a cleanness, a goodness of soil, sun and rain…..the goodness of living flesh that is young once only, and whose health is to be given and enjoyed.

Piqued with their deliciousness, the greed of his hunger could not be stayed, begging and craving to be filled…..gliding up and over the marble of her calves, and then over her knees that were peeking from her smock….. and then under the smock to the secret softness of her young thighs….until finding and gathering her naked hams, he lifted her from the bough into his arms, laying her loveliness like a sheaf of grain upon the ground.

"Wait, Brother of Gold, only a moment, wait. I have something that will make it sweeter."

Hurriedly she stood and went to the tree. Deftly placing her feet on several of the trunk's knots and burls, she climbed up and, without looking found a blanket that was hidden in its fork; even as it had been planted there, like a squirrel hides its store of nuts.

…..the false voices of fear and abstinence at last quiet in their hearts…..a smock lifted, and with it a robe…..the forgetting of long prayers in an abbey, and the long, monotonous vigils of watching bell-tinkling goats and sheep…..left alone now to a loveliness that God's Eye was blind to…… meant only for the crucible of flesh and blood to foment its own miracle…….

* * *

FROM a long way off, as from the dead to the shore of the living…..the faint dull tolls of a bell…….

But in vain; the sleeper did not hear the bell's brazen tongue. Drowned in a blessed dream, a lovely dream garden called *woman*, he was oblivious of all nagging voices of the living.

Brother Maria opened his eyes, and smiled at the voluptuous s pleasures he lay upon. He bent over her sleeping face, like the face of a sleeping Angel, and then brought his lips to her cheek. As she was an idol, and he the grateful idolater, he softly, reverently kissed her breasts and belly, and then the mystic flower to which she had led him; the flower that had lent him a mystery no words could tell.

71

Oh how lovely, tender, oh what a perfect treasure, extinguishing all pain, all need, all want.......

But now this harsh, persisting sound, like a hammer on a smithy's anvil assaulting this dream.....this faint clanging, grating, gnashing......this bell that had now intruded upon his tender worship.....its echoes, like the can-nonades of a cannon, disturbing his dream's blissful garden.......

And then he was awake, and again among the living, having been found and goaded alive beneath the shroud of such a divine pleasure. Again he was a monk, a poor *Brother of Francis*, one dedicated to prayer, humility, chastity.....one who had been sent on an errand hours before, hours that now seemed many years.....an errand, yes, an errand.

Brother Maria leapt to his feet, the bell's last toll scolding like a laughing devil in the air. What was he now to do? He would feign some excuse, yes, some little excuse that his kind brothers would smile upon and believe.....*becoming lost, falling asleep, a difficulty in finding the proper herbs he had been sent to find.....*He would perform penances to redeem his lateness and absentmindedness. He would fast and flog, smear his face and chest with ashes, perform great labors. But first he must wash his face and hands in the brook, even his private parts. He must wash away the smells of love, a woman's love. He would lie to the infirmarian, Father Antonio, and also to the abbot; he would lie to God rather than confess this thing of shame, this senselessly stupid breaking of his vows. He would ask Father Giovanni what he must do; yes, that was it, he would ask Father Giovanni!

Panicking, Brother Maria donned his habit and then started away, only to stop abruptly when the sweet voice called out to him.

"But where are you going? Why are you running away from me?"

Brother Maria turned to the one with whom this thing had happened; his partner in this great crime. She was sleepily awake, and sitting aright on the blanket. Her hair was mussed, and fell long and tangled upon her naked shoulders and breasts. Like the young girl she was, she was pouting, like a spoiled child whose plaything was being taken away from her.

"What is wrong? Did you not like the game we played, the game I do not think you have played before? Please do not go. I know many more games. What would you rather do: kneel before clay dolls on altars, or play more games with me? Come, Brother of Gold, come back to my arms and let us play."

The young girl saw the struggle of his indecision; his wavering. She reached beneath the drape of her tresses, and brought forth her naked breasts, one in each hand. As they were an offering of two fruits, she held them out before her, invoking the god of his need; a god much mightier than his will.

* * *

UNPERTURBED, the abbey on the hill continued its sifting of Time's sands; a tedium that included slapping sandals, cooing doves, and the loud ringing of a bell. It was indeed an hourglass, one whose grains were softly whispered prayers. It was indeed a sundial, one whose shadows, like a flock of swallows, were the coming and going of a flock of friars from their worship.

Yet in the ranks of *Time's* slow, dull, ageless march to that shore Man's creature calls *Eternity*, what a rebellious falling out of ranks there may be, as if the rebel was defiant of *Time's* tolls and *God's* behests; as if he preferred the pain of living, to the reward of dying; as if an abbey on a hill was neither an hourglass nor a sundial,.....but a *mother*, whose arms opened to give her darling license to run, sing, and become lost in the storms of the seasons.

. . . .

. . . .

CHAPTER FOUR

CONFESSIONS

HIS prayer stall was empty at Nones. Ordinarily as punctual as the most punctual among the brotherhood, his stall remained empty through the entire afternoon office of their prayers.

Although unusual, and in most cases a severe violation of monastic rules, it was by no means unprecedented for a brother to be late, or even absent from an office. Fate played its tricks and set its snares behind holy walls as it did in the marketplaces of the world. On rare occasions brothers overslept, or did not hear the bell in a far reach of the fields, making them tardy for their devotions. On other occasions entire offices were missed due to any number of valid reasons: sickness, a snake-bite, a broken bone; a sudden storm waylaying a return from an errand to the mill, the sawyer, or while berry-picking in the forest. Rarer still, there were instances of brothers being robbed and beaten by a ruffian, or found slumped in a stupor, stupidly drunk.

But the curiosity surrounding the empty prayer stall waxed to concern when those who had accompanied the missing brother in the fields had no explanation of his whereabouts. Yes, he had gone to the fields with them, and yes, they had seen him enter the forest to collect herbs for Father Antonio. When the bell had rung for prayers, they had returned to the abbey, supposing he had heard it too, and would not lag far behind; or that he had quickly completed his task, and returned early without their seeing him. When his cell was found empty, concern mounted, and the intrigue grew.

The thing acquired an added peculiarity when Father Antonio, the *infirmarian*, was questioned by the abbot, Father Augustine. Yes, he had sent the brother on an expedition to collect herbs, and yes, the pouch full of the desired herbs had been placed on the table in the infirmary; albeit some of the herbs were very wilted, as they had been picked many hours before. But the brother had not been seen, either entering or leaving the infirmary. Yes, the timetables could indeed align; yes, the two times could match; yes, it was entirely possible that Brother Maria had delivered the sack of herbs while the brothers were at their prayers.

Halting the strict regimen of their routine, after their prayers the abbot ordered the brotherhood to look for their missing member, both in the abbey, and in the immediate grounds surrounding it; a hunt that ended empty-handed and without a clue.

When, at *Vespers*, the prayer stall was again empty, its vacancy was no longer merely curious, but a thing of worry and trepidation; as the stall was inhabited by a ghost; a ghost of one who, for whatever reason no longer could, or wished to worship among the living; leaving only the memories of a lovely golden voice; a voice that had given the drone of their prayers and hymns a lyrical, joyous heart.

There was yet another peculiarity, one that accentuated the silent concern that filled the soft drone of the brothers' prayers; a thing, or rather the *absence* of a thing that in some way magnified the intrigue that had invaded their holy home: *the dull silence that replaced the lilt of the shepherdess's flute.* Its playful trills did not drift through the chapel's window and into the choir where the brothers prayed. Its melodies did not dance among their prayers; the feather of its sweetness did not tickle their hearts and loins. This had the effect of making their orisons seem stale, laborious, and chore-like, as they had lost at once both the flute's trills and the golden voice of their beloved brother.

Instead of retiring to their cells to wait for the day's last office, the abbot bent monastic protocol again, and instructed the brotherhood to police the abbey with greater thoroughness. Darkness was beginning to fall, and teams of lantern bearing brothers went into the barn, granary and stables, and even into the sheepcote and piggery, looking for any sign of their missing brother.

There was only one brother, a priest, who was exempted from participating in this search. With an air of urgency, he was asked to immediately attend upon the abbot in his office. Prompt as he was always prompt, moments later Father Giovanni stood spartanly in the doorway of the office, and making a humble bow, and then crossing himself, entered.

These two men's physical attributes were a picture of great contrariety and contrast. Father Giovanni was tall, youthful, and straightly erect, while the abbot was short, crouched and gnarled with age. Their personalities were also very different. The young priest was quiet, contemplative, and evenly, even stoically tempered; the abbot was simple, gregarious, and like a spark from flint, quick to express emotion. But their offices allowed for these differences, and the young tall priest stood submissively before his squat abbot, like a soldier before his general.

"Father Giovanni, when was the last you saw Brother Maria?"

"At Sext today, Father Augustine."

"And not after?"

"No, Abbot Father, not after."

"And you have no idea where he might be?"

"None. Like the others, I am at a complete loss as to where Brother Maria might be."

"He has said nothing to you whereby you might surmise or deduce some fancy, or some will'o'the'wisp dream in his heart; nothing that would hint at some dissatisfaction, rebellion, even, God forbid, desertion?"

"No Father Augustine. Our brother's absence is as great a mystery to me as it is to all of the brothers in the brotherhood."

The abbot paused, and looked away. His back was permanently stooped, and this made his short stature even shorter, so that he needed an effort to lift his eyes to any he was addressing. It also added to a gnome-like bearing that the brothers kindly jested was about him. His tonsure was snowy white, and his small ears were pointed, and seemed ever pricked, so that when he lifted his sparkling eyes, as he did now to the tall young priest, there was something almost numinous, almost elfin about him. He seemed like one whose true home was not the abbey, but moonlit paths, brooks, and forest haunts; a magical creature in possession of things men's sluggish bloods did not know.

"I ask such questions, my good brother, because I, and I think a good many others know that you have a great fondness, and share a warm friendship with Brother Maria."

"Yes, that is true Father Augustine. But I believe many of the brothers share this camaraderie with Brother Maria. He is special, and I think he touches all hearts in a special way."

The abbot smiled, faintly nodded, and looked away. He then proceeded to make a slow circuit about his desk, before plopping down in his chair with a tired groan and the dead heap of a human toad. Once in the chair he fell into an inner muse; his gaze glassy, abstract, and absent, his hand slowly brushing the bristly, age-stunted beard on his cheek and chin. This meditation was only interrupted by the knitting, and then the smoothing of his brow, and several glances shot like arrows from his eyes to the young priest standing statuesquely before and above him. After a long moment in the twilight of this deliberation, he sighed deeply and spoke.

"*Yes, Father Giovanni, Brother Maria is certainly a special brother, a gifted and favorite brother among us, but you, more than others have always seemed to have a particular liking, a particular fondness for him, as well as he for you, a sort of kinship of soul that seems more than merely casual or courteous; that one might say transcends the brotherly.*"

"*It is true, father, we find it easy to speak of things together. When he has come to me for counsel, I have tried my humble best to lend it to him. As I have said, Father Abbot, I have always deemed him special.*"

"*But how so, Father Giovanni? Are you not referring to something other than his fairness, his blue eyes and beautiful singing voice? We all know that he is a good monk, an apt student, and is quickly maturing into an excellent candidate for the priesthood......*"

"*With your permission, Father Abbot; I am not sure that Brother Maria will ever be, and perhaps was ever meant to be a priest.*"

"*But what is this? There are only a few in the brotherhood that I deem as qualified. His conduct is impeccable: punctual, humble, good-natured..... his studies, well, they are sufficient. Has he confided something to you that I should know, some dissatisfaction of monastic life, some struggle or discontent, something that might help explain his mysterious absence? You are his good friend, but also his confessor, are you not?*"

"*Yes, I am Brother Maria's confessor, as well as one of his good friends, Father Abbot. But it is not what Brother Maria has either confided or confessed that makes me question whether he will continue in monastic life.*"

The abbot twisted the rotundity of his body in his chair, and lifted his eyes from beneath the snowy bushes of his eyebrows to the tall astute priest. The sprightly sparkle had left his gaze, and was now replaced with a child's quizzicality; a nakedness of soul that was full of the vulnerability of love and care.

"What is it, Father Giovanni? As your abbot, I would like you to tell me what you know, or if not what you know, what you speculate, or might even suspect about Brother Maria."

Maintaining his equanimity, after a stony pause, Father Giovanni replied:

"As you know, Father Augustine, the rumors of Brother Maria's early years are scant, and rumor has a way of becoming scandalous, and many times a travesty of reality; but nevertheless, the few stories rumored of his youth are quite unusual. For example, it is said those about him in his youth thieved and did unlawful things. It is said that his mother was very lovely, and she danced and sang in the streets with bears and monkeys to earn their bread.....that she was possessed of a great beauty, one that men found very beguiling."

"Yes, yes, we know that Brother Maria's upbringing was unusual, one might even say unfortunate, that he roamed with brightly dressed bands of storytellers and fortunetellers and the like, and that his mother's reputation was questionable, some say even shameful. But we also know that Brother Maria has given his soul to Jesus Christ, and that his pagan upbringing is long behind him. Why, even my namesake, the great Augustine, as you well know, shirked his sordid youth and gave his soul to God."

"But that is just the point, Father Abbot. I am not sure that Brother Maria has quit his past. I think perhaps it is a thing he cannot do, perhaps a thing in his soul he does not even want to do. I think it still lives in his blood, even as he prays and performs observances behind our holy walls.

You see, Father Abbot, it is not the things Brother Maria has spoken to my ear that gives me reason for doubt, but voices I believe I hear crying in his blood; voices from a deep place in his heart."

"What do you mean, 'voices crying in his blood', and 'things he cannot, nor even wants to do'? We must not judge, and conjecture is a dangerous, even a devilish game the mind may play on us. Brother Maria is a good, pure-spirited, model monk. Why do you say these things?"

"Brother Maria's blood, I mean the instincts in his blood seem heightened and very acute; very alive; as he hears and sees what others do not hear and see. I have sometimes been with him when he hears the screech of an owl in the woods. He screeches back to it, not as a playful child would, but as an owl to an owl, as he is about to fly to it; its mimicry so exact that the owl, as it was his mate, calls back again. When he rides one of our horses, he rides it not as it was a plough horse, but as it was a king's steed; riding it

not like a monk or a laborer, but spurring it like a warrior, as his heels in its sides and his whispers in its ear were coaxing forth an ancient, even a noble strength from the tired beast.

And once last winter, when a pack of wolves howled from the snowy woods, I watched as his face softened, and his eyes danced with a flame that had been kindled in his soul. He went to the window and looked into the dark night, even as though he was filled with sympathy, an inexpressible yearning, as the wolves were his true brothers; as he wished to let forth a great howl, a howl of longing to return to them.

And when the young errand girls from the village and the surrounding fields come to our gates, and Brother Maria answers their knocks........"

"Why do you stop, Father Giovanni? Go on. You have both the ear in my head and in my heart. What happens when Brother Maria answers these knocks from the servant girls?"

"Father Abbot, if I may, Brother Maria is possessed of striking, even what may be called very handsome features, features that he may have inherited from his unknown father, and a pretty, street-wise mother, features that are at once strong and manly, and yet lovely, like a maiden is lovely.....features that strike the hearts of these peasant girls, making them break into blushes and giggles, and a competing desire to speak to Brother Maria.... to sidle near him.....as they wished to touch him.....as they wished to kiss him......"

"Does Brother Maria encourage their behavior? Is there anything flirtatious about his dealing with them?"

"Nothing, nothing at all holy father, and that is the great mystery about the thing, about the fawning coquetry he exacts from these simple girls. He is kind and polite with them, but never suggestive or insinuating; never suave or brash with effrontery. And yet these girls cluster about him like bees about a fragrant lily; as if he was breathing a perfume, a honeyed perfume, one that was meant for women alone....to attract, flutter, and dizzy their hearts.

But Father Giovanni was not able to continue, for like an umpire of fate the bell for *Compline* now crashed over their heads, concussing through the walls and dispelling the spell of the strange things that had begun to rush from Father Giovanni's mouth.

As a spell had been cast over the listener, with the clanging bell the abbot shook his head and smiled a simple, half-senile smile, as one wakened embarrassed from a nap. He rose from his chair, and with his hooped back stiffly made his slow way to the young priest. Placing his hand gently on his arm, he kindly smiled, and motioned towards the door.

"*The bell for Compline. Perhaps we may continue this conversation at another time, a conversation that I must confess seems a little strange to me.*"

But as they were leaving the abbot's office, the abbot stopped once more, and lifted his elfin gaze to the much younger priest towering above him.

"*And you are sure you have no idea where Brother Maria might be, or what might have happened to him?*"

"*No, Father Abbot, I know nothing at all about Brother Maria.*"

As the two fathers walked to *Compline*, Father Giovanni slipped his hand into his cassock's large pocket. The note burned like a live ember in his clenched fist, even as the lie he had told his reverend abbot burned in his heart.

* * *

THE empty prayer stall at the brothers' final office was an object of worried speculation for the brothers. It was now undeniable. After the fruitless search of the abbey's grounds and after his prayer stall remained empty for a third consecutive office, it was now more than certain that something was seriously amiss. One of their Brothers in Christ, the youthful, likable Brother Maria was missing.

A sullen dread enveloped the brothers' liturgies. The empty stall now seemed a coffin, a coffin that contained a knowing eye, one weeping with a tragic fate it alone knew.

Gone was the sonorous voice that swelled their chants, and thundered golden in their recitations. Gone were the blue eyes, the flashing smile, and the broad-shouldered silhouette crossing the courtyard to the cloister after day's last prayers. Gone were the clowning dances before the marble statues of the Madonna and the Saints, and the pauses of their *Brother of Gold* when he lifted his eyes like a keen-eyed hunter, reading signs of the stars, and auguring predictions from the phases of the moon.

Tonight as the brothers silently entered the cloister, and one by one disappeared into their cells a stern, soldierly conviction accompanied their humble obedience: at daybreak they would scour wide the fields and thickets outside the abbey walls for this favorite brother whose vivacity meant so much to their simple, regimented lives.

But all members of the brotherhood that retired into the cloister did not remain in their cells. Less than an hour later one brother stepped forth, and although it was irregular, and a trespass upon the strict edicts of the abbey, he walked with brisk pace and raised cowl past the doors of his sleeping brothers. Still more unusual, when he emerged from the cloister he walked directly back from whence he had lastly come. The brother made for the chapel, but not by crossing the bright openness of the courtyard, rather circuitously, by keeping in the dark of the arcades; as if he did not want to make a shadow; as if he did not want to be seen by any eyes, even those of the stars.

Entering the dusky sanctuary, the brother dipped his fingertips in the font, made the Sign of the Cross, and genuflected. He then walked through the nave to the chancel, and knelt at the feet of the great Crucifix; only to stand, turn and peer carefully about the empty chapel through which he had just walked. As if satisfied, the brother then lit a small altar candle, and walked swiftly to the confessional, steeped in the shadows of the chapel's dark corner. Looking one last, as with a an eye of careful scrutiny about the empty chapel, Father Giovanni parted the curtain, and quickly entered the confessional, candle in hand. After a pause, he softly spoke.

"*The blessings of our Lord, Jesus Christ be upon you, brother. What burden weighs on your heart that you must confess it at this late hour?*"

At which the hooded, faceless penitent immediately whispered:

"*A sin that seems no sin at all; a burden that has given my spirit wings.*"

"*Brother Maria! The Abbot Father is very concerned. The whole brotherhood has hunted each inch of the grounds with candles and lanterns for you. They are prepared to comb the fields and thickets at daybreak. They will bring dogs from the village. Brother Maria, why have you not attended your offices? What has happened? Where have you been?*"

"*I have been hiding in the barn, in its loft covered with straw.*"

"*But why?*"

"*Because I am leaving, Father Giovanni. I am leaving the Brothers of Francis.*"

"*Leaving! What has happened, and why are you hiding, Maria? Not only as your confessor, but as your friend, you must tell me what has happened to you. Please, Maria, you must explain this thing to me.*"

The penitent leaned his hooded face forward, as did his confessor, even as they were two lovers about to kiss, stayed only by the partitioning grille. But they would not be denied. Their kiss passed through the grille, pressing not their lips, but burning their hearts with a passion that paled lesser affections. As the abbey and its brotherhood slept, and the jury of the stars kept their silent vigil, the two men whispered to each other the very meaning and essence of their souls.

"Yes, Father Giovanni, it is true: I am leaving. I am only waiting for the moon to rise, and for a signal to be given me. My mind is made up, and with it, all my heart."

"But what is this that you are saying? The moon? A signal? A signal for what and from whom?"

"I am waiting for an angel to play her flute. And I will go, Father Giovanni, I will escape from these stone walls that have been my sanctuary, but are now my prison. Oh yes, I will leave and go to my flute-playing angel!"

At this Brother Maria suddenly tore his cowl away, fully exposing his face only inches from the grille. His confessor was startled aback, as he was beholding something unnatural, even apparitional in the candlelight. The brother's features were flushed and animated as he had not seen them before; as a winebibber's features are exaggerated after drinking great quantities of wine. His mouth was spread into a smile of blissful idiocy; his eyes, dilated and dancing like leaping flames.

In an instant the mystery was solved and told. As the excited brother sought to find and fashion words, the father confessor spoke for him.

"Ah, yes, of course, you have fallen in love Maria. Yes, that is it. You have stepped into that deep rabbit hole that breaks hearts, even as it breaks the legs of horses, that rabbit hole the world terms 'falling in love'. That is the answer to the enigma; the reason, all in one, for your absence from our offices, for your rash decision and your strange fever. Yes, of course. You are drunk with the wine of a woman's love."

The penitent did not receive these words as a rebuke, but as an affirmation. He brightened the more, even as his spirit would dance like a living flame from his eyes and tongue.

"Yes Father Giovanni, you are very wise! You have read the wonderful secret in my heart! I have fallen in love with a woman, a beautiful angel! I feel as though I have wakened from an ancient sleep, as though I am new-made, as I have never seen the sun and stars, never felt the ground

beneath my feet; never heard the beating of my own heart until now!"

"You make this wisdom you credit me with very easy, Brother Maria. You are drunk with the oldest wine known to man, far older than that wine made from stomping the purple grape; far older, and I think far stronger. Your blood is swimming with the fumes breathed from a woman's charms, and it has intoxicated you beyond your reason."

"Yes, Father Giovanni, yes! You speak words of great truth! I am drunk with a woman's charms, a delicious wine I wish to drink until the day I die! And yes, love has taken my reason away, but it has left immeasurable riches in its stead, riches that make reason seem a child's toy of pinecones and straw! Never has my heart filled with such music! Never has it throbbed with such rapture! Never have I felt so alive, as my feet were roots digging into the earth for the first time, and my spirit, a vine blossoming roses among the stars!"

Father Giovanni saw that his friend was gripped by a spell, one that had besotted him with the dreams and flatteries of lust. He knew that truth is the greatest foe of such spells, and resents the least intrusion. As a drunkard must babble and drivel back to his senses, so must he let his friend burble forth his tale.

"Tell me briefly, Brother Maria, about this thing, this adventure that has happened to you."

"What is there to tell, other than to say an Angel disguised in a peasant's smock led me deep into the forest trees, and stepping from her disguise, shared with me the treasures of her heavenly kind? What is there to tell, other than to say I found in her arms what not all my prayers, chants and penances have given me? What is there to tell, other than to say that the boy who went looking for herbs, has returned a man who found untold riches, riches that he gathered and are now singing in his heart!"

"Who is this girl?"

"No girl at all, Father Giovanni, but an angel in the guise of a simple shepherdess!"

"The girl who tends the sheep in the vale below our abbey?"

"Yes, that precious darling one!"

"She is young, Maria. She is very young."

"Yes, she is young, only a girl, but one endowed with the gifts and the wisdom of a goddess."

"And her name, Maria, what is your angel's name?"

"Her name? I do not know her name. What do names have to do with

love's miracle? We have scarce spoken, at least with words. We have used a sweeter, deeper language to share the secrets of our souls."

"And you plan to steal away with her?"

"Yes, when the moon rises and her flute sings."

"But where will you go, and what will you do? You simply cannot live like bears in the forest. The autumn frosts will soon be here, and shortly thereafter, the winter winds and snows."

"I am good with my hands; a regular potter with clay, a carpenter with wood, a hunter with snares, nets and a bow. I will chop down trees, lift stones, plough fields....hawk, beg, bury the dead, dance in the streets......."

"Dance in the streets, Maria?"

"Yes, even as I have told you many times before, as I did with my mother when I was a boy, with a bear dressed in a skirt and ribbons, and raised on its hinds."

Winded with the excited words that had welled from deep inside him, Brother Maria fell silent, exhausted from his exuberance. Silence once more filled the confessional; a silence so silent the candle's hungry flame could be heard eating its wax. As one breaks a great fast with a nibble of bread, Father Giovanni at last broke the silence with a faint whisper; a whisper that, although unintended, crashed through the confessional like a peal of thunder.

"A hot spark becomes a cold ash very quickly, Maria. This young girl may be only wearing a mask of whimsy and coquetry. She may be married, as are many of the peasant girls at a very early age. The wisdom this goddess owns may have been hard-earned and cleverly practiced. She may have taken others deep into the forest trees to play the same games and to whisper the same endearments. Innocence may also be an artifice, especially when displayed to the callow and unwary. Its pretty mask may also be a snare."

"No Father Giovanni, you are wrong. In this you are wrong! If she has other lovers, even a husband, I will not love and care for her the less!"

Seeing that his friend was deaf to any plea or shout of reason, Father Giovanni became very concerned, even uncharacteristically ruffled. He could see that the spell cast over his friend was very strong, and like iron it was deflecting the truth of his words. He became desperate; not only on behalf of his brother's soul, but with the sudden realization he was in jeopardy, even the stark probability of losing the treasure of his friend's friendship.

Lowering his cowl, he brought his face once more near the grille, so that the two men, only inches apart, seemed to be peering into mirrors, mirrors that were in truth their souls. In these mirrors were reflected two Angels; one solemn, and one drunken; one giddy, and one earnestly pleading; two Angels come to confer and debate, with passionately pounding hearts to defend the souls entrusted to their care.

"*Oh my dear, dear friend, you do not know what has happened to you. You do not know the might of a woman's sorcery, one that makes a whipping boy of a king. There is nothing so strong. There is nothing so false. There is nothing so seductively treacherous for that soul that yearns to return and unite with God.*

You have stumbled into a fool's paradise, my friend, a garden whose glistening fruits are sweet, but cannot satisfy the deeper appetite of the spirit. You may quickly learn to loathe what you now savor; to disdain what you now swear to adore. Oft what seems a candy to the flesh becomes a bane to the spirit; what is alluring to the eye, scabs the soul with blindness; a mere spectacle and parade, and nothing more."

Brother Maria shrank away from the grille, hanging his head, and burying his face in the sleeve of his robe. This had the effect of inspiring his confessor the more, with the hope that his words were finding their mark, and that there was still hope that he might not lose his dearest friend. Father Giovanni felt something break inside him, a dam of reserve and religiosity long since erected and buttressed in his heart. Gripped by fervor he had seldom known, he could not stop the feverish rush of his impassioned words.

"*The pleasures in this garden do not last, but quickly spoil, and will leave you starved and empty. Oh my friend, my dear Maria, this garden is not a garden at all, but a maze that will leave you lost, weeping for the great treasure you bartered for giggles and kisses at its entrance gate.*

Listen to me Maria; you must listen to me my friend! You may learn to resent the goddess of your idolatry. Her caresses may turn to scorpions, the honey of her kisses, to vinegar. Soon you will see this garden's fruits are full of blights and worms. You may one day wake to see you are not enfolded, but smothered by the wings of your angel.....the tale of Eve and the fall of Man is no idle tale Maria....Woman embodies all that is false and vain.....she kindles the brute in Man, and not his spirit.....his loins, and not his soul!"

And now it was Father Giovanni's turn, having spent his passion, to stop his words. Again silence asserted its detached, unspoken rule of equanimity in the confessional. Only after a long moment was that silence violated, torn in two, like the rending of a robe, rent by a whisper muffled in the sleeve of the penitent's habit; a whisper so soft,- and yet more, so queer his confessor was not sure he had heard it rightly.

"*Father confessor, have you ever loved a woman?*"

Only after a strained moment did the priest answer.

"*Brother Maria, as you well know, I am a priest.*"

To which was answered another muffled whisper, but this time stern and measured, as through gritted teeth.

"*Then how, Father Giovanni, would you know the joy throbbing through my heart?*"

Brother Maria slowly lifted his face, but it was not the same face he lowered moments before. Its flush of intoxication had vanished, and in its place was a grim intensity, like a soldier departing for war. Tears had doused the bright happy flames that had danced in his eyes, leaving them smoldering with defiance.

"*Your words are true words, Father Giovanni. I know that. They come from a mind much keener and a character much stronger than mine. They come from a wise man's mind, and not a child's heart, like the child's heart you have always thought beat in my breast.*

But a child feels sweetness, Father Giovanni; and the sweetness that woke in my heart when I was in this young girl's arms was sweeter than anything I have ever known. It was a wound, yes, a tremendous wound given by a sword whose blade was tender flowers....whose exquisite sweetness was an ache that summed all lesser aches into a joy that pales all lesser joys. It gathered my dreams into its arms, and gave them a mother's tenderness, as men's words, even your words, Father Giovanni, could never do.

And yes, yes Father Giovanni, this little Eve plucked an apple from the Garden's Tree, and yes! I ate what she ate, and we shared its deliciousness, a deliciousness that was good, not evil!"

"*......oh my brother, my dear, dear friend, it was an error, a fall, a thing God will forgive! You must only ask.....do not for a woman's kisses dash to pieces your vows, your habit, this abbey's walls.....all that God has given and promised you.......*"

"*To hell with what He has given me! To hell with a God who made such sweetness and called it sin!*"

Far from a soft whisper, these words were an angry snarl, one that Brother Maria spat rather than spoke as he gripped the grille with his two hands. Father Giovanni would always remember this face, this face that had metamorphosed, and was made unrecognizable from the young golden face of his friend; its lyrical beauty now changed to that of a furious, indignant prisoner behind his bars, or a caged creature of the wilds, but with those wilds still living in its blood. He had never seen a face burn so hotly, so passionately, a face so proud of its sin. He had never seen a face burn so true with the fire of its soul.

"*Yes, Father Giovanni, you heard me rightly. If the God you worship is other than the God I find in this girl's arms, then He is not my God, and like twigs across my knee, I break my oaths to Him!*"

And then after a pause, in which both were left startled at the violent outburst, the outburst that left both in a kind of wonder; after this pause, a soft whisper:

"*Father Giovanni, why cannot the God that made us be our mother, as well as our father? Why must His altars be only cold stone with wooden idols, and not also a warm, gently breathing breast with clouds and flowers?*"

And again the face changed, its ferocity transfiguring into another; the defiant prisoner, back into an innocent child; a child who was about to be orphaned, about to trade the salvation of his soul for the dallying pleasures of his flesh; the holiness behind an abbey's walls, for the wilderness of a wicked world.

"*Remember me Giovanni, remember me! In your prayers, yes, but more, remember me between and beyond your prayers, in those moments when you find yourself other than a priest, unencumbered by rites, robes, rituals.....one naked in sun and storm....a man with a man's wants and a man's needs, a man's heart.....remember me as a brother of your flesh, as well as your spirit!.......*

Oh, I will miss you my good dear friend! Oh, my dear sweet Giovanni, how I will miss you!"

And with this Maria pressed his lips hard against the grille and kissed it, its ardency crashing like bells and cymbals in the silence; a kiss that at once froze and burned through the veins of the startled priest.

Dumb of words, Father Giovanni did not even lift his hand with a blessing when Brother Maria, like a shadow, left the confessional.

* * *

LOST in thought, the priest did not walk in the shadows of the arcades as he had previously done. Nor were his steps swift and hurried. Like a surgeon's careful incision, his dark form slowly incised the spacious belly of the courtyard, now glowing marble bright with moonlight; only to have his slow, thought-burdened steps come to a halt near the well.

What was this shadow that had settled its dark wings over his heart, only to weigh on all parts of him like heavy chains? Why did he feel weak and confused, almost dizzied, almost nauseous, as he was about to fall to his knees and retch, and with his retching deliriously weep, as he wanted to purge his soul from the carnal orifices of his body?

And yet he knew perfectly well what was wrong with him. He knew he was sick through and through with the sickness of guilt.

But guilty for what?

Was it that he had broken the abbey's strictures, and stolen from his cell at this forbidden hour? Or was it that he had not divulged his gnawing suspicions to the brotherhood when they had gathered in the Chapter House, suspicions that were more like suppositions about their missing brother? Or was it that he had boldly lied to his abbot, looking into the good man's saintly eyes even as he clenched the incriminating, albeit anonymous note that he had found slipped beneath his cell's door; a note asking for confession; and though unsigned, bearing a signature as it had been signed in his friend's blood?

No, it was none of these; he knew it was none of these. It was a more piercing guilt, one that ached and rankled more deeply. It was the guilt of receiving a treasure, but giving no treasure in return; of receiving a great kindness, but not returning that kindness.

He knew also why his steps had halted here in the courtyard. He knew it was his soul, wrestling with this giant guilt that had halted the beast to which it was yoked. He knew full well that the confessor had been made guilty by the confessed; the theologian by his pupil; the wise man by the child.

He was wounded; yes, that was it, like a hunter wounds an animal; the drops of guilt making bright tracks of his soul's hurt, bloodying these flagstones before the eyes of the stars and the Angels. He was bleeding to death with a wound deeper than any he had known before; wounded with a wound that in killing him had wakened the deepest nerve of his being, that made him want to sing as he was dying; making him want to run crazily about, rejoicing in the arrow that had found him. For this death-inflicted moment he exulted in the wound that bled freely and openly, that was not staunched or hidden by prayers, altars and rituals. In the anguish of this sublime moment he was glad he had been pierced to the quick by the sharpest fang of all; by the fang of love.

Father Giovanni stood transfixed, crucified at once by the riving nails of pain, and the joy bleeding from that pain.

He could easily retrace his steps, and make his way to the barn where he knew Brother Maria was hiding, waiting for the girl's flute. He would not try to change his mind. He would not in any way try to intimidate, restrain, or castigate him. He would only return what this foolish, lust-drunken brother had so freely given him. He would not be the confessor, but the confessee. For once he would speak as a man, and not a holy priest. He would humble his pride. He would tell him how rich he had made his life. He would tell Brother Maria how much he loved him.

Father Giovanni turned, made a step, and then a tentative second one, before again stopping still. There hesitating, as if balancing, like a circus man poised on a high rope, he turned about once more, and made his way quickly, like a shadow back into the cloister.

Once inside his cell he did not disrobe. He did not kneel before the Virgin, or give his back a few perfunctory slaps from his flog. Rather, fully dressed, he simply lay down on his bed and closed his eyes. And yet sleep was much too frail a foe to conquer him. He lay there awake and still, listening to the sounds of the night; the occasional play and whisper of leaves, the bark of a dog and the cries of night birds; the faint shouts and laughter of wine-happy shepherd boys somewhere in the fields below.

He lay there listening to the voices of the night, as he did not remember listening to them before; frightened, as he did not remember being fright-ened before......until, like a knife thrust through his heart, a sharp trill of a flute lifted from the dark forest......as from the deepest, most primitive forest in his soul. Like a murderer made bloodthirsty midst his vengeance, there came another, and then another and another trill, until, satisfied with its grisly kill, the night regained its softly breathing silence.....

......for the remainder of the night the priest lay on his bed with tears streaming from his closed eyes......sweet tears, burning tears; as they were tears that were springing from a deep, very sweet, newly discovered well......

....

....

CHAPTER FIVE

THE CALL OF THE FLUTE

AFTER his farewell to Father Giovanni in the confessional, Brother Maria slipped from the chapel, and keeping in the shadows, even as he too was a shadow, made his way back to the barn, there to wait the moon's rising and the trilling of his sweetheart's flute. Although he climbed to the loft, this time he did not bury himself beneath its loose straw, but instead opened the door of one of its upper windows, and sitting before it, waited for the night to bring love's invitation to his soul.

The night was cool, clear and starry, but the moon had not yet risen. Yet Maria knew what part of the forest from which it would rise. Even now he could see the faintest dawn of its corona.

Oh, how lovely, how very lovely and exciting to be waiting, as she must be waiting, for God's Hand to lift the moon, like a glowing lantern above the trees, as if with this sign of Heaven, God was giving His approbation to their secret love! Oh, how his heart sang, even as he knew her heart must be singing, as they were two birds of the forest, two birds whose breasts were filled with the songs they wished to sing to each other!

And as he sat there waiting for the moon to rise, and her flute to play, Brother Maria fell into a muse.

Did he truly know what he was about to do? Did he truly believe that he would never return?

Yes, he knew, because he knew the resolve in his heart, and right or wrong, he knew he would obey that resolve. He knew he was fleeing from one master to another; from the dictates of the Spirit to a new, at once more savage and more lovely master, one called 'the world'; from the love of an unseen God, to the love of a beautiful woman. But in his abandonment of one master for another, what would happen to him? Where would he go? What would he do? Would he marry this young girl, whose name he did not even know? Yes, that much was certain. Of course he would marry her. He would build a cottage in the forest by a stream, and there through the green, gold and snowy seasons he would live with her and the children she would give him. Each winter night he would gently gather her body into his by a glowing fire, as the wolves howled and the snows drifted, even as he would tenderly wrestle in her lovely arms and legs in the summer moonlight. He would snare rabbits and partridges, and catch fish in the brooks. He would plant a garden, pick wildflowers, strum a lute and sing his beautiful dreams for her.

Or would the stars, these same stars peeking from the sky deliver another sentence, another fate? Father Giovanni had intimated that a dark and dangerous reality might await him, and Father Giovanni was wise, much more wise than he, and often spoke as one who owned a prophetic eye. Father Giovanni was his friend. He had no doubt he would never have a dearer one. He would tell his children about him, about a scholarly priest who had once counseled and tutored him, who had read so clearly the tablet of his heart. Still, in one thing he could not heed his friend's words; for he had intimated that this young girl might disappoint him in some unforeseen way. But what did a priest, one whose life was spent in reading scriptures and kneeling before altars know about the wonderful mysteries of a woman? Woman, and the pleasures she offered was not evil, but innocent and good. Still, there had seemed an irony, almost a mockery, and certainly a rebuke that brooked on being a stern foreboding in his words, as though he was speaking of a probability, even an incontrovertible certainty that he could not understand; as though he was speaking to a little boy determined to catch the dream he had dreamed in his slumbers.

Dark had fallen, and the sky was filling with stars. Were there as many fates for men as there were stars? And how different were these fates, how very different.

One man punished and penalized the flesh, starving it, flogging it until it bled, while another man fed and rewarded its many appetites. One man spent his life preserving and guarding the gifts that God had given him, while another happily spent or squandered them. Father Giovanni would certainly become a Saint, but he would never know the creatures of the forest, nor that great mystery revealed in the arms of a woman. As his friend *would bruise his knees and lacerate his back, giving his heart to the Mother of God, so he, Brother Maria, would give his heart to a mother of moons and forests; a mother full of caresses and kisses.*

Father Giovanni would grow old and die, as all men grew old and die. One day his sandals would no longer slap their feathery slaps upon the flagstones, and his voice would no longer send its thunder and its wisdom from a pulpit, the pulpit with carved vines, flowers and cherubim in the brothers' chapel. His voice would grow faint and feeble, and finally silent. Father Giovanni would die, as the good abbot, the Brother Cellarer and the Brother Infirmarian, and all of the brothers would die. They would be replaced by new young monks, monks whose sandals would slap briskly on the same flagstones, kneel before the same altars, and intone the same hymns. Another scholarly priest would preach from the same beautiful pulpit, elucidating the same passages of the same scriptures. What in truth would change? The swallows would continue to visit, only to leave the bell-tower; flowers would bloom from the melting snows.....ploughboys would hitch their oxen, soldiers march off to war.....shepherd girls would play their flutes in the summer meadows......

And what would happen to Brother Maria? Would he not too grow old and tired, and one day fall like every other leaf of the autumn forest? Would he be killed by a bandit, mauled by a wild animal, be starved or frozen by the harsh elements? Would there be any who would remember him, who had loved him; any who had kept his memory in their heart? Who and what was Brother Maria? Where had he come from? Where would he go? When Brother Maria was gone, would there be another lover waiting, as he was now waiting, for the moon to rise over the forest?

Like an arrow piercing his heart, the flute brought him from his thoughts; its few notes adorning the dark sleeping hills as with a string of pearls; its silver trill the voice of the forest, the voice of the night, the voice of man's heart aching to love and be loved. Yes, the moon was rising, its coppery gold burnishing the dark trees beneath it. *Yes, the moon and the flute.....as if heaven and earth were rhyming, conspiring to create this perfect moment just for him!*

He knew where it would be easiest to climb the wall; in a far corner of the abbey grounds, where the orchard was thickly crowded. He would remove one of the ladders the brothers had used to support the fruit-heavy boughs, and easily scale the high wall. Still, when he heard the flute again, its notes piercing the velvet night like an arrow of blossoms, he smiled this little job away. He tucked his sandals into his cincture, tossed his bag of things over his shoulder, and hoisted himself up into one of the small sturdy trees. As with wings, with a leap he found himself perched atop the wall, the wall behind which he had long enjoyed the protection of body and soul.

And yet the escapee did not at once leap to his freedom. He sat there hunkered, thief-wise with the bundle of his treasure, the bundle that contained the gardener's shoes and soiled clothing. Pausing, he gazed back at the scene from which he was fleeing, as if to engrave it forever on his heart.

And for a moment he was weakened with remorse. Varnished now with the moonrise, the walks, walls, porticoes and rooftops of the abbey gleamed like alabaster. They seemed a sleeping palace, one that was possessed of a royal grandeur and heritage. The bell of the campanile, the crosses on the rooftops, the stone saints frozen in their holy gen-uflections, all seemed the emblems of what is most pure and noble in *Man's* heart. He knew that he would never have such a home again. He knew that his soul would never be again so sheltered, as in a mother's arms, from the wicked dangers of the world. He knew that he was very possibly forsaking the salvation of his soul, and reckless as a tavern sot, he was drunkenly squandering the treasures God had given him for the wine of a peasant girl's kisses.

And still, for yet another last moment he continued to pause, as if reluctant to snip this last thread that held him to all that he had cherished and held so dear. Crouched upon the top of this stone wall, it was as he stood upon a cusp of fate that would determine the destiny of his soul. He felt as his life was here hung in the balance, and that *God* was asking him one last time to make a decision that he had neither the will nor the wisdom, nor even the wish to make; a decision that would somehow brand him for the rest of his days. He felt as though the jury of the stars was smiling a unanimous verdict upon him, but whether their clear cold eyes were sparkling with condemnation, retribution, or happy permission, their silent tongues would not tell.

And Father Giovanni, oh, would he ever have such a friend again? How kind and gentle he had been with him, even at the last, when his heart was drunk with lust, and his robe was filled with the smells of a woman; how with saintly patience, he whose life was dedicated to slaying and sacrificing his senses had listened to his dalliance with a girl's naked body on a forest floor........

.....And then another trill, smiting the quick of his heart more keenly, not as an arrow of flowers, but like a whetted sword.......

Sharp and clear, like the bark of a fox, it contained more than coquetry. It contained the heat of desire, a command that stirred his blood as a fired musket stirs the soldier's blood; a mightier, hungrier plea, a plea that was an exhortation, one whose sweetness makes all subjects its prey.

And still he paused, hesitated, wavered.....and then another trill, speaking like a bird or beast of the forest, calling to the one it had chosen as its mate, demanding it seek out its secret nest or den.

'Come to my arms my darling! Drink deeply of my sweetness! Drink until you are drunk with the milks and honeys I have prepared for you! The moon is bright! Our youth and this night shall never come again! Come to the forest and the arms, breasts and lips that are waiting for you!

And then another, one that at last broke the spell he had called 'salvation'.....a spell broken and forgotten in a fever of the blood that laughed and scoffed at such a silly myth of fear and apprehensions......these few silver notes, mighty as a javelin of lightning cast through storm clouds, dwarfing and dashing the dark world below.....and in that lightning flash, leaving him naked on top of this abbey's walls, his heart, beating like a bird's wings against the cage of his ribs.....crying 'Now! Now! Now! My moment to be alive and free is now! O, I must break from my cage and fly to the forest and my lovely darling now!'........

As a musket blast had felled him, he leapt from the high wall to the ground below. Regaining his feet, he made the Sign of the Cross, kissed and pressed his cheek against the wall, and when another trill echoed from the forest, he spun and sped away to find those arms and kisses that had conquered and dismissed everything he had held dear and believed in.

In the years to come he would be haunted with the memory of this race through the night to his first lover. He would close his eyes and be consoled when he was surrounded with unspeakable horrors: when his nostrils filled with the reek of disease, and his clothes stank with corpses; when starvation was in his belly, and he roasted rats and dogs to stay alive; when his hands were dyed red with other men's blood, and his heart shuddered with the murder those hands had wreaked. At such moments he would close his eyes and feel the crisp leaves, twigs and feathery bed of needles beneath his bare feet. He would see the wheat glistening like moonlit waves, and smell the perfumes of pine and the ferment of autumn. He would hear the trills of a flute, ever sweeter and clearer calling him deeper and deeper into the dark forest, even as they were calling him deeper and deeper into the mysterious forest of his soul, rousing and teasing, enkindling him awake as he had never been awake before.

And then he saw her, glowing, in a pool of moonlight, her dark hair adorned with a large milky flower. And even as he saw her, she saw him, the one whom she had called to the forest and the night with her little flute. And yet the game was not complete, the treasure not yet won. Like an enchantress, she turned and fled from the one she had called from his prayers and vows, leading him deeper still into the forest with a trail made of flute-song and silver laughter, and a body she knew held the feast that her hunter hungered for.

Again, surefooted, she threaded the way to the same great beech tree, its boughs spreading its canopy of burnished leaves over the open grassy place. But this time the young girl did not climb into the tree's fork to fetch the blanket, or gather leaves to prepare a mattress for them to lie upon. This time the blanket had been spread over a mattress prepared before his arrival. This time the mattress had been composed not only of dry leaves, but small pine boughs with soft fragrant needles. This time it was decorated with many flowers, as in a wedding chamber, and not a mere haunt for a secret, momentary tryst.

And this time he went to her, and not she to him. This time he brought to her wild new hungers, hungers piqued by the moon and the night, and with a need that had waked as from an ancient sleep, crying out to be ravenously fed.

He seized and lifted her diminutive softness, roughly, not gently, as if wishing to murder what had come to tease and craze him; that had maddened and mastered him with its perfume and song. His blood was afire, passion having set aflame the straws of reason and conscience; his kisses, not tender, but filled with greed, greed that was a kind of anger, full of beard, teeth and tongue, making the flower of her mouth yield to his thirst.

He was no longer a gentle monk. He was no longer Brother Maria, but an animal of the wilds; she, no longer a young shepherdess, but his prey. Like a hungry bear, he drank the honeys of her mouth, while at the same time lifting her smock to her waist, quickly searching for, finding, and holding fast her second, most secret treasure. But somehow she seemed to be waiting for his attack. Yes, somehow her little giggles told him that she knew he would come to her like a wounded animal, bleeding with the anguish of those desires that she, his huntress, had loosed with envenomed arrows in his blood. Her nakedness was not a prey, but an offering, one she had prepared to sacrifice to a god, her surrender the fruits that she, the sly priestess knew would whet this god's pleasure, and in the end make him leashed and impotently silly with her favors.

He cast her roughly down, and though at first she slapped and flailed, and tried to cry out, he was deaf to her cries, uncaring of her struggle. He knew innately, yes, somehow innately that these things were as much a part of love's ritual as its blushes and whispers, and that her fight was her happy surrender. He lifted and planted her legs on his shoulders, and began to taste and explore with kisses the slender glory of these silky wings that were spread sleekly lovely about him....tasting her feet, calves, knees, thighs, until finally finding the secret hive of her body, his mouth partaking of the honey for which his heart was so strangely crazing.

And as he became drunk with the tastes and fragrances of this honeyed flower, he heard her giggles change to strange, unnatural moans, moans he had never heard before; as they were made of both pain and pleasure, as if their owner was being stabbed by a knife whose blade was at once sharp and flower soft. He felt her wild stress, thrust and fight, and then her final wish to be mastered.....about his face the savage grip and crush of those tender wings that a moment before had so delicately blossomed, now filling his beard with their secret salts and pungencies....and then that guttural, animal cry, like the moan of the dying, and the strange spasm that shivered through her body like a wave of violent fever, or the flesh freeing its ghost......a cry that rent and stilled the night.....a shudder as from the fright of a murder, or the wonder of a birth.

And when her body had convulsed its last, and she was spent and dead of its desire, when she had been purged of the poison of her passion, he continued to hold her trembling and gently moaning in his hands, as if reluctant to quit the miracle that still throbbed with its dews against his cheeks, and filled his mouth with its strange new nectar.

It was then, when she was limp and lifeless, when she was made most tender and most helpless in her ineffable pleasure, that pleasure a man may never know.....when yielding her secret, she had melted to a purr and a smile....it was only then that he laid her down on the blanket, and entered her with that part of him that had been roused, but not blunted, entering her even as her secret tenderness was still quivering.....eliciting sighs of consensual welcome, even as she was wishing to be murdered again, but this time even more sweetly and deeply.

And once inside her, he was possessed with a blind rage to complete his blind need. Like one starved of bread, he could not stop until it was his turn to writhe, convulse and scream out, and in one shiver of supreme sweetness spew what had welled up from the deepest part of him.

And as he lay entangled in and upon her smallness, like a lion on its prey, a sublime peace filled and flushed through him, as though in these animal acts of love all of his needs, dreams and prayers had been answered, and he need seek or know no more.

He remembered once, on returning to the abbey he had seen a stag mounting a doe, and he smiled to think that he had performed such an act, as he too was a stag, a stag who had mounted a little doe. He smiled to think the stag had found it's kind of pleasure in the forest; and he, this kind of salvation in his life.

Yet as he lay in stillness upon her, his wildly beating heart calming, and the sounds of the forest slowly returning to his senses, this perfect pleasure was disturbed by a sharp pang. It was not a pang of guilt, as from breaking a holy vow, for he knew that he would break a thousand such vows to know such sweetness again. It was instead a pang of fear, a fear that he had hurt this one who had most pleased him; that when the fury of this storm was passing through him his strength had made her yield in painful and unnatural ways. He had been blind to her smallness, deaf to her cries. His love had not been tender. He had loved not like a man, but like an animal.

Had he hurt her? She had screamed, flailed and clawed, as if trying to defend his attack. He was many times stronger than she, and though she had cried out and implored him to stop, in the rage of his need he had not heeded her pleas. Like a rapist, and not a lover he had coerced her to yield to his excited strength, demanding her youth and loveliness to gratify the wildness of his desires. Had he hurt her? Had he shamed her? Had he wounded her heart or soul? Would she not fear, even hate the one for whom she had so ceremoniously prepared and given her body's gifts?

With these thoughts he whispered softly in her ear, a whisper that trembled with tears of concern, even contrition.

"Oh my love, my beautiful love, have I hurt you? Please, you must forgive me if I have. You see I am a monk, and I have never been gripped by such passions before. Please my beautiful one, forgive me if......."

But to his surprise she opened her eyes, and they were calm and smiling, like splashes of rain glittering with stars. Like a little child she nestled and nuzzled tenderly into him, kissing his cheeks and eyes, and whispering languidly in his ear.

"Do not be sorry. You did not hurt me. You pleased me very much, my darling, very, very much. You are very strong, but your strength is gentle. You are a lover, a lover as few men are lovers, and though you have not practiced with other women, you made my body sing as it has not sung before. I cried out, yes, and I begged you to stop, but this is love, my beautiful one. It is very strange, a mystery, a mystery that our thoughts may never know. Its games are sometimes painful, even wicked, but in the end, like now, they are full of sweetness."

And without another word they gratefully drank from that sweetest well of all; the precious sleep of lovers. Wrapped in each other's arms, and beneath a robe of sackcloth from night's chill and dew, they slept secure with the precious treasure they had found; oblivious of war, famine and pestilence; of cradles, gallows and coffins; of flocks in sunny fields, and monks solemnly chanting in dark cold stalls; of a wheel of stars turning infinitely slow and sure above them.

Waking some blissful time later, Brother Maria rose up on one elbow and stared at the tender creature sleeping at his side. The moon was only a few days from its full, and high and bright in the sky, it now shown down through the tree's canopy of branches. A bright splash of moonlight fell directly upon their hiding place, illuming this lovely creature who had initiated him into such wonderful new rites and lessons; this young sweet girl whose name he did not even know.

How lovely she was, how very lovely! She seemed to glow, so that he was not sure if the moonlight was illumining her, or she the moonlight. And naked of her smock, how young she now seemed, her young body as unblemished as pumiced marble. She was little more than a child, a child whose cunning had come to be the absolute mistress of his deepest needs, even his soul; making him her grateful slave. Yes, she was little more than a pretty child, but a child made goddess-lovely and sibyl-wise with the mysteries she possessed and so confidently wielded. This was a brow that kings would bend to kiss, and kissing, bend with their kingdoms to kiss again. Behind these eyelids were the dreams of saints, and in these tresses sparkled stars; upon these lips the mother of the seasons smiled.

Again he stirred with the desire to possess such a treasure, but this time his need spoke with different voices. He did not want to grasp and roughly harness her, making her yield to powerful urges that had snarled from the deepest and darkest part of him. This time he wanted to melt into her beautiful mystery, to drown like a wave in the sea, the sea of her loveliness; to die in the countless blossoms of her spring sweetness.

Soft as a falling petal, he brought his lips to her neck and breasts, and on to the sweet little meadow of her belly.....the navel, like a shy, but wise, ever wakeful eye, smiling, as with omniscience, giving its admirer permission to further proceed....down hips, thighs, knees and calves, until in delirious devotion he reached the lilies of her feet......

Quickened, he kissed hungrily back up her legs until he found the flower that so prettily, queenly bloomed in its secret cleft. But this time he was as tender as he had formerly been rapacious with this flower. He laid his cheek, as in submission upon it, even as it was a throne, and closing his eyes, was at peace from all worry and storm.

.....and then she was awake, even as the earth and stars are forever awake.....through all nights, beneath all snows, with a heart forever beating, forever preparing new bloom, song and wings.....as she had never slept, and never sleeping, was ever eager with fertile need, ever secreting the salty moistness of the earth's fecundity.....to strangle with its arms and thighs, to sing with its whispers, thrust with its hips and buttocks......forever hungry with the womb's eternal yearning to be sown by life's loins.......

.....and now he was again inside her, deep and soft and forever, singing and drowning in loveliness without beginning or end. Gone now the great tree spreading its branches above them, the moon and stars, the hills and forests.....prayers, fasts and flagellations.....gone now the serpent sting of sin, the festering thorn of guilt, the vague and airy promise of salvation..... now only this sweetness.....this melting, this drowning and dying.....now only this ripening of a bud prepared to flower in the dark sea of her belly........

And as he felt love's lava foment and begin to rise from the dark bowels of its making, he opened his eyes, only to see and know that she was about to give her final moment as he was about to give his.....that their passions now were not two, but one, and their two small waves were meeting, merging, crashing and making a much mightier one.......

And as she prepared to flower her ecstasy, she opened her eyes. But they were not this young shepherd girl's eyes at all, but a woman's eyes, laughing in the storm of her passion. As in a blinding lighting flash, he knew these eyes, as he had known them since his childhood, for they were his mother's eyes, as he remembered her flickering glances as she danced about bright fires. Yes, his mother's eyes, painted and jeweled, laughing and singing and telling her son that she had not forgotten him, and that it was not a sin to be in her arms and between her thighs, and to give her his seed and his dreams.

"Oh my darling, my beautiful golden one, give me your heart!"

It was not this young girl who had whispered her passionate entreaty into his ear, but his mother. And with her sweetness, the sweetness that at this blind helpless moment he recalled from his earliest childhood, he gave himself fully, happily, shamelessly.....and lapsing into joy, a joy that was his completion, he knew no more.

* * *

THE dew was heavy, and the moon was low in the west when they woke, and with sleepy, languid kisses, left the tree. She led him from the forest to a small shepherd hut of thatch and crumbling stone on the edge of a field, where she told him he would be safe from any intruder. It was cool inside the hut, and there was a small bed of blankets and straw. A skin of wine was hung from a rafter, as for an expected guest, and a small bundle of bread heels, dried olives and goat cheese hung beside it. But the hunger for sleep mastered the hunger in his stomach, and when his lover disappeared with the promise to return at moonrise, the love-drugged monk fell down upon the rustic bed in complete exhaustion. Never had he been so tired. Never had he been so happy.

When he awoke it was bright day. The hut was speckled with sunlight pouring through the chinks in the stone-piled walls, the rotting sticks of the roof, and the blanket hung ragged over its entrance. Still, the hut preserved a pleasant coolness, and was filled with the simple amenities left by his sweetheart.

…..his sweetheart, yes, his lovely sweetheart…….

Yet even as his mind began to flood with the memories of those sweet animal games he had played with her in the moonlight, hunger now attacked those memories, and slashed through his vitals like a sword. He had not eaten for a day and a half, and this, coupled with the eruption of his virgin passion, had left him utterly famished. Filling a wooden bowl with wine, and unbinding the bag that contained the victuals that had been left for him, he lifted the blanket's flap, sat down in the bright sunlight, and leaning against the hut's stones, prepared to eat like a king.

…..yes, a king, a king…..one who had begged, prayed and flogged for love, only now to be given love's riches so easily, so plentifully……a boy who had forsaken the world, now a man who had stepped into that world as its ruler…….

As he raised the wine bowl to his lips, the abbey's bell faintly reached his ear, calling his brothers to their prayers. Not long ago…..*oh, but how long?…..*he had been one of those brothers, but now he was sitting in a crumbling little shepherd hut, his heart filled with the happy memories of the joys a woman had given him. Life was very mysterious; mysterious and full of surprises. But were all of its surprises as wonderful as those that were given him last night? Were there dark and unfriendly surprises as well?

Brother Maria lowered the bowl from his lips, whispered two *Aves* and two *Paters*, and then ravenously partook of his simple feast.

Never had such simple provisions satisfied him so, as if they were feeding a hunger of a creature newly waked inside him; a hunger more keen, and a creature more keenly alive than he had ever known before. Yet after he had satisfied this new creature, he once more felt an insupportable drowsiness, and without stepping a step away from the hut, he crumpled back on the hut's bed, and drank deeply of sleep again.

The day was closing when he woke. This time he felt wonderfully replenished, even invigorated. He stepped outside the hut to watch the green and gold of the afternoon melt into the pink and violet of the eve. His flute-playing lover had told him she would not come to him before the moon rose, still some three or four hours from now. There was plenty of time for a walk in the sweet-smelling pine trees before she would again bring him her treasures. Meanwhile he could reflect upon the games he had played with her, and perhaps think of new games and adventures they could play together tonight. As he was shedding an old skin, Brother Maria removed his habit and donned the gardener's shirt, trousers and boots he had smuggled from the abbey, and stepped from the hut renewed, a new and happy man.

As he began to walk through the giant pine trees, he felt content and lighthearted as he could not remember feeling before; as this wonderful thing called *love* had new-christened him. It was a different kind of love than the love he had known in the abbey, albeit just as mysterious with its kisses and caresses as the first had been mysterious with its candles and liturgies. He did not understand this new love, this love of *woman* any more than he had understood the love of *God*. Both seemed full of tests and lessons for the soul. Yes, *woman* seemed as much a mystery as *God*, but he would not try to understand this new love, as he had striven, only to fail to understand the former. Had Father Giovanni not told him it was better to accept *God's Love*, rather than to question it? The gate to understanding this new love, at least for now was closed to him, and he was glad it was. He wanted only to be happy, as now, in his blissful intoxication he was. He would not question, but only honor its rites and mysteries. He would kneel before its altars and idols. He would accept, and not question this new love, this *woman love* that had fallen into his arms.

Nevertheless, *Woman love* seemed not incompatible with *God love*, as he had been taught to believe by priests and the writings of the Saints. Had he been confused? Had he misunderstood? Was it a myth, as elves and dragons are myths? Or was there something deeper, more treacherous, more insidiously entwined and entangling in the delicious pleasures that woman gave so freely to a man? Were her pleasures a finely woven web, her charms an opium, or even a poisoned candy? Did deceit speak in her smiles? Would her kisses turn to gall? Would he one day wake weak, shamed, unmanned, his soul forever lost and forsaken?

The more he felt his desire grow for this young girl, the more he seemed to be her thrall, her happy thrall. Could this pleasure he felt in her arms be a clever bondage? Were the wings he was feeling, in reality, chains; this palace he had found, in truth be a dungeon? Was the story of *Eve*, as Father Giovanni had said, more than an idle tale? Was there something beyond his knowing, beyond his feeling, beyond this blissful dream that was shackling him even as it was enchanting him? .....And the blanket in the fork of the tree, and the wine and the viands in the hut......as if prepared for him, waiting for him. .....

Or was it as it seemed; a game of the eager senses, a prodding awake of the sleeping children men call *desires*; children that were sometimes unruly and impatient, wanting only to be exercised and played with? Was it not like his sessions of flogging and fasting in the abbey; sessions of endurance, even pain, producing moments of peace in his prayers?

How wise were the Saints and the scriptures concerning *God's love*; but equally how wise, almost omniscient seemed this young shepherdess concerning *woman's love*. With certain smiles and glances, sways of her hips, and certain tones and songs in her laughter had she not enticed him to her arms? And once in her arms, how had she known how to tease and anger his hungers, only to appease and make them quiet again? Like a wise hunter, she had known that by waking and feeding his needs, she could possess the prize of his heart. How had such a young girl attained such a masterful artistry and wisdom? He had been a helpless child in her arms, and no match for such sorcery. Every prayer he had ever prayed were no defense against such might as she wielded. How had she learned so many games, and after the games were completed, the things she whispered in his ear, consoling his capture, even as he lay defeated in her arms?

As he walked beneath the sweetly smelling pine trees, he smiled as he remembered those games, childish and shameless he had played with his young playmate in the moonlight; her sly lures, invitations, tender struggles and rewards; the different ways she baited the hunter of his need into the forest of her charms, as into the enchanted forest of a dream.

Not until now had he realized how different the night was from the day, as if the two were different worlds governed by different kings. What was given license in the shadows of the night was looked upon as wrong and sinful, perhaps silly in the light of the sun. In the night the creatures of one's heart sang like birds and prowled like beasts, but in the glare of the sun these same creatures were hooded, leashed and caged. In the day the *Angels* sang in hymns and prayers, but in the night they sang in moans and whispers. In the night man wandered like a wild creature beneath the moon, but in the day he broke bread, and plowed beneath a hot sun. In the day Man knelt before an altar with icons and candles; in the night he danced before an altar of naked breasts and honeyed kisses.

Suddenly Maria thought of what had briefly flashed before him, that last time as he had been about to complete his passion. He was not sure what it had been; whether it had been a trick of his mind, or something that had welled up from a deep place inside him,, deeper than he had ever known before. What had it meant, this vision of his gypsy mother laughing through his grimacing lover in the climactic moment of their love, inviting him, gently commanding him to give his seed and his dreams, his very soul to her?

Yes, it had been his mother, certainly his gypsy mother as he had remembered her when he was a small boy, her dark hair and her dark eyes, her nose and eyelids sewn with beads, her carmine lips and her ears with their long copper bangles; but now naked, lovely, and terrible as a storm, throwing back her head and laughing a laughter that scoffed at sin and salvation; that asked for his supreme joy even as it was a child's toy.

.....and then the molten eruption from his loins, and the giving of his secret needs and dreams to her. How incestuously profane! How wickedly sinful! And yet how lovely, so very lovely it had been, to quench his fire in that fertile sweetness where its spark had been first conceived!....

He must confess this evil thing that had come into his mind. He must steal back to the abbey, and tell a priest, perhaps even be exorcised. Yet how could he confess what he could not deny had been the sweetest moment of his life, a moment that had given him a new and wonderful meaning? How could he tell Father Giovanni? No, he could not tell his saintly friend about this wonderful thing. He would keep its secret, like a precious jewel he would keep it in his heart, and tell no one.

The sun was now lowering, and the birds had begun to sing their vesper songs. The great pines were filled with night's first shadows, as well as the last glimmerings of day, as their giant boughs were giant arms that were capable of holding the burdens of both. It would not be long before he would play with his little lover in the moonlight again, tousling in love's playful matches.

He must soon make her his wife. They could not continue to steal to each other's arms like thieves in the night. It mattered not to him if she could not read or write. She possessed another, deeper wisdom, one that the lines of *Homer* and *Vergil* could never teach. He would protect her from villains, storms and dangerous beasts. He would hunt and fish, gather, plough and harvest for her. As she played her flute, he would sing for her. Perhaps he would even write poems for her. He liked poems, but he had never written one. He had sometimes been visited by pretty words, and the mystic images they made as he stared into fires, or sometimes as he was falling asleep. He had likened these visitations to flocks of brightly painted birds. He had sometimes imagined catching these birds, not with his hands, but with a quill and ink; capturing them in a cage, the cage of a beautiful poem.

Yes, this is what he would do. He would write poems for his peasant wife, and in those poems he would sing the mysteries he saw in her eyes, and the lovely meadows of her body. Even now, thinking of her naked beauty lying in moonlight beneath the great tree, silver and golden words fluttered through his mind.

.....*the moon, like the golden rose of your face....a brook, like your silver laughter.....the stars, sparkling in the dark night of your tresses........*

They were simple words, but if these simple words were somehow plaited together they might form a beautiful ribbon to be wrapped about his lover's heart. Would she not like such a ribbon of words? Would she not like to be praised, and adored as a man adores an *Angel*? Would she not exchange this gift with secret gifts of her own?

Brother Maria reached a bridge that had been built over a small swift brook. Standing upon this bridge, he had the sensation the brook was running through him with its endless babble. It seemed to be laughing and singing; urging him to come laugh, sing and play with its sweetness. As his heart was a pebble, singing with the pure fresh love that was rippling over it, he thought how lovely it must be for a brook to babble, a thrush to warble.....*how lovely, yes, how lovely it would be to sing, to open one's heart and have melodies, like flocks of pretty-feathered birds to fly singing from it.......*

But it was a song he did not sing, for when first one, then two, then three flute trills pierced the falling darkness, a strange fret struck a chill into his rapture. The call of the flute was not the same as it had been before, when his sweetheart had beckoned him from the abbey's walls. It seemed full of pain, not joy; of love's tears, not its warm desires; of some inexplicable foreboding, not a welcome to its blissful arms.

And when she broke from the forest to the little hut where he awaited her, she did not bring kisses or embraces. Her hair was unbound and uncombed, and not made pretty with flowers, and behind its muss she hid her face. When he attempted to fondle her, she sharply brushed his hand away, repulsing any foreplay of his passion. She seemed not the same lover who had given herself to him in the moonlight beneath the great tree only hours before. She was somehow agitated and fevered; her voice shrill and harsh, and no longer sweet. Shaking her head vehemently, she would not let him bring his mouth to her mouth, or even to look into her eyes. Roughly taking his hand, as it was the reins of a horse, she began to tow him silently and swiftly, roughly away.

Unspeaking she led him, and unspeaking he followed, but this time not to the great old tree. This time the young girl led him deeper, much deeper into a thicker part of the forest. Blindly, silently, deeply she continued to lead him, until reaching a small clearing, one filled with a moon-less darkness, she stopped, turned, and threw herself sobbing into his arms.

The love she brought him tonight was very different than the love she had first brought him. It was not tender or patient. It was not full of games and caprice. It was instead full of greed and rashness, a rashness that brooked on a kind of madness, even rapacity. There was no exploration or adventure, no song of the soul; no precious exchange of secret needs and gifts. It was a taking and not a giving, a theft and not an offering, an act of blood, bone and bowel, and not of the spirit. As if too brusquely proud for words, it spoke none.

There was desperation in this love she had brought to him tonight, desperation more to die than to love, as she wished to be immolated on her utter and final passion. And when he began to lift from her trembling body, she quickly reached and clutched his male part, harnessing it with her small hand; imploring him to not only stay in her arms, but once more to be in her womb.

This was a different kind of lovemaking, one that did not even permit kisses. After a good while Maria whispered in her ear:

"*What is wrong, my darling? What has hurt or frightened you? I heard the tears in your flute, and I feel the pain in your love. But you need not be frightened. I am strong, and I will protect you. I will not let anything harm you. Oh my darling, turn your face to mine, and let me kiss your tears and fright away.*"

But still she lay silent and quietly sobbing, refusing to turn to him. Only when he had gently, but insistently turned her face, and brushed the muss of her hair from it did he see why she had not given him her kisses. In day's last glimmer he saw that her lovely face had been severely beaten. One of her eyes was bruised and partially swollen shut, and her upper lip, cut and full of swell. A great dark bruise covered one cheek and cheekbone. Most cruel, one of her teeth had been broken away; her pretty smile, the pride of her young beauty, never to be the same.

Tenderly he kissed her, and when she tried to turn away, ashamed of her maimed beauty, he held her fast, kissing each of her ugly injuries, as he was ministering balm. As tenderly, reverently as he ever intoned a prayer, he whispered;

"I love you my darling. Nothing can or will change that. Now let me see, let me see the things so cruelly done to you."

Against her proud struggle, he gently but firmly inspected her naked body, seeing at once that more than her face had been beaten. In the dying light he could see the lash marks that a strap or thong had left on her hams. There were places where she had begun to welt from her flogging, and even some where her skin was broken to rawness.

"Oh my love, my beautiful love, I will take care of you. I will take you away from here, far from whatever brute has done these things to you. Not I, nor anyone else shall ever hurt you in such a terrible way again."

But his words and kisses did not console her. Turning from him she broke into yet another violent paroxysm of tears.

"No, no, you do not understand! You must not say or think such things! You do not know him as I know him, either his strength or his anger. He would hunt the bounds of the earth until he found us, and when he did, he would kill both of us in gruesome and torturous ways."

"But I am not afraid, and I am also very strong."

"You do not understand! You speak foolishly because you are a monk, and do not understand the savage hearts some men have!"

"If I speak foolishly, it is because I speak the truth of my heart. And the truth in my heart is that I am in love with you! My love is true, and such a true love cares not if it seems foolish or not!"

"Love! You speak of love, silly man?! But you do not even know me!"

"Oh, but you are very wrong my darling! I know you very well! I know your secrets and your treasures because you have shown them to me! I know your smiles, your purrs and your kisses, and the many games you know how to play. Oh my darling, I want to marry you!"

"Marry me!"

"Yes, of course we shall marry! I will take you far away, and build you a little cottage home. We shall have a garden and a cow, a barn full of corn

and wheat, and many children, yes, many children!.....and when they are asleep in their beds, we will play the games of love in the firelight......"

"You are a silly, foolish man. You have been dreaming and praying behind stone walls on top of a high hill, and think love is a thing it is not, or could ever be! You think love is a mumbled prayer, a counting of beads, a kneeling before plaster dolls of saints, saints with cold stone hearts who have never touched or loved a woman!

Besides, how could I marry you when I am already married?"

Maria winced, her words like a knife in his heart. He remembered what Father Giovanni had said to him in the confessional. Faintly he whispered, his words the blood spilling from that fatal wound:

"Married, you are married?"

"But of course I am married. I thought you could tell by the things I was able to show you. But you are little more than a child in love, and probably did not know that such things come only from much practice."

"Did you not say, even as you surrendered in my arms, that you loved me?"

"Yes, I said I love you. But do you not know that that is also a part of love, as it was a strong wine that often makes one say things that are not true; that love is a wine that makes one drunk?"

"But why then were you so sweet to me? Why did you smile at me, and show your pretty knee to me? Why did you call me with your flute, beckoning me from my prayers and my vows to the flowers of your body? Why did you court and seduce me, and tell me that you dreamed of holding me in your arms? Were all these things a lie?"

"Of course I dreamed of you. You were pretty, like a woman is pretty to a man. I dreamed of you, as any woman who would look upon you would dream of you. You were young and strong, and shone like a golden god among the drab and dirty monks in the fields, and I wanted to play with you, to win you. When I looked upon you the nipples of my breasts rose like rosebuds, and there was the trickle of desire between my legs. I knew at once I wanted to give myself to you, that I wanted to quiver with you deep inside me, to sing in your arms."

"And did these things not happen?"

"Yes, they happened! They happened even as I dreamed they would happen. Perhaps I will never be loved like you have loved me again. Perhaps, no, I am sure I will never give myself as fully as I did when I was in your arms!"

"*Then come away with me. It matters not to me if you are married. You will break your vows to your husband, as I have broken my vows to my God.*"

"*You still do not understand. You have the body and tenderness of a god, but the heart of a young boy, or a monk in a robe. You do not understand, my beautiful golden boy. You do not understand love at all.*"

"*But what is this thing about love I do not understand?*"

"*You do not understand that there are many kinds of love; that I love my husband very deeply, perhaps more deeply than I could ever love you.*"

"*But was it not your husband who beat you?*"

"*Yes, of course it was my husband......*"

"*But how could a husband beat his own wife, and how could such a beaten one continue to love him? You are a woman, not a dog.*"

"*He is a very jealous man. When my husband is very drunk he sometimes strips off my clothes, and sniffs the parts of my body like a dog, to see if another man's smell is upon me.*"

"*But why is he so very jealous?*"

"*Because I have given him reason to be jealous. You see there have been others I have lain with, that I have given my body to in the forest and tall grasses.....but never one like you, such a beautiful one like you; no, never such a strong and tender one like you, my sweetheart, my Brother of Gold.*"

"*Your husband is not handsome, or 'pretty' as you say of me?*"

"*No, he is not pretty. He is old and ugly. He is not gentle like you are gentle. He is lazy, and sleeps in the day. At night he drinks much wine, and when he is drunk he curses and makes me love him in ungentle ways, more like a beast than a woman; like a goat loves a she-goat.*"

"*But you cannot truly love such a man?*"

"*I love him very much. If he beat me a thousand times, and broke all my bones and my teeth I would still love him. I will never leave him. You see sometimes he is kind to me, and it is very sweet. Sometimes a great beauty shines through his ugliness.*"

"*I do not understand.*"

"*You do not understand because you know nothing of love. You know love's words, not its mystery. You are a boy, a monk, a dreamer with dreams in his heart. You want another kind of love, a kind of love that might never be, not even in your prayers. You want a kind of love not contained in a woman's heart, but fools and dreamers are convinced flies through each of them, like painted birds with pretty songs.*"

Composing herself, and as if readying to leave him, she continued:

"I will not forget you, Brother of Gold. I know I will be haunted with your beautiful words, your beautiful eyes, your beautiful kisses until the day I die. But I know they would never be mine; as my husband's ugliness and cruelty are mine. I do not think any woman could ever possess you, even though none could ever resist you, for all will see in your eyes and hear in your heart a wanderer who is saying farewell in his love; whose dreams are one with the autumn fields and forests. You will hurt those who come to love you, because they will not be able to keep the one that gave them such treasures. But as you hurt many, so in return will you be hurt by many. Having, loving, and losing many, you will be lonely as few men are lonely."

Maria did not understand the meaning of the girl's words, but he understood that he would not be able to change her mind. He understood that she loved the violent man who cursed, beat and abused her in a way that she could never love one who tenderly caressed her, and whispered lovely words in her ear.

"Then you will not come to me again?"

"No, I will no longer call you with my flute. We now must part. We played games of love, but these games are like the games children play before they learn to plough the fields and thresh the wheat. Now we must leave each other, for even now my husband is drinking, and he may decide to hunt for the one whose kisses he smelled on his wife's body, whose bites and scratches of passion he found with a candle. You do not know your danger! You must run away, or back behind the abbey's walls. You are innocent; you do not know such anger. He will have horses and many men! He will kill you if he finds you my darling; in some awful way, mutilate your prettiness; perhaps hang you from the abbey's gates!"

And with this, and no further protest from Maria, the girl fled into the night. Stunned and deeply wounded with heartbreak, Maria instinctively sought out and found the great trunk and arms of the large beech tree, as it was a god of silent counsel and consolation. Spreading his monk's robe beneath it, he lay down sobbing, his beard soaked with tears.

But after a short while his misery was interrupted by a rustle of leaves and footsteps, and a form standing over him at his feet in the darkness. Remembering the girl's words about her husband, Maria started, and made ready to spring to his feet with a defense, but at the last refrained, seeing what ghost, meek, contrite and weeping had walked from the trees.

He could see her against the stars, her silhouette silently lifting her smock over her head in one swift, fluid motion, and then kneeling to where he lay. He could feel the swell of her lip in the kiss she brought to his mouth, even as she sweetly whispered:

"I know I will never sing in another's arms as I sang in yours. I know that, Brother of Gold, as only a woman may know such a thing. But a woman needs more than to sing and to quiver like the strings of a lute. She needs to own the lute's player as well. Come, O beautiful player of my body, for it is early, and he has only begun to drink. Come, strum upon this lute, and make it sing one last time!"

......their love beneath the great tree, like a fallen star.....its heartbeat the heartbeat of the silent night....captured, held, tasted and drunk to its sweetest dregs.....rapt in a spell that steals time, and stealing it, stills it..... replacing its theft with Eternity......

.....stirring, kindling, exploring each other ever anew.....entangling, wrestling, drowning, only to gasp for breath in the stars....exhausting their strengths, needs, dreams..... only to replenish, and eagerly renew more battles, battles that were the play of kittens.....until utterly spent and defeated in their victories, they died the death of lovers, falling into the arms of sleep.....as it was their first sleep, their last sleep, as sleep was their temple and their sanctum....as if they never wished to wake again.......

.....and that last time, that sweetest time, before sleep had taken them to its arms.....compelled as with some deeper knowing, when she had wished to expertly mount rather than be mounted.....riding him like a rider rides a horse, her hands gripping tight his shoulders.....her throat and back strained and stretched, arched like a hunter's bow.....her face uplifted, as in an ecstasy of worship.....as in the wailing of death.......

.....and then her hands leaving his shoulders, a rider riding rein-less, saddle-less, like a rider in a circus.....horse and rider racing beneath the stars, across the first silky grasses of the world.....her arms lifting, reaching through the leafy boughs to pluck the silver apple of the moon.....the deepest part of her hungry to be filled, and filled, satisfied......poised and still, ready in the rule of its ride to be fed the spark for which it forever hungers.....to receive that it might beget.....that spark that is offered like a ritual, from the hoofs of the earth into the wings and womb of the seasons........

And after, when she had left without a word, he lay on his monk's robe in fevers of half-sleep, ragged dreams, and heartbreaking images of that loveliness he had adored, but would never be his again.

The night grew chill, and a drizzle began to drip from the leaves upon him, the same leaves through which the stars and moon had sparkled and shone upon his blissful raptures. Cold and sleepless, he rose in the first damp gray of the dawn. He knew not where to go, or what to do. He only knew he would not return to the abbey; not only from shame and disgrace, but from something more, something still hidden, dark and secret inside him; something that now owned and commanded him, as he knew chants and altars could never do again.

He began to bundle up his robe, but then stopped. No, he would not take it with him. This dark thing, this voiceless voice inside him forbade it, and told him to leave it behind. He spread it out on the leaves, even as it contained the murdered body of a ghost, a ghost surrendering to its crucifixion; the nails pounded through it the nails that rot the leaves, freeze the brooks, and decay all dreams of men. His brothers would surely find it here. They would think he had fallen into marauding or murderous hands. And in truth, had he not? Was this lovely thing called *love* not a murderer in disguise?

But as he was about to depart, he picked it up from the wet leaves again. No, this would not do; to be eaten by animals, murdered by bandits or crucified by the rain, snow and sun was too noble to explain the forbidden thing he was doing. He was no martyr. He did not deserve such a noble death.

Wadding the robe beneath his arm, he climbed into the fork of the great tree, and from the fork into the highest branches that would support him. There he bound the habit's hood, noose-like with the cincture, and binding it to a high limb let it hang like a dead body from a gallows. Yes, that was better. His old self would be found, like a *Judas* hung in shame, eaten by the winds and birds.

Stiff and brokenhearted, Maria started blindly away. The smells of his nameless lover's hair and kisses, and the secret places of her body clinging to him with their stale perfumes and sour reek. They were no longer sweet as they had seemed in the delicious heights of love. They seemed now odors of decay, even as the crisp leaves were now turning sodden with the drizzle, exuding a ferment of autumn's first rottenness beneath his feet.

A great gloom, a miasma of pain and misery had invaded and settled in his mind, and the words the young girl had spoken to him spoke from its mists, like disembodied spirits. Their meaning was disjointed and confusing, and they spoke as to jeer and mock him, among which a few echoed like the refrain of a particularly vengeful ghost, stinging him more deeply than the others.

"*You will hurt those who come to love you, because they will not be able to keep the one who gave them love's treasures. But as you hurt many, so in return will you be hurt by many. Having, loving, and losing many, you will be lonely as few men are lonely.*"

The chill and damp reaching now more deeply into his unprotected body, Maria chafed his hands and arms, and forced himself into a brisk walk in the dull leaden light. Another creature, a savage creature inside him began to assert itself and take precedence over the pain in his heart; growling in his bowels, and besting with those savage growls the damp and cold, and the smells and memories left by this marauding phantom called *woman*. He was hungry, yes, very hungry. He must find food or perish.

. . . .

. . . .

CHAPTER SIX

HOURGLASSES; AND THE DEAD MAN IN THE TREE SHADOWS

THE Franciscan Abbey on the hill imitated an hourglass, sifting not grains of sand, but grains of men's prayer, duty and penance; not in walls of glass, but in walls of stone. It sat upon a hill, as it was sitting upon a mantel, and when it had sifted the season of its hour, an invisible *Hand* turned it over, as once more *Time* began to patiently, endlessly sift its grains into the *Timeless. Sin, penance, atonement, misconduct and forgiveness; Postulates, Novitiates, Priesthoods; youth, age, and death....*all continued to pass through it in an endless attempt to measure, and measuring capture the *Immeasurable.*

The grains that sifted through the abbey on the hill were not grains of sand; but in the *Eyes of God*, were as fine, so that grain by grain they were patiently meting out that *Eternity* that is the salvation of all *Men's Souls.*

These grains were not found on shores of seas, but on the shores of men's hearts, and when they fell, gentle as rain, they fell on soils tilled pliant with devotion. These were grains that brought men to frugal meals, gave them duties with quill and ink, plough, spade and sickle; brought them to their knees again and again with prayer. Like a kind nurse, *faith* woke them at midnight for *Vigils*, and like that same nurse, kissed them asleep at day's close with *Compline*. And so the days and nights passed in a divine monotony, like the grains of an incessant dream that was being sifted through the mighty fist and tender fingers of their loving God.

Such a regimen made much more dramatic any event that disturbed this constant sifting of their simple routine. It made such events occurring midst this world of bells, chants and whispers seem the more unusual; the more controversial; the more mysterious.

"He did not return from his errand in the forest!"

"But what of the bag of watercress in the infirmary? He must have returned."

"But why did he not attend prayers?"

"There is more intrigue than reason in this thing, and perhaps more mischief than intrigue! Something has happened to our Brother of Gold!"

In the days and weeks that followed Brother Maria's disappearance, a great search was made for any clue that might shed light on its mystery; or in the event of some terrible accident, to find his remains. The schedule adhered to by the brotherhood, the one prescribed by their Order's patriarch, the *Holy Francesco*, was altered, and although the bell still punctually rang, and the offices of prayer were punctually observed, things that were not of absolute necessity were cancelled or postponed. In their place, the abbot ordered the brothers into hunting parties that scoured in ever widening circles about the abbey walls; hunting parties that over and over returned without a least trace of their beloved brother.

Without proof, conjecture lifted its *hydra*-headed presence in the brothers' hearts, devising many possible explanations, and as many questions.

If Brother Maria premeditated his plan to defect from the abbey, why did he return the sack of herbs to the infirmary; a thing that could risk his detection, and could only impede his escape? And if he returned them when the rest of the brotherhood was at their prayers, how did he leave the abbey without opening the gates? The gates were locked, and the Brother Porter was in the choir, at prayer with the others, the keys snug in his pocket. The gates could not be entered from outside, and although they could be unlocked from the inside, they could not be re-locked once the one leaving had made his departure. Did Brother Maria climb the high wall, both in his tardy return from the forest, and in his mysterious departure from the abbey?

This at least led to a bit of possible evidence, evidence that the brothers found in a corner of the abbey where the orchard trees were thickest, several whose uttermost branches scratched against the high wall. One tree, although old, stunted and storm-broken, seemed to have some freshly injured branches, especially near its crown, and although it would take a great leap of panther-like agility, and would be impossible for any but a most youthful and athletic body, the brothers concluded that the Brother of Gold was such a one who owned the ability to perform such a feat.

But there was nothing more they could deduce. Some felt that he had perhaps joined a band of robbers, who with riches had enticed him away from the poverty of a monk. Others suspected things even more fell: that he had been murdered, his body buried, or cast in the river, bound to its bottom by stones; or that he had been gnashed apart and eaten by wild animals, a pack of wolves or a herd of boars. There were still others who suggested that it possibly was a voice in Brother Maria's own blood that had seduced him away. As drunkards find it difficult to forget the taste of wine, perhaps Brother Maria had not been able to forget the wanderlust of his gypsy past, and he had fallen prey to its cry in his blood.

The fields and pastures were combed, the deep places in the river were dredged with nets, the forest thrashed and picked through in depths that the brothers had never explored before. There were even attempts made to question the shepherdess that had been so fond of the *Brother of Gold*, she who had played melodies on her flute, and sometimes sang duets with him; she who had adorned her hair with flowers and flashed pretty smiles for him. But she now grazed her goats and sheep in more distant meadows, and her flute was seldom heard. She was no longer friendly, and when the brothers approached or hallooed her, she vanished like a skittish dog.

After several weeks the hunt for their missing brother was exhausted. The abbey began once more to freshly sift its grains of prayer, toil, and duty through the stone hourglass set on the mantel of the hill. The empty prayer stall and the golden-voiced ghost that haunted it were now claimed by a brother of solid flesh and bones. The voice that had soared as with wings in the *Angele Dei*, the *Gloria Patri*, and the *Pro Nobis*, lifting the others in its lovely flight, was gone; the one who danced before the marble Saints, and sang minstrelsies of love before the *Mother of God*, was beginning his slow disappearance into memory.

Yet, as it were the dying gasp of this hunt, and as to leave no stone unturned for a second, or even a third time, one morning after *Terce* the Abbot Father asked Father Giovanni to attend him in his office, a thing the astute priest obeyed with his soldierly promptitude.

Standing outside the open door, as the abbot finished conferring with another brother, Father Giovanni could not help but see in the bright shower of sunlight how age was quickly working its ruin on the reverend abbot; twisting, knotting, and gnarling him; mangling him with age's deformities. Yet in some odd way this only enhanced the abbot's otherworldly bearing, as if his flesh was becoming a useless husk, and from this husk his soul was appearing, beginning its escape into Eternity. And more; as his body was shriveling away, his soul seemed to delight and enliven with its approaching emancipation, as the decay of his flesh was fueling the keen flames dancing brightly in his eyes.

Dismissing the brother, and inviting Father Giovanni to step into his office, the kindly, now cane-propped abbot proceeded to gently interrogate him in much the same way as he had in their first interview; with each question cocking his head to lift his twinkling gaze from beneath the bushes of his eyebrows, and with this effort, somehow piercing the tall young priest more deeply than if he was a man of equal, or even taller stature; his stare at once that of a formidable foe and a compassionate friend.

"*As we have spoken at some length before, Father Giovanni, you had a very special friendship with Brother Maria, one might say a great affection for him, did you not?*"

"*Yes Father Abbot, I did. We enjoyed walks and discussions together. We enjoyed each other's company very much, even though, as all know, we were very different.*"

"*Yes, different, you have said this before, Father Giovanni. But could you explain, perhaps elaborate just a little more about this 'difference'?*"

"*It was no secret that Brother Maria showed no inclination towards scholarly studies. It was not that he was slow or stupid; it was just that he had other gifts; his being was fed from other springs, other voices, even as I, with all humility.....well, let us say, I am possessed of other gifts and pursuits.*"

"*Yes, Father Giovanni, all know and all of us are grateful for your scholarship, particularly your Latin and Greek, a learning that proudly represents our Order at the conventions, one that I am not ashamed to say dwarfs my own, and all other fathers, young and old in our brotherhood. But still, tell me, are you sure that Brother Maria did not at any time intimate a disillusionment, or restlessness in his heart, as often infect the*" *younger monks in their first years in the brotherhood?"*

"None; none that I detected, Father Augustine. In fact he seemed very happy and content with monastic life."

"Did he, Father Giovanni, although it is a little difficult for me to ask this thing, being a question of a delicate nature....but, well, was he ever tempted by thoughts of the fairer sex? As you know, Brother Maria's age made him particularly vulnerable to the charms and temptations of that allure; charms and temptations that may easily hop over an abbey's walls with the Devil's cape, and well, even if the light of our Savior shines brightly in the mind, there are always shadows, shadows in which pretty Jezebels may smile, whisper, and invite."

"Abbot Father, I do not recall Brother Maria mentioning any such conflict or temptation in his heart."

"And yet you told me when we spoke before, that when peasant maids brought baskets of provisions to our gates, and Brother Maria received them, the maids acted fancifully, flirtatiously, as I think you said they appeared to want to touch, or even to kiss him."

"Yes Father Augustine, I believe this to be true. The same allure that a beautiful woman holds over men, I believe Brother Maria held over women."

"Brother Maria is certainly a handsome young man, but 'allure'?"

"Yes, allure, Father Augustine. I believe that Brother Maria, without his knowing, breathes forth a kind of enchantment, especially to women's hearts.....even like a rose exhales a lovely perfume."

"Like an aphrodisiac? Is this what you are trying to say?"

"Yes, holy father, even so. But it is more than his handsomeness. It is a kindness, a kindness that is a sincere sympathy women feel he owns for them, as they are at once both his mother and his daughter, and this sympathy makes him irresistible to their hearts. They are bees that know that this is a flower that contains the sweetest nectar, and this makes them drunk, makes them feel as they are more than drabs and drudges....as each is a queen in his eyes."

"His mother and daughter? Bees, sweetest nectar? Drabs and queens? Father Giovanni, I not only think you are a gifted scholar, but sometimes I think you are a poet, perhaps a budding mystic as well."

Here the abbot paused, and smiling wryly looked away, as if mulling over the answers given him, matching the first interview with the present one. But when he broke his pause, he seemed to have altogether forgotten about Brother Maria. He seemed now only concerned with the young priest standing before him, the young priest that would most likely be his heir.

"*And you are continuing the penance you volunteered to undertake, my brother?*"

"*Yes, Abbot Father, I am. Each night after last prayers I flagellate.*"

"*For how long each night?*"

"*For as long as it requires the grains to sift through the hourglass.*"

At this the abbot twisted, and cocked his eye at Father Giovanni, as does a bird into a wormhole, and with a penetrating, wordless, preternatural gaze, asked: why? This glint of supernatural sapience flashed briefly, like a lightning in his eye, only to vanish, and leave the one who saw it questioning whether he had seen it at all. The old abbot turned away, and broke into a tender chuckle.

"*One must have a great need to punish oneself for such long sessions. Oh I know sometimes the least little thing, the least little guilt, like a thorn working into the flesh, may cause a great vexation; rankle one's very soul. Sometimes even the smallest lie, like a live coal buried beneath the tongue, may ignite a raging conflagration through the canals of the blood, until it threatens to consume the citadel of the spirit.*

Ah, to be young again! Believe it or not, I once had dreams of saintliness in my heart. Now I have but ache and moan in this old mortal coil; and sleeplessness, yes, often sleeplessness, with which sometimes I hobble to the chapel to say prayers. I do not know why, call it a wish to consort with the dead if you like, but when I do I am strangely compelled to sit in the shadows, yes, in the shadows, where no one could ever see me, like a child playing hide-and-seek. My abbot-ship lends me that liberty, as you know, and sometimes rather than retiring to my cell after Compline, I simply disappear like a ghost into the chapel's shadows. I sit there silent and stony as a statue, where the keenest eye could never see me.

But no more of this. I am afraid our dear Brother Maria is gone, and for what reason we shall probably never know. I know this must touch your heart very deeply and dearly my brother, but we will pray for God to walk with him, watch over him, defend him. Yes, I am sure God will shower His mercies upon our beloved Brother Maria, and guide his steps wherever those steps lead him."

* * *

The Night

THE fields had been harvested, and most of the orchard boughs picked. Summer had retreated and fled, and with it, the late burning sun that had been responsible for its abundance. This permitted night's shadows to encroach earlier and earlier about, upon, and finally inside the walls of the abbey.

After their last prayers, the brothers no longer filed solemnly across the courtyard to the cloister in bright hot sunlight, or even in lukewarm twilight, but now beneath the cloak of frosty darkness. Instead of a bright sun setting in the west, now the sickle of a young moon, companioned by the evening star was rising above the trees in the east. Now each second monk that issued from the chapel held a candle that had been lighted at the feet of the great Crucifix, lighting their procession that celebrated with silence the end of another day of toil and devotion.

Silently, each of these candle-bearing brothers disappeared into the cloister for their repose; all brothers but one. That one brother and one candle, as if in a refusal of *God's* benison of sleep, departed from the procession, walked under an arcade, and then past the *calefactory*, the *misericord* and the *cellarium*.....at last opening a door to a small room; one filled with darkness and stale tallow smoke; as well as another smell, a peculiar smell whose pungency seemed to superimpose itself upon the darkness. This room, the *penitenziario*, contained a unique reek, a trapped perfume that permeated darkness: the residue of punishment, and the excretions exacted from repentant flesh.

The brother set his candle in a *niche* in the wall, and then proceeded to lift his habit over his head, making naked all but his protected loins. Reaching above the candle, he brought two objects from another *niche*: the first a leather, belt-like object, coiled like a coiled snake; the second, an hourglass, of which he set near the candle, so that its grains began to sift into its empty half. Kneeling on the floor the brother crossed his self, and then as he began to faintly whisper......

.....*Ave Maria, gratia plena,*
Dominus tecum......

......he brought the unfurled strap down over one shoulder, sharply slapping the length of his thin, bony back. Continuing his recitation of the prayer, he then raised the object again, and slapped it over his opposite shoulder, spanking it in the same harsh, stolid, determined manner.

As the candle burned, the grains sifted, and the arms of night enfolded the abbey, the hard slaps of the nail-studded flog began to acquire a strength and rhythm, almost a music of their own, as they fell over one shoulder, and then the other, sharply scolding, and as it owned teeth, biting into the bare lean back surrendering to the mortification.

And as the prayers continued to be whispered by the penitent's lips, two *Ave Marias* followed by two *Pater Nosters*, thoughts sifted through his mind.....even as the grains of sand were sifting through the hourglass..... even as the grains of stars were sifting through the sieve of night.

.....There was a peculiarity about these interviews he was asked to attend with the Father Abbot. He seemed to know more than he was revealing; as he was chiding him; almost toying with him. The abbot was a kind and gentle man, perhaps a Saint, but there was nothing of the erudite scholar or learned theologian about him. Nevertheless, his goodness of heart could compensate for his lack of scholarship, and could lend him insights that others would remain blind to. There seemed to be something both playful and accusatory in his eyes, something that said: "Why are you not telling me all that you know, Father Giovanni? Why are you not telling me about this thing that lodges in your heart like a thorn?"

Still, if he knew he was not divulging things about Brother Maria, why would he not speak directly to him?

The abbot was quickly growing feeble in body, and soon age would blunt and disarm his faculties. Soon he would abdicate his abbacy, either with infirmity or death. He knew that he, Father Giovanni, would be his successor. Was his Father Abbot testing him; his rectitude, his honesty, his purity of heart?

Why did he over and over ask the same question, even to redundancy, about his special friendship with Brother Maria, when it had been long known and accepted by all in the brotherhood that it was so? And why, in this interview did he use the word 'affection'? Of course he knew there were whispers of envy and jealousy among some of the other monks, but there was nothing unnatural, and certainly not scandalous about their friendship. No one questioned its rightness. And why had he asked again, of how the maids fawned on Brother Maria when he received their errands at the gates? Why had he remembered, and found it important, that he had told him that these young girls vied for Brother Maria's smiles and glances, and seemed to want to be near him, to touch him, even to kiss him?

And why had he asked about Brother Maria being tempted by women?

This was not an uncommon temptation; indeed, 'Woman' was one of a monk's greatest foes. Many, if not most of the monks, at one time or the other, and by a lesser or greater degree struggled with woman desire. The daughters of Eve owned smiles that burned into prayers and dreams, impressing promises of lips and feathery touches deep in the minds of many young monks, posing one of the chief threats to their vows.

Why had he said that a lie was like a live coal hid beneath the tongue; that could set fire to the blood, and endanger the citadel of the spirit?

And why had he mentioned that sometimes he went to the chapel to pray in the shadows where no one could see him? Why had he said he sometimes sat in those shadows, like a ghost or a stone statue? Had Abbot Augustine been in the chapel that night when he had last spoken with Brother Maria? Had he seen Brother Maria's unmistakable figure entering the confessional, and with the stealth of a thief slink away? But if he had, why had he not addressed and chastised his lie? If he had, why had he not exacted a harsh penance on him? Or was the penance he was performing now, these sharp bloody slaps on his back the penance that was replacing the one the abbot felt he should be demanding of him? Was the abbot inwardly smiling, pleased with the anguish with which he was atoning for his unprofessed guilt?

* * *

The Clue

THE sudden, unannounced clanging of the great bell broke on the sleepy abbey like a crashing thunder, rending its holy silence to its very heart; and as that heart was made of a delicate porcelain, breaking it into tiny pieces of alarm and hectic frenzy. From all quarters of the abbey brothers broke from the places that occupied and were concealing them; from the gardens, the granary and stables, the cloister, refectory and chapel, all scurrying like mice into the courtyard where, above in the bell-tower the brother was bobbing up and down like a marionette, madly ringing the bell. Last-most, and with his arms supported by a brother on both sides, the abbot half-shuffled, and was half-carried past the well and the marble saints to where the brothers had encircled one who did not wear a gray habit; a *contadino* who labored in the surrounding fields; a man who, transported with some great fear, could but slur and stammer what he wanted to say.

"In the tree, in the tree, high in the tree.....the dead monk hanging high in the tree......"

"What is this? What are you saying? Dead monk in a tree?....Speak not like a drunk man, tell us what you have seen, and what you want us to know."

"In the forest, high in a great tree, a great tree whose leaves hid the terrible thing, like a curtain, yes, like a thick curtain....but now the leaves have fallen.....a dead monk hanging, as from a gallows, dangling from the noose of the rope the brothers use as their belt.....the robe of the dead monk.....without the body of the monk inside it.....perhaps rotted away, perhaps eaten by the birds or by devils......the robe left dangling, as it was a ghost left to swing and moan in the wind......."

Although the story was strange and told in such a drunken, bits-and-pieces manner, the brothers knew at once whose habit was somehow bound and hanging from a limb of a tree. A posse of brothers was formed and directed by the abbot to follow the man into the woods, and recover Brother Maria's habit; as well as with a more serious commission: to hunt about for any hint of their brother's possible remains. Un-chosen by the abbot, Father Giovanni asked with a kind of humble insistency that he be included in this search for his missing friend, and with a wince that furrowed deeper the wrinkles on his trollish brow, the displeased abbot had shaken his head, almost with acerbity, and on this rare occasion denied the father's request.

Chores, duties, and the counting of beads were forsaken, and within moments a group of two dozen monks issued from the abbey's gates, led by the wild-eyed, wildly ejaculating and gesticulating peasant. Quickly they dispatched down the hill, across the newly harvested fields tufted with ricks, thence directly into the forest that thickly skirted them.

* * *

The Haunted

.....Pater noster, qui es in Caelis,
Sanctificetur nomen tuum,
Adveniat reginum tuum.......

Again he commenced to whisper the words, softly, effortlessly, as they were a brook, one whose gentle, stone-carving current was now passing through him; as if his tongue were to be struck dumb, these words would continue from his lips; as if his heart were to stop, they would continue to spill from his dead mouth.

Again he had placed his candle in the *niche*, and again he had removed his habit, baring his emaciated, secretly punished body. Again he had reached into the darkness and brought from it the horny flog, like the wicked tongue of a devil, and with it the hourglass, of which he set next to the candle. Again he knelt, and lifted the weapon of his mortification over his head. Again the whispered prayer, and the harsh slaps down the skeletal leanness of his back; again the lonely season of his penance in simultaneity with the melody of the prayer, the rhythm of the nail-studded slaps, the grain-sifting glass and the star-sifting night. Again, as they were one with all of these, thoughts passed through his mind, as his mind, too, was a receptacle through which the grains of *Time's* worries and cogitations were sifting.

He had found himself seeing him, even hearing his singing voice and laughter as he had gone about the abbey. When they had invoked the 'pro nobis' he had heard his voice soar above the others, not with a commanding might, like thunder, but with a sonorous tenderness, as with fluttering wings.

Sometimes when he walked down a corridor he actually stopped, thinking that he heard his running sandals, swifter and softer than any of the other brothers, thinking that his friend had returned, and full of excitement was coming to ask him about some problem with his lessons, or tell him some great discovery, a bird or a butterfly or a flower he had found in the garden. But standing still, turning, and once even closing his eyes to lend his ears the added keenness used by those organs, he heard only silence, and realized he had only heard a memory, the memory of his friend's sandals, and his feet that he had kept in his heart.

He had looked from a window in the scriptorium down upon the gray and flower-shorn courtyard, and remembered how he had given dance lessons to the old monks, dances he remembered from his gypsy youth, whose heathen roots, in actuality were probably unseemly and licentious, but when taught with his innocent vigor to the feeble, daft and disabled of the brotherhood, pinned wings of Angels on their shoulders; giving them a moment of gay glory. Looking at the courtyard he had seen one of the most elderly monks sitting on a bench, his hands on the knob of his cane, staring a vacant, absent stare, like a frozen troll.

* * *

The Drunkard

AS the man led the monks across the fields and into the forest, it became increasingly apparent how dissipated he was. It was not just that he was a member of the nomadic herdsmen that brought their flocks and herds each summer to the surrounding fields, but even for such homeless, uncouth tribes, he was a sordid and mangy example. He was very drunk, and his steps were unsure and stumbling, and at times he seemed to reel, using trees to support, balance, and keep him on his feet. At times he abruptly stopped before the posse he was leading, and placing a wineskin to his lips without the least regard of the sanctity of the brothers, turned up his head and greedily, shamelessly guzzled.

His speech was as drunken and rambling as his steps, and he sometimes spoke as to the wind, or to ones who were not among them. Either shamelessly irreverent, or drunkenly ignorant of the monks, his language was foul and full of coarseness and obscenities. The brothers, unsure if he was mad, or merely drunk, could but follow with attentive eyes and listening ears, disregarding the abusiveness of his words.

"I know the brother; yes, I know him, the golden brother, the pretty brother, the brother who sang while he worked in the fields. Yes, I know the brother, the one that sang with the shepherd girl, who had a roving eye and a hard cock beneath his robe for her, as by the Devil I am cocksure he did.

Somebody probably murdered him, murdered him while he was a-humping some maid in the reeds....murdered him as I myself wanted to murder him for setting my wife's heart a-flutter each time she drove the sheep afield......and she ready to lay on thorns and nettles, ready to lay on her back beneath the first bush she came upon for him.

I smelled him on her I did. I know a monk's smell when I smell one, full of candle-smoke, ash and soot. A monk is a man, with a fiddlestick like other men, and he knows, like all men know, there is but one place to play his song with it! I smelled his lechery upon my wife, sure as the Devil hates Sunday I did.

No, I did not murder your holy brother, but I beat the whore of my wife who listened to his prayers, and let the bastard have his way with her......."

* * *

Memories

.....Ave Maria, gratia plena,
Dominus tecum,
Benedicta tu in mulieribus......

The candle, the prayer, the sharp slaps of the flog.....the thoughts that he could not stop sifting through his mind......

When he walked in the garden he felt that Maria was walking at his side, or when he sat upon a bench, that he was sitting next to him. When he sprinkled crumbs for the doves, or for the goldfish in the pond, or when he stood still, and heard a new warbler in a rose tree, he imagined his friend was companioning him. He even began to recount the conversations they had shared, conversations he remembered word for word.

Brother Maria had felt that he spoke to him as one who was not his equal. He had resented his insinuations that he might not be destined for the priesthood, accusing his older friend of mocking the mediocrity of his studies. Brother Maria could never have guessed that his friend regarded him not only as his equal, but perhaps even his superior, one that was endowed with an abundance of gifts he would never own; that he was fed by deeper veins of a purer spring, one his heart had never tapped.

.....if he had only told him.....but he had tried, on many occasions, yes, he had tried to tell him......

"Perhaps I will not be a great scholar like you, but that does not matter to me. Perhaps I will be like our abbot, Father Augustine. He is simple, kind and good, but has nothing of the scholar in him. I am confident that I will pass the exams of my ordination. And more importantly, I have a soul both as needful and capable of salvation as yours. I have as much right to be a monk and a priest as you, or any of the least learners in the brotherhood; for that matter, any dullard with a soul.

You always speak as I am not your equal, as my nature is not only different than yours, but lesser, inferior. I sometimes feel there is mockery in your words. Besides, children own wisdom that you scholars could never dream of. I think you thinkers and scholars, you theologians are sometimes arrogant."

"I am sorry, Maria, if I have made you feel this way, and I apologize for

it. Perhaps, yes, perhaps I have been arrogant, and perhaps at times and in some ways I consider you a child; and yes, I think also that children own a great wisdom. I only mean to say that we are different, Maria, as different as night and day, as the sun and moon."

"Yes, we are different, as flowers and birds are different, as each man born from woman's womb is different; but all men have souls, Giovanni, souls that are yearning for salvation, that are yearning to return to God."

"Different does not mean lesser, Maria. It does not mean better or worse; it does not suggest inequality. Yes, all souls yearn for salvation, and all yearn to return to God, but there are different paths to that God. I am only saying that different rivers flow through your soul, rivers that are perhaps sweeter and fresher, perhaps even deeper than those that flow through mine."

"Please, do not humor me, Giovanni."

"I do not. I only mean to say that you draw your nature from a different spring, a spring that feeds Earth's flowers; that feeds man's heart. Natures like mine are fed from springs that run quickly dry; that feed the arid mind. A sweet milk flows through your veins, not a desert wind. Your thoughts are written in dreams, not on a stylus. You live in a midnight garden, and like a nightingale warble to the stars; I squint like a mole in a little splash of candlelight, afraid of the sun.

You have the ability to live and love fully. You love without thought, without hesitancy, with your heart and not your mind. You do not think about life, or even contemplate it. For you, life is not a manuscript to be translated or embellished, but only to be wondered at. Rather than reading of life in the pages of a book, you touch it, taste it, smell it; you leave the book on its shelf, and read the words God has painted with the flowers and the stars. I think that when you become old and gray, you will still be a child, preferring to sing, rather than discuss the musty volumes men call 'wisdom'. You are destined to be Life's lover, not its sage, and although your heart may sustain wounds, you will know joys that the thinker will forever remain ignorant of."

In some of these conversations Brother Maria became impassioned, as if transported, as he was no longer a humble monk in a habit; as he had become a flame that had burned free of all customs and costumes, from the coils and snares of flesh itself. It was at these times the priest most enjoyed, and secretly admired, even envied his young friend.

Again and again he spoke of his mother. Again and again he spoke of how they danced and sang in the streets with the bears; of her great beauty, and the joy and pain that sang in her voice and sparkled in her eyes. Again and again he spoke of her not only as a memory, but as a living, pulsing, singing presence, one that he felt had not died; one that he felt was part of him, that was ever leading, beckoning, and waiting for his return.

"Sometimes I feel as my mother did not die, that she is still calling out to me from the mists of my being, and that like a lost child I am crying out to her, trying to find and return to her. Sometimes it is as though there are a thousand voices waking inside me, a thousand dreams of love, danger, fury and confusion.....like a thousand roaring rivers.....and all are running down a mountainside, rushing and tumbling into a village street where my mother is dancing, singing and clicking castanets, as if waiting for me to join her.....all of these rivers bathing her bare feet with the blood of my heart."

* * *

The Ghost

THE deeper they entered the forest, the more fearful and reluctant the drunken man seemed in his leadership. His reckless slurping of his wine, the wine he had begged from the abbey in exchange for his path-finding, came at shorter, sloppier, more disgusting intervals. On several occasions he fell to his knees, blithering incoherently, only to be coaxed and raised again to his feet by the monks who found themselves at the mercy of a foul-mouthed, nerve-shattered drunkard. As they stepped deeper into the forest, the *bravado* he had exclaimed in the beating of his unfaithful wife changed to unmanly delusions in his muzzy mind, so that at times, speaking out loud, he seemed to be incriminating himself in Brother Maria's death. At other times he seemed no longer sure if he had killed him in his thoughts, in actuality, or not at all. He began to cry, and crying, blubber his words.

"I did not murder him.....at least I do not think I murdered him. You see I drink much wine, and many times I do things I do not remember.

I remember hunting him with dogs and other men. I remember vowing to kill him, and doing horrible things to him.....of cutting off his tongue, hands and feet, of swilling the swine with his cock and balls.....but I do not remember if I did these things or not, or if I only dreamed I did these things.......

I am afraid, holy brothers, I am afraid I murdered him and hung him in the tree for the birds to eat and the winds to rot.....I am afraid his ghost is near that tree, waiting for me.....I am afraid it will haunt my dreams, slit my throat as I sleep.....oh brothers, if I believe in your God, will your God protect me from the ghost of the one I killed.....the ghost hanging from the gallows in the tree?......."

* * *

AGAIN the candle in the niche, the removing of his habit.....the reaching and finding, like a knight his sword, the gruesome battle weapon he must once more stain with his blood.....and with it the hourglass, this tiny cage that had captured the grains of the stars, that had imprisoned each snowflake that had ever fallen.....whose slow soft sifting measured Love's bloody strokes lashed on all men's soldiery backs.......

.....again his kneeling on the stones, his raising of the bloody, nail-studded flog, the whisper of the prayer that began to warble like an ice-melting brook from his mouth.......

.....Pater Noster, qui es in Caelis,

Sanctificetur namen

Adveniat regnum tuum.......

.....and then the slaps that smarted more keenly tonight, the teeth that bit more deeply, more eagerly, more sweetly.....the skin that broke and the blood that trickled more freely from the blades of his shoulders, down the stick of his spine and his jackal-thin ribs, until their runnels dripped like melting icicles from the gaunt stumps of his buttocks.....their drops like the hot tears of a lover, full of pain and joy, dripping with sacrifice to the stones below......

.....The Abbot Father knew his secret. There was something in his eye that lent a whimsical sapience to his words.....indeed, that imbued his questions with foreknowledge.....something that he knew, and knowing, condoned and accepted, as if, as God's steward, he knew God's mercy had condoned and accepted it too.......

The abbot knew his secret, but did he himself know it? Why did it remain a smile on the old abbot's lips and a sparkle in his eyes, and not a truth in his own heart? Did the Abbot Father see some great irony in him, the preeminent scholar of their brotherhood, something he did not see in himself? Did the abbot feel that he was in love, yes, in love with Brother Maria?

Was he?

He honestly did not know. He who lived for love did not know what love was. This thing men called 'love'; this rare bird that flew between men's flesh and spirit, singing to both, making its nest in both, remained a great mystery to him. He had never known this mystical affection; its wine had never intoxicated his heart, and never intoxicating it, he knew that he was safe from the gaudy and giddy, and often stupid intrusion it made on other hearts.

He remembered only once, once only that his heart had fluttered, and he had, as men say, 'fallen in love'......a memory that had never gone away, a memory that continued to live, like a live ember in his heart.

He had never been a handsome or a robust boy. He had been shy, and shrank from the rowdier gangs at the orphanage. It was therefore a surprise to him that one day a plain, somewhat sickly girl approached him on the playground, stood awkwardly before him, and then leaned forward and pecked a kiss upon his cheek. Embarrassed and tongue-tied, he knew not what to do, and was only rescued by a priest who vigorously shook a bell, calling the children back to their lessons.

......Oh, but what a storm of feelings that little peck had incited inside him! How that kiss had burned on his cheek, and burning on his cheek branded like a red hot iron his heart. Oh how, when at night he closed his eyes for sleep, how those dark eyes had peered into his soul, exploring it as no one had ever explored it before. What a lightning struck through his heart when he saw her skip, or heard her laugh, as that little skip and little laugh had given his heart wings.

......And oh, how that lightning changed to a great sword when he saw her borne from the orphanage on a litter, sick and pale and coughing blood, her limbs frail and twig-like, the ghost of death staring from her pretty dark eyes. Oh, how he wanted to smother her pale cheeks with kisses, kisses that she had made bloom from his heart like roses, in return for that precious peck she had given him.

He had never spoken to her; he had never learned her name; and he had never seen her again. She was buried in the corner of the churchyard where the orphaned, the consumptives, and the pauperized are buried; a nameless stone or clump of nettles marking where the wings of his blessed angel were laid to rest.

Was this love? He did not know. He only knew that if he lashed his back ten thousand nights, this memory, like an ember in his heart, would continue to glow. He only knew he had never told her what he had so wished to tell her.

* * *

The Dead Man

THE place to which the drunken man led them was deep in the forest, but not so deep as not having been searched previously by the parties looking for their missing brother. It was just that autumn had shed its colorful garments, and now the forest stood denuded all around them. Even before the brothers reached the place where the man had made his discovery, they saw the habit hanging before them, like a corpse bound to a ship's mast. Indeed, as it was a dead man left dangling from a gallows, complete with the drooping cowl, like the broken-necked head of one hanged, it hung stark and grim, high in the bare boughs that outreached the other trees about it.

Once having led the brothers to this spot, the drunkard quailed fearfully away, and with shivering nerves refused to be of any further help to them. Afraid that the habit might conceal a skeleton of bones, or even the ghost of the dead man he had deluded himself into thinking he might have killed, the man refused to climb into the tree and retrieve it. This was left to the brothers, who, with no little trouble of many failed attempts, finally succeeded in cutting the cincture by which the habit hung, at which the habit, heavy with dampness, dropped heavily through the bare branches to the ground, working the perverse illusion that it indeed contained the corpse of their missing brother.

Meanwhile a cursory look by the rest of the monks about the great tree did not produce what they so dreaded to find; nor did more thorough inspections in the days to come, inspections that expanded into wider and wider hunts about the tree. The brothers found no hint of foul play by bandits or murderers, nor evidence of the savage appetite of animals.

But there could be no doubt: it was Brother Maria's habit that had been hung like a dead man in the large tree; as it was the skin shed by a serpent, or the feathers molted by a bird; as it was a man who wished to be crucified by the many spites of weather, his identity left to decay and break into threads, picked clean by wind and sun, rain and snow.

* * *

Drops of blood; grains of love

HAD he loved Brother Maria? Perhaps; no, certainly he had. But there had been nothing improper, nothing unclean, nothing scandalous about his love. Love's passion was a stranger, an unwanted guest to his heart, one that he had never allowed to cross its threshold, and not crossing it, he had never known the mischief it invariably brought to other men. He had learned to spiritualize the sparks of the senses, their denial a spiritual fuel, smothering their potential rage; tamping and taming them into the pure, steady flame of equanimity and wisdom.

He had heard of scandals in other brotherhoods, of brothers who, becoming drunk, solicited prostitutes in the villages where their errands had taken them; or even more monstrously, had violated holy sisters. Sill other lurid tales had told of brothers found together, naked and in lascivious embraces, or even brothers found fornicating with animals; acts of sodomy and bestiality that resulted in scourging, defrocking, and the expulsion from the Order. But his conscience was not troubled with such wrong affections. No, it was clean and clear, the reflection in its pool was not muddied with wanton hungers of the flesh, only troubled with the lonely starvation of the spirit.

Only once had temptation stepped dangerously into his heart, and that in a dream, and not in his waking.

In the dream he and Brother Maria were sitting on a garden bench, shortly after Maria had received some sacks of flour from the miller's young daughter. He had watched as Maria had given her a basket of bread in return for the flour, and as he placed it in her arms the girl tickled his shins with her bare toes, and then pressing a bared knee between his legs, brought her mouth to his mouth, giving it a lingering kiss.

Afterwards he had watched Maria cross the courtyard, and as he did he had kissed the mouths of the holy statues, in much the same way as he had kissed the miller's daughter; and when he did the faces of the statues, even that of the dolorous Holy Mother blushed and brightened, breaking their stones with living smiles.

When Maria had returned to the garden bench, he had asked what such a thing was like; what was the magic it contained. Was it sweet like honey; like a ripe fig or a berry? Could he, as his friend, taste it too?

132

He had brought his mouth to Maria's mouth, but just as he was about to touch his lips, Maria's mouth had opened, and a flock of golden and azure birds flew forth, singing the beautiful melodies of his laughter; even as the taste of the kiss was a secret he would not tell.

* * *

The Ghost

WHEN the habit had dropped heavily to the ground from the tree's height, the drunkard had screamed out and fled from sight, insanely mistaking its sodden wool for bones that the habit still contained. Out of his mind with wine, superstition, and most likely his guilt of past crimes, he had only cautiously reappeared when the brothers had knelt to examine it.

"Is it his habit? Is it the golden brother's habit?"

"Yes, it is his; it is certainly Brother Maria's habit."

"And there are no parts of his body left in it?"

"It is his habit, and nothing more."

"You are very sure of the thing?"

"There can be no doubt. I recognize this tear in the sleeve, and these soot and tallow stains."

The word *stain* elicited a great frenzy in the drunkard, a frenzy that brought tears, like a whining child from his nerve-shattered dissipation.

"Stains, there are stains? Dark stains.....dark stains as from blood?"

"No; the habit has been rained upon, and has begun to break apart in places, to become threadbare and rot, but there are no bloodstains upon it; no, none at all."

"And no holes where a knife.....you see I wanted to stab him many times in many places....I swore I would stab him in many places.....in hss guts, in his heart, in his throat.....and I had a large knife.....there must be blood and holes where I stabbed him with my knife......."

But when a brother assured the drunk, guilt-ridden man there were no bloodstains or indications of where a knife had stabbed or slashed, the delusional wretch did not hear his words. He was convinced that he had murdered the monk, having vowed, plotted and practiced the thing over and over in his mind; this having lent his cowardice a pathetic kind of meaning, a thing that in the blear of hate and fear in his drunkenness, had won a battle with reality.

.....you see I sometimes forget when I drink strong wine.....and I remember I wanted to stab him many times.....because I had stripped my wife of her clothes, and saw the places where his hands had scratched and his kisses had bitten her when he tumbled the bitch like a dog in the bushes..... and when I smelled her I smelled him upon her, the smell of the golden monk upon the bitch.....the smell of a man's love is as foul as the smell of a goat's piss.....and I had sworn to kill him, even if that meant climbing the walls of your abbey and killing the bastard in his prayers........

* * *

Last Grains

......BUT the question remained: 'Was he in love with Brother Maria?' Yes, but not that love that besots the senses; not the kind that Maria enjoyed with the shepherdess. Still, had his heart not contracted with jealously when his friend had confessed his escapade with the girl? And when he had heard the flute from the dark forest, had their trills not stabbed through his heart like a dagger?

Even now did strange thoughts not steal upon him, strange thoughts that portrayed his friend playing in the meadow grasses with the young silly girl? Did Maria not know he had given his heart to him, a heart that was weeping and bleeding for him? How could he chase after such a silly creature, preferring to roll like a beast on the forest floors, instead of embracing his gifts of scholarship and learning; gifts that were the treasures of his very soul; that Time's moths and rusts would not find; that would not grow old, wither and corrupt, like the soft places on a woman's body?

He remembered telling his Abbot Father how Brother Maria was as beautiful as a woman, and as keen-sensed and strong-limbed as a hunter. It was true; and this coexistence bewitched and infatuated those in his presence, making men desire his company, and women his intimacy.

But it did not stop there; for as Brother Maria had been an exemplar ascetic, there had always seemed something wild, almost pagan beneath that asceticism. Although obedient in every way, there seemed something untamed, something primitive, something that brooked almost upon the savage about him; as he shared as much with the forest animals as with the men who built walls to defend against those animals. His eyes were full of calm and humility, but deeper in those eyes there dwelt one who was ever hunted, who was dispossessed; one who would ever remain a vagrant to all camps and temples built by men; the hunted who owned the fierceness of the hunter.

Maria was possessed of a rare beauty, and he, a priest, found himself envying that beauty, in the same way he envied the holiness of a Saint. Yes, that was it; his envy was his 'love', an envy of something his prayers would never bring him.

* * *

The Corpse

EVEN as the brothers began to depart from the forest, the crazy drunkard did not go near the habit they were carrying, still unconvinced that he had not somehow murdered Maria, and that Maria's ghost still lingered somewhere near. The wretch lagged behind them, the distance gradually becoming greater as he stumbled, and stopped from time to time to swig more wine. And when he did, he shouted at the brothers, the shouts becoming fainter and fainter, but still full of his delusional, self *bravado*.

"*I smelled him on her!....I smelled the pretty golden monk on her body!.....and I stabbed him.....I stabbed him many times when I caught him on top of her!.....humping like a dog humps a bitch, like the damned bitch she is!..... I killed him and I hung him!.....left him for the birds to eat!....*"

Leaving the forest, the monks crossed the harvested field, and started up the hill to the abbey's gates; more like a funeral procession, than a troop of monks. Their discovery had greatly sobered them; made them strangely solemn; a solemnity that had made them impervious to the slurs and accusations that the winebibber had shouted at them, and that they could still hear somewhere behind them, in the darkness that was now beginning to fall..

They had not wadded, or wrapped the habit into a careless bundle, but had treated it with a kind of care, straightening and brushing it. One of the brothers had carried it over his shoulder, as if lending dignity to the one that had so severely erred in sin, or stumbled in fate, but nevertheless had touched their hearts.

Nearing the gates, another brother had taken the habit from his brother's shoulder, and entering the abbey, held it like a corpse in his arms.

* * *

The Moon

.....Sancta Maria, Mater Dei,
Ora pro nobis peccatoribus,
Nunc et in hora mortis, nastrae......

THE last grains had funneled through the glass. He stood, wrapped the flog into a coil, and laid it back in the *niche*. He blew out the candle, only to kneel in the darkness again, unrobed. There, in the exquisite pleasure of the reward his smarting wounds had given him, he waited for the last drops to complete their courses down his back.

He had punished himself more severely tonight. The nails had bitten more deeply, and the runnels they had invoked from his flesh were more numerous, and ran more swiftly than on other nights. Yes, he had punished himself more severely, and he could feel that it had left him very weak. But he felt strong in his weakness, strong and very thankful. The hand of *love* had been remorseless, like a wicked master of slaves, and he had drunk its lashes like a sweet wine.

Yes, that was it: the hand of love had wielded the scourge tonight, and he was glad that it had not stayed its fury; that it had wounded him deeply. He closed his eyes, and when he did he felt the last drops running down his back, singing with gratitude.

Walking back to the cloister, Father Giovanni paused at the edge of the courtyard. A gelatinous tide of moonlight had washed over the walls into the sleeping abbey, its blanket blanketing the gardens, walks, and holy statues like a shimmering snow. He could see the moon, like a goddess's eye gazing through the arches of the bell-tower; as it was a toy of stones left by a child in an ancient race of giants; or an hourglass..... an hourglass that had been forgotten by those giant ones, still faithfully sifting *Time's* grains.

Above, the stars were beginning to burn sharp and clear through the darkness, as they were candles being lighted by an invisible hand;

perhaps the same hand that had wounded his back, and more deeply, his heart.

How mysterious was this Hand; this Hand of Love, at once brutal, bloody and exacting, and at the same time so full of tender and abundant mercies; all the while maintaining its eternal mystery, so that Man could not begin to guess its ways or meanings.

Tears burned his eyes, tears that burned with the same fire that had rained tears of blood down his back. Yes, there had been the downy wing of Love in the scourge. Yes, his heart had received Love's chrism, its kiss; its sacred wound. He had been stabbed to the quick by a young, foolish, reprobate monk, one who had hung his habit like a scarecrow in the top of a tree; a scarecrow that was a cocoon wherein a butterfly had formed and slept, only to flutter away into the world. Yes, if he knew what love was it was because of this gypsy child who had forsaken salvation to play in the arms of a peasant girl.

He lifted his eyes once more to the moon, its silver gaze resting near the bell; as for a moment it was passing through this glass of stones; briefly, as it was winking; as it too was a grain, a beam, a mote being sifted through an hourglass.

Yes, his friend had left, but not before leaving him a gift that had allowed him to taste his Savior's wounds. Yes, this was what he had seen in Father Augustine's eyes. Yes, his Abbot Father knew that he loved Brother Maria, and he approved of that love. Yes, he would be the next abbot. Yes, he would shepherd his brothers until the day he died.

Father Giovanni turned and began to enter the cloister, and as he did he reached into the pocket of his robe, gripping tight what Father Augustine had given him, without a word, after their last prayers tonight.

The brothers had found a flute in the habit that was hung like a dead man in the tree; a flute like the shepherds play in the summer fields.

. . . .

. . . .

CHAPTER SEVEN

NEW LOVERS, LABORS, DREAMS
PART I

FOR the next days and weeks Brother Maria wandered aimlessly through the fields and forests; the refrains of autumn thundering rich and golden as he did. Having no destination, he neither knew nor cared where his steps were leading him. And yet, though all was new and unfamiliar, he was not afraid. He felt a warm welcome from the coloring forests and the drifting clouds, a welcome that helped assuage the pangs of farewell from the life he was leaving behind in the abbey's walls.

......the world with its mystery of forests, hills and clouds stretched endlessly before and all about him......oh, how lovely to lose oneself in this mystery, to be embraced by it, be a part of it.....no longer to debate or wrangle with it, fear or scorn it, deny or hide from it......but to gather its beauty into one's arms, one's heart, one's dreams.....not to slay, but to surrender and be fed by its wildness.....with the brief flame of one's soul, explore and be lost in its forever-ness.......

He imagined himself a sailor that had set sail for exploration and adventure. Having lived a landlubber's life of strict, regimented prayer, self-abnegation and penance, the hills and forests seemed a limitless sea of limitless glory to him; rich at every step with the jewels of singing birds, gurgling brooks and painted flowers. All delighted him; even a sharp wind or an angry thunder. Unmoored into this new sea, all was new, fresh and lavish to the waked children of his senses; intoxicating them with a world burning with autumnal flames, singing with sweet-throated birds, and flowering with sweet fruits and berries. It was as if he had parted a drab curtain, and walked into a shimmering dream that had long awaited his entrance.

Rapt with these new wonders, he sometimes felt guilty that he had left the shepherd girl to whom he had so fervently pledged his heart. At first he had dwelt for long hours on the plaintive words she had last spoken to him. But he soon convinced himself that he would ponder and puzzle the truth of these words out later, perhaps before a glowing hearth when the world was bleak and frozen, and not so lush with its fires and songs. She whom he had sworn an angel soon faded from his mind; preoccupied as he became with his growling stomach, his nightly need for shelter, and his inebriation with such a teeming anthem of earth and heaven. Only for the first day or two had he been sorrowfully haunted with her maimed beauty; her bruised eye, swollen lip and broken tooth. He felt ashamed that it was sometimes difficult for him to remember her face at all; that instead, he dwelt for long whiles on her young body: her slender hips and tapering waist, the arousal of her breasts and the arch of her neck as love's final quiver quivered through her.

At first he had reproved himself. He had whispered prayers to God, or falling to his knees, made the Sign of the Cross, asking forgiveness for his unclean thoughts. He had even resolved to return to this beautiful one that had given him her treasures, teaching him such wonderful things. He had resolved to rescue her from her degenerate husband; if necessary, daring him to a fistfight. But gradually the painted hills and forests dispelled such resolutions, and the pain in his heart was replaced with the joy and curiosity of adventure; her disfigured face fading into meadow flowers and pretty winged butterflies. Only when he closed his eyes for sleep did her features return; sly and cunning with seduction, or contorted and grimacing in the throes of her passion. Only then, lonely for her lovely and wicked embraces, and yearning to cry out to her, did he remember that he had never learned her name.

Sometimes he would walk upon meandering forest paths, paths that would enchant with some indefinable promise, only for that promise to become entangled in impassable briars and thickets. At other times he would walk upon small cart roads, ox trails or goat paths, not knowing nor caring where they would lead. But more times than not he would simply walk through the fields and the forests without path or trail, as if content with continued exploration, and the revelations that that exploration would bring; new meadows, new flowers, new songs of birds and brooks.

He could take no wrong path, because he owned no destination; and he could not be lost, because he was continually new-found in the splendors given his delighted senses. Although he did not understand why, it became his habit, even his instinct to avoid hamlets and dwellings, as if he felt he was now part of an ancient race of nomadic wanderers, one that had been sentenced to make their way apart from the habitations of other men. Or truer to his feelings, he sometimes dreamily imagined he was a creature of the wild, a deer or a bear or a wolf, a creature loosed into the unending fray of predator and prey; the eternal world of the hunt.

But despite his estrangement and itinerancy, he could not help accidental interactions with his kind, as after several weeks of wandering came his way.

At nightfall he seemed to always find, as by some ancient instinct waked in him, a safe shelter for his sleep. Avoiding barns and byres, no matter how deserted or inviting they seemed, he built lean-tos against large stones or forest trees, making his beds of ferns and dry leaves. When he was in the open country-side, he had slept beside hayricks, of which the autumn fields abounded. Waking in the early dawn, he would steal away, avoiding his discovery, and the questions such a discovery would certainly bring.

But one chill dawn he had not stolen early away, having been seduced by the first warming rays of the sun. Instead, his slumber was waked by a sharp prodding in his side. Startled, he woke to find a large, muscular man standing over him with a pitchfork, and a malicious leer in his eye.

"*Who are you, and why are you sleeping here? A thief? A criminal? Perhaps a killer on the run? Speak, and speak quickly and honestly, or I will skewer your bowels with this fork, and leave you for the crows to pick and quibble over.*"

"*I had no place to sleep, and I did not think there would be any harm..... you see, I normally begin to journey at the day's breaking, but the morning was frosty, and the sun was warm, and, well I.......*"

"*This is my field, and I do not like strangers, either thief or beggar!*"

"*I am neither. You see I am one making a religious pilgrimage, a pilgrimage to holy altars, wells, and other places blest by the blessedness of Christ, Mary, and the Saints!*"

"*A likely story. A practiced ruffian could as easily say the same.*"

"*But it is true. I am a religious, and neither a thief or ruffian. See, my cropped hair, and this crucifix about my neck.........*"

"*But you are not from here. You can not be from here. Your skin and hair are fair, as are the people of the north, and your eyes are as blue as the sky.*"

"*Yes, it is true. You see I did not know my father, and my mother, only when I was very young.....we traveled a great deal, in wagons.....*"

"*What would make me believe these things you say are not full of a practiced cunning, and your hair and crucifix a clever disguise?*"

At this Brother Maria raised up on his knees, closed his eyes, and lifting his face to the sky spread wide his arms. Only feet from the man and his pitchfork, readied like a harpoon, he slowly and solemnly recited a *Pater Noster*, not in the peasant vernacular, but in Latin.

His anger assuaged, but not his suspicion, the man lowered his pitchfork.

"*Well, whether you are a thief, killer, dissembler, or a holy disciple of Christ as you avow, young man, you are trespassing on my property. I want you to leave at once. I do not want to see you again. Go!*"

With this the man pointed with his pitchfork to the woods that formed a border about the field, and without a word Maria kissed the ground before his feet, made the Sign of the Cross, and began to make his way in the direction the man was sternly pointing. Yet before he reached the trees, the man shouted out, calling him back again. Returning, Maria found the man softened, and perhaps touched with guilt.

"*Young man, uh, holy pilgrim, you must forgive me. You see, there have been many robbers and ruffians about, well, and I thought.....and my wife and I are very devout, servants of Our Lady. We sometimes make pilgrimages of our own.*

Look, you look a little lean in the ribs and hollow in the jowls, as you could use a good square meal, eh? Come, you have convinced me of your story, whether it's a bit of a yarn or not. Let me give you a good meal before you are on your way, to show you I am not all vinegar and flint. You look like a strong young man, and I have a great deal of firewood to chop before the winds of winter howl.... and well, ha, to tell the truth, I am not as young as I once was......."

Maria smiled brightly at the man, and accepted his invitation. Following him to his large house, he saw that one of the legs of his trousers was empty, that he was missing a leg, but notwithstanding such a deprivation, he appeared bullish strong, using the pitchfork as a crutch to agilely and lustily hobble back through the field.

The man's hospitality stopped short of allowing Maria to enter his house, and he was shown to the barn where he promised a bed would be prepared for the night, and a warm meal brought to him. The man then led him to a wood-yard, showed him the felled timber that had been dragged there, and the axe that he confessed, due to his handicap and age, he could not wield as he once did. Patting Maria congenially on the shoulder, the good old man limped away, only to return shortly before noon, pleased to find a stout stack of firewood that the strong young wanderer had robustly chopped. Good to his promise, the man's matronly wife brought him a good meal, replete with meat, greens and bread. Without a word she had duteously placed it before him, and Maria had ravenously eaten.

Impressed and very pleased with his work, the man asked Maria to stay on, and Maria gladly accepted. After his days of wandering, he was very grateful for such hospitality. The nights were becoming cool, and he welcomed the warm bed in the hay barn, and the generous meals that replaced his diet of berries and bitter nuts in the forests. He also welcomed the routine of this new employment. Waking before dawn, he prayed and washed, and just as morning began to part the curtains of the night, the axe was ringing in his hands.

The work was not work to him, and each morning he went to the wood-yard with eagerness. Wielding the large axe, he felt a delicious exhilaration well up from his depths; the dormant, untested muscles in his arms, chest and shoulders flexing, knitting and singing, as they were slaves set free of their bonds. The more he raised and let fall the axe, the more exuberant he became, and by the mid-mornings his shirt was off and the new child of his brawn was glistening golden with sweat. At times he even began to sing, at first psalms and hymns he had sung each day in the abbey, but gradually other words and melodies, ones he recalled from his youth; songs that he half-remembered, or extemporarily composed as the axe happily rang.

.....*Come to the river tonight,*
When the nightingale woos the moon,
Come to my arms tonight,
And heal my heart's deep wound,

For stabbed to the quick,
And made heartsick
By your beauty fair and bright,
The flower of my heart wilts and swoons.....

The old man was entirely won over by Maria's energy, his cheerful spirit, and the stacks of winter firewood that were sprouting like giant mushrooms all about the wood-yard. He would visit him regularly, and would tell him anecdotal stories with great bellows of hearty laughter. His wife would also come to the wood-yard, and as she was the man's shadow, would wordlessly leave a demijohn of wine and a basket of meat and bread for him. She was as reticent as her husband was blusterous, so much that Maria wondered if she could speak at all. She gave the impression of not only being shy, but also afraid, as she had been threatened, even beaten into her deference, and she never once spoke or lifted her eyes to him.

The man's wife became a curiosity to Maria. Once, stripped of his shirt, when wine and arduous toil were letting his axe ring and his voice sing in a particularly lusty way, he was sure the woman had stopped after bringing him his meal, and in a guarded way, was watching him from behind a tree.

So won over with this young man's golden smile, carefree songs and prodigious labor, after four or five days the old man surprised Maria by telling him he had prepared a bed for him in a parlor of his house, and invited him to begin dining with him and his wife in the evenings; to which Maria beamed, and respectfully, gratefully agreed.

The home of the old couple was very pleasant, and possessed a simple, although not lavish opulence that Maria had never known before; certainly not at the abbey, nor in the house of those that had adopted him when he was a boy. Although comfortable in all ways, there was one peculiarity that seemed a kind of theme of its furnishings.

Before losing his leg, the man had been an avid hunter, and in nearly every room there were trophies of his hunts: pelts of wolves, bears and wildcats nailed on walls and hung from rafters, used as rugs, as well as drapes and cushions for furniture. He had left the heads attached to these pelts, and where the eyes had decayed from their sockets, he had placed pieces of sparkling glass. This had the effect of animating the pelts, as if giving them a living genius, so that one felt the house was a kind of forest with wild creatures alive and ever prowling; ever watching.

But after several weeks, restlessness revisited Maria. He had chopped and stacked a great store of firewood, one that could last the winter through. And although snow was still high in the mountains, and the old man had made a generous offer, even a petition to keep Maria safe and warm under his roof, devising all sorts of odd jobs for him to do, Maria declined his kind offer, professing that he was bound by his vows to continue his pilgrimage. Of course this was a lie, but what else could he say? He could not tell the truth of his desertion from the abbey, a thing almost as criminal as a murder. And he did not want to become a burden to the elderly couple. Besides, confined with the two old people, the winter months would certainly wax long and dull. His labor in the wood-yard had stirred awake a new vigor in him, one that woke new desires to roam and wander; to see and know new things. Assuring the old man both of his gratitude and the conviction that demanded his departure, Maria prepared his few things in a rucksack, and bidding the old couple goodnight, retired to his bed in the parlor, intending to rise, pray and leave before the morning light.

Excited about the new adventures and hardships that awaited him, Maria laid awake, watching the forest of dancing shadows cast by the softly glowing hearth on the ceiling over his head. In this gently dancing forest he saw his friend, Father Giovanni, solemnly kneel in prayer, and

Abbot Augustine, hobbling across the courtyard with his cane, smiling his sweet kind smile. He heard the great bell ring for prayer, and the music of his brothers' softly-intoned chants ......and the great Crucifix hung on the choir's wall, the Crucifix he had kissed so many times. Stricken with pangs of remorse, tears welled in his eyes; but as sleep began to steal upon him, he stole deeper into the magic forest of burning shadows, and as it was a refuge, forgot the abbey, his brothers, and the shameful thing he had done.

.....he saw flocks of brightly painted birds, and schools of winged fish fly through this forest.....and a great horned stag chasing a half-denuded maiden..... a young girl, a shepherd girl running and laughing through the trees.....only to stop now and then, and with the lovely silver trill of her flute, promise the stag its beastly pleasure........

Suddenly Maria was startled from this fantastic forest he had entered before sleep's gates. He was startled from his dream to what seemed another dream. Someone had entered the parlor, but hearing neither the thud or dragging of a crutch, Maria knew it was not the old man.

Sitting up in his bed, he was amazed to see instead his slavish, taciturn wife. In her nightgown, and silent as a ghost, she walked to the hearth, and placed a pillow on the bearskin spread on the floor before it. As she was an apparition, she proceeded to sit upon a chair, and stare into the fire.

Spellbound, Maria watched as the woman, after a long pause, raised up her hands and unbound the bound hanks of her hair; and then shaking them free, let a cascade of silver gray tresses fall down upon her. Even more incredible, she then loosened her nightgown, and slipped it over her shoulders, baring both of them.

And as the breathless moments passed, desire breathed forth its perfume. Deeper and more communicative than words, the mystery of *woman* was singing to the helpless need of *man*, seducing him like a child into her secret world. As an answer to that plea, Maria rose from his bed, and walked the few steps to the unspeaking woman. As she was a phantom, he stood behind her, entranced; afraid to speak and unsure of what to do.

Finally, light as feathers, Maria placed his fingers on her hair. It was not coarse as he supposed it would be, but soft and downy, and like a comb he found his opened fingers sliding down and through its downy ropes until, reaching her shoulder, he let his hand rest lightly upon its nakedness. Feeling his hesitancy and timidity, the woman turned her face and gently kissed it, giving him her silent consent and affirmation. Entranced, Maria let his other hand again comb through her long gray tresses; only to come to a rest upon her other shoulder; at which she gave the same reassurance.

Bending down, Maria returned those kisses, lightly kissing each of her bare shoulders, and when he did he felt a shiver of pleasure, gentle as a smile purr deep inside her. Without once lifting her eyes to him, the woman stood, and letting her gown slip to her feet, stepped nakedly from it; and then lay down on the bearskin before the fire.

Age had been kind to her, and Maria soon found he was drowning in a sea of delights that the years had preserved more than they had diminished. In places age had thickened her, but it had not flaccidly burdened or wrinkled her. It had instead fashioned a matronly voluptuousness; one not imparted to youth, but reserved for an elitist few in age. In her secret places, places the sun had never found, she was still soft, white and delicate; as silky as a flower petal. Her breasts could still

145

be provoked; her fingers were still light and feathery; her kisses, still moist and sweet; her blood still warm, and ready and willing to stir into flames.

Age had also stored in her heart many naughty and passionate desires, desires whose games she had long since played, or perhaps never played with her husband. Her husband had long been a cripple, and more than likely he had demanded that she, like a concubine and not a wife, fulfill him in ways that did not allow her own gratification. Maria found in the older woman a most passionate lover, a mother of seven children who had never been tenderly and passionately loved, ready to answer each show of tenderness and passion, and to give freely of her untold and unused needs.

Maria knew how profanely perverse was this thing, performing libidinous acts with a woman twice his age, even as her sleepless, one-legged husband dragged and thumped his crutch on the floor directly above the rollick of their sins. But her loving was as deep and dark as the night, her games even more clever and cunning than what the young shepherdess had played with him, and despite the cries of his conscience, he continued in her arms until the fire burned ember low.

Shortly before dawn the woman whispered in Maria's ear, the only words she had ever spoken to him:

"Must you leave me, my beautiful darling?"

"Yes, I must leave. I have packed my things….."

"But I could visit you many times, and we could love each other many nights and in many ways through the long cold winter. My husband likes you. You need only tell him that you have changed your mind, and that you would like to stay until the spring."

"But my pilgrimage, my vows……"

"Make your pilgrimage over the hills and valleys of my body. God is also here, deep in my arms and kisses. Stay my young golden one, and let us be sweet to each other, as we have this night."

"But it might be dangerous, for both of us…..and besides, our ages, I am younger, much younger…..perhaps, perhaps younger than your….."

Her voice now changed; no longer soft and languid, but now coarse and strident.

"Then you think I am old, too old to give you the pleasures the young peasant girls may give you?"

"No, I did not mean what I said in that way. You are very beautiful,

and you have given me very beautiful things.......”

"I do not want you to go! I will not let you go! If you leave I will tell my husband that you have violated me. He is as stupid as a pig. He will believe me. He will track you down with dogs, bludgeon you with an axe.....toss you on one of the wood stacks to rot the winder through!"

But then her voice changed again, and like a kitten's purr, she whispered in his ear.

"Did you not like the things I brought to you tonight?"

"Yes, they were very sweet....."

"Then stay my beautiful one, stay! You will not be sorry. I will not let you be sorry. I will give you things the peasant girls do not know. They will only lift their skirts and lie on their backs for you, but I know many tricks and pleasures. I will please my pretty boy as they could never please you."

With this the woman bent over him, and kissing his lips and face, continued down Maria's chest, her face vanishing into the tent of her long gray tresses. Finding his most tender place, she lent him a pleasure he had not known before. Completing her sorcery, she stood and slipped on her gown, only to kneel to him again, and once more whisper in his ear:

"I will have a beautiful breakfast waiting for you. I will tell him you have changed your mind. He is a stupid, one-legged pig of a man. He will not know, and we will be very happy."

And so for the next days Maria stayed on in comfort, lust and danger. The old man was delighted in his change of mind, and gave him an abundance of chores and tasks to engage him. He was delighted not only with Maria's youth and strength, but that he had found a factotum to take care of many neglected repairs.

Each night the man's wife came to him like a ghost, like a member of the dead enacting a ritual it had performed among the living: laying a pillow on the bearskin by the fire, unbinding her long gray tresses, and then stepping naked from her gown. Without a word she would lay down on the bearskin, and Maria would go to her, obedient to her invitation. Often with her husband thudding and dragging his crutch across the floor directly above them, and sometimes holding conversations with his self, they would play many games; sometimes until the fire died, and the first cocks crowed.

During the day the woman would resume her former *persona*, rarely speaking, and servile to the old man; never once giving Maria a glance, brush or smile. Only once did she break from her strict and stoic disguise.

One morning when the old man hobbled to the barn, she suddenly looked at Maria with a steely stare, and silently motioned for him to follow her. His mistress now in all ways, Maria readily obeyed. Upon climbing the stairs she led him to the doorway of her sleeping room; a room that was small, sunny, and sparsely furnished. Still without a word she then led him down the hall to another room, one whose door she opened with a key. It was a room that was large and far more lavishly furnished, but in a state of clutter and disarray. This was certainly her husband's room, evidenced by the stale, unaired residue of tobacco and opium, his heavy boots beside the bed, a hookah on a nightstand, and a row of canes with ornately carved knobs, some of serpents and open-jawed beasts, hung neatly along one wall. Near this collection of canes were hung a number of wolf and bear pelts, as they were a hunter's kill; pelts that had retained the beasts' heads, tails and claws.

But most strangely conspicuous, on the wall above the bed were drawings, strange drawings made with charcoal and ochre. They were simply, crudely drawn, and but for their crudity and depravity, one would think they had been drawn by children: drawings of a bull, a horned stag, and a great-fanged, long-tailed wolf, each with large human phalluses, lolling tongues and great snouts. Each was abusing a naked woman, each in its own wicked way.

Unspeaking, the woman brusquely entered this room, and to Maria's astonishment, even as she had done that first night by the hearth, she proceeded to unpin and shake free her hair, and then to quickly unbutton and slip from her skirt and blouse. Throwing back the blanket on the old man's bed, she lay down, and turning to Maria, said emphatically, coldly: "*Come.*"

This was too peculiar and far too dangerously daring for Maria. He stepped away, a thing the woman did not like. A harshness filled her face, and with it a cold and wrinkled oldness. She snapped her fingers, exhorting Maria to come receive the pleasure she was offering him. But Maria hesitated, and stepped another step nearer the door, a step that elicited a harsher shrillness in the woman's voice, a voice Maria had learned to dislike, if not fear.

"*Do not be silly, my precious boy. Be quick, before he returns. I am not asking, I am telling you to come to me. Remember, I am your mistress, and you do not want your mistress to tell our little secret, do you? Who would he believe, silly boy, his duteous wife of thirty years, or a vagabond counterfeiting as a wandering monk?*

You must surely know how much I hate him, and hating him, how much satisfaction it would give me to know I have enjoyed another man in the very place where he uses me; here, beneath these silly pictures of his lust. Yes, I have been both his wife and his whore for thirty years, performing the things you see scrawled on this wall, even as the one-legged fool drapes himself in pelts, imagining he is a wolf or a bear. Come, Maria, you know you like the things I do for you; you know that you like them very much. Come here at once, it will not take long! I want to make a cuckold of the one who has made me his whore."

After several weeks of this perversely duel existence, Maria resolved to leave the household. The guilt he was feeling, especially in the presence of the garrulous, albeit depraved old man was quickly becoming intolerable. It would not be difficult to leave. At night, before he was visited by his apparitional lover, or after lovemaking with her on the bearskin, he could easily slip into the night and his freedom. Then why, for what seemed interminable days did he stay on? Shamefully, he knew very well why. It was because of the wicked games and exciting adventures this older, half mad woman was bringing him each night; games and adventures that made him feel alive in dark, forbidden ways in which he had not felt alive before.

There was something else, something that at first he tried to ignore, even to forget, but as these strange days and strange nights passed, he simply could not rid from his mind. The morning when the woman had ordered him to bring his embraces to her husband's bed, Maria had seen her naked body in the bright sun, He vividly saw things about this ghostly lover he had not seen when under the spells of firelight and blind, lustful rapture. With a sense of disgust, he realized this was the one to whom he was giving his youthful ardor; one full of moles and wrinkles, with flaccid buttocks, drooping breasts and a sagging belly. Compared to the young, fresh, marble smooth body of the fawn-like shepherdess, she was a hag.

At times now midst their orgies before the fire he felt a nausea, as one caught in a web, a web whose sticky threads were long gray tresses crawling with venomous spiders. Remembering the body he had seen in the sunlight, a body gripped by age's decay, he felt as he was loving death itself, and this, for a reason he could not articulate, held and intrigued him, even in some way atoned for the shame he felt in his desertion from the abbey; that the love for which he had forsaken his vows, was cadaverous; decaying in his very arms; was death itself.

This thing's absurd, perverse reality, of making adulterous love with a woman more than twice his age, directly below the pacing and mumbling of her opium addicted husband, as well as the playacting during the day began to tell on Maria's nerves and conscience, making him at times edgy, and at times uncharacteristically sullen. During the day he began to dread the old man's convivial bluster as much as his wife's deceitful silences; silences that were ever pregnant with threat. He felt as guilty with the old man's confidences, as he did with the woman's duplicity. He began to resent both of them, especially the woman, feeling she had groomed his youth, only to make him her whore; perhaps as a kind of vindication for her husband making a lifelong whore of her. Now when she appeared at night by the fire, and lay down naked on the bearskin, he went to her with a feeling of slavish dread; as his love-making was a sort of duty, one he performed to earn his keep; a duty that was perhaps more strenuous than his chopping of the great heaps of firewood had been.

But more than this, he became increasingly frightened that their secret would be discovered. Once discovered, the old man would surely murder them, especially when he realized his trust had been violated right below his thumping cane and dragging foot, even while he babbled to the ghosts in the opium fumes of his mind.

This intense fear was made manifest one night in a strange dream, one that visited Maria as he waited for the old woman to step from the darkness, exacting his duty to love her. In the dream the bearskin by the fire became animated; gathered, filled and rose into the body of a giant bear, and began to sway and dance on its hinds. And when, midst its swaying dance it turned to him, it threw its great head back, and let forth a great bellowing guffaw of laughter. Spreading wide its forelegs, Maria saw that indeed it was only the skin of a bear, and that the shepherdess, her hair full of flowers, was playing her flute inside the bear's skeleton; as she was imprisoned in a prison of bones.

But there came an experience one night that was more strange and harrowing than a dream; one night after the old couple had bitterly quarreled during the day; a quarrel that he was sure resulted in the man beating his wife.

That night, midst their lovemaking, Maria heard the old man's thudding limp and dragging crutch grow loud, loud as he had never heard it before on the floor above them. Afraid, Maria had bolted upright, but the woman clasped him back into her arms, and with a soothing whisper in his ear, renewed their ardor, only now in more rough, ungentle ways. Affable and courteous during the day, the sleepless man, now filled with drink, opium, or madness, continued to thud, drag and curse into a kind of rage only feet above their adulterous lair; curses that seemed to only fuel the wicked passion the woman had brought him this night.

The man's tantrum seemed to excite the old woman, exciting her into new dares of passion and lovemaking; dares that seemed unnatural, almost beastly, the thud and dragging crutch, only feet from where she was fornicating with one who could be her child, spurring the secret ecstasy of her depravity, as if each thrust she was asking of Maria's love, was a knife she was driving into her husband's bowels.

"Now, like the drawings on the wall.....like the stag and the wolf......come Maria, like the things he makes me do, like the drawings on the wall.....tonight you are the wolf, tomorrow I shall be the bear.....more deeply, hurt me more deeply Maria! Kill me with your love!.....as I imagine killing the bastard with my hate!......"

The great danger and perversity of this thing culminated in a most unexpected way.

One night, charged by the wine he now drank before this aging phantom lay upon the bearskin, Maria felt a surge of hatred for her and her wicked games. Rather than obediently lying down with her, he roughly mounted her, even as the beasts in the drawings, blindly wishing to punish and break the pride of her sly games. Roused to a rough passion, he made her yield to his strength in a way that neither her age nor her venery could tolerate. She let out a long, lust-filled cry, as full of pain as it was of pleasure, only to then crumple limp as death beneath him. Above, like drums in a jungle hunt, the thudding and scraping on the boards, as well as the deranged dialogue came to an abrupt halt.

Exhausted, and stunned with the wickedness that had breathed such an animal pleasure through him, Maria lay on his back, each nerve of his body singing, giving thanks to the obscene act that made possible such a purgation of his lust. The woman nestled meekly into his arms, and whispered in his ear, as one at last tamed, and gone silly mad in that tameness.

"Yes, like that, like that my sweetheart! We will play these games and be very happy!

I will kill the son-of-a-bitch. I will poison him, or stab him with a knife in his sleep. Yes, I will stab him after he sucks his hookah, uses me, and falls asleep. He is a stupid man, a cruel man, a man whose missing leg is more useful than his shriveled cock......a one-legged, cock-less pig who bids me love strangers for his own pleasure......swineherds, stinking shepherds, peddlers of the roads. But you are different, my beautiful golden boy. I like you very much. I will be young and sweet for you. I will love you as no peasant slut could ever love you......I will let you love me in cruel ways....dressed as a wolf or a bear. I will kill him, and we will be very happy together."

With this, as that first night, she kissed his bare chest, and then disappeared beneath the muss of her gray hair, disappearing to show her gratitude, and make him hers.

She had whispered the crazy words into Maria's ear, but their whisper had been loud, as they were meant to be loud; as their perversity was spoken to an ear she was sure was listening. Yes, that was it. The thumping made by the one-legged old man during their lovemaking, as it had been a tribal song of lust, had halted.

Maria opened his eyes, and as the woman was ministering her deviltry, he looked at the low ceiling above them. The firelight enlightened a sizable knothole in one of the boards, and in that knothole there peered what he was sure was an eye, like the eye of a cat peering into a mouse's hole; an eye that sparkled, both with kill, and an obscene pleasure.

....

....

CHAPTER EIGHT

THE GIRL AT THE ABBEY'S GATES

Early winter; the abbey; 1328

AUTUMN had all but fled the hills and vales; the fires of gold, orange and russet-red doused to naked umber and gray. High above, the first winds of winter, like skeins of geese were passing in the cold nights, their wings full of snow, from which they powdered white the mountain peaks.

The weather had changed to damp and cold, but inside the walls of the hilltop abbey the brothers' routines remained unfazed and unswervingly the same. The great bell continued to punctually ring out, exhorting the brothers to their offices; from the midnight bell of *Vigils*, to day's last bells for *Vespers* and *Compline*. As it was the voice of their *living God*, the brothers strictly obeyed the bell, shuffling to and from their prayers; their sandals wearing the flagstones glassy smooth, like a brook polishing its bed of pebbles.

Only mortality would dare to interfere with the brothers' routines; wounding one with a lame hip, one with congested lungs, one with aching teeth; others with failing sight or hearing; still others with enfeebled minds. Like a cat with a mouse *death* played with the brothers, whimsically deciding when to pounce, grip and munch; and then to bury his bones in the dark hole of their crypt; directly below where the living brothers, like soldiers marching to an endless war, continued to intone prayers and hymns.

.....The clanging bell, the brothers praying, working, sleeping..... praying ever and ever again.....young monks, old monks, dying monks......

monks rising in the dark of the night, the mystery of the night, the mystery of death to save their souls.......

The summer had come and gone, and behind its fruit-piled bier the harvest maids of autumn gaily danced, with bright hips and berries in their hair. The wheat, grapes and orchard fruits had been gathered, crushed, pressed and stored in preparation for winter's long cold siege. And still, with inexorable constancy the great bell rang and summoned its small human tribe, their prayers, like the grains sifting through an hourglass, meting out the steps of *Man's* soul to *Eternity*.

Still, there was a thing or two that had changed in the hilltop abbey, and the regimen performed by its holy soldiers. The playful trills of a flute no longer was heard in the vale below, its silver threads no longer drifting in the breezes that breached its high, whitewashed walls. Indeed, the flute had been heard only a few times since the earliest autumn; and when it was, it seemed to lack the lilt of its original sweetness. Its music no longer fluttered like a pretty butterfly into the solemn sessions of their prayers, Even more curious, was the disappearance of the player of the flute. Toiling in their harvest fields, the brothers found themselves looking in vain for the young girl that held such a sensual sway over their austere lives. They could no longer steal glances of her rounding hips and budding breasts, her bared knee or slender, pearl white throat. Consequently, the brothers dreamed less of her voluptuous youth pressing against their lean, penance-punished bodies No longer at close of day did the trills of her flute tickle them like a feather as they lay on their cold hard beds. An older, surly youth now tended the flocks, and when the brothers asked where the flute-playing shepherdess had gone, he only scowled, and snarled some rough words beneath his breath, and walked coldly away.

There was another change inside the abbey's holy walls, one that coincided with the disappearance of the shepherdess and the happy songs of her flute. Tragic or scandalous, it was not a change that was openly talked about. As the days passed it was looked upon as something only to be forgiven, and once forgiven, forgotten; like a deep wound that has scabbed, and then sealed over by an ugly scar. One of the brothers had either ignominiously deserted their brotherhood, or had been abducted, or perhaps even killed by beasts or brigands. Their convivial, much favored brother, Brother Maria was no longer with them. His robe had been found by a winebibber high in a tree, in a dense part of the forest, and although it had not been torn apart or bloodied, it shouted of foul play. It was concluded that, like a snake's dead skin, the brother had shed his holy habit, and for whatever reason, the deserter, or his ruffian killer had hung it high in a tree.

There was one who knew more of these two enigmas, but he had chosen not to divulge what he knew to any other. At first Father Giovanni had been alarmed when Brother Maria's habit had been found, sodden and decaying, hung like a scarecrow in the tree. But remembering their last conversation in the confessional, coupled with one of the gardener oblates declaring that his habiliments had been stolen, he was sure there was more to this story than bandits or wild animals. No, Brother Maria had broken his vows and deserted the brotherhood, but he had not been killed.

A great reproving guilt had settled in the priest's heart for not divulging what he knew. Although certainly a sin to keep such a thing to himself, and not to tell his abbot of Brother Maria's elopement with the young shepherd girl, he had remained silent even when the scandal had burned like a fire through the brotherhood. He was mystified at his reluctance, and ultimately his flagrant refusal to tell the abbot that Brother Maria had forsaken the love of Christ for the embraces of a common peasant girl.

Why had he not told the kindly abbot the story of this intrigue? He was sure the abbot, with his homely wisdom would understand full well. But what had kept him from speaking out the words, even when again and again he had gone to the abbot's office, determined to do exactly that? What was the deeper reason that his reason was not telling him? He knew this untold thing would only gnaw deeper and deeper into his heart until, like a worm in an apple, it would corrupt it whole. He who practiced a strict, uncompromising obedience in all he did was mystified at his stubborn revolt from the same. As the secret were a precious jewel, and he a miser who alone knew where this jewel was hidden, he became increasingly, jealously covetous of its treasure, and anything or anyone who might come near it.

But what was this treasure, this unnamed wealth that this secret knowledge represented to him? Was it something forbidden, something to be avoided, something that his soul feared?

With Brother Maria's absence, the priest realized just how much this young brother had meant to him. He had grown to take a great pleasure in his company, even to secretly cherish it. It had melted a frozen vein in his heart, a vein that since Brother Maria's departure had frozen shut again.

At first he had been greatly surprised, fearful and shy of the warmth he felt in this brother's effusive, carefree presence. He was afraid of the sensual opulence that, like a blossoming tree, this blond brother exuded and showered upon him. He had never felt such a thing before. He was a theologian, a distinguished scholar priding himself in a vast wealth of learning, and Brother Maria, a man-child that had been raised in the forests with bears, wolves and gypsies. Brother Maria would never be his intellectual equal. He lacked such an aptitude, and more than aptitude, an inclination to aspire to such intellectual heights. He was not a creature of the mind, but one of the blood; a soul that delighted more in the voices of the forest, than those of the village; a creature nourished more by moonlight, than the light of the sun.

Gradually his despairing of his friend's absence, and the guilt resulting from his refusal to divulge what he knew about it, began to weigh like chains on his heart. But it was a burden that the priest would eventually, unexpectedly unburden to a most unlikely person, and in a most unlikely manner.

Some four months after Brother Maria's desertion, the Brother Porter sought out Father Giovanni in the scriptorium where, on this wet cold day he was working on a manuscript before a south window, receiving what little light the leaden clouds let forth. The brother interrupted his absorption, informing him that there was a young girl at the gates who wished to speak with him, about a thing she felt was of great importance. She had been informed that it was not possible for a woman to enter the abbey, but if she would like to wait, the father would be informed of her wish. Bundled in a sheepskin coat, and her face wrapped tightly about with a scarf, she had agreed to wait for a reply.

Disturbed from the manuscript, Father Giovanni was annoyed; his first impulse to disregard the request, to have the brother tell the girl he was occupied, and to give the begging child a crust of bread, a few nuts and an apple, and to send her on her way. Heavy rains had come in the late summer, and had continued through much of the autumn, rotting the orchard fruits and mildewing much of the wheat and barley, and from time to time urchins, both alone and in ragged bands climbed the hill to knock on their gates, begging for gruel, bread and apples.

But why would the child climb the hill on such a cold inclement day, as none of the other begging children had done? And why would she ask specifically for him? Those who begged did not care what hand gave bread at the abbey's gate. And of what important thing could she possibly wish to speak?

As he was reading the meditations of the priest's mind, the Brother Porter said:

"If I may, Father Giovanni, she does not seem a begging child. She has no bowl or bag as the other starvelings bring with them."

"And she said nothing more, Brother Gregorio, only that she wished to speak with me?"

"Nothing more; only that it was a thing she felt would be of great importance to the priest, Father Giovanni."

Quickened with curiosity, and a faint, unidentifiable swell of hope, Father Giovanni rose from the table, and left both the manuscript and the scriptorium, and as he did, he sharply, uncharacteristically ordered the brother:

"Fetch me a bag of things from the refectory, Brother Gregoiro.....bread, a good piece of bread, not merely a heel, and also one of the large barley biscuits.....and two or three of the best apples.....bring them to the gates at once......."

With brisk step he walked directly to the abbot's office, where he asked permission to speak with the girl. Busy, even as he was greatly ailing and crippling, the abbot gave his permission, but not without casting a queer look, as if smelling something that smoldered outside the ken of his knowing. Yes, Father Giovanni could speak with the young beggar girl, but only briefly, and only outside the abbey's walls.

Wrapping himself in a hooded cloak, Father Giovanni went to the gate, and after the Brother Porter unlocked and opened it, he stepped outside to greet his mysterious guest; bearing the bag with bread and apples. Nodding to the girl, he motioned for her to follow him, an instruction that without a word was given, and without a word was obeyed. He led her along the path that hugged the abbey's outer wall, a path that suddenly forked into a small glade of larch, alder and red-berried rowan, their autumn foliages long since threshed from their naked boughs.

Although the girl's face was bound in a thick scarf, and like a *Muslim* woman was almost entirely hidden, Father Giovanni had identified her at once. She was slight, but strongly knit; her build ruled by a kind of loping, fawn-like litheness that he remembered as she drove her sheep through the meadows. But more than this, her identity was confirmed by a wooden flute peeking from a kind of leather holster hanging from her pelt coat. Oh yes, this was she, and this an instrument like the one that had sent its songs, delicious as the smell of baking bread, over the abbey's walls into the brothers' prayers. This was a flute, the like of which, with these two dark eyes had pierced his friend's heart, bewitching him away from their holy walls. Father Giovanni winced when he remembered those little trills, delicate as a forest bird that he had heard that fateful night; trills that like a volleying cannon had commanded his friend to forsake his sacred vows, and with them, the friendship he had offered; the friendship that had given him a very special meaning.

A hundred paces into the glade there was a clearing in which the brothers had constructed several benches, creating a secluded retreat for their meditations. Here, Father Giovanni stopped, and gestured for the girl to be seated, a gesture to which she at once complied. The priest nodded, and smiled a wan smile full of stern reserve. And as he did, despite his robe and holy vows, he felt his heart burn with resentment, as in jealous competition against this simple unlettered girl who, with the promiscuous play of her young body had bested his lifetime of scholarship, stealing such an inestimable treasure away from him.

"I am Father Giovanni. I have been told that you wish to speak with me about an important matter. What is this thing of which you wish to speak my daughter?"

The girl did not free the scarf from her face. She kept it tightly bound, so that only her eyes peered from it, as from a bandit's mask. And when she lifted those eyes to him, he was disarmed of his jealousy; his resentment melting at once to sympathy. The wells of her dark eyes were poisoned with anguish, an anguish that he at once recognized, for it was the same anguish he felt in his own heart. This simple girl was the sister of his soul. They shared a common loss. Widowed of love, she was in mourning, as was he; she, openly; he, secretly; perhaps even hypocritically.

When she spoke, her words were soft, and muffled by the scarf that she refused, even now to remove, requiring the priest, in order to hear her, to bend down upon one knee before her; that knee, and the cassock that covered it, buried in the wet, thickly drifted leaves.

"I have come to ask you about a certain brother of your abbey, reverend father."

"Yes? And what is the brother's name?"

As the tears that filled her eyes had stopped her words, the girl looked shyly away. She spoke softly, almost inaudibly, but words that had summed and saved an undeniable reverence in her young heart.

"I am not sure. I did not ask him his name. But I think his brothers called him 'Brother of Gold' when they were in the fields......I think they called him that name because he was fair, like the people of the north. Sometimes I heard them call him 'Maria'; like a woman's name, like the Virgin Mother the monks worship. Yes, I think the brother's name is Maria, Brother Maria."

Father Giovanni raised his cowl over his head, using the cold damp as a pretense to hide in, like a turtle in its shell. From his raised cowl he whispered his reply:

"My daughter, Brother Maria is no longer a member of our brotherhood. He left in the early autumn, and we have not heard from or of him again."

Father Giovanni saw that the girl received his words as they were the prick of a sharp thorn. She turned her face away, as with a great pain, but then turning it back to him the priest saw that her passion was fighting fiercely with the sorrow in her tear-filled eyes.

"But you have no idea, no idea at all where he might be? You see he spoke of you with a special fondness, as you were his very special friend! That is why I climbed the hill and knocked upon your gates! That is why, Father Giovanni, I asked to speak with only you!"

It was now Father Giovanni's turn to be pricked by a thorn, unable as he was to sustain the hurt and importunity in those eyes that he knew was the hurt and importunity in his own heart. But how could he tell this girl, this girl young enough to be his daughter that he was secretly bleeding with the same wound? How could he tell her that they were brother and sister, that they were each other's mirror? He stood, and began to pace, his signature composure discomposed, discomfited and ruffled with her words. But when once more he stopped, turned and spoke to her it was in soft, tender, almost caressing tones; tones that brooked on tears of his own.

"I assure you, my daughter, I have heard nothing of Brother Maria, although I very much wish I had. I, you see......yes, he was my friend, indeed a special friend......and, to tell the truth, at times I sometimes find myself missing him a little......perhaps at times, more than a little. You see, my daughter, beneath monks' heavy robes beat hearts not unlike your own."

The tall slim priest resumed his pacing back and forth before the muffled girl, not kicking, but as his sandals were leaden, wading through the ankle-deep, half-frozen leaves. Despite their differences, the eminent theologian found himself wanting to confide in this common girl, this girl less than half his age; this pagan peasant girl that had never been baptized, and had certainly been promiscuous with her body. He found himself wanting to confide in her as he had not confided in another, even his confessor, to tell her things that he had not told his Father Superior; things that she alone could understand. He was gripped with a desire to unburden his heart to her; to confess to her.

The day was full of smothering damp, drear and cold, shrouding all in a freeze-distilling mist, so that the world seemed constricted, contracting to the two of them; so that, imprisoned together in a dungeon of gloom, the only thing left for the two prisoners was to share the truth of their sorrows. The girl would listen, and would understand what no confessor, and perhaps no *Angel* could. His words broke slow, tentative and frightened from his mouth, but quickly gained strength and swiftness in the current of their escape.

"I sometimes find myself worrying about him, and I say many prayers for him; many before the altar of Maria, his namesake. It may seem strange for one such as yourself to learn that a priest of the Holy Church has such feelings. It may seem strange to you to know that I sometimes lie awake thinking of Brother Maria, worrying about him, praying for him. It may seem silly to you, but there are times I think the echoes of his songs and laughter are still ringing through our stone arches and courtyard, as he was still among us, like a beautifully singing ghost. It may seem foolish, but I sometimes hear his footsteps running to meet me."

The purgation of his words coming to an end, silence thundered about them, deafening all but the cries of their hearts. But it was the girl, and not the holy priest that broke this silence with a brave plaintive whisper; a whisper so simple and poignant, so unequivocally true it smote the austere, erudite priest like a sword.

"I understand, yes, I understand, father. I can see that you loved Brother Maria too; that you loved him very much; that you still love him."

They were words that he had long feared; words that he had long denied; words that he had not even permitted his own heart to speak. But emitted from this common girl's lips, even while walled about by a world of mist and gray, they were a lovely thread of music, one that pushed a great stone from his heart.

He turned to the girl, not with the kindly smile of a priest, but with a man's heartsick gratitude.

"*Yes, perhaps, yes, I think that could be true. Thank you, my daughter, for telling me what I was perhaps afraid, no, that I was certainly afraid to tell myself.*"

And then after an awkward pause, one that was full of indebtedness to this young girl, he softly asked:

"*How did you come to know Brother Maria?*"

She spoke softly, slowly, shyly, each word carefully weighed and measured, as if her heart was a coffer, and these words a dowry of jewels she had shown no one; as they were her life's riches, and she was revealing them only to him;

"*I tended the flock of sheep in the vale below the abbey, the flock that my older brother now tends. From time to time teams of brothers would descend to the fields to till, plant, or reap. Even from a distance I could see that one of the brothers was different, his beard as gold as the wheat is gold, and his smile bright as fire. Even in a far field I could hear his laughter lifted into the breezes.*

I could not stop thinking of him. I dreamed of him upon my pillow, and when one day I saw him enter the forest alone, I followed him. It was then I first knew the Brother of Gold, and he first knew me."

Made shy with what she had confessed, Father Giovanni went to her, and spoke gently.

"*I understand, yes, I am sure I understand. Brother Maria spoke to your heart, and your heart could not deny its song. Brother Maria was different than the other brothers. He possessed a rare kind of beauty, as if the soul of a beautiful queen had been captured and lived in the body of a mighty warrior.....as if at one and the same time he was a loveliest woman and a manliest man.*"

And now the girl's words were not shy or measured, but touched with a living fire. She stood, and like a flame her spirit spoke.

"*Yes, that is it! You say it very well, reverend father! And because you say it so well I know you cared for Brother Maria even as I cared for him! Yes, like his name, 'Maria', Brother Maria is a beautiful woman in a man's strong body. Perhaps you too, like I, cannot stop thinking of him. Perhaps you too are haunted with his sweetness when you wake in the night. Perhaps you too will never love another as you love him!*"

.....there again were the words that he had feared, that he had denied, the dagger of flowers that pierced the core of his heart.....but coming now from this young girl, they were words he accepted and embraced.....as if the thrust of the dagger was a pain that was sweeter than anything he had ever known.......

"But child, Brother Maria is a monk, one who has devoted his life to God. You have stepped between his vows, and his God for whom they were sworn."

With this tears came streaming from her deep brown eyes, tears that bore her words in their rushing torrent. She became wild, and Father Giovanni was amazed to see one so slight, young and shy, and wrapped about in such wretchedness ignite into such a passion; to be so un-intimidated, almost irreverent of his person,

"Yes, Father Giovanni, it is true, I have committed a great sin. I am in love with a holy monk! I gave my body to him, as I would give it to him ten thousand times! Yes, I have sinned! I have sinned because I love him, as I will love him till the day I die! And yes, I knew him but briefly, but in that briefness he touched me more deeply than I have ever been touched! He woke a part of me that was dead. He woke a part of me that your Church, with its idols and its candles could never touch......and when I saw his habit hanging in......."

"You saw his habit in the tree?"

"Yes, I saw it. You see it was the tree where we.....you see I was looking for him, to apologize to him, to tell him I had been wrong.....to ask him to take me with him......."

"Apologize? Why apologize my daughter?"

"Because I was cruel to him. I think I hurt him. He had asked me to leave with him, to be his wife.....to live in a cottage with a garden and a cow, and to bear his children.....he told me he would always bring flowers and poems to me.....but I told him I would not be his wife, that he was only a monk full of foolish dreams about love and women.....but I soon doubted what I told him, and was not sure that foolish dreams are not better than no dreams at all.....that perhaps they are the noblest, perhaps the only truths."

"It was you who placed the flute in his habit's pocket?......?"

"Yes, it was me. I climbed the tree to his habit, but as I was about to remove it, I could not.....I thought that somehow it would be disturbing something not to be disturbed, like the unearthing of a grave....that t he had hung his habit in the big tree as a kind of burial, a burial in the wind

and sun, and not beneath the grass and stones.....that a part of his heart had died, that I had killed it, and I wanted to share that death by giving a part of me that would never sing again.....Yes, I climbed the tree, and left my flute in the pocket of his habit."

"But daughter, are you not married? Do you not have a husband?"

"Yes, father, I have a husband, a husband full of drink and curses and lechery! Yes, I have a husband, but I also have the memory of a monk who once laid his body upon my body, with whispers and caresses and flowers, in a way that a creature like my husband, and I am sure few other men could ever do!"

Greatly moved, and strongly suspecting that the story was still not fully told, Father Giovanni went to the girl and placed his hands upon her shoulders. Though at first she resisted this gesture and looked away, the priest placed one hand beneath her chin and lifted up her muffled face to him. Slowly, as it were a shroud, he began to unbind the scarf that so bound and concealed her countenance.

It was as he suspected. Her young, darling face had been harshly beaten, most surely by the hands of her uncouth, drunken husband; the drunkard who had led the brothers to Maria's habit in the tree. Her pretty nose, as well as several of her pretty teeth had been broken.

Yet despite these wounds that had so marred and scarred forever her maiden beauty, there was something else that spoke in the face that his fingers had unveiled. Although the girl was very young, there seemed a faint, womanly bloom about her. Father Giovanni let his eyes fall to the young girl's waist, then back to the dark eyes that silently confirmed the secret he had guessed at. The mystery of the child's climb to their abbey in the winterish flaw, her insistence to speak with only him, and with such a desperate passion, all were at once answered.

Father Giovanni was unprepared for the girl's sudden embrace. As she was drowning, she tightly wrapped her arms around his waist, and buried her battered, weeping face into his breast. Below he could feel the reason for which she had received such a beating; the cross she was bravely bearing; the cross that was beginning to swell from her thin, beaten body.

"I do not know, Father Giovanni, I do not know if it is his or my husband's, or even perhaps another shepherd man's, but I pray to God, yes, I pray to the God that knows my sins that my sins bear the blessing of his blue eyes and golden laughter.....but if it is, you see, if it is his, I am very frightened......."

With this, even as the girl and the priest were frozen in an embrace, the great bell rang, as it was the voice of a superintending God, concluding the drama both had tried to hide from all other eyes, only to share with each other. Father Giovanni spoke with fatherly, not priestly tenderness to her.

"Now I must go pray, but I will not forget the things we have spoken of. I will not forget to pray for you, you and the monk that both of us are in love with."

As they were about to leave the shelter of the trees, the girl lightly touched Father Giovanni's sleeve, bringing both to a halt.

"Good father, I know that the brothers removed his habit from the tall tree. Do you know what became of my flute?"

"That I do not; but I shall ask. Perhaps I may find it."

It was a lie; another lie, a bold and blatant lie told to the pitifully beaten face of a young girl, a young girl who had entrusted him with the secrets of her heart. *But why? Why? Even now, why was he too proud to tell this child the truth? Was he covetous with his love?*

"Will you do a favor for me, father?"

"If I can, yes, I surely will."

"If you find the flute, and if you see the Brother of Gold ever again, will you give the flute to him?

You see in a few days my people are leaving. We are taking our flocks to warmer meadows, and we may not bring them back in the spring. If my darling returns, give him my flute, and tell him that the one who played it for him no longer has music in her heart. Without him she no longer wants to play a flute. She no longer wants to sing. Without him she no longer wants to live."

Father Giovanni nodded, and blessed her; and then pausing, made the Sign of the Cross over the swell of the burden her young years were so bravely carrying.

Quickly the girl rained kisses on his hands, first one, and then the other, and then with lightning swiftness she stood on her tiptoes, and uncaring of any incorrectness or forbiddenness, planted a kiss on his cheek; and then began to briskly walk away. But after ten or more paces she stopped, and rushed back to him. Bound again in her heavy scarf, her eyes drove like burning nails into his soul.

"Brother Maria loved you very much, Father Giovanni!"

At this the second bell for prayers began to clang loudly. The girl turned and began to pick her way down the muddy, rain-pitted road; the eyes of the priest following her until she disappeared into the wet and cold of the darkening afternoon, the drizzle now becoming the night's first flakes of snow.

It was the last that Father Giovanni would ever see her; leaving him with the sack of bread and apples still in his pocket; and in his heart the arrow of truth she had so openly spoken, and the truth he had not.

* * *

FATHER Giovanni was moved very much by this visit from the peasant girl. As a celibate ascetic, he had never seen a woman's heart so fanned to flames by its love for a man. The image of the girl's impassioned eyes staring from the mask of her scarf, as piercing as those of a begging child, haunted his walks and prayers for many days to come. And he knew why they so haunted him. It was because their hunger was his hunger. He knew that this carefree brother had given his heart to both of them; filling them with its life and sweetness, only to take it away again like a sly, irascible thief.

In the days to come Father Giovanni found himself musing upon, and admiring this young girl very much. How courageous she had been to trudge up the hill, heavy with child, beaten and shamed, and then to boldly ring their gate's bell. How proud in her shame, and how noble in her sin; with what regal majesty she had burned! This common girl had touched him, humbled him, even shamed him, he the future shepherd of Christ's disciples; especially when he had unbound her scarf to her bruised and broken beauty. This child had sacrificed so much, and yet still loved so much! Was he, in truth, capable of a love as pure as she who herded goats and sheep through the fields?

In the days following his conference with the girl, Father Giovanni found that he wanted to be alone; to be apart from the company of his brothers. Again he went to Father Augustine, this time to ask for the indulgence of silence, and again, with yet another numinous twinkle, like a mote of omniscience sparkling in his eye, the abbot had granted it. Unspeaking, Father Giovanni walked through the abbey like a ghost, one that could be seen by all, performing a heavy penance none could guess; a ghost who dragged twin chains of guilt and mourning.

Since his talk with the girl, he had begun to reconsider those contemplations that had brought some resolution to his heart.

Like a ghost he found himself revisiting places where he had seen and spoken with Brother Maria, as if those memories, and not the stone arches and pillars, the altars before which he knelt, the great Crucifix, the iron bell-, as if these things were more dream-like, more ephemeral than the reality of his friend's memories.

Once when he was sure no brother was near, he entered Brother Maria's empty cell. He stood before the one small window, and there imagined his child-hearted friend pondering the glittering stars, the playful swallows, and the sailing clouds in the great caravan of the seasons; the world beyond the abbey walls that had spoken to the dream-smitten child of his soul.

Several times he had strayed into the corner of the orchard where it was thought Maria had made his escape. He stood before the very tree that had been supposed to be his accomplice. He imagined Maria's strong lithe body climbing into the tree, and his cat-like leap to the top of the high wall. He imagined a rising moon, and then a flute's silver trills. In obedience to those trills, and in disobedience to his vows to God, and to the abbey's holiness, he imagined Maria leaping to the ground, and then running into the forest to those dark eyes that had stared at him through the mask of her scarf.

Once he had even slipped into the confessional alone, and relived his final talk with Maria…..*his eyes burning with tears as he pressed against the grille….the sound of his lips fervently kissing it…..and then the words no one had ever spoken to him before, not even when he had been a boy, words that seared his heart…..*"*Oh my dear sweet Giovanni, how I will miss you!*"…….

Sometimes he would lie awake on his bed at night, imagining dangers that might befall his deserted friend. His mind would become a hornet's nest of consternation and worry, stung with any number of terrible fates that could easily lie in wait on his friend's blind paths. What would his dear Maria do, and where would he go? How would he survive the deep snows and bitter cold of winter? He could grow sick; he could starve. Would he have a warm coat, boots, mittens? He could be assaulted by brigands, or torn apart, limb by limb by hungry wolves. His blue eyes might be pecked out by crows; the beautiful dreams in his heart might be eaten by worms.

Or would he return, like the butterflies and the swallows? Would he climb one day up the steep hill to their gates, a ragged, gaunt and weary prodigal son, begging to be readmitted to the brotherhood that he had forsaken? Yes, that was entirely possible; even probable. Maria's nature was too sensitive to be long battered by the scorn and vicissitudes of the world. He would eventually learn that wisdom was life's true treasure, and not the sugary kisses given by maidens. He was too special; too tender; too precious. Such a songbird must be caged, for only in such a cage as was this abbey's stone walls could its rare song be protected.

The thought of his friend's possible return always quickened Father Giovanni's heart with hope, lighting it like the wick of a lamp. If he indeed one day returned, he promised himself that he would not harshly censure him, nor even make mention of the young shepherd girl, and the things she had confided to him. He would not tell him of the child that he had very likely fathered; and the beating the girl had received from her husband because of it. He would calmly hear his confession, and listen to the follies he had committed in his foolish journeys. With strict, but not severe penances, he would forgive him.

He would assert his prestige; more than likely, in the event of Father Augustine's death, the abbacy itself. He would pull strings for him; intercede and make limber the rigid rules for him; he would lie for him. In some way he would win him another tonsure, habit, and three-knotted cincture. He would again hear his friend's golden laughter and see the blue fire blaze in the jewels of his eyes. He would again watch him teach the old monks how to dance, and warble sweet responses to the forest birds. He would again find moments to sit with him on garden benches; to listen to the fancies in his heart, and in return, share with him the riches of his scholarship. All would be as it had been before. All would be well.

But there were other thoughts, strange thoughts that sometimes came to him as he lay awake on his bed at night.

Sometimes he tried to imagine the young shepherdess and Brother Maria together, and the strange, carnal acts they had performed, entangling their naked bodies on the forest floor. He thought of this mysterious fire that had been enkindled in their bloods, the might of this mysterious spark that had raged through them, that neither could resist; that could only to be quenched by the other. He thought of how strong such love must be, this love called *passion*, to call one from one's religious vows, from food and shelter, safety and certainty, from

God; and for the other to risk being beaten like a dog, cast out to the roads and the winds; all to taste the other's kisses, and for a moment be wrapped in the other's arms. Was this love? And if it was, was it not the love of fools, perhaps even beasts; a love that would embarrass the Angels? Or was it also, in some primitive way a part of a love that men cannot understand, that somehow was valid, that somehow was a part of that love that moves the stars and seasons, despite men's codes and strictures?

He had never known this kind of love, and because he had never known it, it held a great mystery for him; even as the sacraments were an imponderable mystery, one that men could worship, but never understand. When he imagined the lovers and their embraces, he had also imagined Maria's holy habit hanging above them in the tree, like a dead man hung for some terrible crime; and this picture represented some symbolic truth that he could not comprehend, and not comprehending, haunted him.

He had kept the flute the abbot had given him, the flute that the shepherdess had placed in one of the deep pockets of Maria's habit hung in the tree; the flute that he had lied to the young girl about. He had kept the flute, even covetously guarded it, like a child keeps a precious shell or pretty feather. Still more childishly, some nights he placed it beneath his pillow. And when he did, he imagined it brought him strange thoughts, and when he slept, at times strange dreams.

At first he thought these thoughts were only tricks of his mind played in that twilight between waking and sleeping, when the real becomes ethereal, and the mundane becomes fantastic; when the mind becomes a theatre of the irrational and impossible. But when the phenomenon continued, he was not altogether so sure. When he placed the flute beneath his pillow he imagined it began to sing to him; to breathe lovely melodies into and through deep parts of him. As the hookah breathes illusions into its smoker's mind, so the flute seemed to breathe melodies full of fantastic creatures and adventures into his.

Once he imagined hearing the flute's song deep in the forest, even as the moon was ripening, and when they did a monk leapt from the abbey walls in answer to its song. But as the monk ran into the forest the monk changed into other creatures; sometimes a bear or panther, sometimes a great owl, sometimes a tremendous stag. He had followed, and reaching the deep place in the forest from which the flute was playing, he beheld a thing that was at once wonderful and profane.

The fantastic stag had raised up on its hinds, exposing its large swollen phallus, a phallus that was not a phallus at all, but a flute, to which the shepherdess had knelt, brought her mouth, and was filling the forest with lovely melodies. And as she played the stag changed into yet another form; its rack of antlers stretching and branching into the crown of a great tree, a tree whose blossoms were sparkling stars.

Once he was visited by a very unusual dream, one that was more strangely wicked than lovely.

In it was reenacted the episode of the girl's visit to the abbey. As before, the day was cold, wet and full of freezing flaw, and as before he had led her to the clearing in the alder and rowan trees. But when their colloquy had ended, and the bell loudly rang, he clasped her tightly in his arms, and refused to let her go. He tore the scarf from her face, only to find it very beautiful; as flower delicate as he had first seen it bruised and broken.

Falling to his knees, he began to kiss the girl's swollen belly through her heavy coat, and when he did he heard laughter, Brother Maria's laughter, as if it was coming from her swollenness. In that laughter a voice spoke to him:

"*Ah, so you too, my dear Giovanni, have heard the beautiful call of the flute, the flute my mother plays.*"

One night, when lying awake in the silence of the sleeping abbey, he was seized by an irrational urge to rise from his bed, and take the flute from the hiding place he had chosen for it. Although he had never played a flute before, and although he knew it was a ridiculously childish thing to do, he stood before his window, and bringing the flute tenderly to his lips, breathed into it, soft as a kiss; as the kiss he gave his Savior's feet on the great Crucifix each day.

In the darkness his heart grew light, and his fingers began to dance up and down on its stops, and he imagined he was making sweet melodies. And although he had never indulged in such silly fantasies, even when he was a boy, he imagined the melodies were flocks of birds, beautiful birds whose magical wings fluttered into the night. Flying from the abbey, he imagined these birds would find the ear of his lost, wandering friend; telling him that he was thinking of him; and asking him to return.

But gradually these strange dreams and midnight caprices faded and passed, and with them the cold bleak winter that melted into the snowbells and violets of yet another spring. Again the armies of the seasons marched through the forests and over the hills in full regalia, slaying the hours, days and years, and with them the memory of a boyishly blithe, gypsy-hearted brother who once prayed and worshipped in a hilltop abbey; the sifting of sands through Time's hourglass, bringing so many toils and duties, also bringing forgetfulness.

The memories of this unique brother faded from the brotherhood. New oblates, postulants and novices had never heard his name, and old monks forgot him with the passing seasons and years; or with the disdain for a reprobate who had broken his holy vows. Even the priest who had loved him with a special love, almost with the fervency with which a man loves a woman, began to forget the one who had once breathed such a fragrant breath through the stale airs of his heart. He no longer entered this brother's former cell, a cell long since occupied by a new brother of the Order. He no longer recalled their conversations on the garden benches, or heard his laughter ring in the breezes. The apple tree in the corner of the orchard, the one brushing the wall, was chopped down. He no longer slept with a shepherdess's flute beneath his pillow, or brought it to his lips in the deep of the night, imagining that he would bring back the blue-eyed child that had once so deeply touched him.

In the abbey on the hill the great bell continued to clang out the hours of prayer, and the brothers continued to be obedient to its punctual commands; their sandals continuing the brook's endless polishing of its pebbles to perfect gems. The roses continued to bloom and fade; the swallows to swoop into the belfry in spring, and to fly away in autumn; the moon to rise with the evening star, and fall with the morning star. Life continued to fulfill its offices and seasons, as there had never been one named *Brother Maria*.

Only now and then on a specially lovely, quiet night would one of the priests, promoted to abbot, stop in the courtyard on his return to the cloister, listening to the song of a night bird, or a gust of wind in the leaves, as in the depths of his soul he had heard the trilling of a flute. Only then would the abbot think of a pair of eyes that had stared from the mask of a heavily wrapped scarf, and another that had burned through the grille of a confessional; as they were a brother and sister imprisoned, perhaps even baptized with the strange fire of human love.

He had tried to find her. He had asked the brothers that worked in the fields to inquire about her, if needs, go to the camps of the itinerant grazers and herders to look for her. Gnawed by guilt, he had left the abbey with the flute in his pocket, prepared to tell her that his heart had been eaten with jealousy; that he was much more guilty than she; that if there was anything he could do for her and the child, he would try his best. But her people had not returned with their goats and sheep to graze the following spring, and those that came with their flocks, knew nothing of such a one.

It was not until several years later, when, several of the monks had come upon the same wretch who had led them to Brother Maria's habit, that Father Giovanni, now Abbot Giovanni, heard that the flute-playing shepherdess was dead. She had hung herself high in a tree in the forest. It was a thing the dissipated man knew to be true: she had been his wife.

. . . .

. . . .

CHAPTER NINE

NEW LOVERS, LABORS, DREAMS
PART II

AFTER Brother Maria had fled the old couple's house that strange, ugly night, he once more enjoyed the freedom of his own wants and wishes. The country-side was now in its full autumn bloom; the forests painted with yellows, reds and russets. The air was cool and fresh, the sky, pellucid blue, and everywhere berries, nuts and fruits hung ripe on stalk, vine and bough.

As it had been with the shepherdess, the memories of the nightlong orgies with the older woman, and the perverse theater the opium-addicted old man made her perform for his wicked espial, faded with the sunny days and starry nights. As before, Maria soon became enamored with the pageantry of Nature all about him; with the richly colored and fruited fields that were now beginning to sing and busy with creaking carts, yoked brutes, and teams of harvesters.

Now wading breast-high into seas of wheat, oats and barley were slow-marching armies, soldiers whose sabers were sickles flashing and swishing in the sun. Behind them was a second army, an army not of men, but of women; gleaners and binders of the rich spoils that the men left toppled in their victorious wake.

The orchards now received assaults of rapacious gatherers, those that came to plunder their summer-ripened riches; some propping ladders in the crotches of the trees, then climbing like monkeys into the boughs in search of ruddy and golden gems. As they were fishers of the *terra firma*, some spread great nets about the gnarled boles of olive trees, as well as about the trunks of hazel, pecan and beech trees; nets that received catches from the barefooted fishers shaking the branches above.

Hillsides of vineyards were freckled with harvest maidens, their hair bound in bright kerchiefs, their bodies draped in sienna brown smocks. Not far away, in the shade of trees were the great tubs and presses, as they were the hives to which these pretty human bees were busily bearing the nectar from the flowering fields.

At first shy of this human invasion, Maria soon grew to seek out its nearness. He wanted to remain solitary and apart, but at the same time he liked hearing the harvesters' songs and laughter as they worked, and even their coarse words and curses as they drank wine, bandied and quarreled. Their voices were a kind of music that entertained and comforted the hours of his lonely wandering.

But there was more; Maria knew there was more. In his aloneness he found himself straying nearer and nearer those harvest teams composed chiefly of women.

It was not that he wanted to speak with them, for he permitted himself no friendly glance or smile, fearing a flirtatious encounter, or worse, a misadventure. When any would chance look at him, he would quickly look away, as if still adhering to a monk's strict vows. Although he had had two adventures with women, one with a much younger, and the other with a much older, *woman* was still a new and mysterious creature to him. Still, he could not deny his fascination, even the enchantment, like a net with which children catch butterflies, that their fairness cast over him.

What was this creature that he had for so many years not looked upon, that he had taken vows of chastity against, and had been cloistered from, indeed, had seldom even been allowed to speak with? Behind this creature's pretty smiles and playful glances was there some awful danger, some treachery? Were these fair, laughing creatures a temptation of evil, or as they seemed, a divine invitation?

His first encounters with 'woman' had resulted in heartache, confusion and disgust. Yet had they not also given pleasures the like of which he had never imagined? Had they not wakened the gypsy days of his youth, exhilarated him as his prayers and chants had never done? Had 'woman's' fingers not reached into the sleeping depths of his heart, exhuming a dusty, albeit golden harp? Did the pleasures 'woman' gave not compensate for the wounds she inflicted?

One thing was undeniably true about this fair creature: She was lovelier than anything that had ever met his eye; lovelier than fields of poppies, or the rising moon; lovelier than the frescoes, marble statues and gorgeous altars that had surrounded him for so long in the abbey. Indeed, though autumn was now arrayed in the banners of its glory, the women he saw in the fields seemed that glory's flower. Indeed, 'woman' seemed the rose of the seasons, as if all other beauties were summed in her loveliness; as if she consummated every beauty; every wonder under the sun.

Maria became enamored with this loveliness that was so dazzling new to his eye, and though at first he felt ashamed that this fascination had so firmly gripped him, he became increasingly hungry to watch these angels as they bent, reached, stretched and swayed in their labors; to see their shapely thighs, hips and breasts; even to hear their voices, sweet as warbling birds, that brought strange new thrills to his heart.

Curiously, he found himself studying and admiring not only the youthful and the comely, but those that were not shapely, and those who were no longer young, as they too were possessed of great charms and sorcery; as they too, as the fair daughters of *Eve*, possessed divine mysteries. He found himself wondering what lovemaking with the homely, the crippled and the slovenly would be like. He became curious of the secrets they would surrender; the kisses of the coarse and the aged; the caresses of the lame and the unlovely. Would the nipples on their shriveled or sagging breasts become erect when they were kissed? Would they sweetly moan, and whisper silly things in their lovers' ears? Naked of their clothes, would they still inspire the male animal in men's loins to play the games of passion? Would they quiver in their fulfillment, and what strange cries would those quivers bring?

At night when he closed his eyes for sleep, his mind would fill with the women he had seen laboring in the sun; the sweat from their toils making cling their smocks to their bodies. Oh, how lovely were these fruits that ripened secretly on the vine of *woman*: their breasts, hams and bellies; the little tufts, like nests of birds beneath their arms, and in his imagination between their thighs. At first he had resisted such carnal thoughts, even rising to his knees to admonish their wickedness with prayers or floggings. But the pleasure these fantasies gave him was irresistible, and he soon not only ceased to punish such thoughts, but invited their visitations.

They soon acquired a dream-like quality, a quality that, however wrong, strange and exaggerated, Maria did not attempt to expel. The teams of maidens in the grape yards sometimes seemed to him gentle herds of gentle deer; the gleaners, flocks of pretty, crumb pecking birds; the orchard harvesters, rainbow-scaled fish swimming through the boughs of the fruited trees. And sometimes in these fantasies, one would turn to him, slyly smile, and then make naked a blossom-white thigh, and with an alluring smile race into the green waves of a field. Enchanted, he would follow her, only to watch as she changed into a dolphin, leaping and laughing, and then disappearing in the golden sunlight.

There were other times when he imagined these teams of maidens were flocks of flowers; their smiles, one smile; their gazes, one gaze/. In some of these twilights these flowers sang and spoke to him; singing of his wandering, and telling him that one day he would return to sleep in their petal soft arms; embracing, forgetting, dying with them, together in the fertile sea and seasons of the earth.

But it was not only that Maria became enamored with the harvest maidens; more and more they became enamored with him. He was a stranger none had seen before; young, tall, and broad-shouldered, with a swift step and a ruddy flush of health. But even more, he was golden and blue-eyed, as they had never seen another man. His tonsure was disappearing, and it was being replaced with a crest of silky gold, even like his beard, and in the bright sun both sparkled flaxen, as if they too were blooms of the harvest fields.

Maria could feel their eyes upon him when he passed. Sometimes near a vineyard one would hap to see him, and would call out to her harvest sisters. Immediately a flock of bright smocks and bandannas would appear in the vine rows, or from behind the mulberry and olive trees where the grapes were trellising. In unison their toil-grimed faces would brighten, and they would look, like a herd of deer, in rapt concert his way. They would sometimes halloo or wave, and as he walked away, sometimes even laugh and blow him kisses.

Some made bold to call out to him, unseen from the olive, fig or apple boughs where they were gathering, and midst giggles, tease and taunt:

"Where are you going golden one? Are you tired? Would you like to climb this tree and rest in the nest of my arms? Or would you like to sing for me? Come, golden bird, do not fly away! Come sing to us, and we will give you a beautiful meal of bread, wine and kisses."

Several times others, when they saw that he did not respond to their halloos, but continued on his way, dropped their chores and came running and laughing from a wheat or grape field. Sensing no danger in his shy, gentle bearing, they became emboldened, encircling and teasing him with jests and endearments.

"*Oh golden traveler, would you not like to rest a little while? I will take you to a quiet place, and you could lay your head on the pillow of my breast.*"

"*Have you a sweetheart, O blue-eyed boy? Or have you many? Is there honey in your kisses, as there is honey-gold in your hair and beard?*"

"*Would you like to be my sweetheart, beautiful one? Would you like to taste my lips as I would like to taste yours?*"

Coaxing only blushes, boyish smiles and glances from his chicory-blue eyes, and captivated by his silent shyness, several dared to bring him flowers, and when they did, they reached up and pecked his cheek with a kiss, before running giggling away from this daringly majestic thing they had done.

One warm afternoon Maria shed his shirt and walked waist-deep into a cold clear stream to bathe. He was startled by a whisper and a titter, only to see three or four young girls that had left their baskets in a vineyard, and had followed him to the stream. As if one was daring the other, several came near the stream's edge, lifted their skirts to their calves, and then to their knees, and then inches above their knees, only to dip their toes in the water, before laughing and running away.

This game of coquetry did not last long, for soon was heard a man's rough voice, calling them gruffly back to their deserted chores.

Maria continued to bathe, but after a moment, feeling eyes upon him, he looked up to see a young girl standing near a tree. Seeing her youth and insecurity, Maria flashed a broad bright smile at her, at which she shyly came to the brook's edge. When she ventured a step or two in the water, Maria spoke to her.

"*My lovely girl, why are you not with your sisters?*"

Frozen with fright and timidity, the young girl did not speak.

"*What is it, pretty one? Is there something you wish to say to me?*"

The girl's lips trembled, and her deep dark eyes glassed with tears, her fright stopping the words she so wanted to loose from her heart. Smiling, Maria brought his finger to her cheek.

"*Do not be afraid. What is it that you wish to say to me? I will not tell anyone. It will be our secret.*"

Still struggling, but comforted with this man's gentle warmth, the girl tearfully and bravely spoke.

"*I, I think you are very handsome, sir, more handsome than any man I have ever seen.*"

"*That is a very nice thing for you to say, dear one. Thank you. I will remember it always. I will keep it near my heart, like a jewel.*"

The girl paused, struggled, and then bravely continued.

"*I have never had a sweetheart, and I have never lain with a boy, but if you wish, and you are still here tonight when the stars and darkness come, I could come to you. I would like very much for you to take me in your arms. I would like very much for you to be the first man to love me.*"

Astonished at the young girl's words, as well as admiring the valor she had summed to speak them, it was now Maria's turn to be at a loss. And as he caressed her face with his finger, softly, as he was caressing a kitten, there came a woman's cry from behind the trees.

"*Lucrezia! Lucrezia! Where are you, you little idler? Mimo will be very angry if you are not in your row, and your basket filled when he returns!*"

The young girl was severely torn, between her duty in the vineyard, and this man before whom she had just offered the treasure of her maidenhood. Compassionate with her youth, Maria gently spoke to her, even as he gave her cheek another caress with his finger.

"*You are very sweet my darling. There has never been another who has made such a lovely offer to me before, but I do not live here, and you are very young.......*"

Again one of the harvesters called out.

"*Lucrezia, come back at once! He is returning! I see his ox-cart on the trail! He will be furious! You know how the son-of-a-bitch is when he has been drinking!*"

Commanded by her duty, the young girl kissed Maria's hand, turned, and began to race away, only to stop and return, her very soul the messenger of her words.

"*There are girls in the village, younger than I who have lain with boys, and men, older men, but none half as beautiful as you are sir! Some have married these men, only to be slapped and whipped by them. But I can tell you are a gentle man, and would never do such a thing. Oh, how I would like your arms to hold me, sir. How I would like to make a golden child with you!*"

"*Lucrezia! Lucrezia! If Mimo is drunk he will beat you! The bastard*" *may beat all of us, even like we would like to beat him!"*

The young girl grew nervous and tearful. To Maria's amazement she hurriedly untied her blouse, and held out her small breasts to

him, boldly, almost proudly, as they were the secret treasures of who and what she was.

"If you would like them, they are yours, beautiful sir. I will come to you with the first stars, and you may have them, and the rest of my woman sweetness as well."

Maria did not know what to say; and knowing not what to say he did what his blood told him to do. As with a show of reverence, he brought a kiss to each of the small, unripe fruits she was so heroically offering him. Blushing, and with her face full of tears, the girl tearfully whispered: *"Thank you, beautiful sir, oh I thank you very, very much!"* and raced away.

Maria did not stay. He did not accept the treasures the girl was promising him. But for the next days he sometimes regretted his decision when he thought of her. He imagined her naked beauty gleaming in the starlight, a child with the buds of womanhood first breaking from her body. He imagined the many ways he would like to play with such a child lover, and what it would be like to lay between her slender legs; to be the first to guide and teach her; to hear her first gasps and sighs; feel her first quivers; enfold her as she first died in a man's arms.

But he thought of her in another way also, a way in which he had not thought of the shepherdess or the older woman; a way other than the frolic and treachery of passion. When he lay about his fire he was haunted not only with the tears that spilled from her eyes, and the small, unripened fruits of her breasts she had offered him, but also with her words: '*Oh, how I would like to make a golden child with you.*'

Deep in the cool autumn nights he would wake and remember the kisses he had given the buds of her little breasts, and there would be tears that came from his eyes, and a great wound, as of an ancient loneliness that would break open and bleed in his heart. As he lay in the dark and cold, he hurt with a realization at once shameful, lovely, and true:

He had never kissed a holy altar, or indeed the great Crucifix after his prayers with such a sincere and tender reverence.

* * *

AND as the autumn mellowed and deepened, and the fields and hills yielded their riches to the sun, so Brother Maria seemed to ripen as well. Changes came upon him, changes both of body and soul; changes that seemed to ripen fruits long waiting to ripen inside him.

Rather than becoming pale and haggard, he became hale and strong from his wandering. The rigors of exercise, and the constant needs demanded for his survival in wild and weather encouraged a wonderful new robustness in him, transforming his delicate features into strong manly ones.

He became leaner, but it was leanness of strength, and not of want or weakness; not like the sickly lamb, but like the hungry wolf. His muscles, long neglected by a regimen of prayers, fasts and penances, now knitted, tautened, and in the correct places swelled. His shoulders seemed to broaden, his chest to harden round and full.

His tonsure that had boldly branded him an ascetic began to melt away into a thick, blond-gold growth that now freely, promiscuously rioted forth. Even his beard seemed possessed of a glossier health. Like a shadow-stunted flower given sun, it now bloomed richer, with a suave and silken flow of waves. Still more, his beard and hair were flecked and veined, as if marbleized with an auburn red, so that when smote by the sun, they seemed afire. This in turn enkindled a brighter indigo blue in his eyes, until they shone like pieces of a bright blue sky.

The autumn days were pleasantly warm and balmy, but as it was a harbinger of what was to come, Maria woke one night to a chill he had not felt before, one in which his bed of leaves could not protect against; a cold that stilled the crickets and hushed the night birds. Outside the small warm ring about his fire he could see the white, creeping ambush of frost, while above him the stars shone clear and cold, as their candles had frozen into ice.

Cold as he had not been since leaving the abbey, he quickly built his fire into a goodly blaze. Too cold to sleep, he sat against the stone in whose lea he had built his night camp, staring into the flames as his face bronzed and his body gratefully warmed.

The weather was changing, as he knew it would. For some days, weeks, or perhaps a month more the sun would be warm, and the air sweet with the earth's honeys. But on the heels of this last shower of golden warmth there would be drifts of snow and howling winds. Autumn's lovely fires would be quickly doused with blizzards and bleakness. It would be very difficult for him to continue his wandering. He could easily starve or freeze, or be killed by wolves or bandits. Until now he had subsisted on a diet of ripe fruits, fish he had caught with his hands, and small birds he had cleverly snared; and even sometimes by singing psalms before lonely cottages, begging a bowl of gruel or a crust of bread. But when winter came the brooks would freeze, and the fields and forests would be bare. It was too late to return to the abbey, even if he could find his way back to it.....and if he did, after deserting its holy walls, breaking his holy vows, lying and playing with women.....no, he could not return. He would rather be gnashed apart by wolves and picked by crows than to kneel at its gates in scarlet shame and defilement. He must seek shelter, and with it some employment, at least until the streams thawed and the hills began to green again.

The idea of seeking out a shelter was not altogether disagreeable to him, not only because of the inevitable, perhaps even intolerable scarcities of the coming winter, but because a hunger, a great and different kind of hunger had developed inside him, one that needed only a pause, and a safe warm place to feed and appease.

As he had walked through the fields and forests certain very beautiful pictures had captivated him, and had been sown like seeds into his heart; storm clouds, songs of birds, flowers, warbling brooks, moonrises; the lovely breasts, hips, and smiles of women as they toiled in the harvest fields. These images had not left him. They now lived inside him, inhabited him like a family of ghosts, ghosts that haunted him with an enduring, voluptuous loveliness. He did not want to lose these ghosts. He did not want to dismiss or forget their poignant sweetness in the mists of the days and hours. He wanted to keep and guard them, like a miser his jewels; a mother her children.

At times these ghosts not only haunted him, but fevered him, invading and troubling his prayers, sleep and dreams. They flooded his mind like swarms of gorgeous butterflies, of which he wanted to capture one or two, to hold their pretty-winged creatures for a moment in his hands.....to give words to a sickle moon, the song of a nightingale, a field of sun-gilt wheat..... to a shy smile, a sloe-eyed gaze, a slender neck or supple knee. Sometimes when he closed his eyes for sleep such beautiful images rushed through him in violent squalls, and he would not fall asleep until the night was very deep; until finally, exhausted with their exquisite pageantry, their beautiful wings fluttered into sleep's shadows.

At times these ghosts became angry in their sweetness, restless to be released, pounding their beautiful wings, hard as fists against his heart, begging to be purged; as if they wished to be exorcised like a priest exorcises devils. They became impatient with the one in whom they were lodged, becoming rebellious, like prisoners in a dungeon. Children of dreams, they insisted he give them the time he gave to the world through which he was dreaming. More and more Maria wanted to free these spirits; to feed their hunger and give them raiment. More and more he wanted to give them 'words'; to make poems with the beautiful butterfly ghosts that fluttered inside him, that maddened him with the glory of their wings.

As he had wandered, lines had risen from deep inside him; simple lines that were playful, silly and adolescent, and sometimes even shameless, but nevertheless lines that lightened his heart, and made him want to sing, like a bird sings its song to the wind and sun.

Once, upon passing a team of maidens in a vineyard, these random lines assembled into a kind of succession, one that was strange, but sweet in his heart, and finally, as melodious as a flute sang on his tongue.

THESE maidens in the grapes, Angel flocks,
That Autumn has given new disguises,
That the eye of ardor mesmerizes;
Their golden wings, now homespun smocks,
Their haloes, rags of red bandannas,-
For the sons of men, celestial brides,
Hives of honey between their thighs,
Their peasant laughter warbling love's hosannas.

Early one morning Brother Maria packed his few things in his knapsack, and started with a new spring in his step: the spring of resolution. His wandering this day would not be aimless, but with purpose. He would ask if he might join a harvest team, those that traveled from village to village, and field to field through the country-side. The work would be hard, and the employment would last only as long as the sun was warm and the wheat stood tall, but it would provide square meals, and perhaps a bearing for the unfriendly weather ahead.

But the first few teams were not congenial to his wishes. Learning he was a monk in pilgrimage, scanning his goldenness and the monastic delicacy that still defined him, the remnants of a tonsure's corona yet visible on his head, they scoffed, and sent him on his way, once shouting after him that he should go pick apples with the women, and not try to wield a heavy sickle with the men.

But upon the third day he was accepted by a band of harvesters without a scoff or snide remark. To the contrary, he was enthusiastically received by its foreman. Several of his workers had become drunk, thieved, and deserted his team, and he was afraid that any day clouds of locusts might appear to devour the precious beards before their stalks were cropped. He was in immediate need of strong backs and arms. A great sickle, albeit old and unsharpened was placed in Maria's hands, like a sword in a new, untried soldier's hands, and shortly he found himself midst an army of men mowing through a frothy sea of golden wheat, their swishing scythes flashing like sabers in the sun.

And yet once among and alongside them, his fellow workers were not without playful, and many times derisive remarks. The tawny, uncouth, slavishly working men found in Maria a great novelty, and that novelty a comic relief to their tedious, sun-burning and back-breaking labors.

"Is the sickle too large for the golden darling?"

"Do you want to return to your hymns and your beads my lovely boy?"

"My sister and my mother are named 'Maria', and I once skewered a nice piece called 'Maria' in a hay wagon, but I have never known a man named 'Maria'.

"His mother named him Maria because he was so pretty."

"Perhaps we should put a skirt on him, and he could join the gleaners."

Unruffled, Maria endured their insults, even at times rebuffing their callous remarks with broad smiles. But more than this, he proved his mettle with a steady and energetic zeal, one whose great swathing swings soon won the respect, even the admiration of his surly detractors. This was augmented when it was seen that Maria enthusiastically shouldered his share, and even more than his share of labor, lending a hand to those who were tired or weak, or those who were suffering in the aftermath of heavy drink.

At sundown when the men retired to their camp, Maria made repairs on the poor sickle he had been given; splinting the curve of its handle until its fit was solid and strong, and sharpening its dull blade with an oilstone until it gleamed silver sharp. Watching his adeptness, several men brought their tired and wounded sickles to him, at which Maria beamed and gladly gave them what repairs he could.

Soon the blond-haired and blue-eyed recruit was no longer nettled with demeaning barbs, but was an integral, even a chief part of their team, one whose labor few could match, and none could surpass.

Nicknamed the *golden lion*, the men began to like him, to smile, jest and laugh with him, and when one day Maria began to sing in a voice as golden as his hair and beard, he taught the others the song's words, and they joined and chimed in with him. Feeling it was not *apropos* to sing prayers or hymns, Maria sang songs he remembered his mother singing as she danced with bright scarves and skirts about a fire.

'O what is in the glance and smile
That dance about the leaping fire?
What sings in the restless heart all whiles,
But the hungry wolf of love's desire?
In the hunt of every lonely child,
Each hunter needs a dark-eyed missus,
The hunt with wine and honey, sweet upon its kisses.'

At night a great bonfire would be built, around which all the laborers, both men and women would eat hot stews served from communal pots. After they ate they would drink wine while they sharpened their sickles' blades with oilstones, and when the wine revived their tiredness, they would begin to play music on accordions, fiddles and lutes, until eventually the music erupted into dances.

Too shy to join them, Maria sat in the shadows, permitting his self only a little wine. After a while he would rise to his feet, and though his ribbing mates urged the *golden lion* to stay, he would politely defer, and depart to his mattress of sheaves, purposely prepared a good way from the others. There he would kneel like a child and pray, and then lie down, close his eyes, and listen to the revelry build and leap like a fire's hungry flames only a short ways away.

He had told the others he was tired, and still adhering to the practices of a monk, he needed to say his prayers. But he knew this was only one of the reasons he left their company so early. He had felt dark, curious eyes dwelling upon him; the sly, curious eyes of women, especially when the wine began to flow through their bloods. He had stirred, and when he did, by a sense unknown he felt them stir as well. He had felt the previous wounds that had been inflicted by this lovely creature, the wounds inflicted by 'desire's' sharp tooth begin to rankle, fester, and sweetly, bitterly bleed.

Maria lay on his bed and closed his eyes, his head swimming with his unaccustomed indulgence of wine.....listening to the music, the coarse, deep-voiced shouts of the men, and the shrill laughter of the women. And as he did silhouettes emerged and stepped on the softly glowing stage of his eyelids.....the silhouette of a young girl racing through a forest, at times making trills on a flute.....an older woman with long gray hair slipping naked from her nightgown, then laying down invitingly on a bearskin.....a one-legged, crazy old man, draped sometimes in the pelt of a wolf, sometimes in that of a bear, mounting his wife in beastly ways, and making her do beastly things......and maidens, innumerable maidens, gay and fair as angels, stomping grapes, binding sheaves, picking fruits from ladders..... sometimes bringing him flowers and little kisses.....and once, small budding breasts brought from a blouse.......

After more than a week scything daylong in the hot sun, and having distinguished himself with his brawn, zeal, ringing laughter and sweet singing voice, Maria's discipline and inhibition began to wear thin. One night as he was about to leave the fire, a number of men tried to waylay him. With the wine beginning to make happy their blood, they shouted out good-naturedly, urging him to stay in their midst.

"Where are you going, Golden Lion? The night is young, and it is too early for sleep!"

"Pray your prayers after you drink one more cup of wine! Your God will not mind!"

"You work hard in the sun, and you need to play a little beneath the stars!"

"Stay just a little more! We like you, Golden Lion. Drink one more cup of wine! Dance with a lady! The night is very young!"

Weakened with tiredness, wine, and their cajolery, he accepted the invitation to stay after his meal, and to partake of the revel. A neophyte with their peasant songs and dances, he found no lack of teachers as he drank a second, third, and even a fourth mug of strong wine; especially many pretty helpmeets who vied to teach him the steps of the peasant dances, so many that a kind of competition quickly developed to give him lessons.

The women were at once smitten with this golden, blue-eyed lion that had stepped from the forest to work among them. They liked his broad shoulders, strong arms and broad chest. They liked how his gold-enness shone in the sun and sparkled in the firelight, and how, even though he was a large strong man, he was light on his feet. Before long each of these olive-skinned, dark-eyed ones, their smiles bright as fire, wanted to have a turn with the *golden lion*. Each wanted to be near him. Each wanted to touch him.

These teachers quickly discovered they had inherited an exceptional pupil, one who learned the steps and the rhythms of the dances swiftly and with alacrity. The dances had only to be shown him once, and he was dancing about the fire with laughter and abandon; as he had danced these steps and twirled these twirls since he was a boy.

Even more astonishing in the nights to come, was the natural adeptness he demonstrated with various musical instruments. Lute, fiddle and accordion seemed to long for his caresses, caresses that unlocked secrets that seemed to be waiting, as in a dusty corner for his touch to uncover. Although he had long forgotten them, he had played upon these instruments when he had been a small boy. Their memories still lived in his fingers. With only a few, stiff, tentative attempts, his fingers began to race up and down the clavier, dance upon the lute, and to kiss the fiddle strings with an eager bow, waking sweet and melancholy voices that slept with pretty dreams in their hearts. Seeing his natural proclivity for these instruments, he quickly became the beneficiary of two of them.

The first was a fiddle. It was old and dusty, its strings loose, and what seemed hopelessly out of tune; its bow of horsehair, fraying and balding. A one-eyed fiddler man had left it behind him when he had become very drunk one night. He had insisted that instead of drink and his clumsy fingers, the spirit of his dead wife lived in the fiddle, and was harshly upbraiding him under the guise of screeches when he tried to play sweetly upon it. When it was given to Maria, he brightened, and after several brief repairs, and several rainy days of practice, the spirit of this dead wife was crooning docilely in his hands.

The second instrument was a lute, given to him when he sat alone, playing this fiddle. It was given to him by a young servant girl in the camp, not more than eleven or twelve years old; a girl hampered with a pronounced limp, and who always wore a yellow bandanna wrapped about her head, the bandanna's tail falling from its knot to the small of her back. Maria stopped his playing of the fiddle at her shy, silent approach. Standing before him, she presented him the lute.

"*I have brought a lute for you, good sir. I thought your hands might make it sing about the fire.*"

Maria looked at the lute. Unlike the fiddle, it was a fine lute, a beautiful lute, one that needed loving care, but no serious repairs.

"*It is a very beautiful lute, sweet one, one that does not seem an Italian lute.....see, .the pegs, the neck with tortoise shell.....and this moon and two stars carved and painted on its face. I know this kind of lute. It was made from a very old, and very special kind of pine tree.....yes, smell, its fragrance still lives in its wood. It comes from another land; a jewel of a lute, one called a 'cobza'."*

"It is my father's lute. My mother gave it to him, my mother who died."

"And where is your father?"

"He is travelling."

"Traveling?"

"My father is a doctor.....he was a doctor in the wars.....and there is now sickness in the hill-villages."

"But it is your father's lute; I could not take such a precious thing from you, even in borrowing."

"My father is old, and no longer plays the lute. He keeps it because he says it reminds him of my mother....as if she is still living in it.....my mother was from another country, the country that the lute came from..... my mother has gone away, dead I think, but still lives in the lute, or so my father believes........

But I must go now.....you see I help prepare the stews and breads for the teams. If you would like, play the lute a little. I think my mother would sing sweetly in your arms."

With this the young crippled girl placed the lute upon Maria's lap, and when she did she lifted her face to his. Her eyes were like deep dark wells, wells that sparkled with stars. They were the most beautiful, and perhaps the loneliest eyes Maria had ever seen; as if their loneliness was far more ancient than the loneliness of others.

As she started away, Maria quickly spoke, arresting her steps and once more turning her face to his.

"Miss, I think it is Katrinika, is it not?"

"Yes, my name is Katrinika."

"I have noticed the bandanna you wear; your yellow bandanna."

"It keeps my face free for the work I......"

"It is a very pretty bandanna."

"It is like the others that the others wear, sir....."

"But it is not worn like the others wear theirs. It is wrapped much more deeply on your forehead, nearly to your eyebrows, and its tail dangles much longer, all the way to your waist....and if I am not mistaken, there are tiny beads sewn in the hem of its tail."

186

"It is a thing I do not think about, sir."

"And the knot with which it is tied.....a different kind of knot......as it was a knot tied by the fingers of a different people, a different people in a different land.....even like this beautiful lute was fashioned by different hands in a different land......"

These observations seemed to make the girl nervous, and with a: *"But now you must excuse me, sir, I must be at my duties. Good day, a very good day to you sir,"*.....the servant girl limped away.

For many hours Maria played the lute, and it was indeed as the young girl had said: *'I think my mother would sing sweetly in your arms.'* As he began to play upon its strings it began to yield its secret charms and dreams, poignancies sweet and deep, as there was indeed a sleeping woman in its strings, one that woke when his fingers were upon it; that sighed and gently moaned, that sang to a deep and tender part in him.

The day was damp, and the beards hung heavily on the drooping stalks, prohibiting the teams from entering the fields. Maria sat apart, playing first the fiddle, and then the beautiful lute, his fingers and his heart hungrily waking lovely melodies from each. As he did he could not help thinking he was lovemaking with a woman; that he was kissing and caressing awake her voluptuous secrets into song. He imagined he was kissing every part of her, even her disfigured hip; even her crutch-like leg. As he made the lute and fiddle sigh and croon, he imagined becoming lost in the beautiful, forest-dark eyes of a crippled young servant girl. A depravity beyond his will, he imagined kissing this young girl's naked loveliness over and over, until she blossomed into a woman in his arms.

The champion of their sun-glaring labors soon became the minion of their moon-glowing revels. He was the men's comrade by day and the women's darling by night. Soon Maria began to dance with a gusto and authority, one that no longer obeyed, but commanded the partners in his arms; partners who began to suggest other lessons, For now in the frenzy of the dances they pressed their bodies into his, branding his inebriation with the treasures beneath their smocks and blouses. Now they pressed their thighs and breasts into him, and laid their cheeks upon his shoulder. They brought their fingers to his hair, playfully caressing and combing through its fledgling comb of blondness. And when they did they brushed his neck with kisses, and brought whispers to his ear:

"I like to dance with you, Maria. I like to be in your strong arms."

"I watch you as you scythe with the other men. I see that you are very strong, and I see that you are very handsome. And when you sing it is as though my own heart is singing."

"Have you ever had a sweetheart, Golden Lion? Or are you only interested in praying to your God?"

"Does a monk ever think of a woman in his prayers? If you were again behind your abbey walls, would you think of me?"

"If you would like, I could come to you after the music and the dancing tonight. You see I felt you stir and harden when I pressed into you. No one would see me come to you in the darkness. I could lie in your arms. I could bring kisses to your mouth."

Under the pretense of drunkenness, some threw themselves into his arms and tried to bring their lips to his at the night's close. But laughing, and sometimes swinging them around in his arms, Maria politely denied their impassioned coquetry. In a stupor of wine, he went to his bed, knelt and prayed.

And so the days and nights passed, with a regimen of lusty labor in the hot sun, and wine and dance in the cool, starry nights. This was a happy time for Maria, when he felt the muscles of his body emerge, bulge and harden, and his skin toughen and bronze. It was a simple life, a good life; a life that nourished parts of him whose hidden hungers were long unfed.

When the dew dried from the wheat, the men entered the fields like an invading army, their sickles gleaming and swishing in the sun, making a battle cry, not of war, but as ancient and mighty as war; the battle cry of survival in a world of extravagant, savage odds; the odds of locusts, famines, and the wolves of winter. The army of men were followed by the barefoot women, like a flock of beautiful birds; with their bright blouses and kerchiefs, and their long ochre skirts lifted and bound on one side by bright red sashes; their backs bent double to the ground as they bound the stalks the men's sickles had felled. This pleased, and even excited *the golden lion* very much, to think that the women's treasures were only a short way behind the men's labors; that the dark eyes of primitive desire followed them. At times he felt these eyes studying him, admiring him, as if his bare chest, strong arms and shoulders were their prey.

But they were days of trial as well, for more and more he felt his blood stir when he danced with the peasant women, some of which were the wives of the men he was scything alongside. Even when he would see one bend or stretch in the sun, or expose a knee at the well, or a slender throat as she lifted her face to drink from a jar, he would feel the animal inside him stir in its cage, restless with its dark hunger. He began to neglect his prayers, and when he closed his eyes for sleep these same peasant women appeared in his wine-dizzied mind, begging to bring their breasts and kisses to him, even as they had insinuated when they had danced in his arms moments before. Several times these dreams became more than dreams, their insinuations more than insinuations when, in the dark of the night, he woke to whispers at his side.

"May I come under your blanket with you, Golden Lion? I could make you very happy. Has a woman ever made you happy? If they have not, I am sure I could. Please, Golden Lion, would you let me try?"

But even then he had denied their offers, giving them an embrace and a small kiss, assuring them of his appreciation, and then sending them back to their own beds, some in which were sleeping their drunken husbands.

It did not take long for the men to notice the spell *the golden lion* cast over the women. They saw the blushes and heard the silly titters come from them when Maria was near. And with this their robust camaraderie faded into grumbles and grudges. When the women competed for him as their dance partner, Maria felt the men's resentment seethe the more. He felt that a bitter contentiousness, even that a fistfight might ensue; so one night, surrounded by the amorous covey that had come to vie for him, Maria surprised all by announcing that he would dance with Katrinika, and no other, a thing that elicited a rousing laughter from all.

All knew that Katrinika, the young girl who had lent Maria the beautiful lute, was hampered with a pronounced limp. She could not gather, pick or bind as could the other women. Made shy with the handicap of her birth, she seldom spoke, and did not participate in the randy drinking and dancing after the meals.

Her shyness was perhaps the reason she never relinquished her bandanna as did the other women, keeping her tresses bound while the others loosed their glossy manes, to flutter and sparkle in the firelight as they danced. And it was her limp, shyness, and the canary yellow bandanna that she ever wore, like a nun her veil, that painted her with plainness, even homeliness in the eyes of the harvesters, making her vulnerable to sharp orders, and occasional callous, unkind jests.

For this reason, when Maria smiled brightly, and held out his hand to the young servant girl, none were surprised when, with a little shake of her head she refused him. Fearing some cruel mockery of her deformity, she colored brightly, and midst a shower of hoots and jeers, at once limped briskly away.

But Maria had intended no jest, and he did not laugh when the young servant girl refused his offer. Keeping his word to dance with no other this night, he declined all invitations to dance about the fire. Strangely moved by the girl's shyness, and a certain dignity embodied in that shyness, Maria sat alone, cradled the lute she had lent him, and let his fingers lovingly caress its strings. After coaxing forth several of its melancholy secrets, he silently stood, and retired to his bed.

Lying awake, he wondered about this thing that had so deeply moved him. Only when the girl had blushed, stammered and limped shyly, but nobly away, did he begin to intimate a possible meaning. Was this not at least part of the reason he had denied the others' amorous advances, even when they had come to his bed in the middle of the night? Was his denial of their pleasures not a kind of penance he was exacting, like a fast or a vigil, one that was begging for the indulgence of this girl's lovely dark eyes to lift to him? When he sang, laughed and danced about the fire, was it not in truth for her, imagining her dark eyes full of ancient loneliness were watching him from the enveloping shadows? Did he not sometimes think of her as he toiled in the hot sun, her plainness and humility, even her limp having stung his heart with a peculiar kind of beauty, one that he would like to hold in his arms? Did he not dream of unbinding her bandana, holding her pretty face between his hands, and then ta taste the kisses she had probably not given another? In this inscrutable forest of 'woman love' that he had entered, this forest where all and nothing could be trusted, and yet all was a possibility, was it possible that this crippled girl, like no other, had in some peculiar way won his heart?

With such thoughts Maria fell asleep, only to be wakened in the night by this very one he had thought about. Knowing it was she, he reached out in the darkness to embrace her.

"Oh, precious flower, gentle doe, my little Katrinika, I am so happy you have come to me! I like you very much, and I want to be sweet to you. Here, the night is cold, come beneath my blanket......."

But she had recoiled when he had reached out to touch her, and even more when he had invited her into his bed. The young crippled girl had not come to be his lover.

"*No, it is not for that reason I have come to you, blond sir. There are others prettier than I, many others who will come to your arms, and give you sweet things.*

I have come to simply tell you 'thank you' for your offer to dance with me. I think you are a kind man, and I could see in your eyes that you were not mocking me. But as all know, I am a cripple. You need to find and ask another to dance around the fire with you, even as you must ask another to comfort you in your bed.

Please, do not ask me again to dance with you, because it makes the others laugh. I like you, blond man, but I do not want you to pretend to like me. When the harvest ends, I do not want to be left with a wound in my heart, a wound that will hurt very deeply one such as me, and may not go away for many winters and summers to come.

Now I must go.....no, please, you must not try to touch me like that. You are strong and handsome, and you need a strong pretty girl to be sweet with you. You would soon tire of one who cannot play like the other girls. Goodnight, blond man, and thank you for the kindness you have tried to show me.

And thank you for playing the lute so sweetly. I hear my mother, the mother I never knew singing sweetly in it."

Never again did the crippled girl come to him in the night. Never again did she lift her beautiful dark eyes to him near the fire. And this had a surprising, even a violent effect on Brother Maria. Knowing there was no chance to win this one who had stolen this dream in his heart, and never having known such a defeat before, his urge to be with a woman was greatly inflamed. He began to drink more wine, and to dance with more abandon. He permitted his smiles to reciprocate daring glances; to tenderly whisper in ears, even to brush the soft napes of necks with his beard. He held his partners as he had not held them before, allowing his hands to slide to their waists, then slyly over their hips; his thighs meeting their thighs, arousing the flame of his manhood, a flame that now wished to be quenched by the loveliness that had excited it.

But all soon changed, and his needs were answered in an unexpected way, due largely to a jealous conspiracy of his fellow reapers.

One night at the urging of the other men, Maria became very drunk, more drunk than he had ever been before. Slurring his words, singing loudly, and even cursing with the curses he had heard the others use, he stumbled to his bed, only to be joined shortly after by one who had been paid in some way to join him, and to show the monk among them another kind of prayer.

A group of men surrounded him as he lay in his bed.

"*Here Maria, I think Lenora will help you. I think she knows what you need! Your prayers have been heard!*"

"*She has had enough practice, haven't you Lenora?*"

"*And don't worry, she's paid for, we've pitched in a hat to buy her this night!*"

"*Now it's your turn to have her, Maria, or what's left of her, for half the men have had a throw of her!*"

"*Maybe now, pretty golden monk, you will keep your hands off the asses of the others you dance with about the fire! Maybe now your horn will be blunted.*"

It had not been all drunken horseplay. Lenora was a whore; probably one who visited harvest teams, giving her body in return for meals. But she was a sweet whore, a loving whore, and as the nights grew cold, and the last days of harvest grew near their close, Maria was grateful for the one the men had brought to his bed. After being loved by Maria that first night, Lenora no longer sold herself to other arms at the end of the day. She was asked to remain as the *golden lion's* bedfellow, one that he prized, and came to guard and claim his own.

She was not old, but older than Maria, and though not unlovely, he had no doubt she had been much lovelier in her youth. But she had long learned to use sex both as a candy and a bane, and this had prematurely coarsened her, robbing her of her natural allure. She was shameless, but in her shamelessness she was polite, and when she had given of her favors, she thanked the one to whom she had given them. But she soon discovered that she did not now belong to one who mistreated or in any way abused her. She had fallen in the arms of one who did not ask for her favors, but rather one she wished to freely give them; one who was kind and patient with her; one who she wished to please. She, who had been scorned and derided by the other women of the harvest, now owned the trophy they had tried to win.

Maria culled bouquets of flowers for her, and sometimes sang songs for her. Once when he found a drunken man trying to molest her, he had roughly thrown him off her. When the man renewed his attack, Maria had delivered hard, decisive blows to his ribs and jaw, ending the confrontation. That night when his lover asked him what he wished of her, Maria asked only that they lie still, and look at the animals in the stars together. The much abused woman, proudly grateful for his defense of her, nuzzled in his arms, and gave her heart to him.

As they were harvesting their last fields, late one gray afternoon a snow began to fall, bending and blanketing the bearded stalks, making their field work impossible. Some in the crews left for their homes, convinced the year and their earnings had come to an end. Others built small makeshift shelters in the nearby woods, hopeful that the sun might soon shine again, and allow them more work and pay. Maria and Lenora were among those that remained.

Lenora was delighted with the opportunity to have her lover all to herself. As the snow continued to fall for two days, the lovers ate, slept and played in each other's arms, relishing these carefree moments that had been given them. Buried in their burrow of pine branches, dry sheaves and blankets, they played like fox cubs in their den, waking only to fuel and quench the other's needs, and to be exhausted back into the peace of their arms.

On the third day the blizzard quit, and the sun shone in a bright blue sky, Birds began to sing, and the earth to slurp the melting snow back into its muddy and rocky mouths. The harvesting of the last few fields was still at an *impasse*, contingent on the warmth of sun and breeze to once more winnow the wheat crisp and dry. More of the men became disgruntled, quit the teams, and slopped the miry ways back to their hamlets and cottages. Of those who stayed in the forest, some remained in languor, some in debauch; and a peasant harlot and her *golden lion lover*, in love.

They had lingered on with blithe hearts, and not with the lassitude and dejectedness that had infected the others. Maria had no home other than the forest, the forest that would soon be drifted with snow and prowled by packs of wolves. Lenora's only home was now her wandering lover's bed and side. Maria was strong, healthy and winsome, and would easily find employment from which they could eke out an existence, at least until the spring. Lenora was duteous, and wanted only to love her golden-haired darling, her protector, and the envy of the other women.

Waiting for the fields to dry, one warm sunny afternoon Maria hiked to the nearby village to purchase a few things they would need at their departure; the departure that he and Lenora would make together.

Lenora went to the icy, but still open brook to wash their clothes. Never had Maria felt so robust and lighthearted, and on his return from the village he whistled and sang, even as he fell into a happy muse.

How long had it been since he had been a gray-robed monk who prayed, fasted and scourged? That now seemed many ages ago, like a tale told to children of a ancient wars and giants. Or had it been a dream? Where was Brother Maria now, the Brother Maria with a tunic, tonsure and beads? That Brother Maria seemed an entirely different person than the one whose steps were now so happily and confidently bearing him.

And yet he knew that it had been only a few months since he had been the Brother Maria who had prayed and fasted, and then had fled the walls that had offered salvation to his soul. Oh, how many revelations had come to him in this short while, revelations that he would never acquire with fasts, chants and prayers! He felt a new vigor in his blood and bones, even as a tree must feel the spring thaw its deepest roots, its warmth shivering through its branches, and tickling its crown with feathery buds. Brother Maria was no longer Brother Maria. His roots were no longer frozen beneath the snow. His blood was rising with a new fever, a wonderful new kind of manhood, and the pleasures so freely offered to that manhood.

What would Father Giovanni say if he now saw him, with his broad shoulders, his brash smiles, and his swaggering ways; with his golden hair and beard that he had not once trimmed or shorn? He would like to see his good friend again; perhaps even be confessed by him. He would like to give him a warm embrace, and look into his dark wise eyes, those eyes that he knew contained secrets he could never guess; wells he could never fathom. But he would also like to tell him that he had been wrong to insinuate that the world was a vain, dangerous and evil place. Yes, of course there were evils. But there were thieves and usurers everywhere, even in an abbey. Death, disease and thievery were not held in abeyance by high stone walls. But the world was full of glories also, glories that exalted the soul to new heights and breadths of mystery and discovery. In this short time since that last night when he had spoken to his friend in the confessional, he had learned to do many things: to hunt and harvest, to gather and snare, to build shelters and sickle wheat. He had learned to dance, sing, and play a fiddle and lute. He had learned the great mystery of how to love a woman, as he now loved Lenora.

He would tell his friend that a woman's loveliness was full of many pleasures, not evils; songs of angels, not snares of devils. He would of course not tell him of the lovely storms of lovemaking, but instead, what a woman's eyes and smiles brought to a man's heart; how they warmed and wakened a man's soul, as if 'woman' enkindled something dry and empty inside a man; her love containing something higher, something blessed; like being enfolded by an Angel's wings, kissed by an Angel's lips.

And if he asked about the young shepherdess, what would he say? His friend had certainly been correct in his prognostication of that outcome; yes, he had proved wise and prophetic about that. And what would he say about his dreams, his strange dreams of the maidens in the grapes.....like a herd of deer, or a choir of Angels beckoning to him with one gaze, one smile, one yearning.....the dancing bear, with the shepherd girl, playing her flute, imprisoned in the skeleton of dead bones....and those impassioned, climactic, shameless moments when he imagined he flooded his seed into his own mother.....a sin, of course a sin, but one that he did not feel like it was a sin at all.......

But Maria was suddenly torn from his meditations by men's loud laughter, and the distressed screams of a woman. They were coming from near the brook that babbled at the foot of the field. At once recognizing Lenora's voice, a lightning shot through his heart, one that gripped him with fright, then with rage, then with a deeper and darker passion, one that he had not felt before.

Bounding over the muddy field and into the thicket where the brook ran, Maria saw a sight that drove a dagger through his happy heart. Five or six men were about Lenora, some unbuckled, knelt and readying to take their turn with her; one having just completed his lust. The men were older than he, mangy and disheveled, and were making his lover submit to unnatural, goatish copulations.

Maria threw his self upon them with a rage that acknowledged no odds. Several were strangers to his eye, but several were not, and as they circled him with flashing knives they pulled from their boots, Maria could see their faces smeared with ugly scowls and murderous smirks, expressions that had seethed with jealousies behind masks of laughter and fraternity in the sunny fields.

But Maria was not ready to die. The one who had once been a humble Brother in Christ, now turned into a brutal fighter. In a kind of awe, the peasant woman beheld her tender sensitive lover transfigure, becoming wild and savage before her very eyes. In a few bloody moments each of her assailants had swiftly fled, struggled away with wounds, or lay in the blood-blotched snow. But more than the feat itself was the swiftness and dexterity with which it had been accomplished; and still more, its terrible, ruthless savagery. Lenora watched as her tender lover continued to kick and maul those he had seriously wounded, even one who laid motionless, moaning and gurgling blood upon the snow.

Dazed from his mania, and the storm of wrath that had breathed through him, Maria turned to Lenora, only to find her cradling one of the men he had beaten away from her. Maria stepped towards her, but when he did she only hugged and cradled the moaning, half-conscious man more deeply in her bosom, as to protect him from the certain murder she saw in Maria's wild eyes.

"No, you must not kill him! He is my husband! No, go away! You are a madman! Look what you have done! You have the blood of the gypsies inside your veins! No, do not touch me! I hate you! Go back to the forest, to the wolves and your dreams!"

A great pain shot through Maria's head. He dizzied, fell, and knew no more.

* * *

At first he did not understand. His pain was too great; the cold, too numbing. At first he did not know why the man was staring at him so intently, so coldly and dumbly, as he was staring through and beyond him.....beyond trees and clouds, summer and winter.....through and beyond him, as if Brother Maria was a blade of grass, a wisp of smoke.....a stare full of emptiness, an emptiness empty of anger, happiness, love...of all things that bloom and die beneath the sun......and yet he liked these eyes, he trusted them.....they were full of a final wisdom, an utmost knowing.....they were awake, open and laughing with Life's final secret, a realization of its futility......as if in the end, death alone had eyes to see, and had earned the right to laugh and scoff.......

He struggled to his side, and dazedly looked at the bloody scene about him; the bright red blotches of blood on the snow, as might be seen about a butcher's door.....the dropped weapons of boards, a ragged coat, a bloodstained knife.....and the dead man before him, staring into the open maw of death, a knife's hilt protruding from his ribs.....the knife that he, Brother Maria, a former monk, had driven as deep as it would reach inside him.

"*Come, hurry, you must flee! They will come for you! They will hunt for you! They will kill you!*"

Maria now heard the voice and felt the hand on his shoulder that had roused him.

"*Are you hurt blond man? Can you stand? Can you walk? You must away at once. The men you have fought will come again. They will bring others. You will not be able to fight them. They will kill you, perhaps in a most terrible way. Do you hear me? Do you understand my words? I am the servant girl, the girl with a limp that you once asked to dance about the fire with you.*"

With the help of the girl Maria managed to stand, but with the horror of death about him, the death he had inflicted with his own hands, he could not speak. Seeing his stupor, the girl tried to push and lead him away.

"*Please, there is no time! The woman's husband has learned that she was your bed partner......that she was giving you pleasure without being paid for them. He is very drunk, and very jealous, and he has sworn an oath to kill you! Please, you must not let him kill you, blond man......I would rather he kill me......you see I like you, I like you very much blond man......here, bend down your head, I will loop the strap of this bag, this satchel over your head....there are two large biscuits, a piece of cheese, a flask of wine in it, and you will need it for other things......now, hurry away at once......I will never forget you, blond man, I will never forget that you asked me to dance, and there was kindness in your eyes......I will never forget that you made my mother sing from the lute......but now, run, now you must run away!*"

Maria began to stumble away along the icy edge of the brook. His head throbbed from the stone that had bashed it, and he could feel the clammy warmth of blood trickling down his cold side. And yet it was more than fear or pain, or the horror of the monstrous thing he had done that made one foot lead the other. It was something ineffably sweet: the wonderful kindness that the young girl had shown him...... *the satchel, the 'cobza', the tender, but firm belief she had lent his heart.*

Maria stopped, and looked back at the crippled girl limping away. The foot she was dragging was making a pronounced trail in the snow, as she was an Angel gallantly dragging its broken wing through the carnage of men; as if it was writing a signature of Heaven's love and forgiveness.

And as he had halted and turned, so the young girl stopped the labor of her lame steps, and turned her eyes back to him.....and despite shyness, pain, the curse of her birth and the cruel dangers that now threatened with such imminence this murderer's life, both retraced their steps back to each other's unspoken needs.

Removing her yellow bandanna, and freeing her secret wealth of her dark black hair over her poor coat, she tied the bandanna firmly about his wrist, even as she was binding her heart about his heart. She lifted her dark eyes to him; as he had always hoped she would, her soul confessing its truth through their lonely windows.

"I love you blond man. I love you very much. I will never love another."

And with this she lifted her two hands to his face, and beckoning it down to her, placed her lips as lightly as a pecking dove on his bearded and bloodied cheek; a kiss full of tears; impaling his soul upon its sweetness.

"Now run away into the forest, blond man, run that you may live for all those that will want to love you."

Maria turned and began to walk briskly, then to jog away; his heart afire as it had not been before. Yes, he had killed a man, and he must run and hide. Yes, for this sweet face and these sweet eyes, and his mother smiling through them, he must live.

. . . .

. . . .

CHAPTER TEN

THE SECRET THE ABBOT KEPT

The Abbey: 1332

THE darkness had come early, falling like a dark snow upon the hills, and on through the naked arms of the forest trees. Creeping from the forest, its tide proceeded to flood the newly gleaned fields, and then swelling and hungering for more, it mounted the steep narrow road until it lapped, breached and spilled its blackness over the high walls; smothering the walks, wasted gardens and shriveled flowerbeds; the pond and arcade, the pillars and cornices; drowning the stone saints, their hands lifted with stone blessings, and the stone *Madonna* weeping her stone tears. Its dark blood soaked each thing it touched; contaminated all with blackness; surrounded like a sea of wolves the candle in men's souls.

Vigils had been recited, and the brotherhood had silently returned to the cloister for their second sleep, the sleep that would endure until the bell rang for *Lauds*. But shortly after the midnight chants were ended, and the brotherhood returned to their beds, a lone monk stepped back from out the cloister into the moonless night. He walked across the courtyard and into the sanctuary again; as in defiance of the strict decorum of the *Hours*; indeed, as in defiance of sleep itself.

The penitent knelt in silence before the great Crucifix, lifting up his face to the carved *Savior* hanging in a sensual, all but erotic pose of anguish upon it. Inherited from an unknown time, and from unknown hands of unknown *Byzantine* monks, the eyes of the *crucified One* were ever full of suffering and compassion for the countless ones who knelt before it; those asking for forgiveness, guidance, deliverance. So did these dark wooden eyes now look upon this one who was knelt in the penumbra of candlelight at their feet.

What did those eyes, those sad loving eyes see?

They saw a very tired and worn man; but one who had become gladly tired and gladly worn for his Savior's sake; a man bowed beneath a great burden, but willing and thankful to shoulder that burden; spending as much time on his knees as on his feet in the silent bearing of its great weight. Beneath his robe, and this invisible cross that he was bearing were thinly fleshed bones, the result of long days and weeks of fasting; and even scars left by a tongue of nails and leather on his skeletal back. The upturned face was gaunt, drawn and pallid, as it was a prisoner starved of sunlight, a prisoner of the spirit, subjected to long vigils spent in prayer and contemplation. Its features were frozen in a rictus of pain; but a tender, most lovely pain, as of a bud in its great, nay, its stupendous struggle to flower and know the sun.

These eyes saw a man neither young nor old, but a man prematurely grave and seasoned with age. They saw a humble man, his humility whittled from a pride of incisive intellect and unrivalled scholarship; a man not strong in body, but vigorous in spirit; a student, not a soldier; one whose hardships and soldiering came not midst battles in field and forest, but midst campaigns in the savage wilderness of the soul.

They saw a man whose heart had shed all trappings, and now burned with the flame of sincerity. They saw a good man; a devout man; an earnest and true man; a man whose deepest wish was to open the gates of his heart to the God he yearned to worship and obey.

And what did this exquisitely carved Savior, bleeding with His wounds on the cypress Cross, hear as the penitent prayed in the silence of his heart?

"Father, I promise to be my brothers' shepherd, but only when Thou shepherd'st me. It is an honor I accept, however unworthy I may be; an honor I accept only on Thy behalf. Guide me. Lift me. Breathe through me with Thy Spirit. Light the lamp of my heart, that, if only for a short while and a short way, I may give my brothers' steps sure guidance through the darkness of this world."

After an hour spent in prayer at the feet of the great Crucifix, Father Giovanni rose to his feet, and walked back through the dusky nave towards the door. But he did not reach the door; or the courtyard and cloister beyond it. His steps were halted by a voice, a voice without a body that, like a faint wisp of smoke, issued from the darkness.

"*You will make a fine abbot; I think finer than the one who is departing.*"

It was as the darkness spoke; as by an Angel concealed in its shadows. It was a faint and weak voice, exquisitely, almost ethereally gentle; a voice that the priest knew, and knowing, honored and loved. It startled the solitary monk, not only because of its speaker's invisibility, but because its speaker had managed to be in the chapel at all.

"*Father Abbot, I thought that I was alone.*"

The voice replied slowly, but sweetly; not like the croak of a sick bird, but like one content, replenished by a fresh new rain. It was weak and frail, but in its weakness and frailty it wielded a tender might, like a song of distant thunder rolling gently over, and as if blessing the hilltops.

"*Can you see me?*"

"*No, I cannot see you, Father Abbot. I can only hear you.*"

"*Good. That is how I would like it to be.*"

The abbot had been bedridden for the greater part of two weeks, and when he had not been, had dragged and struggled about on crutches; with brothers at his side, lest his feeble steps should fail him. He was old, and it had been accepted by all, even the beloved abbot himself, that he was dying.

"*Then for allegorical sake, let us imagine that you are alone, and that there is no one here in the shadows. Let us imagine, my son, that you are having a dialogue in darkness, in the night of your soul so to say; that you are having a chat, perhaps even a debate with your conscience; and if not a chat or a debate, then a confession, a confession to an unseen confessor, an unseen counselor; perhaps even an unseen God.*"

"*A confession, Father Abbot?*"

"*Yes, a confession; one that you are making to the confessor of your own soul, in the silent confessional of your own heart.*"

"*I think I must confess what my confessor has long known.*"

"*What do you mean?*"

"*I mean that I believe my Father Abbot was here that night, that night years ago when I was sure I was alone, when I was sure there was no one else in the chapel.*"

As the invisible auditor had not heard, his reply seemed irrelevant, and out of context.

"*The abbot's bones simply will not let him sleep. They go moaning and a-wandering, like an absentminded ghost looking for where it left its grave.*"

"*I think my Father Abbot sat in the darkness, even as he is sitting now in the darkness, invisible and unseen."*

And then another odd and senseless rejoiner......

"A curse of age, those brittle, rickety bones; one more cross to bear up Calvary, one more to be shirked and buried by brother death I suppose."

"You knew; you know; all this time you have known."

"Who are you speaking to, and of what my son?"

"I am speaking to my beloved abbot; to Abbot Augustine, and I am speaking of that night....."

"......I must remind you, that you are speaking in the dark silence of your soul, not to another, and certainly not to your abbot. Your abbot is not here. He is in his cell, sleeping like a child in its cradle; sleep's cradle soon to be death's coffin. You are speaking with your own soul, and the compassionate God that watches over it. You are speaking to darkness, but more precisely, to the ear and eye, to the light within that darkness."

"Then.....I am sure there was someone else in the chapel that night....."

"What night are you speaking of my son?"

"The night when I spoke to the missing brother in the confessional, even after I told my Father Abbot repeatedly, emphatically that I had no idea where he was, or where or why he was leaving; even after I had lied, again and again lied, face to face to my Father Superior."

"I will admit, yes, I will admit that there were many times when the brotherhood was asleep that your abbot came here to sit and pray in these same shadows. And when he did he sometimes felt as he was an owl, one whose eyes see things that scurry and flutter through the night. He fancied that his sight, and with it his mind sometimes became more keen than they were in the light of day."

"You have known that I have lied to you for years; and yet in the Chapter House, when the brothers cast their ballots in the box, you said nothing."

"An owl, yes, an owl, a sleepy old, crippled old, nosy old owl."

"You knew that I lied, that I emphatically, unflinchingly lied to you when you asked me about the delinquent brother. But worse than a lie, I have omitted it over and over in my confessions. I should have been reprimanded, made to perform a severe penance; to flog or fast apart from the others, in some way be castigated before my brothers, rather than be nominated to shepherd them."

"I speak not for your abbot, for of course your abbot is not here, but for the sensibility of your soul when I say I think you have performed years of severe penance, but one that your conscience, and not your abbot has exacted

upon you. I think you have flogged your heart until its repentance has wept rains of contrition, rains that were made salty, even bloody with your tears."

"But you saw Brother Maria stealing into the chapel, and my coming to him in the confessional, and yet you said nothing about it, even when you knew I was lying to you about his whereabouts. But why? If I do not ask this question of my abbot, then I ask it of my soul, and the unseen God that watches over it. Why? Why? Why?"

"And how does your God answer your question?"

"With silence; a silence that echoes with the same question: 'why'?"

"Then let me try, once more for allegorical sake, to give words that that mumble-mouth, mealy mouthed silence may be trying to tell you. Yes, let me try.

Let us say, allegorically mind you, that God, and His unsleeping Eyes is not the grim fellow we sometimes make Him out to be. I am not sure He sees lies where men see lies; even as I am not sure He sees Truth where others see and are convinced of Truth. I do not think God gives much credence to the appearance, or one might say the dream of things. I think he is much more concerned with the dreamer than the dream. I think he looks into man's heart, and although He sees that it is filled with a jumble of deceits, falsities and fallibilities, He also sees its morsel of goodness, sewn like a golden ducat inside a ragged coat; a seed of wheat cast among a miserable tangle of thorns."

"I am not sure I know what you are saying. I have lied; time and again I have lied to my abbot. It is a great sin."

"Once again, perhaps our unseen God sees no lie where we see lies, no Truth where man's reason is convinced of Truth....no sin where men see, and raise their scornful fists."

"But my abbot knows that I, his elected successor has held, if not coveted this lie in his heart. He has known it since the beginning, when he sent the brothers to hunt the fields and forests for their missing brother."

"Your abbot knows no such thing, and if he ever did, he has long forgotten it. The crotchety old curmudgeon has one leg in the grave, and the other is in his bed, happily sleeping in sacerdotal bliss. Besides, a lie enveloped with love is not a lie, but a shell to protect the precious seed of a truth. You must remember that you are not speaking to a person, only to yourself, your higher, more tender and compassionate self; and it has a counsel and authority that an abbot does not wield, and certainly cannot gainsay. It owns that gift our Savior gave to men; it owns forgiveness."

"My Father Abbot is very good, and very, very kind."

"I think the abbot's successor is very good and very kind, and very conscientious as well. That is why I know he will be a very fine abbot; because he has the capacity to hurt, to suffer and to bleed for love, even as our Savior was crucified for love."

This was followed by a silence; a silence one with darkness, the night, the soul itself; a silence that was at last broken by a whisper, as soft and tender as a lover's whisper, as it was indeed the voice in the dark night of all men's souls.

"You must have cared deeply for this brother, this, uh, Brother Maria I believe his name was."

"He was a very special friend, not only a spiritual, but almost a blood brother, even though we were as different as the sun and moon. You see, I scarce knew my mother. She was sickly, and she died a terrible, unspeakable death in the famine, causing my father to drink heavily, and go mad with grief. When he was called to the military, he wed a second wife. She was a wanderer, an itinerant, and I think she committed infidelities. When she left for another man, or perhaps other men, my father gave me to the Church, and I never saw him again."

"And there was no one else?"

"Only a half sister, a cripple, one that my father's second, unfaithful wife gave him."

"Go on."

"As you know, I excelled in my studies. Although I excelled, I did not enjoy camaraderie with my fellow students. I avoided them; I shunned them; I had no friends. I did not intend for my learning to characterize me as aloof, but it did, yes, my scholarship made me arrogant in others' eyes, because I knew more Latin and Greek, more dates, conquests, coronations, more Aristotle and Pliny than they did. Brother Maria was not a student. He did not care about Aristotle or Pliny, about Greek or the coronations of dead kings. In some inscrutable way he befriended me, his natural innocence seeing through, or perhaps uncaring of the arrogance that others saw in me. Never having a friend or a brother, this was a great flattery, almost a marvel to my heart."

"Inscrutable? Marvel?"

"Yes; as if this brother of inferior learning gave me things I had never been given before. His senses were alive, like a creature of the wild. He was awake to the wind and clouds. He opened my mind by somehow touching

my heart, his carefree laughter singing to it like a sweet-throated bird. In some way he completed me."

"Completed you?"

"Yes, completed me. You see we only seemed to be different and incompatible; but more deeply, I think we were each other's complement."

For brief moments my heart came from the clouds of its darkness and shone like a moon, a moon that was full and gold. He gave me back what I had lost, the childhood joys of which I had been deprived. For the first time the dust of my heart brought forth a beautiful flower."

"Have you heard from this brother?"

"I have not."

"And his habit that was found in the tree? Many of the brothers surmised that he fell into wrong hands, wrong hands and a brutal end. Do you have any idea where he might be?"

"I think he left God's Hands for a woman's arms."

"A woman; or perhaps a young girl, a young girl that once played a flute in the meadows?"

"But how did you......"

"It is not another, but your own soul that knows these things. Remember, you are speaking in the dark night of your soul.

Do you know where this girl is?"

"No, I do not. But I have heard she is dead, that she took her own life."

"Please, my good dear brother, go on."

"I do not know where Brother Maria is. I do not know if he is even alive. As you know, there are great dangers outside our holy walls: famines, pestilence, bands of bandits and mercenaries that now wander at will, factions with or against both the emperor and the papacy....and he was not strong, but delicate, an artist or a poet, with the soul of a child......

.....I believe I knew him very well, because he owned what I did not have. He was fed not only by deeper springs, but brooks from higher mountains. He knew life's garden with his senses, not his mind, with a soul that presented a special appeal, one might even say a special charisma, especially for......"

"Yes, you and your abbot spoke of this thing on several occasions; how maids delivering goods at the gates were often coquettish before him. And I am sure such flirtations were difficult for such a brother not to respond to. As I remember, he was a strong, handsome, very likable young man, one that could win any man's or maid's heart, and with it, his or her favors. Yes,

this answers a hundred questions. With a wink and a smile, a peasant girl may lead a prince through the world, and perhaps a monk from his vows."

"Through a fool's paradise, do you not mean?"

"Perhaps. But are we not all, in the end, fools? Is our quest for truth not simply a whittling away at the falsities we have not only armed ourselves with, but in our bluffs of pride, convinced ourselves that we were not hiding behind? Perhaps this malingerer, this defrocked, this dasher of holy vows and playfellow with the fair sex, perhaps he turned his back to God, yes, sinned and turned his back to God to know something deeper inside his self. Was he right to do such a thing, to break his vows and go philandering into a fool's paradise as you say? Certainly not, at least with the ideals the Church first gave him. But perhaps these ideals, and not the man was wrong; their dream, however lofty and noble, perhaps too lofty and too noble to be achieved and earned,- only in another way that the wisest cannot see; that only God, and not man's sluggish creature may know......

Love swaddles all errors and mistakes. It blesses all wounds; makes them blister, fester, hotly burn; only to heal them into tenderness and health."

"But this brother turned his back on his brothers. He broke his vows. He rejected the Saints, the Virgin and her Blessed Son."

"Again, the Eyes of God do not see what the eyes of men see. Men look through a glass darkly, while God looks not through a glass at all, and sees each pebble glowing like a star on the shore of Eternity. We see a breaker of vows, an iconoclast, a fornicator, perhaps a robber or a ruffian, or even, God forbid, a murderer. But that Eye that never tires nor sleeps; that sees in darkness, peering through the window of the humble and compassionate heart may see a stumbling, albeit an earnest Angel.

Perhaps there are two wildernesses in life: the wilderness of the world, and the wilderness of the spirit. Both are full of dangers. Both are full of temptations. Both are full of the snarls of that beast that men in their fear call death. The soul must adventure through both of these wilds. It cannot hide behind high, whitewashed walls, or in the incense and candlelit airs of a chapel, even as it cannot hide in the gluttony and licentiousness of a tavern. It must step from darkness; stand naked in its own light; be bleached pure of its disguises, until the stumbling Angel stands splendidly aright, burning in its divine flame.

Perhaps knowing this young monk made your soul more human. Perhaps, as you have said he completed you; in some 'inscrutable' way he has humbled you. Perhaps this is why God gave him briefly to your life, to ripen you for the stewardship that has been bestowed upon you, even that fate that has been unanimously, and I think rightly voted upon in the Chapter House. You are a good monk, Father Giovanni, but an even better man; and I have the sincerest belief that you will be an excellent, and the very best of abbots.

Soon your abbot's bones shall be laid in the crypt directly below where we, like spirits, are now speaking in these shadows. In moments such as these; in silent moments, prayerful moments, moments of communion with your soul, listen; for his bones shall be crying from death itself: 'Love, my dear brother! For our Savior you must live, guide, die for this precious thing men call 'love'!'

These were the last words of the dialogue; a dialogue between the penitent monk and darkness; a dialogue between his heart and the speaking silence of his soul.

But there were sounds that ensued in that darkness and that silence; whispers of a *Pater Noster* midst dragging steps, and the methodical thuds of a crutch, like a wounded ghost opening a door; leaving the chapel to return to its bed; a bed that it knew would soon be its bier.

And in that darkness, and the eternal lingering of that silence there were sobs; sobs that came from beneath the carved *Savior*, and the kind eyes that looked down from the *Byzantine* cross upon which, like that *Lover* slain for the sake of all lovers, it so beautifully and heroically hung.

* * *

LESS than a fortnight after the dialogue between this penitent and the anonymous, compassionate voice spoken from the shadows, the old abbot of the Franciscan Abbey was stricken with a seizure. He no longer made nocturnal jaunts from the cloister to the chapel, for he could no longer walk. He no longer joined his brothers in the recitations of their offices, even when the brothers carried and gingerly propped him in his choir stall, for he could no longer speak.

Death held him in its grip; one bony hand about his throat, the other slowly squeezing his sparrow frail heart. He could but stare; a stare that did not blink; that neither smiled nor frowned; that was incapable of telling his needs, or speaking his blessings; that could not form the words of a final confession; that could not weep the tears it so wanted to weep.

And as these bony hands continued, day and night to grip, and inexorably squeeze the heart that had spent its life bravely, cheerfully awaiting this noose tightening about all men's necks.....even as Extreme Unction was administered, and the Brother Cantor chanted over him.....the new abbot, Abbot Giovanni, knelt for hours on end, praying at the dying man's feet; at times holding them; at times kissing them.

. . . .

. . . .

CHAPTER ELEVEN

THE MANY KISSES
IN ONE MOTHER'S SMILE

(1331-1337)

THE MAY sun fell upon him, warm and gentle. It fell upon him where he lay in the green bloom of grass, munching the biscuit and slices of spiced apples the two dairy girls had given him. He knew that when he had smiled, and told them how pretty they were, that they would return with things for him to eat. He also saw that the older, plainer of the two sisters had blushed when he had picked a flower and insisted upon braiding it in her hair, and that it was she, and not her much prettier younger sister who had given him the neat bundle of biscuits, apples, and a piece of dried fish when they had returned. He had seen that she had prettied herself in the interim, tightening her smock in such a way that showed her slim waist, and with maiden pride, her modest breasts.

He knew this smile, blush, and silly laughter that had quivered through her when she had given him the repast she had neatly bundled in a kerchief. He knew this scent that the flower of her sex exhaled. Yes, she was plain, but it would be very nice to taste the honey in her mouth; and then to lift up her skirt, and explore her secrets. He would like to help her plainness flower its secret passion, to have it sigh with pleasure when she surrendered in his arms.

The warm sunlight fell upon him through the freshly leafing boughs, thawing the winter from his bones as it was thawing the long winter from the forest trees. Yes, he was like a tree of the forest, the sap of his blood new-waked and rising, hatching its bloom beneath the sun.

Yes, he was a tree, the roots of his flesh nourished by the earth's fertile goodness, a goodness married to the sun; a deathless goodness briefly given, and briefly partaken of by all that lived and died.

Yes, it would be lovely to play in her arms, to make her plainness bloom its secret flower from her curious heart; for a moment to lie together, joined, forgetful of all, stunned still in the playful miracle of their answered needs.

He plucked a tasseled blade of grass, placed it between his teeth, and closed his eyes. He frequently gave himself to these lapses of reverie and dream, these dalliances of introspection that filled his idle moments; moments that he once regarded full of vice and sin; that he once thought the dangerous playground of the Devil. And perhaps they were. After all, did not the images of many women visit him in these idle moments, smiling with sly invitations he had more often than not accepted; the virginal, the matronly, and even the married? But he was no longer ashamed of idle moments and memories of amorous embraces. He had made his peace with the Devil. The Devil was not such a bad fellow after all, at least no worse than was he. He had proved to be a good, reliable traveling companion.

But there were times when his idle moments were filled with more than love's adventures. Sometimes other things would visit his idleness, things that seemed even lovelier than the women he had played games of love with. Sometimes these moments were filled with words, simple words that painted simple scenes of beauty: a cloud, a butterfly, the flight of a swallow or the gallop of a horse; a peasant woman hanging laundry on a bush, her breasts and buttocks tautly full, as they too were fruits that the earth had ripened beneath the sun.

The words that delighted him were simple, and he would play with them, as one plays with a grape upon the tongue. He would play with them as he ambled or toiled, giving them rhyme and variation, even melodies. When the wine flowed richly strong through his blood he would sometimes sing them as he played a lute or a fiddle in a tavern. Sometimes he would sing them to a maid shy of his charms; one who was busy in a garden, or combing in a window, or in a kitchen whose window he passed. He had learned that women liked poetry, and that it helped bring their prettiness to his arms, like crumbs bring a sparrow to a child's hands. With these words he would make lovers sigh, purr, and give deeper of themselves. Sometimes, like a lullaby, he would sing them as they slept at his side.

.....When I look at this beautiful manuscript
Some master poet placed before our eyes,
How fine and fair, how perfect the penmanship
Of the stars that sparkle in your hair,
The perfume of rich roses in your sighs.......

The Brother Maria who now lay back in the soft grass, dreaming in the sun, was not the same Brother Maria who had once been a Franciscan monk. The years had changed him greatly. Gone were his robe, cowl and sandals, and in their place were a sheepskin coat, wolf-hide boots, and a rustic's tunic bound at his waist with a scarlet sash.

Near his side lay a satchel of rain and sun-worn leather, not so very different from the satchel he had once taken to collect herbs in an abbey's forest. It was a satchel that had been given to him by a servant girl he had once met at a wheat harvest; and for that reason it had become very dear to him, and he carried it always, even as it had become a part of him.

Instead of herbs, this satchel contained a collection of keepsakes, keepsakes that he had not the heart to discard: polished shells, ribbons, combs, painted barrettes.....sachets of rose petals, curls and coiled tresses of hair.....snippets of nightgowns and undergarments. Completing the sum of its contents were scraps of paper neatly rolled about a spindle of wood, a broken handle of a broomstick he had found. Upon these scraps were words he had scribbled when he sat alone in inns and taverns, or in moments, lonely moments when he sat before a fire in his wanderings.

But more than his dress and his few belongings had changed. His features had changed as well. The spare leanness of his monastic years had acquired a stronger, hungrier leanness, one earned not by austerities, but by vigorous exercise and the punishing elements. The muscles had gathered, knitted and tautened tight on his bones. His chest and shoulders had swollen and greatly broadened. His was no longer a leanness of one who begged, but one who prowled; no longer that of a fasting penitent, but of an animal whose hunger was continual, and must be continually listened to and obeyed; at any cost or risk, fed.

His skin, and in particular his face was flushed with health, so that no trace of a former paleness could be seen on it. His color was still fair, but a fairness that had been made tawny with the sun, that could quickly flush ruddy with wine, choler or mirth. His face was still boyish, but this boyishness was now being bartered, if not forfeited to the hardihood of manhood.

His beard was a golden blond, a blondness that was marbleized and set a-sparkle with veins of auburn red. His tonsure had long since disappeared, and in its place had flourished forth a luxurious mane of gold, a characteristic that distinguished him more than any other. In it was a suave wave and rich curl, and he had allowed it to grow and fall halfway down his back, so that it seemed that of an ancient Nordic warrior, or that of a beautiful princess in a tower; a thing that caught the eye, and envy in the hearts of the women who saw him.

But if his hair was his most distinguishing feature, his eyes were the most soul-telling. They had not lost the azure of his youth; indeed, their blue gems appeared to sparkle more brightly now in his wind-burnt and sun-tawny face. As they were the amulets of a gypsy, they mesmerized those that looked into them; the facets of their jewels reflecting different qualities to the different ones before which they shone.

To those first looking into them on country trails, village streets or in randy taverns, they were full of mirth and open friendliness, at once touching and warming the stranger's heart. To those he fell in dispute or scuffle with, they were filled with fire, glaring at his adversary with lashes of lightning. To the opposite sex, they were beguiling as were no other eyes they had ever seen; as kind as they were keen. They probed a deep, hidden part of their hearts; as they were sympathizing with the frailty, the tender secrets of womanhood itself. And this sympathy at once stirred, wooed and won those caught in the tender sparkle of their spell.

When he was alone these blue gems told other stories, stories that told of great storms that had passed through him since he had left an abbey on a hill; stories that laid bare his soul, and baring it, told naked truths that others did not see.

At times their crystals seemed to cloud as he stared into a fire, or as he mused in a dark corner in a smoky tavern; at other times when he stopped to look upon a flock of flowers, the flight of a bird, or a comely maid, they seemed to spark and sparkle the more. Still at other times their blueness became milky with abstraction; as if the one looking through these eyes had forsaken the world in favor of another world; a secret world that only he knew and had access to; one that only he wandered in.

But there was something else, something that those who met or came to know him seldom guessed, for there were moments that a great loneliness filled these eyes. It was unlike the loneliness of other men, for its torments seemed resigned, even reconciled with its solitary prison, knowing that the one seeing through them would never share a kinship with others; a ghost that was doomed to wander in cold places, never to warm at a hearth; an animal that was born to flee or stalk, but never to curl at a master's feet.

This loneliness told of an unutterable sadness, not for itself alone, but for all it beheld. Behind the sparkle of their mirth was a melancholy; a sadness that knew the seasons held no lasting joy, that all was impermanent, and must surely and irrevocably wilt, fade and die; that the garden of the excited senses, and the flame that burned in the loins and sang in the heart,- the sweet-throated bird of love, even the promise of salvation were fleeting, futile, and entirely illusory things; that life was autumnal, its splendors not a greeting to its passer, but a farewell.

The sum of these characteristics had joined to create a very unique man. Gone were all traces of the ascetic; his asceticism having been dispelled by the fledging wings of a rugged might none of his former brothers could have guessed slept dormant inside him; as if a deer had run into a forest, only to run back as a lion. His brawn, height and broadness at once demanded a masculine respect, and once set to a task, even adulation. Once seen, his blondness and blue eyes were not forgotten, especially by the opposite sex. For as a rugged vigor had emerged from this one who had once been a counter of beads and a repeater of prayers, so equally had blossomed a most handsome, even sensual beauty.

Brother Maria stretched comfortably in the grass, the sun melting the cold and dark from his bones. Perhaps winter would never come again, or perhaps he would die before the knives of its north winds once more stabbed through his coat, driving him hungry and lonely through an inhospitable, desolate world; like a lynx or a wolf. Yes, he would surely die, as every summer flower blooms and dies. And yes, the winter would surely come again to smother the fields and hills with its cold, merciless blanket. But now the meadows were afire with poppies, and beneath the chestnut and beech trees the violets and cyclamens were blooming. It was spring, and he was alive; his heart was abloom with hill and cloud.

It felt good to be seduced by the sun's warmth, even as it was a great delight to be seduced by a woman. It felt good to lazily dream, as it was a reward for the hardships of his wandering. The sun thawed, soothed and consoled him, as its beams were kisses a lover was raining on his face in the aftermath of the great war of passion.

This was one of his favorite times, when, half-awake and half-asleep, he felt he was not estranged, not a stranger to the world of men through which he passed, but shared in the equality of life; its fertility and song. He was a living, pulsing part, a leaf or blossom, a warbling throat, loved not more or less than all other things by the earth and sun; at peace with the knowing that he would live, die, and be forgotten, remembered only in the grass and flowers he now lay upon.

He heard a flute, followed by laughter in a far-off field. He smiled when it brought back the memories of the shepherdess in the meadows beneath the abbey, the young girl whose sly cunning had initiated him into love's mysteries....the first taste of her mouth, the smell of her neck and breasts, the damp of her belly....the first time her arms and legs opened with invitation, and he entered, a frightened child into the secret forest of her love......and then the burning miracle that had flushed through him, blazing him complete, and making of him a new wondrous thing, a creature new-waked from the dust.....a man.......

.....He had sometimes felt a great shame when he could not recall his lovers' faces, when he could remember very well the ripeness of their breasts, the roundness of their hips and the slenderness of their thighs.....freckles, scars, secret moles hid from the sun..... navels, toes, the little tufts about the flowers of their sex.....the smells and textures of their skins.....the purrs, sighs and strange little screams that passed through their arching throats..... their heels digging into his back, like a rider into a horse's flanks, spurring his thrusts, and urging him deeper and deeper into their softness.......

.....And more times than not he had forgotten, or had not even asked their names.....

Was the great fire in the heart and the loins, the fire men call 'love' in the end such a trifle, such a little trinket purchased with a few words, glances and kisses? What would become of them, the givers of these trinkets; these lovely princesses and priestesses that had revealed so many mysteries to him? Would they grow old, wrinkled and fat, and lose the prettiness that had so beguiled him? In the years to come, would he want to play in the straw and moonlight with these nameless lovers again?

.....And what would become of him, Brother Maria, in the great mystery of Time, and the great claws and beating wings of its seasons?....

Much had changed since the callow monk had fallen into the arms of a young shepherd girl, and thence into the arms of a stormy, predatory, and for all its hungers and wicked dangers, lovely world.

......He remembered seeing his reflection, that first time after he had wandered the autumn, winter and early spring, when he had knelt to drink at a brook's still pool......a face very different than the young monk he remembered.....a face he had not seen before, but one he had known somehow in some vague beginning.....a face Time had starved and coarsened, and yet had given flower to its starvation and coarsening....as Time was a clown painting a fellow clown with a new disguise......the mask of an ascetic changed to the mask of a forest hunter.....the stubble of his tonsure, now a leonine mane....the gentle eyes now full of primitive fear, need and cunning.......

Would Time's hand not continue to paint other, less handsome masks..... gray and wrinkled and sleepy masks, perhaps even scarred, diseased and cadaverous masks?......Was life a jest that Time played on all men, that instead of painting new masks, it simply removed old ones, like unwrapping the bandages of a mummy.....until the last flatteries of youth and the last disparagements of age were removed?......Who and what was this clown, this Brother Maria without a mask in the carnival of Time?....When the last mask was removed, would his blue eyes be pecked away, and their hollow sockets be laughing at a fool they had watched gambol through a meaningless world, performing clownish antics and fooleries for all its days?........

.....His appearance had greatly changed since his defection from the brotherhood, but his inner change was commensurate with his outer. For was it not true that he now seldom prayed, and when he did, only apathetically, insipidly, halfheartedly? In truth could he say he still believed in God, before whom he had become stupidly drunk and brazenly degenerate, before whom he had perversely fornicated, and even shamelessly adultered, without the least guilt or remorse in his heart? No, the face that was now reflected in still pools could not say such a thing. This face knew his heart. It was its flower. God was for the sedentary; those who slept safe, warm and pampered behind cottage and castle walls, with sheep in their folds, flour and hams in their pantries; or for those who had retreated behind abbey walls, counting wooden beads and kneeling before plaster dolls.

What had God to do with the growling hunger in one's bowels? What *had God to do with the great animal struggle to survive in storms and cold, in the lonely wilderness of life itself? What had God to do with that fire in a man's loins, sparked on the flint of a woman's smile; that fire that forever sought to be extinguished between a woman's legs?*

No, he knew he no longer believed in God. The face he saw reflected in still pools was a coarse and wild face, but nevertheless an honest one. It no longer believed in a God of promises and prophecies, of guilt and sin and redemption. It now worshipped at other altars, and with other prayers and vows. It now looked upon God as a drunkard's tale, a fairy story told to children; a promise of health to one on his deathbed.

But without this fable was there no treasure or trophy to be won in life's uncertainties and punishments; nothing that gave meaning and significance to one's miseries and wanderings; no verdant garden at the end of one's dusty dreams? Nothing that could be held sacred? Nothing to believe in?

This was a question he had often posed to himself, one that, at first with shame, and then with an amused pleasure he had answered in the same way. Of course there was a meaning and a reason. Of course there was a treasure to be won in the famines and battles of the world, a treasure that wrapped its arms and legs about one's lonely needs and dreams, and for a timeless moment purged one's soul clean; fed its hungers, rescued it from dangers, sheltered it from all uncertainties of the tomorrows, from the predators of death itself.

He had quickly found that women liked him, and that he liked them very much in return, and in this secret world of the sexes he had quickly learned their language; a language that was a kind of poetry whose words were not words, but smiles and glances, blushes. feathery touches, fluttering lashes.....a flower behind an ear, the twisting of a loose strand of hair..... bared knees, untied bodices, playful toes beneath a table.....this poetry providing a moonlit arena in which the womb could quiver its plea to be warmed and filled.

He had learned to hear the tones in their voices, tones full of innuendo and insinuation, full of guttural dare and throaty, purring play. He had learned that this language was very vast, that the words and ways of woman's love were as unending as the flowers of the field: for many were the ways women gave , told, asked for or demanded their love.....many their invitations and denials, their challenges and retreats, how they wished to play or not play, to conquer or be conquered.......

He learned this language quickly and easily, not only because he found in each woman he loved a wise teacher, but because he was an apt student with an eagerness to learn, accepting like a child love's provocations, invitations, and hidden promises.

Woman was a different creature, sometimes more skittish, sometimes mightier, but always more sly and inscrutable than men. When they entered his presence he felt their strengths and vulnerabilities, the reserve or quickening of their needs, and either a defense or welcome at having the den of their womanhood discovered. In turn he became obedient, a disciple and devotee of their wishes; at times their child, father or hunter; at times reverent or wicked, patient or provoking, innocent or shameless; a noble knight or sordid rake in their arms.

And for a brief moment life and all of its hardships and perils was given a delicious reprieve; an exalted meaning; a simple burning reason. His wounds were healed, and his hungers, fed. For a moment he was forgiven and redeemed, his loneliness found out, welcomed, and warmly filled with a fruity wine. For a moment the lightning of pleasure dispelled life's darkness, blinding him with rapture; filling love's hour with Eternity.

And yet after love's frolic, what was the dull ache that often ensued, as if cheapening and discrediting it; leaving him more empty than before.....
as he was a fool placed in stocks, an object for cruel jests and ridicule? Why did his lovers sometimes seem frivolous and coarse, even loathsome, when only moments before they had seemed sublime? Why in the aftermath of love did their sleeping smiles often seem sly and wicked, as they had completed a larceny? Why did the secret places he had desired, when once known, explored and enjoyed, sometimes seem repugnant to him?

Was love always so short-lived; a firefly, and not a star, leaving lifeless and dead what only moments before had been brightly kindled? Did the plucking of its sweet flower always result in the wilting of that flower in one's hand? Was love not what it seemed or promised to be; rather a snare, a sweet tasting poison.....a sin, perhaps the original sin?

Still, over and over he let himself be seduced back into women's embraces, regardless of which one opened her arms to him: the young and old, the virginal and the slatternly; the dainty, the coarse, the homely and the comely.....the widowed as easily as the married, the married as easily as the spinster.....for once in their arms, each became beautiful, and he felt as he was being wrapped in the wings of many angels, many angels that were one.......

What was this beckoning he could not deny, this beckoning not only to the wild beast of his flesh, but to the lonely child of his soul, a beckoning deep, sweet and poignant......asking with smiles and gazes, with the wine of kisses and the cries of the womb......an endlessly winding river that whispered in each gentle bend a promise, a maternal encouragement to return......and he a curious child, a lost child, a wanderer passing through the green and golden hours of the suns and seasons......smitten with the romance of the winding river and the playful breezes, the romance and the eternal song and death of longing....a nostalgia for an unremembered beginning, one that all sought to reclaim, although none knew what it was........

He started awake from his slumber. But why? A leaf had fallen on his nose.....no, a gnat or a fly.....no, it was a feather tickling his nose, a feather in the hand of a girl with brown eyes, dark unbound hair, and a fire-red poppy tucked behind her ear. Her smile was tender, and shy of the very secret she had brought him.

"Sir, I saw that you were sleeping, and I had prepared a few things for you to take on your way......a biscuit, some pickled olives, a flask of wine..... and I must be driving the cows home soon, and I thought......"

Maria placed his finger on the girl's lips to stop her words, and then tenderly cupped her cheek in his large hand, bringing her face gently, like a dew-heavy flower to his; and with her face her lips that he began to tenderly press with his own in the introduction of a kiss. At once he could feel her unpracticed, but eager curiosity. At once he could feel that she was starved for passion's mysterious fruit.

Gently and patiently, as he was picking a ripe berry, he fitted his mouth to hers, introducing his tenderness, and then little by little making known his strength and wisdom; tasting the sensual softness, that like the pulp of a peach must surely permeate all parts of her. But to taste the peach was not to be satisfied with the peach, and he proceeded to press, knead and coax open the flower of her mouth, until it surrendered to his asking, and yielded the sweet nectar guarded by its young dry petals. Finding her shy tongue, afraid and hiding like a pretty worm in that flower, he tickled it awake, inviting it to play.

The girl, wakened to this joy, whispered:

"I am not as pretty as my young sister. I saw her smile at you, and you smiled back at her."

"Those smiles were for you, not her."

"I do not understand. You smiled at my sister, as you wanted her kisses. Did you not want her to bring you her kisses?"

"No, I wanted something more, something I hoped her older sister would bring to me; something that I do not think she has ever given, and is perhaps too shy to give."

With this Brother Maria rose to his feet. He placed the lunch the dairy girl had brought him in his satchel, and looping its rope over his shoulder, prepared to leave. He had slept longer than he had intended, and the sun that shone so pleasantly down upon him was now beginning its descent. He knew a barn where he could sleep tonight, and there was just enough light left to light his way.

But when he thanked the girl for her kindness, insisting that he must go, and then turned to take his leave, the girl's fingers snagged the cuff of his coat, and when he turned back to her he saw that her plain face was flushed with the kisses he had given her, and that his kisses had woken another, deeper hunger in her heart.

"Please sir, teach me! I brought you the thing you wished for, but I do not know how to give it! The thing is yours if you would like it, for I do not think I will ever know a man like you again, so tender and so golden beautiful......and the cows are heavy with milk, and can find their way back to the barn without my switch. The dog's a good dog, and will nip their heels home. The older sister brought you what you hoped for, sir; I am sure she did; and she is only a little shy to give it completely."

Un-harnessing the satchel from his shoulder, he knelt back to her. Bringing his mouth to her mouth, he lifted the hem of her smock, and caressed with feather softness up the marble of her young leg, and then over the marble-smooth mound of her young hip. Mesmerizing her with his kisses, his hand found the undefended tuft between her legs, and enfolding and gently pressing it with his hand, he felt her deepest nerve stir awake, sending a shiver through the young meadows of her body. With her fingers clenching fists of his hair, he laid her back in the soft grass; and a blanket of twilight and first stars spread over them.

A short while later, when he walked away and entered the darkening forest, his mind teemed with thoughts,

.....Would he remember her sweet plain face, or would he forget it as he had forgotten so many others?..... Would it too melt into all other faces that had flushed, and playfully dimpled or pouted at him, only to grimace in the throes of passion, becoming an entirely different face, a face of storm, not kindness, as it too was a mask.....a mask as terrible as it had been lovely?

.....Was this little, juvenile, cat and mouse game all there was to love's great mystery?.....soft sighs from a child whose name he did not know, and did not ask, whose body's tender places he had briefly caressed, and for a moment stirred, explored, brought into flower.....whose face he would soon forget, and that he would never see again?......And her words; would he forget her words also?..... "I love you golden sir. I will love you forever. I think you are very beautiful, and I love you with all my heart."...

But these were things he would think about at another time. Night had fallen, and the forest was now dark about him. He must hurry if he was to find the small shepherd barn in which he would sleep tonight.

* * *

(two years later)

HE had grown very tired and heartsick. His infatuation with the hills and forests, and the kaleidoscope of the seasons had dulled and numbed, and there were times he felt the flame in his heart, so strong and steady with youth and health, flicker as with a cold draft of winter wind.

More and more the great romance and freedom of his wandering was heckled by frets and doubts, and the constant need to find food and shelter; these the unsavory companions that would nettle and nag him after he left a lover, a drinking carousal, a day of lusty labor or a tavern fight. He had become increasingly moody, and his moodiness at times made him out-of-sorts or glum, at times lazy and cynical, at other times cross, argumentative, and quick to lash out with anger.

And in his tiredness these dark companions whispered dark thoughts into his heart. 'O aimless, shiftless wanderer, where are you going, and what are you doing? Who is Brother Maria? Is Brother Maria a ghost?'

In truth, had his dreams made him a dissipated, threadbare vagabond? Was he slowly growing lazy, old and mad? Had his spirit grown as worn and ragged as his dress? Was it not time for his dreams to bear a flower, to give their little worth to the world he was passing through? Was it not time to give back some fruits to that plenty from which he had taken so many?

The weather had not been good, and he had reasoned that this had been a contributor to the deep sadness that was shrouding his heart. There had been long weeks of drenching rains, rains that had swelled the brooks, made marshy the forests, and sloughs of the tillage. This had resulted in the mildewing and rotting of much grain, and when these rains were followed by spells of hot sun and drought, the harvests were greatly diminished, and in places ruined. Blights and rusts had contaminated and shriveled orchard fruits, and murrains had infected many herds and flocks. Everywhere people feared a return of the famines; the famines that still haunted their memories.

Although hunger and starvation had made no firm footing in the country-side, scarcity had, and it had become more difficult for him to find work at plough and seed-times, and even more at times of lambing, shearing or sheaving. In addition the winters had been extraordinarily long, bleak and harsh, and their cold and dark had for the first time lingered in the warm blood of his young years, shivering through it with the morbid harbingers of age. He had become increasingly sullen and morose in the barns, stables, and deserted shepherd huts where he sought shelter; at times excessively dreamy, at times sleepless and edgy in his forest camps; unduly boisterous when he drank wine; ready to curse or fight if one disturbed his sulking meditations in a dark corner of a tavern.

There was another sign that indicated a growing scarcity in the land, one that was even more keenly poignant, even more telling than sodden wheat and rotting grapes, and the swelling knots of paupers begging before village gates. Brother Maria felt the fear and want of this scarcity in the women he loved.

He felt a need, a desperate need, one he had not felt before; a need his lovers abandoned in his embraces. Their fingers dug more deeply, their legs wrapped more tightly. Their kisses seized his lips, rather than nibbling and teasing them. As if drawing from a deeper, more intense well of passion, their moans and cries vented a greater hunger, as they were pleading for life itself. Their surrender was more immediate and more complete, and rather than little gasps, sighs and spasms, the crescendo of their passion swelled and often finished with fury, not sweetness.

And when they had given their needs, they continued to cling to him, to his strength and vitality, as he was life itself, as what he had given them was more than love; as it was breath and bread. When he would prepare to leave them, either early in the morning or deep in the night, their arms would wrap tightly about him, as they were drowning; begging him not to go away, *to love them again, that they might be fed and sheltered for a little longer in the dream of passion.*

But there was another peculiarity with this lovemaking, over and beyond the desperation and fury of his lovers' passion, one that he only gradually began to recognize.

Although many wanted to be loved by him many times and in many ways, none insisted he be their permanent lover. Maria did not know why this was so, but as time passed, he was filled with suspicions. Perhaps the young girls felt guilty, and were too shy to show this older and wilder one with whom they had been unchaste. Perhaps the prettier ones felt he was too ragged and poor, even uncouth, and although he was clever, and one who had kissed and caressed them as no other had, they did not deem him the best catch. Perhaps wives retreated to cruel husbands, preferring their blows to his endearments because of his vagabondage, a homeless, shiftless wanderer of roads, forests and dreams. Perhaps this in the end was the critical truth in all of them. His lovers saw in him something that could not be tamed, something that could not long abide the flowery reins of their charms; something that in the end, after he had given them his poetry and love, would forsake their arms to hunt, roam and sleep, and finally die in the forest.

But there was something that was born in him during these hard months and seasons, especially in the bitter sweetness of autumn, and in the long cold bleakness of winter; something that not only helped to keep kindled a spark in his heart, but to keep flesh hanging on his ribs.

Several of his peasant lovers had given him musical instruments to play, to while away his time upon; lutes, fiddles, a flute and an accordion. It did not take long before each was singing, sweetly and obediently in his hands. In long days of cold, snow and damp he played and practiced on them, sometimes from morning until night. Making them sing came easily to him, even as loving women had come easily to him; indeed he considered the two things very much the same. He had learned to caress and make sing different women's bodies with the same tenderness with which he caressed and made sing these different instruments. In his arms each surrendered, at times softly, shyly, demurely; at others, lustily and brazenly. Like an adoring mistress, in his arms they yielded melodies long sleeping in their hearts; treasures waiting to be discovered, that they had yielded no other, and had saved for only him.

There were those who chanced to hear his bow kiss the fiddle's strings, and his fingers dance upon the lute's: herdsmen, tillers, carters, as well as the keepers of public places; and when they heard his sonorous voice accompany the melodies he evoked from their instruments he was asked to play in cottages, barns, and eventually small inns and taverns. In return he was given food and drink, articles of hand-me-down clothing, and even nightly roofs over his head.

Accentuated by his blond and unique handsomeness, and his boyish, winning personality, plus the spellbinding melodies his hands would magically bring forth, he was soon invited to play not only in smoky taverns for bread and ale, but at country dances and weddings, at grape and wheat harvests, even at funerals. As he had learned to make all of his lovers sing,- the timid, the sad and the lusty, so it was easy for him to caress and coax each sort of mood from the instrument he held in his arms; from the merry to the melancholy, the jig to the dirge; and finally songs of exquisite, romantic sweetness.

His playing and singing provided not only a means to stay alive, but brought another unforeseen consequence as well. It fueled the infatuation of the women that heard and saw him, and this in turn enkindled and fueled a flame in Maria's despondent heart.

Filled with drink and mirth, and often pain and pathos, there were often arms full of need and lips full of kisses in the wake of his playing; those that would seek him out, wherever he had made his bed. And it was not only those whose waists he had held in the dances, or those whose eyes had sparkled when he made the fiddle sing; but there were those for whose weddings he had played, who came to him a fortnight later, secretly longing for a second bridal night; and there were widows who forsook their mourning, who removed their black veils for the sweetness in his arms.

He had found something that helped keep him alive in the increasingly frequent spells of cold, rain and dearth; something that lifted his heart, and often gave him woman-pleasure. But these times were left to dice-rolls of luck and chance, and were nothing to be depended upon for his survival. And there was something else, something these opportunities did not reach or amend; something inside him that seemed one with the worsening weather and the increasing scarcities; a deep apprehension, a dark chasm of foreboding; a gnawing hunger whose cries were heard and felt, but not fed.

Neither lute nor wine, nor the charms of women succeeded in eradicating the specter of despair that had invaded him. They could not staunch the ache and trickle of its festering wound. He grew increasingly, more deeply lonely, a loneliness recognized by lovers, who, despite their sweetest favors, looked in his eyes after those favors were given, and knew they had not freed him from the dark, possessive mistress who clasped him with iron arms.

And although Brother Maria wanted to free himself from these dark arms, he knew that to struggle was vain; that their embrace was inextricable. This was another kind of lover, another kind of loneliness, a timeless and eternal loneliness, one with the wind and stars; one whose kisses fell off the human heart like rain from stones. It was the loneliness of all men who know they are a brief wild creature, and at any gust of wind or fork of the path could perish in the jaws of a mightier creature, a hungrier creature, a creature that relentlessly stalks, and in the end picks the bones of all things.

Brother Maria grew accustomed to this disenchantment, this disenfranchisement, this banishment in which only he and this jealously clinging mistress existed. Its pain, even more than the flights of love, felt honest and true to him; its anguish gradually becoming a show of dearness and affection. He grew to like the unequivocal certainty that he was alone, and that he was the prey of a relentless hunter whose arrow he knew would one day pierce his heart; the lover who would one day be his killer. He grew content with the realization that he must die, and with this realization came the license to laugh, curse and fight more freely. He could not be intimidated by the one in whose arms he knew he would be poisoned. Possessed by such a fateful lover, he could only more freely, shamelessly, prolifically love.

He wanted to give this great loneliness a voice, a simple, brutal, lovely voice, a voice naked of the flatteries of the lute's strings and the fiddle's reels; a voice that would contain the rave and rage of the banished and the madman; a voice that would make sing the tortured prisoner of his heart.

Acquiring quill, ink, and scraps of parchment, he began to scribble out strange thoughts and dreams that had fevered him for many days and nights. At times too drunk and despairing to sleep, at others, too cold, with snow and frozen forests about his fire; and at still other times with a peasant lover sleeping at his side, he began to cloak this unseen, unknown need with words; words that appeared like wicked and lovely apparitions conjured from the blank sheets before him.

Passion was his only theme. It had become his sole meaning, the only thing that gave his ragged and wayward existence a reason. For passion he drank wine and ate bread. For passion he made the fiddle sing and mourn. For passion he wandered homelessly through the seasons.

.....*Sweet lady, let me play upon your body as it were a lute.....in my hands let me make you sigh, sing, cry out your secret song, as I shall mine.....songs that only we and the Angels shall hear and know......for this straw and this blanket, and this brief hour is the humming hive of life's beginning.... the warm heart of the frozen forest......the first, last heartbeat of the night.....without our love earth and heaven would not be...the stars would end their fires.....the dream of life would be no more.......*

......*They say the mad rave, and see in the wind things only madness sees.....harlots riding giant wolves, blood-drizzling moons, corpses hanging from gallows.....and yet I am seized with another kind of madness in the knives of these cold winds, one in which hang ripe the succulent peaches of your breasts.....and the honeycomb of your mouth, sweeter than the nectar harvested by the slaves of ten thousand bees......and that other hive, your sweetest hive.....that meadow of clover in which I beg to enter, sing and die........*

Many of these little thoughts he had wrapped about the broken piece of the broomstick in his satchel, but there were many others he had given to lovers; leaving them on their pillows, in their boots or in pockets of their smocks, even though he knew many could not read.

Once, upon stealing away one morning, he had been seized with a strange desire to gently place one of these thoughts upon a sleeping lover; as it was fig leaf clothing her nakedness.

......*I am your hunter through the seasons, my Beloved, through the green and golden, and the bleakest hours of the sun.....but the pebble of my sling misses your pretty feathers when You fly through the fir and poplar trees, as do my arrows when like a deer You run through the flowering meadows.....as does my song as You harvest the apples and the barley.....but oh, my Sweetheart, when the dreams of Summer and Autumn end, shall we not play like rabbits in moonlight, deep in drifts of snow?........*

....

....

CHAPTER TWELVE

THE CITY

Siena, 1338-1340

IT was early summer when at nightfall he entered the city, when the streets were sweet with the smells of blossoms, herb gardens, baking bread and roasting meat. The roses had begun to make festal the arches, and to embrace the lonely windows high above with their jeweled arms. The falling darkness was peopled as with ghosts: the unseen, bodiless ghosts of laughing children and singing lovers; ghosts that bantered and quibbled, others that played lutes and lazy mandolins. In some candlelit windows and on some twilit balconies sat lovely, sloe-eyed maidens, like beautiful exotic birds, preening with combs and mirrors, gardenias in their hair. He was very dusty and tired, and very drunk, and as he passed through the streets his heart beat against his chest like the erratic drum of a child.

But as Brother Maria continued to walk through the streets, he felt rather that he was the ghost, and not the forms and voices in the darkening dusk, as if it was he who had become invisible to the living. Unnoticed and unaddressed, he walked through the streets, wrapped in the mist of the aloneness and dishevelment of which he was now long accustomed.

It had been many years since he had entered a city, and the flood of human commerce and fraternity at once swam through him with rich sounds, smells and textures of forgotten memories; things of which he had not heard or seen for many years. In the quickening night the arches, towers and spires rose into the darkness like a race of giants rising from the ancientness of their sleep, and with them a waking, sculpted brood of beasts: lions, wolves, lynxes, serpents, and with them angels, both benign and malignant; these stone creatures crouched or watchful, or slinking free in cornices and arches; some holding torches, like sconces in their jaws and hands.

Surrounded by the darkness, and protected by these giants, the city welcomed only a part, and not all of him; the ghostly, not the fleshly part. Far from cheering his loneliness, it made it the more stark and forsaken. A deep melancholy filled him, a longing for the living from which he was no longer a part; a nostalgia for something he had once been, but was not sure he could again be; like the dead wanting to drink wine, dance, and resume the struggles and battles that had felled them.

But why? He knew he had been a favorite among his religious brothers, and a favorite among those he labored with. He knew that women sought his embraces and the words he whispered in their ears. He knew his laughter stirred laughter in others, and that a strum on a lute or a scurry up a fiddle stirred those about him into rollick and revel. Then why this aching chasm of loneliness carved in his heart? Why this passing through the ways of men, and the wheel of the seasons like a ghost wrapped in a mist; a ghost whose invisible cloak no laughter of a friend or kiss of a lover could penetrate?

Night fell, and Brother Maria continued to walk through the spider web of streets. As he did his heart became more and more heavy with regret and remorse, as one who had lived but had not lived, who had loved but had not loved; whose prayers had been hollow, and whose dreams had only been dreams to confound his soul. He felt alone as he had never felt alone in a winter forest; the sounds and sights he passed salting, and not salving his hidden wounds.

The laughter of playing children pierced him most deeply; a knife stabbing his heart with a guilt-sharpened edge of ruined innocence. The shouts of drunken debauch, the smokes and tart smells of the taverns, even the manure and urine reek of the stables stung him with regret, a regret of having no lasting friends to laugh and bicker with, to honor and curse; to live, fight, love and die with. Both the street whores, and the young virgins on the balconies filled him with sadness; the former because he knew he was their sordid brother, and the other because he knew he was a thief who had pilfered their sisters' treasures. Even the lovers, arm in arm on bridges, or pressed together in doorways called a deep remorse from his heart, for though he had given the flame in his loins to many, he was not sure he had once given the flame in his heart. As candles began to be lighted, shutters to close and chimneys to let forth wisps of smoke, he felt sad and alone as he had never felt before.

He stopped; leaned against a wall steeped in dark shadows cast by unchecked vines. As one winded from a great climb, there he rested with closed eyes, his spirit suddenly exhausted from bearing a load he had not known he had borne until now. He drank from the wine cup he had begged outside a tavern, but its taste was falsely sweet, and he cast it away, not wanting to dilute the pain that was poisoning him, bitter as wormwood; the pain that was his life's only honor.

There came a soft tug on his sleeve, and he opened his eyes to a young, dwarfish woman at his side. Her face was gaudily painted, as if she wished to disguise her youth and compensate for her shortness, and although she had tried to paint it away, the degradation staring from her sunken eyes.

"Would you like something sir? I know a place or two we could go; a stable with fresh clean straw, or beneath a bridge few folks walk upon, or here in the shadows if that would pleasure you. It would be cheap, and as quick or long as you would like. You could call me your sweetheart's name if you wish; or if you've no sweetheart, the name of one you wished would be. It might be a help to both of us sir."

Brother Maria tried to smile, a smile that for once refused his asking. He shook his head, and looked away, as the young woman was an angel, one too blinding bright to look upon; one that had not come to tempt, but to soothe, but with her soothing, to ridicule and scorn.

"I saw you, but you did not see me standing in the shadows when you passed. I stand there every night. I've learned to read men's faces; the tavern drinkers, the loners and such. I saw the great pain written on your face, the great pain from some great pain in your heart.

I could help you feel better, sir. I've only to kneel, or pull up my skirt, here in the darkness of the vines if you like. You see I know pleasure tricks, tricks the taller girls do not know. I'm cheaper than most, and will do your bidding, short of cruelty that is. You'd be on your way, and feeling better shortly."

Brother Maria reached into his coat pocket, and placed whatever coins he found in the girl's hands. She brightened and nodded.

"Come then, in the shadows here; it will not take long, and you will be on your way."

But instead Maria gathered her into his arms, holding the young street girl's small, dwarfish body tightly, as a frightened child clings to its mother. Midst his shivering sobs he whispered:

"I have been looking for you! But where are the horses, dogs and wagons, and where are the monkeys and the bears? Is it time to dance, mother? Is it time to sing and dance, and walk the petticoated bear over the barrels?"

The girl wrestled free from his arms, and looked at him with a queer wonder, throwing the coins he had given her at his feet. As she recoiled out of his reach, she spoke with an indignant pride.

"No, I will not! I give my body to drunkards and the old, to the big-bellied and the one-legged, but not to madmen! Madmen may hurt. Madmen may kill! Monkeys, bears, horses and wagons.....you are mad!.....I've my pride, and I'll not pleasure a madman, not for gold will I do the things a madman wants me to do!"

Ghost-like he continued to wander through the streets, aimlessly, listlessly, wandering through a world whose ways his soul had long forsaken, like a dead man among the living; through a world that was at his fingertips, but he could never touch; whose ear was ever deaf to the screams of his heart; *through arches and narrow tunnel-ways, beneath arcades, steeply climbing and plunging stairways.....a labyrinth of darkness, stone monsters and wicked angels.....a labyrinth of eternal darkness.......*

.....Mad, yes, he was mad.....mad from his long wandering, from his silly dreams, from his wallowing between the thighs of women.....'cheap and quick, in a stable or beneath a bridge'......monkeys and bears, yes, the beautiful bears, and the dancing with castanets, candles and drums in the squares for bread.....the wounds in his heart, like starvation written on a pauper's face, murder on a murderer's......

.....mad, yes, the Angel had told him he was mad.....a ghost, yes, a ghost......a mad ghost that was a pathetic fool, one full of rave and false glory.....who had forsaken a holy abbey to whore with other ghosts in a dream of meadow flowers and moonlight.....who had run from the sun, and all of the treacheries it had gilt and brightly painted.....that had danced the wooden smiles and pretty ribbons of its puppetry before trusting eyes.......

He continued to walk, even when the streets emptied, and their estuaries filled with the deep dark tide of night, drowning the sights and sounds of the living; leaving only the smells, hues and echoes, the faint memories of their burlesque and puppetry; as they too had been false; as they too had never been real. *.....Darkness, only darkness, and the* *ghosts lost and wandering in that darkness…..* He did not look for a place to sleep, either on a bench, in a cart or doorway. He did not want to sleep. He did not want to be wrapped in the false arms of forgetfulness. He did not trust sleep, and the myths of its glittering dreams. He only wanted this darkness and forlornness,, the just wages and honor of the wretched dissoluteness of his wasted youth.

Suddenly the tolls of a midnight bell struck above him, concussing its loud, judgmental thunder through the narrow, sheer-walled ways where he had strayed. Its loudness at once deafened his thoughts and froze his heart; murdering him with its cold, solemn holiness. Leaning against a wall he closed his eyes, somehow thankful, amazed that Time had not ceased its march, advancing the beating drum of death against the pitiful madness of men.

Continuing a hundred steps up the steep narrow way, he discovered he had reached a convent on the village's height. It was adjoined to a chapel, one whose door was left ajar, even at such a late hour, an invitation to the devout to participate in the sisters' midnight worship. He was too tired to return, too weak to flee. *Where? Who?* Without a debate, only tears in his heart, he entered the door into the chapel's dusky airs.

Inside, its hallowed goodness smote him with an excruciating pain, its silence, smells and images like nails of remorse and regret driving through each part of him. Oh, how tenderly, voluptuously, preciously sweet! The candles, the incense, the stately columns and lovely frescoes! The altars dressed with beautiful cloths and flowers, the polished vessels and idols glittering in the candlelight!

What had he done? Where and why had he gone? Oh dear God, if indeed there was a God looking at him through the glazed eyes of these clay idols, and those painted on these Saints and Angels in these gorgeous frescoes, what a wretchedness must He see!…..Where had he been?…..Why had he gone?……..

Overcome with drunkenness, exhaustion, shame and remorse, he knelt and wept, even as the unseen choir of sisters intoned their midnight prayers behind the grille, piercing him through and through, like archers with their arrows; arrows sharpened with consolations of sweetness and purity.

They too were spirits invisible in the darkness, even as the voices in the streets had been invisible spirits of the night…..these virgin sisters, the same as the coarse and frivolous, the greedy and gluttonous, the drunken and the licentious.....as the little street girl that offered to please him......spirits of the night's darkness, spirits of the dark dreams in his soul.....Angels that could be heard, but not seen....drunkards, harlots, devils, disguising their voices as Angels, as Sisters of Mercy at their midnight prayers.......

What had he done? Where had he gone? What madness had possessed him to climb the wall, run to the forest, and give the salvation of his soul to a shepherd girl's arms?.......

Brother Maria woke, but why and where? Slowly, groggily he remembered.....the candles, the altars, the chapel and convent on the hill of the city.....the virgins' hymns.....hymns that were no more, their melodies and the phantoms that had sung them stepped and faded back into the dark and the silence, the dark silence from which they had come......*Had they been real, or were they also a dream.....kindness, tenderness, love, a flattering, trustless illusion?.......*

"Sir, are you well?"

Brother Maria now felt the hand upon his shoulder, the gentle hand that had woken him from his sleep.

"The Abbess Mother told me to ask if you are well. She saw you as we prayed, from behind the grille, and grew concerned. She said you seemed as you were gripped by some great pain of body or soul. Are you well sir? Do you need assistance? Mother Abbess knows doctors. Even at this hour she could send for one if you would like."

Her gentle voice was as tender as a smile, her hand that touched his shoulder, like a leaf fallen gently from a tree. Maria stood, and turned to behold the one who had waked him; but his pain, his exhaustion, his surprise at the veiled face leaning near his own, robbed him of words, and made his tongue a stone.

"Sir, good sir, are you well? Mother Abbess asked me to ask you if you are in pain. If you wish to pray, the sisters welcome your prayers. But if you are not well, if you are in some great need....."

"Thank you, sister, I am only tired, very tired. You see I have travelled long.....for many days and weeks, perhaps years, yes certainly, years.....you see not only my body, but my soul is very tired....but I feel much better now, and I have no need, other than such a holy place as is this to kneel and bend my head in prayer."

"Our door is always open. You may climb the hill and pray in our chapel any time you wish.

But now I must go. May God bless you, my brother. May Christ and the

Holy Virgin be in your prayers and bless you always."

And with this, the veiled sister disappeared, as if indeed she had been a ministering Angel; one that had stepped from the darkness only to show him this kindness.

* * *

BROTHER Maria stayed on in the city. He played fiddle music in a tavern, one called the *Sickle Moon*, for which he was given a sleeping room above it, as well as meat, bread and drink. There were many other taverns and tiny inns, and with time it was not difficult for him to find work in some of these as well. It was not long before he had earned the reputation of a beautiful singer, and one whose fingers made his instruments dance and tearfully croon. He was often referred to as *the golden-haired gypsy*, a name he did not refuse, and only garnished when his tongue and fingers, and sometimes his feet were made nimble with wine.

Gradually, and unexpectedly a strange peace came over him, one that he had not felt before. For one thing, he quickly grew to like his lodging over the tavern. He who had been solitary for so long, a traveler across such vast swaths of lonely hills and forests, welcomed the noisome conviviality and ribaldry, and even the seeping of tavern smokes and stenches through the gaping cracks of his plank board floor.

He had taken care, with the sartorial help of a sweetheart to have fashioned a new suit of clothes; a suit that included a rich velvet coat of forest green, and a fine shirt of pale yellow. He began to take a close interest in his grooming, combing the lush mane of his hair until it shone with a golden luster, and brushing and neatly trimming his beard. To embellish his appearance the more, from one of his ears now dangled a silver earring, one shaped like a crescent moon and star; the star's heart a piece of lapis to match the blue of his eyes.

It was a life he liked very much, one in which many times he slept the mornings away, when the tavern was not yet loud and boisterous . After religious life, and his subsequent wandering, the large city was like a giant circus to him, and he a child given permission to stroll through it. During the day he whiled away the hours by visiting its countless sights and places: the shops and markets, the winding and climbing streets, the promenades, the green grocers, butcher stalls and fish sellers;

jewel smiths, glass blowers, puppet shows and street jugglers. At night he played a lute and fiddle, sang, drank wine, and became drunk in the taverns. In idle and drunken moments, when he found himself alone, he composed bits and pieces of simple, and more times than not, incomplete poems full of random words and phrases.

And the women?

Although there were many who wished to be his lover, at first he received the favors of but a few, a thing that he himself could not entirely understand: a seller of flowers, a mender of coats, an aging widow whose two sons had gone to war. However, he had become more selective; more suave and practiced, more daring with the few he chose to speak with; his innuendo only thinly gowned with words in the smoky dark of the tavern; his blood afire with wine; his thoughts with seduction.

"Is there a man in your heart?"

"There were two; but when you smiled at me, one has become a boy, and the other a stupid brute."

.....and again, to another beauty that had danced before his singing fiddle.......

"Are there other men who seek your riches?"

"I let them seek, but they do not find. My hidden treasures are for one who caresses my heartstrings like the strings of a fiddle."

Some would wait in the shadows of doorways and alleys when the tavern closed, and with darting quickness pull him to their breasts when he passed.

"You play sweetly, gypsy fiddler, as there are angels in your fiddle."

"There are; sleeping angels that wake when they see your slender throat and waist, and the peaches of your breasts.....beautiful peaches asking to be harvested."

.......to flower girls and shop girls, and girls kneading dough, with flour on their faces in windows he happened to pass, he waxed boldly poetic, offering bold flatteries and compliments.......

"I burn with jealousy, yes jealousy of the other men who pass this window.....and the sun, that villain that kisses your blue-veined arms! I am jealous of these roses that climb about this window, only to make a garland about your prettiness. I am jealous of your blouse, and how it touches your velvet softness.....I am jealous of the wind that tastes your lips.....the very earth that is softened and kneaded by such pretty feet!"

.....after drinking much wine, he would boldly tap upon the shutters of

sleeping lovers, asking to be loved by them again......

"*Your face is like a moon appearing from dark clouds. It illumes the night, and makes darkness a cloak of glory.*"

.....and again.....

"*You are sweet, very sweet, so sweet the bees think you are a honeyed blossom. O little moonflower, can you blame me if I am once more thirsty to sip your nectar?*"

He had a great liking for the furtive, those he called *brides of shyness*, and he became very fond of some he did not court or try to seduce; content to receive only their smiles and blushes. One such one was a simple girl in a bake house, several streets below the *Sickle Moon*. Lowering a pole and basket from an upper window to the street below, a basket with bread that in turn received the customer's payment, the bake girl remained coy, and altogether inaccessible to the flirtations of his smiles and playful words. She remained obscure to his eye as well, half-hidden by the cherry-red kerchief that bound her hair, and by her reluctance to step fully into view, extending and retrieving the pole and basket a step away from the open window.

Brother Maria was charmed with this little game he began to play with her, passing the bake house window often, buying biscuits, and pleading for her to show her face fully in the window. He even placed flowers, and sometimes ribbons with his payments in the basket with which she had lowered his biscuits. Busying to and fro before the window and its bright green shutters, her kerchief matching the bright red geraniums in the flowerboxes, Maria imagine d she was a forest bird, one with a red crest flitting here and there in waxy green leaves.

Laughing in the little square below the window, his golden hair, silver earring and blue eyes sparkling in the morning sun, it became his habit to call out to her; as if her reticence had charmed him like no other; her sweetness somehow familiar, as if he had been charmed by it before.

"*Come to the window, my little red-crested bird! I want to see your pretty feathers and your pretty face! I want to hear your pretty song! Men knew how to sing before they knew how to talk, and they knew how to love before they knew how to sing. Come little red bird, warble your song for me, like this......*" And with a laugh he imitated with remarkable exactness the warble of a bird.

On another occasion.....

"*Why are you so shy, my princess of biscuits and bread? Princesses are too beautiful to be shy. Why do you not take off your kerchief and lean from the window? Let the morning adore you with its golden kisses!*"

Or again.....

"*Your biscuits are the sweetest I have ever tasted, as I am sure are your kisses! Ah, my princess, my shy little red bird! To hear the melodies of your song, to have your wings flutter into my arms! This flower, and with it my heart is in this basket you take back into your window!*"

But there was a peculiar reason, something that made him sometimes forego those who freely offered their favors and begged his embraces. It was something that came to confuse him; something that as the days and weeks passed began to tease, then to stir, and eventually to vex and haunt him.

Foolish as it seemed, he could not forget the veiled sister in the city's hilltop convent. He could not forget her kind words; and more than her words, her tenderly sensuous voice, and the hand she had laid softly on his shoulder. Without reason, he was seized with a desire to know the face behind this veil; to caress it with his finger; to kiss it.

Many were the times he climbed the hill, kneeling in the shadows of the dusky chapel, and listening to the sisters sing their prayers; hoping that upon their completion the same sister would again come to him; a thing that never happened. When their office ended, the gate of the grille was unlocked, and after each sister knelt and kissed their Mother Abbess's feet, the sisterhood entire filed out the postern door, like a troop of ghosts, silently, and with draped veils.

When he arrived early for their prayers, it was much the same. The bell rang loudly overhead, and after a short moment the prioress unlocked the grille's door, and the procession of silent, veiled sisters entered the choir. After again locking the door, the sweet voices of their liturgies began, as if both in solicitation of and competition with the angels.

This coming and going of the veiled sisters in the dim-lit chapel gradually adopted an otherworldliness in Brother Maria's mind, and upon returning to his room above the tavern, he was sometimes eager to try to place this sensation into words.

.....Maiden soldiers of the midnight deep,
Combating demons with thy sacred hymns,
A flock of Angels in the dusky airs,

At midnight's chime, risen to vanquish sin,-
O mercenaries of Eternity,
Midst your sweet intercessions and forgiving,
Do you not hear the screaming prayers
Of those knelt at your feet,
with longing of the living?.......

These fruitless visits only piqued his wish to see the one, who, masked in a veil of purity, had once touched his heart with an angelic voice and hand. In moments fevered with loneliness and discontent, when great swells of his old yearning came upon him, he would write out lines meant for this phantom that had touched him in his hour of need, whose memory had come to so haunt, and haunting, challenge him.

.....Would it be such a sin to lift thy veil,
To show these eyes the vision of thy face?
Would it be such a scarlet shame of Grace,
The secret of such sweetness once to tell?
Oh virgin pure, meekly sweetly rare,
Is it irreverence
To wish what pleads like thunder in my prayers:
Thy lips to dare with mine,
and share the wine of Innocence?.......

And this mystery he wanted to look upon, the one that had spoken to him with such tenderness from behind a veil, was greatly fueled by the splendors he began to imagine beneath her habit entire.

What had begun as an idle fascination, gradually gripped him with the talons of his curiosity, until he developed a strange, and even an obsessive need to look into the eyes of the one behind this veil. He even timed and positioned his visits to the hilltop chapel so that, knelt in shadows, he was near the postern door where the sisters solemnly came and went from their offices. Although all were veiled, he was sure there was only one who matched the height and youthful step of she who had spoken to him in that dark hour of his soul. Slim, erect, stately, and with a voluptuousness her habit could not hide, only teasingly flatter the more, she glided with the grace and regality of a swan amid her flock of solemn sisters. Despite its wickedness, Brother Maria began to yearn not only to see the face behind her veil, but to know the secrets beneath her holy habit. He began to feel more like a wolf in the chapel's shadows, than a penitent.

He had lived in the room above the *Sickle Moon Tavern* for nearly two years now, and he had grown gradually tired and dissatisfied with the regimen that had come to be his daily routine: his aimless jaunts through the streets, his playful flirting with bread girls and flower girls, his nightly carousals; waking on dice boards, his pockets plundered; and many times in strange beds, more often than not with undesirable playmates, even other men's wives at his side. He began to regret when he had played the last song on his fiddle, and the taverns closed; those silly creatures that waited for him, freely offering him kisses and their other woman favors; ploys that seduced him into acceptance; drink having painted as goddesses what waking revealed as little more than hussies and harlots.

He grew more and more dissatisfied, and more than dissatisfied, he began to feel threatened, as he was in jeopardy of being tamed, of being clipped of his wings. The city had gradually become a cage of his soul; his days grown stale and starved of dangers, adventures, hungers. At times he felt as he had been imprisoned, as he was slowly turning to stone, like the stone lions, wolves and gargoyles he daily passed; that he too was being sculpted and frozen into stone; that he too would soon open ferociously locked jaws, silently roar and writhe, forever trying to twist free of these stone walls. He waxed increasingly lazy, melancholic, temperamental. The old loneliness returned, and like a jealous lover, wanted him back in her cruel, selfish, death-dark arms.

In his growing discontent, the veiled sister in the hilltop nunnery assumed a metaphorical significance, one that came to symbolize, and to promise freedom from the fevers of his pent-up needs. He knew that it was foolish, a foolishness that made trespass into the profane, but as he yearned more and more to break from the cage of his domestic imprisonment, so more and more he was compelled to know the secrets of her veiled loveliness; as if behind her veil was kept the hills and forests of his happy freedom; as if behind her veil was the face that summed all faces waiting to smile at him from gardens, orchards, and village windows; and with those smiles, waiting with sweet kisses and fragrant breasts in the tender moonlight. Irrational as it seemed in the light of the sun, to lift this midnight sister's veil became a kind of compulsion, a challenge, as to a prisoner planning his escape, a challenge that stirred and woke him from his torpor, his bondage; that spoke to the *wanderer* in his heart.....*to wrest her secrets.....to know her face, her heart, her womb.....to be free, like a forest animal again.......*

He began to climb to the nunnery more often, more times than not drunk and full of lustful loneliness, even denying willing lovers for this phantom one. He began to receive a perverse, vicarious pleasure as he knelt humbly in the shadows, dreaming of unclothing the virgin beauty of this sister's body; to be not only the first, but the only one to know her secrets. When he bowed his head and closed his eyes, there were often lurid imaginings that filled his prayers.

Oh, how he wished to kiss her, and more, much more, to violate her sacred mystery! Oh, how he wished to feel her body quiver with its final pleasure, to see her face yield its deepest secret in the anguish of its ecstasy..... to wrest from her what she had vowed to God......to take her from God's arms.....to conquer her, impale her with his passion.....to know her utterly and completely.......

And eventually she began to acknowledge him, or at least he imagined it so; her veil ever so slightly, all but imperceptibly nodding at him as she entered and left with her sisters. And this recognition, albeit as slight as a trembling leaf, fueled his longing the more, so much that once on his way back down the hill he purchased a prostitute, and asking her to drape a scarf over her face, even as it was a veil, spent his needs in different, unbridled, even wicked ways; profanely imagining this Bride of Christ's surrender; at last owning her secrets.

There was yet another peculiarity that had become a part of this strange fetishism. In his dreams, both in his waking and his sleep, the faces of former lovers began to appear behind her lifted veil; as her mystery was an eternal place where each woman he had loved still smiled and lived. Each time he lifted the sister's veil in this dream world, another former lover appeared: *one with golden leaves, another with a sprig of red berries, another with a sunflower in her hair.....one with a gardenia tucked behind her ear, another with moonlight trembling on her lips.....others nibbling cherries or apples with pretty white teeth.....forgotten whispers and laughter, pouts, and dark eyes.....as each was a part of the mystery this sister withheld behind her veil.....as her loveliness summarily embraced, contained, and gave answer to them all.....as this mystery was their mother.......*

He composed lyrics that gave voice to these strange and wicked fantasies. Gripped more and more with his disenchantment, and given more and more to bouts of drunkenness, one night he climbed the hill not to feign prayers, but to court this phantom's heart. Full of drink and heartsickness, his fiddle filled the little square before the nunnery, and the midnight silence that surrounded its high walls with the pain and longing in his heart. At intervals the fiddle music stopped, and he half sang, half recited words he had written.

..... *'Lady of purity, virgin of grace,*
Masked by the snowy curtain of thy veil,
Does kindness not wear a face,
As Spring sings through the nightingale?
Do Angels ever hush their harps
In the carnival of light and dark,
Giving more than music, to those with wounded hearts?'.......

He knew how absurd and perverse it was to sing before a nunnery's gate, but touched with the madness of the thing.....*his dreams of being the first to taste her lips and breasts, the first to lay between her snowy thighs*.....he also knew that it was not a Bride of Christ with whom he was smitten, but a phantom, a spirit, one that could assume any or all faces. Still, unresponsive to his ploys of prayer and courtship, he wrote a poem for this veiled ghost, a ghost whose name he had long ago learned was *Giulia*. Knocking on the convent's gate one late afternoon, he placed it in the Portress Sister's hands, and humbly asked if it might be delivered to Sister Giulia.

> *To The Angel Behind Its Veil*
> *WHY do you not lift up your veil for me,*
> *And let me glimpse the keeper of such kindness?*
> *Why pray, sing, nod in anonymity,*
> *And leave my gratitude in abject blindness?*
> *The midnight heavens, blanketed in cloud,*
> *Sometimes are torn by breezes at a seam,*
> *Whereby the moon peeks from their heavy shroud,*
> *Smiling thru night with love's enlightening.*
> *Oh, even ghosts and phantoms own a face,*
> *Whereby their seers spy their airy essence,*
> *Features that define their spirit's presence.....*
> *Then why not Sisters of Mercy, love and grace?*
> *What then is reason's Reason? Why kneel and pray?*
> *If not to doff all masks, donned in Life's masquerade?*

One night some weeks later, as he stood in the courtyard outside the nunnery, softly strumming his lute, he heard the jangling of iron keys, and the opening of its gate. Like an invoked spirit, a veiled sister stepped out and began to walk swiftly and directly towards him. His first thought was that it was a waking dream, one in which he was frozen in wonder and disbelief. But as she crossed the courtyard towards him, and her habit, wimple and veil became more distinct, dream melted away, and he was sure it was she his heart at last had conjured.

Stopping short of where he stood, she nodded her acknowledgement of him; and then with another nod, signaled to follow her. After several hundred paces from the nunnery's gates, the sister stopped, turned to him, and spoke through her veil.

"I have received your poem, sir, and I have read it several times over."

It was the same sweet voice he had heard that first night, the voice that had haunted him ever since with erotic dreams. *Or was it?*

"O Angel, how you have filled my dreams! How you have touched my heart with your sweetness!"

"I have thought of you as well. I have felt your eyes upon me as I come and go from my prayers…...."

"It is dark here. Lift your veil! Let me kiss you! You have no idea how I have dreamed of seeing your beautiful face, how many times I have dreamed of tasting your lips!"

"Ah, so that is it. You want to kiss me, to know my mystery, to have what I have never given a man?"

"Yes, sweet angel, on my knees, my beggary full of a thousand prayers!"

"Then I shall answer your prayers and your beggary. If you like, I shall give you what you want."

Slowly and gently, all but ceremoniously the sister's fingers lifted her veil, but what she unveiled was not the soft, unblemished face he had so wished and imagined. Stepping from the shadows into the soft blaze of moonlight, she revealed a face of grotesque disfigurement; as it had been diseased, or burnt by flames: with a twisted, harelip mouth, a missing eye, and a deep scar furrowing her cheek.

But this was not all. As she was a feral animal discovered in its lair, her silky voice became shrill and strident, her words a kind of hiss fraught with fangs.

"Now you may have your kiss, depraved, stupid man! Now you may have your kiss, or if not, never climb this hill again, hoping to pluck a

virgin's rose! Sister Giulia, the angel whose lips you wished to taste, left our sisterhood more than a year ago!"

Retreating back down the hill, Maria was stung by the mocking, hyena laughter in his heart, the ridicule of his conscience that was howling, '*Fool! Fool! Fool!*' Reaching the *Sickle Moon,* and then climbing the alley stairs to his room, he at once sought out, like a winebibber his wine, the friend that would most sympathize and console him; the one that could speak to his mad heart, and drown it into a delirium of forgetfulness. Exchanging his lute for his fiddle, he went back down the stairs and into the sleeping streets.

He was very drunk, and he had no idea where his steps were leading him. He only knew he wanted his hands upon the body of his fiddle, to make it naked in his arms, to caress and ravish it.....make it surrender.....tenderly and violently wrest its sweetest favors....give it his heart as he knew he had never given his heart to another.....breathe his soul into its voluptuous arms, and let it sing his pain to the night.

But where could its strings sing? Where could he go? He knew the alleys where were cockfights and dicing. He knew the haunts of the whores. *No, no, this was a deeper, darker, sweeter pain.....he wanted no rowdy companion or paid lover, only the one he cradled in his bosom..... only she would cry with the beauty of his sorrow.......*

He wandered through the streets, past several windows where with only a little knock he knew he could wake a lovely sleeper, a sleeper in whose arms he had played before, and would be eager to play again. He knew they would know his secret knock, and with a sleepy smile they would unlock their door, and without a word lead him to their beds. But would they not think he was silly if he refused their arms, and told them that he only wanted to softly play his fiddle at the foot of their beds.....to make love to their heart, and not their body.....to give his soul, naked in all its anguish to them?

He knew he could not escape to the sympathetic ears and arms of the forest. Warring dangers were afoot, wars that he did not understand, nor did he want a part of.....wars of nobles, knights and barons.....wars pitting hilltop city against hilltop city. The gates were locked, fortified and heavily guarded, and although the night had spilled its million diamonds in the darkness above, he was confined, trapped like an animal in these stone walls below.

Who would listen? Who would share his loneliness, his gypsy loneliness as timeless as the hills and forests.....that wanted nothing of the habits of men, the worship of a rebuking God, the lust for blood and war.....the reducing of love to little spasms and silly titters.....a loneliness wishing only to be left alone, to love and to wander, to sing one's heart.....wounded with death as all men's hearts are wounded with death....to sing, and singing perish in the eternity of the never ending dream of the seasons.......

Maria found his self in the small square called the '*Piazza Lucia*', the square that was surrounded by houses, including the great old bake house he had passed on so many mornings, calling out cajoleries to the bake girl in its high window. He could see no candle behind the closed shutters, but he knew that the ovens were kindled early, and that those tending them were often awake hours before the sun rose.

Was she awake, the common bread girl with a red kerchief? Would she hear the lovely pain of his heart, and hearing it, would her heart sing with him, like a bird of the forest as he once asked her to do? He had never seen her face. She had never spoken to him. Yes, he would sing to her shyness, and the pain of such shyness.....he would make his fiddle sing of the heart's pain and shyness.....like a ghost singing to a sister ghost, he would make his fiddle sing to her.

He stood before the great old house and brought the fiddle to his shoulder, and then the bow to its strings. As tender as a kiss, the bow touched the strings, as if nuzzling his beautiful lover from her sleep. And at his touch she stirred, woke, and responded to his caresses. Soft as a whisper she moaned a deep sigh of passion, yielded and consented, and gave herself to his needs.

.....and once playing, he knelt on his knees and continued to play before the window where the bake girl had sent down her baskets of bread, as if plumbing a deeper, sweeter depth of his heart, one that he had not explored before.....a passion that reached for and found a deeper passion, that smote the ears of sleep and night, bringing some in gowns and nightcaps to doors, windows and balconies, their annoyance arrested, changed to tenderness as by a spell, a spell of something deep and ancient.....something that was hidden, but with this music at last spoken in their hearts.......

For the last hours of the night he knelt and played, unburdening his heart to the old bake house, and the closed shutters of its upper window. His fiddle spoke new depths and breadths, surrendering the pain of its love with an abandon it had never sung before.....as its melodies were melodies played not with a man's hands, but deeper, by the passionate hands of a man's soul.....until at last the player of these melodies stood, and as dawn was breaking, left with an exhausted, but a much lightened heart.

And as he did, like the moon peeking free from a bank of clouds, a face appeared in the crack of these same shutters. In its moon-eyes were tears; and on its moon-lips trembled a glimmer, as of a smile that was too sweet to smile. In its moon-heart was a candle, one that illumined the night.

....

....

CHAPTER THIRTEEN
THE ORPHANAGE

1342; but consisting chiefly of memories of 1315-1322

Duty

BEFORE he had lifted to him his eyes, his gentle brown eyes sunken deep in his gaunt, bearded face.....before the soft, hesitant, child-timid knock on his door.....before he had descended from the choir, kissed the Crucifix of polished cypress wood, and returned briskly from his morning prayers to the dry brazier warmth of his study.....before his uneasy sleep, in which he had wrestled on a rack of frightful dreams, pelted as with sharp needles by the sound of the unfriendly, unrelenting rain.......

.....before the Curia's coach had brought him up the hill those many years ago, and as a novice he had first prayed, fasted, flogged behind these holy walls.....before he had become a monk, a postulant, a student.....before he had become a man, when still a boy he had known the meaning of this stare in this brother's eyes.....the soul-rending purport of those words readied on his tongue......

"They are very thin, pale and ragged, Father Abbot, and terribly draggled from the rain and the muddy walk up the road to the gates......."

.....Yes, he knew. He knew in his very bones this stare, these stumbling words, this weak whisper that was a mighty cry of the soul, screaming like a man burning to his death:

"Bread! For the love of God, a piece of bread!"

.....a need, a need of something that could not be satisfied, that could not be quieted; a need whose ghost still lived inside him, haunting him,

because it had once harrowed him. He knew this ghost, this ghost that was a terrible animal that had been driven from the ruined fields and sodden orchards, from empty pantries and depleted cellars to inhabit the cage of men's ribs. He knew its growls and unappeasable ferocity. He knew it was a creature that did not sleep.

"They are huddled with their bowls beneath the ilex bushes not far from the gates, father, huddled and draggled wet......shivering like cold rabbits they are......."

The rains had not ceased for four consecutive days, and before that, the greater part of the summer. Their constant pelting, dripping and drizzling had permeated the thatches, the hay, the wool of their sheep and the rows of their gardens. They had soaked the brothers' capes and sandals, their cowls and their robes. They had drowned their flower-beds, made ponds of their fields; laid siege to their frescoes. They had permeated their hymns and prayers; their waking and their sleeping; their fears and their faith. As they were vermin, they had gnawed into their bones with a cold dampness; seeping deep into their flesh; jeopardizing their very souls with their sharp wet teeth.

......Yes, he knew why the brother had come to his study......he knew because he remembered......

"Father Abbot, they have climbed the hill, even in such a miserable gloom and cold wetness as the day is......three or four of them......another passel of their poor creatures a leg or two behind. There is little more than nakedness on their backs, and a terrible want and misery in their eyes; a patchwork of ragged wretchedness they are, Abbot Father."

"Thank you, brother, I will go at once. Bring me bread from the refectory; and a few nuts and apples. I will attend to them."

"The flour is dwindling, the barrels of apples not more than three or four now......"

"Bring what we have. They would not have climbed the hill unless they were starving. God will provide."

And he knew what was about to greet him. He knew what awaited him as he walked, hooded and bundled across the flagstones of the courtyard, the bread sack hung from his shoulder; past the drowning roses, the beaten shrubberies, the mud-milky pool of goldfish; past the marble, stoically suffering saints varnished with yet another tribulation......and the Virgin weeping now not from her eyes alone, but from each fold of her veil and gown. He knew what he would see when he slid open the little door of the judas-hole. He knew he would peek at a horrible story that, once again, was being told throughout the country-side.

.....He knew because he remembered. He knew because it was impossible for him to forget.....

And yet when the Brother Porter opened the gate and he stepped outside, it was as he had not known this thing at all: as if such 'want' and 'need' forever gave their beholder a new wonder.....as they were things that their prayers had been insufficient to assuage, a hemorrhaging they had not staunched.....as if they had never, nor could ever die......filling the soul with an ever new wonder of horror......

The brother had spoken true. The children were indeed wretched, some shoeless, hatless and jacketless, their hair matted to their scalps, and their drenched clothes to their bony limbs. And as the first stepped shyly from the large dripping bushes, others followed, made courageous with their need, all making the Sign of the Cross and smiling wan, forced little smiles.....some with jaws beginning to hang, and strange stares beginning to fix unnaturally in their eyes.

.....yes, he knew, he knew these stares and hanging jowls, these stingy, contrived smiles.....he knew because he remembered.......

He set down the bag at his feet. Kneeling, he reached inside it and began to twist and tear apart one of the two small loaves. One by one he placed the paltry offerings in the bowls the children held out to him; a piece of bread, two nuts and a shriveled apple in each; offerings that the young, encircling beggars politely, and with a sense of ceremony accepted; his hand receiving in return kisses, like pecking bills of doves from each one of them.

When the loaves were divvied out, and the bag emptied, he blessed the squalid pack knelt crescent-wise about him, and then made to reenter the gate. But as he did he felt a tug upon his sleeve. Turning, he saw a young pale girl knelt at his feet. She was holding the bundle of a child, and from the scarf that wrapped about her face she was staring up at him with sunken hollow eyes. She did not speak, but only brought her hand timidly to the bag. Understanding what she was silently asking, he opened the empty bag and held it out to her. At once the young mother plunged her arm into its deep bottom, scavenging the crumbs with a swiftness that brooked on madness.

For days to come he was greatly troubled with this last scene. He could not rid it from his mind; not when he was engaged with visiting prelates, or with the Brother Cellarer in his office, or again with communal matters in the Chapter House; not when he ate; not when he flogged; not when he prayed. He could not forget feeling the girl's scrounging hand, even as it had become detached; even as it was dismembered from her arm; as it was the feeding frenzy of a school of fish in the bottom of the bag.

He could not forget her hunger-filled face; a face that had certainly once been bright, pretty and winsome, but now was pale and emaciated, quickly becoming skeletal. He pictured this face flushed with health, a shepherd's flute in its mouth, playing melodies that once drifted over their abbey's walls.

* * *

Rain

THERE were days, even weeks when the hungry children did not climb the hill and ring the bell at the abbey's gates. There were days when the sun shone brightly, and the rain-drenched wheat, barley and millet began to dry, and many of their beaten stalks began to gallantly rally, rise and half-stand again, giving the brothers hope that their prayers had been heard; and that a part of the harvest would be salvaged. The sheep, goats and cows were again let out to graze. The garden vines were rescued from their harsh trouncing; as they were the broken limbs of soldiers, bound and fastened to the splints and crutches that their nurses in gray habits tenderly gave them.

But as there was a war in heaven, one that pitted the throne of the sun against the armies of rebel storms, these truces of sun and warmth were soon broken by great swarms of bruise-black, thunder grumbling clouds, clouds that gathered and grimaced angrily, unleashing yet more artilleries of winds, sleets, and unseasonably cold rains.

And when the sheets of rain came to beat down the crippled, half-risen stalks again, dashing the hope in their stewards' briefly lifted hearts, the abbot was invariably summoned to perform his errand of charity at the abbey's gates. When the heavens spoke with rain and thunder, the sons and daughters of the itinerant herders and grazers would again make their hungry pilgrimage up the steep hill. Hearing the jingling of the gate's bell, Father Giovanni would leave his duties, go to the gates, and peeking first through the judas-hole at the swelling tide of starvelings, proceed to dole out pittances from his bag.

These rains and the subsequent visits by the begging children began to tell on the abbot's nerves. Normally stoic and unruffled midst the most urgent and calamitous events, the abbot began to be at times unsettled and disquieted by the rains. He had become distrustful even of the most pleasant skies. On his solitary walks he would sometimes abruptly halt, and then pivoting slowly in place, as on a wooden leg, look warily in all directions. He began to take a peculiar notice in scurrying vermin, flocks of crows and wheeling hawks. He began to look at circles about the moon.

He began to hear rain in the chirps of birds and the song of crickets. He began to hear the bell at their gates ringing in his prayers. He began to dream of famished children at the abbey gates; not with bowls, but with knives in their hands; not with hunger, but with murder in their eyes.

He remembered; he remembered very well. He remembered when the snows, sleets and rains came, and the sun shone only in furtive fits, and when it did its eye scoffed, rather than smiled; leered rather than encouraged. He remembered when the dark days did not go away, when they made damp and cold the orphanage; when cabbages replaced fish and tripe....when he ate bulbs and roots and snails.....when he had eaten boiled grass, and the moss pulled from the churchyard walls....when he had picked through dunghills.

* * *

Childhood

IT had been said the orphanage had been converted from an almshouse, which in turn had been converted from a Lazarus, and before that, a foundling house, attached to the long disused skeleton of a former Greek church. It was the collective suspicion of those who came to be its young inhabitants that it had originally been a large, communal granary and stable of an early Lombard hamlet, a hamlet that had spawned a market village; that village that had come to grow in the vale below it. The old building had grown over the years from the many needs and uses the people had thrust upon it, until its cobbled parts had reached and latched onto the church's wall of rusticated stones, like a decrepit gripping the arm of the strong. In truth he remembered it as being a good part of all of these previous facilities, its walls attaching leech-like to the ivy-clinging, rook-infested walls of the church, once irremediably burned and gutted by vandals, and through the long years abused by camps of infidel armies.

Its monstrous relic was administered to by priests and a few nuns from a nearby nunnery, many of which were grim and severe, while others were gentle and kindly. He remembered it as being miserably ill-lit, moldering, and almost always drafty, creaky and wind-moaning; some parts of its hastily constructed walls but wattle and daub, providing homes for swifts and pigeons, and in the warm months, busy colonies of wasps.

But more than any of these things he remembered its dismal rooms pervaded by the ubiquitous spirit of 'death', and death's co-conspirators of hunger, disease, and lunacy. Its pall and reek filled each corner of its rambling edifice, speaking with terrible ghosts who owned many terrible voices and faces, especially to a child's eye and ear; for as it had disjointedly grew to attach itself to the derelict church, when the famines came it no longer accommodated children alone, but older unfortunates as well, those crippled and sick, as well as those blasted of their reasons.

Its dark being spoke in croaking whispers, puling whines, racking coughs and violent retching. It spoke in groans inspired by the anguish of corrupting flesh and raging fevers. It spoke in the many tongues of madness: in the screams, howls and giggles of idiocy, of those suffering in the horrors of their tortured consciences and their unclean dreams; wickedly cursing those who had wronged them, and begging forgiveness from those they had grievously wronged; those calling out for lost wives, husbands, children, confessing and repenting jealousies, adulteries, murders; begging for the embraces of lovers, both from those whose affections they had won, and those from whom they had been spurned.

It spoke in the smells of thin, insipid pottages and porridges. It spoke in the trapped stenches of vomit, urine, excrement, damp straw and fetid feathers; from the sundry exudations of decaying flesh, smells that joined and melded into that one most peculiar and pungent smell of them all, so nauseous it was almost sweet, that dormant smell waiting to bloom from the end of all living flesh.....from all victims that lay limp in the hands of the strangler that strangles all. 'Death' blossomed its dark glory from the rottenness that the orphanage embraced, and strong as a priest's swinging censer, gave the fumes of its flower to all.

It came to speak in the children's eyes as well; behind their many stares that became one stare.....the stare of a beggar gone witless mad from the creature that was eating it alive.....sometimes pale, like a ghost, or frightened like a stray dog, sometimes blank, as the soul had fled the house of its body. Sometimes their eyes seemed not the eyes of children at all, but glazed and glassy, like the button eyes of dolls, or fish on a fishwife's table, blind and insensate to the world of the sun....or suddenly becoming fierce like feral animals, filled with growl and threat.....as they no longer wanted to beg, only to seize.......even to kill.

.....As it had been in the beginning of the famines, so it was now..... the drenching rains, the fields languishing in ruination of flattened stalks and mildewing beards.....the certain omens of the coming of the winter's sickness and hunger.......

.....the bell, the peek through the judas, like a peek into an anteroom of hell.....the opening of the gate, the nuts and puny apples, the twisting and tearing into little pieces the bread loaf brought from the bag.....the frenzy of little hands, like crazy spiders in the bottom of that bag........

And so also the flood of memories that the dry, sunny, intervening years had not succeeded in tamping into forgetfulness. As they were one with the assaults of the leaden skies, he could not stop them from rising from the graves in his mind.....not in his abbatial duties, not in his prayers to the Saints; not in his flagellations; not in his sleep.

.....the rats and crows, the scavenging dogs.....the corpses, pickers, fleecers, wailers, diggers.....this mad, promiscuous, incestuous beggar of Hunger multiplying his demented, damning grin on more and more lips..... his animal growl in more and more bowels, his scowl in more eyes, his desperation in more and more teeth and fists......

.....the bell, the shrill, grating bell no longer being rung furtively and hesitantly, no longer a shy polite jingle, but now harshly, stridently.....as the children's hands had reached deep inside him, and were shaking shrill his nerves, his nerves that still held memories.....becoming more impatient, insistent, angry.....no, they would not go away.....not the rains, not the children, not his memories....even when he intoned his prayers.....even when the nail-studded scourge slapped sharply, its teeth biting deeply, as it too was hungry.....the blood running in red rivers, one with the cold rains down his back.......

.....his mind began to blur and swim with horrid scenes, as in the dark throes of an illness. He began to burn with fever.....the cold and drear, the

*thinning soups, their dwindling provisions, the ringing at the gates now a
knocking, an insistent knocking on the gates.......*

*......and something else, something deeper......some anguish of the
soul......something that the brother had said to him today in passing.......*

* * *

The Bell

*HE began to hear it in closing doors, leaf-fluttering breezes, even in the
screeches of owls. He heard it in the hits of hammers, the rustle of a chain
or a horse's bridle. He heard its jangling in the breathy wheezes of the older
brothers in their prayers.*

*He was no longer sure whether he was in truth hearing it with his ear,
or only with his mind. At times it seemed to ring through his bones and teeth
like a slow march of lepers, or chain-rattling prisoners. He could not will
it back to silence, for silence was the playground its mischief disturbed to
play in. Prayer offered little defense, for a sharp fear had breached his faith,
creaking like a broken shutter in his heart. Even sleep was no sanctum from
the dread of its menace, for sometimes its ring seeped into his dreams like an
evil laughter.*

*In one such dream he seemed to hear the bell as the brothers were
chanting in unison their early prayers. Filling with panic as it continued,
and seeing that none of his praying brothers seemed to hear or heed its
ring, he rose from his stall and walked out the chapel and across the wet
courtyard, only to hesitate and suddenly stop before the gate. The bell had
ceased to ring; as if its ringer had heard his approaching steps. Made curious
at this silence, he cautiously slid open the judas door, stepped up on his toes,
and brought his eye to its small window......only to look directly into the
bloody-fanged maw of a wolf.*

*It was a dream that came to repeat itself, but with dreadful variations
when he pressed his eye to the gate's small window; this window that brought
its stare to his dreams, that peered laughing and jeering through them like
a harlot's painted eye; a wicked, garish eye that mocked him, commanding
him with the knowledge of his own fears; the abbot of an abbey's fears.*

*Sometimes he saw a crowd of hungry children, their stomachs pro-
truding, their backs twisted and grossly hunched, their callow faces goatishly
bearded. Some of their heads were not children's heads at all, but bloody-*

251

beaked birds; others, savage beasts with tusks of boars. Another time the children held knives above their heads, poised like archers, their eyes riveted beadily upon the tiny target through which he was peering.

* * *

Fever Dreams

HE touched the wick of his candle into the one burning in the brass candlestick before the Virgin, and after genuflecting, climbed into the choir with the rest of the brotherhood.

This was his favorite office of prayer, the last office of the day, when, other than their recitations, silence was obeyed, and only with a most urgent need, the symbolic language of their hands was used. His duties of the long day were done, and just as importantly, so were his words.

At the sign from the Brother Cantor, he began to sing the Vesper hymns he had sung since he was a young man. But it was difficult for him to remember all of the words tonight, and even more difficult to concentrate and give his heart to them.

The rain beat down hard on the roof directly above, echoing loud through the cavernous stone hollow of the chapel. It deafened the drone of the brothers' voices, deafened and devoured them like whirring locusts, or a great rushing wind...like the Voice of their God rebuking their iniquities.

The roof was now leaking in numerous places, even here in the choir, and there was an indefensible damp that had invaded the entire sanctuary, that threatened altar cloths, vessels, idols, anything it coldly breathed upon. A leak had trickled slyly down a wall, and noticed too late, had excoriated a part of one of their prized frescoes.

The brothers sat in their stalls, hunched and shivery like rabbits, their cowls uplifted, and their hands stuffed deep in their sleeves. For days most of the brotherhood had been crawling on top of the spongy roofs, thatching and re-thatching, trying to stop heaven's tears from spoiling the shelter built in its honor. They were tired, wet, and beneath their show of faith, very frightened.

He burned with fever, a fever that filled him with strange thoughts, but as when he was a boy and the rains came, he would tell no one of these thoughts and the terrible shapes they assumed. He would instead quietly recite, and while reciting, remember. Even as the Brother Cantor directed,

252

and the murmur of the brothers quailed in meekness beneath such supernatural wrath, he would remember......even when the rain was pounding its fists over their heads he would remember how their God had once rent the bellies of the clouds to vent His angry spleen.......

But why? Why was his heart so insistent? Why must he remember?

NOT long after the first fits of cold and rain, he was assigned his first duties outside the orphanage, duties that helped justify and pay for the keep of those left in the care of the Church; at least those who were able and healthy enough to do a day's labor. With few exceptions, the orphans were eventually adopted, but most were not embraced like true sons and daughters by their adopters. More times than not they were treated like indentured servants, servants that, treated kindly or unkindly, remained servants, and these first assignations away from the orphanage were like an apprenticeship of the life of servitude the boys were more than sure awaited them.

These duties were not altogether unwelcome to the orphaned boys. They offered an escape from the dark, despondent, sickness ridden airs of the orphanage, and the cramped, confining playground, bounded on two sides by the church's crumbly walls, and on the other two sides by its forsaken churchyard. The duties were manual chores, chores that included sweeping streets, collecting dung and animal carcasses, and any other refuse littering the ways. Sometimes they accompanied sawyers into the forest to help load and unload their wagons of wood. Sometimes they did the same with the masons, accompanying the muscular, wine-drinking men and their oxen into the gorge-like quarries.

These chores, although at first exciting and venturesome, soon proved slavishly miserable. But it was not due to the strains of their demanded labors that made them so. They became miserable because more often than not the sun did not shine on them. Working daylong in gloom, cold and penetrating damp, the boys would trudge back up the hill to the orphanage at nightfall, only to receive a piece of bread and a small bowl of gruel, huddle about stingy, sickly fires, and then go to cold beds to shiver their famished bodies beneath threadbare blankets.

.....but why, why after all these years must he remember?......

.....AS their prayers had incensed, and not appeased the wrath of Heaven, when the office concluded the rains redoubled their punishing assault, making it necessary for the brothers to file through the subterranean tunnel to the cloister, instead of crossing the open courtyard....his legs weak and unsteady, his mind, swimming; his body, burning. He felt as though

the dark, narrow passageway was a catacomb, his brothers, fellow ghosts in that catacomb......

HE *remembered how, in the first days the men lifted their collars and grumbled, resenting the unyoking of their beasts, the rusting of their ploughs, the loss of time in the fields. But as the days became weeks the grumbles waxed to worry, worry to curses, and from curses finally to prayers. Many were seen with uplifted faces, surveying and prognosticating the thinning or the thickening of clouds, the flights of birds and the nimbuses of the moon. Knots of men began to gather andconverse in stables, or beneath the eaves of shop roofs, their voices gruff, grave and low with concern.*

And as days became weeks, and weeks, months, it became clear that a second consecutive harvest would be drowned before it had ripened. In late summer the crops were blighted with smuts and mildews, and as autumn neared, the fields of wheat, barley and rye became little more than sloughs. Herds and flocks contracted flukes and murrains, and it was not uncommon to see a dead sheep or goat, even a dead horse or ox monstrously bloated and rotting in the fields, providing invitations to great crowds of feasting crows. The orchard fruits blighted, and dropped stunted to the wet ground..... collected only to be swilled with mash to the swine. The grapes shriveled to rottenness on spindly, rain-strangled vines, guaranteeing a second year when they would offer no luscious clusters to be stomped, and the giant casks would remain empty of their purple juice.

That is how it had begun, branding a young boy's mind with wonders that turned to horrors.....And now he must remember them.....as the miser must pass his filthy coins again and again through the sieve of his fingers, and with them the lies and crimes that made them his......so he must pass such morbid riches again and again through the burning sieve of his fears.... the rain, his fever.....the thing the brother had said to him.......

......ENTERING his cell he blew out his candle, crossed himself, and said one last 'Pater'. He lay down on his bed, the rain drumming on the slates and thatches above, and on the mud and stones, deepening puddles and swiftly gurgling rivulets in the courtyard below. Although the rain had abated to gentleness, it seemed a dark, evil gentleness, one that like a dark laughter seemed to delight in rushing and plashing through each part of the abbey; through each part of him.

Although he burned with fever, he did not remove his wet habit. Gripped by delirium he knew he would not sleep tonight. He knew he was mastered now by fear, not faith, that he must lie awake in the night like a flame in cold snow.....buried alive, yes buried and burning alive....not that he might forget the living, but that he would always remember the dying....

IT was after the second failure of the crops, and the second harsh winter that followed on its bare bleeding heels that grimmer signs began to appear.

More foundlings were found and given to the orphanage. The former church, and the sanctity still ascribed to its derelict walls, as well as the mercy shown by the priests and good sisters reached out to unfortunate mothers and their secret, unwanted burdens. Bundles bearing the cries of new life were stowed, and later found in small trees near the orphanage door, out of the reach of vermin and dogs, or wrapped in rags or sacks, laid in baskets high on stone sills. A significant more were deposited on the steps and altars of the churches in the village by anonymous hands, ghosts whose breasts were too dry to feed the mouths they had born, and in a last act of compassion, wanted to free them from death's arms.....the less compassionate smothering their scrawny burdens, and then scratching out graves for their corpses in the pauper-yard, and if not in the pauper-yard, beneath bushes or in the muddy rear of gardens......graves that were too shallow to be true graves.....little more than a shoveling over with dirt to keep them free from rooting pigs, or the packs of hungry dogs.......

As the rains continued, friendly faces became hard, pinched and cold. Replies to simple questions and exchanges became sharp, choleric, ugly; quick to turn contentious. There was a general callousness and guardedness that came upon the people, caused by the scarcity and rationing of oil, cloth, bread and meat; the fears of their want choking the natural compassion in their hearts. Many of the stares in people's eyes were dazed and apathetic; others became distract, witless mad with deprivation; still others became inhabited with slyness and meanness, things bred in desperation, not to be trusted; and still others with a blankness that was almost peaceful with surrender, a surrender that was a kind of perverse hope of their souls, to know they were about to leave this world that would not give them bread.

And as the third and fourth years were barren of harvests, madness, the mongrel child of want and need began to infect the people, and infecting them, to possess them. There were those in the streets who began to speak to spouses long dead, to the phantoms of sword-bearing devils they alone could see. Some began to drink to drunkenness, and to rave or laugh without reason; others to languish and to stare with idiocy; still others to squint or cock cold eyes with stares that did not seem their own. There were young girls in the streets that, in desperation not to starve, began to give older men inviting smiles, offering their bodies for bread. There were packs of lean dogs that could not be easily kicked away, only beaten with clubs or goaded with the sharp tines of pitchforks......or as the famines continued, killed, roasted and eaten......

.....HE knew these rains, their evil laughter and their gnashing teeth. He knew the rancor contained in their gentle-seeming drops. He knew that inside their tender song howled the wolves of hell........

......remembering what he had seen, what he had heard, what he could never forget.....this knocking on a door, this insistent jangling of a bell..... the judas, like the harlot eye of his own soul.....the words the brother had spoken to him today.......

THERE were noticeably more vagrants in the streets; ragged, filthy, prowling, jackal-thin and hunger-eyed, sleeping in doorways, and rooting like pigs through garbage heaps; gathering in small knots at corners, before church doors and bread shops. In the morning an ever swelling crowd of beggar-kind milled and huddled outside the village gates, some made indolent with want, others, seething with its pangs.....some with malice, even murder written over their distorted, hunger-twisted faces.

In the wet fields there developed camps of these roving wretches, as they were malingerers of a beaten army; those whose stomachs had driven them from hut and hamlet to a widening compass of country-side. Over their fires they roasted pigs, sheep or goats they had freely taken from folds and fields not their own, or had broken down doors of barns to steal. But as the livestock thinned, and they were driven to further desperation, they had begun to slaughter oxen, mules and horses, eating even cats and dogs; even the weasels they caught with their hands. It was said some fought with the crows and wild dogs for the carcasses of dead animals.

BUT it was not until after the first snow fell over the fourth ruined harvest that death joined in full force with these grim happenings; when hunger waxed to carnage with its lunacy, and made even a more horrid show of Heaven's displeasure.....a man found hung from a piece of harness in the churchyard, frozen stiff, half-naked and half pecked apart by carrion birds. His wife, frozen in the snow beneath him, dismembered and decapitated, eaten to the bone by animals. In a small cottage a starved mother was found with her babe at her breast, the scrawny creature vainly trying to suck the shriveled breasts that death had squeezed dry of life's last drop.... these the first of countless, endless others......these perhaps not victims, but the fortunate........

.....*HE knew these rains.....their gnashing teeth, their hideous laughter......the sickness and madness they brought......he knew that the living could become the dead, and the dead could become the living.......*

CROWDS *of the pauperized moved herd-like over the roads and fields, foraging for roots and bark, burdock and nettles, or digging on their hands and knees in barren fields for vestiges of vetch and turnip roots.....under stones for grubs, slugs, worms.......*

.....*the gentry, starved from their castles and their velvet liveries, joined one with the beggarly and wretched.....the honest turned to thieves, barons to paupers, nobles to pickpockets.....men turned into beasts, the last shred of their dignity surrendered to the primacy of their need.....their bare hands now claws and hoofs, digging and pawing through mud, ice and snow for green blades and the meat of worms.....those who roasted dunghills, and imagined them bread.....those who exhumed corpses, cracking open skulls to find the brains still soft inside them.......*

.....*hands that had fleeced pockets for silver snuffboxes, now searching only for crusts of bread, and finding no crusts, for crumbs.....the dead, fallen in the roads, in the mud beneath bushes......without coffins, without tears, without prayers.......*

.....*THE rain, the incessant, accursed rain.....and in that rain the battering upon the gate, and the jangling of the bell that had become the rattling of swords.....its ring no longer a ring, but now the sharp bites of a chisel chiseling at the abbey's stones.....chiseling his very bones.....the cries of the children that had become the growls and snarls of wild beasts.....beasts rebelling against, and wanting to eat their human masters......*

THERE *were many who wandered alone, aimless and demented, the invisible monster of their hunger cannibalizing them even as they wandered.....as flesh was being eaten to its skeleton before men's very eyes.....their jaws hanging, their faces sallow and blotched with disease..... their gaits drunk and stumbling.....the stares of madmen, idiots, ghosts in their eyes.......*

There were others who took to the wilds.....bands of the starving that were armed with picks and heavy clubs. Reduced to barbarity, their unshorn hair and beards making them seem as they were as much the progeny of animals as men. No hut, cottage, byre or barn was safe from their needs. Cellars were robbed of their wine, shops rifled of all they contained. Even the dead were not exempt from their banditry, for digging up and dashing apart their coffins, they plundered corpses' ornaments; bracelets and necklaces, brooches and jeweled crosses laid upon decaying breasts; cutting off the fingers still adorned with precious rings.....bartered for a piece of meat or a crust of bread.

Packs of wild dogs, fierce as wolves, began to roam the country-side, packs that found the unburied dead, tearing them piecemeal apart..... leaving hands, arms and legs in their wakes.......

Yes, that is how it had been, how the howl of hunger deafened reason into madness.....the rains, the blight, the famine.....men, women and children on all fours digging for roots and worms....those weeping and wailing into the wind, begging not for bread that they might live, but for death that they might quit the hell of living......

.....things he had seen that he knew his prayers had never, would never, could never rid him of......the gentle rains full of gnashing teeth, lamentations, the wails of human madness.....the endless knocking, the accursed jangling.....the scratching and clawing, the children's teeth gnawing like rats......the harlot's eye of the judas, smiling, as it knew the secret in his heart.......

* * *

The Judas

HE had been sleeping, dreaming.....yes, sleeping and dreaming.....the rain, the jangling bell and the knocking on the gates.....and the children's voices, discordant and angry, one with the angry sheets of rain slashing down upon the slates......he must go to them, yes, even at this hour and in this heavy rain he must take bread and go to them.....he knew their hunger..... he knew the animal waked inside them....he knew that death, madness and murder were the incestuous offspring of its hunger.

.....and the eye of the judas that stared in his dreams, like the meretricious eye of a courtesan, one that knew the secret that burned in his heart.....teasing him, taunting him, making him remember something the brother had said to him.....something that had touched him very deeply with a deep fear......

He did not don his cape; no, he would not allow himself such comfort, even when they had climbed up the muddy hill, naked and cold in the pelting rain. And he would not wake any of the brothers, not even the Brothers Porter or Cellarer. He knew where the gate's keys were kept. He would go to the refectory alone, place whatever bread and apples he could find in the bag, and then go to them alone.....the knocking....the bell, like a racking cough....their many little hands clawing, their sharp teeth gnawing....as they would bore holes in the walls.....as they would kill to be fed........

.....THE people were forced to eat moldy grains, rotted fruits, disease-dead animals.....sometimes pieces of leather, the droppings of pigeons, the manure of dogs, horses, pigs......sometimes in hunger's madness chewing on their own arms and legs, like a dog biting at its fleas. People replaced flocks in the fields, not grazing, but scavenging on their hands and knees in mud, snow, rain.....in the streets picking through refuse, corpses, dunghills.....or gathered around fires and cauldrons in which were being boiled pet cats and dogs, their favorite songbirds........

......the rain, the knocking, the bell, like the death rattle of the dying......and in that rain and rattle what the brother had said to him.......

.....yes, he would cross the courtyard......he would bring his eye to the judas-hole, to the harlot's gleaming, knowing stare.......

.....and the words the brother had said to him today.......

..... "Not man nor beast could live in such a foulness.....nothing but thieves, starvation and disease.....and that poor brother who deserted the brotherhood some years ago, that kin of the gypsies......you knew him, did you not, Abbot Father?....alive or not, I sometimes wonder about the poor creature......."

.....those lying dead in the mires of the streets, in the pieces of rags that still clung to their bones, in the wastes of their diseased bodies.....wrapped in rags, horse blankets, or abjectly naked, stripped and eaten by death's minions.....looters hung in trees, or starving to skeletons in prisoner baskets, dangling above the streets.......

.....stepped over and around by passers-by, fleeced by pickers and sniffed at and pissed on by dogs.....under carts and in garbage heaps.....feasted on by wild dogs, picked to the bone by crows.....or disappearing frozen beneath the snows, their carcasses grimly smiling with the poppies in the spring....frozen in death, not delivered from it.......

..... "Not man nor beast could live in such a foulness".......

.....the rain, the knocking, the bell.....the clawing now not only at the gate, but on the walls surrounding the abbey......an army of children with raised knives.....

......the people becoming deformed, disfigured and demented with a

want to which God showed no mercy, and Man owned no answer.....horribly blotched and scaled, covered with pustules.....bleeding with open sores and ulcerated bowels, bleeding from their eyes and mouths and anuses..... their limbs rotting from their bodies.....typhus, scurvy, pellagra, ergotism, dysentery......death dressing its victims with its hideous costumes......

.....“nothing but thieves, starvation and disease”.....

......he had been too young to see such things, but the doctor man who had taken him from the orphanage insisted he accompany him.....things he could not forget.....his mother eaten alive, her flesh torn from her bones by the fangs or knives of the starving.......

.....their eyes unnaturally bulging, as to dribble their jellies from their sockets.....their tongues coated as with fur, their teeth falling from their mouths.....the beards now on both men and women, like the beards of wild goats.....shaggy growths sprouting from the pits of their arms, like unchecked weeds from their genitalia......

.....“that poor brother who deserted....that kin of the gypsies?......”

.....stomachs and limbs monstrously bloated.....spines twisted and grotesquely humped.....apathetic, lifeless, idiotic.....twitching, scratching, biting, like monkeys in a cage....violently convulsing, retching, giggling.... crazy and screaming with fires of fever raging through them.....

.....before the gate and the judas.....the judas that seemed at once a harlot’s eye, a harlot’s navel, a harlot’s filthy vulva........

..... “you knew him, did you not, Abbot Father?”.....

......those that had rushed upon the hanged, to eat the broken bodies still twitching on arms of gallows....those that had eaten each other in their imprisonments......those that had slit the throats of their children, rather than have them know the spite of hell, these lies of God.

.....“I sometimes wonder about him”......

.....standing on his toes and pressing his eye to the judas to see, and at last to know.......

..... “you knew him, did you not, Abbot Father?”......

.....the eye not a harlot’s eye, not an evil eye.....but an eye blue, and sparkling with laughter.......

* * *

The Bell-Tower

FATHER Giovanni started awake. He lay motionless, stunned in his own waking; as if returning from a great blow to his head; as if being born from the dark dream of the womb.

He lay stone still, listening to his gently beating heart, it's wildly drumming finished, having driven the fever from his blood, and with it the terrible beasts of his memories and dreams.

As from a sip of strong wine, warmth coursed through all parts of him; the canals of his blood now freed of their freezing ice. His eyes moistened, and a tear of mild sweetness rolled down his cheek into the coarse cold thicket of his beard. The tear was a prayer, thanking God for the passing of his fever, that he might live, and continue his shepherd-ship of his brothers.

The storm of his fever had passed, but what had woken him?

As he lay still, he heard no slapping sandals, no cantor in the hall with his psaltery, no croaking of a dawn bird. No, he had been waked by something else.....something more august.....a voice more benign, more dear.......

The rain had stopped.....yes, that was it, he could hear no more pelting on the slates and walls, or on the courtyard below.....the rain had stopped, leaving in its wake a silence more deafening than its fury.....and in this silence he lay alone, as on a desolate shore, his heart gently pounding, faithfully bleeding with the great wound of its birth.....crying to the Ear of this silence with the wonder of its song..... "I am alive! I am alive!".......

Leaving the cloister he walked towards the chapel, intending to pray and give thanks at the feet of the great Crucifix. But crossing the courtyard he halted his steps near the well.

The wet night lay heavy on all, heavy and deathly still.....its drench of silence intimidating, suffocating the barks of dogs, the riffle of leaves, the chirps of crickets. In the stillness he listened to the song of his heart; this creature that was bleeding in the sacrificial ecstasy of its own dying. Naked of God and belief, it cried not for mercy, but with gratitude for the miracle of its own tenderness.

He placed his foot on the first step of the bell-tower, and with a kind of humble proud submission....at once with defeat and victory....at once like a prince to his throne, and a villain to the gallows.....began to mount the dark stone steps to the belfry.

......He had been frail and weak as a boy, made sickly from the mal-

nourishment caused by the famines. He had been befriended by none, not by a mother who had known a terrible death, or a father gripped by drink, who, unable to sustain such grief, had given him away.....not by those of his own age that he had outshone with his scholarship.......

.....loneliness, not the famine, had eaten him to the bone.....his memories of the orphanage, and the scenes of the Great Famines less harrowing to his boyhood than his aloneness.....yes, that was it.....a precocious student of God's love, his soul had been starved of human love.......

THE giant bell hung above him, stony as a sphinx, the riddle of its secret, the promise of some eternal blessedness sleeping in its cold iron.....a secret that, however cryptic and unknowable, was both the eternal lure and the eternal fate of his faith.

As he was the captain of a ship, from here he could survey far reaches of the country-side.....the fields and forests surrounding the abbey's walls like a dark sea.....a dark sea full of ruined harvests, starving flocks, the boil of storms.....the monster that the mariners of men, in the tiny coracle of their flesh call 'death'.

'.....not man nor beast.....nothing but thieves, starvation and disease.......'

Here and there he could see small fires that had begun to sputter and struggle forth in the shepherd camps. It had begun to once more drizzle, and the drizzle to congeal into tiny droplets of rain, droplets that were colder than snow, that threatened to change all bloods to ice.

He had heard of prophets, pagan prophets called 'astrologers' that read in the stars an even harsher rebuke, a more punishing punishment that would be sent by heaven.....that would pale the famines, and the misery and destitution left in their wake.....that would make them seem the calm before a storm.....a harvest of death unlike anything men had ever known..... mowing man's creature like the sickle mows the wheat.......

'.....and that poor brother that deserted the brotherhood.......'

He had not thought of him in years. He had thought he had forgotten him; his youthful memory long since buried beneath the cares of the brotherhood, and the ever pressing affairs and duties of the abbacy he had inherited after Father Augustine's death.

But he had been wrong.

'.....that brother that was a kin of the gypsies.......'

.....Did his mouth still warble forth its golden laughter, his blue eyes still flash with boyish dreams? What horses had he ridden? What flowers had

he picked? What songs did he sing with the sweetness of a bird?

'......you knew him, did you not, Abbot Father?.......'

Or had death, with its cold eye and indiscriminate heart claimed him too?

And if it had not, had this one who had dashed his holy vows to dally in the arms of women......this reprobate, this self-defrocked, this one who had turned his back on God......had he ever once thought of him?

....

....

CHAPTER FOURTEEN

THE YELLOW BANDANNA
PART I

Late Spring, early Summer, 1340

*HE had intended to leave, yes, he remembered, he had intended to leave.....
to briefly sleep, pack his few things, and at first light leave without goodbyes
to friends or kisses to lovers.....without reminiscence or regrets.....without
a destination, ambition, care.....yes, he had intended to leave, and leaving
to wander, sing, hurt, starve, perish.....unnoticed and unremembered,
walking like a ghost from the city's gates back into the endless fields, hills and
forests....into the dream of the seasons, the pretty dream, the cruel dream,
the dream of blossoms, wolves and knives, of endless games played with
women's eyes, lips and bodies.....the evanescent, swallow-winged dream, the
dream whose only waking was a farewell.......*

*.....yes, he had intended to leave the city as ghost-like as he had entered
it.....leave the glut and stupidity of the living.....the butchers in their
bloody stalls, the fishmongers gutting the glaze-eyed fishes.....the begging
urchins and the galling hawkers.....the knights sharpening their swords
for war, the women smiling fatuously from their windows and loggias.....
the wine, the taverns and dice houses, the slatterns that lured him to their
beds...leaving the stink and greed of the human animal...the rot of its greed
and its reasonless reasons.....the endless walks, smiles and dreams inside its
prison walls.......*

*.....he had intended to sleep in his room until day would break, but as
he had begun to mount the stairs, arms seized and wrapped him about.....
lips violently pressed his throat and mouth, and a hand unbuckled and*

sleekly found, held and tenderly harnessed his maleness......arresting him midst perfumed flurries of kisses and silly laughter, and whispers breathed like a smoke of opium into his ear......

"No, it is much too early to go to bed! Come back to the Sickle Moon, my golden gypsy! Come play and sing as only you can play and sing! And after, yes, after, you will have what you wish to have, and what I wish to give! Oh, I have seen how you look at me when there is wine in your blood! I have seen the hunger in your eyes, even as you have seen the promise in mine. Come and sing for me! Let your hands play on the lute as I will let them play later upon my body....after, yes, after, you will have the prize of your pleasure. It is our time. That fool of my husband has gone hunting in the forest, and tonight I am yours to hunt and to have!"

....he had intended to climb the stairs, to sleep, and then to leave, but her body pressing into his, the tongue in her kisses, the promises she hotly breathed into his ear.....and how her hand had found and held him..... tenderly yoked him, roused him, sweetly slyly owned him......

.....he had been led away, like a calf to an altar, obedient to those hips, that clever hand and that promise that tugged at the leash of his heart..... back into the temple of straw, oyster shells, tallow smoke....pelts, tools, barrels and wine casks......the visceral bowels of human mirth and dreams..... where man's beast goes to forget, to be purged of its' hurts and failures......

.....and then playing and singing wildly.....drinking deeply, very deeply, as he had seldom done before.....playing lute and fiddle as he was ravishing, not loving a woman.....as he was making, not asking her to yield..... hurting her, not pleasing her.....like an infidel at his savage sport.......

.....singing, drinking, dancing, his hands exploring waists, hips, breasts, even as they explored and danced upon the lute's and fiddle's strings.....his mouth tasting the mouths of all that fell laughing and pressing into his arms.....as he was kissing each flower that had ever bloomed, each smile that had ever smiled.....kissing them for the first time, as it was the last time.....as death was his mistress, and she was alive, promising immortality in his arms.......

.....he had intended to leave, even then, after the tavern's close, to climb the stairs, briefly sleep, and then to leave.....the taverns, the littered streets, the whore-haunted promenades.....the meaningless maze of endlessly monotonous ways and days, stairs, alleys, gargoyles and ghostly arcades..... to step into the wilds where he belonged, where he ever yearned to be.... where he might hurt and bleed alone beneath an audience of cold uncaring

stars....*where he might fall like a leaf to the silent forest floor....a soldier falling quietly, namelessly on the sword of his defeated dreams.........*

.....but she had waited for him in the darkness with her thirsty kisses, and he had pressed her against the wall, as to immolate her giggles with his need, as to kill what had teased and waylaid him....her breasts bared, her skirt raised, her legs lifted, wrapping tightly about him, even as his hands clenched fists of her nakedness beneath him.....and her whispers, whispers he had heard countless times before in meadows, barns, doorways.....in beds of leaves, feathers, straw and snow....'O my beautiful darling, how I love you!'......

......and then the hands upon his shoulders, tearing him from the pleasure she was offering him, from the only thing that gave his meaningless life a moment's meaning.....tearing him away with curses, and a great clout to his head that felled him in the darkness...... the rain of hits from boards and kicks from heavy boots, savage kicks to his sides and his legs and his face....kicks that woke something inside him that he had always feared would wake inside him.....that he feared slept in the dark forests of his heart.....in the first memories of his blood.......

......the ecstasy of love melting to the ecstasy of murder.....the pleasures of the flesh giving way to the rage of killing it.....lifting the large man from his feet.....and then casting him over and over, blindly, darkly, ex-ultingly against the stone wall, disarming and breaking his will with the giddy abandonment of his fury.....even as the one who had been about to give him her favors screamed desperately at his side.....a cry he had heard sometime and somewhere before.....another lover begging for his love, only to accuse it of being beastly, as if the one contained the other: "Stop! Stop! You are killing him! He is my husband! No! Stop! You are a madman! He is my husband! You are mad and savage! You are killing him!".......

......But he could not stop. He could not stop because he did not want to stop, because something that had long slept in his blood had awoken, filling him with a new delicious pleasure......Oh, how small and petty love seemed beside these brutal blows! How silly were a few kisses in a dark alley compared to this exultant match of life with death....no, he would not stop, not for a woman's sugary kisses and the little trinket between her legs......not for the silly things she whispered in his ear......

.....and then the rush of other shouts and screams, the many rough hands upon him, and a storm of blows to his ribs and his face.....a storm that woke him, possessed him with yet a fiercer fire, a fire that was a kind

of ecstasy......as a Saint must feel upon receiving the bleeding wounds.......
......as he had never been a monk, a player of lutes, a writer of childish poems......until he was no longer Brother Maria, but an animal whose heart had beat in the shadows of prayers, kisses, dreams, only now to lunge and be the thing it was meant to be......one that had waited, lived for such an exultancy......the exultancy to kill......the hands that had counted beads and softly sleeked over women's bodies now doubled into hammering fists.... fists that summed his loneliness, shame, beggary and endless wandering into savage blows delivered to his hunters in the dark....hunters that he was felling, that were bleeding and groaning at his feet.......
......only at the last to fall upon the fallen, with the knife that had entered deep into his side.......

* * *

.... A dark, drowning underworld of pain, washed over by sweet breezes of the living....a lovely smell, one that salved and soothed, tempering that pain with deliciousness......calling the dead back to the sun.......
......and then from pain and struggle came the march and blaze of living light......at once both an intruder and a friend......its army avowing at once to save and to sack, to kill and to nurse......an army of bloody, blinding, crusading light whose soldiers were voices, voices that were not angry with the hubbub of war and assault, but soft with excited whispers of health and goodness..... "Father, there is a customer in the street, the one who buys the rye, and not the barley biscuits"..... "Yes, daughter, I know, but I can not find the damned basket!"..... "You moved it from its place when you and the other men brought him home last night"..... " It's like a curse, this muddle-headedness of mine" ..... "You are an angel of mercy, father, but one that was filled with plum wine last night......and please, father, speak more softly.....as you know, the doctor said the knife went very deep, nearly to its hilt, and he must rest, and not be disturbed"... "Yes, Katrinika, I will whisper for you and our wounded Achilles......and I suppose for that pathetic, misfit of a drunkard that some call a doctor......."
......there came not only the voices of light's army, but also the cadence of its soldiers' feet......not the quaking march of boots, but a tender shuffling of slippers......pattering and scurrying, like rabbits in their warren....playfully busy, but in no way menacing.....the steps and voices making a beautiful music midst the throes of his pain....the feet of one rabbit unevenly dragging,

limping, yet delicate and dainty, like a gently falling rain.....and familiar, yes, familiar, the lovely scrape of its step....even as the whispered name was somehow familiar.....'Katrinika, Katrinika'...this name, the music of these uneven steps, and something more.....a hand, a tender hand that had laid upon his brow, softly caressed through his hair.....even as he had wrestled with death's monster......

* * *

HE woke in a large bed in a small, sparsely furnished room, a room of old wood with a high ceiling and two very tall windows on one wall, allowing a golden river of sunlight to flood inside it. In one corner there were colored rocks, painted beads and polished shells set neatly upon each of three tiered shelves, like the what-not collection of a child. Against the wall nearest the foot of his bed was a simple table, upon which was a bright blue vase holding a small bouquet of fresh, assorted flowers, and a candlestick with a spent, all but completely guttered candle, giving the impression that it had burned long, nightly hours.

On the wall above the table hung a simple wooden crucifix, the length and breadth of a man's forearm.

On the roughly hewn rafters overhead were pots of gillyflowers, bright and glad, like a parti-colored choir praising the rich sunlight. The windows' curtains were of a creamy, chintz-like cloth. They were gathered about their middles by cinnamon-brown sashes, each one of them gathered and bound back in a pretty bow, so that they offered no restriction to the golden river flowing past them.

The vista the windows offered lent an initial, albeit bewildering clue to the whereabouts in which he was waking. Like a hillside of meadows, meadows whose grasses were dove-gray stones, terra-cotta tiles and tawny thatches, tightly packed roofs sloped steeply downwards, like loaves of bread tumbling into a blue sky and distant, emerald forests. Here and there towers, arches, bells and belfries rose with smoking chimneys above these rooftop meadows, as here and there on the stone slates were grazing goats and small flocks of pecking chickens. As they were feathered acrobats of the clouds, swallows swooped and careened above these meadows, playing in the azure airs.

Slowly and vaguely, he came to the conclusion he was on a great height of the city, looking down upon its roofs cascading to its surrounding walls, and the fields and forests beyond.

But it was another corner of the room, a corner with an osier-woven chair, one with a green, velvety-covered seat that greeted his return to consciousness with a most surprising, most endearing pleasure. Upon the floor near this chair were leaned, like delicate figurines of glass, the fiddle and lute he had played in the Sickle Moon; the sunlight falling brightly upon them, as if strumming them with the golden fingers of its beams. And even more friendly and more dear, his satchel was hung by its strap over the chair, the sun finding the scars of its leather face, like the age-weathered countenance of a fisherman.

Despite the room's frugality, there was an overwhelming opulence that filled and sweetly ruled it. Its few furnishings were neat and ordered; varnished immaculate by the strong morning light. Even the motes of dust seemed to sparkle happily, as if dancing in this cove of human civility and care.

Making pleasant, and pervading all, were sweet aromas swimming through its air, mingling with the sunlight, and giving the room a kind of domestic sanctity; blessing it with the smells of baking bread. These smells, with the sunlight, conspired to seduce him like a narcotic, bidding him close his heavy eyes, but not fully releasing him to sleep, so that with a dreaming ear, he dreamily listened.

.....the door left partly ajar, admitting the luscious smells, passing steps, whispers.....occasional flights of warm, buoyant laughter.....words his brain could make little sense of in the underworld of pain, fever and dream.......

...... "Father, you must take Federico to the early market tomorrow morning, when the millers send their wagons from the river. You must load him with bags of flour. Dough needs flour, papa, even like bake houses need bread.....oh, and a bundle of the good oak and hickory faggots, and the rowan kindling the 'contadini' bring...... "

...... "O the devil, that mule is as stubborn and lazy as I am! Either he will be the death of me or I will be the death of him."......

..... "We need to eat papa. We need to keep both you and Federico stubborn, and with that stubbornness, alive."......

"Why alive?"

"So that you can kill each other!"

"But that is so very early, daughter, no one about but the crepe-draped widows praying for the husbands they harped to an early grave. Besides,

the gates won't open to the millers if there's a Florentine seen snoring in the bushes, for as you know a snoring Florentine is no less than an arrow in the back."

"I think my father is out of sorts this morning, because I think my father drank wine until the moon climbed the mountains last night......."

"I like plum wine, and for that matter I like the moon climbing the Apennines. It makes me feel young. It makes me want to bray and kick like Federico. It makes me think of your mother."

"It makes your head full of webs and dreams....."

"Age has nothing more than webs and dreams."

"And plum wine?....."

"Have I told you how.....?"

"Once for every biscuit I've burned my fingers on since I was young enough to get them burned!"

....."How your mother and I would watch the moon rise over the mountains and into the stars in that window, that very window in the parlor near the hearth....."

"Yes papa, and how you kissed and danced....."

...... "And then proceeded to happily play and maul......"

"I think you are a depraved old man, one who drinks plum wine until it spills from your gills, until you are tottery and silly, and who I worry to no end about returning through the streets and climbing the stairs when the taverns close."

"Plum wine and my depravity gave me an angel of a daughter....."

"You mean the angel with a sway hip and a limp?"

"I mean the one that teaches Heaven to sing, and for whom I will wake early tomorrow morning and take that stinking, flea-bitten, thoroughly abominable creature, stubborn as Jove, to the market for."

"Oh, that angel! The one with the broken wing, that loves her papa more than anything else in the world!"

And again, waking to sunlight, the swimming aromas of baking bread, and the happy banter and chatter of words.

...... "Papa, you were at the taverns late again last night. I heard you climbing the steps and serenading mama's ghost when I woke to stoke the ovens."

"I like your mama's ass, always have, even now, after she's been dead for all these years."

"Papa, please be serious. I was worried."

"What can I say? I like plum wine, and looking at plump pretty things."

"Mama's ghost, papa, she could be listening. Besides, I do not like to be left alone with our patient. He's slept for two days, and what if......"

"Yes, and you've looked in on him each five minutes, day and night for those two days. You're an angel of mercy with a flour-pasted face. And as far as your mother's lovable old ghost, she knows my wicked heart. She married it and proceeded to dog it, only to foolhardily forgive it a million times over. Ghost, or a box of bones, she knows she's the only one I could ever love. Her memory has made a eunuch of me.

Besides, daughter, if I had not been in the tavern three nights ago, that whore haunt of a tavern hole where you found me, I could not have brought the gypsy fiddler home with me. He may have bled to death in that hell-hole of an alley."

"Still, I think I will be afraid when he wakes. They say he is very wild, very wild and strong, that he lived in the forest for a long while, that he can be very savage....."

..... "and very sweet. I have heard him play and sing in the taverns. He plays any instrument given to him. Makes them purr like kittens and warble like golden-throated canaries....growl like bitch dogs when he wants them to: fiddles, lutes, mandolins, citterns, accordions. Why the good fellow even sings....has a beautiful singing voice.....and he can dance.....the women always vie to be his partner........

And as far as wild and strong, 'bravo'! One man against six in that wretched alley, like Daniel in the lion's den, only he, not they, was the lion den that left the bastards chewed and mauled. Even the knife did not stop him. They say he continued to break heads against walls even with its blade stuck in his side, like a harpoon in a whale. Ha! A Daniel, a lion's den, a harpooned whale all in one!"

"O papa, he is one who has lived his life in the hills and forests. Just look at his beard and his long hair....."

....."thick and gold, to make a Roman courtesan pine....."

....."And he has the worst kind of reputation, a reputation of seducing many women, even married ones."

"Pah! What some of the jealous hussies call seduction, others call flattery and courtship. Besides, he is the seduced, not the seducer. The women flock to the fellow like moths to a flame."

"Well, I still do not understand why you brought him here, why one of the other good Samaritans could not have......"

"…..*You know very well why, daughter*….."

"*Father, please, he may be awake. He could even be listening.*"

"*I brought him here because I recognized him as the man who called out nice pretty things to you from the street when he bought biscuits, even warbling like a bird and asking you to come sing with him!*"

"*I do not remember such a one…….*"

"…..*and played his fiddle in the Piazza Lucia not more than a week ago…..played it till dawn, directly below the bread window, with a sweetness to make the angels swoon…….*"

"*I do not remember……*"

"…..*made the damned gargoyles weep with its tenderness……*"

"*O father, please, he is vulgar, a shameless skirt-chaser, the rake and wife-stealer of the city.*"

"*Yes, a vulgar, shameless skirt-chasing rake of a brute that brought a blush to my daughter's cheek and a sparkle to her eye.*"

"*It is even rumored that he has tried to seduce a Bride of Christ in the hilltop convent.*"

"*Good! I am sure God would rather have his brides plucked, trussed and happy, than unplucked and shrewish!*"

"*Papa!*"

"*A roll in the hay would do 'em good, give 'em something to cluck and cackle about in their prayers!*"

"*Papa, we must prepare the oat cakes for Signora Bertoldi. You know how she complains if her cakes are not ready when she comes.*"

"*To hell with Signora Bertoldi! If the old hag bickers and banters again she'll receive horse-bread instead of oat cakes…..maybe even a chamber pot, one flavored with plum wine!……I'm talking about the shameless, winebibbing, womanizing…..you know, that 'savage' fellow with good red blood running like good red wine in his veins…..who sings for my angel and pays for his cakes with ribbons and pretty words…..the one who caterwauled like a rutting cat beneath our window in the middle of the night, singing and strumming a fiddle with enough pain and sweetness to wake the graves…… takes a hell of a heart in a hell of a man to be that alive, to feel that kind of pain*"……

"*Father, please; I do not want to have a barbarian for a sweetheart.*"

…..*"that handsome golden lion with a six inch wound in his side sleeping on the cliff of death, and probably perdition in the room above…*"

"*Papa, please, you know what such men, this one in particular…..*"

"Yes I do, and I applaud him! Proud to have him under my roof! Hope he's tickled a thousand pretty bellies........"

"Papa, your wicked tongue! Mama's ghost!"

"Fiddles! She's cheering me on, knowing how brief, and tenuously precious is this little promenade beneath the sun and stars! This is a bake house, not a nunnery!

"Neither is it a brothel!"

"My daughter's no nun....."

"No, she's a drab!"

"By God an angel!"

"A crippled mangled one, who fell to earth for a happy spinsterhood, to take care of the child of her papa in his drunken dotage!"

"You shy like a horse, or better yet, like your kind. Did you not tell me you thought you once knew this man?"

"I do not remember. No, I think I was mistaken."

"Did you not tell me that you thought he might be a kind man you met when I was called to that devil bloody battle.....one who had nicknames like 'golden lion' and 'blond gypsy', whose real name was a common name, a religious name, a woman's name... .. 'Maria' I think it was?"

"Papa, that was many years ago, and I am no longer sure."

"The man you said you lent your mother's lute to, who played it sweetly, so sweetly you heard your mother singing from it with her tears."

"Besides, he was a kind man, but also a brawler and a womanizer."

"Look me in the eye and tell me the truth, a thing your gender seems to struggle mightily with."

"The truth is that I am a cripple, not a nun, a whore or an angel. The truth is that you and mama's ghost are badgering and bullying me. The truth is that I want Signora Bertoldi out of my hair....and yes, I think I may have once met this man many years ago.....and he made mama sing from her lute very sweetly, so sweetly that I.....and yes, like my incorrigible sweet papa, I think he has a special heart."

.....He did not know whether they were the voices of fever or dream, of the dead or the living.....the quips and banter of their dialogues, the homely goodness of the man's tender gruffness and the young woman's gay flights of laughter.....washing over him, intermingling with the smile of sunlight and the tender smells of baking bread.....the pain in his side tearing him apart like sharp teeth.....and yet soothed by a human loveliness......a human acceptance and embrace.......

.....the bread, the bright sunlight, his lute and fiddle, like loyal grooms standing ready and polished against the sunny wall, duteously waiting for their master's return....his touch that would make them live again.......

..... 'Katrinika, Katrinika'.....he did not remember one with such a beautiful name as 'Katrinika'....a cripple with a limp named 'Katrinika'.... or did he?..... yes, now..... snow, blood, the dead man at his feet.....her dark eyes and her pronounced limp, a young girl, a creature broken in body, but burning true.....and a yellow bandanna, her yellow bandanna that she had worn like the women he remembered in his youth......the bandanna she had unbound from her hair and had given him.....that he had kept in his satchel.....the satchel that was now hanging from this chair........

.....the dead man, the man he had stabbed with his own hands staring through his soul, as with laughter.....and the dark eyes swimming with sweetness, that had not condemned him for it......and the words, the sweet words she had said to him, that had entered his soul with the little kiss she had given his cheek.....even with the man he had murdered at their feet..... words that had come from her young prettiness.....words that had touched him very deeply.....words that he could not remember........

.....but now he must sleep.....the pain, the sunlight, the smells and whispers of comfort and goodness.....yes, he must sleep......and then perhaps he would remember what the young girl had said to him.......

* * *

IT WAS on the fourth morning that sleep and delirium made their retreat, and his consciousness victoriously returned to sunlight, the aromas of baking bread, and the dull, patient, aching throbs of pain in his side.

But there was more than pain and hunger that had woke him. As he had at last breached from the depths of fever back to a world of sun and clouds, he had heard something, or rather *felt* something about him, something that he would come to remember as a kind of whir and rustle of wings; a kind of music, as bees droning about nectar-heavy flowers.

Without lifting his head from the pillow, Brother Maria opened his eyes. His disjointed memories, now gathering and assembling, now telling him where he was: *a sunny room, safe with his lute and fiddle, and his bag of things; a room filled with sweet smells, sunlight, and a warm, genuine friendliness.*

Not lifting his head from the pillow, or in any way stirring, he saw at once that he was not alone. A piece of bread, a small bowl of gruel, and a cup of water were at his bedside, and the one who had brought them was now very near, standing on a chair, tautly stretched and reaching, carefully watering the bright-faced flowers above him.

It was the kitchen girl, the same that he had cajoled and teased when she had lowered the basket with his biscuits from the window with the green shutters. Yes, it was the same girl, his surmise punctuated true by the bright red kerchief binding her hair.

He remembered hearing her father call her '*my angel*', but it was a pet name coined in a father's fond heart, for there was nothing of the angelical about her. Still, this was not to say she was uncomely, but rather without a flamboyancy of beauty; as might seem a daisy at the feet of a garden's bed of roses.

She was dressed neatly, cleanly, freshly, in a dun smock and a milk-white blouse, whose bloomy sleeves lent the illusion of feathers about her arms. This was accented by the geranium-red kerchief binding up her hair, of which only a few strands had escaped to tell of their raven dark truth. In the first haze and blur of his waking, she indeed seemed a red-crested bird among the bright flowers above him.

She was more slight than voluptuous; modestly, and not richly or sensuously endowed. As she stretched to the flowers, he could see that the swells of her breasts were small, as they were the nests of wrens, not doves. Her shoulders seemed broad and strong, like a young boy's, and although her loose-hanging blouse cheated the eye of her waist, it did not cheat it so much that he could not see that her back tapered trimly into its hollow, before giving way to her hips: one that slightly bulged, attesting the defect of her birth.

Stepping down from the chair, and then deftly placing it back in its place, she went to the windows, and stood in the butter-golden sunlight. Having no idea that her patient was awake, this gave the patient the leisure to more closely study her.

It was her face that the eye fixed upon, but this too was plain, unadorned by either nature or by the hand of vanity. The brow was nearly concealed by the kerchief, but her ears peeked free of it, rabbit-like and dainty. Her cheeks were slightly raised, slightly Slavic, and her nose, although not grossly, was distinctly aquiline; canceling her from those of regal or sculpted beauty. In the bright wash of the sunlight could be seen otherwise unseen freckles, as if the last vestiges of girlhood were reluctant to take their leave of her. Her skin was more bronze than olive, a bronze that the sun would probably ripen into a soft brown with age.

There was nothing lush or sensual about her mouth, but in conformity with the rest of her, her lips were velvety full and carnation pink; and there was that about them that told of never having given or taken kisses; and yet in no way would be afraid of them. They were simple, honest lips, lips that knew no tricks, and would not be persuaded into learning them; warm, not cold, but like a flower receiving rain, in no way unwilling to receive the gift of kisses.

Her lashes were long, dark, and daintily filliped; her eyes deep, dark, and glossy, as if moist with a dew of tears that would not dry. The genius behind them was not quick like a bird's eyes, but still as pools; not aggressively hunting the world before them, but in their quiet stillness, receiving its secrets and its wonders.

She was altogether plain, plainness so plain it seemed to speak a deeper beauty, one that spoke candidly, truly; not in flattery to the eye, but in a pleasant colloquy with the heart. Standing in the sun she seemed a rapturous bird, for there was a music that warbled through each part of her; as if she had captured the passing moment, and it was the reason of her being to pour it back to the green leaves of the forest. Though statue still, she fluttered; though silent, she sang.

Her modesty was her gown and jewels, and this was the child-like appeal, the charm that breathed forth finer humors. Her beauty hid from the eye, exhaling fresh breaths, not a sensual perfume; a beauty not displayed, but waiting to be found. There was something of the noble, even the heroic in her, as if despite the defect that had made her life's straggler, the pride in her struggle gave her victory in its races, There was a presence about her, one that no adornment could make its own.

The sum of her plain features, with the pathos evinced by her defect, enshrined her with sweetness, even a kind of glory the heart could not be blind to. Her sweetness urged pursuit, but promised no finding; as there was no end to the echoes of such a simple song.

Yes, of course, he remembered her.....yes, now it came back to him..... she was the servant girl that had lent him the beautiful 'cobza', the lute that was decorated as he remembered the lutes of his youth......one and the same, she was the bread girl, the one that he had flirted with in the window with green shutters.....the same young girl that had urged him away after his fight with the woman's husband, and the other men with cudgels and knives in their hands........

.....yes, she was the crippled servant girl he had once asked to dance, that young girl now the young woman standing before him in the cascade of sunlight....the same that had given him his satchel, and then urging him to flee for his life.....and he racing away, only to return to her, as she to him......the unbinding of her yellow bandanna.....and the peck of her kiss on his bloodied cheek.....and her whisper, like that of a grateful beggar child, one that he remembered, nay, treasured as he fled and wandered through the forests....somehow more poignant having come from such young lips:..... 'I love you blond man, I will always love you'.....

He began to lift his head from the pillow, his effort eliciting a soft involuntary moan, one that startled his nurse, and turned her quickly to him with a face unlike the face he had watched bathe in the sunlight. All traces of its simple plainness were gone, and it was now a-boil with sentiments too many and too ardent to be at once discerned; shyness, fright, worry, embarrassment, compassion, duty; its simplicity plundered by a storm of conflicting elements.

"Oh, sir, you are awake! I must fetch father! You must not move, the doctor said you must not move! I have left bread and gruel at your side..... you must be hungry, yes, very hungry.....are you not hungry?.....You see you have slept for nearly three days.....I will fetch father.....but you must not attempt to stand, the doctor gave strict orders that you must not try to stand....."

She said these things as she circled the bed, and made ready to depart, and as she did Maria realized what had been the sound of whirring wings he had imagined. Although the encumbrance of her defect was pronounced, there was a certain petite-ness, even a lyricism in her steps, so that she seemed not to limp, but to skip and dance before the audience of the eye; as she was buoyed by her spirit more than she was bound by her body. Rather than a hopping, broken winged sparrow, she glided like a swallow, each part of her rhyming with every other part; her handicap the jewel of her perfection.

"Please, miss, a moment please....."

And with this she halted her departure, and without lifting her eyes, quietly paused and partly, but not fully turned to him.

"You see, I do not know where I am, or how I came to be here. I do not know who has been, and continue to be my caretakers."

Rather than with a direct gaze, her reply was interspersed with quick, furtive, sidelong glances.

"It is a house, sir, my parent's house, a house where bread is baked and sold. That is the smell I am sure you smell, the smell from the bread baking down the stairs in the ovens."

She paused before speaking again, as if the patient both wanted and deserved to know more, and although she did not want it, the obligation was for her to further explain.

"My father and some other men brought you here. You were greatly hurt, sir, cut very deeply with a knife. It was four men who brought you up the stairs. A doctor's hands cleaned, sewed, and bandaged your wound. He said you were very fortunate, sir, and that you were strong and should mend with rest and time."

Seeing it was his turn to fill the awkwardness, Maria spoke.

"Yes, I suppose I was very fortunate at that. The knife missed my heart, or so it seems......but I think I was more blest than fortunate to have been placed in such kind hands. Your father, and I think his daughter are responsible for saving my life. As soon as I am strong, perhaps tomorrow morning, I will leave, but I will be forever grateful."

To this the girl, without lifting her eyes, replied with a soft, almost inaudible gasp.

"I do not think that very wise, sir, perhaps not even possible. You see the knife went very deep, and there was a great loss of blood."

"But I have no money to pay you for my keep. You see I earn money by making music in the inns and taverns.....I have a room....."

With this the girl stepped from the door and began a circuit of needless busying about the room. As she spoke Maria saw that her eyes welled with tears, a show of her heart she was helpless to staunch. *Yes, these were the eyes, the dark eyes he had looked into that day in the cold and snow, their deep still wells mirroring a depth as vast as seas and stars.*

"No sir, you must not sir. The house is very large and now that my brother has gone, and my mother is in Heaven, only my father and I live in it. We have a garden, chickens, a goat and hutch of rabbits. We have plenty of bread, meat and greens to eat. You may stay here until you are strong."

"But I have a room."

"Respectfully sir, you do not. My father went to the tavern where the incident occurred, and paid the small outstanding rent you owed on the room you rented over it. The keeper is a good man with a good heart, and

said kind things about you, but he told my father he could no longer rent the room to you, fearing further bloodshed and incident on and about his property. Father took the liberty of collecting your few things from the room, and brought them here....the kind keeper making a gift of the lute and fiddle for you.....because he said they would never sing for another.....they would rot with loneliness and sorrow for the hands that had taught them to sing, I think were his words......"

"You are very kind, and I am indebted to both you and your father."

The girl looked away, and in the ensuing pause made pregnant with the familiarity both were unsure the other recognized, or if they did, were afraid to admit, there came two soft sharp raps on the door, followed by the thin, good-natured face of an elderly man.

"Well well well, look at the rowdy one, too rowdy to stay in the grave!"

Brightening with the comic relief, the girl rushed to her father as he entered the room, and lifted a kiss to his bending face.

"Father, you must not say such things! They are irreverent. He is our guest, and still weak with his wounds. You must be nice, and not full of your needling little jokes. And mother, remember mother......"

"And you must remember Signora Bertoldi. The old harridan is in the street, as usual, honking and hissing beneath our window. The fat old goose wants her crumbs to peck."

And then under his breath:

.....״either that or to be peckered."

Hearing, but pretending not to, this flustered the girl, as she was torn between the probity she wished to show the convalescent, and the allegiance she must show her customer. After a quick skipping step towards the door she stopped, and looked for the first time directly at the bedridden; her face now suffused with a tender, almost a supernatural care and softness, like snow melting into sunlight.

"Please sir, you must not feel obliged to leave.....it is not wise.....and you are no burden to us at all.....we've bread, chickens, a garden.....and mind not my father, his tongue is waspish, though its sting is sweet......"

"Daughter, the honking old harridan in the streets....."

"Yes father, of course father.....Signora Bertoldi.....the doctor, well, he will look at your wounds now that you are awake sir....and I will come with more bread and soup and any little thing you need.....there's a bell at your side......"

"Daughter, the hag's almond cakes, and if not almond cakes, a mess of

sow thistle.....I'll stuff it down her throat with my own hands....."

"Oh father, please......."

"The hag, daughter, the hag......."

And with this the girl looked one last desperate time at the patient, her face full of fret, hurry and genuine concern, and with want of words, words that she had neither the composure nor the time to form, rushed out of the room.

The man went to the door, and as preparing for a private confidence, closed it tightly shut, after which he returned and stood at the foot of the bed, directly over his patient.

He was tall, thin and erect, with wild wisps of moustache, and a thick crest of gray uncombed hair. His face, unlike his speech, was entirely free of causticity, and his eyes looked with a gentle, penetrating benignity down upon him.

"Have you pain?"

His voice was tender and intimate, and at once disarming with friendliness.

"Some, yes, but if I lay still....."

"Are you bleeding?"

"A little I think, yes, a little."

"Your color is good, and your eyes are clear and bright. I will see to it that the doctor will inspect and re-dress your wound shortly; that is if the rascal did not become too drunk and lecherous in one of his whore haunts last night."

"I must thank you sir for the things you have done for me....."

"The bastards had it coming. An ugly, brainless, ball-less bunch of louts. Ha! You throttled a litter of 'em, son, left 'em carved and groaning, peppered the bastards good."

"I must confess I was drunk....."

The man good-naturedly shook his head and chuckled. He turned to the window, and stood precisely where his daughter had stood, the sun showering the gray wilds of his hair with a golden glory. His speech suggested an educated mind, and was colored with levity.

"All for that little bauble beneath a woman's skirt.....not to say I've not sued a knee to its mystical throne myself.....ah yes, that little throne that men kneel, beg and wage monstrous wars for.....the same old story, you know the one that launched a thousand ships to bring back that Helen bitch and her sluttery.....as if the flower each fellow goes a-maying for was the whole damned Roman empire..... No, I've gone soldiering for the same

little queen myself. Silly and ridiculous, but ridiculously valiant in its own way I suppose, a thing in a man's blood he must obey, to sail seas and climb mountains, even die for......its prize the holy grail of every son of Adam..... crusaders as well as thieves, kings as well as beggars, every last damn one of our male kind....'Bravissimo' my boy! You left the bastards carved, shamed and sorry, and I suspect at least one of them, cuckolded."

"But how is it that you found me and brought me here? I do not understand, and I do not think I know......"

The elderly man held up his hand, stopping him mid-question, even while continuing to look serenely out the window.

"It was not I, but she. After your caterwauling serenade of lovely drunken madness beneath our window some nights ago.....well, she somehow heard.....you know the hearts of women, smell mischief like a wolf smells blood.....she somehow heard of the brawl and fetched me in a nearby tavern.....a sordid little nook with a few benches and barrels, and a few sagging old hussies, looking more for what's in a man's pockets than to crow the rooster in his loins. She was full of worry, a woman's prescience, and a heart that all the gold in Solomon's mines could not buy."

There came a pause, one in which wry humor was replaced with reverence, the mask of jest lowered in the bright sunlight, leaving a thin aging face awash with a father's love. From that unmasking came a whisper that brooked on prayer.

"Do you know what a miracle a beautiful woman is Maria?.....may I call you Maria?..... a beautiful woman whose beautiful heart keeps the memory of a man in it through the harsh weathers and wicked turns of this accursed world? She gives a man's heart a song. She gives it a reason. She gives it its place and moment beneath the sun."

After another pause the old man turned to Maria, his face as animated as it had waxed stony with homily.

"Now let's have a look at that nasty wound. You see I did not drink too much plum wine last night, and man to man, although I've lusted for a thousand sluts and sirens, the only woman I have ever lain with was my wife.....and, well, you see I learned a thing or two about surgery in the bloody bishop's bloodthirsty army, and I thought as long as I cleaned your wound, sewed it shut, and bandaged it with my own two hands, your doctor might just have the temerity of having a little peek at his handiwork."

. . . .

. . . .

CHAPTER FIFTEEN

THE YELLOW BANDANNA
PART II

Late Summer to early Winter, 1340

THE first days and weeks of Brother Maria's convalescence were very pleasant. After the many years of his desultory wandering, and his two years of dissipated tavern life in the city, it felt luxuriously good to be so waited upon and cared for. For the greater part of a fortnight he was bedridden, and was attended to by the bake girl, Katrinika, and her father, the wine-loving, former military surgeon who had expertly stitched and dressed his wound.

In the large sunny room he was given time to leisurely dream, and like a miser fearful of losing his riches, to count those dreams with the memories he was afraid he might lose: painting his mind with remembered moons, storms, and lovers. He played his lute, and more and more hummed, or softly sang songs he remembered from his childhood; songs that seemed to appear from an unknown part of him, stepping from his past like old acquaintances.

He did not see his custodians often, but when he did they were entirely polite, kind and gracious. The old doctor examined and redressed his wound daily, and was very encouraged about the gash's rapid healing, all but marveling at Maria's hardihood. His visits were normally in the mid-morning, and they were filled with wry humor and scurrilous anecdotes about rascals, drinkers and murderers, as well as spicy tales of lechers, cuckolds and adulterers. After the nights he drank to drunkenness, his visits came in the afternoon, and his manners were rusty and glum, but never rude. He never spoke of his daughter again, nor made any allusion to the former alliance between her and his patient.

Katrinika was rarely seen, and when she was, she remained distant and taciturn. Many times she brought trays of food and the incidentals of his requests to his room, but more times than not, when he was sleeping, or when her father was examining him. When he was strong enough to stand, she discreetly left his things on a table just outside his door, without entering the room at all. Some days he did not see her; and others only when he feigned sleep, and with a peeping eye watched her tidy about the room, like a linnet fluttering in its cage. When they spoke it was brief; polite, but not warm; sincere, but not engaging or committal. Neither made mention of the bloody episode that had introduced them, and had consequently, wordlessly bound them to each other; perhaps thinking, if not hoping the other had forgotten it.

He was no longer privy to the currents of their whispers, or at least to the greater part of them. Now that he was fully conscious he supposed his hosts were more cautious, speaking out of earshot, or only when his door was fully closed. Still, there were times when he could not help but be an eavesdropper, when sometimes late at night the rants and songs of the drunken doctor broke through all cautions. At first Maria was sure it was a guest the old man was addressing with rue and tears, but he eventually concluded it was the beloved ghost of his departed wife.

"Georgiana, the moon is rising, climbing the mountain like a shiny shekel into the forest of the stars.....the forest full of your sister Angels! O Sweetheart! Let us dance before the window as the pretty moon rises......"

At times they seemed a conjuration.

"Come to me my lovely! Step from the shadows to my arms! Your beauty makes a gown of death's shroud, roses of death's webs! Come, I need your sad sweet face to lie upon my shoulder! Oh, what is the sun, the sea....what is God without you my beautiful darling?......."

At other times they seemed a passionate confession, one full of heartrending tears and a knightly love and honor.

"I've ever been true, Georgiana, I swear, even in the war when the others bought whores in the alleys and on the wharves, even when the tarts sidled up to us in the taverns and the tents, offering their bodies for bread and porridge.....oh, how could I grunt with a swine after I have sung with an Angel?........"

One night there came a hubbub that neither doors nor walls could successfully muffle. It came from the large kitchen with the bread ovens, almost directly below Maria's room. Hearing his name in the heated bluster, Maria struggled from his bed, knelt down and pressed his ear to the floor, that he might hear each word. The doctor was extremely drunk, and though his daughter tried to calm and quiet him, he would have none of her consolations, and continued to rant about things that touched Maria dearly.

"….*But why do you not speak with him? He is not a brute, a wild Etruscan come from the caves and forests!……*"

"……*Father, please, it is late, and you have drunk much too much wine! He will hear you!…..*"

"…..*he's not a leper with boils and a bell!…..*"

"…..*No, he is a brawler, a drinker, and a silver-tongued seducer…..*"

"…..*Then for God's sake, why not be seduced?……*"

"*Papa, please go to bed. There is no moon, and mama's ghost does not want to dance tonight! And she will not be happy if you wake your patient…..you must remember she did not like you to drink so, and she did not like for you to shout and curse…….*"

"*O Georgiana, our daughter, our beautiful daughter, our little Katrinika, she whose face is your face, that is the moon itself…..I'll not have her wed a squeaking mouse, a cracker nibbler, a whey-faced eunuch…..no silly, grinning, fearful wag of a thing….no piping peewit…..I'd rather have him be a concupiscent dog of the alleys than a pet weasel crawling over the ivory shoulders of a Caesar's concubine……*"

"*Papa, please, you have had too much to drink…..*"

"…..*rather he have a dream in a broken heart than greed in an itching palm, fire in his loins than good-mannered cunning in his pate…..rather have him have a heart with a man in it, mad and barbarous, than be some circus bear dolled in ribbons…..and our angel, our Katrinika…..I'd rather she be a scullion mating with a soldier in a pantry, a milkmaid with a stable boy in a stable stall, a tavern fiddler…..*"

"*Father, no!*"

"…..*than to lay on her back for a lumbering, monkey-brained fool……rather he have fangs, growl and bloody kill in his heart than a tail wagging between his legs, and that with a pretty ribbon tied to it……*"

"*Papa, the moon is rising, and mama is waiting near the window to dance. She has combed her long hair, and has a beautiful flower in it. She is waiting to fall into your arms.*"

There was another phenomenon that began to occur during the first weeks of his convalescence, randomly at first, and then with more frequency. It was learned where the gypsy fiddler of the *Sickle Moon* had been taken after the bloody brawl; that indeed he was alive and healing in the tall old bake house in the *Piazza Lucia*. This news was embraced not only by those who had slept in his arms, but by those anonymous ones who had given kisses to him in the dark of alcoves, arcades and doorways; even by those who had once laid their heads on his shoulder as he had danced with them, or who had dared once to bring playful toes to him beneath a table; or whose hearts had quickened when, passing beneath their windows, his blue eyes and golden smile had fallen upon them.

When with knocks on the bake house door these affectionate ones were told that the convalescent could not be disturbed, they balked, and refused to be denied. They proceeded to make requests for breads and biscuits beneath the window, and when the basket was lowered with their requests, it was returned with both their payments, and tokens of their hearts as well: flowers, earrings, ribbons, gloves, amorously perfumed notes, tresses of their hair; even silken slippers that, like vases, held little bouquets, or as often, a beautiful rose.

When the old doctor would learn of these offerings from these in-fatuated women, he erupted into great guffaws of laughter; and when he made his morning visits, he seemed flushed through and through with a ruddy humor, and with a strong smell of wine upon his breath.

But his daughter was different; remaining courteous, but inacces-sible. Although it was she who brought the gifts with his food, or placed them separately on the small table outside his door, she did not speak of them, or only with the fewest of words, and they, without the least hint of sentiment: '*Sir, a visitor brought a gift for you*'; or, '*This ribbon was placed in the basket with the biscuit money today. I think it was meant for you, sir;*' or '*When the signorina paid for her oat cakes, she placed rosebuds in the basket, and they in a silk slipper. I think they are for you, Maria sir.*'

At the insistence of his kind hosts, Maria stayed on at the bake house, even after he had left his bed and had begun to walk about; up and down the steep flight of stairs, and even into the streets at nightfall. He was very grateful for the kindness that was being shown him, for although his wound had closed, and was healing steadily and surely, its seriousness had left his side very tender, and his strength still lacked its full robustness. He was not yet ready to play his fiddle in raucous taverns, nor was he prepared to endure the wandering he was resolved to resume. The first cool nights had come. He knew he was yet unfit to endure winter's hardships that were soon to follow.

A new solitude settled over him. He stayed a great deal in his room, composing rhymes and lyrics, and playing melodies on his lute. When he left the house to walk in the streets, it was always as night's curtain was falling. He avoided familiar places and old acquaintances, especially the taverns where he had caroused and fiddled. He did not visit the women he had loved, or those he knew were desirous of loving him. He wanted to be alone; alone with the world that had slept beneath the hot sun, only to wake with the evening star; a world full of towers and arches, mazy streets and stairways, a world waking with a vast creature-kind of lions and griffons, angels and gargoyles, all waking, trying to twist free from the sunny tombs of their stone prisons.

His desire for solitude and anonymity led him into the far skirts of the city, and eventually the country-side. It was a time of truce, and the guards, some of which were old drinking companions, let him pass for an hour outside the gates. It was good to see open spaces again; to see and smell gardens and orchards heavy with ripening fruits, frothy fields of grain and starlit meadows with sheep and horses.

On one of his expeditions he ventured farther, drawn to a field brightened by several great fires, and ringing with loud laughter and song. Approaching as near as he deemed wise, he saw a camp of vagrants, vagrants with wagons, tents and horses; vagrants that spoke another tongue. He learned that it was a band of wandering folk that pitched their camp each year in this very place, mending baskets, tools and kettles, and working in the fields until the frost came and the harvest was completed. Fascinated with these wanderers, one night Maria climbed a tree, from which he could see their flamboyant dress and uninhibited revelry more clearly. A great thrill passed through his heart. This was his kind of dance and music! Its abandon resonated with a deep part of him.

Smitten with autumn, the harvest, and this gay tribe of wanderers, one night he returned to his room in the bake house, and wrote down a few random words. He titled them: 'Harvest'.

.....THE bearded wheat, the ripe red apples,
The press, the threshing-floor, the maidens' feet

Dyed purple sweet, dancing in
the grapes' dark blood,
An offering, a surrendering of
A season, a moment's reason lain before
A mother's smile, the sickle moon
Her earring, silver sparkling,
All dreams before her sweetness swooned,
Begging love's wound be pardoned,
As the seeds of stars, forever bleeding, falling,
Replenishing, like tears of spring,
Upon the fertile furrows of grave and garden......

There was still another development that came in the weeks and months of his gradual convalescence. One early evening there came a knock upon his door, and the doctor made an entrance, one that was uncustomary for that hour of the day. He came with an unlooked for invitation.

"Maria, would you like to drink some plum wine with me tonight? I know some little taverns, some little kennels where we could spend an hour or two unnoticed. You spend a great deal of time by yourself, dreaming and mooning about. As your doctor, I think it would be good for you. We could have a nice little chat."

Maria warmly thanked him, but declined his request. In respect to his deferral the old man nodded politely, and without further urging left. But two nights later there came another knock on his door, and when the doctor stood before him and began to utter his same invitation, Maria smiled, and agreed before the words had escaped his mouth.

And thus began a new chapter in Maria's recovery, and indeed his life, one in which he was no longer alone, but now befriended by a good-natured, witty, although highly unlikely companion. Their friendship and outings served a number of purposes, not the least, providing a shield from the amorous advances of women. Thinking Maria was with an elderly friend, or even his father, his would-be wooers demurred, and though their eyes lingered and played upon him, they respectfully stayed in the shadows, and without overture, left him alone.

He felt comfortable with the old doctor, as the doctor obviously felt comfortable with him. After all, it was the old man's tender, practiced, albeit palsied hands that had saved his life. This friendship led to unfettered conversations; conversations that touched upon sundry subjects.

287

As the wine warmed their bloods and loosed their tongues, Maria confided to the doctor things he had never told another. He told him about the life he once led as a monk; the breaking of his vows, and his dishonorable desertion from the abbey. He told him of his friend, Father Giovanni, a friend he had loved, and often thought about, even now. He told him of his wanderings; his hungers and hardships, his many toils, fights and lovers.

In turn the doctor spoke of his childhood, youth and education, and his conscripted duty in the military. He spoke tenderly and passionately about the courtship of his wife, and his absolute devotion to his daughter. But more than even his love for his wife and Katrinika, when the plum wine had set his blood afire he spoke of an era when he was a young man, an era that he spoke of with uncharacteristic gravity, even grisly horror.

"*There was nothing, nothing, nothing! We ate horses, dogs, rats, mice, worms......we ate goddamned nettles, bark, the droppings of dogs and the manure of pigs.....we dug with our fingers for roots, grass. slugs.....there were those who opened graves and fed off the bones of the dead.....cracked open skulls on stones.....ate the brains of the dead as they were bowls of polenta ......*

.....and then that thing.....O Georgiana my love, forgive me!.....a thing not all of the prayers of the goddamned Holy Church, the arrows of Angels, the care of her drunkard husband protected her beautiful soul against.....that drunkard husband then going mad, giving away his own flesh and blood.....his very son.....you see I was haunted with her severed parts, dreamed of her beautiful head torn from her body.....and I tried..... you must believe me Maria, you must believe me I tried to find him, my flesh and blood that I had given away.....but he had been lost in the famines, and all of the illegitimates and orphans they had bred......."

On one occasion when the wine had set fire to the sleeping horrors of his memory, and he was worked into a rhetorical fever about the things he had seen, he paused, bent down his head to the table, and then like a corpse resurrecting from a grave, slowly raised it back to Maria.

"*.....and the wars, the fucking wars, O my son, Maria, Brother Maria, may I call you Brother Maria?.....Madonna!.....the mother-fucking wars!..... worse than famines......barons, nobles, knights, the blubbery, fat-assed bishops!.....one neither knows what side one is fighting on, or what one is* *fighting for......what crusade, family, city, emperor, pope.....Guelf or Ghibelline, Tatar or Saracen or Christian......a Charlemagne or Barbarosa, or the effeminate flummery of an Avignon pope....if your sword sheds blood to save some count's favorite chamber pot, or if in the end it is only to save one's own cock and balls......."*

And another time deliriously drunk, so drunk he bared the deepest treasure of his heart.

".....and how may such a lovely flower defend itself against such madness, against such fucking armies of bloodsucking sons-of-bitches?.....I am an old man, Maria, an old man with terrible ghosts tramping in his head.....you must protect her, Brother Maria.....you must protect her from the mad monster men call God!...yes, the flower of my heart from the bloody monster men kneel to, bleed and die for, that in their fear and bloody idiocy they pray to, worshiping a throne as airy as a summer cloud!"

These drunken, incoherent, fulminating rants, more times than not culminated their nights in the taverns. But on their walks through the empty narrow streets back to the bake house, the doctor became possessed with another spirit. He began to speak and sing to the ghost of his wife, even as he saw her in the dark windows, or on the balconies and *loggias* they were passing.

"Georgiana, O my sweet Georgiana, come to my arms my angel! Come again! I did not mean to leave you, to let you walk home alone! O God, forgive me! Forgive me my love!

And you stone lions and stone angels that watched the barbarous thing, but in your stone pride did not save her from such fucking dogs of barbarity! O you fucking, stone-hearted beasts and your fucking stone-hearted God!..... Forgive me Georgiana, forgive me my dearest love!"

There was another ramification of these drinking bouts with the wine-addicted, nerve-shattered old gentleman. They lent Maria nearness with his daughter.

She did not sleep before her father's return from the taverns, even though she rose before each dawn to fire the ovens and begin the morning flatbreads. When she heard their approach in the piazza, and particularly her father's serenades to his wife's ghost in the stairwell, she hobbled down the stairs, and without a word helped Maria guide the old man up and into the spacious kitchen. Refusing with a tantrum of curses and adolescent pleading to go to bed, the girl removed her father's hat, coat and boots. Sitting him before the fire she began to pet and fuss with him, sleeking the unruly crest of his hair with her fingers, kissing his cheeks, and as he was a child, coddling him with nonsense.

"Yes papa, mama knows that you love her. She knows that you did everything for her.....that you tried to save her.....that you killed dogs and cats, that you dug roots with your bare hands.....it was not your fault papa, and she does not blame you.....she is happy now, yes, her ghost is happy..... mama's ghost is no longer hungry, and she is very happy.....see, she is by the window, smiling, promising to dance with you tomorrow night when the moon climbs over the big mountain......"

The kitchen was always neat and clean, and softly aglow with the day's last embers in the two large ovens. Maria sat at the table; the doctor hopelessly lost in the superstitious wilds of his mind, and giving himself helplessly to his daughter's doting. It was these moments, softly aglow with the ovens' last embers and a daughter's love, that gave Maria the opportunity o study more closely the girl that had been such an enigmatic angel in his life.

He saw clearly that she was no longer a girl, rather a full-bodied woman, not so very many years younger than was he. Although she was ever wrapped in smocks and shawls, and her hair bound in kerchiefs and bandannas, there were moments when her endowments were not entirely concealed. When she leaned to kiss and pamper her father, or even when she placed a piece of bread or cup of milk on the table, Maria glimpsed the cleft between her breasts; its gentle river disappearing with mystery between the gentle hills it divided. In the ember-light he could see the swan-like slenderness of her throat, and once when her shawl slipped away, he saw how this slenderness rhymed with the slenderness of her shoulder. Once when she was knelt before the hearth, raking the embers into flames, her night skirt had lifted, exposing a delicate calf and knee. Sensing his stare, and realizing the thing that had fascinated him, she looked at him as she had not looked at him before, and in an instant almost lost to the eye, blushed; not like a simple servant girl, but like a woman whose modesty had been pleased, as much as it had been insulted.

Sitting in the shadows, he mused upon this lovely selfless creature as she nursed her father, the handicap of her limp being borne by the buoyant wings of her love.

What was her unassuming, but undeniable allure? It did not tease or prettily invite, but softly, patiently burning, thawed the heart awake with its warm presence. It neither riled the blood, nor taunted the beast in the loins. It spoke to something deeper, rarer, so that one could only think of honoring, and not molesting or possessing it. With the fragrance of a flower it invited one to bend to it, to drink its delicacy; but only at the beck of its perfume. It was not brazen, but shy; a plumage not brightly gay, but one that was painted in oneness with each season of the forest. She burned with a flame, but one that was veiled in a blush, a blush that told of something very kind; a smile that the eye could not see, and the soul could only vainly guess, and guessing, believe.

Free of her draperies, what were the shapes of her thighs and breasts? Where were her moles, scars, freckles? Had the nipples of her breasts ever been pricked awake by a man's hand or lips? Were the tufts in her secret nooks coarse or silky? And her lame hip? Did it own a special sensitivity, one more delicate than the other parts of her body? Had it ever pillowed a cheek? Had it ever been kissed?

.....What would it be like to know such a creature?.......

.....the perfumes of her body, the gentle reeks of the damp places beneath her arms and between her thighs.....the tastes of her toes, ears, navel.....Was her skin course, like a cat's tongue, or soft as a peach?.....How would sound the purrs and moans of her pleasure, the music of her whispers.....sighs of her dreams? breaths of her slumbers?.....What mystery was contained in the moist pink cavern of her mouth?........

There were some nights that the old doctor did not feel well or strong enough to visit the taverns. On these occasions Maria would depart from the bake house alone; taking long, solitary walks through the stony wilderness of streets. Upon climbing the stairs after his late returns, he would find a candle burning on a table, and with it a cup of milk, a biscuit and a piece of cheese laid out for him.

One night when he went out alone he drank a greater quantity of wine, waking his blood as it had not since his tavern fight. The wine woke deep, lusty desires inside him: the need to sow and be harvested; the need to love and be loved by a woman. He walked by several doors where he knew his knock would be welcomed by arms and kisses, only at the last to refrain from those knocks. He started towards the brothels, but soon turned about, preferring to climb the steep old stairs to a candle, a biscuit and a cup of milk; and the lovely, unseen presence he was sure placed them there. It was then that he wanted to run back into the *piazza*, bend back his head and howl at the closed shutters of the bread window above him: *"I am lonely for you, beautiful lady! Yes, this savage man has a lonely heart, and he needs your heart to fill his loneliness!"*

But the thought of going to her room, and with a soft knock and whisper confessing his need to hold, and be held by her sweetness was a thing he could not do. No, not for anything could he do such a thing. Instead, he sought out another lover. He went to his room, and returned to the parlor and its pale firelight with his lute. There he began to gently strum and softly sing.

.....she would tell her lovely woman secrets to him.....yes, by softly caressing her strings, she would give him her dreams, even as he would give his to her......he would caress over her naked body, and she would yield her secret dreams to him.......

In the ensuing weeks, when summer began to bid its farewell with cool nights and crisp leaves, this scenario continued. On those nights when he caroused with the doctor, and the old man returned drunk and muttering to his daughter's doting care, Maria would sit in the shadows, dreaming in the lovely web that this girl's plain young beauty had spun about him. On those increasingly frequent nights when the doctor was abed, Maria returned from his lonely walks, and climbed the old stairs to a repast set neatly on a table for him; and after, the strumming of his lute by the low fire in the parlor.

On one such night he began to sing:
....."O *maiden pale and fair,*
Come to the window, where,
My heart may sing its pain of love,
When all things under and above
Join in my lonely plea,
Your eyes and dove-soft breasts to see.....
O maiden lovely fair,
With moonlight in your hair,
Your beauty the music of the stars and seas........"

Maria suddenly stopped. Upon the wall before him was a shadow, as from a conjured spirit. Turning, he saw Katrinika standing not five paces from where he sat. She was in her nightgown, and wrapped thickly in a shawl; her hair bound in her red kerchief, as if hastily, so that dark strands of its secret escaped, and hung like a vine's tendrils down her neck. Frozen in the moment, she neither stepped into the bronze light of the fire, nor retreated back into the dark of the shadows. Nor did she raise her eyes to him. And when she finally spoke, the tenderness in her voice, a tenderness seasoned by shame and shyness, smote his heart like a sword.

"*You play and sing very sweetly, Maria sir.*"

"*Thank you, Katrinika. I hope I did not wake you.*"

"*No, you did not wake me. Besides, when I hear you sing I feel as I am sleeping; as the words and melodies were my dreams.*"

"*That is a very kind thing for you to say. It is also very kind of you to leave milk and biscuits on the table for me.*"

"*It is nothing, Maria sir. I do the same for papa. After your long walks and outings and such, I am sure you must be hungry.*"

She did not once look at him, and in the ensuing pause Maria could not stop his eyes from wandering over the gentle gifts of her body. She felt his ardor, and it quickened her with fright.

"*Goodnight, Maria sir.*"

With this she turned to go, only to stop when Maria spoke.

"*Katrinika.*"

"*Yes?*"

"*Thank you again for your kindness.....what you and your father have done for me.....the table of things you leave for me.*"

"*It is our pleasure, Maria sir.*"

Again she turned to leave, only to again have her steps arrested when Maria spoke her name again.

"*Katrinika.*"

"*Yes?*"

This was answered by a pause, a pause filled with the storms and poetry of both of their hearts, and not the politic words of their mouths, and only after this pause did Maria speak as he had spoken to many others, but not so sincerely for any.

"*I think you are a very lovely woman, Katrinika.*"

This was again followed by a silent pause, one in which their hearts screamed in vain through the prison bars of their ribs, only at the last to be denied their pardon by the cold jurisprudence of words.

"*Goodnight, Maria sir. A pleasant goodnight to you.*"

In the following days Maria grew afraid that he had frightened her away. As she had been a little bird, he was afraid she would not come again to peck the crumbs he spread for her. When he accompanied and returned with her besotted father, she was always waiting anxiously at the base of the stairs, but when he ventured out alone, and then played his fiddle or sang with his lute before the fire, she was not to be seen. Although the table was always prepared for him, the hostess responsible for its preparation, like a spirit, was nowhere to be seen.

Yet a week later there was left a sign that she had not entirely fled; that she still listened from deep in the shadows of the great old house. When Maria entered the parlor where he played and sang, he found a lute leaning near the low-burning fire. It was the *cobza*, the *Rumanian* lute that she once lent him to play years ago, when he had labored among the harvesters: the same tear-shaped body, the shell inlaid neck, the same moon and stars carved into its wood. Remarkably, the pegs and gut strings were still sound, and after an hour spent in tuning it, it was singing in his arms.

Yes, how it sang with his caresses, like a tender lover responding to his every want and need. Oh, how it yielded, surrendered its secrets for him! Oh, how he imagined when playing it the lifting of a smock, the unbinding of a bright red kerchief, the invitation of those ancient dark eyes.......

A few days later she appeared again; like a timid deer at the edge of a forest, and only after a pause, shyly stepped from the shadows into the coppery light before the hearth. As before, she did not look at him, but rather stood staring into the burning embers as he sang, as if in them were vistas she alone could see. Afraid of frightening her away, Maria did not speak. He continued to play, and sometimes softly sing, and in a part of an hour she turned, nodded with gratitude, and silently went away.

These nocturnal visits were repeated; their encounters seldom including words, or if they did, but a sparse and politic few.

"You play very nicely, Maria sir, as nicely, or more nicely than the bright dressed men in the square and by the river. I think that is why some call you the 'golden gypsy'."

"You say kind things to me, Katrinika."

"I say them because I feel they are true, Maria sir."

"With such an instrument in my arms, the one I think you left for me to play, it is easy to make sweet music, as if the melodies had been sleeping inside it, and were only waiting for its player's hands to wake them."

At this a pause, a hesitation, and then......

"My father says my mother still lives in the lute. He says that her spirit still yearns to sing."

"You had a very beautiful mother, to have such sweet melodies in her heart."

Another pause, another critical hesitation.......

"And where did you learn such sweet tunes?"

"I played them in the streets when I was a small boy. We had bears and monkeys, and I sang and danced for bread and other gifts, with my mother, my mother that I lost, even as you lost your mother."

.....Once more a pause after this strange admission.....

"Did you like the barley biscuit, the one sprinkled with almonds?"

"I liked it very much, Katrinika."

"I am glad; very glad that you liked it. Goodnight, Maria sir."

Although these midnight interlocutions were curt, polite, and without courtship or confession, Maria found his self speaking to this simple girl with a passion with which he had never spoken to another. He sang the ardency of his waked needs through the strings of the cobza and his fiddle, and the words he composed to fit the gypsy melodies he now fluently played upon them. He imagined they were arrows made of roses, and they were being loosed to the heart of a kitchen maid who baked bread.

> *..... 'O maiden fairest rare,*
> *Come, breathe the jasmine air,*
> *The night sky full of stars,*
> *A crown of diamonds for you are;*
> *Night's breezes pining to caress,*
> *To tenderly kiss your breasts,*
> *O maiden young and fair,*
> *Steal to the garden where,*
> *The jasmines fill the midnight air'......*

But these sessions evoked no resolution, and the transcendent, passionate professions of their hearts ended each time with only a polite etiquette of words.

"Goodnight Maria sir. Sleep well, and thank you for the lovely songs."

"Thank you for giving them your ear. Goodnight Katrinika. and thank you again for the kindness that you and your father have shown me."

As autumn cooled and deepened, and Maria healed and regained his vigor, he was visited by more urgent desires, desires that had slept, as if patiently waiting for his returning strength. Like the *cobza*, he needed more than a few sweet words. He needed a lover's touch to wake the songs that had fallen asleep in his heart.

Like spring flowers, his senses once more lifted their heads from their dormancy, and though as delicate as blossoms, were wild as any creature of the forest. When he would see a bare calf or knee, he imagined the thighs and hips draped above them. When he saw a pretty smile, he wanted to taste the secret honey deep in its mouth. When he saw tears n lonely eyes, he wanted to extinguish their pain with the flame of love's pleasure.

The old hunger returned; the hunger that only a woman could satisfy. As the days and weeks passed, Maria realized how vain his hope for an amorous liaison with Katrinika. Although she deeply stirred him, he felt that any overture to her, other than the ballads he crooned by the fire might prove unwise, even incendiary beneath her father's roof. Although sweet, the chill of her aloofness had never melted. She had never brought her dark eyes to his; and in those eyes, the lonely stories and entreaties of her heart.

One night a woman waited for him in a street outside a tavern where he had imbibed deeply. Maria knew her. He had felt her eyes cast upon him from many shadows in many taverns. She was neither young nor old, and neither pretty nor homely; slatternly, but without the scars or talismans of a whore. Feigning an accidental stumble into his arms as she walked out the tavern, she had nervously and falsely laughed:

"Pardon me sir.....perhaps, yes, perhaps it is the wine.....but excuse me, are you not the man with the golden hair, the earring and the beautiful singing voice, the one who played a fiddle at the Sickle Moon?"

Maria heard the ploy and the thinly disguised invitation in her voice. Without a word he brought his mouth to hers, not tenderly, but greedily, punishing its false smile until it surrendered to his hunger. As he kissed her neck he breathed into her ear:

"Yes, I am the man with the golden hair, and you are the woman who has ever wanted to please him! Come, here, to this dark place, this doorway.....you may please him now!"

Without waiting for a reply, Maria brusquely pulled and half carried the woman to a dark, nearby doorway, and there roughly clasped and pressed into her. Pinned by his strength, the frightened woman whined:

"No, please, not in this way!....Yes, you may, and gladly, but not in this way!"

Maria pressed even more strongly into her, and when he did her sluttishness breathed into him: the smells of meat, garlic and onions, of tavern smokes old and tartly new, the staleness that comes to live in long unlaundered clothing, as well as the cheap perfumes that try to stifle the exudations of poverty and the smoldering of age. Oh, how he had missed these smells! O, how intoxicated they made him feel!

As he kissed her neck and breasts he hotly whispered:

"*Do not be afraid! I want the sigh of your pleasure, not the scream of your pain!*"

"*Sir?*"

"*Have you dreamed of me?*"

"*Yes, perhaps, I think I perhaps have.....dreamed and fancied you. I thought perhaps, perhaps it would be very nice.....*"

"*.....very nice? How do you mean, 'very nice'?.....*"

"*.....to give you favors, and be favored by you in return.....*"

"*.....and how favored?.....*"

"*.....by pleasuring you as a woman pleasures a man.....*"

"*And you have had many dreams of me?*"

"*.....Yes sir, I have dreamed of you many times.....*"

"*.....and in many ways?.....*"

"*.....yes, many ways and with many pleasures......*"

"*You are not lying to me?*"

"*No good sir, it is not a lie that I have dreamed of you many times, and in the ways a man and a woman play and pleasure each other..... and you such a strong and beautiful man, as never before I had in my arms.*"

With this Maria roughly lifted her skirt, and finding her rose, held it firmly.

"*Show me.*"

"*Sweet sir, I have a room and a bed, ...there I could give you many things.....let you enjoy what you now hold, and no payment asked.....I've asked money from others who have sought out my pleasures.....I will not say I've not.....but I would not from you, no, not a thing for pleasuring you.....*"

He pressed into her more emphatically, squeezing more tightly what he had captured, even as it was a flower whose petals he was threatening to crush in his hand.

"*Here, now, in this doorway, give me the pleasure of your dreams!*"

"*.....I do not live far from here......*"

"*.....Here! Now!.....*"

"......*but like this, against this wall?.....*"

"......*yes, like this.....*"

"......*if you wish then, sir, only a little deeper in these shadows.....and you may have what you wish of me.....and what I wish of you.....*"

"......*No! Here, now!.......*"

Maria did not go back to the bake house that night. The woman proved a proficient lover; at times reckless and daring, and at others, docile and tender. They played the night through, Maria spending his newly waked, long-starved needs, and the woman being loved as she had not been loved before, even as her two young children slept in a loft above them. As a testimony to his debauch, when Maria returned to the bake house late in the morning, he was sullen and exhausted. Without a word to either the old doctor or his daughter, he went directly to his room, and without taking off his clothes, drank the oblivion of a daylong sleep.

This venting of his desires only whetted them the more, until their sparks were fevered into flames. More and more he exchanged darting glances from smoky shadows. More and more playful fingers tarried on the nape of his neck, and playful toes visited him under tables. More and more invitations were whispered in his ear, invitations that promised pleasures he could not refuse.

He began to leave the bake house at twilight, when the first dewy stars peeked from the darkness above the stone ways of walls and towers. He began to walk through some of the better streets, where in windows, on balconies, *loggias* and terraces women sat with mirrors, combs , zithers and looms; sometimes singing; sometimes with pet birds in gilded cages.

Maria quickly learned that he presented an object of great fasci-nation to these elegant women, not only because of his golden hand-someness, but because of the dwindling number of the city's suitors. The wars had either killed, or garroted many of the young men in strict duties, stationing them outside the city walls, or even sometimes in other provinces. Seldom did such a man such as Maria pass by the lairs of their beauty, and still more seldom without stopping to compliment and court such displays with flatteries. Their vanity stung, many laid down their combs, harps and mirrors when Maria passed them by. Forsaking the webs of their coquetry, they called out, and sometimes let fall roses on his head; those who had lived to be pursued, suddenly becoming avid pursuers.....*and once coming from their perches to the streets below, like fluttering birds, Maria opened the golden cage of his heart, and they were his........*

"*Sir, handsome sir, I saw you passing, and I.....*"

"*Ah, how pretty you look tonight! I see the evening star, like a sparkling brooch in your tresses! I hear nightingales in your voice!*"

.....or.....

"*Why do you look at your mirror to see your beautiful face, when the stars reflect its loveliness across the mirror of heaven?*"

.....or.....

"*Oh, pretty bird, have you no one to sing to? Come sing in my heart, and for your song, I will cherish you with kisses!*"

And there were others, more humble, with tasks in hand, that also gave him their hearts as he passed them by.

.....flower girls, laundry girls, scrub and oyster girls.....bringing him flowers for his hair, kisses for his lips, ribbons for his wrists......

More and more he slept in other beds and other arms, and not in his room in the bake house; sometimes for two or three consecutive nights, and once for a week. His drinking became heavier, and his sleep later in the day, sometimes until shadows began to fill the narrow ways.

On those nights when he returned to the bake house alone, either after long solitary walks, or passionate sessions of lovemaking, a great gloom and darkness enveloped him. At the top of the stairs a candle would ever burn on the table, and before it would be set a biscuit, a slice of cheese, and a cup of milk. It seemed a religious altar; one that his wastrel depravity had made him unworthy of; and he would leave it as he had found it; ashamed to partake of its offering. This had the effect of waking a deep regret in his heart, a melancholy for something once known, but never to be known again; once possessed, but forever lost; a longing to return, as a blind hunter dreams of returning to the hunt.

Bringing the *cobza*, and more times than not, his fiddle to the parlor and its dying fire, he would play and sing melodies more plaintively than he had ever played and sung them before; forgetful of the hour, the approaching winter, the pain in his heart.

Sometimes this deeper ache and profounder need of his soul conjured the shadow on the wall. Katrinika would step into the firelight, her hair loosely bound in her red kerchief, and her shoulders wrapped in a woolen shawl. She did not look at him, and often did not speak to him; their hearts, and not their lips vainly speaking to each other. After an enchanted spell, and then a few words: "*The day will break soon. I must rake and fire the ovens*", she would leave, as if indeed she had been an apparition, one that had been invoked from the shadows by a need to know a mortal sweetness.

But there were exceptions to this routine; exceptions that broke the silence, and the airs perfumed with a combination of virginal uncertainty and carnal need. Sometimes the apparition would halt before its disappearance back into the mists of sleep, or the drudgeries of baking bread, and brief dialogues would ensue.

"*Your songs are very beautiful, Maria sir, even more beautiful, if I may say it, than I believe they were before.*"

"*Thank you Katrinika. It requires a special ear to hear that, and if I may say, a very special heart to say such a thing.*"

"*Goodnight, Maria sir.*"

On another occasion......

"*There is a great beauty in your songs, Maria sir, but there is also a great sadness.*"

"*Yes, there is a great sadness in my songs, for there is sometimes a great pain in my heart.*"

"*Does your wound still give you pain?*"

"*Yes, it still gives me pain, for love stabs deeper than knives.....stabbing through flesh and bone to the very soul.*"

"*A pleasant night to you, Maria sir.*"

On still another occasion, after a first snow had fallen.....

"*I think, Katrinika, I will be leaving soon.*"

"*But the first snows have fallen in the mountains, Maria sir.*"

"*Yes, I think that is true.*"

"*Do you know where you will go?*"

"*Like all men, into the dream of things....*"

"*The dream of things?*"

"*The dream that the fields and forests dream beneath the sun, full of wolves and Angels, thorns and berries, winters and summers....the dream that all men are born to dream.....to sing, ache and perish in.*"

"*You need not go. Father says the winter will be very harsh. You are welcome here.*"

"*My side has healed. I do not want to overstep the great kindness you and your father have shown me.*"

"*Father likes you very much. He likes to drink plum wine and tell old stories to you.....even to sing to mama's ghost with you.*"

"*And his daughter? Would his daughter miss a shiftless gypsy man ever yearning for the lips and arms of a beautiful woman, a woman who does not give her dark eyes full of their lonely stories to him?*"

"*Your songs are very beautiful, Maria sir. I will keep them in my heart. As for the dark-eyed woman, there are many such in the paths of the world. I do not think you will have trouble finding such a one.*"

"*But one that has captured my heart.....*"

"*If I may, you have had much wine, Maria sir, and the hour is late, and well past the call for sleep. Shortly the asses will be braying and the carts creaking, and there are many chores in the kitchen to be performed before the shutters of the bread window are opened. Goodnight Maria.*"

But this time when she had disappeared in the darkness, Maria's words brought her back into the firelight.

"*I want to thank you, Katrinika, for always having a table prepared for me upon my late returns. It is a kindness I shall not forget, given by one whom I shall not forget.*"

"*It is my pleasure sir. We always have biscuits from the day's selling, and milk from the goat and cow.*"

"*But, well, the nights I do not return from my walks.....*"

"*It is not a bother at all.....if you have interests that keep you away for a day or two......*"

"*You are far kinder than I deserve. I think you are very beautiful, Katrinika.*"

"*You have a great deal of wine and music in your blood tonight, Maria sir......You are speaking to the dreams in your fiddle, or perhaps a shadow on the wall.....*"

"*Or perhaps it is your mother singing from the 'cobza'*"

"*My mother?*"

"*Yes, and she is singing an eternal melody, the eternal melody of love.*"

"*I bid you goodnight, Maria sir.*"

But it was several nights later when they exchanged a dialogue that would prove climactic, and bring the simmering of their emotions to a full boil. Maria had gradually grown frustrated with her defenses, and the lack of any reward for which he was seeking. Casual lovers had not answered his needs, for his heart had woken a hunger his body could not satisfy. His undeclared feelings were tormenting him. He could not go on this way. At any cost he must tell her plainly his heart; and either win her amorous favors, or leave the house at once. The winter in the mountains was now sending its cold army into the fields and forests; the wolves even now howling outside the city's walls. He must clasp her in his arms, or leave the city.

He had made his decision. One night after drinking a great stoop of wine, he climbed the stairs to his room, and removed from his satchel the yellow bandanna that she had given him on that terrible morning years ago. Going to the fire, he again began to plaintively play the *cobza*, at which she again stepped into the firelight, sat down, and as if charmed by the beautiful song of a bird, listened. But after a time he stopped, and without her seeing pulled the bandanna from his pocket. Draping it brightly over his shoulder, he laid down the *cobza*, stood, and went to the tall window near the hearth.

"*The moon has climbed the mountain into the forest of stars.*"

Lifting her eyes to him, she at once saw the token she had once given, and he had long kept. Her heart fluttered, and she at once recoiled, as the bandanna was an animated thing, a serpent or a living flame. She stood, and with a nervous "*goodnight, Maria sir*", began to depart. Maria did not object, but keeping his face to the moon and the snowy night, only softly spoke.

"*Did your father and mother not once dance in this window; before such a moon?*"

"*You must ask my father that thing, Maria sir.*"

"*And does not your father, even now, sometimes dance here with your mama's ghost?*"

"*Papa is old, and when he drinks much wine.....*"

"*Your father must have loved your mother very much.*"

"*Please sir, it is a thing very tender to my father's heart and mine. Please excuse me, but I must fire the kindling.....*"

"*Katrinika, will you dance with me?*"

At this there was a silence, one that was made loud with the cries from both their hearts.

"*Will you, Katrinika, here, even as your father once danced with your mother?*"

"*I bid you a pleasant sleep, Maria sir.....*"

"*You refused me when I asked you long ago, when you were a young girl. Remember, about the fire at the harvest camp? You are no longer a young girl.*"

"*The men would have laughed at the cripple girl dancing with such a one as you.*"

"*The moon is not laughing. It smiles; it understands; and with its understanding rains down silver roses of its approval.*"

"*Please Maria, you are a kind man, but boldly said, you may do much better than to dance with a bake girl with a crooked hip and a dragging foot.*"

"*I am not asking a bake girl to dance. I am asking an angel who has taken care of me these long weeks, burning a candle for one who has caroused foolishly deep into the nights. I am asking one who knows me as no other knows me, who pledged her love to me even when the man he killed was lying at his feet.*"

At last turning to her, he brought the bandanna to his lips, kissed it, and then held it to his heart.

"*It has ever been a ribbon, here, about my heart.*"

Her eyes sparkled with tears as she stepped back a step into the shadows.

"*No Maria, please....it was a thing long ago. I was a girl, and you were a strong beautiful man, even as you are now. I am.....as you see and know......*"

"*Flower of my heart, Katrinika, will you dance with me?*"

Maria held out his arms, but conflicted and confused with the great debate in her heart, she shuffled another step back in retreat, and with a last buttressing of her will, refused to fall into them.

"*Come, be the ghost in my dreams no more.*"

And then, about to shy and run, she turned, and slowly, with the great burden she was bearing, came to him; her spirit lifting her shame and coyness, her eyes shy as a nun's, proud as a queen's.

And when she came to his arms, she did not fall, but alighted in them, like a blossom shed from a bough. And alighting, she fit perfectly, like a hand into a glove; not in the least disturbing that glove; as if indeed she was a spirit of the dead that had returned to retrieve it in the exact place where she had let it fall.

.....The smells of her body, the tenderness of her breaths, her touch caressing his heart into music.....her body waking his, not by pressing into him, but by virtue of its delicate being.....exciting him as the greed of others had not.....as her body held a deeper loneliness, and in that loneliness, a deeper and greater storm.......

.....he brought his lips to her neck, and kissed up and down its slenderness, even as he had dreamed of kissing it a thousand times.....at last feeling its silk, and smelling the rich fertility of her skin.......

.....the strands of her loose hair, like tendrils of unseen, celestial roses..... her ear, like a shell washed from the sea, into which he breathed the passion of his heart, the meaning of his soul.......

"Katrinika, my little nightingale, how very beautiful you are."

She did not shy, either from his words or his kisses, but neither did she tenderly answer them. It was only after he had kissed the other side of her neck, and whispered in her other ear: *"O my love, my love, my beautiful love"*, did she bring her cheek to his shoulder, as it was a bird returning to its nest, its wings weary from some untold, unimaginable flight over seas and mountains.

But although she did not speak, or kiss him in return, Maria could hear the great cries of her soul. Like a rain so gentle the hearer is not sure it is rain at all, he could hear the sobs of her soul spilling on his shoulder. Never had he heard such pain. Never had he heard such sweetness. Never had he heard the melting of such a cold loneliness.

He undid the knot of her kerchief, freeing, and with his hand helping to let fall the wealth of her glossy secret down upon her breast and shoulders; and it was like a dark forest full of flowers, singing birds, and sparkling stars, a forest that at once charmed and claimed him.

"O Katrinika, my angel, do you not know how I have longed for you..... to touch, smell and taste you?....how I dream and burn for you? Oh my love, give me your tears, your sighs, your secrets.....give me the treasure that each night I dream of.....I will be gentle, yes, very gentle, and we will be happy, so very happy."

But he had overstepped the bounds of propriety's seduction. Instead of turning her face and lifting a kiss to his begging mouth, she sharply broke from his embrace, Stepping quickly away, she spoke with her back to him, her voice thick, and all but choked with tears.

"I should have known, and if I spoke the truth of my conscience, I 'did' know. Oh, you use pity like a sword, a sword to rend the helpless heart of a cripple and make it a trinket for your pocket! But I will not be made a conquest by your pity! I will not be another whore you call your angel!"

"Katrinika, no, please, it is not like that at all."

"We both know it is. Have you no shame? Do you not know the kind of reputation you have earned in the streets and shops, the reputation of a

drinker, a brawler, a shameless rake? Do you care, or have your dreams made you beyond the reach of care? Do you think father and I do not know why you are gone for nights and days on end; that you have found yet another kitten to make purr, another tavern darling to play in a stable with? Do you not think I have listened as you charm women in the Piazza Lucia, beneath the same window where you once chortled and chirruped like a bird to a bread girl?"

And now she turned to him, her dark flood of hair falling in a rich opulence to her waist, and midst that opulence, her face burning like a flame. It shone full of tears and rage, but more intense, a rage whose tears glistened with an unutterable pride.

"I was a girl, a crippled girl to whom a kindness was once shown. I kept that kindness. I treasured that kindness. I clung to that kindness, like a child clings to a toy.

It is not your fault, Maria. It is mine. You are only obeying the voices in your blood. My curse has made me vulnerable to both desire and pity, and they, more than anything are things I distrust and repulse. I am one who cannot play like other women can play. I am one whose bed you would soon tire of and desert. I am one, beautiful golden gypsy sir, who was not made for love."

"But you told me on that morning in the snow, that morning after I had committed the terrible thing......"

"O Maria, I was a girl, a lame lonely girl who had lost her brother and mother....."

"Where is your brother, Katrinika? Is he in the city?"

"I do not know where my brother is. I do not know if he is alive. My father gave him away to an orphanage when he was very young, after the thing that happened to my mother.....after his wits were blasted."

"What happened to your mother, your mama's ghost that your father is always speaking to?"

At this Katrinika stepped even closer to Maria, her face upturned, bronzed with firelight, fierce as a lioness protecting her young.

"My mother, my first mother, my mother who was not my mother was eaten alive, Maria sir! Yes, eaten alive! During the famine she was attacked when she was alone in the streets, attacked, torn apart, dismembered limb by limb.....and, and she was eaten.....yes, eaten!.....whether by starving dogs or starving men, we never knew, for man and beast had become brothers.....both starved with one and the same hunger!

A girl once loved you, Brother Maria. It is true. But that girl, a crippled girl, is now a crippled woman with a kind, but half-mad, heartbroken father forever seeking the ghost of his wife, a wife whose bones he gathered like faggots with his own two hands! That crippled woman has no desire to be a little prize of a monk turned rakish seducer, one who is ever seeking another pleasure garden to sleep in!

Goodnight, Maria sir, a pleasant goodnight to you."

And with this she turned, and stepped back into the shadows; limping with steps before which Maria wanted to prostrate.

Maria went to his room, his heart broken. Gripped by a compulsive need to leave, he numbly packed his satchel with his few things. He would leave both his lute and his fiddle. He would leave the beautiful *cobza* near the hearth where she had left it for him. He had stayed too long. His dreams, like a spider, had woven a web about his heart; and with its weaving forged chains of misery too heavy for him to bear.

He lay on his bed, tormented as never before. The flowers on the rafters above him, those that he had seen Katrinika caring for that morning when he came from his fever, seemed now to wilt and weep with their once happy faces. Unable to sleep, and hearing the first cocks crow, he stole from his room and down the stairs. He would leave without an apology, without an explanation, without a farewell. It would be better that way.

He knew Katrinika and her father were awake. He could hear their banter about the ovens, the doctor refusing to be hushed by his daughter's pleas. Descending the stairs, he stopped at the door, listening for the last time to the one who had teetered on love's cliff, only to despise him; the one who had waked his heart only to murder it.

"Father, do not raise your voice, you will wake him! He came home very late last night. He is sleeping."

"Damn it! I will raise my voice when I want to in my own house. I'll ring every bell in Siena, and wake the churchyard graves if I want to! My daughter has not slept, and I think she has been crying!"

"O papa, do not be silly, I have not been crying!"

"Then Noah did not see a flood! Your eyes are red and swollen, and there is a great pain and dark cloud about you!"

"Father, we must wheeze the ovens......"

"Did he hurt you?"

"Papa, sssh, he is sleeping!"

"Did he make you sleep with him?"

"Papa!"

"I hope the hell he did! By Jacob and his ladder of Angels, I hope to hell he did.....made you sleep with him, and brought the tears of a woman from your eyes!"

"Papa, how could you say....."

"Because you are a grown woman who needs to be loved, and because you have dreamed of it ever since we brought this gypsy drunkard, brawler and wicked, lady-charmer scoundrel up our stairs! Because the tears of your eyes are not from oven smoke, but from love's purest flame.....because my daughter has never appeared more beautiful in her father's eye's than she now does, no, not if she was wearing wedding flowers in her hair.....for she is now wearing a gown full of the pain of a heart breaking in two with love.....yes, love, a thing she has ever denied and run from!"

This was answered by muffled tears, and a succession of sobs that brooked on thin high shrieks, like a widow keening at a grave; and midst that interlude of wails, those terrible wails of which he was the cause, Maria stepped into the first faint grey of the cold morning. No, he would not return. He would never return. He had been a fool, a shameless fool a thousand times over to stay, to dream a dream that he and a kitchen maid could share, body and soul.

Snow had begun to fall with a great conviction; the wind biting with the raw bite of winter's teeth. Maria stopped and leaned against a stone wall in a small dark cleft between two buildings. He had not slept, and he was hungry, and his head throbbed with the great quantity of wine he had imbibed. And yet these wretched groans and pleas of his body were drowned to faint echoes by the anguish in his heart, and the scalding tears pouring down his face.

.....Where was he to go? What was he to do?.....Had he not asked himself these same questions many times and in many places.....when he had left the abbey.....when he had left harvest teams, closing taverns..... lovers' arms?.......

.....What had become of him? Katrinika had spoken the truth when she had said he owned a most sordid and disgusting reputation. She had spoken the truth when she had said his dreams had outreached his care.....Would any of his lovers, or those he had brawled, diced or become drunk with..... would God Himself care if he was to drive a knife through his bowels in this dark place, and be frozen and covered over with a cold crust of snow?....And

Giovanni?.....Did he not once have a friend named Giovanni?....oh, if he knew he lay frozen dead in the streets, kicked and fleeced by the tramps and paupers, smelled and peed on by the dogs, would even the friend of his youth, Father Giovanni care?......or would he rightly reason that he had received the wages of his sins?.......

Maria stood aright, stretched out his hand, and gently knocked upon the degraded boards of the shutter before him. This at once elicited a response of soft quick steps, the unlatching and cracking open of the shutter, and then the plump face of a slovenly woman with a nightcap, one who peeked timidly from that crack, candle in hand.

"Why, master Maria, is that you? Why are you standing in the cold, and the snow beginning to fall and mount....."

"Forgive me for waking you, lady Eleanora....."

"Oh, not at all, not at all master Maria, with the kindling and the wheezing.....the porridge and bacon and the young one still taking suck..... not at all, not al all..... I've long been from my sleep......."

"May I speak with your son, Salvatore? I have an errand I would like him to run for me, one that shall win a copper for his pocket."

"Why of course, of course. I'll stir the lazy creature. He's greatly fond of you master Maria, and he'd run to Jericho and back again, and that on crutches, and that for no copper at all to do a thing for you.....a moment, a moment, but a moment and the little rascal's yours....."

A moment later the young boy was in the window, so sleepy-eyed and mealy-headed Maria was not sure his senses were awake.

"Salvatore, my old friend Salvatore. It is Maria. Are you awake 'amico'?"

Unsatisfied with the grunt of his reply, Maria filled his hand with snow and pressed it to the youngster's cheek. At once the boy started awake and sheepishly smiled, as if the proposition of waking was a game.

"Salvatore, listen to me carefully. I have a favor to ask of you, and a copper to pay for that favor.

When the sun rises I want you to stand beneath the bake house window, and to order two biscuits, the ones with the pudding that you like so well. When you place your payment in the basket, I want you to also place this yellow scarf, see, tied like a present. Here is the coppers for the biscuits, and here's one for you."

"Are you leaving, master Maria? You look as if you are leaving."

"Yes, for a few days I am leaving. But when I return I will again tell you stories, and give you lessons on my lute and fiddle.

Here, let me kiss your cheek, and then give that kiss to your sisters and your mama. Tell them it is from the gypsy man. God bless you old chap, may God bless you always."

A short while later, when the streets, roofs, and the stone towers were being buried white with snow, Katrinika shut and locked her door, and unbound the yellow bandanna to words that were to carve deeply into her heart.

YOUR Soul a lovely swan that gently glides
Through life's foul weathers, and foreboding straits,
There is a grace that in your heart abides,
That harshest winds serenely navigates.
The bounty that you sail is in your eyes,-
Dark seas that fill the depths of heaven,
Their tears a treasury of diamonds,
That sparkle bright the deeps of midnight skies.
No, Nature has not cursed you with defect,
But given gifts that richly few endow,
A royalty, before which Princes bow,
Making damozels, handmaidens at your beck.
O darling one, think not you have a broken wing,
Your soul, a lovely swan, more regal than a queen's.

* * *

IT was very cold; cold, sun-less and bleak. Maria walked past bundled men squatted about small fires in slab huts, drinking and roasting bits of meat on sticks. The guards, rusty with drink and stiff with cold, upon recognizing him, brusquely opened the gate and let him through with admonishments of a few words.

"Not a good day for a journey, fiddler man. Be careful. The 'Sickle Moon', and the other taverns do not want to lose you, and especially the tavern vixens, eh? Be careful. There are Florentines about, more dangerous than wolves they are, smelling the air for blood, Sienese blood......."

The snow was now falling heavily, the flakes no longer thin, but in thick blotches; the road that led down the hill into the first stand of naked trees vanishing beneath its quickly gathering shroud.

Where was he to go? What was he to do?

He stopped a hundred steps outside the gates, the snow mounding halfway up his boots. Here he wavered with the temptation to reenter the gates. Although he could not return to Katrinika and the bake house, nor to the *Sickle Moon*, he could easily find lodging above another tavern, or with any number of lovers he knew would welcome him. He could resume his playing and singing in the inns and taverns for food and drink. He could seek out new lovers to play with, perhaps a widow who would buy him a new suit of clothes in exchange for flattering her age and pleasuring her bed. The winter would be long, long and harsh. Although he was not old, he was no longer young. He could while it away with dice, cards and fiddle songs; wait until the hills began to thaw and the brooks began to run before he departed.

And yet the bleakness before him invited more than threatened him, as if its snowy cold was somehow the home of his soul; its first and last, its only home; not chattering streets, warm blazing fires, and soft bodies to lay upon; to grow weak, satisfied, and to die upon. Its bleakness and forlornness seemed to beckon him, to pique awake his blood as the cold must stir the blood of its native son, the wolf. This cold bleakness was his home; the home from which he had been lured; the home that he must never again leave. The wolves were his brothers; their howls were his howls, howling through the deepest part of him.

He had long shed the sedentary dream of God, and now with it, the human playthings of hope and love. He must discard these toys for dearer wants and needs. Yes, he would hunt for food and shelter. Yes, he would lay in the grass with women he did not know, and then leave after his brief gratification. Yes, drunk with wine and madness, he would lift shouts and fists to the cold stars. Yes, if needs, he would kill again.

Where was he to go? What was he to do? Was there a Brother Maria in the world, or was he a ghost, a memory, a dream? And when that ghost had fled into the wind, or that memory or dream was smothered by the winter snow, frozen dead like the forest leaves, would the bare boughs mourn or laugh, or only indifferently sigh at the vain importance in the dead dreams of this Brother Maria' broken heart?

Maria began to descend the hill into the first trees of the forest. What was he to do? Where was he to go?.....

.....to perish, yes, that was it.....to hunt, love, kill, perish, like all things perish.....to know the madness of trying to escape, to find a meaningless

meaning in one's certain end.....to madly howl, stalk, mate, kill......only in the end to bleed to death with the wounds of one's silly, fruitless, childish dreams....and then to have these dreams freeze, decay and fall, like leaves from a tree......to perish into a larger, colder, even more uncaring dream....yes, that was where the ghost of Brother Maria must go, and what it must do.....where the ghosts of all men must go, and what the ghosts of all men must do.......

.....Oh, but the horrors that were to come before he escaped this dream,.....horrors that no man had ever imagined, no army of Angels could defend against.....as earth was no longer earth, but a lower realm, a darker realm....oh, what horrors, what hell of horrors never seen beneath the sun.......

....

....

BOOK II
A DARK SUN

CHAPTER ONE

BEDTIME STORIES,
AND
THE END OF THE WORLD

I

Ryazan, Russia, Late Autumn, 1337

VLADIMIR opened his eyes; his nose, cheeks and glossy curls peeping out from the bearskin blanket, like a weasel peeping from its hole.

He had played this trick on his mama and papa many times before, this trick of pretending to be asleep, when he was not asleep at all.

Each night after tucking him and his younger, three year-old sister beneath their blankets, his mama and papa would sit at their bedsides, and tell them stories of things that happened long ago; of princes and princesses, of forests where the animals spoke like men, and where bright-feathered birds warbled of things to come. Sometimes his papa would place his hands above the lamp, and cast shadows on the ceiling above them. The ceiling had many large beams, and it was in this forest of large rafters where Vladimir first saw these magical creatures roam.

When he and his sister became very sleepy, his mama and papa would kiss their cheeks, whisper *goodnight*, and taking the lamp softly leave the room. They would go to the parlor that was still warm and glowing with the fire. They would leave the bedroom door partly open, so that the firelight would faintly enter it, and they would not become afraid in the dark.

Sometimes, when he played his trick, Vladimir would lie awake, listening to his mama's and papa's voices. They would drink the plum wine his papa brought from the cellar, and with whispers talk of many things: the short summer and long cold winter; the beans in the garden, their fields of rye and wheat; their cow, goats and chickens. Sometimes they would talk of the strange people in the village; those with squints, limps or humps, and those they said cast wicked spells. Sometimes their voices would become so hushed that he could not hear their words and meanings. This would sometimes be followed by his mama and papa breaking into a loud laughter, and then a clapping of their knees and hands, as they were crashing cymbals. At other times, when their voices became very low, the tone of their voices was not happy, but dark and serious. He knew then that they were talking of the men they called *bandits*, men that stole pigs, sheep and horses.

Sometimes they would tell bedtime stories for grownups. Their voices would become low, like the voices they used when they spoke of the *bandits*. They were different kinds of stories, stories that made him afraid, so that he buried his head beneath the bearskin, only to peep it out again when his curiosity made him brave.

And sometimes when he was brave, he would do something his parents knew nothing about. He would slip from his bed and walk to the door, where he could hear their voices more clearly. One night he heard his mama crying, and his papa trying to comfort her. Standing at the door in his nightshirt, he felt something colder than the dirt floor his bare feet were standing on, or the wind that had frozen the pretty roses on the garden gate. He felt something like a cold claw take hold of his heart.

"*They say they have the bodies of men, but the heads of savage dogs. They say they bark and howl, and roam in packs through the fields and forests. Long-haired, partly or entirely naked, sometimes they are upright on their feet, like men, other times, on all-fours, as they were a kind of half-human, half-brutish creature.......some with tails and hoofs and horns..... some without heads upon their animal bodies......*"

"*Annushka, we cannot be sure if these stories are true. The people have suffered greatly from hunger and disease, and many are filled with strange dreams.*"

"*They say these man-dogs have fangs, Fyodor, and there is kill in their eyes, blood on their muzzles.*"

"No wife, I am sure these are but stories clothed fantastically by their tellers, like the stories we tell Vladimir and Sophia."

"They say they abuse young girls they find alone in the fields. They mount them as a beast mounts a beast. They say that sometimes these girls bring forth dog-headed children, and that sometimes these rape mothers strangle the monsters they have issued, only to go and hang themselves from trees. Other times, most incredibly, they join these packs, and roam disheveled and half-naked with them, as they had become the whores of these monstrous creatures."

"Please Annushka, we must go to bed; we may wake the children. You are tired, and the wine has fermented long, and is very strong......"

".....and the armies of the short savage men, they and their swift horses and strange weapons.....they who climb walls like monkeys, mutilate and behead, burn whole villages to the ground......"

"Please sweetheart, no more. I will look in upon the children to make sure they are not awake. I will close their bedroom door a little more; I am afraid we will wake them."

At this cue the sly little eavesdropper slipped swiftly and silently back into his bed, pulling the bearskin up to his nose, and closing tight his eyes. He felt his papa stand over his excellent disguise, the glow of his candle making golden bright the backs of his eyelids, and his rough, callused fingers softly brushing away the bangs of his hair; after which his papa left the room, ignorant of the espial he had made.

But long after his papa left the room, and the whispers of his mama and papa died in the parlor, Vladimir lay awake with his eyes open, staring at the forest in the tree trunk rafters, illumined by the parlor's firelight, still spilling through the cracked door.

But now the magical forest was different. The beautiful birds flew away through its branches, and the talking bears and foxes, with the winged rabbits and deer disappeared. These frightened creatures were followed by strange men with tails and the heads of dogs, and some without any heads at all. Some ran on their feet, and some, like dogs, were running on all-fours. Some held feathers of birds between their jaws, and others, arms and legs, as if torn from men's bodies. There were women also, naked, like he had once seen his mama when she was bathing. Their breasts hung down like gourds, and some were riding the giant dog-men. Some were bearded, and the hair beneath their arms was like muddy weeds, matching and becoming one with the hair that dangled like dead vines down their naked backs and legs.

For the first time Vladimir was afraid of this forest in the rafters. He pulled the bearskin over his head, but in the darkness beneath the bearskin there were more dog-men with naked women on their backs. There were also men with terrible faces, men who rode small horses that seemed not horses at all, but giant wolves of the forest.

Beneath the bearskin Vladimir was frightened with a fear that he would not forget, not even when he was an old man; having been saved by his mama in the hiding place she had made for him; beneath the boards of the kitchen floor.

* * *

With the passing of a few days, these terrible creatures left, and once more the magical forest in the rafters was filled with rainbow-colored birds, flying rabbits, and talking bears and lions. Nor did Vladimir sneak from his bed to listen to his mama's and papa's whispers. He was afraid to hear his mama cry. He was afraid of the dog-men and the women that rode them. He did not want them to invade the rafter forest, and then the forest of his dreams.

But as the apples ripened and the autumn deepened, Vladimir heard another story, one told by his schoolmates in the play-yard. They told a story that did not happen long ago, like the stories his mama and papa told, but only several nights before. It did not happen in another land ruled by another king, or in a magical forest with talking birds and beasts, but outside the gates of their own village; *Ryazan*.

The boys said that only several nights ago a real witch had ridden on a horse, back and forth before their village. She was filled with madness and evil curses, and she was shriveled like a ghoul. A crowd of men and women, some in their nightclothes, gathered at the gates to watch her crazily ride, at which she began to cackle and scream before her audience.

"I and my people demand a part of the goods of your village! A part of your horses, pigs and goats, your flour and candles and oil.....your beautiful rugs and woven cloths, and the things made by your goldsmiths and silver-smiths.....much of your monies.....many of your virgins!......"

Some believed her a madwoman, others a sorceress, but most regarded her but a crone gone crazy with age and drink. Soon the rider and her wild demands elicited a great raillery of hoots and laughter from the crowd, as they had come from their beds and taverns to be entertained by a spectacle.

Some began to throw stones at the witch, and as that did not stop her from screaming her outlandish demands, more and more were rained upon her, until one hit her in the head and knocked her from her horse. With a great '*hurrah*' a group of men rushed to where she had fallen, and surrounding her, quickly lifted her ragged clothes on a stick above their heads. When the mob of men parted, and came back inside the gates, the witch was left completely naked to the eyes of all.

So angry with what the men had done to her, she had neither a regard for the cold or her nakedness. She instead walked nearer the gates, so near that the crowd's torches illumined her. Many became fearful of her ugliness, as there was something supernatural about it; as she was indeed a withered and shriveled hag, one who brought a curse from hell, at which not a few recoiled and covered their faces.

"*For doing this to me I will bring an army of men from the forest, and they will enter your village with swords and fire! They will rape each of your daughters and your mothers, and that with their bound fathers and husbands made to watch! They will mutilate your men, and fill casks full of their ears, noses, tongues, and then swill them to the swine! They will kill each man, woman and child in Ryazan! They will burn to ashes your village! I will return with an army of horsemen, filling these hills like locusts fill the sky!*"

Now when his mama and papa left his room at night, Vladimir would open his eyes from his pretended sleep, and look with a new excitement into the magical forest in the rafters. He had become braver, and each night he imagined new adventures in these shadows. Sometimes they were filled only with the gold and silver birds, winged rabbits and talking bears and foxes, but on other nights these wonderful creatures fled from the dog-men and the women that rode them. But now there was another adventure in this forest, one that excited him very much. Sometimes an old lady entered it, naked and shriveled, and with ropes of gray hair hanging to her feet. Behind her an army of wild strange men came through the trees, mounted on the giant wolves of the forest. Vladimir would cover his head with the bearskin, and when he peeped it out again, they had passed through the forest trees, as they had been ghosts.

319

There seemed to be no end of these fairy stories. Several nights after the naked hag had cursed the village, Vladimir heard once more his mama's muffled sobs in the parlor. Once more his curiosity bested his fears. Once more he slipped from his bed and made the daring expedition to the door to listen.

"The astrologers say they have seen comets streaking through the heavens, like the burning fingers of God writing the wrathful signs of a dark doom!.....And have we not been waked in the night, our house trembling with the thunder deep in the earth's bowels?"

"Calm yourself, Annushka, calm yourself......."

"The torrential rains, and then the droughts, and the clouds of locusts that blot the sun, making night of day......."

"Yes wife, yes sweetheart, I know. We will consult the priests, and say prayers with the others......."

"And these things the merchants tell of, Fyodor, terrible things they have seen with their own eyes and heard with their own ears......"

"No more Annushka, it is late, the plum wine is very strong.....and the children......."

".....these things that the Silk Road merchants tell about the eastern lands......rains of frogs, lizards, serpents, scorpions......hailstones so large they break the skulls of horses......sheets of fire, burning men and beasts alive!.....the earth opening to swallow entire villages......"

"Please darling....."

"......and these strange dog-men, the barbarous horsemen.....this witch cursing our village.....I am afraid, Fyodor, in my heart of hearts I am very afraid!....."

Vladimir became afraid too, afraid and excited with these stories. Now his nightly adventures in the magical forest would be visited by fires, and rains of frogs and serpents.

One night late in autumn Vladimir woke to a wonderful surprise. The door was partly open, and he could hear the soft laughter of his mama and papa in the parlor. But the light in the tree trunks above him was brighter, and it made the forest sparkle as the firelight had never made it sparkle before.

Once again the adventurer slipped from his blanket and his bed, but this time he did not steal to the open door, but past his sleeping sister to the window. There he saw a great miracle, just as his papa told him one night there would come a miracle; a miracle of snow brought by the wings of the angels. The full moon was rising above the dark forest, and with the snow it was making a fairytale of the world; the glimmering blanket of snow covering the garden's stakes and trellises, and half burying it's lonely scarecrow. It had frosted the gables and chimneys of the houses, and the fields and forests beyond!

The stars were bright and clear. They were another forest, a sparkling forest that Vladimir liked to dream among. His papa had shown him the special groups of stars, and he liked to look for them, as the heavens were not only a forest, but a great circus with many animals, giants, and other surprises: *the Bear, the Big Wagon, the Twins and the Soldier with a Sword; the seven holy Sisters, clustered together and praying for the souls of men.*

From this forest of stars Vladimir looked to the dark forest that surrounded their village. His papa told him stories about this forest too. He said there were *bandits* and *gypsies* that lived in it; and there were deer, swift as swallows that ran through it. He said there were also giant wolves, wolves as large as small horses that lived in its heart. Vladimir knew this was a true story. When the moon was full, like tonight, he could hear the wolves howling.

Tonight Vladimir became very excited when he looked at this dark forest. Rather than listening to a fairy story, he seemed to be *watching* one. The trees seemed to have uprooted their roots, and like giants, they had walked closer to the village, and now were on the hilltops surrounding it. He became even more excited when he saw they were not giants or trees at all, but the giant wolves his papa had told him about; and that each of these big wolves was mounted by a rider.

A great thrill rushed through Vladimir. *Of course! Of course! It was the army the witch had promised to bring!*

Vladimir then did something he had done only once before, once when he became sick with colic. Excited with the fairy story he alone knew about, he went to the open door, and after hesitating, bravely walked into the parlor where his mama and papa were whispering. His papa was the first to see him.

"*Well, well, well, look who has come to visit his mama and papa by the fire tonight!*"

And then his mama.

"*Why Vladimir! The floor is cold, and you do not have your slippers on. Is there something wrong, my darling? A tummy ache? A bad dream the bad fairies have brought?*"

And then his papa's strong arms lifted him into the garden of his lap, a garden smelling of tobacco, plum wine, and the smoke of the fire, and the peculiar smells that all old people have. His papa laughed, squeezed him, and kissed him with his bristly beard, and when he laughed, he saw his papa's chipped and yellow teeth that his moustache tried to hide in the daylight.

"Here old chap, have a seat by the fire with your mama and papa, and tell us what we have done to deserve such an honor. The stage is yours, my prince, tell us why you have come from your bed to visit us."

Vladimir flushed with the attention his mama and papa were giving him, especially at this midnight hour. Timidly he spoke his great secret.

"It has snowed, like you said it would snow papa. It has made everything white."

"Has it old chap? Well, then that means tomorrow we must sled down the hill where the birch trees grow. Does that not sound like a business you could manage old chap?"

The idea of sledding down the hill in the snow excited Vladimir very much. It made his next words much easier to come from his mouth.

"And the big army has come from the forest, papa!"

"Oh has it now? The big army from the forest, eh? And what army is that?"

"The army the crazy woman said she would one day bring!"

This elicited a clicking of tongues, and a gentle moan of reproach from both his mama and papa, as he had talked of something forbidden.

"Where have you heard of this crazy woman, Vladimir? From the boys in your school? Oh, I see. No, Vladimir, this is but a story, one that is not true."

"But papa, it is a true story! The dog-men, and the men without heads have come from the forest, and they are riding the giant wolves you have said live there!"

His father chuckled warmly.

"Well, no more of these stories now.....no more of crazy old women, dog-men and giant wolves. Off to bed you go, for you must be rested, old chap, when we go sledding through the birch trees tomorrow."

With this his papa stood, and cradling and kissing him in his arms, began the journey back to his bed. But Vladimir refused to be quieted.

"But I saw them from the window, papa, the army of dog-men and wolf riders! It is a real fairy story, like the ones you say happen between the armies

of kings in other lands! They are on the hills around the village! You must look out the window to see them!"

"*And if I look out the window, will you promise to go to sleep, and not only close your eyes and pretend to sleep, like I think sometimes our Vladimir does?"*

"*I promise, papa. I will go to sleep, and tomorrow we will go sledding down the hill with the birch trees."*

His papa pulled the bearskin up to his chin, and then tousled his hair with his hand, and bending, gave him a tender, bristly kiss.

"*All right, old chap. I'll have a look at your army of dog-men and wolf-riders."*

His father went to the window, and with a smile of paternal tenderness looked out at the snowy night, now glistening bright beneath the full moon. But as he did, his look of paternal tenderness quickly changed. It became a terrible mask, one that Vladimir had never seen his papa wear before.

.....Yes, there were wolf riders, an army of them. In the light of the moon he could see the sparkle of their swords......

In the morning the sun did not rise over a village made pristinely white with the year's first snow. It did not rise over a hill of birch trees with children sledding down its side.

It rose instead over a blanket of whiteness blotched with great stains of blood, and littered with arms and legs, and the heads of the dead staring from garden stakes, and hung in windows and doorways of the houses.

Circling above, and some roosting on the fences and roofs, some alighting on the corpses, and the dismembered parts of those corpses, were great flocks of large birds. In the storm of their caws, and the feast they had found, was the cackle of a witch.

II

Issyk-Kul, Kyrgyzstan, Summer, 1339

SHE felt him stir, foment, and his seed begin to angrily rise. She felt the thrusts of his horn madden and butt with greater fury. She felt the moment of his helpless potency, and how he was crazed with the flame now set wildly ablaze in his loins. She felt him begging her like a child to free him, to extinguish this flame, to douse its wrath, and receive the boiling drops of his hunter's strength.

She felt his need for her to lift her legs, and though wrinkled and stubby, to wrap them about his strong back.....to squeeze him tightly, and thereby squeeze the venom from the angry serpent he had loosed inside her...to hear his cry, and hearing it, to feel this serpent spit its spew.......

And then it was over; and he laid limp and panting heavily upon her, like a sea urchin washed ashore by a storm, its gills gasping vainly for air.

This moment was very sweet for her, this moment when she knew that he had returned from the hunt, and as he had done a thousand times before, once more given the need he had saved for her. In this moment she was reassured that he still needed the pleasure she gave to him, and receiving that pleasure, be satisfied; be stilled.

Only one thing was different this time. When he had finished, he did not nuzzle her cheek, or murmur love words in her ear. He did not stand, and as the act had invigorated his manliness, go outside to shoot his arrows at the rabbits and squirrels, and the birds in the trees. This time he only sighed deeply, rolled leadenly off the top of her, and quickly lapsed into sleep.

Kelka kissed her husband's shoulder, and then rose, dressed, and began to prepare their midday meal. She smiled as she did. It pleased her to have her Kutluk stay sleeping in their bed. It pleased her for him not to go to the taverns, shoot his arrows, or feed the hawks and falcons in their cages while she was preparing the meal.

She looked at her husband sleeping naked on their bed. His hair was thinning, his beard, graying, and his stomach, swelling. But he was still a strong beautiful man, perhaps the strongest in the village, even among the young men and the brawny. The muscles of his shoulders, arms and hams were still firm, and like a lion's, were knitted into a beautiful, graceful might.

As the years were not hunting him, but he was hunting the years, his eyes and ears were still keen, his muscles, strong, and his steps, swift and steady. He was still the leader of the hunts of bear and elk and wolf, like the one from which he had just returned.

Kelka knew that her Kutluk sometimes laid with other women on these hunts. She knew that his words and his smile, even in his old age cast a spell upon women. Kelka knew that this was probably the reason that Kutluk had not kissed her after he had made love to her. Kelka smiled. She was sure he had found a woman he had loved many times, and this was the reason he was now asleep on their bed.

When the meal was prepared, Kelka went to wake Kutluk. She smiled to see him still fast asleep, and to think that even as an old man he had played so vigorously with another woman. She smiled to think that even Kutluk, the great hunter, could be so exhausted with the little games of love.

She kissed his shoulders, then down his back, and then his muscular haunches, but Kutluk was sleeping very deeply, and did not wake. Lying down by his side, Kelka then kissed her sleeping husband's chest, and then the mound of his belly, and when that did not wake him, she began to tenderly kiss the pride of his might: that cluster now hanging limply beneath his belly.

As his manhood was a pet bird, and she a child holding that pet bird in her hands, she began to cherish it; to caress and tenderly kiss it; to speak to it.

"*Oh, why is my mighty hunter still sleeping when the sun is high? Was my mighty hunter naughty on the hunt? Did he find a young pretty doe that wanted to play with him? Ah, but the great lion has returned to his Kelka, has he not? He likes Kelka best of all, does he not? Wake, great hunter, wake my Kutluk, your Kelka has made a beautiful meal to celebrate her mighty hunter's return!*"

Slowly and groggily, her husband groaned, as her kisses at last tickled him awake. He opened his eyes, but did not smile or speak, and when Kelka brought her face to his face she saw that his eyes were smoky, and he seemed to only partly recognize who she was; as he was looking at her from a dream. Softly Kelka whispered in his ear.

"*Come Kutluk, your meal is ready. I have prepared the rabbit that the falcon caught yesterday.*"

When Kutluk had dressed and came to his meal, he seemed uncharacteristically silent, and not full of his usual anecdotal brag. But when he began to eat, and found what Kelka had prepared for him very pleasing, he became animated, and narrated several adventures of the hunt. He even laughed when Kelka teased him about his deep sleep after their lovemaking.

"*I think my husband hunted more than bears on this hunt. At last, after forty years, the hunted has slain the hunter.*"

Kutluk smiled wryly, as his secret was known, before replying.

"*Woman is that creature a man's arrows may never slay, not if he has ten thousand in his quiver. She is like the wind, and the dreams and whispers the wind brings. Still, knowing this, the hunter continues to hunt the dreams and whispers of the wind.*"

But after this brief play, Kutluk seemed to alter again. His few words became slurred and disjointed, and trailed off before completing ideas. When he pushed his unfinished plate of meat aside, and abruptly began to stand from his chair, he suddenly paled, groaned and convulsed, and then violently retched on the floor. Ashamed, he wiped himself, mumbled, and without another word walked outside their hut.

Concerned, Kelka watched her husband. He went to the cages of the hawks and falcons, as he did after all of his meals, feeding them the rats and snakes the children caught for him. He then took his bow, fitted an arrow upon its string, and loosed it as he always did into the target of his favorite tree. But stretching back the bow's string with a second arrow, he stopped, laid his bow and arrow down, and walked back into the hut. Once in the hut, he went directly to his bed, and without uttering another word, went to sleep.

A short while later the sleeper broke into a sweat and fever. When Kelka tried to rouse him for their supper meal, he muttered unintelligibly, and then angrily cursed her. A short while later when Kelka helped him remove his clothes, he broke into laughter, and spoke as he was not speaking to Kelka, but to someone who was not there.

"*Oh, so you want to play again with Kutluk! You want to give Kutluk your flower, do you not? Yes, Kutluk is married, but he is married to someone wrinkled and ugly, not young and beautiful like you. Come, let us play. I want to pick your pretty flower again!*"

Her husband's night was long and troubled, full of fever and senseless ejaculations to friends and enemies, women he had loved, and those long dead. In the morning Kelka discovered two swellings, sprouted like mushrooms from her husband's body.

One was egg-shaped and egg-sized, and had appeared in one of his armpits. Another was the size of an apple, and had appeared between his navel and his male part. Tenderly probing this larger, blackening lump, Kutluk screamed out with pain, unable to sustain Kelka's most feathery touch. Kutluk the great hunter, who had killed countless bears and lions on countless hunts, rolled over moaning on his side, and again lapsed into a fever-haunted sleep.

As morning reached noon, and noon grew into the afternoon, a worried Kelka watched as her husband developed new symptoms of this mysterious distemper. He began to cough, even in his sleep, and when he did he gurgled forth thick knots of bloody sputum into his beard and upon his pillow. Several more black tumors appeared: one on his throat, and still another on his groin. His body began to smell, filling the hut with a sharp, malodorous stench. Kutluk the great hunter, was rotting before his Kelka's very eyes.

* * *

AS night began to gather, Kutluk lapsed into a delirium, one that was neither sleep nor waking. Sitting at his side, swabbing his body and vainly trying to clean him of the blood he was discharging, Kelka heard the strange visions ejaculated by the terrible spirit that had taken hold of her husband, the one he had brought back from the hunt.

.....men hung naked from trees, dangling by their feet, their tongues and their scrotums.....wild men running through forests, mating with beasts..... young girls fornicating with wolves and stags, knelt with open mouths to the phalluses of giant bears.....those burning in furnaces and in cauldrons of boiling oils and lards, or drowning in sloughs of excrement......men on racks, impaled, pulled apart by horses.....jackals eating the hearts of the dead.......

As the second day reached the third, Kutluk no longer waked from his deliriums. Kelka could no longer adequately sop the blood that spilled not only from his mouth, but from his nose, ears, eyes and anus. Her champion was dying in her arms, but in the most wretched of ways; a way that made the great hunter unrecognizable to his devoted wife. Helplessly, Kelka watched as her handsome husband donned a mask of hideous grotesqueness.

......the prodigiously swollen, bruise-black lips.....the tongue so swollen his mouth could no longer contain it, emerging like a black snake......so swollen he could not swallow a drop of water.....his eyes bulging from their sockets, as they wanted to escape the house in which they had been planted, so that even in sleep the curtains of his eyelids could not close.....the tumors growing and multiplying, and around them blackening and gangrening...... the discharges of his blood soaking the pillow and the bed....crusting his beard, throat and chest......the reek of death bringing crows to the trees

outside their hut, their eyes sparkling avariciously at the preparation of their feast......

Kelka had become a Christian when she was young. She had been baptized by a missionary priest when she was a girl, and had become a member of the Nestorian faith. She brought the crucifix from the little altar she had erected in the hut's corner, and began to pass it slowly up and down the length of her husband's dying, hideously corrupting body.

As Jesus ordered evil spirits to flee from men, she was ordering the evil spirit that was living in her husband's body to leave, the evil spirit that strangely gurgled, as if hissing like a devil when she touched the crucifix to the black tumors swelling from his body.

* * *

KELKA woke to the silence of the night. She woke in the bed where, as her husband's concubine, she had given her body so many times; where she had caressed and spoken tender words to him; where she had conceived sons and daughters for him.

Kelka woke to the night strangely pleased and at peace. Her Kutluk was no longer moaning or coughing, and the great struggle heaving and rattling in his mighty chest was gone. Like Jesus, she had exorcised the evil spirit from his body, and in its fleeing, the spirit had broken his flesh, and had ended his life.

.....It was over. Kutluk the great hunter was dead......

She was strangely happy lying next to the body of her dead husband; its growing coldness; its rottenness; its rancidity. She had heard of women who had raved in madness at their husband's death; others who insisted on being buried alive, nailed in the same coffin, and lowered into the cold ground rather than to go on living with their unbearable sorrow beneath the sun. She had heard of some who had cast themselves from high rocks, or into the sea, or into flames of a fire. Yes, she was happy. It was an honor to lay in the bed with Kutluk, the father of her children, and the greatest hunter of their village.

Kelka was also happy because she knew the devil that had fled her husband's body had entered into her own. She felt her lungs begin to burn, and her tongue to chalk and swell. She had felt and seen the black swellings emerge from her breasts and groins. She had begun to grow hot and thirsty, and her mind to blur with the rages of a fever.

But waking from her brief sleep to the still night, lying next to her husband's body, her mind was awake with a sweet, perhaps last lucidity. She heard the forest full of cricket-song. She heard a child's laughter, and a love song sung by a young girl. Her God seemed indifferent with the passing of Kutluk, the great hunter, as He was perhaps indifferent with the passing of all men, Kelka thought that perhaps this indifference was a *compassion*, a *compassion* that smiled on both the dead and the living; as men were very small in His eyes, as small as these crickets chirping in the night.

Kelka opened her eyes, but she did not see the animal pelts, the spears, or the bags made from goats' bladders hanging above her. She saw instead beyond the hut's ceiling into the limitless forest of the stars; the forest where her Kutluk had now gone to hunt.

Yes, that is where he had gone. Kutluk the hunter was too mighty to die, and there he had gone to hunt with his spear and arrows among those sparkling trees. There he would fly his swift falcons. There he would kill bears and lions. There he would lay with many women, having won them with his smile.

Kelka knew that she would follow her Kutluk into that forest. She knew that she would await his return from his many hunts. She knew her Kutluk, the mighty hunter, would always return to her arms.

III

Feodosiya; Ukraine, 1343-1347

ITS ancient Greek name was *Theodosia*, but when it had been gathered in by the southern arm of *Mother Russia*, it had been changed to *Feodosiya*; and when the *Mongolian* armies had won it, it had been changed to *Caffa*. It was in no way considered a treasure to the barbarians, that, with a great army mounted on stubby horses had come from somewhere far away on a sea of tall grass to possess it. It was a lonely, rocky, wind-swept and sun-bleached village on the *Black Sea*; little more than a fishing village, a hub for bands of nomads that came with their flocks to barter and suck hashish from hookahs.

But its sleepy insignificance was to change in a most dramatic way. The irrepressible pluck in the *Italian* blood, and in particular, the *Genoese* blood was here to attain a firm foothold, and begin to climb the unexplored mountains of this part of the world. Granted permission by the *Golden Horde* itself, *Genoese* financiers and merchants made their way to *Caffa*, and at once the alchemy of *East* and *West* worked a great miracle in this rocky crucible nestled on this desolate coast.

It did not take long for the enterprising *Genoese* to reap a wealth of rewards. *Caffa's* location proved not only an ideal port for ships, but an ideal trading center for herdsmen and caravans alike; an eye of a needle threaded by many empires: *India*, *Syria*, *China* and *Russia*, and countless cultures in between. As they were stone mushrooms, within a few decades towers, ramparts, steeples and minarets cropped up, and by the 1300's the quiet little fishing village had been transported to a thriving city with mazy streets, and a population speaking many tongues. It had become an opulent threshold from which the *Silk Road* began and ended its interminable meandering to and from the *East*.

Almost overnight it became a cosmopolitan thoroughfare trading in the most accomplished and cherished commodities known to man. Its markets, bazaars and streets were filled with valuables and exotic goods, most of which had never been seen beneath the Ukrainian sun.

.....*Fruits of all tastes, colors, shapes.....sweet with a warmer, richer sun......honey, rice and teas, and the seeds of Italian grapes, the precious seeds for future generations of vineyards, whose harvests could be pressed, stored and fermented into delicious purple wines.......*

.....*Bazaars devoted to all patterns, textures and dyed colors of wool, flax, cotton, silk and damask......skins, raw pelts and lushly combed furs..... carpets and curtains, rugs, blankets, tapestries woven with lions, fantastic birds and many-headed gods......bazaars devoted to spices.....cinnamon and ginger and turmeric....fragrances and perfumes.....jewels inlaid in silver and gold.....coral and ivory and amber.....stalls filled with ceramics and glazes from Samarkand, blown glass from Italy, delicate snow-white porcelains from China.....vases, bowls, decanters.....stalls with horns and elephant tusks, polished turtle shells, figurines of glass, rosewood, jade and ivory.....on the quays, hills of timber from Siberia.....tools and weapons of iron with which to farm, or take to war......*

.....*cages with wide-eyed monkeys, brightly colored parrots, royal little singing birds.....snakes and great lizards, long-haired sheep and silky goats.....cages of bears and leopards, tigers and lions.....great rows of sleek proud horses, and sleepy-eyed camels.......*

But *Caffa's* most prized commodity was its slaves; slaves of all races, all sizes and ages; men, women and children. Bound on their owners' leashes, they would stand half naked, stoically burning in the sun, or freezing in the cold, inspected by traders and prospective owners with an eye for domestic servants, field workers, whores and concubines. The prospective buyers would run their hands over the muscles in the men's backs, arms, haunches and buttocks; sometimes taking their testicles into their hands to ascertain their virility. They would undress the women, and run their hands over their naked parts; sometimes tasting their kisses; sometimes fondling their breasts; sometimes pressing their vulvas to see how willing they were to be aroused.

Exultant with the glorious success of *Caffa*, the *Italians* expanded to a second village. In a short while they began to trade and merchant with *Tana*, another small village on the sea whose fortuitous location was also ideal for a lucrative port. It too would be an integral stop on that vast, serpentining route for camel, horse and caravan: the *Silk Road*.

But here the ambitious *Genoese* would encounter a snag in their quest to partake of the world's illimitable riches; a snag that since time immemorial had halted the greatest kings and armies: the snag of a *qyarrek*.

Tana became *Caffa's* twin brother. It too boasted bazaars of exotic abundance. Its streets also became filled with incessant bickering and bartering from frenetic sellers, buyers and barterers; at times pitting not only goods and seller-ship against each other, but also race and religious beliefs; beliefs that often butted heads, and ran against the grain of other beliefs. Sometimes caviling would break into arguments, arguments that would heat the blood, double the fists, and place sharp knives in those fists.

.....The Muslim merchant lay in a pool of blood in the sun-baked street, blood that poured from the mouths of his wounds in his abdomen, chest and throat, and gurgled deliriously from his mouth......then kicked over and over by a dozen of his Christian foes, trampled by the hoofs of a horse and the wheels of a cart.....waking the wrath of a dragon, a dragon that was an army, an army that had amassed the greatest kingdom ever known to man.....an army that was the living legacy of the great Khan himself.......

Realizing too late the rashness of their folly, and the immeasurable stakes with which they were playing, the *Italians* found themselves embroiled with hostile foes that outnumbered them twenty to one. They made a gallant, but retreating defense, only in the end to flee to their ships; leaving a world of riches behind, but midst storms of arrows, escaping with their lives.

The race was on; one praying that propitious winds would fill their sails, the other that the thundering hoofs of their horses could out-speed those sails. The gods decided to favor the former, and the *Italians* reached *Caffa* before their pursuers, suing for the asylum that was granted them behind its walls, A grudge still lived in the hearts of the natives, a grudge full of tales of the barbaric *Tartars* razing their village and raping their women. *Caffa* closed its gates, and like a dog baring its fangs, insolently growled at the army of armed horsemen that came to surround it.

It was a siege that was to be successfully withstood, It was 1343, and for the first time the *Khan's* great army was stymied and balked, not by warriors and weapons, but by great stone walls, and a port that could continue to feed and supply the imprisoned. Their savagery waked and irked, the *Mongolians* shot showers of arrows over the walls, arrows full of fire or barbed with poison, arrows that fell harmlessly inside the safely bunkered city. Two years later, the *Khan's* soldiers did the unthinkable. Grown tired and bored, and humiliated with being so repulsed, the *Tartars* decamped, leaving the surrounding hills deserted, charred and denuded from their futile stay.

Faith had championed over barbarism. God had heard their Christian prayers. *Caffa's* gates were opened, and the breath of heaven, full of the perfumes of peace and flowers, once more breathed into them.

But these peaceful airs were to prove only the calm before an uglier and more uncompromising storm. Incensed at their inability to break down the walls of their own city, the *Tartars* returned with reinforcements, and a vow to slay, mutilate and burn each living man, woman and child behind *Caffa's* walls.

This time they brought more than rage, a city of tents and whores, and those who would engineer and build their catapults. They brought a mightier foe, a deadlier foe, a foe that like an army of ghosts could not be impaled or decapitated with swords; a foe the eye could not see; a traitorous foe that killed their own.

In the weeks and months in which the *Tartars* entrenched themselves about these impregnable walls, the tide of a mysterious disease crept into their ranks, one that would wage combat with, and smite the bravest and bloodiest warriors the world had ever known. The combat was swift, and almost always fatal, pitting *the seen* against *the unseen*; first fevering its barbarous victim, then blotching, blackening, and infesting him with stinking tumors. Within hours or days its victim, a mighty warrior in the *Golden Horde*, was rotting in a heap with rotting others.

The tide of the pestilence flowed through the *Tartar* ranks like a sieve, killing at will, and filling their camps day and night with violent coughs, retching, moans of untold anguish; shrieks of those being burned in fires and dreams of fever. The blade of this unseen foe was keen and swift, and in a matter of only a few months the siege began to weaken, thin, and disperse. They who did not know fear, sickened with fear, deserting this battle fought with bodiless spirits; spirits whose general's eye grew increasingly merry and thirsty the greater was his slaughter.

Watching from the tops of their parapets, the *Genoese* rejoiced that once more the God of *Abraham* and *Isaac* had heard their prayers. Their God had intervened. He had dispatched his hosts of Angels, and their golden arrows had littered their foe's camps with the slain.

But this was a foe that cared not for the arrows of Angels, and a God that smugly flouted them. Filled with the rage of defeat, the ridicule cast on them from the tops of their own walls, and death's smoking sword that mowed through their ranks, the *Tartars* devised a way to retaliate: casting death itself over the walls at those that so mocked and scoffed at them.

Instead of casting stones with their catapults, they would lob their corpses, naked and hideously corrupted with disease. Attaching this new ammunition to their machines, they would catapult the dead with their flailing arms and legs into this city that had defied them.

The catapults were inched closer to the walls, and there loaded with those that Heaven's hosts had slain with their fiery arrows. Soon the diseased and decomposing bodies of the dead began to breach these formidable ramparts, thudding inside on roofs, and splattering grotesquely apart, like melons in the streets; dismembering and spilling their contaminated viscera, brains and rottenness into *Caffa's* sanctuary. Those whose trajectories were not sufficient, hit against the walls, creating a ghastly moat of carnage below them.

The bombardment of these naked corpses caused a pandemonium of horror among those who had considered themselves so divinely favored. Their safe asylum suddenly became an inescapable prison, their prison, a charnel house. The rain of corpses brought with them an effluvium of death and decay, a putrescence that seeped beneath doors, permeated clothes and bedding, breathed its foulness into the lungs of man, woman and child. Teams were assigned to collect and shovel the gore and body parts into barrows and wagons, and in designated places bury them. But a great part of the enemy had died, and the survivors were now in possession of a great arsenal of this ghastly ammunition, so that the constant lobbing of corpses day and night out-sped all efforts to collect and dispose of them. Soon hoofs, wheels and boots became filthy with *Tartar* guts and blood.

Great clouds of carrion birds gathered, roosting on trees, walls, roofs and towers of every kind. No blast would fright or discourage them, for their eyes looked upon a feast they had not seen before. As incestuous as snakes in a snake pit, the city was now invaded by another army; a verminish army that bred in offal and carnage; the scurrying, swarming, four-footed brothers of the winged scavengers above them; that gnawed with death, rather than picked at it.

And as the assault of the dead continued, contagion began to take hold and spread behind their protective walls, breathing its fatal fumes through their streets and into their houses. As if death's spirit did not discriminate between *Tartar* and *Christian*, between those who prayed on their knees and those who slew with swords, they who had prided themselves in their God's clemency also began to fever, swell, bleed and blacken; and agonizing, quickly perish in the most ghastly fashion.

* * *

SEVERAL years later, exhausted of corpses to pitch over *Caffa's* walls, the four year siege ended, and the *Mongols* retreated, decimated, but victorious, into the greening hills and the bloomy sea of steppes beyond.

Those still living among the *Genoese* rigged and manned their ships, and set sail for their homeland, thanking God once more for their deliverance from such horrors.

The breezes, fresh and moderate, filled their sails....a genial sun, and a gentle sea. But although they were freed from death's prison, death refused to be left behind, wanting also to smell the salt of a richer sea and to feel the beams of a richer sun. This prison mate clung to the escapees like leeches.....

invisibly it supped and tippled with them, prayed with them.....was their bedfellow...its laughing, drunken, lust-crazed ghost preparing to step ashore at Constantinople, Marseilles, Sardinia, Corsica.....Sicily.......

These returning ships were laden with thankful sailors, and cargoes of many exotic treasures.....among them a monkey than ran up and down the decks, chattering, even as it was laughing, even as it knew it would be the end of the world.

....

....

CHAPTER TWO

BLIZZARDS

Morning; early winter; 1340

LEAVING *Siena* that dark, cold, snowy morning, Brother Maria walked deeper and deeper into the gray woods that stood solemn and naked before him. He began on a carter's trail, but under the heavily falling snow the trail quickly blurred and became indistinct, and soon disappeared into the white blanket that was blanketing all. Soon he did not know whether his steps were bearing him towards, or away from the sun, or indeed if they were leading him in delirious circles beneath it. Gripped by a pain greater than cold or hunger, he did not know *who* or *what* he *was*, nor, as the victim of such a blind pain, did he care.

After walking the morning through, he paused in a small clearing, and for the first time tried to assess his irrational departure from the city, marching like a deserting soldier into the wilderness stretching gray, snowy and endless all about him.

The snow was thickening in the air, deepening about his boots, the drifts sometimes cresting about his knees. He knew night would bring a bitter cold, even as he had begun to feel it in fitful, stinging bites and buffetings of gusting wind. He had brought no food. He had no flint to make a fire, and even if he had, it might be difficult to find and collect armfuls of dry fuel. Leaving his fate to blind, irresponsible luck, he might stumble upon a farm or cottage, but if he did not he would have no choice but to spend the night in the forest. He had a knife, but no gun to defend himself against dangerous enemies, either man or beast. His gloves and coat were warm, lined with furs of rabbit and squirrel, and his boots were of wolf hide, but they would

336

not be impervious to an entire night of snowy, knifing cold; a cold that was even now finding his ears, feet and hands, as if it was a poison making its slow, numbing way to his heart.

If he would turn about, he could still reach the city's gates before nightfall. The guards would recognize him, and they would admit him, regardless of the curfew. In the city there were any number of sheds, stables, and tavern nooks, and if he wished, the bodies of lovers to keep him warm. In a day or two the moon would change, and the weather would lighten and clear. The paths and roads would again be made visible by the traffic of sleds, carts and horses used by the trappers and country marketers. Remaining in the city for a few days would give him time to ask of roads and directions; perhaps places for employment; perhaps inns or almshouses on his way.

This, beyond all else, was certain: the night would come early in the forest, and if it would find him with its ambush of snow, cold and wolves, he could very well perish.

And yet, after a short pause with these dark meditations, Maria turned and continued his blind desertion from the hospitable into the inhospitable; away from the amenities the city walls offered, into the cold hostility of the forest.

.....but why, why was he so rashly leaving.....no, not leaving, but fleeing?......

As he walked on, Maria began to consider causes of this strange madness that had gripped him; reasons that were fueling his aimless, death-tempting, scoffing steps; the flame inside him that was braving the darkness of the forest, the drifts and winds of the blizzard; making his vulnerability so careless and fearless of all possible dangers he was boldly provoking.

As he continued he became convinced it was a thing that was beyond the reach of reason; something in which reason had no play or part in. It was instead an instinct, an instinct that was a response to a raw pain, like an animal wounded by a hunter, driven deeper and deeper back into the wilderness from which it had come, into which it wished to die; a savage wound that threatened his heart and broke his dreams. It was a rawest anguish, unrelenting and unforgiving, a dark primal hurt that scorned the pettiness of any justification or compassion; a wicked thorn in his heart, whose abscessing had infected every part of him. It was not a thing to be reasoned with, or in any way tempered. Madness was its only friend and comforter. Anguish, not bravery was demanding him leave, charging him headfirst, blindly and soullessly into the storm. The pangs in his stomach and the fears in his mind......death itself was insignificant compared with the open bleeding of this gash in his heart.

It was a pain he had not named, a meaning not given words, a mystery he had not lent an identity, thus one he could not parley with or defend against. No, it was something more primal than words, some wordless thing that was consuming him, and consuming him it had become a permanent part of him. It had become his fire, food, weapon, shelter. It was the lover he would make love to as the winds and the wolves howled; the lover in whose arms he must die.

It would walk with him through all fears; bleed with him in love; freeze with him in death. Its thorn had lodged in his heart, and unable to extract it, he must learn to live with its rankling. One with the first hunters, gatherers, warriors, he must embrace the wilderness of his loneliness; resolve to live, love and die in his cold estrangement.

But how could such a bitter irony be his lot? How could he be lonely when he was so admired whenever he touched the lute's or fiddle's strings; when he sang in a tavern, laughed about a fire, smiled at a maid in a garden? How could it be that he who had been told by so many that they loved him, was exiled by the authority of his own heart, as if he was forever destined to seek a greater, deeper, more barren loneliness; as if he was a creature whose wildness was given human intimacy, only that he might spurn and shun that intimacy; fearing the protection offered him by the walls of cities and abbeys, even the tender arms of mistresses more than he feared cold and hunger, death itself?

What kind of man had he become, or indeed had he ever been; one who lived only to love and be loved by women and by dreams, but somehow remaining starved of the treasures both laid at his feet? What was it about his pain that seemed so bitter, and at the same time so sweet, that seemed to lend a kind of encouragement and validation to his spirit? Why did he feel he was meant to live apart from all others; that it was at once his curse and his blessing; that although so many women wanted to fondle and play with him, none wanted to keep him, and keeping him, share in his banishment? Why did they leave him in the early mornings for boorish ploughboys, or husbands that were cruel louts and drunkards?

And yet was he not as guilty as they; just as inconstant, uncaring; devotion-less? Was the pain his heart incurred by lovers when they left his arms not quickly forgotten with new smiles and new kisses; new frolics in the hay? Did he not leave the arms of one lover only to fall into the arms of another?

And why did he remember so few? And why did courtship at times seem to assume a kind of routine, a kind of predictability; prescribed seasons, almost a pomp and ceremony of welcome, play and farewell? Why were there times when he seemed to tire and cloy with the games he played with his lovers, even the most eager ones? Why did his heart warm and sing, only to grow cold again? Why at times did he feel defeated in the wake of love's sweetest victories?

Yes, his loneliness had consumed him, like the snow and the forest were consuming him.....its despair telling him again and again that he was a vagrant in life, one who had culled none of summer's flowers, even while others had knelt to gather great assortments for their baskets....a forlornness in a wilderness, a forlornness that was a deepest ache, an ever bleeding wound that would not close, that pleasures salved, only to salt the more with their absence, with their fleetingness.......

Gradually the cold began to invade his thoughts. Gradually the furies in his mind began to fade as the sluices of his blood began to shiver; as both were congealing into ice. Maria stopped and stood still, as if suddenly slapped awake, filled with the premonition of a danger that now starkly confronted him; one that mocked all other dangers; a danger men call 'death'. Night, the stealthiest of predators had crept through the forest trees, stalking him, and now with the wind and bitter cold on its flanks, had inescapably surrounded him. Like a pack of wolves it howled at his human smallness and stupidity that had walked into the lair of its eternal darkness; a howling darkness that forever laughed, that forever hungered.

The snow had become heavier, its flakes grittier, as they now contained tiny stones, no longer whisked by a playful wind, but now driven through the teeth of a crueler, more vengeful one. The hurt of his flesh began to overcome the hurt of his spirit, and for the first time he thought how foolish he had been to imagine he would stumble upon a cabin, a barn or hamlet, even as he had always imagined that youth and love lay inexhaustible at his beck; that in his roaming there would always be another shelter, and with that shelter another lover whose arms would beckon to his needs and dreams.....bathing in a brook, picking meadow flowers, dreaming wistfully at a gate.....that he, a spendthrift with eternity in his pockets, would bring a song to their hearts and a kiss to their lips.

But with the quickly falling night, and the un-abating wind and snow, there was no shelter of hay, or a woman's warm arms to comfort him. He felt instead other arms begin to enfold him; sly and cold, not warm and consoling; arms wanting to embrace him with that embrace that awaits all men; whose tenderness grows strangling tight.

He slipped his knife into his glove, but the knife was cold, and it only made his hand the colder, so that he was not sure if his numbing fingers gripped its blade or hilt. He could build no fire, and something like a cold iron chain squeezed about his throat, preventing him from screaming out. Like a forest animal, he burrowed into a thick fir tree, digging his way to its trunk. Its boughs would be his shelter; its needles, like a porcupine, his defending swords. No, he did not want to die. He did not want to be strangled by this lover who was stalking and seducing him, whispering dark erotic possibilities to his soul; asking him to play with these twin playmates of love and death.

.....the darkness, the quickening snow and wind, the approach of the night all around him.....the cold poison inching nearer and nearer his heart.....as it was the last heart, the last warmth in the forest....as its precious treasure had been entrusted to his keeping, and he must protect it, or else the last human dreams would die, and never sing again.......

He would remain standing through the night; if needs, be attacked, flayed apart and eaten while he stood; he would stand rather than lie down and, flake by flake be buried.....be as honorable at his end, as he had been a fool with all of the prodigal chances he had squandered in his life.....like a soldier, he would greet death, that little jest that God plays on men.....he would stand at the last with defiance against those dreams whose trinkets God had flattered and burdened him with.....he would prepare to kill the hungry wolves of this God's Angel army.

The snow and darkness had imprisoned him, joining forces, uniting, locking arms, as if night and snow were not, nor ever had been two, but one, the interwoven cords of the same hunter's net. In the last failing gasp of gray fading light he saw the tracks that led to this tree; tracks that were sifting full, drifting over; erasing their maker's existence. Whose tracks had they been, that no hunter or lover would ever find or follow?....Whose these drops of blood dripped from a wound in a heart, a wound that no doctor could stitch, and that time could not heal?

.....No, he would hold his satchel to his end.....be buried with its treasures of slippers, ribbons, tresses and earrings, little pieces of under-things he had removed from peasant girls, tavern girls, harlots. He would guard them to his end, and with them the memories of giggles, moans, deep sighs of surrender.....he would keep their secrets, the secrets they had whispered

in his ears...he would keep them safe, or be buried with them forever.......

.....Who had been this one named 'Brother Maria', and what had been his dreams?........

He would pray the night through....no, not pray...he would not be a hypocrite at his end. He would instead dream the night through....dream dreams of women, yes, dream as he was praying before holy altars, altars made of silly laughter, kisses and pretty naked bodies....even at his death, he would dream of their bodies, and the many pleasures they gave with their prettiness.....not the solemn altars with candles and dead clay idols that they had long replaced.....that he no longer believed in.......

.....women he had seen or known, running naked in the snow before him.....their breasts and buttocks like ripened fruits, their smiles like summer roses, their hips and thighs like loaves of warm bread.....all of them, like beautiful rabbits, beckoning him to their warrens...inviting him to lie on their warm bodies.....drink the wine of their kisses, know the silky ferns between their legs.....be blanketed by their arms and perfume-heavy tresses......

.....and the sister, the holy sister with the veil, standing in the snow as he remembered the statue of the Virgin in the abbey's courtyard.....begging him to come to her, to drink from her breasts.....to kneel at her feet, lift up her habit's skirt, and taste the warm honey of her holy mystery.......

But he would not go to her. He would not go to any of them. He would stay burrowed in the tree's thick branches. He would preserve his little warmth, this last and only warmth.....He would cradle his satchel in his breast, and preserve the warmth of his dreams........

He would watch these rabbit maidens tumble and play in the snow until the dawn came. They would keep him alive until light chased them back into the dark forest. Another night, when the storm had passed, and death no longer held a knife to his throat, he would play with them, many of them in the snow and moonlight.

* * *

Two years later;
Early winter; a hilltop; 1342

THE morning spoke of snow. It spoke in the grayness that had settled through the bare branches of the forest like a smoke. It spoke in the rags of clouds that raced fugitive across the early sky, then in the thicker, darker clouds that, in tumbling avalanches fell from the mountaintops; their sleight-gray underbellies swollen, as they were udders full of icy milk.

It spoke in the stillness that now gripped and intimidated all with suspense, so that no rasping reed, no chattering squirrel or pecking bird could be heard; as if nature's breath was held, and all was deafened and drowned, awed by a presence mightier than itself. And in this silence the great secret was imparted to the bloods of creature-kind, lending a premonition to their knowing; that knowing seen in the quiet eyes of goat and horse, in dog, mouse and bird, even the fish that lay cold and still, like sleek stones on the beds of the brooks.

It spoke to *men* as well. It spoke in the knife that no garment could stay, the knife that entered the heart with a sharp cold chill, telling *man's* blood it was no better or worse than the blood of the forest creatures; that it too would grow cold and freeze, and when it did, the creature that had been permitted to warmly dream would become slow, numb, and be forgotten forever.

When Maria felt this cold knife pierce the vital place inside him, he did not wince. Yes, the snow would come. Yes, this tiny hammer pounding in his breast, ringing with so many sunny dreams and songs, this tiny hammer that was no stronger than a violet would grow cold and numb, and quitting its little beats, would freeze into forgetfulness. Yes, the snow would come. Yes, he would die. Yes, Brother Maria would be no more.

All morning he was busy collecting his nets from the half-frozen brook, baiting and setting his traps, and pounding tall stakes so that he would not lose them beneath that flood of whiteness that he knew was bursting its cloudy gates. He made sure the stable was supplied with oats and hay for his horse and goat. He piled high the wood stack near the door, and brought many armfuls to his hearth. He covered the cracks in his small cabin as best he could with blankets and pelts.

As he went about his chores he felt tiny flecks fall into his hair, eyebrows and beard, and then melt in the fragile warmth into which their white seeds had been sown. He felt cold little nuggets on his cheeks and hands. He felt the cold slyly, thievishly creeping through his boots, and the sting of the air, deft as a pickpocket poking and fleecing blindly through his coat; as its hand was greedily searching for the little bird that still sang in the cage of his ribs.

And as he went about his chores in anticipation of the storm, a great pleasure filled him, a pleasure not of accomplishment or possessions, but rather of his infinitesimal smallness; as he was a blade, a husk, a petal, whose smallness was part of a perpetual, endless farewell to the sun; his dreams about to be buried, his dreams that were no more than a chaff, a chaff he once fancied the flourishing of trumpets.

It was not only that he was glad with his insignificance, but with the honesty with which he accepted it. Still, more than feeling his proud heart was about to be buried, he felt befriended, as he was not alone in the great wilderness of life. The fires and thunders inside him at last could commune, wrestle, dance and die with kindred spirits, with brothers and sisters of birds, beasts and flowers, all of which forever wage, and forever lose the battle with the crushing foe of their own mortality.

.....and he would lose life's sweetness as well, those little sips of summer's honey, like the sips the bees steal from the flowers.....their sweetness taken to a hive that shall never wake to spring.....those little sips of sweetness that had gradually become a nuisance, an incessant, laborious toil and thankless dream.......

For did not the pleasure offered in courtship and lovemaking prove as brief as it was sweet; its truth, never to be trusted? The frolic and warfare of the sexes often left one feeling foolish, futile or deluded; the moans in the dark, the spark in the loins, the tender whispers in the ear more often than not, when they had died away, leaving one empty, doubtful, and even disdainful of the treasures that had been won or given away; as love had not been a moonlit sea, but a fevered dream in a pitch dark prison.

With the approach of the low gray clouds, his first impulse had been to go to the village, little more than an hour down the hill. He knew such storms called many to the warmth and hilarity of the taverns. There would be many women in these taverns, some whose smiles he had never kissed, and whose breasts he had never held. In addition he knew that he would not be left to stumble back up the hill's snow-drifted paths. There were any number of lovers, former, present or future that would wait for him when the taverns closed, begging him to stay, and to play the games their smiles and eyes had promised to play with him.

Maria had long since learned that women sought out his nearness; that there was that in his long blond hair and clear blue eyes, in his deep swells of laughter and the melodies of his fiddle's strings that they could not forego, like bees that could not forsake autumn's last roses. He had known it since his youth, since he had first left behind the abbey, his vows, and his good friend, Brother Giovanni.

And as the years passed, this original attractiveness did not diminish, but changed to a more charismatic one, one that touched the secret, most vulnerable place in all women's hearts; from the maidenly to the matronly, the virginal to the slatternly; the homely to the comely; the shy, the widowed, the married. The years of hardship and roaming had seasoned him, lending him the keen eye and ruggedness of manhood, but leaving intact the last bloom of his youth. His body had retained its leanness, but now was as strong as it was lean, and as agile as it was strong. One glance from his eyes, one chord from his lute, one finger on a cheek or caress up a calf, and love was conquered and made his. Many were the times that, without a word, strange women brought their mouths to his mouth, their thighs to his thighs, or taking his hand, led him to a place where they were prepared to surrender in completeness.

But there was something more than his strong, romantic appearance, something that separated him from rakishness; something that only the deeper, more delicate sense of a woman's heart could recognize and know. Women knew that this was a lover who wanted to satisfy, as much as he needed to be satisfied; to give as much as he received. He was not ungrateful of the tender gifts given him. He did not treat the ones he loved flippantly or brusquely, but with veneration, even the plain, the meek and the homely. The giver was given to feel the receiver cherished her gifts, and cherishing them, she entrusted them to his keeping, and wanted only to give him more. He obeyed his lovers' every whim and wish; those of naughtiness or childish flirtation; to play like kittens, or more roughly, like dogs. He listened to that mysterious language in women's hearts; when they wished him to be patient, reckless, or devious; when they wished him to rule rather than to capitulate; when they wished him to make them sing fully, as no lover or husband had ever made them do.

Gentle or wild, with the strength of a lion or the sweetness of a warbling bird, women felt the deepest part of their womanhood stir when they were near him, and at once they wanted to give their heart as they had never given it before.

But as the storm grew near, Maria felt a strange reluctance, and then more strongly, a firm resistance to the delightful seductions and adventures that he knew awaited him at the foot of the hill. He would not go to the village tonight. He would not lose himself in wine, dance and song. He would not play the games of smiles, glances and kisses. He would not sleep in the dark forest of a woman's arms.

But why?

It was not yet mid-afternoon, but with the absence of the sun, and the massing swirls of meshing clouds, dusk had begun to fall, and with it a more earnest fall of snow. The gray and brown quilt of the forest floor was quickly being covered, and with it the tawny reeds and berried bushes that hedged the brook. As they were giants being mummified for eternity, the trunks and naked branches of the trees began to be draped, as with burial shrouds. The high parts of the mountains were beginning to whiten, and whitening, vanish into the low clouds, so that earth and sky seemed to be joining into an indistinguishable oneness.

The snow was now such that his boots were making deeply pronounced tracks, tracks that after his errands in the stable, at the brook, and to his small woodshed were completely covered and erased when he returned from them. This seemed to produce a further calm in Maria's heart, a further pleasure, and something deeper than a pleasure; some whimsical irony, some sublime amusement his reason could but wonder and guess at.

Was he not too being buried, buried in simultaneity with the meadows and the forests, with summer's brief flowering? Were his dreams, and the deep and lovely meanings he had given them not being admonished, jeered, interred beneath this cold white confetti softly drifting down from heaven? How small and vain were his visions of moons and hillsides, of sheep and horses and children running through garden paths. How brief and vain those games played in women's arms; how foolish the words of love he whispered in their ears.

Returning from his errands, and in his wake the disappearance of his tracks beneath the gathering storm, Maria had the sensation he had made no tracks at all, that he was not a thing of flesh and blood.....but a ghost, yes a ghost, a spirit of the dead, a bodiless wanderer drifting through the vague mists men call 'life'.....as unsubstantial as are dreams of love and beauty that flattered their ghostly dreamer with the brush of downy wings upon his lips and heart.......

.......Perhaps this was part of the reason why he did not want to go

to the village tonight, to seduce and be seduced.....perhaps he knew too much.....perhaps he knew that love was no more than a tedious, monotonous ritual, or more than a ritual, a dream.....a jaded dream that aging wisdom was too wise or tired to shoulder and endure.......

Were there not times when an indefinable tiredness, an inexplicable futility, an autumnal melancholy welled from deep inside him? He had felt these things with particular poignancy at the times of lovemaking. Watching his lovers unclothe in candlelight, or before a glowing hearth, he felt at times the moments of intimacy, excitement and mystery had been reduced to a mechanical rite......the gown slipped from their shoulders to the floor, the unbinding and letting fall of their tresses.....their smiles and titters, their little sighs as they lay back upon their beds.....the opening of their arms..... the lifting of their legs.....the revelation of their secret flower.......

......it was a ritual he had participated in countless times.....to kiss and whisper, to caress and be caressed, to gratify and be gratified......for an instant to be purged, and perish in the soft sweet flames of arms and thighs......for a few brief moments the pain in the heart to be pampered, consoled, forgiven.....as if love's need was a sacrifice to a larger need, a greater want, a greater starvation.....as it was a piece of meat thrown to a lion in a cage, that the feeder knew full well could never tame its hunger, because its hunger was the endless hunger of the forest from which it had been captured......the eternal hunger of death itself.......

.......What was this ritual men called 'love'?......this blind greed to ravish and be ravished......to blindly grope, and groping touch some deeper, darker, throbbing nerve of undiscovered pleasure?......some dare of the soul, some nursing of the flesh, some promise of a serene finality......whetting a craving that it had promised to blunt and dull......

.......Beneath the tent of love's tenderness was not love a victim, its purity murdered by an assassin's dagger through the heart?......Were lovers not creatures of the night that were ghosts in the sun.....creatures whose dreams left no tracks in the snow.....that wandered forever, forever hunting a new and sweeter prey.....incestuously hunting what they had engendered..... forever wishing to lay with the children of their own dreams?.......

His chores completed, Maria prepared a mush of meal and meat scraps for his dogs, and then taking a long swig of wine from the goat bladder of wine that hung from a rafter, he stood before the open door, looking into the whiteness of the snow that was conspiring with the approaching darkness to smother the world.

He could no longer see the stable or the woodshed, no more than fifty paces away. He could not see the birches, oaks and pine trees of the forest, their white beards now changed to white shrouds. He could not see the mountains. He could not see the sky. He could not see the tracks of his dogs, or the tracks of his own boots that had led to the place where he now stood. Looking at his snow-crusted coat and trousers, and feeling the snow that had coagulated icily in his hair and beard, he felt that he too was disappearing; that what he thought he was, was soon not to be, or indeed, had never been; that perhaps the woods, the mountains and the stars had been a hallucination, one that had lived in the smoke of a hookah, and that was now dissipating and being forgotten; that all that was left in the world was this faint warm pulse in his breast; a last singing bird, one that for some inscrutable reason he had felt it his duty, as if his unique obligation to cherish and defend.

How beautiful was this snow, this whiteness, this quenching of the sun, and blotting of the woods and mountains! Oh, how he wished he could be drowned by it too.....dissolved into its beginning-less end, its endless beginning......to walk into its white glory until his flesh fell, and broke apart and joined its whiteness......or to become a wild bear, to hunt and mate, to die and decompose as a bear dies and decomposes, its fur, teeth and claws feeding the spring flowers.....or to hang oneself from a tree, as many years ago he had hung his holy habit from a tree, there to dangle, freeze and be pecked apart like the hungry birds peck the juniper berries..... pecked to the bone.....pecked free of reflections, memories, all promises and desires........

As Maria shut and bolted the door, he thought how much he was like an animal burrowing in its den, his warm blood and beating heart enveloped safe, safe and forgotten, like a corpse quit of the world; or as he was a bear preparing to hibernate, a hibernation that no spring would wake.

And as he looked up at his cabin's ceiling, and placed the stool in an exact, as if prearranged place, he thought of how small, how vain, how meaningless were these dreams he had so jealously guarded, and how lovely it must be to forsake them for a greater dream, or no dream at all.

.....Yes, now he remembered this is why he would not go to the village tonight. This is why he would forego the pleasures of the fiddle, wine, and a woman's arms.......

He stepped up on the stool, and as he did his thoughts continued.

.....*What had his heart tried to say, and why had this brooding given as much sadness as it had sweetness; some indefinable shame, some unful-filled longing, some forlorn wanderlust of the soul? Why had he thought that this whiteness that was smothering the world, ending the world, killing the world, was but a lover's whisper in his ear?.......*

Reaching, he gripped the rope; its end tied into a secure knot about the thick beam upon which its coil was laid.

.....*Could it be that there were gray hairs in his beard, that he was no longer young, and that he was preparing to accept the inevitable, that the game of smiles and kisses was over, and in his acceptance and forfeiture to the inevitable he was laughing in the face of death's unanimous verdict, like an idiot child in the face of a blusterous bully?......*

He placed the noose about his neck, pulled tight the two knots; one about his neck, the other bound to the beam......yes, they were ready..... yes, they would hold.

.....*Was it that the endlessly wandering ghost at last understood that its wandering could find no meaning, because there was no meaning to be found, because there was no beginning and no end to life's perpetual illusions, illusions of life and love that were forever flowering, wilting, dying?.....that there were only endless taverns with endless dice and brawls, endless abbeys with endless chants and candles, endless arms of women whose endless wiles wanted to tame and own the animal in his blood?.......*

Yes; the rope and the beam; they were strong enough; they would surely hold.

Maria built hot the fire, and exchanging his snow-covered things for a fresh change of clothes, he hung them near the blaze to dry. He poured a mug of wine from the wineskin, sat comfortably down, and stared into the fire's leaping flames. As he was a priest making a libation, he brought the mug to his lips, and then let long, deliberate swallows send their gifts down his throat; the strong wine trying to burn away the last defenses of the decision he had made.

.....*but no, no; it would be better this way.......*

Staring into the fire, Maria broke into a paroxysm of tears.

......*And with his tears came a rush of painfully accusatory thoughts he had neither the will nor the desire to stop.... the snow, wine and hearty blaze collaborating to thaw the ice that had formed about his heart these many years.......*

What indeed had he to show for himself since the breaking of his vows and his flight from the abbey? A much worn satchel, one full of lovers' gifts, and with these trifles, random sketches and scribbling of his dreams?

.....he looked at the statchel's bleached and battered ox-hide hanging by the bladder of wine......in it a collection of keepsakes that lovers had given him, lovers whose names he had forgotten, or perhaps had never known.......lovers whose faces he could not clearly recall, that had blurred and faded, dissolved in fumes of wine or the fogs of lustful rapture, dissolved as the mountains and forests were now dissolving in the snow and dark. Were these then to be counted the treasures and trophies of his life?...... ribbons, combs, slippers and brooches, tresses of hair, snippets of sleeping gowns......What had he accomplished, other than to heavily drink, dice, brawl, play a fiddle......romp with love-starved women in barns and fields?

.....Had he the courage to toss it in the fire before he stepped upon the stool? Or would he let it hang beside him from the same beam, or still more, bind its strap about his neck, like a second noose, letting its bag of silly trinkets hang down upon him, its ribbons, laces and cheap jewelries hung fresh and primrose sweet upon his corpse, the corpse that had so treasured them........

Images began to parade through his mind......images that a man dangling from a pine beam would not remember.....beautiful images that kept the tears freely flowing from his eyes.......moons and mountains and valleys, gardens and lovely meadows....scarlet leaves of autumn, trellis-works of summer roses.....an abbey with marble saints, sleeping in glowing moonlight......images that he had promised to sketch or paint, to place in rhymes and verses, to capture in some little vial of endearment what he could not bear to lose and leave unsung........

.......and then the faces he had held and kissed.....that had yielded their hearts to him.....playful pouts, frowns of hurt and need, grimaces of passion.....yielding and sharing secrets of which there were none deeper or sweeter they could give.......

.......oh, the pain of many partings in moonlight and gray dawns, in cold sleets and pelting rains....from garrets, taverns, stable lofts, wheat fields and carts of hay.......oh, the pain of this beauty that he had imagined he had held, that he had given the fire of his needs, but had passed through the sieve of his arms like the snow that was falling through the limbs of the forest trees.....through the ribs and eye sockets of skulls, burying all.....this Dream he could not keep.....this Beloved he could clasp but not hold.....oh, the pain of the ghost child eternally longing to place the sun in its pocket, the

moon beneath its pillow.....the ghost child that became the beggar child of its own dreams!........

Yes, it would be better this way; the stool, the beam, the noose. Life was too sweet, too sweet and too cruel, its sweetness the cruelest lover, cruel because even midst its kisses, it had never meant to be one's own.

* * *

HE did not know how much time had passed, only that the fire had died down considerably, and he could hear the fists of the blizzard flailing harder against the roof and walls; its mania trying to break them apart and smother the spark of warmth that it knew they shielded. Beside the hearth his two dogs lay sleepily stretched, like guards who had fallen asleep in the dereliction of their duty.

The cabin was still tolerably warm, no doubt aided by the drifts of snow that he was sure were mounting up against it, forming a defense against the same foe that had so violently driven them there. As the night and the storm had devoured the bounds of earth and sky, so now, like winds of a desert, they seemed bent on washing over the civilization of time as well.

......a ghost, yes, a ghost......a ghost timelessly wandering and dreaming.....that owned no body, left no tracks or traces.....that had no reason other than to know the pangs in the mazes of its dreams.....a ghost that would hang itself, that would be claimed, shrouded, given to and forgotten in whiteness........

Still, Maria felt sure it was not near dawn. Struggling from his chair, he raked, fed and built the fire anew. He filled his mug again from the zburied alive, he wanted to cherish, to hold tightly in these last moments those dreams he had dreamed beneath the sun. He stepped upon the stool, as he had practiced a hundred times before. He reached for the rope, placed the noose about his neck; and returning it to its place, stepped down from his makeshift gallows; not with cowardice, but with a firmer determination.

.....He was ready; willing. Yes, he would do this thing he must do; not with bravery or fear in his heart, but with proud resignation; with duty......

He brought a candle to his small table, and sat down before it. Like a child with his toys, he placed a sheet of parchment, and a quill and ink horn before him. Taking several long, deliberately slow drinks of the strong wine, and feeling his mind swirl and yawn awake, he dipped the quill in the ink and began to haphazardly scribble, even as he resumed his morbid meditations......meditations that would be his last.

He did not believe in God. He was no longer sure he ever had, even during the ascetic devoutness of his monastic days. He was not sure he ever could, without his heart accusing his heart of cravenness, or worse, hypocrisy. Strangely, wickedly, honestly he did not feel the need for belief. He was impartial, unbiased; a disinterested non-participant, a veritable ghost in this great debate waged in the world of the living.

God was an intangible, an irrelevancy, a crypt of intellectual darkness he had no desire of exploring. He neither accepted nor rejected God, and this ambivalence preempted belief, rendering it useless; a tinsel trapping, a show that was fine for others, but not for him. He did not scoff or scorn the notion of God, and he was not bitter with a God who had allowed famine, disease and death to live and freely rollick in the world; for this God had also created flowers, the rising moon, and women's sparkling eyes and tender bodies. These few lovely things had been enough for him. He had no desire of worshipping lifeless idols, or reciting monotonous litanies. For him, prayer and worship, all of his ambitions, hopes and dreams had been answered and fulfilled when he had lain upon a woman's body; all of his pains extinguished into this brief moment of blind pleasure. Woman was the blessed altar, the salvation in the wicked wilderness that this cold-hearted God had given Man; she was the summation of Man's hunt, the reward given to Man's toil of dreams.

As these thought had raced through his mind, Maria had sketched on the parchment he had laid before him. He had crosshatched a simple altar and candle, and opposite them he had sketched a woman's naked breasts; their nipples roused, like rosebuds about to bloom.

Fascinated with the juxtaposition of the two sketches, Maria continued, sketching a cruciform idol beneath the altar, and beneath the naked breasts, a woman's naked haunch, and then the flower of her sex.

Had he not been left disillusioned by one as much as by the other? As both were a regimen of rituals, had not both become insipid and routine, depleted of their original allure and promise? Were not both vainly idol-atrous: one with idols made of wood and painted plaster, the other with jewels and painted smiles? Why did men blindly worship such things? Did Brother Giovanni sometimes feel ridiculous, almost foolishly stupid after kneeling before idols that were little more than a child's dolls, even as he,

Brother Maria sometimes felt a childish fool in the wake of passion's silly games? Or was it the birthright of this ghost, the ghost of 'man', to be the idiot of his needs; a ghost that like a nag plodding after a bobbing carrot, hoped of something other, something more, some remuneration beyond the objects of his dumb adorations?

He had continued to dawdle and sketch as he had mused, and laying down his quill he held these sketches before him, studying them as he had drawn the pictures of his soul. Beneath the altar was a column of images recalled from his religious youth: a cross, a chalice and censer, a string of beads, a prayer book; icons depicting various Saints. Opposite these was a pornography of images: a woman's buttocks, thighs, belly, a man's and woman's genitalia; faces distorted in the carnal heights of their passion.

He was not ashamed, but rather curious of what his hand, as with the permission of his soul had drawn. Quite the contrary, he felt an honesty and correctness, even an unburdening, as he remembered feeling after he had confessed to a priest, or after he had first lain with the shepherd girl so many years ago.

And were these sketches so very different than those he had made when he was a small boy, the sketches of vines stretching and flowering from a man's phallus to a woman's breasts and vulva? Was the ghost that had wandered so long over hills and through forests, that had prided itself in fistfights, drinking bouts, fiddle playing and lovemaking.....was the ghost sitting at this table so different than the child that had first drawn these things?

Leaving this strange purge of his soul, he began to pace back and forth across the cabin, like an agitated bear in its cage; a cage not only of these four walls, but of his vain dreams from which he could find no escape; sometimes stepping on the stool as he passed it, reaching to the noose, only to step down again; as this too was a ritual; as the bear had been made a clown, one that performed tricks, even the trick of death.

As the storm howled and pummeled at his tininess, he paced; as if the blood of the wolf, stag and boar had become *his* blood, as if he was a creature that knew to be captured, to be deprived of its hunger was to die of another hunger. Made drunk with the wine that he now drank greedily, and pierced through with pains of remorse for a youth wasted, and dreams shattered, he waxed giddily mad, a madness that was the truest and loveliest song of his soul, a song that he screamed to these rafters full of nets, pelts, and the noose of a rope that waited like an evil, laughing eye for his end....and beyond these things, into the heart of the storm.....into the icy heart of an uncaring, unmerciful God.

With a violent kick, he kicked the stool aside! No, he would not be buried by this snow! No, he would not bear the slavish chains of other men! To hell with God and the rising and falling of the sun and moon!.....no, he would not burn his satchel!.....for a little while longer he would carry it proudly, like a soldier his sword.....carry it, covet it, die with it.......

He began to speak aloud, as to spirits in the air.

.... "Ah, my little princess, why so sad? Come, bring your sadness to my arms. Give me your hurt. Let me heal your wounds. Life is very short, and I will make you forget there are such things as pain, sadness and death in the world. Love is a beautiful garden; come, let us taste its fruits together......."

And again.......

.... "The moon will be very big and bright tonight, signorina. Come let us play deep in the tall wheat. You know how I so love to kiss your feet, your hips, your firm round breasts! Oh, how they glow like polished marble in the silver moonlight! You know, yes, O yes you know how your gypsy lover thirsts for your sighs and kisses!....."

And this night, oddly, to the father he had never known.

.... "Papa, mama told me that you smiled through my eyes and sang in my voice! She told me I rode a horse like you! She told me that your wildness was your kindness. She said she gave you her heart, and giving it, she gave it to the winds and thunders. I have your eyes and voice, papa, and I have mama's heart that she once gave to you. I will take care of mama's heart, papa! I will sing with it until I die!......."

In his drunkenness he spoke to death.......

.... "I knew it was you, yes, beyond your veils and shawls, behind your smiles, your swaying hips and the baring of your breasts. In moonlight, dark doorways, lofts of hay, I knew that I was loving you, signorina 'death'. You did not trick me with your disguises. I knew that it was only death I was serenading beneath a window, only death from whose body I was caressing off her clothes.....that I was becoming a sot and a fool for a skeleton of bones. But you see I thirsted for your kisses! I wanted you to surrender in my arms, to quench the seduction in your eyes.....to hear your sighs, your moans, the whisper of your eternal sweetness, your eternal need!......."

And to God.......

.... "I do not ask your forgiveness, but instead, it is I who forgive You! Yes, I, Brother Maria, forgive You, O great God of men's dreams and myths!

I forgive You for sowing this world with the seeds of pain and death, for You have also loosed the maiden of Beauty to run naked and laughing through its fields......the maiden that runs from Your scowls and from Your wrath, into meadows full of flowers!......"

Maria stopped his impassioned shouts before the table, and stared at the sketched caricatures that had erupted through his quill. In his intoxication they seemed the playthings of a child: playthings of sanctity and vulgarity spilled from the toy box of his soul; one column filled with sacredness, the other with profanity. In his intoxication they seemed not different, but the same; as they were twins; as they were the two sides of one coin. All were dolls; some made of wood and plaster; the others of pretty, fading flowers; all full of the same deadness, the same withering.

He crumpled the sheets of sketches in his hands, and tossed it in the fire. Returning to the table he again sat down, placed another parchment before him, and with his quill and ink sat silently still; now strangely, suddenly sober, suddenly poised, like an animal crouched to kill.

He felt at once calm and fevered; as if each of his nerves was a sword, each raised, still and keenly sharp, prepared for the execution of one swift fierce act, some commission of his soul that his soul had not yet learned of. He felt possessed of an unnatural keenness, as the owl must see, the wolf must smell, as the lover senses his mate in darkness. He felt that he was ready to wickedly seize, or to humbly confess; that he must at last make known the truth that had lain hidden in his own heart.

Gone was the cabin, the fire, the bladder of wine. Gone were the wind and snow, and an inhospitable, moody, windswept world of loveless days and nights; a cheating moon and a pitiless sun; a stool, beam, rope. All that was left was this candle, this quill and parchment, this precariously precious, timeless moment that he had never known before, and that he would never know again; a ghost, yes a ghost, weeping for the mercies of the living, whose world of snowflakes sifted through its arms, burying all.

All of the secret pains and joys of his heart......his gypsy mother, the savage hunter of his father.....Brother Giovanni and the abbey, the countless hardships of his wandering, and the countless kisses and caresses of lovers......wanting now to give some voice, some flower, some meaning in the meaningless shambles of his life.

.....a dumb man about to speak, a dying man about to confess..... Maria dipped his quill into the ink, and wrote in a fury of words what was aching to be spoken from the deepest part of him.

The Blizzard

THE
Wind and cold, the snow,- the fury of night
Drowning the forests, meadows and mountains,
Angel battalions, blinding men's sight,
Their mad wings smothering earth and heaven;
The storm's fists flailing 'gainst the cabin walls,
Its sharp fangs gnawing with sleet and dark,
Encircling, like an army of starving wolves,
This last warm fortress guarded in my heart.
A goat's bladder of wine; a candle, ink, quill,
This stalking and creeping,- freezing ever nearer......
Your memory lovely in the fire's mirror......
Your sweetness, peeking over every windowsill.....
Oh, how could ghosts flee, surrender to death's sighs,
When the stars and seasons smile, so warmly in your eyes?

* * *

MARIA raised up his head from the table, where, as it was a pillow, he had laid it on the words he had written.

The candle had guttered out, and the fire had burned low. His dogs were stretched out, sleeping, their bellies bared to the warmth the hearth still offered. Ice clung to some of the boards on the walls, where like a cold transparent mud it had oozed through cracks and knots. There were places on the floor, and several more on the nets and pelts in the rafters where the snow had successfully infiltrated, having sifted through boards and thatches to construct settlements of small white drifts.

What had wakened him? He was sure something had wakened him.

It could not be a bear or wolf, or any other kind of wild animal, for his dogs slept on, and he heard no commotion in the stable as he did when prowlers from the forest came near, and his dogs barked and his horse frantically neighed, reared and kicked.

Regaining his senses, he determined he was waked by no disturbance at all, but rather by a gentle thunder; the thunder that sings in the trough of all waves, and laughs in the trail of all winds. He had been waked by *silence*.

Yes, that was it; silence had wakened him. The wind had ceased its tantrum against the walls, and its howls and shrill whistling in the chimney and thatches above. But there was more. Like a show of mercy, like a covenant after such rapine, a splash of silver-shimmering light shone on the dark half of the cabin's floor, having found a window pane free of rime and the snowy scurf through which it could gleam. The night was still deep. The storm was spent. It could only be the moon.

Maria unbolted the door, and with a considerable effort shoved it partly open against a waist-high drift. Wedging outside, he waded into the new snow, the night now as still and crystal clear as before it had been mad with the blizzard's holocaust of fury.

He was greeted with a world of pristine whiteness, stretching from his cabin door through the forest, up the mountainsides to the very stars. The moon was rounded gibbous full, and like a lamp illumed the great blanket of purity into an incandescence of a silver blue fire. In the absolute stillness, he had the sensation that he could hear the echoes of *Time's* wails, whispers, songs; the last echoes of summer; the last cries of the dead in their tombs, bidding the sun their last farewells.

.......falling leaves, whirring wings, whisking tails.....the moans of the dead and the cries of the unborn.....the secrets of seeds, the secrets of wombs, the secrets of dreams.....the secrets of every lover that had been spurned, and those of every lover that had ever yearned to be loved.......

.......a bright-dressed gypsy woman, laughing, whirling like a dervish over the mountaintops, clicking castanets and disappearing into crystal canyons of silver-limned clouds, leading a train of costumed monkeys and gaily lumbering and dancing, petticoated bears........

Deep in the forest a wolf howled, a howl that thrilled the deepest part of him. Both the wolf's blood and *his* blood were enkindled with the same fire; the moon's fire. In the brotherhood of earth's creatures, they were both hunting, both wandering in their loneliness, the first loneliness, the eternal loneliness of life together.

When the snows would melt, the brooks, babble, and the flowers lift their bright gay faces, he would leave.....neither to conquer nor to surrender, but like a ghost, to wander with the dream of waking from its endless dream.

Yes, this wolf was his brother, a brother who was filled with hunger and howls, as a ghost named Brother Maria was filled with hunger and howls; both of them, in the great wilderness of the night, crazed with this great mystery of 'death', and its sister mystery of 'love'.

He returned to the cabin, and taking the poem from the table went to the low-burning fire. But only for a moment did he hesitate, before dropping it in the burning embers. In an instant, a very brief instant, it burst into flames, and then shriveled into ashes.

. . . .

. . . .

CHAPTER THREE

THE FISHERMAN'S COTTAGE

The coast of Sicily; Autumn; 1347

MAMA nun mi, mannan all' acqua sulla,
Picciutta sugnu e mi mentu a ghuicari,
Pri strata mi casco la tuvagghiula,
C' un picciutteddu mi l'happi a pigghiari......
Toinella toina! Toinella toina!

THEY came over the hill, the four of them, arm in arm and singing gaily. It was a song they knew very well; a song they had heard their papas sing in the vine arbors; a song they said came from the big city, Palermo; a song in which their papas freely improvised when they drank much wine. On this clear quiet day their young voices rang like trumpets.

"*Mama, today I lost my kerchief I had on,*
A fine young boy found it on the way......
Toinella toin! Toinella toin!"

They were the best of friends, and they had been ever since they could first remember. Arm in arm they marched over the small rocky road like a squadron of happy soldiers, one whose brash youth would vanquish any enemy they would confront.

"*And there he said to me, your neck is sweet,*
I would like to kiss it, your favor given,
And if another time we chance to meet,
I'll make you call on all the saints of heaven!
Toinella toin! Toinella toin!"

And then singly, three of the four shouting improvisations of the song's ending.

"*Struggle though you may, the angels will not save you!*"

"*The Saints have your soul, and now the Devil wants his due!*"

"*Here in the olive trees, where God eyes cannot see us!*"

And then, as they had sung the song many times before, all joined in with the last refrain:

"*Tointella toin! Tointella toin! Tointella toin!*"

The boys reached the crest of the hill, and reaching it let go their embraces, seeking out the shade of a small tree, and the dusty rags of its few dusty leaves, the remnants of a century of storm, sun and sea still clinging to these rocks. The morning was growing old, and suddenly feeling the sun's stoked fire, their exuberance had turned to despondency. One of the boys wandered off behind some bushes to pee, while the others sat listlessly in the sparse patches of shade. After a moment one of the boys called after the boy behind the bushes.

"*Hey Ignazio, why do you always pee behind trees and bushes? Are you ashamed of your little pecker? Are you afraid we will laugh at it?*"

This enlivened the three boys, bringing a shout from a second boy.

"*Even dogs do not try to hide their peckers! They'd pee before the Pope!*"

And then from the third boy, Edwardio:

"*You cannot hide it forever. You may be married one day you know, and that's a thing, try though you may, that is hard to conceal!*"

And again, the first boy, *Cologero*, the pack's leader, shouted good-naturedly at the one invisibly peeing behind the bushes.

"*Do you think Alesandro will hide his from Angelina when he marries her in a few days? It might make his bride, the beautiful Angelina very sad.*"

The boys then jested among themselves; *Edwardio* quick to kick it about.

"*I think Angelina will have seen Alessandro's pecker long before their bridal night.*"

And then the second boy, *Felice*.

"*If my parents had arranged a bride like Angelina for me, I know mine would have been set a-crowing very early!*"

This elicited a general laughter among the three boys, even as the younger boy, Ignazio joined them from behind the bushes. He was several years younger than the others, and had not yet matured into their brashness. *Cologero*, the oldest among them at fifteen, stepped from the tree and embraced *Ignazio* compassionately. He kissed both of his cheeks and held him tightly to his breast, like the older brother that in truth he was.

"*We are only joking, Ignazio. Your pecker is fine. Come on, let's go talk with Federico. We will talk to him about his nets and his boat, and how many fish he caught this morning. Maybe in that way we can see his 'bella-donna' daughter, eh? Come on, his cottage is not far away; only a few more hills, 'filio mio'.*"

Their jest and brief rest beneath the tree seemed to have revived them, but more than these things the mention of *Alessandro's* marriage to *Angelina, Federico* the fisherman's daughter. Their fraternity was inspired by the mere mention of her name. They continued on the small dusty road, among occasional cries of gulls and the sea-waves gently lapping against the rocks.

With the mention of their friend's marriage, their rollick waxed to a more serious tone; each imagining they would soon have a wife and romantic adventures of their own. This seemed to stir the young manhood in each of them, and with it the dreams of what that manhood would do and accomplish. One by one they told the sun, rocks and sea their ambitions, and as they walked on their lifelong comrades lent attentive ears.

"*I will not marry Agostina, the shoemaker's daughter like my parents say they will make me do. She is ugly, and she will only become fatter and uglier, like her mama with the years. Beak like a crow. Ass like a horse. I'll bind a millstone to my neck and jump in a deep well before I will go to bed with her. But I will be a pirate before I will drown myself. I will sail to many lands, and I will kiss many pretty women in each of them.*"

Felice finished the *bravado* of his life's dream, and *Edwardio*, the jokester among them, solemnly commenced his.

"*My mama said I must marry Nina, the butcher man, Eligio's daughter. She said that way we will always have plenty of sausages to eat. Nina is sweet, but she does not have big teats. I want a wife with big teats. What do I care about sausages? What do I care if it rains sausages when I have a scarecrow wife with a face like polenta, and teaties like stunted potatoes? Maybe I will come with you, Felice. Maybe I will be a pirate too. When I serenade beneath Nina's window I feel as I am singing to a skeleton, even if she has the smile of Maria. I would rather have a wife with big teats, than one that smiles like the mother of God!*"

Felice doubled over with laughter at his friend's drolleries, and after regaining his composure asked *Cologero*, who had smiled, but had not laughed.

"*And you Cologero, what will you do? Will you be a grower of melons like your old man, or come with us and be a pirate too? What kind of wife for you?*"

Cologero, the elder statesman among them, assumed a judicial, even a grave demeanor, as if his wisdom was called upon to answer one of life's great questions.

"*I do not know if I will be a pirate or not; and my parents have not yet chosen a wife for me, although I have heard them mention a few candidates. But you see I do not really care what I do with my life, whether I am a grower of melons, a mender of shoes or a milker of goats and cows. I only want a wife that is as sweet as the wife Alessandro has won; a wife as sweet as Angelina. If I knew a pirate ship could help me find a wife as sweet and beautiful as Federico's daughter I would sail the seven seas, sail to the end of the world until I found her.*"

This very heartfelt admission had sobered the joviality among them. Even *Edwardio's* clownery changed to graveness; as if all now recalled the mission they had set out on this morning: *to catch one more glimpse of the 'belladonna' before she lost her virginity on her bridal night.* Suddenly in concert with the words of their older and wiser leader, *Edwardio* chimed in.

"*Yes, Cologero, I agree. It would be worth a ship of jewels to have a wife like Angelina. When she dances in the grape tubs at harvest, with grape leaves in her hair, and other grape leaves fashioned into a crucifix on her back, I cannot take my eyes from her, even though the others have lifted their skirts to their knees, like hooks to catch the other boys. Even the eyes of the old fiddlers stray to Angelina, ogling with lechery at her shapely breasts, and her ass like the ass of an Angel.*"

And now *Felice*, in full and enthusiastic agreement.

"*All of the guys vie for her kisses when they bring their grapes to her tub. It is a tradition as old as the sun, to receive a kiss for one's bunch of grapes, but like a queen Angelina breaks that tradition, and gives her kiss only to Alessandro when he brings his grapes to her tub.*"

And again, Edwardio:

"*I would kiss her feet if she would let me. One by one I would kiss and suck her little grape-stained toes, and count myself a king.*"

"*And only three nights ago*", rejoined Felice, "*when we came with the others for the 'bride's flouting', when we paraded past her window, throwing kisses and begging for her hand ....oh how her eyes sparkled in the torchlight! Oh how I wished to kiss the rose of her mouth! But she only laughed, and shook her head at me as I passed, dressed as I was. like a soldier marching to war.*"

To which, *Edwardio*"

"*As she rejected me, dressed like a knight with a sword and helmet, sealing my doom with a sausage lady with a Virgin Mary smile, a sausage lady with scrawny teats. What are the Crusades and the Cross of Jesus compared with the beauty of Federico's daughter?*

And you, she rejected you too, Cologero, dressed as you were, like a beggar of the roads...... "

"*All are beggars before such sweetness and such beauty. That is why I dressed as I did. Alessandro has been blessed by Heaven!*"

Cologero's quick, but somber reply resulted in a silence among them, a kind of reverence demanded by *Eros* and their pubescent worship of nature's *feminine goddess*. To break that silence, *Cologero* stopped and returned to his younger brother, lagging twenty paces behind them. Smiling, he placed his arm around *Ignazio's* shoulders.

"*Ignazio is the only one among us who knows for sure what he will do, and who he will marry. Since he was a small boy he has wanted to be a priest, and make the Church his wife. Is that not true Ignazio?*"

Cologero tousled his brother's hair, and kissed him on the cheeks, at which the shy, simpleton boy of few words smiled brightly and nodded with adoring enthusiasm.

Attaining the crest of the small rocky hill *Felice* called out:

"*We are here! There is Federico's cottage!*"

"*Yes, and he has returned from Messina. There is his boat on the beach, like always.*"

Happily their troop approached the simple little cottage, halting their steps a stone's throw from its door, *Cologero's* face brightening, but soon clouding over with pensiveness.

"*But where is Federico? He is normally mending his nets and cleaning his fish at this hour. And where is his wife and children?.....and the birds, the many crows, some even on the cottage roof.....a fisherman and his catch attracts swarms of gulls, not crows......*"

This, followed by *Felice*.

"*And the smell, the smell! What kind of fish is Federico catching in his nets that smell like that! No wonder he complains about not being able to sell fish at the markets in Messina!*"

And then *Edwardio*, unable to restrain the joke on the tip of his tongue.

"*Angelina will smell when she comes to Alessandro's bed, but on the other hand, what a little price to pay for such a treasure!*"

"*Federeico! Federico! Federico the fisherman, we have come to see you and talk with you, and perhaps help you mend your nets!*"

Cologero shouted out at the small cottage, but in return there was no reply other than a fluttering and carking of some of the crows that, more avaricious than scared, quickly fluttered back to the roof, and even a few brave ones to the ground before the open door. At this the other two youths began to take turns yelling.

"*Federico, we are Alessandro's friends! We have come to talk with you!*"

"*And perhaps eat breakfast with you, if it does not taste as badly as your dead fish smell!*"

"*We have not come to steal your daughter away! She flouted us three nights ago when you were in Messina!*"

"*And who does your goat think he is, King Saul, walking in and out of your cottage door like that?!*"

But these shouts and jests to the gentle, good natured fisherman elicited no response, and the four boys were left in silence, staring at the crow-infested cottage, its door open, and a goat moseying unconcernedly in and out of it.

"*This seems strange. There may be something wrong....the open door, the goat and crows, the smell.....stay here, and I will go have a look.*"

Cologero started to walk towards the cottage, but stopped at the words of his young shy brother.

"*No; let me. I will go tell Federico that we have come to visit him.*"

Cologero knitted his brow, and returned to his young brother, his seldom uttered words and their conviction stirring him deeply.

"*You wish to go to the cottage, Ignazio?*"

"*Yes, I will go. I will lift my hand and make the Sign of the Cross before the door, like the priests do. Cristo is in my heart. I am not afraid.*"

Cologero could feel the great step into manhood that his brother was trying to take. He could feel his courage waking from his shyness and his handicap; the rites of passage that he was endeavoring to undergo.

Cologero smiled warmly.

"*Yes, Ignazio. You go. Federico is probably sleeping in his bed. You wake our friend, the lazy old fisherman.*"

Ignazio looked deeply and meaningfully into his older brother's dark brown eyes, and then solemnly, as with mission, turned away and walked the hundred dusty steps that brought him to the cottage, even as the others looked on silently, with a mixture of heightened curiosity and dread. They watched as the young boy halted before the goat and the open door, raised his hand, and made a slow pronounced Cross in the air, and then without hesitation, walked into the cottage.

But having entered the cottage, *Ignazio* seemed to have been swallowed away. After his disappearance into the cottage there came no boom of welcoming laughter, no cry of friendly surprise; no sound of any kind; only a silence that seemed to snicker with the secrets it did not wish to divulge.

After a long, interminable moment, *Cologero* cried out:

"*Ignazio! Ignazio! Is Federico in the cottage, Federico and his wife and children? Say hello to them from us, and to the bride-to-be, the bellissima belladonna, Angelina!*"

But oddly, *Ignazio* did not respond, either with words, or by stepping back into the sunlight from the cottage.

This was followed by several more moments of puzzling silence, moments in which the watchers became more uneasy and concerned, even the clownish *Edwardio*. He shouted out, his normally bold voice quavering in the still blue air.

"*Ignazio! Please, Ignazio, say something! Those things we said about your peeing behind trees and bushes, and your......they were only jokes, Ignazio. Are you trying to have a joke with us now? Please, Ignazio, say something. You have had your laugh. You win. It is no longer funny.*"

But the silence endured, and no cry from the boys could break it. The cottage was small, and in a moment could be surveyed. *Cologero's* head began to dizzy.

......The open door, the goat, the crows......no happy Federico singing and mending his nets.......the smell, the awful smell.......and pretty Angelina, where was Angelina?.....the angel he had kept hidden in his heart since he was a small boy.....

Cologero prepared to enter the cottage, just as his younger brother stepped slowly, half-stumbling from it; his face, pale, and his eyes, strangely dazed; the goat lazing at his side. After five or six steps the young boy fell to his knees, bent over, and violently retched.

Cologero raced to him, and kicking away the goat knelt at his side.

"What is it Ignazio? What is wrong? What is it that you have seen?"

But *Ignazio* did not reply. He could not reply. Perhaps he would never reply to a question again. He was consumed with retching his innards out, and with his innards, trying to purge what could not be purged; what he had seen, and what he would always remember, even in his dreams.

Cologero raced into the cottage, the cottage that was no longer a simple fisherman's cottage, but now a charnel house full of *death's* carnage.

.....Federico on his bed, his wife and children on the floor.....all bloated and blackened, all decomposing......and Angelina, his sweetest Angelina.....near the window where she had once smiled at him when he had returned with Federico and his catch...her face and toes eaten away by rats.....Alessandro directly above her, hanging from a noose........

. . . .

. . . .

CHAPTER FOUR

THE CONVENT

Part I

Leaving

Early spring, 1343

HE told no one he was leaving; not the woodsmen, the hunters or trappers; not his fellow carousers in the taverns; not his lovers.

Only his horse, goat, and dogs knew. Looking with deep, dark, loving eyes they saw the farewell in his heart. They saw that a perfumed breeze was charming him away. Only they knew he would not remain their master; that he had become a slave to a master of his own; an invisible master, one more stern than he. Only they knew that lovely vistas had visited his dreams, and new songs had thawed awake in the rivers of his blood, making him toss through the nights like a sweet infatuation.

Only they knew his human kindness would go away; his soft pats and scratches on their ears, the chestnuts and apples in his pockets, his gentle whispers in angry storms. Only they knew his leave-taking was at hand. Only they knew they would not see him again.

The snow had not completely left the forests, as though jealously clinging to the strongholds it had claimed through the long winter. The brooks had only begun to break into gurgling freshness, starting their great labor of sending mountains of ice to the valleys below. Spring's army had only sent its first, frail, effeminate scouts, the first tender violets, hyacinths and anemones through the damp rotten leaves.

On such a day, early, with only a satchel slung over his shoulder, Brother Maria left his cabin on the mountain; on foot.

It was a thing he had to do, and yet it had not been easy. He had imagined leaving when the sun was warm, the hills, greening, and the fallow fields, ploughed and sown. But he knew it would be more difficult then. Captured by spring's rapture, he would descend the hill to the taverns to drink, gamble and play the fiddle, and be hunted by pretty smiles and sparkling glances. The sun would reach into his heart and loins. It would seduce him; make him lazy; make him dream of days that would never come again; of valleys stretching into setting suns, rather than those leading to rising moons. These dreams, and the reminiscences of life's golden morning were for the aging and the sedentary, and the sedentary was a creature he did not want to be; because it was a creature he feared more than the wolves of the forests; more than death itself.

He did not want to become satisfied. He did not want to be relegated to a serf or a vassal; one yoked to a plough or a wagon of stones. To feed, dazzle and delight his senses was all that mattered to him. In their eagerness life throbbed its truest pulse; beat its wings; cried, bled, and sang its song; and without that song life wilted, withered and died. Age and idleness was a musty book, one that told tales of lusty adventures, but was good only to lay in one's lap as he drowsed by a fire.

He did not want to languish in a cage. He did not want to be kept, fed and gently sleeked. He did not want a sharp hook in his mouth, and then to be tossed in a basket. He was unsure of what he wanted; only that he did not want the comfortable hearths, the useless knickknacks and fripperies of the world. He had seen what had happened to the burghers, how wealth beguiled them only to fatten them, burden them, and in the end, imprison and unman them. He did not want to wax slow, stiff and lazy. He did not want to become the tavern braggart, or the village's storyteller. Beyond all else, he did not want love to become a circus trick, a casual, practiced performance. He wanted it to remain a quest, the endless quest he knew it was; with pain and pleasure, full of risk, ache, treachery and defeat; the mystery of a hunt that had no end. He wanted it to remain a rare jewel, hidden in its hiding place; undiscoverable, unattainable, yet ever dazzling bright.

He left more from fear than longing; and more than fear, from the tantrum of the child in his heart. He had no fear of dying, but he did not want to die with these fists flailing against the walls of his dreams; wanting to break free of their chains; to know the excitement of being lost, and in that excitement the thrill of a crazed flight. Too restless to yawn, gossip and whittle, Maria left when the cold winds had not yet been bested by the warm.

And quickly, in the first weeks and months of his departure, he once more became brown with the sun, lean with a frugal diet, strong with the ardors of his wandering. His dormant senses awoke, and shook the sleep from their eyes. Once more he became alert, keen and hungry, like a forest animal; ever ready to mate; ever ready to fight; ever ready to kill.

But this time it was not as it had been before. This time he bore the armor and weapons of a new maturity. His body had acquired the strength of a wonderfully strong manhood; his mind, now ready and savvy for any challenge. He was no longer callow; no longer a novice; no longer a boy. He was no longer a stranger in life's wilderness, but an indigenous creature that was welcomed by it; that like a native son, was part of it.

He had become conversant in the languages of the world. He now knew how to beg, hunt, steal; how, whether with roasted mutton, or with roots and berries to fill his stomach. He knew how to find shelter, how to protect himself from the night and the ugly moods of the weather: in barns, stables, forest caves; and when the taverns closed, in the arms of women. He knew how to defend against life's adversaries, to be wary of predators that ever crouched in wait to rob or maul him: to build fires and wave firebrands at packs of wolves, to wield knife and cudgel, to kick, swing his fists, and sink his teeth into a dangerous foe. He knew the language of the seasons; of the south wind and the north, of vernal hope, summer's plenty, autumnal sadness. He knew the feasts and hungers each season brought; their troubles and felicities, their golden harvests and their frozen scarcities.

He knew the languages of taverns and dice houses, of cockfights and brothels. He spoke their curses and their lies; their gallows humor and their thieves' slang. When needed, he knew the language of church and cloister, of rectitude and scripture. He could curse as nimbly as he could pray. He could speak with a monk with the same ease that he spoke with a whore.

He also knew the language of the night, those strange dialogues that awoke when sunlight fled from the world. He knew the anthems of the forest; its snarls and mournful whines, its piercing screeches and sweet warbles. He knew them because they were part of him, dwelling in the primal darkness of his blood. The darkness of his soul was the darkness of the forest, and these voices emerged in the solitude of his want and need; and in that darkest of all nights: the night that invades and freezes the soul; the night of loneliness.

But most importantly to him, he knew that language that, without its knowing, made all others of little or no consequence. He knew the language of '*woman*'.

This was his greatest prize of learning, of which he was both pupil and teacher. Without this precious literacy there would be no need to wander the hills and forests; there would be no reason in the wheel of the stars and the journey of the seasons. Like songs played on a lute, each *woman* he loved had yielded to him another melody, new lyrics, added another cryptic lesson to his *repertoire* with which he armed himself against life's futility; its brevity; its death. This language gave him a reason. It gave his heart its song. It sustained him; it nourished him.

He had learned that this language seldom used words, and when it did the words were used as foliage behind which the world of the senses strummed harps of paradise. It was a deeper, richer language, one in which the soul breathed fragrances from exotic flowers; and sang its dreams, like a nightingale to the moon.

It was a wordless language; a language of blushes and titters, pouts, dimpled smiles and sparkling eyes; a finger twisting a strand of hair, a stumble on a path, a flower in a bodice; the lifting of a skirt when drawing water from a well. This silent language rendered the heart vulnerable; telling its fears, hopes and possibilities. It told of a curious eagerness to dare and play, or a shyness that must only pine and wish; the heart's decision to recoil and refrain, or to be a willing, uninhibited partner in love's dance.

It was a wordless spell, one that raised a tent about the lamp of desire, and when Maria entered that tent his voice assumed another voice; one with melodies filled with warmth and invitation. Gentle as a caress, and pregnant with insinuation, often these sensual purrs undressed their hearer, making her blush, and a shiver to run up her spine; leaving her naked with shyness, with a quivering womb, and ready for his arms and his flame.

And it was this language, this wordless language that women heard and were drawn to, like bees to a honeyed flower; that hypnotized them like an amulet, promising them sympathy and consolation. It spoke directly to their hearts, hearts they opened when they heard his secret knock upon their doors; when they let enter this charming guest, and became his loving servant.

And to his golden, leonine beauty that smiled at them through the blue eyes of an eternal child, they stole from their beds in the dark of night, flouted richly dressed suitors, committed adultery and risked being beaten by a husband, for they recognized in him one who understood them; one who would not only flatter, but patiently listen to them; making them want to please him in any way they could.

He loved his lovers only as they wished to be loved: at times chastely and reverently, crooning love's lullabies in their ears, and giving kisses soft as dew to their eyes; while with others he would do shameless things, things that would make the angels cover their eyes with their wings. He gave himself wholly, and in his arms each felt loved, not used; as his love had been a gift, not a theft. He made each feel beautiful, and in return he became their darling. He loved each separately, separately and as one; as all were one lover with endless needs; endless needs that when answered, gave endless treasures in return.

Courtship and loving gave his ragged existence a royal meaning. He had no interest in acquisition, ownership, or ambition of any kind. Money meant nothing to him. He did not grow envious when he passed magnificent castles on hilltops. He knew he possessed riches they did not. He knew their palatial halls did not contain the tender embraces he received in alleys and hay carts. He knew he was rich, while the dwellers in these marble mansions were poor. The play of the sexes, and the brief arena in which they played was all to him. It gave his sojourn through every hardship his significance. The longing of desire, its smoldering anticipation, and then its sudden spark that fanned into a momentary flame, blinding him to the world's treacheries and precariousness, stilling time and the great, never resting hunt of death,- these were the things that gave his life its reason; its salvation.

But there was something that nagged at his heart. He often wondered if his homelessness, his lone wolf existence did not have something to do with women's great attraction to him. They knew he came from the forests, and that he would return to the forests; a consorter with wolves and gypsies; a vagabond full of sweet words, smiles and caresses. Was it because he was a vagrant, and they knew even the strong wine of love could not make him drunk enough to stay; that he could be seduced, but not tethered? Was it because they sensed something untamable in him, something they could not possess, and not being able to possess, they felt no shame in trying to do just that? Was it in part the age-old human idiocy of wanting something they knew they could not have? Did they coddle him for an hour, because they knew he was the property of the tomorrows? Was he their plaything, a plaything to be outgrown and discarded?

He sometimes became sad when he realized this beautiful bird that flew to his heart in the night, fluttered away in the morning. He became very sad when he saw this delicate flower that seemed to sum earth's and heaven's beauty so quickly fade, wilt and die, leaving no lasting trace of its preciousness. More and more he saw in love's courtship it's tearful farewell. More and more he saw in love's smile something impermanent, something autumnal, something darkly veiled and grieving. More and more he felt a doom waiting behind love's brief excursions into eternity.

At times he became pensive and sad to think this sweetness was so fleeting, that the flame kindled in his loins and the spark sown in his heart were so quickly spent; that the arms that passionately clung to him would soon loosen and dissolve into air, as if they had never held him at all.. He became haunted with night's beautiful ghosts that brought him treasures, only to vanish again into the forever-ness of that same night from which they had brought them.

* * *

Wandering

ONCE more the wide world stretched out before him. He no longer wanted to hide behind a cabin's walls, burrow in sulking meditations and sorrows; hang the children of his dreams from a gallows' beam. He wanted to explore the immensity of fields, forests and mountains that stretched to the reach of his eye; to the brim of the blue and starry bowls of heaven. Its sky was his sky; its hardships and horrors, his hardships and horrors; its dream of beauty, pain and death his dream of beauty, pain and death. He knew he was a part, a tiny part of its cruel and lovely song. He was small, small and brief, a firefly blinking in a forest of stars. This little voice inside him, so full of joy, hope and anguish; this spark, this tiny singing hammer in his breast was all that separated him from the eternity of darkness; between Brother Maria and the hunger of worms, the spoil of wolves, and the moans of winds.

......*My heart a lighted candle,*
Burning, bleeding, knowing,
Its spark, soon to be no more.....
Kissed, only to be strangled.....
Bones dreaming, singing in the dark,
Guttering in their glowing.....
A Breath that snuffs the sun, and with it,
The tiny candle of the heart......

He continued to wander aimlessly, indefatigably; out of step with the cares and toils of men, but somehow in lockstep with the march of the seasons; a child hopelessly entranced with the kaleidoscope of their changing moods and colors; green summers and golden mornings; the scowls of storms, the silver smiles of moonlight. He wandered from forest to forest, through the endless prison bars of day and night; from one woman's arms to another's, shedding lovers like one sheds a coat in spring, only to greet the next as she was holding a new coat, readied to warm him when the first frost crept upon the flowers.

.....*Through the hours and the seasons,*
Bleeding with doubts, fears, hungers,
With arrows and with cherries,
Without a hope or reason,
Like a ghost in the wind, sighed and wearied......
Hungry, grieving, madly bound,
Ever lost, ever fearing,
never wanting to be found.......

He wandered as much with the wounds and dreams of a man, as with the wounds and dreams of a ghost. And as he did he came to see that there were refrains in nature's many moods and confusions. Winter melted into spring; summer wilted into autumn. Again and again ploughboys plowed the fields with oxen, as again and again flocks of maidens bound the harvest sheaves. Again and again the gentle hour of love bloomed, and was spent, and then faded into cold and bleak tomorrows of aloneness; only to be enkindled again in an unexpected moment; a glance, a smile, a titter.

......I followed thru summer fields,
And autumn forests russet-gold,
Winters melting to wilding springs.....
Entering some cyclic dream,
That quickening, gathered me
Into its cruel and lovely, mothering wings......

The violets would bloom their purple bonnets from the receding snows; the leaves would fall; the rivers, melt; the song of birds would return, only to leave the hills and forests sullen at their departure. At nightfall youths would stand beneath lamp-lit windows, listening to singing maidens, and the maidens would accept their courtship, grow fat with babies, and then grow coarse with age. *And Brother Maria? Yes, he too was part of these refrains.* He would beg, dice, brawl, become very drunk. He would take women into his arms, feel their lovely warmth and lonely greed; hear their secrets in his ear. He would feel their bodies stir, excite and struggle until their struggle grew into a crisis, only to briefly quiver, sigh, expire, and be rendered still in his arms.....as if their hearts had been a sacrifice.....as if his love had killed them.

.....the evening star was in her hair,
A mandolin in her arms,
But only when I fell upon my knees,
And closed my eyes with tears,
Did her gentle kiss,
Like moonlight press my lips,
Only then did maiden 'death'
Whisper: 'I am yours, forever yours my dear'......

And there were seasons of one's heart that matched these seasons of the streets and forests, tides that washed over and through him, drowning his heart in dread and despair, then in hope and happiness, and then again and ever again in deeper, darker storms of despair.

.....and always the killing frosts, the first flakes of snow, the leaving and farewell into the lonely, death-brooding mystery of things.....to be lost again, only to dream of spring and pleasure, and be renewed again.....compelled to step, as with a criminal's expulsion, a kind of blind madness into the jaws of vastness.....the prey of jackals and black-frocked crows, death's deputies waiting to pick his bones and peck his eyes, to glut his beautiful dreams..... Small, very small.....a few sinews stitched to a few bones.....a breath in

a breast, an ember in a brain.....brief, very brief.....a dream imprisoned in the walls of its own illusion.....a caged bird whose only friend was its song.....and yet he would dare this vastness again.....daring to be torn and gnashed apart, to be swallowed, to be consumed.....to pass through the dark entrails of eternity with wicked fight, song and giddy laughter.....something savagely compulsive, something that could not be seduced by warm fires or women's arms.....something that was doomed, but that rebelled against that doom.....brief, very brief.....raging like a fever that could not be tempered, that laughed at balm and poultice......that would rather grow mad and distract.....that would rather die than be bled, bandaged, healed.......

.....Rising, the moon's harlot eye,
Over the parapet of the world,
Silver, beautiful, merciless,-
Rags of clouds, like silk gowns hurled
From ravished angels scudding by.......
A goddess with a cruel smile,
Stirring the lynx's guile,
Murdering all lovers in their beds.....
Calling the wolves of the heart
To howl in laughing circles,
in the ritual of 'the dead'.......

* * *

Spring, 1345

HE had been wandering more than three years when he came upon a city in the south, one about which the olives, dates and vineyards flourished, and the nightingales returned to the gardens each spring. He had made it a practice to avoid larger cities, to ask shelter from cottagers in their barns; or to simply sleep in the fields and forests. But on this mid-May morning, when from a hill he saw the sun smiting gold its towers, cupolas and other ramparts, he was smitten with its majestic, metropolitan grandeur, and he entered its gates to walk its splendid streets.

It felt good to have so many sounds, voices and pictures of human endeavor move and bustle about him, to be gathered and mingle in such a humming hive of human commerce and fraternity. It was another kind of forest, one made of stones, not trees, and after all, though he knew the ways of the fox and the owl, was he not one of its native creatures? It felt good to hear the squalling babes, the screaming urchins, the hawkers and bantering fishwives. It felt good to walk by butchers' stalls hung with fresh lamb, pig, and sides of beef. It felt good to see ownerless dogs, stumbling drunkards, gamesters with puppet shows and mummers with clown faces. It felt good to see pretty maidens batting their lashes, and combing their beautiful hair on balconies.

Brother Maria walked through the city all morning. He bought bread, cheese and ale in an inn, and after a small rest in one of its corners, he began another walk in the first shadows of the late afternoon. It was time for prayer, and the cathedral bells were calling the faithful. He could see them, like fish fighting a current, swimming upstream through the busy streets, through the crowds of sellers and barterers, the worldly ones mindless of these unworldly fish fighting to return to the sea of their salvation.

He suddenly felt the poignancy of his aloneness, and in that poignancy envy for both of these conflicting crowds, neither of which he was a part of. He found himself envying those who were hungry for their prayers, who had found meaning in their devotions, and a promise to liberate from the world of death all about them. But he envied the others equally, those that were gripped by gain and ambition. Their blindness and their ignorance seemed another kind of innocence. They knew no better, even as they committed acts of gluttony, stupidity and criminality, perhaps even murder with the ingenuousness of a child. He admired the self-importance and meaning they had come to assign their sly and slavish ways. He envied their shallow love, their deceits and their lies, the wily schemes of their greed. Both the spiritual and the worldly had an identity and honor, an integral place in life; neither of which he claimed or owned.

He walked past the cathedral whose bells were loudly pealing overhead, and whose giant doors were open to the flock that was obedient to them. Stung with nostalgia, nostalgia for his youth and his cloister days, he stopped, listened wistfully, and then walked on; only to return as the giant bells were slowly quieting back into their iron stillness.

Struck, as with a spell, Maria loitered in the street; stood in a doorway, bought a fruit at a cart, knelt to pet a dog.

He had come from the hills and forests. He was a dusty and ragged vagrant; his beard and hair, shaggy and un-groomed. He had been drunk and debauched. He had cheated at gambling boards, only to promptly gamble away what little his cheating had gained. He had thieved and brawled. He had fornicated with tavern girls and men's wives, the last whose husband had apprehended him in the arms of his adultering wife, and from whom only with a desperate fight he had been able to escape.

But his sins were *his* sins. Their filth soiled *his* soul; their blood stained *his* hands. They were *his*, and he did not want to beg for their forgiveness. He would beg for food and shelter, but not for forgiveness from a God he did not believe in. He would beg, or ask a sweetheart for a crust of bread, but not God. As one who had volunteered to carry an orphaned child on his shoulders, his guilt was his responsibility; one in which only he endured; one in which only he was accountable.

No, he did not want to feign giving his heart to God; no, he did not want to confess things to a father he did not truly love. God had made the world badly. He had filled its garden with the noxious weeds of famine, sickness and death. He had poisoned the apple of man's heart, corrupting its sweetness with the worms of deceit and greed.

Breaking the spell, Maria moved on. But as he did the music of a choir, a choir of nuns drifted from an open window.

'*Te Deum, laudemus;*
Te Dominum confitemur,
Te aete mum Patrem,
Omnis terra venerator…..'

He stopped, and listened to the hymn he remembered so well from his cloister days; the words, as if etched on the tablet of his heart. Not with his mouth, but with something much deeper, he joined the hymn.

'*Tibi omnes Angeli, tibi caeli et*
Universae potestates,
Tibi Cherubim et Seraphim,
Incessabilli voce proclamant,
Sancti, Sancti, Sancti,
Dominus Deus Sabaath…..'

Memories welled up from deep inside him, and he was smitten with many sweet sad pictures.

…..the abbey's gardens, its walks and arcades…..the solemn chapel with its candles, altars, clouds of incense…..his kind, hooded brothers, their

slapping sandals, their kind eyes....the frescoes, the idols in the niches......
and his friend, Father Giovanni, oh, dear sweet Giovanni!......

Maria turned, climbed the large broad steps, and quickly slipped into the giant cathedral, not to fall at God's feet, nor to repent for the dissipation of his soul, but to be filled with the memories of his lost youth that had been so full of innocent dreams.....and to pray, yes, to pray for a gentle soul, the soul who had perhaps most truly loved him.

......the sweet sacred tones, cadences and antiphons.....the nuns' voices
behind the grille lifting and soaring, climbing and reaching up the rungs of
this sordid world that they might join the Angels in their garden.....praying
for those groveling below.....the gross, the wicked and the slovenly, the
black-veiled widows, the hungry children.....those he had seen thronging
the streets today.......fishwives, drunkards, hucksters and hawkers....the
wretchedly ragged, the avaricious and conniving.......

.......And for him? Were their beautiful, exultant voices singing,
praising and imploring their invisible God for a shiftless one such as he?.......

......for one who had wandered through the fields and forests, shirking
responsibility.....one who diced and brawled, drank to drunkenness.....one
who had lain with many women in stables, orchards, wheat fields.....only
to leave after love's embraces, alone and homeless.....empty, not filled.......

......'oh Giovanni, oh my dear sweet friend, I was wrong, very wrong,
and you were right, oh so very right, noble and wise!'.......

He was among the last of the worshippers to stand and leave the cathedral. Outside the shadows had grown, and now inhabited the chasms of the highly walled streets. The solemnizing effect of the hymns, along with his memories had left him feeling lighter, newer, but also sad, and somehow aged; not the age of an old man, but that of knowing he would one day soon be an old man; one with empty pockets and an empty heart.

As he began to depart he saw the sisterhood leave from out the postern, they who had intoned such exultant hymns behind the choir's screen, stirring him to his very depths. They were veiled, and in the late afternoon sun they seemed to glow, as they were a flock of visiting angels. A young, prettily dressed child stood with her mother near the garden path upon which the holy sisters were passing. At their approach the child stepped forward, and with her mother's encouragement held out a fist of flowers to the first sister, presumably the abbess. The sister stopped, lifted her veil, and resting it on her head leaned down with a wan smile, accepting the gift from the child's hands.

Of a sudden Maria forgot his worries of becoming old and lost. He instead determined to amend the ragged filthiness of his vagrancy. He must have his coat cleaned, brushed and mended. He must bathe, and have his beard and hair cut, trimmed, and pomaded. He must find a place to stay, a tavern in which to play a fiddle for his meals. He must join the faithful, and when the bells rang loudly, punctually come to the cathedral to say each day his prayers.

.....*He remembered that loveliness, that voluptuousness her robe could not conceal.....that he had played a lute and written poems for.....that he had climbed up the steep hill time after time to see.......but only now had been lent a glimpse of the exquisite beauty hid behind its veil.....yes, oh yes, he could as soon forget the moon and sun.....this was she, yes, this was she!*

His moment of solemn piety had passed. He was no longer tired and lost. He had a reason, the promise of a salvation. He must bring his mouth to her mouth, and taste her kisses; *Sister Giulia's kisses; yes, he remembered, her name was 'Giulia'.*

....

....

CHAPTER FIVE

A CHATTERING MONKEY,
AND
THE EGGS OF SPIDERS

September; 1347;Messina, Sicily

THERE was a great excitement that spread through the city; first near the water and the wharves, then in the winding streets that led into and from them; quickly inflaming the city entire. This happened each time ships appeared in their harbor, the merchant ships that anchored here on their journeys, laden with cargoes, most of which were rare cargoes not native to their dusty and rocky land; things brought from the *Crimea, Egypt* and other places in *North Africa*; from the other side of the world; from *Syria*, **China**, and *India*.

Whether night or day, when a merchant ship appeared in their harbor, horns were blared and bells were rung; and the citizens were roused and gladdened. They were at once gripped by an air of festivity, and quitting their meals and toils, fields and taverns, and even their sleep, prepared for the happy event; great crowds coming to the shore with excited expectations to see the treasures that these giant floating chests had brought to their port.

....*"The ships! The ships! The perfumes! The silks they say are woven from the spittle of worms!.....the great ivory tusks!......the chalcedony, rosewood and the amber!.....the white squirrels and the brightly-feathered birds!.....and the jewelry!....the silver and the gold and the jade!.....yes, they are friendly ships, see the flag of the Genoese!......."*

Arriving in their bay, the *Messinese* would wave bright flags and scarves at the sailors, or if it was night, as it was now when these ships were anchored before them, they would build great bonfires upon the shores, and fill the shoreline with waving candles. Scantily clad maidens would wade out into the water, and then with flowers in their hair and between their teeth, push baskets of fruit and garlands before them; with raised nipples and quivering wombs swimming like porpoises to the sailors and their ships; their brown skins bronzed by the sun, or as this night, silvered with the light of the moon.

Happy were these sun-tawny, labor-toughened sailors to see these sleek maidens swimming out to greet them with fruits and flowers, and in turn it was their custom to hang many lanterns from the masts, sprits and bulwarks of their ships, reflecting the friendliness that was being offered them. For this reason it was unusual that only two lanterns were hung from the galley that had first entered their harbor this night.

"But why only two lanterns on the ship, when normally they are decorated with them? Surrounded by the night, they seem like two pale eyes, more sad than happy.....and see, the second ship just appearing, with only a single lantern burning.....they are Genoese, yes, Genoese, but they seem to be limping, not sailing into Messina.....something sad, yes, something sad, not happy as all the times before......"

And indeed when the first maidens reached the ships, they did not meet happy sailors hungry for their fruits and kisses, men whose pent-up needs wanted only to inseminate the sleek bodies swimming to them in the moonlight. These fruit-laden welcomers were greeted not by lusty sailors seasoned by sun, wave and wind, but by those who seemed to have never seen the sun, who were the victims, not the victors of terrible storms. The maidens were greeted not by those laughing, but moaning; not by the living, but by the dead and the dying; those who had no interest in kissing their mouths or sowing their bellies; but by ones who tried to stop their beautiful eyes from seeing the unspeakable horrors that were upon them.

......those on their hands and knees, retching like sick dogs, those stumbling, wandering and raving.....those covered with growths and black boils, turning their faces away from the beauty of the living, like lepers ashamed of their hideousness......those lifting dead others, bound on planks, or wrapped in blankets or great coats, or nothing at all, lifting them to the sides of the ship to drop them to the water below, fulfilling their promise to

bury their dead comrades on their native land, knowing that the tide would wash them ashore…and if the birds, fish and salty waters did not eat them, perhaps a Christian burial in the hands of the compassionate…….

……the maiden porpoises swimming back to shore, swimming in the same moonlight that had gilded them with joy, now stinging and biting them with horror…..bringing not kissed lips, but harrowed hearts….. maidens too terrorized to talk, having seen things their eyes had been too tender to see…..or if they spoke at all, in stuttering starts and stops, as what they had seen was strangling them…..and when they managed words, they spoke only of the death that rode upon the ships…..and the death they were frightened now clung leech-like to their bodies……

"…..a great sickness on the ships…..the sailors being eaten alive with sores and terrible boils…..begging for help, for mercy, their corrupted faces looked upon me…..they reached out and touched me…..like blind beggars in the streets. They were raving, they were frothing…..oh, I am afraid, very afraid that whatever sickness is upon them is now upon me, and my loveliness will turn to their hideousness…..I have never seen what I saw on the ship…..like a glimpse of hell….I am afraid, very afraid……I must go and give myself to the Madonna and the Savior……I must pray death is not upon me……"

…..And as the morning began to break, and the tide was sucked back by the waning moon, corpses, like dead sea urchins lay upon the shore…..a few struggling their last struggles on their bellies…..death, like crushing tortoise shells on their backs…..corpses bloated and blackened with disease, scarce recognizable as men……as their foulness had been belched forth by the sea's bowels, only to be beached on their native rocks…..flocked about by gulls and crows, sniffed at and pawed by dogs……others having found no rock or sand to rest upon, taken back out to sea by the tide, as the cruel sea mother, like a dog its vomit, would once more devour what it had disgorged…..their ribs and skulls found in the years to come by crab-hunting boys…….

…..the horrified, but good-hearted Messinese collecting the corpses in carts, dressing them and giving them coffins, giving them funeral rites in their churches, and burials in their churchyards…..and those of the living that swam, reaching their shore mad and staggering, drunken with disease and fright…..cared for by caring hands, given this good people's beds, homes, love…..even as death, like an invisible monkey rode and chattered sassily on each of their backs……and with spiders behind their chattering general, an army of spiders that had swum ashore to lay their eggs on every threshold,

before each hearth, upon each altar and inside each cradle.......

......a shriek from a window, a terrible, heartrending shriek....and then another from one racing in derangement through the street.....and still other hysterics from one beating her head against the altar of the Madonna..... those who had borne fruits, garlands and kisses to the sailors, swimming like silver porpoises in the moonlight, now distract with what they had been given in return.....their sleek and slender loveliness now swelling and blackening with hideous boils......

......It was too late.....Though the waving candles of welcome on the shore had changed to flights of burning arrows, and platters of fruits had changed to the teeth of swords.....it was too late.....although the ships of their brothers, of the Genoese, the merchant ships that were laden with riches from the far corners of the world.....merchant ships that were now 'ghost ships' had been turned away, driven from their shores.....it was too late.......

The poison had been spilled, and now was left to seep and trickle to all places, and in each place spawn its evil. A monkey chattered in every wail and moan, jeering at the throwers of peanuts by mortal fools. The spiders had crawled onto their shore, through this good people's very legs, over their feet and into their streets.....scurried with invisible legs up the walls of shop, home and church into their windows, into their beds, into their dreams and prayers.......

......It was too late. The spiders had laid their eggs, and with those eggs the monkey would chatter on.....and God would curse the world as He had never cursed it before.

* * *

THEY had been told too late, the prophetic signs and prognostications..... told too late from the priests and the soothsayers.....the unseasonably hot winds from the south, the falling stars, the stranded whales.....the column of fire above the papal palace at Avignon..... the quakes reported in Pisa, Padua and Naples......the blood in baked bread, the souring of wine in their oaken casks, the worms infesting the hazel nuts......

......Signs, yes, there had been signs.....signs that had been heeded too late, too late.......

Quickly, in the next days and weeks the eggs of the spiders hatched the monsters of their young; the bitten fevering, frothing, raving, dying; the lustiest corrupted, shriveling like worm-infested fruits. Once bitten, within hours the noble became wretched; the most beautiful, blighted and cadaverous; the creeping, scurrying, hatching of these spiders crawling over all; sparing none. Babes shriveled where they sucked. Priests crumpled where they prayed. The streets, homes and churches filled with wails, moans and shrieks, and as the city was crawling with a sea of spiders, and the chatter of a monkey drowned the pealing of every bell in *Messina*, there was a great exodus of the living from the walls that had been invaded by death and its dead.

But it was too late. The eggs of the spiders had hatched. They had spun a web of death over the city. The *Messinese* fled without thought of property or belongings, often without the thought of children, spouses, mothers or fathers. They fled from this unseen enemy whose bites were eating them alive. They fled to save their souls.

But it was too late. The spiders had laid their eggs in the refugees' shawls, blankets, cuffs and pockets, and when they reached the friendly walls of *Catania*, begging for mercy, the arachnids spilled death's foulness into its healthy streets also. Soon their neighbors' open arms closed; their love changed to fear and swords, and like fang-baring dogs, they barred their neighbors from entering their gates.

Bells began to clang, as in an alarum; holy hymns were thunderously invoked, and the bones and the holy veil of *Saint Agatha* were removed from their sacred place in the cathedral. They were sent to march in procession about *Messina's* walls; to purge the devils that those with second sight saw as man-headed dogs. But it was too late. These dog-devils would not be driven away. They could not be exorcised. Their evil had been unleashed by their dark master; a monkey that had skipped down a gangplank of a merchant ship, only to run through the streets, chattering its laughter at prayers and rituals, mocking the relics of ancient Saints, as they were the toys of children.

It was too late. The spiders had laid their accursed eggs. Within six months half of Sicily, like a blighted field, would lie withered and dead.

And when at last the spiders were spent of their venom......long after, in the songs of birds, shepherds' flutes, serenades sung beneath lovers windows......there was yet heard the echoes of a chattering, a chattering that was a laughter in all of them.

The galleys had left, yes the galleys had left, but they had left hell in their wake; their sails filling with an evil wind that would take them to a hundred other ports.

This was only the beginning.....a beginning that had been too late; yes, it had been too late.

....

....

CHAPTER SIX

THE CONVENT

Part II

MARIA found a sleeping room not far from the cathedral. It was in a dilapidating house abutting a small market; its gable decorated with a faded, paint-peeling sword and escutcheon. Cajoling the landlord and landlady, he told them he was penniless, but assured them that his rent would be paid in double when it came due the following week.

"*You will see, you will see. It will be in your hands, and you will have a roomer that will pull roses from his sleeve, and throw the dice as the devil was in his heart! He will read your fortunes in the stars, or in your palms if you like, and play fiddle-songs that will lull the moon asleep, its silver cheek pillowed on your rooftop, weeping silver dews upon your garden flowers!*"

He at once made a pilgrimage to all of the inns and taverns in the streets about. He smiled brightly at the tavern girls, and garrulously ingratiated himself with the keepers, inveigling his way into their hearts.

"*My mother was a gypsy, you see, and I learned to play, sing and dance at an early age. We danced with bears in the streets! We dressed them with skirts, capes and caps, made queens and princes of them!.....danced and rolled barrels with them in the village squares! We told fortunes and swallowed fire. Yes, I know my hair is as golden as the harvest wheat, and my eyes as blue as the sky in which the lark soars, but you see my father was not one of those brown-skinned, black-haired, chicken-thieving rovers. Ha! He was a wild man from the mountains, and like a wind from those mountains one day he swept down on his horse, saw my mother, and whoops! made blue-eyed, golden-haired, devil-may-care me!*

Do I have a lute? Fiddle? Accordion? No, but that's a trifle for a musician the likes of me. They will not be difficult to find. Once your clients know I can play the way I can play, they will bring their own. You'll have an arsenal before long.....lutes, mandolins, bagpipes, flutes, I play 'em all, even the 'cobza' and 'zongora', one as well as the other. And when they hear me sing, like the nightingale in a summer garden, and see me dancing the maids off their feet, why your guzzlers and your gamblers will treble in a fortnight!

I see doubt in your eyes. Do you have a lute? My hands hunger for a lute, like the knight for his sword! There is music in these hands; gypsy music, music of the mountain winds, the howling wolves and the warbling brooks! What, no lute? Then I will sing for you, yes, here, sing and dance before you now! Come, pretty one, be my partner! Ah, the stars are in your eyes, and what a slender waist you have, slender and smooth, like the curve of a fiddle. Have you no sweetheart? No husband? No one at all to hold you in their arms and make you sing?

My name? My name, pretty one, is Brother Maria. Yes, Maria, like a woman's name, like the mother of God. Ah, how you dance! And your waist, how slender, it fits into my arm like a glove! Are you sure you have no husband that tells you so? No suitors beneath your window, on their knees with roses in their teeth? Let me sing just a little, in your ear.....lay your head on my shoulder so that you may hear the song I shall hum for only you.

Payment? No, I will accept no payment.....other than perhaps a sausage, and a little kiss, here, on Brother Maria's cheek."

After a few days Maria had completed a circuit about his sleeping room above the small market, introducing himself to all of the inn and tavern keepers, as well as butchers, fish sellers and bakers, leaving friendly, salutary words with each, and special flatteries with the maids. He wanted nothing of the tedium and drudgery of labor, but he could play a fiddle, croon, cajole, beg; and he had kept an eye open for where he could steal. And there was ever a card he kept up his sleeve, an ace called love. He saw the admiring smiles and glances about him. With a suave and knowing hand, it would not be difficult to untie purse strings at one and the same time as he unbound bodice strings.

In the weeks to come he established a reputation as one with music living like wind and thunder in his fingers, throat and feet. Seeing that his threadbare coat was beyond repair, a seamstress lover made him another, this time of rich, forest green velvet; adorned with brassy buttons and a collar trimmed with lacework. His boots were repaired and polished. His beard was trimmed, and his hair, although left to luxuriously flow, was trimmed and sleekly combed. He began to wear bright silky shirts with bloomy sleeves, as beautiful as women's blouses, and often wrapped about his head a magenta red scarf whose tail fell to his waist. In the firelight where he played his fiddle, his earring sparkled, twinning the sparkle in his eyes. The young man who had once a shaven head and a monk's robe, had fledged flamboyant wings. He had become the gypsy that first, last, and foremost he was.

But this was a gypsy who appeared to have a Christian heart. Each day he attended morning and evening prayers at the cathedral. And more, each day found him in the little garden that separated the cathedral from the convent, when the sisterhood filed in and out of the postern door. As their abbess was a duchess, and he, one of her homage-paying subjects, each day when she passed he was there, neat and bright in the little garden; placing roses before her on her path; kneeling, and bending his duteous head.

But not once did she pause, or give any indication of recognition of his show of devotion. She stepped over the roses, and even once upon one of them; in Maria's mind more purposely, than accidentally, and continued to the cloister.

Why had he stayed? He could not hope to have a love affair with a nun. She certainly recognized him, and as she had coldly spurned him before, so was she spurning him now. She was inaccessible, not only unseen as she sang litanies in the choir, but securely cloistered behind a convent's walls. She was a Bride of Christ, whose veil protected her like iron bars. She had given her life to prayer, her soul to God, renouncing all things of the world. She had starved, and rid the appetites for courtship, marriage, men; for love's embraces and the mother cry of the womb. Then why had he developed this infatuation, praying on a hypocrite's heathen knees, when he could not even see her, talk to her, flatter or try to court her; when he could only glimpse her, veiled and robed, walking queenly before her sisters, as they were not her sisters, but a coterie of her minions?

Maria did not know the answer to these questions. It was an enigma that often perplexed him, at other times stung him with arrows of frustrated desire; at still others made him feel like an abject fool. But there were things he thought he *did* understand, and as the days and weeks passed, he began to piece together bits and pieces of the reason that had tied him to the abbess and this city; if not with iron chains, then with a silken thread, like those children bind to the legs of their pet birds.

She was beautiful, in many ways the most beautiful woman he had ever seen. Her complexion was olive, but a bronzed olive, as if aglow with firelight; her features, as if chiseled by the hands of angels; her lips, full, ripe, and coral pink. Her skin was as bronzed as his was blond, her eyes as inky dark as his were azure blue. Glowing in her wimple, her face was like a cameo, inlaid and raised on anything it passed. She was his sensual equal, his manhood's match; the antagonist that was his complement. Her beauty was its own pedestal, and it was displayed as for him alone to adore.

There was something royal about her, something of the countess; as such a one had donned the veil in a fairytale. She was certainly not the daughter of a peasant or a commoner. Nor was she one pushed from parents into religious life because of a limp or twisted spine, a harelip, stutter, or a silly simple mind. It was well known that the nunneries were sanctuaries for the slow and the misshaped, but were also virtual prisons for some that, for whatever reason, were forbidden to marry; their beauty left to languish and wither in penance and prayer. Many were the comely daughters given over to the Church, and with them handsome dowries. They were given almost as the pagans offered sacrifices, to live and die a virgin, that foregoing the marriage bed, they might give a virgin's prayers to Heaven; an appeasement to a temperamental God.

Maria thought this possibility very likely, especially when her regal beauty so outshone all around her. It also lent another kind of explanation, one that shed a possible light on his motives; motives too blind and irrational for him to at once know, only to slowly puzzle out.

His lovers had been almost exclusively peasant women and tavern girls, those who had never known the luxuries of coaches, furs, silks and other fineries. This Sister Giulia was different, She was not one he had courted while she sweated and toiled in a field; or one who, drunk with wine, had given him kisses in a dark street, or had played lusty games with him in a stable. Her beauty was aristocratic. It had been groomed, schooled, pampered. It was noble.

In addition, he had seldom made a pursuit of one of his lovers, and if he had, only for a flirtatiously short and passing moment. Women came to him, not he to them. It was delightful, albeit fanciful to think that such a refined and beautiful woman, especially one gowned in the habit of a Bride of Christ, would one day surrender her woman favors to him; the treasure she had reserved for God, given instead to him. He was smitten with the intrigue, the dare, and although profane, the hunt.

Was his infatuation with the sister, then, some kind of challenge he was presenting to himself......the hunt of a prey that once eluded his arrows?

Maria was sure he saw a flaw in her sublime beauty; a flaw that both repulsed and attracted him; a flaw that not even her holy habit could disguise. Although her features, and what could be guessed of her shoulders, breasts, hips and legs seemed slender and sensual, there was an air of aloofness about her. There was something cold that belied her life of prayer. Maria had learned that she was the abbess, as he had first supposed she was. She indeed seemed possessed of an abbess's sternness, and seemed fully capable of ruling over the sisterhood with an iron hand. She seemed an angel, yes, but one riding a stormy stallion, whip in hand; or a goddess, with quivering nostrils smiling upon a smoking battlefield. She seemed disdainful of lowly ones and lowly things; the marble of her beauty discolored by a vein of arrogance. Her beauty exuded a cold haughtiness; and this excited Maria very much.

In exotic daydreams he imagined melting the ice of her hauteur by composing passionate, even erotic poetry, imagining moonlit nights when he sang these poems of plaintive longing in the convent's garden. In these dreams she would come to his arms, and lay her head gently on his shoulder. He would lift the veil from her face, and she would lift her mouth to his, giving him the fig of her kiss, and with it the doves of her breasts.

In other dreams, irritated and frustrated with her aloofness, he imagined violating her, sometimes on altars before holy icons. Against her will he imagined breaking her will, making her yield to his needs in rough, even beastly ways, even as the eyes of Saints, Martyrs and the Holy Mother watched; until her stern coldness was broken, and her struggle was surrendered. He imagined her brittleness submitting to his wolfish needs, of entering the deepest part of her, at last touching and waking the sleeping tenderness of her deepest nerve.

Not in daydreams alone did he imagine breaking the brittle glass of her beauty. In the climactic moment of lovemaking with other women, he shamelessly imagined it was a holy Bride of Christ whose face was grimacing with ecstasy, yielding, sighing forth its virgin lust; its marble breaking to the soft petals of a flower. It did not matter who his lover was, even the lewd, the homely or the drunken. Her body became the voluptuous body he imagined beneath a holy sister's robe. The fingers that dug into his back became the fingers that counted rosary beads; the kisses that seized his lips, the lips that softly intoned midnight prayers; love's most prized, often casual favor, became the treasure that had been promised God.

Once in a particularly impassioned session, when the face beneath him surrendered in the height of pleasure, he saw the whites of his lover's half-opened, lust delirious eyes, eyes that revealed another woman, a lovely wicked goddess woman who had lifted the veil from her face to rule with lightning and storm. In this instant he saw the beautiful, brittle face of the haughty abbess break to the bruised face of a common shepherd girl.

Spring passed to summer, and there was no change. This came as no surprise to Maria. He had long realized the absurdity of the thing, long known how implausible and entirely impossible such a courtship was. He had not received a word or a nod from this duchess with a veil, let alone a smile. Besides, he had not remained as faithful as he had first avowed to be. Late hours and heavy drinking at the taverns, as well as his many love affairs were not conducive to a routine of morning and evening prayer. Many days he either slept until after noon, or was made a truant by gamesome lover. On other days he was sour, ill-tempered, out of sorts from drinking bouts; an enemy of dogs, men, cheer and sun. On still other days he was gripped with a melancholy deep and dark, and his only mistress was his fiddle, a mistress that with tender mourning did her best, but not always successfully to soothe and console him.

The beautiful face remained behind its holy curtain, and the desire to see it gradually faded, even as Maria gradually accepted the futility of its pursuit. Amused, he thought he must seem a silly harlequin to this regal sister, one that she laughed at, and likely sneered at behind her veil. It was probably very evident to her that the roses she stepped over or upon signified more than a pilgrim's devotion. She was a virgin, but she was not a fool. She had no intention of becoming a gypsy's whore.

Oddly, this did not matter to Maria, and although he conceded his defeat, he did not receive it as one. The lovely figure that had walked past him woodenly, stonily a hundred times at arm's length in the convent garden, remained; even more intimately near when his thoughts conjured her. It was not her body that he had so sought to unclothe and lay with, but its mystery; not her lips, but the angels that had moistened them with their tears.

Again and again he was driven to make his thoughts tangible, to paint them in ink on sheets of parchment. When dark moods of dread, despair and futility gripped him, he would not go to the taverns to play his music, or even attend a lover's tryst. Though charismatic and liked by all, he earned a reputation for shiftlessness and occasional laziness; a certain undependability that irritated his employers and lovers alike. He would stay in his room above the market, make some false excuse to his landlord, and with an uncharacteristic moping that sometimes waxed into gruffness, tell them on no account would he tolerate being disturbed.

When he painted words, time went away; and with time, the false pageantries of the world. All that was left was a pure, simple essence, like the flame of a candle, one that kept the wolves of want and need from encroaching upon the small warm circle of his moment; one that like a gleaming sword kept at bay the great dance of death. All that was left was life's hunter gripped by his endless hunger for song and love; a hunger of the soul, not the body. All that was left was a ghost, pausing as it passed through the night of eternity.

He was sure the fear of death was the reason man tried to create beautiful things: statues, paintings, poems, altars, churches. It was this fear of death that made him want to challenge the winds and seasons, to leave something of his existence in the path of the transitory; some relic in the wake of its plunder. Man shuddered at life's constant sickening and withering, its wasting away; at its ashes and its graves. He grieved to see its lovely flowers murdered by frost, to feel his dreams rot to bones in his heart; to hear the hoofs and wheels of a hearse bearing love away. Man grieved because he knew he too was a flower, a flower whose hour would be cropped by a mowing scythe; crushed by the trudging boots of inevitability.

He thought that all art, whether a poem, a fiddle song, or a majestic cathedral must contain the same contrarieties that life itself contained. It must be a war; as bloody as it was holy, as cruel as it was sacred; as reckless as it was planned; a war that life was perpetually waging. In this war were spring and autumn, storm and sun, courtship and betrayal; the bones of an endless end, and the flowers of a beginning-less beginning.

One must give one's all to these children of one's heart, these mercenaries of one's soul, full willing to have them stand before the dreadful march of time; to die in the singing of their song. Full of the wounds inflicted by life's futility, these children soldiers must return one day to their mother, *to death*, and though defeated, lay upon her breast their dreams that had lived and vainly died for her.

Maria knew these words that he was compelled to write in fits of moody madness, these scribbled flights of thought that men called *poems* were a submission, a fatal devotion to this mistress-mother. He also knew that the best that man could do with his most magnificent creations,- sculptures, paintings, manuscripts, cathedrals,- was to reveal glimpses, reflect hues, echo faintest echoes of an inviolable mystery whose veil no hand could lift; not from a flower or the song of a bird; not from an ornate altar; not from a woman's smile.

Oh, why could he not capture it, and like a rare bird, place it in a cage? He would cherish and covet it. He would not harm it. Would there not be a time when this mystery was known, when it would sing for him, thrill him with its secret exultancy.....as when he was giving himself to a woman? Was there not a time, when, delirious with pleasure, he would burn through and through upon finding its deepest, warmest essence? Was there not a time when life's womb would hum like a golden hive, and blind to all, a whisper would whisper in his ear: 'Yes, oh yes, sweet one. Now you have found me. Now you know what I am. Now you know the flower of all yesterdays and all tomorrows!'

As the summer deepened, Maria knew that it was this that had attracted him to the abbess. He was not in love with a beautiful woman, but with a beautiful, aristocratic phantom draped in a veil. He could as well love the moon as the abbess, and yet he could court the moon. He could flatter it, woo it, pine for it, let his heart sing like a drunken nightingale to its silver mansion; and by praising its mystery he would praise the mother mystery of the fields, the forests and the stars.

Returning from drink and love early one morning, he happened to pass the cathedral. Outside the convent's gates he saw a young veiled sister, watering the flowers. Approaching her, he asked if he might have a word with her. Silently nodding, she politely consented.

"Good morning, holy sister. Oh, I see. You cannot speak, because of a vow of silence? Yes? Well, that is fine. It will be a little game then. I will speak a few words, and you may answer with a nod, a smile or a frown, or

maybe a hit from those mighty fists of yours, eh?"

After a pause, one filled with the sparkle in Maria's eyes, a shy smile crept behind the sister's veil, and stole across her young face, and Maria continued.

"Would it be out of place for me to ask a favor of you? You see I have something of a little importance that I would like to be given to your Mother Abbess. Do you think you could place it directly, confidentially in her hands for me?

Yes? Thank you, sister, I would appreciate that very much.

I do not have it with me now. I was running an errand, and I happened to see you watering the beautiful roses…..and they are very beautiful, indeed, like the face of the sister I am sure is hiding behind this veil, pure and sweet and fresh…..but I could bring it tomorrow at this hour…..no, not tomorrow? The day after tomorrow? The day after that? Yes? At this hour? Fine, I will bring it to you, holy sister, before I attend morning prayers, three days from now, and we can play our little game again."

Spent from his carousal, Maria climbed the stairs to his room and threw his self, fully clothed upon his bed. But sleep would not come to the rescue of his exhaustion. His brain was teeming, and after an hour he rose, and began to compose his courtship of a duchess ghost that stepped over, and sometimes coldly upon the roses, *even as they were his heart*, that he had left on her path. Entering the forest of words, he began to seek the eternal enigma he knew he could never find.

…..Fair Lady, when your fingers raised your veil,
And th' golden sun found what was hidden there,
Your features, like the facets of a jewel,
Enlightened life's each corner with your beauty rare;
Then did a ray strike like a sword my heart,
And woke me to a second, lovelier Light,
Lifting, with your hand, a shroud of dark,
As an Angel, appearing to a Saint at night…….

The young sister was in the garden on the day and at the hour as she had indicated she would be; this time unveiled. Maria greeted her.

"Ah, a flower watering her sister flowers! Are not the roses jealous of such beauty, and all unveiled to receive the morning sun? Do you remember me, holy sister? Yes? And do you remember the favor I asked of you, to give your Mother Superior something from me? Do you remember that I asked that you, and you alone place it in her hands?

See, it is only this, a little message. Slip it up your sleeve, so that none of your sisters will see it. Can you do that for me? Will you be watering your garden, here, in three more days? Splendid! Perhaps I will see you again, holy sister. Such a fresh and pretty face, the rose of this garden's roses, no longer hiding behind a veil!"

But when Maria returned in three days the sister offered no response of any kind from her abbess; shaking her head in silence. He thanked the sister courteously, and left her with a compliment:

..... "Your eyes, sister, are like deep dark pools glimmering with long-lost treasures in their depths.....You make the morning glad to discover such riches......"

Maria reasoned that no response was not a bad response. He also reasoned that a woman's vanity is stronger than any vow, even to God. He would invoke his muse again. He would assign him a more daring, if not an outright devilish duty, one that would again be delivered to the sister gardener's hands.

.....Is there an Angel beneath your robe?
Behind your veil, does Heaven smile?
A lightness guides and rules your steps,
A buoyancy of grace, un-beguiled.....
More like a princess cloud, than chains of flesh.
Beneath your habit, a glory traced....
O! Only Heaven's creatures step with steps so mild!
A week later, again he greeted the young sister in the garden.
"Ah, the morning star, driving night from the world!"

Maria learned that again the abbess had sent him no response. Again he left, partly dismayed, partly amused, but wholly and eagerly emboldened.

Was this not, after all, what he had secretly wanted? He had more than enough lovers, and after all, she was an abbess, a regal one on a throne, and he a defrocked monk, one who had become little more than a beggar of the roads, one who danced and fiddled for his suppers. Should he not be honored to write poems to a queenly phantom behind a veil, one who received them with neither scorn nor praise? Was her mystery not more beautiful in this way, sealed against all smiles and censures? But why could he pour his heart out to a phantom, one that was cold and aloof, as he had never done to God? Was God not also a mystery? Was love a thing as easily found in wine fumes as when one knelt before an altar; courted as easily with fiddle music in a smoky tavern, as with requiems of prayer?

And why now when he imagined her in his arms, was he not tender? Why now, making love to other women, was he sometimes seized with something dark and blind, almost wickedly rapacious? Why sometimes after lovers had reached and screamed out in their crisis, did he whisper in their ear?

"Are you mine now, oh angel hiding behind a robe and veil?"
And again:
"Is it not sweeter to give your treasure away, than to keep it?"

Why did he once tear the blossoms of many roses apart, only to sprinkle their petals on a lover's breasts, and then on her sex, before he lay down upon her? And why, after love's embraces, did he ask this lover to kiss a rose, even to lick it like a kitten, imagining it had been stepped upon by an abbess's cold haughty step.?

There were several times he wrote to her spurred by wine and unchecked lust. At those times he became prurient, and flagrantly bold.

…..But even queenly Beauty needs repose,
As roses need the night to crown the day,
When starlight sends day's toils away,
Does such a sacred mystery disrobe?
Ah, but to be your Angel guide,
To see in darkness, where mere men are blind,-
The muffled queen, at last a gown-less bride…..
To secretly adore, what from the sunlight hides……

And so the summer went: Maria writing poems, many of which were improperly erotic, delivering them to the sister gardener, and receiving no response in return. It became a kind of game, even a pastime. He knew it was dangerous, but receiving no threat or rebuke, he was encouraged, and continued to write to this aristocratic phantom, this beautiful queen whose palace was a convent.

There were only a few changes in the game; the first being that his poems became more impassioned, no longer brooking on the profane, but boldly making trespass upon it.

….. *"Ah, to unveil such precious loveliness.*
Receive its sacraments,
Worship with eyes, hands, lips…..
To kiss, and kiss, and kiss
Beauty's sleeping, sensual, naked blessedness."

Another was the change that came over his eager message bearer. Urged by one of Maria's flatteries, one morning a gay silver titter broke from her avowal of silence, and when this happened again on another morning, words followed; whispered words, spoken only behind the wall where no eye from a convent window could see.

"My name is Sister Celestina. I am a novice. I have only been in the cloister a short while."

"Do you like it here, Sister Celestina?"

"It does not matter if I like it or not. I have three older sisters, and my parents did not think they could find a man for me to marry. You see most are at the wars, or are dead. My parents have much land, and provided a large dowry for the abbey. This is where they want me to be."

"And the abbess? Do you like your abbess, Sister Celestina, the one you give my missives to?"

"I am breaking my vows by speaking to a man. It would be even a greater sin if I told you things that perhaps I do not like about the Mother Superior."

"But I was once a religious too, a monk in a monastery. That is how I acquired my name, Brother Maria. I know how sacred is a vow, and I avow to you that I will not break my vow to never tell a thing your cherry lips impart to me."

"Here, near the wall. I sometimes feel as if the convent has eyes, her watchful eyes.

She is stern, very stern, Brother Maria. She rules the sisterhood like a general rules his army. She does not speak often, and I do not think I have ever seen her smile. I sometimes feel I do not live in a convent, but in a prison, and she is the warden."

"I saw her once with a lifted veil, Sister Celestina. She is very beautiful."

"Yes, she is very beautiful, Brother Maria, but there is a vein of ice that runs through that beauty. Her heart is like marble."

"Well, I will keep your secrets, good sister. You have my word. I will return when you are next in the garden."

"Brother Maria....."

"Yes, sister?"

"You are very nice. You say sweet things to me. I like talking to you very much."

Maria brought his finger to her cheek, and gently brushed it in a tender gesture of affection. As he was removing it, the sister suddenly seized it, and as she was a bird hungering for crumbs, profusely kissed it.

As the summer ripened, there was yet another incident that marked this fanciful, enigmatic, highly dangerous game of a gypsy courting a holy abbess; this beautiful, albeit icy ghost behind a veil.

On one bright morning when Maria saw the sisterhood walk from the cathedral to the convent, a bee had worked its way behind the abbess's veil. She had lifted the veil to whisk it away, and as she did the sun shone directly on her face, exposing it in a way Maria had not seen it before, even on that day when he had first seen and recognized her, when the child had given her a bouquet of flowers.

He saw at once that, beyond any figment of his imagination, she was truly beautiful, as few women are beautiful. But he also saw that her beauty had begun to age, that the first signs of its fading were upon her. Whisking the bee away, he saw a scowl spread a shadow across her face. Her beauty suddenly appeared dark, a bit ashen and shriveled, even cruel; but also pitiful. Conscious of her regality, and knowing it was dwindling behind a convent's walls, she had grown cold, perhaps bitter; perhaps even shrewish. This stung Maria very deeply, inspiring an urge to save what was left of her special beauty; to rescue it; to make love to it. He wanted to hold it tightly in his arms, to wrest its sublime secret, and make it once sing; to adore what she was taking unused and unloved to her grave.

The lines that this glimpse of her aging beauty inspired, and that he gave to Sister Celestina the following morning, at last prompted the abbess to respond.

...... Your garden's roses are most beautiful,
Yet one day they shall hang their gorgeous heads,
Like weeping widows, shedding their maiden petals,
And like a phantom from this earth be fled.......
Neither rain nor sunlight shall revive
Glad Summer in sad Winter's memories.
Beauty is meant to be adored, alive,
Its moment not mourned for eternity.
Therefore be not vexed by a bee,
It hums where sweetness glows,-
Like lips that yearn to kiss, not sting, the loveliest rose.......

These lines at long last prompted a reply from the ghost behind its veil. Sister Celestina pulled it from the pocket of her habit as it was a great prize.

"*The Mother Superior told me to give you this, Brother Maria.*"

"*Ah, I see. Thank you Sister Celestina.*"

"*I hope it is a nice letter.*"

"*Yes, I hope so too, Sister Celestina.*"

"*Brother Maria, if I wrote you a letter, I would say nice things. I would tell you I like you very much.*"

"*And I would respond that I like you also, Sister Celestina.*"

"*Brother Maria?*"

"*Yes, Sister Celestina?*"

"*If I had not taken the veil, I think I would ask you to kiss me.*"

The note from the abbess was simple and direct, and yet cryptic:

"*Sir,*

The Sisters of Mercy are allowed to have conversations with men, but only through a curtain or grille, and only if the sister is wearing a veil; and only for a brief while.

Come tomorrow, at two o'clock in the afternoon. I will free a moment. I will speak to you then.

In God, Sister Giulia

The note stirred conflicting emotions in Maria. It intrigued and made him curious to speak with the ghost of his idolatry, if only through a grille and from behind a veil. It also made him wary, but for what exact reason he was not sure; as it was some sort of snare, a web woven by that cruel beauty he had glimpsed unveiled in the garden. But it also satisfied him greatly, to think that his poems had perhaps broken through her glass heart, and would be rewarded with an exchange of words, however brief or reproachful.

He washed, barbered and oiled his hair, and with a brushed coat and polished boots he arrived promptly at the time that, more like an imperative command than an invitation, the note had told him to come. He was led by a short, squat, waddling sister down a hallway to the convent's *parlatorio*, a small white-washed room adorned only by a cross hung on one of its plain white walls, and a curtained window on its opposite one. Before this window was a simple chair, and silently gesturing for Maria to be seated, the veiled sister waddled away.

After a moment the curtain was pulled aside, more sharply than slowly, revealing in great contrast a matching room flooded with bright afternoon sunlight, sunlight that was blinding to Maria's eyes. A few feet away, on the other side of the grille, sat the phantom he at last had conjured. She was veiled, but the eyes hidden behind the veil were not hidden in the cold, brittle, stridently smoldering words that came from it, setting its holy cloth ablaze with a fire of *animus* and resentment.

"*Good sir......*"

"*Abbess Giulia.*"

"*I have received the poems you have given to Sister Celestina, as I received the poems that I presume were penned by your hand when I was with the sisters in Siena. I have received them, read them, and immediately, you may be assured, burned them.*

I am a Bride of Christ. This robe and this veil are the wedding gown and veil that I will wear to my grave. I will not be courted or seduced by another. Christ is my husband, and I will not commit adultery with a brightly dressed gypsy who sings in taverns, has a reputation for sleeping in beds other than his own, and writes profane poetry to sisters in a nunnery.

Do you understand me? I will not be your mistress. I will not be your whore. This game of yours disgusts me. Never write me again! If you do I will take measures to have you removed from the city, but not before you will be harshly reprimanded, and not with words alone. Do you understand? Well?"

Silence punctuated her words, a silence left in the wake of their cold thunder. Maria was left staring at the same immobile phantom, behind whose veil he knew the beautiful face had twisted into its bitter twin. Slowly he leaned to the grille, and tenderly whispered:

"*Your heart has been imprisoned. I hear its wings beating against its cage. Let me open your cage's door. Let me teach you to fly.*

Tonight, at midnight, by the garden wall. Come to me. Bring me your kiss; but one kiss, and you will not see or hear of the tavern gypsy again."

To which the stony abbess coldly replied:

"*I have duties to perform. Leave the convent at once. Let my words be both an admonishment and a warning. Go with God, and ask Him to forgive your degeneracy.*"

With this the conversation ended, the curtain was drawn, and a bell was rung. Maria was led out of the convent; soundly chastised, but happy.

....

....

CHAPTER SEVEN

A STOWAWAY MONKEY,
AND
AN EVIL WIND

Early October thru Mid December,
Messina to Genoa; 1347

*HORROR bested compassion, and within days those that the Messinese
had festively welcomed to their shore, were driven back to their ships with
stones and spears, and then escorted with rains of burning arrows from their
harbor; their unloaded spices, silks and parrots, and sundry other precious
goods a sacrifice to appease the angry sea god: to keep the fumes of this
terrible death from their land.*

*But it was too late, too late. The dark seed had been sown into the
fertile womb of these grapes, olives and golden sands. The laughing devil of
this chattering monkey, riding piggyback on these frothing, knock-kneed,
disease-drunken mariners, its laughter full of a wickedness men had never
known before, was ashore, and with it the hatching eggs of countless spiders
beneath their very feet.*

*.....Within weeks not only Messina and Catania, but Syracuse and
Trapani, Agricento and Sciacca were aflame with death, as well as the
fishing villages and the shepherd colonies in the remote, pastoral greenness
of their land. It had been too late. The chattering monkey had laughed at
the prayers of the devout, the holy water of the priests, and the bones of dead
Saints. In the wake of one autumn half of Sicily's inhabitants had been
buried, or lay rotting beneath a pitiless sun.*

The goddess wind that had swollen their Genoese sails, befriending and rescuing them from the long siege of the Mongolian monsters and their corpse-casting catapults, had whisked them safely away. And yet the gentility of this propitious breeze soon proved worse than any siege, for now the breadths and depths of a boundless sea, and not mere stone walls of a city surrounded the liberated crews; and surrounding them, rendered their escape impossible. Death had boarded their ships, and happily chattered its hideous laughter in their hulls and on their planks.....climbed nimbly up and swung merrily from arm to arm of their masts. Those who believed they were escapees, were prisoners, prisoners whose master ate peanuts at their feet, and perched chattering on their shoulders.

What had appeared as white-winged, treasure-laden angels skimming the blue waves, bringing its Genoese children back to safety, soon proved no angels at all, but dark swimming serpents that spat their venom into each port in which they anchored. Fateful these serpent-angels as they fluttered and slithered along the Black Sea coast, and then through the Dardanelles, leaving Gallipoli, Eceabar, Cannakkale sick, reeling, dying, spewing their fatal venom into Greece, Bulgaria and Romania. Most fateful of all was a serpent-angel's anchorage in the bay of Constantinople, where within weeks two thirds of its Byzantine population would be heaped in stinking piles, rotting without rites in the sun, the feast of dogs, birds and vermin.

And fateful, most fateful these serpent-angels slithering through the Dardanelles, and into the open Aegean, these slithering soldier serpents of a punitive God having found a chink through which He could bear His Wrath to a drowsy, falsely proud, unsuspecting world. Man had not learned the lessons he was to learn. The biblical plagues that had rained blood, toads, locusts and serpents on his wicked race had not been sufficient. This was a God that wanted more than first-borns and virgins, whose vengeance knew no compromise.....a fury hurled by a punishing hatred that did not differentiate between the believing and the unbelieving, the humble and the haughty, the sober and the besotted. This was a God that wanted nothing less than to murder races and kingdoms; a God that would make His victims beg for the death they had so feared or mocked, that their gaudy priests had promised to protect them from.

It was too late. The monkey, the spiders.....death had been smuggled into their midst, and the world that stretched eternally fallow and sleepy before them, would never more be the same.

Still, even death and its messengers needed the brawn of the living to spread its dark message to all corners of the world. Death's ships needed living crews to plow their keels. Figuratively, literally, apocalyptically, the crews that brought these serpent-angels into harbors were ghosts and skeletons, and if they were to set to sea again, they must be replenished by those still robed in flesh. Knowing that death was aboard them, the remaining crew members were full willing to stagnate in the harbors where they had anchored, casting their dead overboard to pollute these cities' shores, unless they were given strong bodies with which they could sail away.

Prisons were emptied, and the prisoners, shackled in chains, were driven by goads and whips, not to a block or a gallows, but instead to a ship in a harbor; the prisoners to serve out their sentences in a dungeon of disease and death.

From Sicily, up the peninsula of the motherland the serpent-angels slithered, fluttered, staggered and chattered, envenoming Naples, Corsica, Sardinia, Morocco, Marseilles.....breeding death wherever they chose to sink their fangs and scurry ashore their soldiers.....ships aflame with hell.....ships that were not ships, but dungeons.....crews made not of the living, but of the damned......invalids and madmen too weak to throw the boil-infested, vermin-eaten dead overboard.......

.....the sick and the crazed dreaming one dream, the last dream..... the dream of the dying.....the dream of dying on their native land....the land of palaces, beautiful women and incredible opulence.....in Genoa and Venice, and the green hills and meadows of their spacious kingdoms.......

. . . .

. . . .

CHAPTER EIGHT

THE CONVENT

Part III

Late Autumn, 1346
To early Autumn 1347

THE night turned windy with fits of rain. The first breaths of autumn ruffled the fig and olive leaves, tickling their pale bellies that had been hidden the summer through; the moon, in its last quarter, was shrouded by a thick blanketing of clouds. When the great bell struck midnight, calling the sisters to their prayers, Maria was standing by the wall in the damp, wind and darkness, having forsaken the taverns early, and all persuasions and promises that begged him to stay.

But long after the bells had died, the convent gates remained closed. She had not come. The little game was over. He would return to the taverns, or knock upon a friendly shutter to find consolation in other arms. He would become drunk. He would imagine the skirt and blouse he was lifting over his lover's head was a holy habit. He would imagine that the one who wrapped him in her arms and legs, and dug her nails into his back was a beautiful Mother Superior of a convent. He would imagine his lover's face a cruel face, one that melted into sweetness; her harshness into purrs of tenderness and surrender.

As he was leaving the garden, Maria saw a form step from behind a tree, and then go and stand by the wall, near the very place he had waited. He did not know how, or for how long she had been standing there, but like a thief wrapped in shadows, he was sure it was she.

She was veiled, and as he approached she spoke with the same cold, coarse, mocking tone as when she had spoken through the grille.

"*Are you not afraid? I could alert the constables and have you arrested you know.*"

"*No, I am not afraid. Are you, mother abbess?*"

"*Of what would I be afraid?*"

"*Of what many, if not most are afraid: of love.*"

"*Love? My entire life is given to love.*"

"*To the love of God, but not to the love of a man. They are different, you know, one tasting and embracing pleasure, the other praying to deny and forsake it.*"

"*You are audacious and repulsive. You disgust me. You flatter your women only to use them. How could you think of me in such a sordid way?*"

"*I do not think of you; I dream of you. And those dreams take me away from this petty world with their lovely wings.*"

"*Leave at once. Never come back with flowers, poems, or your gypsy flagrant ways.*"

"*I will do as you wish, and I will vanish, even from your reproaches, if you but give the little gift I have asked of you.*"

"*Go I say, or I will ring the bell, wake the sisterhood, summon the constables.......*"

"*Go ahead. Wake the damned village and the country-side! Shout your indignation to the stars! Tell all that I have molested you, not by coercing your body, but by caressing awake your heart from its cold tomb of sleep, loneliness and spinsterhood! Shackle me in chains, but know the one in chains but begged an instant of pleasure in this pitiful world, an instant that both of us could enjoy!*"

"*You are surly. How can you speak such words? Why are you here at all?*"

"*Why are you here, Abbess Giulia, but for your heart to hear such words and drink the sugars of such surliness?*"

"*I have only come......*"

"*Why, beautiful lady, why? Why have you stolen at such an hour from the bed of your sleep and the walls of your holy fortress?*"

"*Not to be profanely insulted. The night is cold and damp. I should not have come, even to scold you. I must return.*"

"*Have you not brought the gift I asked of you, the gift you have kept, and perhaps have never given, a gift you fear you will take to the grave unless you give it to the one who has recognized your beauty, and is begging*" *for a favor from that beauty, here, in the dark of the night where no other could see, when even the eyes of the stars are veiled with clouds?!"*

"May God forgive your base despicable soul......."

"And as part of the forgiveness of such a despicable soul, pray lift your *veil, O beautiful lady, and give this little present from your lips. The Angels will not tattle the thing, and if they do they will only tell a benign, all-forgiving God."*

At this she turned sharply, and walked swiftly away, only to stop abruptly, statue still, without turning back to him; and in that frozen moment there was no shrill retort, only the wind rustling through the roses and the skirts of the garden trees. Slowly, as they were bearing chains, Maria saw her hands begin to lift from her sides, and then continuing, reach and lift her veil, slowly, as she was lifting a corpse's shroud.

Maria went to her, and looked into her unveiled face. Her eyes were cast down, and when he tenderly lifted her chin with his finger, she closed them tightly. Her mouth was also tightly closed, as her lips were biting each other; her whole demeanor stubbornly, stonily wincing, resigned and readied as for a sacrificial punishment.

Maria brought his mouth to these tightly, bitterly closed lips; brushed them, pressed them; asked them to come and play; begged them to skirmish. But they did not answer his entreaties. There was nothing of the soft petal or the sweet cherry in them; nothing of acquiescence or invitation. Cold and dry as husks, it was indeed as the veil had been a shroud, and he had kissed a corpse.

Pulling away, the abbess opened her eyes, not with the soft daze of one who had received a tender gift, but as a fierce animal in its den. And when she spoke, there was the dagger of hatred, colder than steel, colder than the kiss she had not returned in her words.

"Are you finished? Good. Then be true to your word, and never let me see you again, gypsy man."

With a stare, not a smile, Maria nodded. The abbess brusquely lowered her veil and swiftly walked away, proudly, triumphantly. She unlocked the gate, slipped inside it, and re-locking it, quickly disappeared into the sleeping cloister; leaving Maria stunned; stunned that such sensuous features were so frozen of feeling. Her kiss had held no honey. It was dry as ashes.

He began to leave, but as he did he heard the keys in the gate again.

Turning, he saw in the darkness a form, *her* form; but this time it was not walking with queenly pride. This time it was running, as with fright; as with a desperate need. For an instant Maria froze with fear as she ran towards him, fearful that her guilt had armed her with a knife, and that distract with shame, and the vow he had cozened her to break, she would try to kill him.

But it was something else that had made her run to him, something deeper than a want to kill. She was gripped by remorse, a remorse for something she had never had; a child of her heart she had orphaned, that she had left to starve and die. Tearing, not gently lifting up her veil before him, Maria saw that her beautiful face was contorted and running with tears. Her words, choked with sobs, rent his heart.

"*Teach me Brother Maria.....I want to know......you see my parents, they were wealthy.....grapes and horses and dye houses.....and I had sisters, older sisters......I had suitors, many suitors, rich suitors, but I was not allowed.....teach me Maria......teach me before it is too late, how to be sweet, how to love.....teach me how to.....you see I do not know, I have never.....I, I do not know how to give a kiss.......*"

Maria wrapped her in his arms, and let her sobbing face press against his shoulder. He leaned her into the thick ivies of the wall, their waxy leaves drizzling down upon both of them, so that tears and rain intermingled, as if baptizing them.

He placed his hands about her trembling face, and gently kissed the tears falling on her cheeks. He touched his bearded lips to her brow, nose, chin and eyes, and then to the thirsting flower of her mouth; bringing his mouth to those lips that had never opened to a kiss before. As he had once been taught by a young shepherdess, he now patiently and tenderly began to teach this older woman the wisdom her life of prayer had deprived her of.

His lips taught her lips how to seize and desist, and at times how to linger; how to tease and urge and play; passion's ascendancy, and its tender adieus; how to ask for more, and how to oblige; how to explore, ask permission, seek deeper adventures; how like a hummingbird hovering before a lily, to sip and savor love's nectar, as if suspended, buoyed in eternity.

Over and over, for hours he kissed her in the ivy leaves, as over and over she asked for the sweetness she had been denied through the long years. At last, exhausted with this first lesson of passion, she pressed her cheek upon his shoulder, and whispered:

"I must go my darling. It will soon be time for prayers. Oh, but you must not leave me, no, you must not go to the autumn forests to live with the birds and wild animals. You must come to me again, many more times again! You must give me your kisses, as I promise to give you mine!"

* * *

IT had started this way; as a dare and a game, a dare and a game that grew into something far more than a dare or a game.

These rendezvous in the dark garden, after the sisters had retired from their midnight Vigils, were dangerous for both of them, and both were acutely aware of the dangers; the abbess perhaps more than Maria, who thought love lacked its mystery without a risk, that love was not love without peril brooding in the shadows; that love and death were the siblings of the night.

An hour after the sisters' midnight prayers, she would steal like a ghost from the gates; and in the shadows near the wall find a place that dripped thickest and darkest with ivy. As they were plush pillows, she would lean back into the leaves, inviting him to join her, opening her robed arms like wings. He would go to her, press, fit and become one with her, enfolded in the mystery that had captured them both; a mystery of love made somehow sweeter by the sin and dangerous jeopardy it contained.

She would bring him her kisses, but she would also bring him her fears. She had first tasted love, a love the Church had never given her, and she was afraid to lose it. Such a pleasure seemed a snare; one set by angels, not devils, but nevertheless, somehow a snare. She was deathly afraid of being found out, and the unbearable consequences that could ensue from such a scandal. She felt as this pleasure, this new and secret pleasure that was rife with risk, this pleasure called love that preempted her prayers and vows was making her mad, rending her soul in two, and more than once she told Maria that unnatural, desperate thoughts filled her mind, even her prayers.

"I sometimes think the only way would be to end my life, to hang myself before an altar, with a letter begging for God's forgiveness pinned to my robe. But then I think of leaving you my darling, and I think I would rather be smeared naked in ashes, or be driven into the world with stones and thistles than to forsake your kisses, your words, the jewels of your eyes.

Oh speak to me my darling. Your words are like golden birds that flutter from your mouth. Let them flutter into my heart. Let their songs fill me. Let them dispel the dark clouds of my fear!"

Maria had deep concerns as well. He was worried that those he consorted with in the taverns would discover his profane escapade, or indeed, that some even now suspected its truth. Several times when the taverns closed, women pulled him into corners, petulantly whispering their displeasure at their invitation being declined.

"Why, Maria, will you not come home with me, like you have done other nights? Did I not play as you wanted me to play? Did I not satisfy you? Or is it that what some say is true, that you sing serenades beneath the nunnery's walls? Oh sweetheart, come home with me, and I will do lovely things for you that virgins have never dreamed of doing, not on their pillows, not in their prayers."

Unfulfilled desire also began to gnaw at him. The abbess brought him her thirsty kisses, and with them her eyes, cheeks and hands, and without her wimple, her cropped hair and the swan-like slenderness of her neck; but no more. The press of her breasts and thighs came from behind the protection of her heavy habit, and the least attempt of his to explore beneath it was gently, but strictly halted, as its pleasures were forbidden, and must remain unknown.

She stirred his blood, but never stilled it. This resulted in him sometimes failing to appear in the convent garden, and at other times, late and drunk, and smelling of the perfumes and kisses of other women, scents that hung on him like a robe of smoke.

"Why do you run to other women when you know I have given my heart to you? They are tarts, and I am not. Oh, why are you so naughty and so bad, and why do I love such a bad naughty one? The treasure that I have promised God, I have thievishly taken back from His altar, with the hope, nay, the fervor of giving it to you. I have broken my vows, and now want to give you what I had promised Him. You may have what you want, my darling, and what I will gladly give, but not here in these leaves and shadows, not while I am dressed as God's bride. Yes, you may have, but you may not take; and you must be patient before it is freely given."

Once when he arrived late and very drunk, and she had been waiting in the ivies for a long while, she threatened him with threats that seethed with something much darker than her kisses; much darker than her love.

"Where have you been, Maria? You have made me feel like a whore on a quay, waiting for sailors to come ashore. If you come to me like this again I will tell the village officials how you seduced and molested me, made me give you favors against my will……I will lie, yes lie, and then laugh when they shackle you in chains…..oh, who would they believe, the Abbess Giulia of the Sisters of Chastity, or a homeless wanderer and tavern fiddler?…… But what am I saying? It is I who break the vow of chastity, steal from the convent's gates and sneak to you like your concubine in the night. Oh, here are my lips, my breasts….yes, please, you may hold them! Come take what I beg you to take! Kill me with the sweet dregs of your love that you have not spent on your harlot others!"

More and more these rendezvous began to tire him, to vex and trouble him. More and more he felt ashamed of their shamelessness. More and more he resented the abbess's threats and possessiveness, and feared the madness his kisses may have awakened in her heart. What was more, as his hands had explored her he suspected that she was older than he had first thought she was. The breasts that she now wanted him to hold were small and soft, not large and firm, as they had lost the ripeness of their prime. When the moon was bright, and her wimple removed, Maria glimpsed the gray in her cropped hair, and wrinkles beginning to crack apart the porcelain beauty of her face. When he pressed into her, he felt the brittleness of encroaching age wrapped in her thick robe.

But it was one cool autumn night that made him more deeply regret his infatuation, and the courtship and lovers' trysts that had followed.

For a week or more he had not stood hidden near the garden wall after the sisters' midnight prayers, waiting duteously for a ghost to steal from the convent gates. It was wrong. It was tempting unknown, punitive dangers. Besides, he had found gratification playing in a younger woman's arms. He had made up his mind, at all risks, to be quit of the beautiful abbess.

Well after midnight he had returned to his room, exhausted, and throwing himself on his bed, he had at once fallen asleep, only to wake a short while after, sure that someone had entered his room, and was standing near the door.

"Who is it? Say something. I see your coat, but not your face. Is it Bernadette? No? Then Lucianna? I am sorry I did not come after the tavern closed, but it was very late my love, and I was afraid I might wake your

father. Come here my sweet girl, the night is cold. Come to my blanket and my arms. Here, I will light the lamp......."

"No! Do not light the lamp!"

The voice was shrill and piercing, and struck a great fright into his heart.

"It is not Bernadette, or Lucianna, or any of a half dozen other of your whores! It is one who is old enough to be their mother, and who counts herself their queen. It is one who wants to give you what they give you, so that you will have no need to go to them; one who wishes you to be hers, and hers alone!"

Startled, and not with a little terror Maria rose from his bed and went to her. She had removed her wimple, and passed through the streets disguised, like a man, in a hat and a long coat.

"Giulia, my love, sweet Giulia......"

"Tut, none of your frippery, gypsy boy. I will give what I wish to give, but I will not be seduced."

He brought his mouth to hers, but she turned away. She brusquely unbuttoned the top button of her coat, and as she firmly clasped his hands and brought them to the second button, spoke in a cold, shrill, unlovely way:

"Here, the rest of the buttons are yours. I think you know, better than I, how to undress a woman."

Under the fear of her commands, Maria unbuttoned the buttons of her coat, only to discover a shift, and no habit at all beneath it.

"Oh my angel, come to my bed.....let us be sweet........"

"Here!"

Her voice was strident, and her body, cold and rigid, as she stayed by the door and quickly untied the top part of her shift. Slipping it to her shoulders she roughly, angrily removed her breasts, holding them out to him coldly, resentfully, one in each hand, as they were alms for a groveling beggar.

"Here, take them, they are yours, as I have promised you they would be. If you like, you may kiss them Maria. Yes, you may kiss them."

Obedient, and half afraid, Maria kissed her breasts. It was as he had guessed; they were no longer lovely, even less lovely than they had seemed beneath her robe. They had lost their firmness and roundness, and now hung like summer fruits, spoiling and shriveling on the vine of her former beauty.

"And now the other; hold the other Maria."

"Other? I do not understand......"

*"The other that you hunt in others, like a dog hunts scraps in an alley.....
the treasure I once promised God, but am now begging you to take.....the
treasure that will buy you, if I cannot win you. Here, it is yours!"*

And with this she roughly grabbed his hand, and then sharply led
it down her body to her sex. Once there, she firmly held it there, as if
shackling it to its nook.

*"Is this not want you want, my gypsy darling? Is this not what the others
give you? Hold it in your hand; hold the little treasure I hoarded for God,
but now I openly give to you.....It is yours.....you have my word, Abbess
Giulia's word.....it is your own little toy to play with when we escape the
prison of this city."*

Afraid of her madness, Maria knelt and twisted the hem of her shift
into one of his hands. Slowly lifting it, the other hand tenderly followed,
caressing up the calf, knee and thigh that with age had withered in
the dark closet of her thick robe. Reaching the bony hip, and then the
pouch of her belly, he hesitated, and when he did the shrill voice, the
voice that was so used to rule and imperiously command:

*"It is the present I have promised you. Hold it in your hand, Maria. Do
not be ungrateful. My treasure, the little toy, is yours."*

Maria placed his hand over this hidden flower of her aging body. Its
tuft was small, like the deserted nest of a wren; cold and forgotten, as if
the songs of summer had left it long ago.

*"Do you like the present the Abbess Giulia has brought her gypsy child,
the pretty flower that one day soon I will let him pluck? It is yours, Maria.
You may hold it, cherish it.....yes, you may hold and cherish it.....you may
even kiss it if you like."*

Against his will, Maria complied, and when he did a faint shiver ran
through her body. But it was not a thrill of warmth, rather a shiver of
cold; a shudder, and not an arousal; not of sensual, but some avaricious
pleasure. He felt her hand lightly touch his hair, her hips weakly move,
and then the sigh that was not a lover's sigh, but one that seemed an
obligation, as if her lust was contrived; as disingenuous as had been her
love.

He stood, and at last she brought her face to his. She was heavily
perfumed, and even in the dark he could see that she had painted
brightly, like a lady of the night, or even more inexpertly, garishly, like

a clown in a circus. She fumbled for, found, and weakly tethered in her cold fingers the mate of what he was still holding in his, even as she brought her painted mouth to his ear, breathing in it her madness; the madness he had so foolishly loosed with his kisses.

"*I will arrange everything; the horse, the carriage, the hour and place....I have money, much money. I know where we can go. They will not find us. Marry me, or make me your whore, if only one among your sluttish many.....help me escape from that accursed convent, Maria, help me, and a great wealth, as well as that little trinket you hold in your hand is yours.*"

* * *

AFTER she had left Maria could not sleep. She had not come to his bed. She had not even completely removed her coat. She had only let him touch and kiss her secret places. She had only stolen through the night with the promise to be his whore, if in return he would help her escape from her imprisonment in the convent.

Unable to sleep, Maria left his room and walked the streets, his mind whirling with a hectic storm of self-accusatory, even fearful thoughts.

.......It was his fault. He had blown on the ashes of her heart, and it had flared its loneliness into flames, flames that had fevered into madness. She was old.....her body stiffening and withering with age.....he did not love her, no, he resented her, hated her, even feared her....as there was something venomous in her passion......something snake-like, ever ready to wrap and coil about him, to strike out and kill what it had kissed in the ivies, those ivies that had been full of poisonous leaves.......

Returning to his room at daybreak, he wrote a short, apologetic letter to her, asking her forgiveness. He had been wrong. They must not see each other again. If this was not possible, he would leave the city at once.

He prepared to go to the cathedral, but then stopped, and went back to his desk. The young sister, Sister Celestina, had been very sweet to him, and invaluable in her role as a go-between. If this affair with the abbess turned dangerously ugly, he might not see her again. As a farewell, he would compose a few lines for her.

Quickly the words flowed from his quill.

.....WHY when you blush do your eyes look away,
As if my smile was savagely un-tame?

412

Shyness is no sin, no scarlet shame,
Rather life's royal queen in love's array.
When morning smiles upon the garden,
And pardons night with golden grace,
The rose does not wilt, but lifts its lovely face......

He walked with resolution through the streets and the early wakers to the convent garden, where, as so many other mornings, he saw the familiar figure of Sister Celestina tending the flowerbeds. She saw his approach, and casting up her veil, brightly ran to him.

"*Brother Maria! Where have you been? I was afraid I would not see you again! You, and not the Saints have filled my prayers, and now they are answered. I have missed you very much!*"

Tears welled and stood ready to fall in her beautiful dark eyes. He could feel the fervency of her heart in her words.

"*I have missed you also, Sister Celestina. How could one not miss such a pretty smile? But the world has many hooks and hands to snag my coat as it passes by, and so it has now. I have only come this morning to give you this missive to be given to your abbess. Could you do that for me, my little flower?*"

Somehow disconsolate, she received it from his hands with a kind of resignation, if not reluctance, and tucked it securely in her pocket. She lifted her eyes back to him.

"*And here is another, one for Sister Celestina, from Brother Maria.*"

She looked at him, and in the dark wells of her innocent eyes he saw that she did not understand.

"*It is a little poem I wrote for you, for the rose of the convent garden.*"

The sister received it, instinctively kissed it, and held it to her heart. Her eyes brimming with an adoration of tears, she said:

"*But you are not leaving, are you Brother Maria? You will come again and speak sweet words to me?*"

"*But of course, my pretty one, of course.*"

The convent bell began to loudly ring, announcing prayers. As their deafening tolls were small and unimportant, and could not be heard in the impervious spell that now held her pounding heart, the young sister continued to fix her gaze upon him. Her eyes full of tears, and her lips trembling, she summoned a great valor in her heart to whisper; "*I love you, Brother Maria*"; words that like a pantomime, were drowned by the bell, but thundered loudly in Maria's heart.

As the ringing died, she turned to walk away, but after eight or ten steps she stopped, and ran back to him.

"You see, Brother Maria, I know about your love for Abbess Giulia, and her love for you! I have been bad. I have been wrong. I have read the beautiful words you have written to her, and I have stolen from the abbey, (there is a way without a key), and I have watched from the shadows as you have kissed her for long whiles in your arms, here, in the ivies of this wall. You may think I am a silly girl, but I have kissed the leaves of these ivies when I have come to water the roses......

Oh, why do you love her, Brother Maria? Her beauty has fled. She is old, and she is cruel. There is ice in her heart. Why do you not love me? Beneath this robe I am a woman, one who is fresh and young, and not old and cruel. My heart is not ice. It is a bouquet of roses, one that I lay at your feet, Brother Maria!"

The peals of the bell had died, and in the silence of its interdiction. Maria was left wordless, holding this young girl's heart in his hands, as with tear-streaming eyes she turned and walked briskly towards the gate. She was very lovely, and his eyes fell upon the loveliness that her robe could not conceal; the loveliness that in sharp contrast to the abbess's aging body, promised voluptuous secrets and adventures.

She stopped, turned, and saw what his eyes were delighting in. Running back to him she reached up and seized his bearded face between her hands.

"Yes, there is a woman beneath this robe, a woman who wants to give all of her woman softness and sweetness to you!"

He bent, and gave her mouth what it was so sweetly hungering for; a kiss that seized, lingered, and then seized and lingered the more with a greed both had been trying to deny.

"Sister Celestina! Come, it is time for prayers!"

It was the abbess. She had stepped from the gates, and was staring directly at their amorous embrace. Her voice was not shrill, but evil in its artificial mildness; and there was a strange wildness, as of laughter in her eyes.

* * *

MARIA was very concerned about Sister Celestina. He was concerned that she would be expelled from the sisterhood, or that she would receive some terrible, shameful penance, too terrible and shameful for her delicate youth to bear. When he saw that she was no longer in the garden in the early mornings, and that another sister had assumed her duties, he dared one day to enter the convent and ask permission to speak with her. But the faceless sister behind the grille told him that it would not be possible.

"*Then on what day may I speak with her, and what hour?*"

"*Sister Celestina may not have visitors.*"

"*But for how long? Days, weeks, months?*"

"*Sister Celestina is undergoing a penance. Only our Mother Abbess knows how long that will be.*"

"*Then may I please speak with the Mother Abbess?*"

"*I am sorry. The Mother Abbess is very busy.*"

"*But it is very important.*"

"*You may tell the sister sub-prioress of your concern, or if you wish, you may write your request, and I will convey it to the Abbess Mother.*"

Maria knew that Sister Celestina had not been stripped of her habit. He knew because he saw her coming and going to prayers with her sisters each day. Although the sisters were always veiled, Sister Celestina was at once recognizable to his eye. Her figure was slight and slender, and her step was young and light, although Maria thought not as light as it had been before; as she was attempting to disguise some discomfort, even the hint of a limp.

One day Maria attended afternoon prayers, and then boldly, in full view of the abbess and the sisters, appeared in the garden to watch their return to the convent. Midway, and only a few steps from where Maria stood, the abbess stopped, and whispered something to Sister Celestina. Giving her a key from her pocket, Sister Celestina returned alone into the cathedral, even as the abbess and the sisterhood continued on, disappearing in the cloister, Seeing that Sister Celestina would be alone, Maria retreated back through the garden, and stole into the cathedral with the hope of speaking with her.

But he was a moment too late. He entered the cathedral only to see the sister complete her genuflection before an altar, unlock and enter the choir, and then relock its door behind her. Here and there were worshippers still knelt in prayer, preventing him from calling out to her before she vanished into its inviolate darkness.

He waited in the shadows for a quarter of an hour, and then for the best part of a second quarter. Finally, when the last worshipper left, he rushed to the iron bars and loudly whispered:

"*Celestina! Sister Celestina! It is Brother Maria. I want to speak with you!*"

But although his whisper sounded through the empty cathedral, there was no response. And only after a prolonged silence did he whisper again.

"*Sister Celestina! Answer me! I know that you are there. Come, my little morning rose, let me see you. I need to talk with you.......*"

Like a conjuration, she appeared in the shadows, a ghost shy of the living; standing a good distance from the bars, veiled and unspeaking.

"*Sister Celestina! I have tried to see you, to speak with you, but they have not let me. Come, sweetheart, near the grille, now, while we are alone!*"

But remaining in the shadows, she offered no reply. Maria reached his arm through the bars, pleading, like a beggar begging for bread.

"*Please, Celestina, come! You must tell me what she has done to you. I will protect you! I will break down the damned convent doors and take you with me if in any way she has harmed you!*"

At this the unspeaking sister shook her veiled head, and retreated several steps back into the shadows, like a spirit that fears its conjurer. But Maria would not be denied. He went to the choir's door, and violently shook it, rattling it like a maddened prisoner. He thrust his arm to his shoulder through the bars, and shouted:

"*What has she done to you?! O dear God, what has the madwoman done to you?!*"

Silently shaking her head, the ghostly sister faded farther in the darkness. Maria's shouts filled the cathedral.

"*Celestina, lovely Celesina, come back! O my beautiful child, you must tell me what she has done to you!*"

Pressing his head against the bars, he closed his eyes, and exhaustedly whispered:

"*Please, darling, I will not hurt you. I wish only to help you.*"

"*You must go away. You must never try to talk with me again. Mother Superior has sent me here to pray, alone. I am not to speak. She will punish me more harshly if she sees me speaking with you.*"

Maria raised his head to see the young sister standing before him; almost close enough for his reaching hand to touch.

"*Then my angel, she has punished you harshly? Please, lift your veil, I want only to see your beautiful eyes. You once said you liked speaking with me, as I like speaking with you. We must speak a little, here, now. Trust me, Celestina, Come my little flower."*

She turned to leave, hesitated, and then stepped back to the bars. Her veil was trembling, and from behind it sounded a soft moan, as if she indeed was a moaning ghost, one imprisoned in its own grieving. Thrusting both hands through the bars, Maria clasped her face, and then bringing it to the bars, pressed a passionate kiss to the veil that hung before it, seeking the lips behind its curtain.

"Please Celestina, my darling, you know that I care deeply for you, and you know that you may trust me. There is no one here. No one will know. Give me the key, Celestina. Here, in my hand, please my love, give me the key!"

Slowly, numbly, as indeed he was communicating with the dead, she reached into her pocket and placed the key in his outstretched hand.

Quickly he unlocked, entered, and relocked the choir. He led her away from the light into a small back room, a kind of vestry where robes and vessels were kept. There the young girl stood, trembling in a fever of fright, shivering like a wet dog before a warm fire. From behind the veil came a voice, one transformed from all recognition of the happy voice he had spoken with so many mornings in the rose garden.

"Mother Superior was very angry.....Mother Superior said she would cut out my tongue, and chop off my ears and nose. She said she would do a terrible thing to my woman's part.....that she would make sure I was a virgin for all my days.....and then she ordered, Mother Superior ordered the sisters......"

"The sisters? What did Mother Superior order the sisters to do?"

"She made them go to a field to gather briars and thistles.....and one by one take turns using them like whips upon my naked legs.....and after...... after the sisters had gone, and I was alone with Mother Superior......"

"Dear God, what has she done to you?!"

"Mother Superior made me lift my robe higher.....to my waist, to my belly.....and she, alone, for a long time.....Mother Superior whipped those parts above my legs......"

Slowly, tenderly, Maria brought his hands to the hem of her veil, and as he did, the lines of a poem passed through his mind.....but what poem, and written by whom?......by a lonely man, a lost man who once walked through forests, through a dream of nights, days, autumns, springs.....by a ghost that men had named 'Brother Maria'.......

.....'What then is reason's Reason?

Why do men kneel to pray?

If not to lift a veil, lowered in life's masquerade?'

But the face he unveiled, although welted from incessant crying, and though leeched of its sunny brightness, was not bruised or broken. Maria kissed the young girl's tear-swollen cheeks, and wrapped her in his arms.

"*Oh my love, my little precious love, I will take you with me. I will protect you.*"

He felt the trembling of her body, afraid to seek the strength of his; as if the chill of death had entered and possessed her, prohibiting such compassion. And in her fear he felt some secret hurt she was guarding, hiding, making her afraid, deathly afraid that it would be discovered.

"*Let me see my love, let me see what she and the sisters, with their thorny whips.....you need not be afraid. We will play, for a moment, just a moment we will play that I am the groom and you are the bride, and I may see what our marriage permits you to show, and me to see.*"

Maria knelt before her, and then slowly, tenderly, as that tenderness was dread, began to lift her robe up over her naked legs.

They were beautiful legs, slender and lithe, and newly freed from the coltishness of youth. They were legs that were not meant to bend and lift with heavy labors in the fields, but to run and lightly dance, to open and close like the wings of butterflies with the one chosen to play between them; their porcelain, lyrical beauty making all the more gruesome the raw bloody wounds that had gored them, from her buttocks to her calves.

And as he brought caressing hands and kisses to the terrible wounds inflicted on their loveliness, he whispered:

"*They will heal, Celestina. We will salve and bandage them, and they will heal. They will be slender and beautiful again, and they will carry you like wings, like the princess you are. I will take you away. She will not do this to you again.*"

Suddenly there was a great commotion in the cathedral, and a great rush and tramping of men's boots. A voice cried out, a shrill woman's voice that smote the solemn silence, and sent daggers of betrayal through both of their hearts.

"*I saw him enter the cathedral, the gypsy man with the bright scarf and the jewel hanging from his ear....the one who plays a fiddle in the taverns....they are in the choir, I am sure they are in the choir, that is where he seduces our brides and makes them perform lewd acts, in the very place where we pray and sing our hymns.....the novice sister and the gypsy who has come from the forests, that is their secret den of sin.....I have proof.....a poem that he wrote for her, as well as many he wrote to me.....arrest him! Here, I have another key! He is a seducer! He uses our innocent brides for his lust!.....He has even tried his trickeries on me!.....Arrest him! You must arrest him!".......*

Maria heard men's feet approaching, like herds of beasts through the nave and the transepts; and then a key, a second key unlocking the door of the choir.....the male rush of heavy boots and angry bodies. There was no escape. It had been a trap.

....

....

CHAPTER NINE

THE KNOCK AT THE DOOR

Genoa and Venice,
Mid-December; 1347

BUT they were not welcome. They were not welcome because it was too late. It was too late because the people knew their native sons were bearing the chattering monkey of 'death' upon their shoulders, a monkey whose rumor had taken wings on the wings of the wind, through the valleys and hillsides of wheat, grapes and olives of their land......warning them not to trust, because it was too late to trust.....because it was too late to pray.....because it was too late to hide......for 'death' laughed its chattering laughter before all altars and into all fears.......

.....forbidden from their ports, all galleys arriving from the Crimea, Cypress, Constantinople, Tunis, Sicily.....no galley from the East or the South allowed to bring its crews or merchandise ashore.....there was a monkey climbing up and down their masts, swinging from their yard arms.....and though this monkey laughed, ate peanuts and gamboled like a silly clown before an organ grinder, it was full of a dark evil.....a strange, dark, godless evil disguised in its silly capers.......

.....no jubilation of music, masks and torches.....no ringing city-wide of cathedral bells.....no priests swinging censers, and with upraised hands blessing their sails as they were the gentle wings of holy birds.....too late, it was too late.....no choirs singing praises in convents.....no parades of drums and bugles, clownery or confetti.....too late, too late.....no bankers and usurers salivating at the florins held in the ships' holds.....no courtesans painting their faces, preparing couches for the homecoming of their sea-

weary, woman-starved clientele.......

.....there was no welcome, because it was too late.......

.....instead, only the volleys of belching cannons, and flight after burning flight of arrows loosed by legions assembled on the shore.....archers, rather than trumpeters, lighting the night sky, quenching the stars......some of these missiles landing successfully on the decks, as their senders were willing to burn their riches, rather than to die......the flaming sallies scattering these giant chests of wealth back to the seas and lands that had first contaminated them.....back to the hell that had uncaged such an evil monkey.......

But at this the monkey's chatter stopped, and its laughter died......its heart contracted with bitterness.....its monkey eyes changed to an adder's eyes....their carnival merriness to a diabolical leer.....to be so rebuffed, so spurned, so denied the opulence it had so longed and lusted for.....the delicious dreams it had so wished to poison.....to be so unwelcomed on the verge of its coronation....

But it was too late. It was too late because the monkey knew the weakness that lived in the blood of the living.....because death knew it was more sly and clever, and far more potent than this frail genius of breath, blood and brains that even kings and princes owned. Compassion would be the soil that the Devil-monkey would use to skip into the magnificent streets of Genoa and magical Venice, and into a sea of flocks and fertile lands, and an innocent people beyond.......

.....Gangplanks were lowered, and the sick, the staggering and the dead were at last given over to tender mothering arms......the monkey running into the gorgeous streets unseen, its razor-sharp teeth frothing with rabidity.....full of avarice, and the bloody bite of revenge......

Never had the monkey seen such lovely gardens and such glistening fruits.....gardens of palaces and cathedrals, royal arches, loggias and towers, canals and lovely esplanades.....and never had its army of spiders bred in such promiscuity, laying their eggs in pockets of silk and velvet, in purses of counts and countesses, beneath pillows where the heads of such gorgeous tresses lay.....indiscriminately, dispassionately, in the beds of the rich and the poor, the virginal and the lascivious.......

Never had death seen such fertility in which to cast its seeds. Never had the monkey seen such royal rites and rituals to despoil, such beauty to defile, such pomp and vanity to infect and corrupt....never had it seen such a grandeur in which to toss its peanut shells and to happily urinate upon........

Too late, too late.....fate's seeds were sown, and within days the streets were filled with screams and wails of anguish, an anguish sprung from a compassion that would curse its race for generations.....death was afoot and abloom, laughing in every ear, heart and dream.....its laughter full of chatter, its chatter full of a hiss louder than drums and bells: 'too late! too late! The Great Mortality is among you, and it is too late!!'......

. . . .

. . . .

CHAPTER TEN

THE DUNGEON

HIS first thoughts were not thoughts at all, but sharp, piercing shards of knifing pain........

.......a pain that blurred, poisoned and disjointed his thoughts into fevered figments of a dream.....a dream that ate all other dreams, and with it the memories of a lost child that once owned them.....prayers, embraces and gamboling bears and singing gypsies....all left on a forgotten shore beneath a forgotten sun.......

.....the pain a man must feel when stretched on a rack, or as he is slowly being impaled .....the pain a soldier must feel on a battlefield as he bleeds to death in a blazing sun.....the sword's cold steel lodged through his entrails like a monster's fang.......

.......it filled him, nauseated him, punished him.....from his wrists bound tightly behind his back, up the lengths of his arms, into his shoulders, neck and head, throbbing down into his chest and the extremities of his back, legs and feet, joining each muscle of his body into a twisting knot of anguish....these, the results of the savage kicks to his ribs, abdomen and face, even as he had lain defenseless before the rain of boots and the butts of cudgels.......

.....neither did the return of his consciousness bring relieving salvos of hope......but like a hangman's dawn, only damp and cold, and the reek of decay and sour ferment in some deep dark bowels beneath the world of sunny fields, flowers and happy faces.....his mouth filled with the flavors of life's dregs and spoilage.....the grit of dirt, the salt of blood, the bitterness of shame and defeat.....his tongue, once the dainty epicure of kisses, and glib with song, poetry, the flattery of women, now swollen at his miserable end to

a chalky, loathsome slug......

.......most pathetic, most miserable, the memories in these fever dreams.....memories that like the cold eyes of fish swam by the wreckage of his life.......

.....fragments of things he had cherished like he had cherished no altar, no belief, no God......the dowry of his soul, bequeathed to no one.....pretty butterflies in flowering meadows.....green hills, flocks of clouds, galloping horses.....the naked bodies of women in tall orchard grasses, hay carts, stables and doorways......the lilting of a flute, and the leaping from an abbey's walls, deserting bells and prayers for a young girl's kisses.....smoky, noisome taverns, and fiddles singing in his arms.....the bloodcurdling screams of a man as he was being dismembered in the cage of bear....'Ohai! Ohai! Come back Ohai!.......

.....these his treasures, his sum, the trophies of his ruined life that he had kept, clung to in these, the dark bowels that now claimed him.....those wretched bowels he recognized as his 'death'......

......oh, he had been a fool, a wicked, wretched fool a thousand times over!.....the gruff shouts and shrill shrieks, the torches that exposed him, alone, with the young sister, as if he was violating her.....his tenderness twisted, corrupted into obscene abuse....."Did he lift your habit's skirt, sister? Did the gypsy seducer kiss your nakedness?"......and the poem, the incriminating poem he had written for her....and those lurid lines he had written for the abbess....."Yes, that is the man, the man who wrote me pretty words, wanting me to be his mistress, a mistress that would be his whore!".....the realization that the silly dare of his desires had snared him in an inextricable web.....oh, he had been a fool, even at the end when he had fought so ferociously, throwing constable after constable off him, only in the end to be garroted and shackled by their overwhelming numbers.....the abbess's shrill voice somewhere above his bondage: "Yes, that is him! The fornicator! The one who has tried long to make harlots of God's Brides!".......

......and now as consciousness began to break upon the pain and misery of his fate, not through his blindfolded eyes, but through the blinding darkness of his soul, he remembered things his captors had said, those coarsely speaking, uncouth ones that the prelates had given him over to, to be led from their tribunal through the streets to another place, a darker, lower place, a place of imprisonment that he knew was nothing other than the anteroom of his doom.....

......They had roughly, and with a dark joviality pushed, goaded and

drug him down stairs and through narrow stony ways, his eyes made blind with a tightly bound rag......and once out of earshot of his judges, they had rained upon him jeers, and curses spoken with mouths full of food and drink... and with them the sharp prods of boots and pikes, the slaps of their hands, and the stinking breath of their laughter........

"So, you've been caught with your fiddlestick where your fiddlestick should not've been, eh fiddler man?....although I am sure it has fiddled merrily many a-time and in many a-nook in its day!"

"The tavern whores were not good enough for you, eh?"

"Have you something against what is good enough for the rest of us?"

".....a common wench is not tender enough for your tastes?"

".....not seasoned enough with prayers?......."

"He is a lover of tender meat, virgin meat, and not old tough goats like the rest of us are left with."

"Tell me man, what it's like on the lap of a virgin?"

"Yeah pretty lady man, does she recite 'Aves' for you?"

"How many holy brides did you marry?"

"Roll in the bridal bed?"

"Send plucked to their prayers?"

"Why, the rascal picked their maidenheads like a child picks berries in a berry patch."

"Tell me truly, chap, how many were true virgins, and were not first a shepherd's throw?"

"Oh, you and your fiddlestick, made the sisters sing their devotions as they had never sung them before!"

"Sung from their hearts....."

".....and the place below their hearts....."

....."made a brothel of a nunnery the fiddler man did....."

......and then midst their prods, their coarse gibes, jeers and laughter, and their foul breaths upon his blind face came the iron jangling of keys and the opening of a door....and then the rough casting of him down on an earthen floor, one that stank of the sour rottenness of roots, grapes and apples.....the barbed sallies of their cruel words and laughter unexhausted, even here.......

"Here is your new home, pretty man."

"Do you like it, even if the bed is a bit hard, and without a window, but for one poor little one?"

"Through which when daylight peeps, a man's ghost might watch a man's body hang."

"And sorry, there are no whores, with or without a holy habit here for your enjoyment."

"No visitors at all, mister pretty lady man."

".....except for rats......"

"......and maybe a priest at the break of dawn....."

".....as all prisoners have before they are led to the gallows."

".....and sorry about binding your ankles tight like this.....but we wouldn't want you to run away to another nunnery to say your prayers......."

And as they closed and locked the door, their voices forsook jest and jocundity, becoming more gutturally and cynically malicious.

"Sleep well, pretty lover, for as I am a man, it will be your last."

"Pretty man will soon have his prettiness picked apart by crows."

"That should teach you to keep your pecker from a-peckin' between a virgin's legs."

And with this the heavy door was closed, and there came the iron rattle of keys locking it. But several long moments later the keys rattled in the iron wards again, the door opened, and a single pair of slow, heavy, dragging boots entered in the darkness before his bound eyes, and with the boots a stolid, colorless voice.

"I'm leavin' a bowl of water on the table. I am sure even men with nooses about their necks become thirsty. Ye've got no hands, so ee'll have to just slurp it with your tongue, like a dog.....like the dog you are."

At this Maria had desperately moaned through his gag, and the boots stopped as they reached the door.

"Why, I quite forgot. Ye're gagged. Even dogs need mouths to lap a drink of water I suppose."

The boots returned, the man knelt down to him, and with large, roughly callused, stubby fingers clumsily removed the gag that had been cinched tightly through his mouth, granting him a chance for speech. As the man rose to his feet, and began to leave again, Maria had managed a weak show of words, words that trembled on the verge of tears.

"Thank you.....thank you for that, and for the water you have brought me."

The man made no reply, but again with the great drag of his limp began to leave and close the door. Knowing that this would probably be the last person that would enter his imprisonment, if there was truth to be had in the men's ugly jests and threats, he had called out with fear and panic.

"No, please, wait! Do not go good man! Could you find it in your heart, friend, to also remove this blindfold from my eyes? For as men nearing their death may still thirst, so they may want to see one last time the world they are about to leave."

But this did not stop the rattle of the iron keys, and the locking of the door behind the man's departure. Still, in the awful silence of the place, Maria did not hear the man's heavy boots scrape and drag away, and he could only deduce that the owner of those boots had paused, and remained standing just outside the door.

He ventured no other appeal, other than the pleading of his heart wildly pounding against his ribs. Only after its drum had pounded for several long moments, did he venture a weak whisper of utterbeggary to the man that he was sure still stood behind the closed door.

"Please, kind soul, for the love of God, in my last hour, let me see."

As the words had created an intrusion on the plutonic place, they were quickly drowned again by its rule of silence, silence more deafening than any thunder. Still, he did not hear the boots step away in that thundering silence, and after the suspense of a few moments the key rattled in the iron wards, and the boots entered again; slowly scraping with their owner's pronounced and heavily dragging limp.

As before, the man had knelt down to him, but only after long moments of anticipation, anticipation filled with the wheeze and reek of a liquored breath, did Maria feel the man's abnormally large hands reach out and roughly and clumsily untie the rag about his eyes. This completed, the man remained hunkered before him. Free of the blindfold, and first blinking and squinting in the pale light cast by a candle on a small low table, Maria looked into the face of his bene-factor; he who had granted him this show of kindness, as if wanting to show his prisoner the grimness of his dark predicament. . Inches before him, Maria studied what it was not possible for him to look away from.

It was by no means a handsome or kind face. It was greatly pocked and pitted, as from a former disease; gnarly, and furrowed with great lines that spread like the intricacies of a spider's web in all ways over it; not fine lines, but deeply carved ones, and whether the lines were from great cares, weather and sun, or the abuses of drink and dark doings, or the sum of all of these, he could not tell. But there were several deep pocks, as if gouged more deeply, deeper than the work of sun or dissipation, and these at once he recognized as scars, scars that suggested awards given to rough deeds. The face was tawny, leathery like a sailor's, and although it was not fully bearded, it was bristly with the scurf of filth and neglect, a neglect second only to the man's long shaggy hair hanging greasily and dog-like about the disgusting picture of his horrible countenance.

But it was the man's eyes, those windows of the soul whereby the heart tells its truest story that made a great impression. They were small, very small, like the eyes of a pig, and when he looked at them, hoping for a spark of warmth that had moved his hands to acts of compassion, that spark was not to be found. Small, beady, and half-hid by errant vines of his hair, the eyes showed hints of neither warmth nor coldness, but rather were leaden with a dull resignation, like a slave that had been long beaten and conquered by whip and toil. It was not the stare of one that had tired of the living, but one that had long ago joined death's team; that had learned to ignore and trivialize life's reasons and it's trophies; the stare of one who had traded the sensitivity of life for the coarseness of its abuse.

Maria ventured several words to this unsavory, unlooked for, invaluable giver of kindness.

"Thank you, friend. Thank you very much. I am very grateful."

But the man was not only expressionless; he seemed to be wordless as well. Boring him through with his keen, pig-eyed stare, he sighed, and with a groan that must surely have long accompanied some former wound or broken bone, in a crippled way he managed himself to his feet.

He was a monstrous man, and indeed, from where Maria lay on the floor, seemed a giant. Once on his feet, he stoically turned, and with a limp that matched his giant-ness, but refused the support of a crutch, walked the several steps to the table, lifted the candle from it, and made for the door.

"Please! Must you take the candle? Friend, I beg of you, leave the candle for these eyes you have so kindly un-bandaged!"

At this the huge man stopped, but instead of replacing the candle back on the table, continued to hold it, as once more he returned, and with a groan once more slowly hunkered down before him. Again he stared with his small pig eyes, eyes that seemed to have exhausted tiredness itself; lazy and blank of any discrimination between pain or kindness; the candle revealing even more of the grotesque masterpiece that was his face's inhuman ugliness. Again he did not speak, so that

Maria wondered if he was one who had had his tongue cut from his mouth. Only after a long, interminable moment looking into that hideous visage, was his wordlessness broken by a slow drawl of words, words that were as soul-less as his eyes were swinish.

"*You want me to leave the candle, eh?*"

"*Yes, please, it would be a great kindness.*"

"*And you would like me to be your friend?*"

"*I sense a kindness in your heart......*"

With this the horrible face broke into a broad, filthy, tobacco-blackened and teeth-missing smile, one that only augmented its hideousness; loosing from that smile a husky laughter, as if indeed he was a giant laughing in a hashish dream.

"*Of course I'll be your friend, your last and only friend, a friend like no other, even as I've been the friend of too many to count.....thieves, drunkards, murderers, the innocent and wrongly accused, those caught with their pricks playing in places where they shouldn't have gone a-pricking.*

Yes, I'll be your friend. I'll free you of all your pains. At dawn I'll bind a bag over your head, and then a rope about your neck, and with a kick of my boot take the earth from beneath your feet, and with it every fear and worry that the head beneath those pretty golden curls has ever had. After all, what are friends for? Yes, I'll be your friend. I'll break your neck and watch you thrash and wriggle. I'll watch mister death tickle you and make you dance. And after I'll go to a tavern, tumble a moll, and pay for that tumble with what I earned from hanging 'ee. Yes, I'll be your friend, as at the end death is the friend of us all."

The words had in no way livened or excited his eyes; and the gross man had stood with a slow, groaning effort back on his feet, only to remain standing before where Maria lay. After a long moment, his large boots inches from Maria's face, he spoke words that perfectly matched that soul-less soul from which they were borne.

"*Go to hell pretty man. Go to hell with the rest of us!*".'.....and then with lightning swiftness, swift as his gait and speech had been slow, one of his bootssavagely kicked Maria in his chest, sharply, brutally, and he had known no more.*

* * *

MARIA opened his eyes. He opened them to a dark, dingy, terrible place; as what he looked upon was a mirror of his soul.

The hangman had left the half-burnt candle on the table, to be sure more from mockery than any show of kindness, knowing that it would burn out in a short while. In the glow of its little light Maria saw at once the wretched hole of his captivity. It was a small, damp and low-ceilinged room,, its walls and floor a degenerate, moldering work of crumbling dirt and caving stone, and here and there live roots that had succeeded in invading it. It was a cellar of some sort, and the residue of sodden straw and rotting fruits inhabited it; and more, the sour stale smell of urine, as he had not been the first to know its wretchedness. Too buried to afford heaven's light, except one small iron-barred, vine-strangled window near its ceiling, its only other aperture was a small judas-hole in the massive door, one that, whether closed or open, admitted only a deeper darkness, and perhaps a watching eye, like a pernicious owl from that darkness. There was a low table, and before it a stool, like a common milk stool. On the table's top burned the stubbish candle, and beside it, a water bowl and pannikin.

With bound wrists and ankles, Maria made a great struggle to painfully sit aright, and then braced his back against a wall. This only brought him more anguish, for here he could more clearly see his doom, the doom that his many careless pleasures had led him to. For indeed, he knew that it had not been only his amorous dallying with a Bride of Christ that had cast him to this dark place and dark fate, but countless other dalliances and caprices, countless other rolls of the dice that his heart had brazenly flung across his paths. Those that he had long consorted with; thieves, ruffians, drunkards, whores,- they who had been the happy comrades of his degeneracy, had in the end been conspirators, conspirator that were his jailors.

A parade of ghosts began to troop across his mind, even as he imagined them filing phantom-like across this small foul place; stepping from the darkness of one earthen wall, and for an instant being exposed in the arena of the candlelight, smiling and bowing, as from a performance, before vanishing into the darkness of the opposite wall.

......*faces he had cursed, spat at, hit with his fists, fought with, knife in hand.....simple faces he had cajoled, tricked, cheated.....pious faces whose goodness he had deceived, disregarded, disappointed.....faces of lover after lover, young and old, fresh and jaded, sweet and wicked, some of whom he had seduced and sworn to love, others that had been the seducers, vowing their love for him.....all left unloved in his aimless, shambling wake.........*

.....and in the parade the face of a dead man staring through each......a dead man in the snow, his glassy eyes impaling his soul, smiling.....as if he at last was exacting his revenge.......

In utter despair Maria found himself agreeing with his captors. He had deserved the ugly fate that awaited him at dawn. He deserved to hang from the gallows, his broken dangling body cheered by a drunken rabble in the streets, and then circled and picked by a crowd of crows. The heartless hangman had spoken the truth: *'Yes, I'll be your friend, as at the end death is the friend of us all'*.

It was a just punishment; one that he must surrender to, like a deer with the hunter's arrow lodged in its side. And he must pray, yes, he must pray for forgiveness, for turning his back on goodness and holiness. Yes, now at his end, with death's noose about his neck he must pray for forgiveness, for absolution. He had not recited a *Pater Noster* for years, but he must try to remember the words he had recited so many times in his youth. Yes, for the salvation of his soul, he must try to say them. He had been a fool. He should never have left the abbey. He must try to remember and say the words.

'*Pater Noster, que es in coelis,*
Sanctificatur nomen tuum,
Adveniat regnum tuum, fiat voluntas tua......'

Yes, the words were still there, like polished pebbles in a brook, but the one reciting them found them bitter, and did not want to use them. He did not want to ask for forgiveness at his end, not when he had lived a life so recklessly undeserving of it. He who had been a faithless idler, a shameless rake, even a killer, wanted to claim this one last act of heroism. Even though he must die defiant and unrepentant, a guilt-reeking criminal in the eyes of men, he did not want to die a hypocrite in the eyes of his heart. He had turned his back on the mythology of God, and at his end he would not buckle before the throne he had so long been deaf and blind to; the myths that he had so long forsaken and resented.

Without belief he must be brave, face the inevitable.....remember things told him in the cloister, told him in his youth, things the commonest know.....the man at his plough, the woman at her churn.....the smithy at his forge.......

'Death will come when it will come', 'each leaf in the forest must wither and fall', 'the midwife meets the pallbearers passing in the hall'.....yes, he had heard these words many times before, but now when death had hung its heavy chains upon him, and was leading him to its open maw, these simple words woke like sleeping thunders with the awful might of their significance.

.......Yes, he was about to fall like a leaf in an autumn forest, and that forest would be no better or worse for his falling. Its trees would continue to sleep in winter and wake in spring. Trout would continue to swim through its streams, and birds continue to warble in its branches. Hunters would come to hunt, sawyers to chop. Children would pick its berries, and lovers seek its depths to hide their secret kisses. Life would go on without his creature wandering with lonely, pretty dreams through its green leaves.......

Despair seized him, clutched him; not only in the dungeon of this cellar, but in the dungeon of his soul. He had not been a good person, but a bad, and sometimes a very bad one; in the eyes of the world a drunkard and fornicator, a thief, and yes, a killer. Had not the friend of his youth told him he owned a different nature, a worshipper of the moon, and not the sun? What had his friend meant by those words? Were they poetry, like the words he had sung when he played a lute? Or did they contain some deeper meaning, some deeper truth? Had his friend seen a dark fate, a dark curse smeared like blood upon his soul.....a curse of Cain?........

Again he felt the need to pray, but not to a Father he knew he had rebelled against, whom he had both deserted and been banished from; to whom he knew he could never return, even if it meant the salvation of his soul. Fathers were stern; full of rigidity and wrath. He must pray to the Mother of God, his namesake. She was a woman. She was mild, and would understand. He would conjure her from his memory, just as he remembered her when he was a monk, the beautiful marble statue in the courtyard, her face filled with a sad sweet smile; a smile that was kind and understanding of all things; a smile that knew the mystery of suffering, that had watched her Son nailed on a cross. Yes, she would hear his prayers; she would be kind to one who had been named in her memory, and had called out to her in his hour of need.

.....An 'Ave', yes, perhaps if he recited an 'Ave'.....but did he remember the words, and would they be spoken from a heart of sincere devotion, or only from selfish, desperate need?.......from a penitent who was giving his heart

to her, or from a hypocrite who was asking only to keep it for himself?.......

'Ave Maria, gratia plena,

Dominus tecum, benedicta......'

But no, no; this too was no good. The words were there, but when he spoke them they tasted false, somehow befouled, like a stale wine. No, he could not pray, even to his namesake, even to the Mother of God. No, he must die motherless and fatherless, resolved to answer for his abject wretchedness alone; resolved to give his soul to the beaks and gullets of crows.

He would miss the world, but would the world miss him? In truth, would anyone mark or miss his absence? Would any but a few tavern girls or peasant women shed a tear when they saw the one they had given their embraces dangling from the gallows? After a few short prayers and days, at most the passage of a winter or a summer, would he still live in any heart he had angered or tickled? Would anyone remember his blue eyes, his laughter, the melodies of his lute or the earring that sparkled beneath his golden hair? Would any of his many lovers remember the dreams he had whispered in their ears? Would he be forgotten when their arms wrapped tightly about another lover?

Again, welling up from a deep place inside him, the same questions, the same haunting refrains of his soul.......

.....Was he a part of a dream, a pretty-colored leaf felled by an autumn breeze, only to be gathered in the infinitely greater dream of the sun and seasons, of life's perpetual, meaningless song of flower and decay? Was there nothing more? Was life a thing so easily withered and casually spent, and with a change of the moon, coldly forgotten?

He looked about him, and felt overwhelmingly sad to know that in such a pit of degeneracy, in rags, ropes and bruises he must end his voyage, a voyage that had once been so full of hope, promise, and lovely dreams.

.......Dreams, yes, this hidden treasure of his heart would be the most difficult to relinquish; the pretty singing birds of his dreams that he kept in the cage of his breast, that sang to him in his needs and his loneliness, that nourished and sustained him.....that he told no one about, even his sweethearts....these would be the most difficult to leave behind, to forsake and forget.....these dreams lent him by another dream, by another mother.....a sweeter and more tender, and yet more exacting mother......

They were his children, and like a loving caring parent he was not prepared to leave them, to let them languish and die before they had reached

*the maturity of their bloom. No, he did not want to leave his beautiful
dreams. He did not want them to perish. He could turn his back on God,
on His altars and His prescribed ways of holiness, but he could not bear to
orphan these children of his soul. Although he had committed countless sins,
they were innocent. They should not have to pay such an inglorious price.
They should not be left to starve, to be forsaken, to be eaten by worms. He
wanted to nurse them, to shepherd them; he wanted to watch them grow,
to give them the milk of his heart; let them go to battle in poems, frolic on
fiddle strings, sing in the hearts of lovers.*

*He looked at the small window near the earthen ceiling, and thought he
saw a spark....yes, a star! a star whose sparkle pierced him like a dagger.....
oh, no more to be a wanderer beneath that star, and its countless brother
and sister stars.....no more an adventurer of the seasons, an explorer in the
endless wilderness of days and nights.....never to watch the milky oxen till
the fields, the moon to wax and wane, the green forest to grow gray and
drowsy, and fall asleep beneath a blanket of whiteness.....no more to break
bread or drink wine, to taste a nut or apple, to smell the sweet perfume
of clover.....no more to come to a woman's arms in moonlight, to know
her throat and breasts, the sweetness in her mouth, the dark forest of her
body.......*

*His heart breaking with sadness, Maria hung his head and sobbed, his
mind swimming in a maelstrom of pain, humiliation, regret and farewell.
And in those great welling sobs he thought of his youthful, well-ordered and
peaceful days in the abbey. He thought of Father Giovanni, of his upright-
ness, his learning, his purity, and when he did he was glad that he had
known such a wise, simple goodness that had found a fertile soil in which
to take root and blossom. He was glad that he had known this man, this
man much nobler and wiser than he could ever be; a man that had perhaps
fought greater odds than he. He was sure his friend was a Saint. He was sure
that he was what the wise called 'holy'.*

*Did this good man, this beautiful friend of his youth still think of
him? Did the picture of a young monk named 'Brother Maria' still pass
in moments of reflection through his mind? Did he still remember his eyes
or laughter? Or did he, like all the others he had diced, drank, fought and
whored with, did he too, this Saint in an abbey forget him, as he had been
a phantom that had faded into the dream of the endless tomorrows?*

*Was Brother Maria a ghost? A voice in the wind? An autumn leaf
fluttered to the forest floor?.....oh, it was a pain too great to bear, to leave*

the sun and hills, the moon and stars, the weeping and singing children of his dreams........

.....the pain too great for his heart to bear, he lapsed into a darkness darker than night.....no longer wanting to think, no longer wanting to remember, no longer wanting to feel.....only to expire and be extinguished.....to forget, and by forgetting, be no more........

......But in the darkness in which he fell, a dream came to him, a dream that was half memory......a half dream and half memory of his childhood that he had not remembered until now.....a memory of his mother........

......They had made a new camp, and after nightfall she had led him away from the music and the fires, the wagons, and the cages with the bears. She had led him silently, as in a solemn initiation into the large trees, her painted and jeweled feet surefooted, like a marten or a fox on the narrow paths before her. She led him deep into the forest, with neither words nor glances, the foliage purple-dark and deep, at times so densely dark that though she was only a step before him, he followed with his ear alone....his mother a phantom, a phantom with the rustle of a skirt, with tinkling bracelets and anklets.....with the perfumes, whispers and music of motherhood. Touching his cheek and hair with a light caress, she had reassured him:

"Be not afraid, Ohai. You are a hunter, like your father was a hunter."

They reached an open place, the darkness giving way to a light that, like silver flakes of snow fell from an unseen moon. In the middle of this space was a remarkable tree, its giant trunk twisted and burled; its boughs, like great arms that had broken free of the earth, spreading broadly wide all about it, as if the moon was an apple, and they were stretching to reach it, to pluck and eat it.

......then down a hill midst drifts of moonlight, until they came to a swiftly rushing river, and in that openness the moon filling the gorge carved by its cold knife, its silver-bleeding wound flowing from the mountain's heart.....

He watched as his mother did something he had never seen her do before. Removing her clothes, she then unpinned her hair, and shaking it free, let it fall beneath her waist. Clothed only in moonlight, and her long dark hair she stepped into the river, deeper and deeper, until its dark swift current had submerged all but her breasts and shoulders, at which time she turned and called to him.

"Come, Ohai. Come to me. The water is cold, but I am very warm.

Come to me, my darling hunter. Do not be afraid. I want to give you my love!"

He had obeyed, removing his clothes and stepping into the cold stream. Yet approaching her, he suddenly felt the river's hunger, its current binding its icy arms about his waist, and lifting his feet from its sandy bottom....as it wanted to eat him, to swallow him in its insatiable throat. Laughing, and reaching out to him, his mother brought him to her arms, and he clung to her midst the cold darkness rushing all about them. He bound his child legs tightly about her waist, and his child arms tightly about her shoulders, his cold nakedness clinging to her warm nakedness.

.......the river passing like swords about and through them, he clung to her beautiful mother warmth and all its songs and laughter of sweetness.... and clinging to it he felt his young body rouse and burn in the river's coldness, a flame that wanted to join her flame.....to give its secret to her secret...... its warmth to her warmth......

.......he felt her softly take his swollen part into her hand, holding it as with a harness of flowers, patiently waiting, encouraging it to grow, to blossom......and then her mouth pressing against his mouth, its kiss breathing the great mystery of 'Mother'.....the mystery of the forests, mountains and the rising and setting moon into his blood......

..... "This is love, Ohai, this is love....."

.......and when the milk of his loins spilled into her warmth, his heart spilled into her as well.....and he knew he was now part of life's smile and its wisdom......that for a moment he was part of the stars and flowers, and the dark cold river flowing all about them......

.......but opening his eyes he saw that he was no longer a child, no longer a man at all, but a bear with claws, snout and great teeth, and when again the fire came into his bowels, and he sought the warm nest in the warm belly in the cold river below him, he felt his mother quiver, and her throat growl with pleasure, a she-bear joining his own pleasure.....at which he lifted his head, and filled the night with a savage roar.......

He started awake, came back from the strange dream, opening his eyes to the abject hopelessness of his imprisonment. He came from this strange lovely dream back to decaying walls and the stub of a sputtering candle, to aching wrists, shoulders, ankles; to the certain death that hung about him like a suffocating smoke.....to the moments that soon would bring rattling keys and the opening of a heavy door; bringing from darkness life's grinning devil; moments that would bring a dragging limp, a noose, and a crowd of crows.

And yet he now burned through and through like a flame; like the flame that had burned in the cold dark river of his dream.

'.....Be not afraid, Ohai. You are a hunter, like your father was a hunter.....'

......His gypsy mother, yes, his gypsy mother as he remembered her, with her bright skirt, her jeweled arms, ears, nose, eyes.....her long black hair, bright smile, flashing eyes.....clinging to her sweetness in the cold river, even as the cold darkness of death flowed around, past and through them.......

'.....Come to me my darling hunter. This is love, Ohai, this is love.....'

Tears poured from his eyes; warm rich tears rising from the cold darkness deep inside him. He did not want to die; not yet, no, not yet. He did not want to be swept away from his mother's warmth and sweetness, devoured by the cold darkness flowing all about him. No, not yet. Let him be a brawler, a drinker and an adulterer for a little longer.....he and the children of his dreams were not yet ready to swing in the wind, be eaten by kites, no, not yet.......

'.....a hunter, like your father was a hunter.....'

Yes, he would pray to God, but only on his own terms, not for salvation, only to continue his ways, the ways of a shiftless, careless wanderer, preferring dice and drink, and the kisses of silly women for a few years more..... whatever the consequences, he would accept them......but not now, not yet, he was not ready to leave this world with all of its snares of treachery and dangerous arrows.....he was not ready to leave his beautiful dreams that sprouted like flowers that sprouted from the ribs and jowls of death.

But how was it possible? He was certain that he was to hang at dawn, and with bound hands and feet how was he to make any show of a fight? Even if his limbs were free, it would be difficult, perhaps impossible against the odds and press of their numbers. And if he escaped, where would he go? What tavern crony would hide him? What lover? He would be a marked and hunted man, and to abet him would be a crime as worthy of hanging as his own crime. He would be hunted not only by the constabulary and the Church's officials, but with the offer of blood money, by the entire citizenry.

The abbess's heart was stony cold. The poison of jealousy had been dripped into its well, and she would have her revenge; his kisses spoiling to venom on her lips. He was sure she would not intercede for one who had stirred, only to spurn her aging beauty, but instead gloat at his hanging from a gibbet, his neck broken and his blue eyes pecked like berries by the birds. Besides, the scandal would be known by all. The outrageous news would be known, told a thousand times over, minced and elaborated upon, exaggerated and condemned, about the violation of a Bride of Christ by a tavern fiddler, and that in the choir where the sisters prayed. It would be gossiped through the streets, even beyond the city walls, like a fire raging through dry wheat. The Bishop was hard-hearted, and even if he was not, his hand would be forced by the abbess's lies.

And Sister Celestina? No, she could in no way plead for his life. He had heard of punishments exacted on fornicating nuns: each sister in the sisterhood made to take turns flogging their sinful sister's breasts and hams, her tender places shaved bald, her vulva branded with a red-hot iron, her tongue cleft.....forced to wear a girdle of thorns, stigmatized with a red scarf or sash, forced to pray apart and alone.....often stripped of her holy habit and sent into the world to beg, scrub or whore for her bread.

And the turnkey that doubled as the hangman? He had brought him water, and then unbound his mouth and eyes. No, he had looked in his eyes; the creature was heartless and soul-less. He may as well ask the Devil, or death itself to pardon him.

Then how? Who? There must be a way! His mother had made him both a hunter and a ferocious bear with her love....he must thrust his arms from this grave, climb the great tree, reach for the apple of the moon.....no, he would not let death, God or the Devil take him without a furious struggle and fight!

The priest!.....had not the debauched men needled him about this one last guest that would gain admittance to his cell? Yes, of course, a priest would come, however briefly, to receive his last confession. Apprehended by the Church, the Church would be obliged to grant him this last grim visit, even as it did the coldest and bloodiest of murderers. But could he throttle, perhaps even kill a holy priest? Had he not held priests in the highest esteem, even venerated them? Did he not once aspire to be ordained? No, yes...O the horror of the thing!

Still, it came back to the priest. The priest was his only possible salvation, not of his soul, but of his legs and lungs and heart. If he could kill the priest, he might take his robe, and beneath its raised hood and flowing skirt walk from this accursed hole. The rest would be left to chance, his wits and his brawn, and more, his instincts, yes, his gypsy instincts! He would find his way from this catacomb of death. He would break heads and ribs. He would *slit throats. He would flee into the streets and fields and be free again!*

Yes, he would kill the priest. If he was to live, it was a thing he must do. He did not want to die. He was not ready to die. He wanted to give himself to his mother many more times in the dark cold river. He wanted to see the moon rise over the forests, to sing in taverns and grape arbors, to kiss beautiful women, and feel their bodies shudder with surrender in his arms.......he wanted to feel cold and hunger, to be lost and lonely, to flee from this tyrant called 'God' with knives and fists, and the shamelessness of love......no, if it was possible, he must do this thing.....even at the expense of a dead priest, he must not die!

But to do so he must free his hands and feet, yes, that was the first thing he must do. The candle was guttering, but it was still alive, and that aliveness told him the night was not yet spent. He had time. If he could find a protruding stone in the wall, one that perhaps had a jutting edge......yes, whatever the cost in pain and blood, even if he would maim himself, even if he would cut a hand clean from his wrist, he must try!

Slowly he began to inch about the perimeter of the small room, careful to feel and judge, examine each stone with his fingers. But completing a round of the cellar, he did not find a stone that could expedite his plan. With a great effort, and several painful failures, he made himself stand, proceeding his search in the same way on his feet, only this time a span higher about the walls. Still, with bound ankles, making another slow, inch by inch circuit about the room, his search did not find a stone's sharp tooth that could gnaw through the tightly knotted rope.

For a moment he stood there aching, panting with the great effort, his body throbbing numb with pain, a fatal gloom flooding his mind. Was this then his end? For an instant he thought again of praying....but no, no, to hell with God! To hell with the Saints!.....he would rather rot here in his bonds, swing from a rope, be eaten by rats! Still, there must be a way, some other way. The worm-eaten stool and table were of no use, nor was the candle. Nearly spent, it would not sear the rope, and besides, he could not risk an accident. He needed the precious light, at least until he was freed.

Again he slid to the floor, and began his inching about the wretched little space of his captivity. But this time his search did not prove fruitless. A short way after his renewed effort had begun he found a cavity in the decaying wall, one that had spilled loosened earth over a stone, a sharply hewn stone. By scraping the earth away, he could uncover its edge, of which its cold bluntness was as precious as a whetted knife, upon which to begin the desperate chafing that could mean his life.

Difficult, and painful beyond his sense to feel, he employed the stone to stubbornly work his emancipation, and within an hour, and at the candle's final spark his hands were free and his own again. Or were they? They were numb and raw from their bondage, and even more from the release of that bondage to exercise in any useful way; or even feel, his wrists worn to the raw meat of his flesh, and when he attempted to unbind his feet with them, they fumbled uselessly with the knots of the ropes still binding fast his ankles.

But in the dark he rubbed and chafed them, as they were frozen with cold, and he was trying to coax warmth back into their icy blood. Again and again he tried to untie the knots, but again and again pain and numbness rendered his hands incapable of what he was telling them to do. Still, as life trickled back into them, he succeeded at last in untying the ropes, and in the darkness he sat with freed hands and feet, gratefully aching with a pain that sent its throbs to his very soul.

Slowly in the pitchy dark he came back to himself. Slowly, though filled with the teeth of pain he felt the gladness of his two hands and two legs, with which he must try to make his escape. Slowly, there in the dark he meditated his murdering of the priest, and his escape from this dank stifling place back to sunlight and freedom. His will to live now paled the pains of his body, laughed at the guilt his deed would bring. There would be time to be healed, to be salved and bandaged, to run from, hide, and forget his guilt..... but first the priest, the grim, but necessary business of the priest.

Several things were now in his favor that had not been so before. His hands and feet were free, and with them, he was now in possession of a rope, a rope with which he could quickly and quietly strangle the priest. Yes, that was good, especially the rope he had freed from his ankles. It was long enough, and not short and frayed like that piece he had broken in two from his wrists. Another thing was that his eyes were accustomed to the dark, as the eyes of the priest would not be. This too, was an advantage, one that could not be denied. And the table and the stool could be used. He would kneel behind the table, his hands behind his back; the stool at his side. When the priest would stand over him with his blessing, it would not be difficult to spring to his feet and bash his head with the stool, or even the clay water bowl. And if the blow did not immediately kill him, he would pounce and strangle him with the rope, or perhaps with his own hands.

There was yet another card in his favor. If there would be a struggle, bringing the guards to the door, he would use the Latin he had learned from *his cloister days to emulate the voice of the priest. The rough men would not dream he could speak the Church's mother tongue. Yes, it might work; no, it 'must' work!*

He practiced in the dark, crouching behind the table, and then springing to his feet, first with the stool, then with the rope. Once in his practice the stool fell to the floor, the noise magnified in the cavernous place, and echoing as far as the silence would carry it. He listened with bated breath and a wildly pounding heart; for an interminable instant standing still in the darkness, like a ghost afraid of being apprehended by the living. But the noise had waked no danger, and after a few moments his thoughts returned to his desperate plan.

He began to walk back and forth, five paces comprising the breadth of his cell;.....one, two, three, four, five.....back and forth in his small confinement. He must stay awake. He must not become sleepy. Sleep was his enemy. Sleep was death. He must stay awake, awake as he had never been awake before. If needs, he must never sleep again.

'......a hunter, Ohai, a hunter.....'

He did not know how near dawn was; the darkness, timeless here where heaven never smiled, but he did not think it was far away. Again and again he stood still, or pressed his ear to the wall, listening for any hint of day, any heartbeat of the world above him....a creak of a cart's wheel, a bark of a dog; the crow of a cock......but he could hear nothing, and he would resume his pacing, like a wild animal, like a bear, yes, like a bear restless in its cage....one, two, three, four, five.......

......yes, that was it; that was what he had become. Brother Maria was now a caged animal, one who's every nerve and muscle was taut with the need to pounce and survive, to crouch and be ready for the kill.....to again be free in the forest. No, Brother Maria was not a ghost, but a wild beast. And the more he paced the more the dread of this horrible act he was determined to perform fled from him.....the more calm he became with the meditation of what he was to do.....one, two, three, four, five.....Oh, what had happened to the lazy roamer of the wilds, the player of lutes and the lover of women? What had happened to the young golden youth who wanted only to pray, and strive for the examples of humility and purity? He was now an imprisoned criminal, one about to murder God's servant, and that without guilt, but with a kind of excitement, a strange kind of exultant rapture.....with the taste of blood whetting awake and quickening his soul......

But now, suddenly, the silence was intruded upon, its lower kingdom disturbed by steps, human steps, and in simultaneity, somewhere above him, in the realm of the living, the faint shrill crow of a cock, the crack of a carter's whip.....There were voices outside, a short way from the door, their graveness muffled, half inaudible; and then their approach, the jangling of the keys and their turning of the wards.......

......the crouch behind the table, the stool at his side, the bowl and panikin.....his hands with their weapon behind his back.....the opening and closing, relocking of the door.....the candle's brightness, the priest standing above him. He bent down his head, doubled his fists about the rope, resolved, and more than resolved, strangely thrilled to do this thing that might free him to the wind and sun again.

"May the blessings of our all-merciful and all-knowing God be on your soul my son."

"Thank you, father."

His words came faint and dry, like a whispering reed. Still he waited. Was the priest's blessing his cue? No, let the guard walk away. Could he do this thing? He tautened, poised.....yes, murder, like love, sang in his blood..... their courtships were the same.....perhaps as were their pangs.......

"The hour of death is an hour that comes to all men. No man may flee or hide from it. In the name of Jesus Christ our Lord and Savior, I have come to hear your confession. All men are sinners. All bear darkness in their souls, darkness in the many forms of sin. It is not too late, even at the last hour to expel these shadows of darkness, to ask for light, to be forgiven my son."

Maria did not answer. Behind his back his fists tightened about the rope. He hung his face low, so that the light of the candle could not find it. No, he must not listen; there was no forgiveness, or if there was, he did not want it. He would not be threatened by salvation.....he must only listen to this hammer pounding in his brain: 'Kill! Kill! Kill!'

"For the salvation of your soul, my son......."

Maria sprang from his crouch, seizing the priest by his throat, driving and pressing him against the wall. He would need neither stool nor rope. Although the priest struggled, Maria's hands were more than strong enough to complete the grim business; to kill that he might live! But as his hands began to do the rope's work, from beneath the priest's cowl came a raspy, half-strangled whisper from the one he was strangling.

"Maria, no, it is me....Giovanni."

So surprised at these words, Maria's hands lessened their vice-like grip, but still held the man of God helplessly pinned to the wall.

"Maria, Maria, it is Giovanni.....your friend.....Giovanni."

Incredulous, Maria loosened his hold about the priest's throat, and with a brush of his hand removed the bag of the cowl from the face it was concealing. Wide-eyed and harrowed with disbelief, unsure whether he was dreaming these features or no, he stepped away from this gaunt and severely kind face, kind even in the stress of its struggle against death, this kind dear face he remembered from his youth.

"Father Giovanni!"

The friend of his youth looked at Maria, and managed a smile from his ascetic, aged, but gentle friendly face.

"Yes, Brother Maria, Father Giovanni; but more precisely now, I am called Abbot Giovanni."

"But have I hurt you? Dear God! You see I was prepared to kill the priest that came to confess me, and then to take his robe......."

"Yes, friend, and I am sure in another moment you would have done just that. No, no Maria, I am fine. You see my robe, and this thick tunic I have worn over it has been good for something more than the show of holiness; it has protected me not only from the damp, ha, but it has saved my life from your strong hands."

There came a stir at the door, the small door of the judas-hole sliding open, and a man's voice speaking through it.

"Good father, there is no trouble? I thought I heard a commotion......"

Father Giovanni walked swiftly to the door, and spoke to the man through the grille of the judas; his voice unlike the one that had been nearly strangled, or that Maria remembered from his youth, but now firm, masculine, authoritarian.

"No, there is no trouble at all. Please, you must let me have these moments with the prisoner. They are his last. He is confessing; asking for the forgiveness of his sins. He is giving his soul to God."

"But of course, of course father confessor, I am a Christian man.....one who respects how these things are done at a man's end."

"However long it shall take. I do not wish to be disturbed. The prisoner wishes to make a complete confession......"

"But of course, father. The man's soul.....and a great list of crimes on the brigand's soul I'm sure of it. The day has not yet broken, and the spectators only now beginning to trickle and gather, setting up their booths of grog,

rabbits and eggs, pickings from their gardens......give the man his confession, and if his sins stretch from here till tomorrow....I'll not bother your Christian duties, I'll eat a mess of onions if I won't."

And with this the small door of the judas closed, and Father Giovanni turned to Maria, shrunken out of sight in the corner, away from the judas's dangerous eye. Turning to the prisoner, Father Giovanni's voice was low, soft and kind, and asked to be answered in the same tones.

"Come Maria, that will give us a little time. Here, let me see your hands. Sit here, near the candle. Let me at least try to cleanse them with this water and the sleeve of my robe. Oh, these are terrible wounds! The ropes must have been very tight; they have bitten deep into your wrists. You must have worked very hard to free yourself from their bonds. You must have wanted very much to be free, to live."

"Yes, Giovanni.....may I call you Giovanni?......I wanted to live very much, so much that I would kill a priest and risk sending my soul to hell, only to save these hands and eyes, and not swing from the gallows."

"You want, then, even now, to live?"

"Yes, I want to live."

"To atone for your sins? To start anew?"

"To start anew, yes, but not to atone for my sins, only to stumble and wander on, perhaps to create more of what you call 'sin'."

"And you were truly prepared to kill me?"

"Yes, with this stool, or with this rope, or with these two hands. You see, it would not have been the first man I have killed a man."

This elicited a silence from the priest, but one that did not endure; as if this too was understood and accepted by his kindness.

"I have come to confess you, you know."

"I will not confess! You must not ask me! If there is a God He knows my sins, I need not tell their sordid tale! This God of yours has been deaf to countless prayers lifted to him, from widows and hungry children, from the lost and the wayward! Why would He care for the confession of a vagrant who is about to hang? If there is a God He knows my heart. He holds it in His Hands, and may weigh its ugly scars against its noble dreams. No, Giovanni, no, you must not ask for my confession, a thing I will not do."

Father Giovanni offered no plea or argument, but continued to bathe and daub Maria's wounds, using the water in the bowl.

"There, is that better?"

"Yes, Giovanni, I think so; yes, thank you. But you must tell me, because

all seems a dream to me: how has it come to be that you are here? It surely can be no accident, and my appearance, my hair, my clothes, the many years....I must look so different than my cloister days."

Father Giovanni paused, and as he washed Maria's wounds, in the light of his candle looked at the friend of bygone days; days before he had become an abbot.

It was true; the last time when he had seen the much harried, beaten prisoner before him he was a young, thinly bearded monk with a tonsure and shaven head. He had been bright and winsome, full of laughter and exuberant youth, the singing bird of their solemn cloister, delighting every heart that heard his carefree song. The man now before him was very different. The stubble of his tonsure had rioted into a tangled harvest of golden, shoulder-length locks, and from one ear dangled a jeweled earring, such as a savage, seafaring sailor might wear. A brawniness had conquered the former litheness and delicacy of his young body.

The boyish face had grown a thick beard, one as flaxen gold as his hair, flecked with auburn, and here and there with a lonely sprout of gray; a face bruised and bloodied by his cruel captors, and a bit pale, as if shadowed by the wing of death that now hovered above it. Looking at this face, the abbot could not help but wonder at how many sharp winds had driven against it, or how many fists had hit it, or how many women had caressed it. All of these things, and many more were written upon it, but in a different language, a language that he could not entirely decipher, that his Greek and Latin could not help to translate. It was a language that told the secret story of his soul; as if time had carefully written its adventures and mysteries upon it.

Still, there was something the same about this face, something that had not changed; something that Father Giovanni remembered, that had not been eroded or buried by the years. Behind its ruggedness there was a flame, a flame that had not been touched by the wickedness of the world. The eyes were still blue, and amid the face's beard, bruises and scars of dissipation, their windows were lighted with an innocence that still sparkled; a boyishness that had not fled the man, and the many arrows of the world's many hunters that had been shot into the boy's heart.

"There is not time to tell all, Maria. As an abbot, I must visit many cloisters, monasteries as well as convents; and I must attend many conferences, some that take me many days' journey away from the abbey, even as the one I have attended here in the city. There is always business to do.

Leaving a meeting last night I heard a row, and saw the men taking one bound and blindfolded away. And though it was dark, and though the torches did not light his face......well, I heard one or two about me mention 'Brother Maria', and at once I knew it was you, knowing that no other could own that name. I went to the Bishop right off, and asked if I might be your confessor.

You see, old friend, the Mother of God, your namesake, really has watched over you."

Maria hung his head, and offered no reply. It was Father Giovanni who again broke the awkward silence.

"*And what is this crime that has brought you here, Maria? What have you done? The men told me only that you were apprehended in the cathedral, that it had been a great scandal, and that you had received a grim sentence. Were you stealing......*"

"*Yes, stealing!......stealing the treasure, the very dowry of a Bride of Christ, one she had sworn to keep locked away from men. You see I have not only killed, but I have also seduced. I am not the same person I was in my cloister days, Giovanni. I am not the person that you, or any of the old fathers wished or thought I would become; not even that young monk that confessed to you in a confessional that last night before leaping from the abbey's walls to a shepherd girl's arms. I am not like you. I am not like you at all. I no longer pray holy prayers, but in their place dream unholy dreams, and do unholy things. I have changed. Look! This dark wretched cellar is the proof of that change.*"

"*But Maria, my brother, each one of us bears the heavy yoke of our sins; each is imprisoned.*"

"*Yes, some in an abbey on a hill, with marble statues and gorgeous frescoes, with flower gardens, goldfish and linnets singing prettily in gilded cages, and others in a cellarage, smelling of urine and rotten fruits!*"

"*But as you must know, Maria, there are not only well-trodden roads, but rambling sheep walks that lead, even the saintly to salvation.*"

"*Salvation?! What is that Giovanni? I neither hope nor pray for salvation! I do not believe in such a thing, and if I did, I do not think I would strive for it. Why should I pray, fast, flog, perform all sorts of penances, hoping for an hour that may never come, when Brother Maria's heart beats now? Time is a fleeting thing, Giovanni, but it is also an endless thing. I only wish to tear off a tiny piece of its cloak as it passes by, and call it mine, not God's!*"

"*These are very strong words, Maria, words that at this hour and in this place perhaps you do not mean......"*

"I mean them as they were a brand upon my heart! I flee from this thing you call 'salvation', this phantom that accuses the needs of my flesh and blood of poisoning my soul. I flee from the voices and footsteps of men, and the promises they promise. My blood is not tame, nor have I any wish to tame it. I accept the great wilderness of the world, its dangers and pleasures; a wilderness in which I do not try to escape, only to explore, like scholars explore the wilderness of books and knowledge. Salvation? No; it is a word only, one I broke like a twig over my knee long ago."

Standing, he walked to the wall, and there paused, turned, and walked back to the intently listening abbot. He continued, his eyes alive and dancing with passion, even as death's noose hung about his neck; passion that the abbot remembered from his friend's youthful days, and remembering, had touched and won his heart.

"Giovanni, you are a good man who strives for noble ideals. You have become an abbot. You have become the leader of a holy brotherhood, a brotherhood I am sure obeys and reveres you. But I have no wish to revere and obey, however right and noble are these ideals. I have no wish to lead, or be led by bells and offices. I am not like you or other men. I want no goal, no mission. I detest these things. I detest order and responsibility. I obey only the rivers of my blood, and the storms in my heart. I have no aim, other than to probe what is before my steps and eyes.....playing a fiddle, kissing a pretty smile, seeing the moon rise over the forest trees. Salvation is a dream I no longer dream; a truth I have long rejected. It is for good men, noble men, righteous men, but not for me; not for Brother Maria."

"But are you sure, very sure you know what you are saying Maria, and at this, your life's most crucial hour? This is no time to be whimsical or rebellious, a dreamer or a poet. The fate of your soul, Maria, may very well be balanced upon these words."

"I know what I am saying, yes, I know, because I am listening to the voices of my blood, the first voices, the most happy and hungry voices; voices that echo the first cries of the hills and forest. Oh Giovanni, dear friend, I would rather live and die like an animal, the teeth of another animal in my throat than one of your sages, martyrs or Saints, they who spent their lives fearing and hoping of what shall come!"

Again his words ended, falling into the silence whose listening ear was all about them; a silence that seemed to embrace the two men's littleness, their briefness; magnifying their insignificance before the monstrous audience of time itself, pausing its march of nights and days, suns and moons to listen to the drama being enacted on their souls.

Maria knelt before the abbot, and stared into the face he had known in his youth, a face that had also aged and changed. It was a kind face, a gentle and honest face, one whose rigors of prayer and penance had carved and starved all falseness away, until only the pure flame of the soul burned and shone like a lone candle from its dark quiet eyes; a candle that found protection in the niche of these ascetic, haggard lovely features.

"I remember words you once spoke to me, Giovanni, words that I have kept in my heart, that I have coveted, that have even haunted me through the years. I remembered them because I have learned their strangeness to be true."

"Words? What words were these?"

"That our natures are very different, Giovanni; that you worship the sun, and I, the moon.

You may think I am lost and foolish, drunk in my madness. You may think the man you shall soon see dangle from a rope had a lost soul, or gave it to vain dreams, puppet shows ruled by the puppeteers of devils, but you must understand that as you kneel before the wooden idols on your altars, I too have had idols before which I have knelt, idols that are unholy in your eyes, but holy in mine."

He stopped for an impassioned instant, the abbot listening with stern face and widened, riveted eyes; despite his faith, stunned to a kind of spiritual awe. Maria had bowed his head, as one exhausted, as one whose surrender was a last rally cry of bitter defiance against the doom to which he now must submit. He lifted his face again, as if proudly, like a pagan prince, and when he did there came a whisper from his mouth,- no, deeper, from the depths of his soul, and in that whisper the sum and meaning of who and what he was.

"I cannot imagine what it is to adore one of your holy idols, Giovanni, no more than you could imagine what it is like to be embraced by a woman. Both perhaps are a bit silly; the play of children in the eyes of this unseen God of yours. And yet for you and I, children made of dust and blood, they are not silly at all. They are part of our lives, their rituals things we must, and are meant to perform. They are not only the idols, but the sacraments with which the child worships, and in its childish way tries to know life's mystery; you, a father's approval, and I, a mother's acceptance."

Once again, allowing his words to flow unhindered, Father Giovanni *was struck dumb with how he spoke with passionate conviction, even at the very hour of his death.*

But the spell, though strange and deep, did not last long. It was interrupted by the judas being suddenly opened, at which Father Giovanni went to the door and listened to the nervous whispers of the turnkey, whispers hushed, excited and greatly liquored, whispers that were meant for him alone.

"Pardon me, father. I am not one to interrupt holy shrift, but it is just that it is market day, the carts are arriving, and with them a crowd of people gathering for the spectacle.....the hanging that is.....jostling close to the steps and the arm for a good feast of the eye.....like a kind of stage......before they mill the streets, have their whirl so to say. The early ones are setting up their tables for ale, pickle and cheese, baskets of eggs and crates of conies..... and the day full of gray and drizzle.....and, well, the man who is paid to do the job, the man who wields the axe, and for prisoners like this 'un, slips the bag and noose....well, he is a man of many responsibilities.....many tugs at his sleeves so to say......

"You must let me finish. It is a man's soul, and not a cockfight. You must let me do the work of my office. What is a moment or two more when eternity is before the soul?"

"Of course, of course holy father. I am a Christian man, me and the missus. She counts her beads each night, kneels and prays before the Virgin on the holy days.....take another moment or two, but you see the hangman when he has had his drink, well, sometimes is quarrelsome, and his wife no less a quarreler, and a colicky child to boot......and the day a foul day, and it being market day in the streets.....and the crowd anxious to see the varlet hung, to be done with the thing, and wet their feathers as little as they can in doing so."

"Only a moment more. I will knock on the door when I am ready."

"Yes, holy father. I would not interrupt a man's confession for the world, not for the stars and seas would I."

The peephole closed. Father Giovanni turned back to Maria, now standing before the table. He bent down, and picked up the rope that had bound Maria's ankles, the one that Maria had readied to strangle him with. Standing aright, he looked at Maria.

"I must do this thing, Maria, fulfill my priestly duty. As a servant of God I cannot let your hands be free when they come to take you away."

Understanding his words, and the meaning of the rope he held stretched before him, Maria nodded and placed his hands behind his back. Binding the wrists he had just washed, Father Giovanni bound his friend's hands, but not so tightly as to pain them like they had been pained before.

"Oh Maria, my dear Maria, you.....you do not know what this......."

His voice cracking, Maria was startled to feel the priest kneeling on the floor behind him, and then his bearded lips, wet with tears kissing the hands he had just bound.

"Oh Maria, Maria, my dearest, sweetest friend."

Father Giovanni stood and faced the one he would not see again. He raised his hand over his former Brother in Christ, now kneeling again on the floor below him.

"God bless you my son, my brother. God bless you, and forgive the sins that cling to your soul. God bless you, Maria......I, I, you see I have never, I am a priest....I am not a worldly man......God loves, no, both God and I, Maria.....I have always, since our youth, more than words can tell. You have been a singing bird in the dark night of my soul......I will never forget you, never my dear friend, never......."

His voice faltering with the swell of emotion, Father Giovanni bent down as to kiss Maria's brow, but stopped short, straightened and turned, and walked swiftly to the door.....yet at the door he froze with a bowed head, only to raise his hand, and in an excruciating show of will, duty and resolve, rap the door three sharp cold times.

"Guard!"

There was a jangle of keys, the judas opened, and the grizzly, ale-flushed face appeared. Authority, not tears were in the words the abbot spoke to the man.

"One moment more. And when I leave I must not speak; not to you, not to anyone. I will be continuing my wordless penance, a vow of which I only broke to hear this man's last confession. Furthermore, I would have you allow the prisoner to say his last prayers before you lead him to his judgment. You must give me your word you will give him a last moment, alone and undisturbed, before you lead him to his fate."

"Of course, of course father, a moment more; but only a moment. The hangman and his drink, the crowd, and the morning with a heavy drizzle, and the cold of the changing moon and all. Of course, and you must not be afraid of your holy penance being disturbed.....I am a Christian man, and my wife counting her beads as she shells, sifts and bickers each night by the fire......."

"*It will not be long.*"

With this the drunken man closed the judas-hole, and in one swift motion Father Giovanni strode swiftly to where Maria stood by the table. Quickly the abbot untied his hands, and then hurriedly slipped from the hooded tunic he had worn over his habit.

"*But, I do not understand.....Giovanni, what are you......*"

"*Sssh! Be quiet Maria. Here, slip this on, this I luckily wore against the morning's damp.....and the sandals......hurry!*"

"*I cannot Giovanni! It is a thing I cannot do!*"

"*As it is a thing I cannot do to watch you hang. Come, slip this over your head, and as you do, listen to my words:*

"*But I cannot.....*"

"*Do as I say! We have so little time!*

Walk from here without a word. It is dark, but they will guide you with torches. Once free of the gates bear right into the small streets. It is market day, and they will be congested with booths and tables, and the market animals of the marketers. There it might be possible to mingle into the pressing crowds, and then, with the will of God work somehow free of the city's gates.

Yes, that is good. They will not see your face in the cowl. Here, take this money. It is not much, but you will need it. And this cross, take this cross with you.....here, bend down, let me place it about your neck."

"*But what of you Giovanni?*"

"*They'll do nothing to me. I will tell them you throttled me, that you did to me what you had intended to do to another priest. They will not hurt me.*"

"*But why, Giovanni?*"

"*Here, with my cincture tie my hands, tie them firmly behind my back. Quickly! Do as I say Maria!*"

And now the voice of the gross man from behind the door.

"*Holy father, is it almost done with the prayers you are? The drizzle, the man with the bag and the noose, and he with hungry mouths to feed, a colicky babe and a hell harpy of a wife.......*"

"*Yes, one moment more!......Now Maria, hit me in the face. Hit me with your fist!*"

"*I cannot!*"

"*Hit me I say. Bloody my lip, break my nose!*"

"*I cannot.......*"

"I will lead you from here to the streets. I respect the holy life. I am a Christian man, baptized, raised on the rites like a horse on oats."

"Hit me Maria!"

"But......"

"Like this, damn it!"

Giovanni's fist met Maria's jaw, not like a child's or woman's fist, not with delicacy or timidity, but solidly, with the strength of his religious conviction.

"I'll open the door now, father confessor. I'll respect your wishes; leave the prisoner to a few moments of prayer. But even death must obey the movement of the stars, father. The cocks are crowing a new day, and well, life goes on, even when death takes it away."

"For the love of God Maria!"

The blow came solid to his friend's jaw, but softened at the last by his reluctance, it did not buckle his knees and knock him from his feet. The keys jangled from the jailor's pocket, and began to clumsily feel their drunken way into the wards.

"Again, Maria, harder!"

Another blow, this time to the other jaw, spinning and doubling him over.

"Again!"

This time the blow came crashing with a greater force, square and flush to his friend's jaw, tumbling the priest to the floor. The door began to open. In one motion Brother Maria blew out the candle, and then knelt in the darkness to the bloodied face, and pressed his mouth to its bloodied lips with a passionate kiss.

"I love you Giovanni! I love you and I will not forget you!"

The door creaked open.

"As I said, father confessor, the gawkers become impatient, it being market day and the cold drizzle and all, and the hangman, well he's a man too.....sour as green rhubarb with his bad rum.....and, well, as I am a Christian man, and my lady counting her beads every night as she shells the peas, doing her nagging and haranguing as women do.......

.....well, right this way, father, you needn't say a word to break your fast of words.....I'll lock him in just so, we'll fetch the poor devil shortly, bless the poor wretch's soul.....fetch him to hang him like bacon and be done with the terrible thing that justice bids.....the Lord bless us all.....come, father confessor, I'll show you the way.....dark as night, ha! Dark as a dungeon

down here, is it not?......and that hooded coat of yours, it is good that you wore it, very good indeed.....for it has begun to rain more lustily now......."

Wordless, and with his head bent and buried in the bag of his cowl, the counterfeiting priest was led by the gabbling turnkey, and joined by several other torch bearing guards. Reaching the daylight breaking wet, chill and dismal above, the streets filled with booths, crates and market animals, the unspeaking priest walked into the bustle and banter of the congested marketers, only after a short way to leave them by veering into a very narrow street. After several windings of this narrow way, not large enough for a horse and cart, the priest stopped in a nook, and knocked on a shutter. It was answered by a sleepy lady with a nightcap, who after a moment, brightened, and then leaning out from the window, grabbed the priest's cowl between her hands, and gave him a sensuous kiss.

Two days later, buried in a cart of straw, Brother Maria left the city's gates; what his friend had done for him, burning like a flame in his heart.

....

....

CHAPTER ELEVEN

TWO BEASTS

The length and breadth of Italy entire,
1348

TWO beasts, separated by lush gardens of olives, grapes and figs, by rivers, mountains, sea breezes......by fiefs and kingdoms, princes and pontiffs, serf and gentry......two beasts that were born as one beast......twinned, wrapped and clinging tightly in the womb......inseparably, as if lasciviously entwining in each other's arms......only to be pulled apart, torn into two from the one......one beast halved into two beasts......two beasts that became divided, but ever yearned to be one again......to once more twine like serpents, caduceus-wise......a brother and sister beast forever longing to incestuously mate, and to be one profane, monstrous thing......

And although great vastnesses divided them, they lifted their snouts to the wind, and when they did their nostrils quivered, their beast eyes gleamed, their beast blood quickened......for smelling the other, their bowels began to boil....as the smell they exuded was a musk, a musk that was the delicious fume and reek of decay.......

And smelling the other's reek, their need was stirred to possess that reek......a need that once waked, would not sleep, but become ever the more hungry, ever the more tormented and fevered......until the two divided beasts began to rut and rage......to writhe, froth and kill as they rutted and raged......with blind beastly greed moving towards their satisfaction...... glutting all in their paths as they did......farms, villages, cities......desiring only to be filled, spent, slaked......uncaring if the culmination of their lust meant the murder of entire lands and cities.......

And so it was that smelling each other, they were consumed with the need to mate with each other.....to be one as they had been born to be one.....and so it was they began to crawl and slink, and then to robustly, recklessly romp and rage towards each other.....their blind dark lust for the other driving them on.....over mountains and rivers, through streets and arbors, into the hearts of the peasantry, the royalty, the religious..... smelling the other's awful reek, the reek that grew ever more deliciously pungent the nearer they came to each other.....their approach becoming more unlicensed, more savage, more wickedly riotous as they continued.... carousing and drunkenly swaggering.....as they, this brother and sister beast neared the terrible profanity of their wedding night.......

.....one slinked, raged and rollicked from the sands and rocks in the arid south, from Sicily.....the other from the fertile heights in the north......from Genoa and Venice.....the two wanting only to mate with each other..... drunk with Death, giddy with Death, crazed with Death.......

* * *

* * * * *

THERE had been signs, or so it would come to be said; signs read by those who read the stars; men called astrologers; men who studied the language written in the heavens, a language portending the approach of some pro-digious calamity.....an ancient, prophetic language of blood-red moons, eclipses and conjunctions.....comets whose burning tails blazed across the frozen fields of heaven.

There were others.....seers and soothsayers and wizards......that peered into crystals, inspected men's stool, interpreted dreams and the flights of birds; those who could hear Death's footsteps in the night, feel its cold breath upon their faces, hear its howls in their blood.....and those professing cisterns had turned to blood, that milk had curdled in the udders of their goats and cows.....those that were sure some among them were the perpetrators of this strange contagion, cursing all they looked upon with the Evil Eye.

And as the first wails, groans and shrieks invaded the sleepy streets, there came reports of rains of blood, shrouds and coffins flying in storms, armies of spirits waging battles in fields and clouds.....great howls in churchyards, and those dredged from graves who were now walking among the living, half decomposed, or wrapped in unnatural flames.....serpents coiling about cradles.....corpses so bloated and blackened, and some so animal-eaten, that *they were scarce recognizable to the lifelong friends that found them.*

These signs, dreams and visions formed the first terrible rumors, these terrible rumors a dreadful possibility.....this dreadful possibility becoming, quick as a conflagration, a diabolical reality.....as here and there the presence of this death-hungered beast was evidenced in the horribly disfigured corpses found in fields, streets, homes.....hanging in barns and from forest trees.....

Like bees preparing for winter, frenzy swept into and through these streets so timelessly asleep with roses, mandolins and amorous glances. They now teemed suddenly with a new crop of shops and shopkeepers, as well as peddlers, hawkers and necromancers; those selling nostrums, pomanders, exorcisms, and an inexhaustible variety of potions, plasters, runes, charts and charms, all professing to defend against this pollution creeping like a dark river through the country-side.

Most of this sudden crop of small, makeshift shops were easily identified by illustrative signs hung over their doors: stars and crescent moons; wizard wands and hats; mortars and pestles; animals of the zodiac; and for those who could read, inscriptions: 'Astrologer', 'Fortuneteller', 'Charms', 'Physics', 'Lancing and Plasters', 'Poultices and Caustics'. Chalked above some were human figures holding long serpents, their heads held in one hand, their tails in the other. Above others were drawn toads with long spitting tongues, some with erotic, half naked maids mounted on their warty backs.

Sundry were the palliatives and curatives sold by these necromancers, apothecaries, soothsayers and conjurors; amulets and ointments, powders ground from the horns of unicorns.....pigeon hearts and goat urine, dead toads and lizards, the meat of roasted snakes; concoctions of wormwood, garlic and zedoary. The midwives informing of sweats, diets, routines; the astrologers telling of the portents of comets, eclipses and conjunctions; the fortunetellers, the meaning of dreams, and divinations acquired from palms, birth signs, and even the colors and qualities of urine.

Nor were these soothsayers, fortunetellers, and the palm-itching pre-tenders the only ones to which the frightened turned; for zealous clusters of the citizenries began to gather about men of great faith as well; men who had stepped down from their ornate pulpits to preach in the dusty streets, warning of God's rebuking wrath that was even now entering their streets; those they had gathered listening to their every word as each word was a token of salvation.....as each word was the last piece of bread they would ever eat in this world.

"He who holds the winds tight in His Fist, bidding them to sleep, may

in a trice unclench that Fist, and loose flocks of tempests that may quake the valley and topple the mountain! Fierce as bloody wolves, His Angels may make drunk their arrows! Make barbarous their swords!.....Fill their wings with scourge and vengeance! Such a time has come, a time when that Fist has let free the terrible winds it has long enclosed!"

.....Day and night, tirelessly, they passed from shop to shop, and door to door, the streets now their cathedrals.....shouting like roaring lions, their righteousness turned to a savage ferocity, their meekness turned to tumults of madness.......

"His patience is the patience of Eternity, and it has been stirred, provoked by men's wallowing in irreverence, by the banquets of his gluttony, avarice and licentiousness! The rod of His admonishment has turned to His sword, His sword to rains of scorpions, His scorpions to the stinking breath of Death breathed into all places, upon all faces, and into all souls.....even as men bury their shekels, drain their tankards, frolic like sluggards in sties of painted harlots! Man now stands on the brink of his grave, not only at the end of his days, but at the end of the world, his soul teetering between Heaven's glory and the maw of Hell!"

But no barricade could stay the beasts' hunger for each other; not walls; rivers, not hills or forests.....not shops with charts and amulets.....not the priests screaming their exhortations.....not bonfires, prayers or flagellations. Death breathed its fumes into each field, hut and palace; poisoned each well; screeched its fiddle beneath all windows. Its Angels' arrows killed where they fell; their aims impartial, undiscriminating, unmerciful. Venom-tipped, they found the hearts of the priest and the virgin with the same marksmanship with which they found the fornicator and the drunkard.....and before each arrow fell, a thousand others were poised in the bows that had shot them.

Nothing could deter it. It marched over the valleys and mountains of the peninsula like a conquering army. It was a beast that could not be defended against, or in any way challenged by the living....It passed every door, pausing only long enough to contemplate knocking in the sunlight, or with its own key to enter in the dark of night; for once waked, Death's beast was a beast whose hunger was never sated, whose eye never slept, and whose vengeance was never forgotten or exhausted.....a beast whose wrath was like no other, because its lust was like no other. It smelled the approach of its sister-brother half.....and when it did it scoffed at men's faith, walls and swords as they were straws.

And as these two beasts began quickened towards each other, to smell and taste, crave more the other.....devouring from south to north, and north

to south this kingdom of Saints, richly fruited fields and ocean breezes.....
moans, wails and shrieks of anguish and horrid affliction arose where they
passed......choirs of lamentation that would crack the hardest heart, cries
punctuated by the daylong, nightlong clanging of Death's bells. Incessant
and full of the twisting screws of unbearable pain those, who, behind doors
daubed with large, scarlet painted crosses......as they were the bloody signatures of hell.....vented the sufferings of Death's victims midst the prisons
of their terrible ends!

Penned like swine behind boarded up doors and windows, were those
condemned to die the most piteous deaths with their fellow prisoners:
mothers, fathers, children, servants. In these dark, cramped, fetid dungeons
of Death....some with trapped fumes of pitch and brimstone, with goats
tethered to their doors to ward off the pestilence.....in these dungeons were
suffered woes beyond the bounds of human faculties to fathom.....beyond
the bounds of sin to know or faith to tell.....things men's eyes were not
made to see, their nerves not meant to endure, their souls not given sense
to know.....those sentenced to die even as they watched their loved ones
retch out their bowels, go mad, fall into ghoulish decay.....sons, daughters,
parents.....hideously disfigured, shriveled and blackened, eaten alive by boils
and swellings, some the size of bladders.....the torments of a tormenting
God that had become blind to His children's anguish.....deaf to their bloodcurdling wails, cold to their prayers for forgiveness.

Some, demented in their dying, stood at windows like beasts in cages,
struck dumb, or piteously howling their insufferable sufferings.....their
reasons having fled to lunacy, their hearts wrung dry of hope.....wailing
themselves to hoarseness, then to numbness, then to senseless idiocy.....
some, lapsed to animal madness, chained to doors and bedposts, there to
be given reprieve only by the executioner of grinning Death.....those, who,
in a desperate attempt to flee Death's horrors, and their own grotesqueness,
stood upon beds or stools, and in the throes of their madness, played both the
hangman and the hanged.....briefly twisting until they dangled still, and in
that stillness, freeing themselves from the horrors of hell.

And in the streets and country-side there were those who were unafraid,
or having become crazed with fear, had become numb to fear.....plunderers
and pillagers, looters looting cathedrals, wine cellars, bake houses, barns and
granaries.....those that cast a cold eye on Death, and a burning eye only on
the plunder that Death left behind.....their hearts now callused, and no
longer with the tenderness of the living.....

As Death fueled, and gave license to darker depths of depravity, orgies were enacted openly in fields and streets......in their hilarity women giving their bodies freely to strangers. Stages were erected upon which men copulated with beasts, and with other men dressed like women; young boys and girls sodomized for the sport of the most depraved.

And of those who clung to their consciences, many woke in the night to devils or Angels standing over their beds, the devils with horns and whips, the Angels with blood-soaked swords and robes......the air spawning apparitions that stepped forth from the unforgetting, unforgiving past......only then to retreat back into, haunt and live in deliriums of guilt and fear. As death's tide crept through their streets and seeped beneath their doors, many were the shapes seen in clouds, the howls heard above churchyards......many the ghosts of the wronged that visited the dreams of their wrongdoers....those whose tongues were forked with lie and slander......hands that reeked with the foulnesses of larceny, adultery, unrequited murder.

But there were no asylums for the guilty; not clenching beads, reciting prayers, or cradling idols before altars......not in confessionals, not in penitence, not in depravity. Like claws, guilt raked through the dunghills of their hearts, and Death scoffed at their tardy repentances......bringing howling devils from each pin and prick of remembered sin. Impending Death, and the horrors of its repertoire haunted the malfeasant with thefts, adulteries, murders, and a thousand other misdeeds he had committed, and with visions of hell brought braggarts, killers and seducers whimpering to their knees. Their consciences stung raw by the wasps of guilt, sleep barred shut its gates, and let the one so stung writhe in anguish, or end his shame with a dram or knife, a noose or a bullet through his brains. Some, either too brave or too afraid to die, went about the streets like public criers, naked, or in sackcloth, or smeared with ashes, or with live coals upon their heads, screaming out long hidden sins that were hung like heavy chains upon their souls.

......those staggering like drunk men, death riding on their backs and laughing in their eyes, spurring their victims on like jaded horses......the fevered and the delirious pleading, giggling, debating with ghosts in the air......those shouting execrations at God from abandoned consciences......those who walked with eyes uplifted, babbling to the wind and clouds...... the dazed and the aimlessly wandering, their wits blasted and their souls robbed......now but mindless, soul-less slaves bound by their masters of guilt and dread.......

......those that were partially or completely naked, who had broken from

their bonds and their caretakers, running crazily about as they were being whipped by devils.....those that attempted to escape from the captivity of their quarantines.....to claw out, tunnel beneath, leap from the windows of their incarceration.....mothers bearing dead babes in their arms, still trying to give them suck, unwilling to give the cart or the grave their dead treasures.....babes aborted by mothers that did not want their children born into hell.....those that could but dumbly stand, blankly stare, coldly shiver.....beyond all care and knowing of this world.....waiting, like the sputtering stubs of candles, for their extinction.......

.....those that could no long stand, but remained doubled up and retching, as if attempting to purge the evil spirit from their bowels.....some that crawled on their hands and knees through the streets, barking and snarling, frothing from their mouths like rabid dogs.....grown men crying for their mothers.....those that leapt from bridges into rivers, drowning in their vain attempt to allay their fevers.....bawling children running in senseless circles about their parents' corpses......

.....those that pounded their heads against stone walls, trying to dash out their burning brains, as if to cheat Death of its pleasure.....proud, beautiful maids turned hideous hags in an hour.....the owners of silks, velvets, diamonds, ending in their own vomit and excrement....the wise and scholarly, reduced to blithering.......

.....those that laid lifeless on church steps, in streets, alleys, doorways, with unclosed eyes and unshut jaws.....beneath bushes, in fly-swarmed heaps in fields, now food for birds, dogs, wind and rain.....priests deserting their parishioners, constables their offices.....friends fleeing friends, parents their children.....dogs and swine becoming feral.....sane men becoming savage mad.......

.....those whose swollen tongues would not let them speak, or only hoarsely rasp with Death's fire in their throats and lungs, holding in their hands knives and pistols, begging strangers do what they could not.....those that faltered, swooned and fell where their death-drunk steps had taken them......or abruptly dropped as they ran, like deer felled by the hunter's arrow.....their bodies fleeced, stepped over by passers-by, sniffed by dogs and the snouts of pigs.....of no more regard now than a pitch of dung.......

.....Two beasts, two beasts that had been one beast, lusting to become one Beast again.....and nothing in their way, not stone or fire or prayer to stop them.......

CHAPTER TWELVE

THE HOWLING WOLF INN

Late Autumn, 1347, Central Italy

I

Worries

A FORTNIGHT after the prisoner's escape, the abbot and his retinue, including guards assigned by the Bishop, rode out from the city's gates; the sky blue and bright, and the forests painted red and gold with autumn.

There had been, and was still an ongoing hunt for the escapee, but he was elusive of their capture. Considering the seriousness and profanity of the crime, a great bounty had been placed on his head. A ransacking of his haunts was made. The inns, taverns and gambling houses where he drank, diced and played his gypsy music were searched, his lovers, questioned, and then searched and questioned again; but this one named *Brother Maria* was not to be found.

The scandal was great, and told with many variations and vulgar interpretations, the most popular being that the gypsy had had his way with many of the holy sisters, and had turned the convent into little more than a brothel with his frolics. He had attempted to molest the aging abbess, a thing that she herself professed. As if that was not enough, the prisoner had raised a fist against his priestly confessor, and after harshly beating him, stole his habit, and used it as a disguise to escape his place of imprisonment at the very hour he was to hang.

Several days after his escape, the young sister who he had violated in her place of prayer was found dead, hanging in her cell. The entire sisterhood was confined, and at the order of the Bishop, was performing a collective penance. The sisters no longer filled the cathedral with the beautiful harmonies of their devotions. If it happened that one was briefly seen, she was veiled, and did not speak, her face bent before her steps. Candles and censers burned day and night in the choir, where the violation had taken place.

Outside the gates the departing party of clerics was greeted by crowds of paupers, their swelling numbers pressing against the city walls like the tide of a ragged sea: beggars of every sort, age, deformity and craft: tinkers, slapdash tailors, smithies and boot-makers, children hawking sugared apples and dolls of sticks and twisted straw. A second summer of torrential rains had ruined great parts, or even entire yields of the wheat, oats and barley, mildewing the stalks before they could bear their fruited beards. The grapes shriveled and rotted on the vines, and the orchard fruits were stunted and wormy, and fell inedible to the muddy ground, gathered only to swill the swine. Even the herds and flocks seemed to grow gaunt and listless, as they too had begun on the sure road to starvation.

It was late autumn, and famine was now gaining a stranglehold upon the people and their fields, preparing for a second winter with little or nothing in their granaries and cellars. A tide of misery and apathy had seeped over the land, and settling stagnant upon it, showed no sign of leaving. Here and there could be seen crude tents, swayback sheds and caving huts where men and women, hollow-eyed and spectral, like human jackals huddled about struggling fires. All were slovenly, clothed in rags that did not cover bare knees and bare elbows, and often, shoeless feet. Made faint with hunger, mothers knelt on the roadsides with the pretense of no longer being able to give suck to the bundles in their arms; bundles that were moribund and too weak to cry, or in their vain attempts had become tiny corpses. Some were not babes at all, but armfuls of grass used as sly tricks of their beggary. These mothers' faces were piteous, but behind their piteousness lurked another face, a face more savage than piteous; a face ready to kill with a soldier's cause; life's first and final cause; *the need to eat*.

But on the day of their departure the weather was fair and blithe-some, the autumn stretching unseasonably deep into the year. The forests were a bloomy gold, the meadows, flowering, rhyming with the straw-gold of the ruined harvests. But as the travelers began their return, the abbot's heart was filled with thoughts of worry, doubt and confusion. The brooks, although happily plashing, seemed to wail as they were in chains, and the trees, although fluttering their bright gowns in the breezes, seemed to lament, grieving the passing of summer. There seemed to be another, stronger, underlying melody, one dark and sinister, an undertow of darkness that was sucking this hymn of gold-enness into its maw.

......*He knew the badges of starvation. He knew their filth and rags and madness. He knew it whittled away man's pride, stripped him naked of his dignity.....made a wild beast of his civility, a madman of his reason, a whore and murderer of his innocent heart.......*

......*He remembered when he was a boy, when the heavens opened and the rains came. He remembered the women on their hands and knees in the fields, scavenging for dock and nettles, digging for roots and worms. He remembered seeing corpses in the alleys, fleeced by thieves, pawed at and gnawed upon by dogs.....the rumors of prisoners eating prisoners, and of those, desperate beyond hope, who dug up graves to eat the brains of the dead......he remembered the thing that had happened to his mother......*

.....*Oh, but now this other thing that he had heard of, that no plentiful harvest could feed, no overflowing barns and granaries could appease.......*

At nightfall, on the second day of their journey back to the abbey, they reached an inn where their horses were unsaddled and stabled. Made tired from the day's long ride, Abbot Giovanni prayed, ate lightly, and retired early. He lay down on his bed, but his eyes would not close with sleep. He tried to count his beads and pray to the Saints, to *Francesco* and *Augostino*, but soon found that his soul had as little appetite for devotions as it had for repose.

The weather had suddenly, sharply turned from the day's mellow warmth, and a chill, pitching wind now gusted in the thatches, threshing the leaves from the fig and olive trees, driving them in a tirade of madness against his window. If a snow would come from the mountains they would not continue tomorrow. The abbot rose, fed the fire, and then sat down before it. Although no bones had been broken, one of his jaws and cheeks still wore the badge of a dark, swollen bruise, a bruise accompanied by a dull ache; the results of the hard blows given to him by the escaped prisoner.

As the fire built, and he looked into its bright flames, faces appeared, faces that had opposed his sleep and devotions; that had refused to stay behind the city's walls, insisting to ride with him on his way. They were faces whose eyes burned his soul like live embers, pierced it like sharp needles.

After it was realized Maria had slipped through their fingers, brushing past the guards, and then through the mob that had gathered to see him hang, a great hunt, manned by the joint forces of the Church, the constabulary, and the bounty-hungry citizenry had ensued. Many of those that had known the criminal were brought to the Bishop's lawyers for interrogations, interrogations in which he, a victim and central figure in the intrigue, was allowed to attend, make crucial questions, and participate in any way he saw fit.

Many of Maria's comrades and cronies were interrogated; those he had consorted with in the taverns, dice houses, and his other haunts. Most of these men were poor and uncouth, if not unsavory; drunkards and gamblers, specimens of the city's riffraff; most probably more ruffian and criminal than the criminal they were being asked about. And yet when they were asked about Maria, it seemed to call a kind of nobility from their degeneracy. All spoke of him as a man of great humor, but one given sometimes to dark moods. All spoke of him as a magician with any musical instrument placed in his hands. Yes, they had seen him wage fistfights, even knife fights, fights that he had won. And yes, it was undeniable; the gypsy fiddler had a great fondness for women; and women had a great fondness for him.

But most of the faces the abbot saw in the fire were women's faces, for many, if not most of those questioned had been women; women that had known Maria intimately; that intimated having shared embraces, if not their beds with him, and as they openly confessed, their hearts with him.

There were not a few, and they varied greatly from each other. Some were Maria's age, while others were younger, and still others, significantly older. Some were very pretty, some, homely, while others owned a slovenliness that brooked on the slatternly. Some were fresh, others worn, sickly and jaded. Some had shapely figures, others did not. Among them were the shy and the brazen; the dissolute and the innocent; the unmarried, the married, and the widowed. Many were tavern maids, scullions and poor ragged street girls, but among these humble ones were several with means; widows, and the wives of rich merchants.

There were commonalities that bound their differences, and it was those commonalities that now stared at the abbot from the eyes in the flames; eyes whose earnestness had, like a red hot iron left such a brand upon a deep part of him.

It was obvious that Maria had touched each of their hearts very deeply. When asked about him, each of the women, even the most brash and brazen, softened with a deep sincerity, as they were in a confessional confessing the secrets of their souls. Each was earnest, none, flippant. Each avowed, none prevaricated or denied. All spoke of Brother Maria, the fiddle-playing gypsy with tenderness, and what could only be called a lover's idolatry.

Some told of how he had drunkenly clowned and danced, pulled little baubles from his sleeves, or had sung beneath their windows; others, of poems he had slipped beneath their pillows, in their pockets or slippers. Several confessed that when their love for the gypsy was discovered, they had been harshly beaten by their husbands, but that they had found opportunities to go to him again, risking yet another beating. Most peculiarly, when Maria had left one for another, none seemed jealous or resentful, only sad, as at losing a treasure that was not meant to be kept; one meant to be shared, not owned.

There were two other women's faces that visited these flames. One was the sister who had hung herself in her cell. Although the abbot had not seen her, when he had been young he had seen others who had hung themselves in the famines; their eyes bulging and their tongues spilling. And yet when he imagined this ghastly scene, the sister's eyes were staring with the same sincerity that he had seen in the other women's eyes, even as it hung from its noose; as if she too, still loved this golden gypsy.

The second face was very different than the others. It seemed cold, unnaturally cold, even though it had finely honed features. Appearing before the tribunal, the face of the holy abbess had not softened when she spoke of Maria. Her lips tightened, and her pupils narrowed when she told her story. He had not liked this face; its features tight and coarse, almost feral. It was the only face that was not beautiful in the flames; even less beautiful than the face he imagined hanging, strangled in its noose.

He could not sleep. He did not want, nor did he feel the need to sleep. His mind was one with the sleet and winds of the storm; stormy with strange, violent thoughts that had never swept through him before.

Standing before the window, he looked into the darkness. The wind was now driving leaves, twigs and chaff against its panes with a greater fury, and in the rain were tiny rocks of ice. The wind was bringing snow from the mountains. The snow would cover the fields and forests, the brooks and bridges and roads. It would invade the darkness; smother it with its blanket of whiteness. The abbot fed and stoked the fire again. He would not sleep tonight. He would sit before the fire, his heart heavy with the thing he had done, the thing no snow could drown, no sleep could make him forget.

He had abetted a criminal, one charged with a terrible crime: a dishonoring, perhaps even a deflowering of a Bride of Christ. They had arrested him with a sister in the cathedral, in the very place where the sisters intoned their holy prayers.....and the reverend abbess.....she had said he had tried to kiss, even to violate her.....to take the treasure that was God's alone.......

He was certainly a seducer and adulterer, those he had adultered with had shamelessly, almost proudly confessed the thing. He was a drinker and a dicer, a consorter with the depraved and the promiscuous. And a killer? Was Maria, the young Adonis monk he had once befriended, a killer? Yes, probably...no, most certainly, he was a killer. Had he not admitted ii?..... And had a killer's strong hands not gripped his own throat in that cellar, choking him, to the very verge of squeezing the life from his breast?.....And the fist that had given him those hits, the blows that still swelled his jaw...... that was a strong and practiced fist, one that had surely thrown many such blows against many foes........

This was not the same Brother Maria he had known so many years ago, the boyish Brother Maria with a tonsure and habit, prompt at every office, kissing the great Crucifix, and reciting solemn litanies with the brotherhood. This was a different Brother Maria; an entirely different person; a shiftless wanderer, a charmer of women, a brawler of the streets and taverns..... He did not want to think how many other jaws his strong fists had hit, or against how many throats he had pressed a knife's sharp blade..... And the poor young sister, the tragic fruit of this terrible scandal? They had found her dangling in her cell, as she could not live with her shame.....shame that her vows had been broken in the arms of this seducing rake.

Why had he helped free him? Why in God's name had he done it? Or had he? No, no, it must have been another, or it was a horrible dream he could not shake free of. It could not have been him, no, not him, an abbot whose responsibility was to govern forty God-fearing Brothers in Christ; who had been elected the representative of his Order, the Order of Holy Francesco. It could not have been him, Father Giovanni, who had acted against his moral judgment, against his abbacy, against God's Church itself. It was another Father Giovanni, one that had forgotten he was a priest, and in his forgetfulness had condoned, nay, had been integral in the freeing of this convicted reprobate.

But it was no use. To deny the thing in his mind was only to admit it in his heart. If he would live to be as old as the mountains, as magical as a wizard, as hidden as a hermit in a cave, it would not alter what he had done. It could as well be carved into every tree in a forest, or painted across curtains of clouds. He had been in full possession of his faculties when he had freed a dangerous criminal.....and if Maria would kill another, or others?.....his abetting, his complicity......the great sin of the thing would bloody his own hands, and weigh like a millstone on his own soul.....forever.

.....Or if Maria would be caught, racked and tortured until the incriminating truth was forced or bribed from his mouth.....he would be stripped of his habit, his abbacy itself, and naked of these things he would wither with ignominy in a dungeon.....perhaps one day be led from that dungeon to a gallows exactly like the one that had been prepared for Maria. If anyone would ever find out.....but what was he saying?....he knew, yes, 'he' knew! His soul was the accused, the rightly accused......by his own conscience accused......

And how could it remain a secret, when God's eye saw it plainly written upon his heart? He could not keep such a thing concealed, locked away in a corner of his devotions. He must confess it to his confessor, or go mad with the gnawing rat of guilt.

Or must he? Was it not possible to bribe guilt with a sugar, and keep it from the eye of the sun? Did not every man, perhaps even the Saints, take secrets to their graves, secrets that neither shame nor valor had admitted? Beneath his robe, did he not bear as many sins as other men? Did not even Father Augustine take their mutual secret to his death, the lie that he had repeatedly told; the truth he had repeatedly withheld in the confessional itself? Or did that lie still live, like a noxious weed, albeit sealed in the crypt below their prayers? Had not that weed, un-plucked and un-scythed, lifted up its wicked thorns in this awful crime Maria had committed in the cathedral? Maria bore terrible misdeeds upon his head, including murder. Had he not enabled, even protected such a one; his escapes, first from the abbey, and now from the Holy Church? Was he not this criminal's accomplice?

Oh, conscience was a sword for the noble, a staff and lodestar for the holy, but was it not a whip and goad for the weak? Was there no respite ever given to that little whisper, that airy, unseen voice that was both the arbiter and accuser of man's heart? Such a thing as he had done would be forgotten; his integrity never suspected, questioned, challenged......only by this little unseen thing, its littleness bloodily pricking him to his grave.

No, He whose eyes were in every star and every blade of grass saw what he had done, however deep and dark it was hidden, like the den of a mole from the scrutiny of the sun. He had seen and He had known, and there was no darkness dark enough, no snow pristinely pure and innocent enough to hide this black grain that was now embedded, soiling his heart.

Maria had been a special friend. He had loved him as no other had; in a way that no mother or father had. He had reached through the solemn sacraments of the Church to tickle his ribs, and for a moment make him break into tender, human laughter. Maria had loved him as a man, not as a priest, and bearing an indebtedness to this love, he had tried to return it to this one who had been a model monk in his youth, but now was a feckless seducer and debauchee; and yes, from his own mouth, a killer.

Man's love was very different than God's love, and he, an abbot, was like a child in the former's arena. Man dressed his love in whatever costume he saw fit to court his lover in: a minstrel, clown, warrior, prince or beggar. Man's love was permitted to thieve, loot, cheat and kill, even to strangely weep like a lost child in the summer moonlight. It was a soldier of fortune, devious, even bloody that it might do its king's or queen's favor; a jigging fool that it might win a wink or a smile. It courted what it eternally preyed upon: that prey the illusive, unpredictable creature of the human heart.

Still, what was the thing that made the heart do love's bidding, at whatever cost; to build temples, sail seas, wage bloody wars? He knew the answer to this timeless question, but he was ashamed to know it. He knew that as a priest he should not be lonely, that the abundance of God's love should fill him; content him. But he also knew that there was a hunger in the heart that asked for something other than candles, idols and chants; more than a promise of salvation. Loneliness was that mighty throne in this world that brought love to its knees. It was loneliness, an eternal loneliness that man, like the curse of Cain had wandered with since his beginning; that the savage wolves of love encircled, smelling Man's helplessness, as frail as a crippled fawn; peering at its vulnerability; desiring to lay with it, to howl with it, to taste its delicate throat.

Loneliness was love's food and nourishment; its milk and blood. It was love's mistress, whose cold breast was ever demanding to be warmed. It was a throne before which Man was born to serve, and serving, in his end curl at its feet and die. Without loneliness, love was but a withered leaf, the sticks and straw of a child's discarded doll.

A young monk had once touched his heart, and touching it, a spring had sweetly gurgled forth, making green its dusty desert. If this gypsy, robed in a monk's habit had not once loved him, he probably could never have thrown himself with such completeness at God's feet. Man's love seemed the journeyman of God's love; an apprenticeship that was a discipleship; a prerequisite to a higher knowing.

No, he could not have let this wicked child swing in the wind. He had lied over and over to fellow priests, to the Bishop himself about the thing; and he knew he would do it over and over again. He would rather be scourged before the gates of hell than have never done this crime.

Maria had once reached through his ribs to caress awake his sleeping heart, a thing that his prayers, a thousand years on his knees, could never do.

* * *

HE could no longer hear the drone and drunkenness of laughter below him in the inn, and therefore he knew it was very late. Still, his thoughts showed no sign or wish of sleep. He left his room in search of the keeper, walking past those who were either too drunk or too frightened to dare the storm, and now were driveling on benches, or sleeping on tables midst flagons, greasy cards and half-eaten plates of food, like dead fish washed ashore in the flotsam of a storm. Finding a young servant girl still awake, he asked for a mug of wine. She had politely complied, and thanking her, he had returned to his room, prepared to continue his grim, worry-filled vigil until dawn.

Once more he fed the fire, and then stood before the small window. The wind and storm showed no sign of abatement, as the consternations in his mind showed no sign of leaving him. The rain had changed to sleet, and now the sleet to icy flakes of snow. Although the snow was still allowing glimpses of the frozen, half-buried silhouettes of courtyard and gate, the stable beyond and the haycocks beside it, they were but tiny morsels in the giant mouth of the dark night, stark reminders that man was only a little moment being swallowed into the voraciousness of death. Retiring to the fire, he once more sought meditation and counsel in its flames.

Death, yes death; did its wolves not howl in the courtyard below all windows? Did its skeletons not one day come to play their fiddle in all men's dreams? Death came to all men, its sword whetted equally sharp for peasant and for king. Thus the Savior came to save Man, to give him life beyond this world.

But did the Savior know the ghoulish masks and horrid habiliments death could wear in the streets of this world? Did He know hell would regurgitate the worms in its bowels, and those worms would corrupt the prettiest smiles and the noblest dreams? Did He know not only Man's soul would become a snack for the Devil, but his flesh would become scraps for dogs? Oh, these stories, these terrible stories from Messina in the south, and now Genoa in the north, dwarfing his guilt and his worries, like the snow was burying the fences and the gardens into crumbs of insignificance.

At first they had been just that: stories; stories that seemed as fantastic as their tellers professed them to be true. If they had been told to him by any other than the monks that were clutching their crucifixes and kissing the hem of his robe, he would have given them little or no credence. But as the abbot stared into the flames, the eyes of Maria's impassioned lovers became the eyes of these impassioned monks, monks that had fled for their lives from the south, over the strait from Sicily. They were the same eyes; eyes inflamed with a same intensity and conviction; as if love and death were the same fuel that had built their bright blazes.

Whatever these monks had beheld, they were things unspeakable, horrors too great for their tongues to aptly describe. And yet they had tried.

.....ships, unanchored and un-crewed, limping into the harbor to flounder like poisoned birds......manned more by the dead than the living.....some with men's bodies lashed to the mast or yard arm.....dying men, but not dead men when they were bound.....diseased men, left to deliriously shout their last cries to the sea and sky.....their last struggles picked to the bone by gull and kite.....bulwarks hung with strings of others, as in a vain hope death might ward off death....corpses turned to skeletons by the rays of the sun and the salt of the sea........

This is how, wild eyed, these monks said it had begun, death crawling from these ships, like a hideous monster from the sea, filling the streets of the living with its wrath; breathing the fumes of some potent pestilence into all faces, all bloods, all places.

The stories were too horrible to be true, and yet he knew they were true; as they were testimonies of those who had walked through hell.

.....oh, what had he done, and what was happening to the world as he had done it?......he was a priest who had committed a great crime, even as he was most needed in the abbey with the brotherhood.....oh, the storm, and his friend wandering somewhere in it, among the winds and wolves..... or if he had been captured, hanging frozen in it.....he must pray, yes, he must pray.....but the wine and the fire, the long ride.....he must sleep, yes, he must kiss his crucifix, and sleep a little.....yes, just a little.......

* * *

STIFFLY he rose from his chair, where, if only for a short while he had slept. The fire was low, and the storm's wind had invaded his room, as its freezing wings wanted to smother the pocket of its warmth. There were drifts of snow on the floor; yes, snow even upon his habit.

It was still night, and he looked out the window into the great maw of the night's darkness. Only a few hours ago the world was warm, golden and inviting, but now it was cold and inhospitable. The world was being put to sleep by a hand as soft as it was stern; beneath a blanket of snow; without a promise that it would ever wake again.

.....But were Heaven's Hands blanketing the child of the world, or smothering it in its cradle? The times had grown strange, so strange the wet nurse might wear the gloves of the assassin.....the changeling left at one's door, though sweet, might be the progeny of either an angel or a devil.......

.....and these eyes, the eyes of monks, and the lowly drabs and tavern girls that had stared at him from the fire's flames.....this passion of the heart that stood upon a cliff's edge.....staring from the flames of hell......the eyes of the miserable and the starving, those begging on roads, at bridges and at village gates.....huddled in hovels, crawling through fields, crouched and shivering like dying rabbits beneath bushes.....a want of bread, a want of God, a want of love.....but in the end snowed over, left cold and desolate, eternally alone, eternally forgotten.......

.....this great crime he had committed, and the guilt that would never leave him.....this paupery caused by the famines.....this strange contagion that was eating through the land.....his mind grew worried and

muddled.....agitated, all but reeling with unwonted doubt and fear, uneasy sleep and a terrible dread.....the eyes of a sister hung in a noose staring through his soul.....almost as he was dreaming.....yes, dreaming, he must be dreaming.......

There came a soft knock on his door, disturbing and retrieving him from his doze and troubling dreams. It must be time for early prayers, and a brother had come to wake and join him.

But the abbot opened the door not to find one of his brothers, but instead, a servant girl, the same that had kindly fetched him a mug of wine. She was shy and deferential, and she spoke in a soft whisper:

"Pardon me, father, I know it is very early, but, is it possible that I might have a word with 'ee, a private word? You see there was a man came in the storm last night, and he has told me in private he wishes to speak with you, and only you."

Shot through with terror of the intrigue he had so lately left behind, especially coming on the heels of his nightlong contemplations, the abbot responded in a way that could not entirely hide the fears of his apprehension.

"A man? In the storm? Wishing to speak with me? Please, come in my daughter."

She was a simple girl, nervous and fluttery, her eyes excited and dancing. As she spoke she wrung her apron in her hands, and she continued to whisper, as she had forgotten that she was now speaking behind a closed door.

"The man told me he wished to speak with you, holy father, but only in complete secret, so that no one else would hear the words he wanted to tell you."

"Is he a religious, child? Does he wear a robe like mine, or an official's uniform of any kind?"

"No, he does not wear a robe like you and the other brothers, father. Nor does he wear a uniform, or bear a sword like a soldier, or any other manner of official. He is one with a heavy coat and boots, and they of fur and hide."

"Isabella! Isabella! The men are waking.....the floor must be swept, the tables scrubbed and straightened.....and there are still eggs to be gotten, birds to be plucked and trussed....."

".....and a silver earring, one shaped like a moon....."

"We must ready the breakfast! You know how sour they are the morning after their drinking and their gambling!"

It was the innkeeper's wife in the inn below, her voice as shrill as a rooster's crow, uncaring if she woke all of the sleepers in the inn. As there was severity in its shrillness, the girl turned to leave at once.

"He will speak to you tonight, holy father, as he has written in his note....."

"Isabella! Isabella! Where are you? Come at once you skittle scamp! There are a dozen others to do a chore as well as you, you know. The drinkers are waking, full of groans, like a graveyard at the last days.....and they full of bitterness at their losses, as drink and the Devil, and not the oafs of their own selves made them bet their purses.....kings made fools with the tumble of the dice!"

"I must go, father, she is such a Tartar, and my father has gone lame in his hip, and the fields drowning, the cows not giving, and the sheep coughing and falling with the murrain.....we're struggling poor with the rains and the famine and all....and a job with a Tartar, though a curse, is still a job......."

"But where is this note you speak of daughter?"

"Oh, good father, forgive me! And that was the reason I stole to your room! Here it is, in my apron's pocket, if it was a snake it would......."

Giving him the note, she began to open the door to leave, only to stop, close the door, and turn back to him, as she had felt his concern.

"If I may, holy father, I do not think the man means you harm. His eyes sparkle blue as never I've seen a man's eyes sparkle blue before.....as they were jewels, jewels as clear as the sky without a dark cloud, and the larks singing in them."

With this the girl rushed from the room, and the abbot sat down once more near the fire to read the note. It read:

"Abbot Giovanni, I know your fears, and the part I play in them. We must indeed be careful, for the inn is a stop for many who travel to and from the city.

Tomorrow, if you see me, give me no recognition, as I will not give it to you. Late in the night, after the inn is asleep, I will come, and, with your permission, we will briefly talk. Your brother, M

PS...Fear not the servant girl, Isabella. She is a sweet girl. She has given me her word of secrecy. I trust her, as I am sure you may also.

But more than this note, the servant girl's eyes burned in his heart. They were the same eyes he had seen in the fire.

* * *

II
The Discussion

THE next day the snow continued to thickly fall, and it was unthinkable that the party of clerics would continue on their way. They were snowbound. The roads, especially those in the hills, would be impassable.

There would be no travelers waylaying at the inn today. Still, the inn was thronged with men, local men that the storm had pardoned from their cottages and labors, giving them an excuse to drink, roll dice and play cards. It gave them yet another chance to commiserate with each other on the scarcities left in the wake of the wet summer, and to discuss the quaking of the hills, and the showers of light that had been seen in the night sky; agreed by all to be portents of troubles even more dire to come. The large parlor of the inn's tavern was congested, smoky and loud. But it was not loud with debauch, rather with fraternity; a collective concern of the winter's abrupt arrival, the growls of hunger in their children's stomachs, and how they were to live until the spring melted the snow, and the sun permitted their ploughs to once more turn the soil.

At intervals the group of brothers left their rooms. Like a timid flock of quail they sat together in an alcove away from the others, speaking softly and nibbling on light repasts. This gave the abbot the opportunity to search, find, and observe the blue-eyed stranger who had sent the servant girl to his room. He alone of the brothers knew of the note, as well as the note's sender. He alone among the brothers knew this man's appearance, an appearance that was not difficult to at once apprehend.

Even buried in shadows, he was conspicuous, like a candle in a dark room, his cascade of blond hair and silver earring, his broad shoulders, the prepossessing silence that magnified his solitary presence; distinguishing, defining and marking him. He sat alone and away, his back turned to the conversations that drink and concern were fueling. He drank slowly, not indulgently; eating frugally, not vigorously; as the years had not succeeded in eradicating the last vestiges of his asceticism.

Father Giovanni studied this young, boyish monk he once knew, and this wild, virile, flamboyant man he had now become. He noticed how the tavern girls took special notice of him, and gave him sidelong glances when they passed, and how before they passed they straightened their skirts and blouses, and tucked loose strands of hair behind their ears. When they went to his table, he saw how they flushed and quickened; their eyes, brightening, their nostrils, dilating. Through the gruff voices of the men he heard their voices soften and sweeten, sing like songbirds when they attended him. He saw how they bent over his table so that their breasts were displayed, and how, upon the pretense of picking up things they let fall on the floor, they bared a calf, or even a knee before him.

And the more he did not return their glances or smiles, or in any way address or engage them, the more they would try to capture a sparkle from his blue eyes; to stir him; to woo him. They were like bees that had found a fragrant lily in a field of thistles, and they hummed and hovered about this precious flower, vying for a sip of its nectar.

Only several times was he called from his quietness. A young man was having trouble stringing a string of his lute, and became frustrated when he could not. Without a word Maria had taken the lute into his hands, and quickly and agilely restrung it. As a proof of the repair, he let his fingers dance several times upon the strings, as nimbly as a spider on its thread, a thing some in the inn noticed; stopping their talk to see and hear.

Another time two men at a table became involved in a heated argument, one that had brought them to their feet, their hands doubled into fists. Maria had quickly stood and leapt from the shadows to part them. One of the men was very drunk and blusterous, provoking Maria with curses, and then swinging at him with a vicious, albeit sloppy blow that Maria easily eluded. Seizing the surprised man's collar, Maria dragged him to the door and threw him roughly outside into the snow, a thing for which the inn broke into a loud applause.

Without a word he had returned to his table in the shadows; as if he had latched a rattling shutter. Refusing all mugs of wine sent by the inn's appreciative clientele, the abbot saw how the tavern girls found excuses to fuss near him, as if wishing to be close to his manly strength and heroism.

On still another occasion one of the servant girls had a problem with her shoe. She was the least pretty among their crew, her face full of frown and coarseness, and several times the abbot had heard her lash out with sharp words. Maria asked if he might look at her shoe, and when she scowled at him and walked away, he pulled a chair out from the table, and gestured to her to place her foot upon it; a gentlemanly invitation to which she returned, and warily, sourly obeyed. Removing the injured boot from her foot, Maria quickly made a makeshift repair of its strap. But as he was ready to give it back to her, he made the girl place her foot back on the chair, at which he tenderly caressed the sole of her foot before slipping it into the mended boot. Amazed quite from her harshness, the girl's face softened, as with tears.

In the early evening the abbot had napped in little fits, each fit being brief, uneasy, and unsatisfactory to either his nerves or his fatigue. At last he quit all attempts, and began to pace across the room, stopping now and then to listen to the men's voices in the inn below. Little by little the droning murmur had swelled to a boisterous hubbub through the day, at times breaking into guffaws, curses and arguments; drink proving victor over their sober concerns. Only gradually, at nightfall, did it begin to lessen and die out, as their numbers thinned, and the men returned to their huts and wives.

Shortly thereafter, there came a knock on the door, and the abbot rushed to answer it. But it was not Maria. It was the servant girl, Isabella, holding in her arms a bundle wrapped in a towel.

"*The master thought you might want a bite of biscuit, holy father, and with it a few olives and greens, and a bit of fish. He's a hard man, but one not beyond the gesture of a buttery heart at times.*"

"*How kind of him; thank you; may God bless......*"

The abbot reached to take the bundle from her arms, but eluding his hands, she instead stepped silkily into the room, at which the abbot closed the door. The girl set the bundle on the table, and then turned to him.

"*The truth is, father, that the traveler wanted me to tell you a thing, and well, when the keeper mentioned that you had not taken a sup tonight, and wondered if the drink, smoke and strong talk of the drinkers hadn't kept you from it, well, I said I would bring these victuals to your room, and with them, the thing the man with the long hair and a jewel hanging from his ear wished to tell you.*"

"*That was very kind, but also very clever of you, Isabella. And what is it that the man wishes to tell me?*"

"*A simple message, father. The man with the earring and the long golden hair told me that he will come when the inn is asleep, but not before. He asks you not to lock the door. He will climb the stairs when all is quiet.*"

He will talk to you before the cocks be at their crowing."

"*Yes, of course. But has the man with the long golden hair a room?*"

"*No father, I do not think he's the means for a room. But the master likes him tolerably well, because he helped pile the firewood today, and he's been kind to the sharp-tongued mistress, as one might be kind to a mongrel dog I suppose.....and he told him he may sleep on a table in the corner this bitterly cold night.*"

"*Your master is a kind man.*"

"*With some, father, but not with all. He's taken a liking to the traveler, as have some, if not most of the others.*"

"*And are you one of the others, Isabella?*"

The girl flushed, the violence of her feelings betraying her will not to show them.

"*He seems a kind man, father, a kind and gentle man.*"

Father Giovanni looked closely at the embarrassed girl. She seemed somehow prettier than the first time he had seen her this morning. There was a pin of polished shell in her neatly combed hair, and a simple necklace of matching shells about her neck. There was a touch of pink upon her cheeks, one that was a natural blush, and not an artificial paint. She was young, and the first flowers of her maiden charms were only just now beginning to peek from the sleep of their innocence. The girl seemed more a woman, yes, that was it, more a woman than she had seemed this morning; as if she had wakened; as if she had flowered.

"*You work very hard Isabella. You were here well before dawn. Now it is late, long after dark, and you are still here.*"

"*Well, the blizzard and the blocked roads, and the men of the village coming to drink, smoke and play cards, to discuss the famine and their hardships......*"

The abbot interrupted with a paternal smile.

"*And perhaps to talk with the stranded traveler, the kind traveler.....*"

The girl looked shyly away, and at once Father Giovanni regretted having made known the secret so coveted in the girl's heart.

"*Respectfully, I must leave now, holy father, or my master will become cross, and my mistress, vexed to wickedness.*"

The girl walked to the door, but stopped just as she was about to open it. Without turning to the abbot, she said in a soft voice full of a tender emotion, an emotion as delicate as a violet that was struggling to break from the cold ground.

"You see, holy father, the visitors of the inn are good men, but they are sometimes a bit rough and burly with their toils and drink, shepherds and drovers, ox-drivers and carters and the like, and sometimes they treat me as they were, well, as they were cuffing or kicking a dog."

She paused, allowing her welled emotion to give her thoughts a chance to collect and arrange the important words of her heart. She spun about to the abbot, the melting darkness of her eyes swimming with tears, tears that were burning with an intensity that one could not have believed lived inside her; eyes that were the sisters of those the abbot had seen in the fire's flames.

"The man with the long hair, the earring and the blue eyes is different, holy father. He is kind. He speaks gentle words to me. He told me I was lovely, and that he would write a poem for me. And when I told him I could not read, he smiled, and said that he would then sing it to me, like a serenade, for indeed the words he would write would be a serenade to a princess, the princess of my heart."

Fighting with her emotions, she paused, and then looking directly into the abbot's eyes, she spoke with the pride and temerity of a queen.

"Yes, holy father, I like the traveler very much!"

And without a word more, she left the abbot's room.

Left to himself, and the probability of waiting hours more for his secret guest, Father Giovanni removed the towel from the bundle the girl had brought him. It consisted of a small trencher neatly arranged with two barley biscuits, a piece of goat cheese, olives, and a piece of dried fish. There was also a small flask of wine, from which he poured out a measure, and then sat down before the eager fire.

.......Once more, in the flames, faces appeared.....faces plain, simple, sincere.....faces homely, pretty, haggard.....faces of shepherd girls, tavern girls, street girls.....the wretched and the comely, the shy and the shameless.....the wild-eyed, the hollow-eyed, the lonely-eyed.....like faces of ghosts pressed against a window, mutely trying to tell of death's world..... and of things for which their hearts still ached and pined, but sadly had left behind in the streets and gardens of the living.......

* * *

Father Giovanni awoke from the doze induced by the potent mixture of his fatigue, the fire and the fruity wine. He awoke to find a figure,- tall, lean and broad looking out the window, a few paces from where he was slouched. If it were not for his height and broadness, he would have thought it was a woman, for the figure had a long flow of golden hair, and a jeweled earring dangling from one ear.

The abbot stood, and Maria turned to him.

"*Ah, you're awake. When I received no answer to my tap on your door, I invited myself in. It is very late, or I should say early. Even the keepers are asleep, and the drinkers sprawled on the benches and tables.....well, when I saw you sleeping in the chair, brother.....rather, Father Giovanni, I fed the fire and......*"

"*But have I slept long?*"

"*No, only a short while. It is still hours before dawn.*"

"*As you can well imagine, I am very surprised, and at the same time very delighted to see you, Brother Maria.*"

"*And perhaps a little afraid?*"

"*Well, perhaps; yes, a little.*"

"*.....as understandably you might be. As we both know, I have a healthy bounty on my shaggy head.*

But yes, well, you see I knew that you would soon return to the abbey, broken jaw or not, and that the Howling Wolf would be a convenient stop along the way. After I escaped from the city I made my way here, and camped in the forest. And then, as you know the weather turned sharply, and the snow came, and......"

"*I am happy, although a bit puzzled that you did. I am very glad to see you, Brother Maria, and under much different conditions........*"

"*You mean above the ground, rather than below it....prepared to run, rather than to dangle? Yes, it is good to see you again too, Father Giovanni, and yes, in a little merrier circumstance!*"

The abbot saw the eyes of a youth resurrect and dance, if only for an instant in the bearded, all but mangy face, even as they once did in the face of a rosy-cheeked monk. In the wilderness of hard cares and toils that had grown up about those blue eyes, there were still glimpses of a boy.

"*But do you not think it is dangerous?*"

"*I do not think it is. We are two days' journey from the gates, and the snow has halted all travel on the roads. There will not be a coming and going of guests, or dogs and posses.....and besides, at this hour the inn is asleep. No one knows I am here.*"

"And the girl?"

"Isabella is a princess. She will not say a thing. I have written her a poem. Our meeting is locked away with that poem in her heart, and she would rather die than give another the key."

The abbot paused, and Maria turned away to the window, not to look at a storm of wind and snow, but at a storm of thoughts that had blinded him of the words he had come to say. As with a mutual understanding, both men became silent; a silence that was not awkward, but strangely comfortable, as is only possible between old friends; as both were giving the other a pause to prepare the few pithy words that in these brief moments must sum and suffice for the many stored in their hearts.

And in that pause, bounded by the firelight, the two figures presented a portrait whose contrasts could not be more starkly defined; the firelight a cage that had caged two animals: one, a gentle creature of prayer and scholarship, docile as a deer; the other, a creature of instinct and ferocity, savage as a lion. Strangely, both the deer and the lion owned an equal strength; both, an equal timidity.

The abbot was spare and gaunt, emaciated by a life of austerity; the gypsy wanderer, broad and leanly strong, seasoned into a kind of wolfishness. One was cleanly shaven, his hair cropped in a dark tonsure; the other was thickly bearded, with a mane of golden tresses that fell on his shoulders and trailed halfway down his back. One was a servant of God, the other, a creature of the taverns and the forests. They were two warriors of opposite camps, both mighty in their own rights; both with mighty swords, but tempered with different validities.

Where had life's roads led them, and how had their journeys changed them since their monastic days?

One had dedicated his life to prayer, penance and the holy sacraments, the other to wine and debauch. One was living his life that he might reap salvation beyond it, the other, living each moment as it was his last. One was an abbot with great responsibilities; the other was a shiftless vagrant who disdained any and all discipline. One believed in God, the other, only the songs of fiddles, and the kisses that hung like cherries on pretty smiles.

And yet beneath their appearances they were kindred; they were brothers; and somehow both knew they were. Both shared those rare essences that mystically mingle to make a man a man. They both knew who they were, and although contrapuntal, were rooted in their identities; one as wild and reckless as the other was austere and tame. They were different trees bearing different fruits, but both had twisted their roots into the same rocky soil to withstand many harsh winds. Loftier, and somehow richer than others, both whispered in breezes and thrashed in storms other hearts did not feel. Both caught, and for a moment held the stars that passed through their high branches.

It was Brother Maria who broke this prolonged, mutually respecful silence.

"*I needed to thank you for saving my life, and a life of not much worth at that.*"

"*Maria, I assure you......*"

"*Please, Giovanni, I must.....let me continue.*"

Maria held up his hand, halting the abbot mid-utterance. He went to the fire and stared into its flames, as what he had to say needed to be given, like an offering, to something more ancient, more primitively sacred.

"*It must have been very difficult for you. I cannot imagine the conflict, even the guilt that has resulted in your heart. It went against all you believe in. It went against your vows. It went against your faith in God.*

It is a thing that I, in your position, perhaps could not have done. Thinking of my own neck, I probably would have let such a lout hang. You are a bigger man, and a much better man than I will ever be, Father Giovanni. That is why I waited in the forest for you. That is why I came to the Howling Wolf in the blizzard. That is why I am here; to tell you that I am forever indebted, forever grateful for what you have done for me, for saving the rags of my miserable life.

But I am also here to surrender, man to man, my wrists to you, and with those wrists, my life; for I would rather swing from the tail of a rope and be eaten by crows than to live, knowing I had caused a great crack in such a noble heart as yours."

And with this Maria abruptly turned from the fire, knelt before the abbot, and held out his wrists. The surprised abbot, after understanding Maria's gesture, pressed his hands together in his own, and gently raised him back to his feet.

"*No Maria, no. I did what I did because I chose to do so. It is I who need to surrender his wrists, lifting them in prayerful surrender to however God wishes to bind them. Give it no more thought. You see I believe it was a kind of repayment......"*

"Repayment?!"

"Yes, a repayment, for sowing life into my dead heart long ago."

"But I do not understand."

"Nor need you, nor even could you. Think no more upon it. I know you are grateful, and that gratitude is worth ten thousand words."

The two men paused, looking into each other's eyes; the lion respecting the deer's strength, the deer respecting the lion's frailty. Brother Maria bent down, gently kissed the delicate hands that held his much larger and stronger ones. Softly, like a rustle of a small bird's wing, he whispered:

"Thank you, Father Giovanni. Thank you my dearest friend."

And with this, as to hide the shame of his gratitude, Maria abruptly broke their embrace and turned away to the window. After a protracted silence, he whispered:

"The storm has passed. In a day or two you will be able to travel."

"Yes, in a day or two we will leave. And you, Maria, what will you do?"

Maria continued to look out the window. There was the slightest shrug of his shoulders, and a pause before he softly replied.

"Me? I will leave before dawn breaks."

"Dawn?! But the cold and the snow, Maria; and the famine. You have seen for yourself the people's hunger. This hunger will make beggars of good men, thieves of beggars, and cutthroats of thieves. The country-side is full of dangers. There are rumors of bands, lawless bands, men made mad with starvation that loot and plunder, and commit the most terrible crimes in churches, on travelers and upon women."

Maria continued to look out the window. Waiting for a response, but not receiving it, the abbot earnestly continued.

"Maria, would you consider returning with me? Some in my retinue would surely suspect, but they would not know for certain who you are; or we could make a disguise for you, yes, a disguise! The Bishop has assigned us guards, and being clerics, I think we may travel in relative safety and impunity the rest of the way back to the abbey. There is hunger in the people's eyes, but I do not think there is yet murder in them; or if there is, it is still wary, intimidated by our habits and the large crucifix we carry as our standard. Their hunger is great, but I do not think it has yet devoured their fear of God; but soon, yes, I am afraid soon that will be brushed aside, and eaten too."

Maria turned from the window, squatted before the fire, and stared into its flames. He gave no response, and this encouraged the abbot to continue.

"Listen, please Maria. I am an abbot now, one of no little stature in the province. I know the Bishop well. He is a good kind man, one full of godliness and compassion. I will speak on your behalf to him, and he in turn to the Cardinal. I am confident I can convince him to allow you back into the brotherhood as a lay brother, as a kind of penance for your crime. You will be safe there. You will have food and shelter. You see I have heard things, things that have made me very afraid, afraid the famine is not the worst hardship the winter is bringing. There are rumors of a most dreadful pestilence set afoot upon the land, some dreadful retribution of Heaven, mowing down the men before it like the harvester sickles the wheat. If you wear a holy belt, a cincture, the law cannot seize you.....you see you might.....and it would hurt me, hurt me very much if......."

Maria's soft whisper rescued Father Giovanni's faltering voice. He stirred the fire with a faggot, even as he continued to stare into it as he spoke.

"There are no women in the abbey, Father Giovanni. There are only men. I cannot live on prayers. I would starve like those ragged ones you saw in the fields and on the roads. I need women to nourish me, to tell me I am alive. I need them to laugh, play, and be silly with. I need to hold and be held by them in the parade of the days and years, even midst these dangers you profess are coming our way. Women are all to me, Giovanni. Their kisses and laughter are my sacraments, all the salvation I seek. I do not want to live without them, even as you do not want to live without your altars and idols."

"This kind of love is very brief, Maria......"

"Brief, yes, very brief, and it shall fade, wither and fall like leaves of the forest trees. But it contains joys I can taste and feel; that I can hold to my breast as I cannot a recited prayer or chant. I pick the flowers at my feet, flowers that raise their heads through the bones and rotten cloaks of a thankless dream, a dream that like a fisher's net your God has cast upon this world. I press them to my heart, and for a moment savor their sweetness."

"You must not mistake lust for love, Maria. The two are not the same."

"No? Is not love born of lust? Is not your Angel of love my angel too, albeit he has come to play in the muddy ways of men?"

Maria had spoken softly while continuing to stare into the flames.

But his words, although but a whisper, were so strange that Father Giovanni was taken aback, and did not know how to respond to them. Feeling his suspense, Maria rose to his feet, smiled shyly, boyishly, and then turned his gaze to him.

"It is true, Giovanni. It is who I am; who I have become; who I want to be. I can speak with men; I can drink wine, dice and wage fistfights in the streets with men, but I cannot bare my soul, and play the games of love with men. I need to chase the flight of a woman's prettiness. I need to be her hunter; to court, stalk, beg or seduce her loveliness to my arms, and for a moment hear and feel the wings of her sweetness flutter and become still upon my breast. I need to follow her glances and smiles and tender kisses. I need to play and be defeated by her foolish little games, and if she leads me to a deep dark river, I must leap in and drown as she commands me to do. For a brief moment, in the death and darkness of this world, I need to hunt and be hunted; I need to cherish, and be cherished."

After a pause, the abbot spoke.

"It is true, Maria, that this world is full of death and darkness, but a woman's embraces are no escape. They will fall away, like the rose of summer shedding its scarlet petals; beauty's swan, becoming bones for vultures. But God's love will not die. It will not fail you. Patient with Eternity, it will be the same tomorrow as it is today; the same today, as it was in man's beginning. With its wings and sword it will gather and protect you as the arms of a woman could never do."

Unfazed by his friend's sincere homily, Maria softly continued.

"Women know love as no man knows love; even a priest; even a Saint; perhaps even God.

Woman is the tree in the center of earth's garden; her arms are full of love's fruit, her breast, love's milk; her lips, full of flowers for her playful children. Man is bound to her sweetness as he is bound to no God. And though when he leaves the garden he sows, hunts, reaps and conquers, he is left with an ache for this first sweetness; a warrior forever seeking to return where he has begun, and give back the treasures of his journey; returning to the tree beneath whose branches he was born, and beneath whose branches he must die; the tree that alone has understood him."

The abbot's brow wrinkled with his friend's strange, but lovely, half-pagan words. After a long pause he continued:

"Maria, please, consider my offer. There is war, famine, sickness, and a great lawlessness afoot. The abbey's walls will protect you from these dangers.

I will find a place, perhaps a room with the lay brothers where you may write poems, perhaps even make music with a fiddle. You need not take the formal vows. You need not attend all of the offices. There, at least until these great dangers have passed, you may have a quiet safety. I am the abbot now. If needs, I will bend rules. I will protect you. I will see to it that your desertion from the abbey is forgiven."

Again the abbot paused. He felt that Maria was listening, drinking his words to his very heart. This encouraged him, and with a crescendo of desperation, one that was bearing him into higher and higher crests of passion, he continued.

"You have entered a forest that is a prison of the human soul, Maria. There is no way out, only a deeper entrapment. It is an endless maze that endlessly confounds, with fruits that promise, but quickly disappoint and spoil. It is a wine that makes you giddy and gives you romantic dreams, only to pollute you, leaving you to writhe with pangs of remorse when you wake."

His words had indeed found their listener's heart; a deep nerve in his heart. Maria waited for the abbot to end his passionate plea, and then spoke with a passion of his own; their passions clashing, as they were the swords of two mighty champions on a battlefield.

"You presume that I am lost, Father Giovanni, lost in a forest of false desires and false pleasures, and that with the passing of each hour and each season I am only lost the more; foundering, confused, estranged, until I will stumble into the forest's heart, a place girdled about by wicked thorns. Perhaps you are right, Father Giovanni, yes, perhaps I am an errant child, one who has become lost in the forest of the world.

But I do not think I am any more lost than the thinker who wanders in the forest of his thoughts. Oh yes, there are lovely fruits and flowers in this forest, but there are dangers too; wicked thorns, and serpents underfoot. Men's thoughts may stray down many paths whose sunny invitations fork and meander into dark and endless ends. Perhaps a thinker is even more deluded than the man of the spear and the plough. His pride congratulates himself on moving a troublesome stone, only to find beneath that stone a nest of vipers, multiplying its troubles that wriggle through the grass in every direction. Not so with the man of the plough and spear. He accepts that he is a wanderer, a wanderer that is a riddle beneath the stars; one that time has not, and perhaps will never solve.

Both men bend to pluck the flowers that sweetly tempt them, and both are pricked with the hurt of their enchantment; one bleeding with the thorn of guilt, the other with the thorn of farewell.

Thought presumes that it alone is the owner and guardian of truth, that it alone gives truth its hat, cloak and sword. But perhaps this thing men call truth is a naked child beneath the sun, its nakedness its cloak and armor. Perhaps it runs shameless through the streets and forests, free of any garment men try to give it."

Uncharacteristically stirred, the abbot defended his belief.

"But these are a poet's words, a pagan's words, a heathen's words, Maria. Man is not a creature of the savage wilds; he is a creature endowed with reason, a reason to interpret life's miracles, and to pick his way through good and evil with his faith."

Maria smiled wryly, and with irony in his voice, retorted.

"What is this reason you speak of, but flights of a child's arrows that fall at a jeering enemy's feet? You cannot melt the sun or batter down mountains; you cannot part the seas or the heavens with your reason. You men of thought send the soldiers of blood and bone from your fortress, while all the while you philosophize with polemics about a God whose face none has seen, but you imagine has told all to do His bidding, all the while remaining safe and secure upon the throne of your faith, neither living nor loving life's battles at all."

"Then you no longer believe in God, Maria?"

"God? A God that smites the earth with curses of famine, disease, and the carnage of war? A God that leaves His children but skeletons of want and need, that baits them but to blight them, promising them pleasures but to shackle them in chains; yoke them to drudgeries, humiliate them by binding them to an ox-cart of guilt and shame? Yes, I believe in such a God, and I abhor that God of my belief."

"But your soul, Maria, your soul and this contagion that even now is crawling through streets, seeping beneath doors, contaminating beds and cradles.....Man is small and brief, and undefended against the uncertainty and gaping chasm that awaits him.....that sure fate that stalks his footsteps, looks in his windows, poisons his dreams."

Maria's reply was now a whisper, as gentle as his former words had been heated.

"Most fear death as a bloody killer, or a mad reaper with a sickle, but I see death as a gentle mistress, a mistress that is a mother; life's mother. Most believe it comes in the night to stab and strangle, but I believe it opens night's shutters, and smiles with the dawn; its anguish, a courtship, a call of

mating, like a flute in the night, to drown in its embraces; its pain a lullaby; its leaving a return, a surrender to its arms.

I am not afraid of death. I am only afraid of the living, who, wearing masks of pomp and greed try to interfere with death's kindness, poisoning its cup of wine, making it bitter as wormwood with threat and fright."

Maria ended his impassioned words, without a reply from the abbot, leaving the two men surrounded by the silence of the room, the silence of the hour, the silence of the snowy night that stretched to the forests and the mountains. Magnified by this silence, there came a timid knock upon the door, startling both; as if something otherworldly, something other than men's great battles with love and death had eavesdropped upon their words, and unconcerned with such trifles, had come to summon them.

At once Maria drew his knife, and pressed against the wall. But answering the knock, Father Giovanni was greeted once more by the servant girl, who had evidently slept in the inn through the night. There was tiredness in her eyes, but her hair was combed and softly flowing, and in it, pinned like a barrette, a golden leaf and red berry.

"Pardon me, good father, but the traveler asked me to tell him when dawn was near, when I heard a first cock a-crowing."

Hearing her voice, Maria went to the door, and the abbot stepped away to the window to allow them a private moment. But he could not forbid his ear from listening. He *wanted* to hear; he *wanted* to hear the tender music of their voices.

"Yes Isabella, thank you."

On seeing Maria, the girl brightened, and her tiredness fled.

"The nights are growing long with winter, and though it is still dark, the morning is near, sir. The keepers are stirring, wheezing the fires..... the peeling and trussing and so on....the sleepers rousing on the benches. Soon keeper and wife will be about, their sharp tongues prodding me to my chores."

"Of course; thank you Isabella. I will be only a moment more. But tell me, where did you sleep last night? Is there a room they provide for you?"

"I did not sleep, sir. I wrapped myself in a blanket, and sat by a little fire, and sang over and over the poem, my poem that you made and sang for me."

"That is very nice of you, Isabella, but it concerns me that you have not slept."

"*I did not need to sleep. I did not want to sleep with such sweet words in my heart. They were my pillow; they were my warmth.*"

"*You are very sweet, Isabella. I will not forget you. Perhaps I will come again, when the trees are green and the meadow flowers are in bloom. Perhaps we could take a walk together.*"

"*I would like that, Brother Maria, I would like that very much. I will ask the Virgin to thaw the brooks and break the buds early.*"

Father Giovanni heard Maria begin to close the door, only to stop, and ask the young girl who continued to stand just outside it.

"*Is there anything more, Isabella?*"

But then came different words and a different voice, a different music full of both tenderness and anguish, of both tears and song; a music that strangely, deeply pierced the abbot's heart; a music not of God's love, but, fleeting and foolish, of man's; that poignant music reserved for lovers alone; that lovers have earned, and alone have the privilege to know: the bitter sweet music of farewell.

"*I did not want to hear the cocks crow, Brother Maria! I did not want to hear them at all! I did not want the day and the sun and the world to ever come again. I only wanted to see you sitting by the fire as you have done these past days, and to bring you grog and biscuits, and a smile, both of my lips and my heart, as I have done. I only wanted to know that you were here, at the 'Howling Wolf', and from time to time to hear you speak the words you wrote for me.*"

"*You are a beautiful young woman, Isabella. I do not want you to forget that, because I assure you, I will not.*"

With this the abbot's eye became as disobedient as his ear, and he stole a glance at Maria touching the girl's cheek with his finger, and then bending to kiss her brow. With impetuosity she could not control the girl threw herself in Maria's arms, and choking with tears, burbled in his breast.

"*You are the kindest man I've ever known, Brother Maria! I love you, and I will ever pray for you, on my knees I will, I swear I will!*"

Tearing herself away, she tried to compose herself as best she could, wiping the streaming tears with her fingers from her face.

"*I must go now. I will prepare a bag of viands for you, as full and best as I can, away from the keepers' eyes, and in it the love of my heart, your Isabella's heart.*"

Maria closed the door, and came back near the fire. Both men were silent, neither knowing how to say what was in their hearts; not knowing how to say goodbye. At last the abbot spoke.

"*Then you are firmly resolved not to return with us Maria?*"

Without a glance, a word, a shaking of his head, Maria's silence told him '*no*'.

"*The day will be breaking soon, and I want to be gone before it does. There are kind people that once afforded me shelter a day's journey from here. They have a barn where they once allowed me to sleep. There's plenty of hay, and a horse, cow and goats to keep it warm. The snow will slow me, but I think by dusk.....and I must pack my few things, thank the keepers..... say goodbye to Isabella. It is time, Father Giovanni, it is time for me to be on my way.*"

Maria began to walk towards the door.

"*One moment more, Maria, there is something else that I feel obliged to tell you.*"

The abbot paused, and Maria turned to him.

"*Do you remember when you left the abbey many years ago, that night in the confessional when you told me that you had fallen in love with the young shepherdess, the one that played a flute in the fields? Do you remember when you told me you were forsaking your vows for her embraces?*"

"*Yes, I remember; I remember very well.*"

"*Shortly thereafter a young girl climbed the hill, knocked on our gates, and asked to speak with me. It was she.*"

Maria peered inquisitively into the abbot's face. Never had the abbot seen such loneliness in a man's eyes; the loneliness of a wanderer lost in a primeval forest; a wanderer who, with these few words, had been found.

"*She was with child, Maria.*"

As these words were a sharp knife entering his side, a silent gasp rushed through Maria's body, and he turned and pressed his brow against the door. After a pause, the abbot continued; his voice now made unusually, humanly tender with compassion.

"*I know nothing more, Maria. I did not see her again. I do not know about the child, whether it was a boy child or a girl child, or if indeed the child was born at all. I made several, unsuccessful attempts to find the mother, but her family was nomadic, and with their flocks, followers of the sun, fair weather and good graze-lands. She was gone.*"

Again the abbot paused, as Maria continued to silently press his brow against the door.

"You see the girl was distressed when I spoke with her, not only with her condition, but from the ruined crops, the floods, the sick and famished flocks and herds. The country-side turned wild and unsafe. I think she was hungry, and I think the hand of a husband or other man had sorely mistreated her. You see the famines brought more than starvation; they brought fever and pestilence; they brought typhus, scurvy and dysentery......and she may have been among those that perished."

Maria walked back across the room to the window. There he peered into the darkness like an animal of the night; as he was peering into a forest whose shadows were filled with yesterdays, yesterdays that held the secrets of tomorrows; tomorrows that only his eyes could see.

"The child will not know his father, as I have never known mine. He will be a wanderer, as I am a wanderer, seeking his beginning, while being careless of his end. It will make him strong. It will speak strange wisdoms in his heart, and sing strange music in his dreams. He will know the nights and days and seasons with my heart. He will sing its song in the meadows and the forests.

But this you must remember, Giovanni: that bruised, beaten and half-starved girl that climbed the hill to speak with you was the same girl I spoke of in the confessional that last night, the same girl that, like a glorious angel gave her heart to a young monk deep in a forest."

He paused, and then abruptly spoke with a changed tone.

"I must go now. I wish to be gone before the day comes. I ask you to give me your blessing, Father Giovanni."

And with this Maria turned briskly from the window, and knelt before the abbot, at which the abbot raised his hand, slowly made the Sign of the Cross above his head, and gave him his blessing. Maria kissed the priest's hand, but did not look into his face. He rose and walked to the door, and was about to leave when he halted.

"I will never forget you, Giovanni. How could I, when my heart will cry its cries, and sing its songs only because you have allowed it to cry and sing?"

With this Maria slipped from the room without again looking at the abbot, or giving him a chance to reply.

Their meeting left Father Giovanni strangely moved, and confused with conflicting emotions. He had the strange sensation that it was he who should have knelt, asking this reprobate for his blessing; and yet exactly why he should do so, he could not reason. He felt sharp pangs of remorse at Maria's departure; remorse for the many things he had not told him. He too wanted to say that he would never forget him. He too wanted to say that he had given his heart a song. Several times he walked determinedly, with a kind of desperation to the door, only at the last to refrain from opening it, curbing his impulse to descend the stairs and tell this shaggy vagrant that it was not he who had saved his life from the gallows, but a gypsy named Brother Maria who long ago had rescued him from another kind of dungeon; another kind of death.

Father Giovanni heard the great heavy door of the inn open, and then roughly close. As he had once heard the trilling of flute in a midnight forest, it was like a death knell to his heart. He rushed to the window, not as a priest, but as an impassioned lover, only to see the one he loved wade out into the drifting waves of snow.

Seconds later he heard the door open again, and then saw the servant girl, naked of scarf, boots and wrap race from the inn into the cold and snow. Like a sword piercing his heart, he watched as she threw herself into Maria's arms; this young, unlettered girl giving her heart in a farewell that he had neither the courage nor the humility to do.

The abbot continued to watch as Maria's figure crossed the inn-yard, and then began to wade knee-deep in the snow out through the gate. He watched as he began to fade into the gray and cold of the morning; the wilderness, made white and boundless with the snow, gathering him, as if embracing him with limitless arms. He watched as he began to fade into the uncertainty of those tomorrows that some men call death, some eternity.

He had given him his blessing, but he knew, like a carnival's confetti, that that blessing would become soiled, and fall from his shoulders. Like dust on a soldier's epaulets, he would brush it away. But he also knew that the angels ministered blessings that no man could brush away.

The abbot watched the figure trudge directly for the forest, like an animal un-caged, instinctually returning from whence it had come; the snow as pathless for his feet, as his passions were pathless for his soul. It was a lawless, foolish way he was choosing, one rife with snares, pitfalls and delusions, a pathless path that only a criminal, a fool, or a child would choose, obedient to dark drives and fires of the blood that ever raged, but were never quenched.

Could it be that God's finger had drawn a path in the snow for him, a path only a few could see? Was it perhaps more courageous, even nobler to abandon one's self to the dark evils and treacheries that passed all doors, crouched in all shadows, winked and laughed in all wine-cups; to wade unarmed into the wilderness of life's dangers, rather than to hide behind high walls, thick robes, whispered prayers and polished vessels, as if playing hide-and-seek with death? Was this child's path perhaps more honest, more human; its sins more innocent? Was it not a greater, perhaps even holier feat to live and die with a curious heart, rather than a doubting one masked with hope?

A soft knock on his door brought the abbot from his meditations. Answering it, this time the abbot was greeted by one of the brothers in his traveling party.

"Brother Antonio, good morning."

"Good morning, Father Superior. The keeper has told me the wind is sweeping down from the mountains, and he thinks it wise to make no plans for travel for the next few days. He said not to worry about our rooms. With the wind a'howl, and the roads and bridges drifted shut, and the forests full of hungry wolves and brigands, there will be few or no guests, and no need to pay him but only a little, or not at all. He asks only that we remember him in our prayers, especially on the days of the Saints, and the days of Our Lady."

"Assure the keeper that he and his wife will be in the prayers of the entire brotherhood, and that I am sure God will reward him for his kindness."

The brother hesitated, before next speaking.

"And, well, there is this, Father Giovanni."

The brother held out a large bundle, what appeared to be some sort of leathery sack or bag.

"What is this, Brother Antonio?"

"A satchel, Father Abbot."

"A satchel? Why, whose is it? How did you come by it?"

"Shortly before we left the city, a woman with a veiled face, a soft voice and sincere eyes stopped me in the streets, and asked if I would not give it to you. She said to place it in your hands, and yours alone, not before, but after our departure. Forgive me, Abbot Father, but with the travail of our journey, and then the storm, and the various hubbubs in the inn, I quite forgot about the thing until this very hour."

When the brother had departed the abbot laid the satchel on the table, but as there was a kind of sacredness about it, he did not open it to see its contents. It was very worn and weathered,, like an old saddlebag, its strap and pouch mended over in many places, and the abbot at once recalled the episode of the maid servant and her broken boot.

.....a woman with a veiled face.....a soft voice and sincere eyes......the eyes that stared in the fire's flames......the eyes that had once stared from a girl that had knocked on their abbey's gates.....the eyes that stared from the sister hanging in a noose.......

.....It could only be Maria's......

Without opening it, the worn and weathered satchel told a story, a story of enchantment and mystery, like a fairytale told to a child. It told of moonlight, and butter-golden sunlight; of snowy forests, and meadows that were frothed with flowers. It told of hunger and begging, scavenging and stealing; of women giving their love in tall grasses and under the candles of midnight stars.

It told of a wanderer; one who was aimless and homeless, a boy that would never become a man, and a man that few boys would ever learn to become. It told of one who believed he was an outcast, but in truth was no outcast at all, but who walked in lockstep with the hours, days and seasons. It told of one who had turned his back on God, who had broken his vows, and defiled God's holy laws; and of a God who had never forsaken the dreams in His defiler's heart. In its bleached and battered leather were blue eyes, a boyish smile, and gentle songs that death had permitted it's bearer to sing as he walked through the dark world of its rule.

The abbot returned to the window, and looked out into the first grayness of the dawn. The snow had stopped, and the wind now blew only in swirling fits and gusts, the elements of snow and wind now being arrested and replaced by a biting cold.

For as far as his eyes could see the world was white: the gates and stable-yard, the surrounding fields, and farther, the bare thickets and the dark naked masses of forest; and then the gradual ascent of the hills, like snowy, un-swept stairs climbing, merging and finally disappearing in the mists of the patiently waiting, father-gentle mountains.

Man was a little thing in such an infinite wilderness; a little thing, a brief thing, a wild and untamed thing; a littleness that could not comprehend God's ways and reasons, any more than the ant could comprehend the heavy boot of its executioner.

Like a wolf Man only knew he was a hunter hunting for prey; that he thirsted for blood as much as he thirsted for spirit; that he needed, and would do anything, even kill for this tender creature called *love*.

The abbot watched the small figure fade in the grayness, and then smaller and smaller, dissolve and disappear into that infinite wilderness men call *the world*.

Did this figure know he had stolen a thing very dear to him, to the abbot of an abbey; a thing he had never given in his prayers, or to an idol on an altar; that he had never given to God? Did this ragged, shiftless one have any idea that he was bearing a piece of his heart?

.....but the lie, the lie.....the terrible, sinful thing that he, Abbot Giovanni had done......

It would be his secret, his and God's alone. He would live with the gnawing teeth of his guilt, and one day he would sleep with it safely ensconced in a crypt. He would wear the lie as he slept in death, hang it proudly, like a soldier's medal on his breast.

Besides, there were far greater things afoot, far greater things than a lie, or one man swinging from a gallows, far greater than love itself that he must tend to. He must return to the abbey. The brotherhood would need him. He had seen the face of famine, but this thing that the monks had told him about, this scourge, this contagion, this godless monster.....no, this was another thing.....he must return to the abbey as quickly as he could.

As the abbot was turning from the window, his eye caught a tiny speck in the snow below. Studying it more closely, it seemed a leaf, a golden ivy leaf with a red berry; as it was a treasure that the snow was burying, gathering in its arms.

....

....

CHAPTER THIRTEEN

A LOWER REALM

MAN had stubbornly insisted that his God was a merciful God. But as to scoff at, and sweep aside this age-old belief, his God had sent a merciless, uncompromising scourge; one that slew without warning, without remorse, without discrimination.

God's Silence had at last spoken, and when it did it whispered not with love, but thundered with untold rage. As heartless as the bloodiest foe, Man's God punished with a rod of vengeance; a rod that crawled over His children like a sea of scorpions. Assembling His armies of Angels on the world's edge, He commanded them to let fly arrows of fire into men's wicked hearts.

.....a Spirit that never slept, that walked undeterred through the days and nights.....passing through locked gates, stone walls, through the strong and pious with the same rapine it passed through the weak and the dissipated.....that could not be arrested by swords or edicts, parleyed with by reason, appeased by prayers.....a Spirit deaf to supplication, blind to sanctity.....wise to every artifice, and intimidated by nothing.....moving through the living like locusts through wheat.......

.....Now the nights were too short to bury the dead, the days too long to witness such carnage.....the carts and buriers too few, the pits too shallow, the dying too wretched for the living to behold.....all vastly outnumbered, overwhelmed by this dark tide drowning the harvests and trophies of Man's making.......

......Now Earth a lower realm, one no longer of smiles and laughter, but of wails and tears.....no longer perfumed with flowers, but reeking with carnage.....no longer governed by a golden sun, but by a pall that dimmed *the sun's goldenness.....a realm, a lower realm ruled by a God of darkness, that men had thought a God of Light.......*

.....Death was now priest and midwife, bride and pallbearer..... poisoning bread, wine, kisses.....blighting wombs, loins and cradles..... Death grinning in all windows, stomping grapes in all vineyards, playing its fiddle in all dreams.....tossing saint and drunkard in the same heaps, carts, graves. Giddily singing, Death mowing all that wailed and prayed before the mad swaths of its sickle.......

.....Something unimaginable, incomprehensible, something too terrible for eyes to see, Man's mind to know.....this disease, this wrath, this insatiable Beast hungering and murdering, even as it had been sent to end the world.......

. . . .

. . . .

BOOK III
A WRATHFUL GOD:
A MERCIFUL MOTHER

CHAPTER ONE

OF WOLVES AND ANGELS,
AND
THE HUNTER OF BOTH

Late Autumn and early Winter; 1347

THE SNOW was deep and heavy, but arriving prematurely, it would prove only a forerunner of the storms to come. On the fourth day after Brother Maria had left Father Giovanni at the snowbound inn, the skies became clear and sunny, and winter's blanket began to melt back to the dregs of autumn, and the measly harvest it had smothered.

Maria had not been able to build a fire. Time and time again he had failed, unable to find any quantity of dry faggots from which he could sustain flames hardy enough to warm him, or bright enough to protect him. After several wet and sleepless nights, he had resorted to begging the pity of peasants, who, after some prayerful petitions, had allowed him to make beds in their barns. It was then that Maria first felt something strange, something he had not felt before, and though he gratefully accepted these beds of hay, his sleeps were uneasy sleeps, sleeps in which he mistook creaks of the wind for unfriendly footsteps.

There was something begrudging in the hospitality he received, something full of suspicion and reluctance, and offered not at all with the good-heartedness to which he had grown accustomed. When he had knocked on doors the men had answered with cudgels in hand, and dogs leashed at their sides; their wives and children huddled behind them. They had been brusque and cold, unwilling to chat or converse, only to ask him if he was alone, and for what reason he was traveling. They made it clear to him that he could shelter in their barns for one night only. They had given him a crust, but had offered nothing more; not a cup of wine, or even a small bowl of warm milk. They had brought him blankets, but rather than placing them in his arms, they had draped them over posts. In the morning they had not told him goodbye, or offered him another crust of bread. They had not offered any blessing of the Saints, or any other good words for his journey.

After fitful sleeps Maria was anxious to depart at first light. Leaving the blankets neatly folded where he had slept, he would steal away into the grayness like a ghost. One morning, after he had crossed several fields away from the barn where he had slept, he had an uncomfortable feeling that there were eyes upon him. Stopping and turning, he saw that the man in whose barn he had slept was not far behind him, accompanied by another man. Both were armed with cudgels; both had dogs. Instead of a smile, or a hearty wave of goodbye, there was only a stare of distrust and unfriendliness in their eyes, one that told him he was not welcome to visit again. There was something hostile in their eyes. There was something feral.

Maria soon discovered the reason behind these stares. He soon discovered why, everywhere he went, the people had become wild, afraid, and wretched; as they were forsaking their humanity, and had become part savage, even part animal.

The country-side was now firmly gripped by yet another famine, a practiced taskmaster capable of exacting from its victims the last twists of their nerves, and the last pangs of their stomachs. Hunger howled through the people's bowels, its howls an evil laughter drowning the myths of God, Faith, and Heaven. It had made them its abject slaves, slaves whose sole duty was to feed the teeth that were gnawing apart their innards. The cruelest of masters, it made beggars of laborers, vandals of beggars, and gathering these vandals into lawless bands of thieves and looters; changed the hunger in their bowels to murder in their hearts. It plundered sanity, civility, and simple goodness, and in their places left apathy, distrust and the wiles of madness.

At earliest dawns and latest dusks Maria had come upon leper colonies in his wanderings, their members appearing from caves and thickets; made shy with their hideousness. He had stumbled upon them bathing in brooks, or eating behind the windbreaks of large rocks. He had smelled the decay of their bodies. He had seen their hands covered with festering sores, gnarling and slowly rotting from their wrists. Watching their limping and dragging steps, he knew their feet were decaying in the same manner from their ankles, leaving but stumps and bone pegs to hobble upon.

They had hid their faces and tried to turn away, but not before Maria had glimpsed their ghastly features, so diseased and distorted he could not tell if they were men or women. They were being eaten alive; their ears, noses and lips becoming one mass of corrupted flesh; their features, and with them their identities being blotted, coagulating into a ghastly mask of death.

But the faces he now saw in the fields he passed frightened him as the lepers' gruesome faces never had. The lepers had been stricken by death. They were its slowly decaying victims, and ostracized and sentenced to confinement, they were resigned to their doom. Like timid sheep, they were chivvied away from the living. But many he now passed were more like wild wolves than timid sheep. They were ones not ready to accept death, but rather to resist it; if need be inflict it on others to avoid it. The healthy and the robust were not their masters; they were their prey.

Many were the working tenants of farms, who, victimized by severely poor, and sometimes completely ruined harvests, were dismissed, sometimes driven away by their masters, who themselves were on the brink of indigence. Faced with the option of either starving in their huts of daub, stick and stone, or fending for themselves, many had left to hunt and forage in the wilds, or to beg on their knees in the village streets.

He saw them, the starving and the homeless as he passed on the paths and small muddy roads; wrapped in filthy blankets and coughing dredging coughs; huddled about small smoky fires in lean-tos, or in dens of plaited brush. Some stood stony-eyed in the fields, gaunt and mangy, like scarecrows; shivering like wet sheep, a thinnest sheet of flesh clinging to their bones. Starved to the precarious precipice of death, the men were long-haired and long-bearded. They were hollow-eyed and pale, and flaccid flesh hung from their jaws, as from the jowls of blood-hounds. Some of the women were balding, some goatishly bearded, as they were transforming into hags of hell. Hair had emerged from their armpits, and had grown promiscuously from their private places; as if the more they were starved, the more this hair thrived, overtaking their shriveling flesh like unchecked weeds.

Some of the women were on their hands and knees, digging in the mud with their bare hands, or scratching at patches of snow, searching for edible roots, or bits of burdock or nettle, or perhaps even slugs, beetles or worms. Seldom did they speak; neither to him, nor among themselves. Sometimes they would send their emaciated children to beg from him, but having nothing to give, the children would walk listlessly away, their brief hopes dashed.

These were victims of not only one ruined harvest, but the victims of many. Starvation was not visiting their bowels, but with all of its fears and needs, was making them its permanent abode. Their wretchedness had not been given, but as they had performed a prolonged penance, it had been wretchedly earned; their hunger making them animalistic, not only with filth and slovenliness, but with their gaits and stares; as if gradually turning them into boars, wild goats and wolves.

The sheep and cattle had become blighted with murrains; murrains that poisoned those whose hunger could not forbid them from eating them. After killing the last creatures grazing the fields, these bands resorted to roasting dogs, cats, weasels and vermin, even death- bloated sheep and horses, for which they battled the flocking crows.

Death was inside them. It had invaded and conquered them. It stared out from their eyes. Laughing, it screeched upon its hideous fiddle, a fiddle that was called starvation. Its music was not sung, but growled and snarled, wailed and cried, or like a crazy cat, mournfully whined. It sang in every eye Maria passed.

.....*weak stares, lonely stares, despondent stares, dull and indolent and blankly empty stares.....stares resigned and enslaved by the hideous fiddle that now had come to screech, wail and laugh day and night inside them, its horrid music playing through their bowels and dreams......the fiddle music of hunger now deafening all cares, all prayers, all hope of their tomorrows.......*

......*hungry stares becoming dangerous stares, bloodthirsty stares..... stares not to be tempted, humored, trusted.....a stare replacing all pleasant-ries and all kindnesses.....stripping the soul naked of worship, conviction, conscience.....a stare to be wary of, to be feared....a stare that without blinking could kill with teeth, claws, knives......a stare that like a mirror reflected the stare that was beginning to creep from his own eyes ......*

As the days and weeks passed, and the winter crept closer, Maria felt more and more a part of the destitution he saw all about him. His ribs began to bulge, and his stomach to cry out for food. Grown weak and faint with hunger, he had no choice but to beg in the village streets, singing and dancing before taverns, and in squalid little squares for the paltriest bits. When he was not passing through a village, he approached the bands camped in the fields and forests, asking the starving if they might feed the starving. But they were not interested in the pleas of his beggary, no matter how ingratiating his words, or how lovely the gypsy songs he sang. They had become greatly hardened, and even less giving than the niggardly villagers. They refused him with blank or hostile stares, and sometimes with stones or cudgels raised in their hands.

But finally he found admittance into one of these bands, and then into others, through a path that had opened so many adventures since he had left the abbey.

He came upon her walking alone before him, laboring with her arms full of the firewood she had gathered in a thicket. She was young and thin, and terribly pale, dirty and disheveled. Hollow-eyed and hollow-cheeked, starvation held her in its arms, squeezing the vitality from her young body. But it had not yet completely strangled her. Maria could see the vestiges of a maiden loveliness that was still clinging to her emaciation; proudly stubborn, despite its gifts having been greatly wasted away.

Running lightly up behind her, Maria introduced his self.

"Please, may I help? You have far too much to be carried by your pretty arms."

Not hearing his steps, and fully surprised at his words that had disrupted her heavy chore and broken into her sad thoughts, the girl shrank away with fright.

"No, go away! I do not know you! No, please, I will cry out!"

"But I only wish to help! I am much stronger than you, and I do not like to see a lovely young woman struggle with such a mean chore. Where are you taking the wood? Would you, lovely lady, not allow me to lessen the heavy load from your arms, and perhaps help you take it to your camp?"

"Go away! Please, let me alone! I do not know you! You are a stranger, perhaps a thief, or worse, a molester of women, one of those who only wander and loot, or force women to give them pleasures! Please, even if your asking is honorable, which I fear it is not, I can manage, I assure you."

Seeing that he frightened her, and that any entreaty of words would be futile, Maria plucked a late-blooming poppy, ran before her on the path, and there knelt with the bright red flower between his teeth. Her face hardened into a scowl, and she looked away as she passed him, at which Maria dropped the poppy on the firewood in her arms. Plucking another poppy, he ran ahead of her again, and once more knelt, clownishly with arms akimbo, the poppy between his teeth. Again she passed him by, with a grimace and an averted gaze, at which once more Maria stood, and dropped the poppy on her load.

But the third time was the charm. Stopping before him, she lifted her eyes with the frailty made by her burden, her hunger, and the curiosity of her sex.

"They are a bit heavy, and I do have several fields to walk, and if you could, good sir, indeed bear them just a hundred paces or so......"

Maria went near her, smiled, and softly whispered:

"I will gladly help you, but only if you first allow me to make your prettiness a little prettier."

Without giving the young girl a chance to make any kind of protest, especially with her arms still full of the faggots, Maria threaded the two poppies resting on her bundle in her hair, and the other in a buttonhole of her blouse. Standing away, he appraised her.

"Yes, that is better. Now, lovely princess, my arms are ready to serve you!"

And with this, he let the girl gratefully tumble her burden into his arms. Firmly gripping the bundle, Maria abruptly turned, and without a word began to walk down the path. A bit flummoxed, the girl was at a loss for words, and leaving the poppies in her hair and blouse, she ran after him.

Slight, and much shorter than Maria, from time to time the girl looked up at Maria as they walked on, but he did not answer her look, nor did he offer any prelude of conversation. Feeling awkward, as well as grateful for this unasked, unforeseen favor, the girl started one of her own.

"Where are you from, sir?"

Without once looking at her, Maria answered, while they continued on their way.

"I am from where the winds sleep, the moon rises, and the violets first peek out their purple faces at the spring sun."

This strange answer somehow fascinated the girl, and fascinating her, engaged her. Softening, she looked up at the tall, blond, handsome man being so kind to her.

"*But where are you going?*"

"*To the hills, pretty one, to the green hills.*"

"*Ah, are you are going to Siena, or perhaps Gubio?*"

"*No, not those hills, the hills beyond; the hills with sweet red apples ever ripe in their orchards, and angels disguised as maidens singing in the wheat and the grapes.*"

Intrigued and amused the more, the girl eagerly continued.

"*Are you a soldier, or perhaps a pilgrim; or maybe it is a poet you are?*"

"*I am both a soldier and a pilgrim, returning from both the defeat of battle and the defeat of worship. And yes, I am a poet, singing the defeat of all men that go to battle in the dream of things.*"

"*Are you returning to your wife?*"

"*I am married to the sun and moon, for no other will have such a defeated one.*"

"*Perhaps to a sweetheart then, one who has waited for you for many days and weeks, perhaps years?*"

"*Yes, to a sweetheart, one that I have never met, but has waited for me since the world was young, when there was thunder in the mountains, music in the forests, and angels singing in every smile.*"

And with this Maria began to gently hum, at which a soft smile spread over the girl's haggard face; a smile that brightened even more when Maria began to sing.

"*I come from battles ageless old,*
From dawns and dusks, and barleys gold,
From all that's weary in men's souls......
To find and forget, in moons of the west,
Where sunny valleys with green hills wed,
Apples gold and autumn-red,
O to find and forget, at last be blessed,
To dream on the pillow of my mother's breast."

The girl quickly became charmed with this stranger's soft warm voice, so full of melody, whimsy and adventure. She had never heard a man sing so sweetly, as there was a beautiful bird that warbled in the cage of his heart. She felt as though a spell was being cast upon her, a spell that she welcomed like a pleasant dream.

Who was this strange man? Where had he come from? Where was he going? Other men were mean-spirited and wild, or sick and dying, but this man seemed not like any other, this man with blue eyes, and hair more beautiful than a woman's hair, and a voice like a warbling bird's; a voice that was sweetly singing, and gently wooing her heart. It was all very lovely. This handsome man had placed red flowers in her hair, and was carrying her wood. He was singing a beautiful song, a song that made her sad heart flutter, and her pale cheeks flush and burn.

The path emerged into a clearing, one that was full of late autumn sunshine and warmth. The girl, strangely altered, looked to Maria, her face soft and dancing, animated and enamored.

"Do you not wish to rest sir? Our camp is still a distance from here, across this large field, and I fear the faggots grow heavy in your arms.

We could rest, and talk a little. I like to talk, and it is very dull, sad and tiresome in the camp. They only wish to talk about the famine, and the coming of the winter and the wolves. If you like, you could sing another song for me. As I said, I like to talk, and, well, I think I like talking with you, sir, yes, I think I like talking with you very much. O please, just a little, sir, upon this slope where the sun is warm and pleasant, and the grass is dry and soft."

The slope that the girl led him to was indeed warm and pleasant, the tepid sunlight finding here a place to gently burn into a glowing warmth, as to preserve the year's final embers. Maria tumbled the wood from his arms to the ground, and removing his coat, spread it out for the girl, at which, surprised at the gentlemanly courtesy shown her, she sat down with a, *"thank you kind sir"*, wrapping her arms about her thin legs, and letting her chin rest on her raised knees.

Maria laid down beside her in the soft, straw-dry grass. He closed his eyes, and gave himself to the tender magic the sun brought to his heart and blood. The girl attempted to make Maria speak, but she soon found that after singing his little song, this handsome blonde man did not want to speak. He wanted only to listen, and if not listen, to sleep a little by her side.

But she did not care if he was awake or asleep. She had found someone, a very handsome man who would listen to her. She was lonely for such a listener, and she began to free her heart of the many things that had been imprisoned inside it.

"This is the second year we have lived in the woods, the second we have wandered from our home with a band of the others. After papa left, or disappeared, or died......some say in a knife fight, and other wicked tongues,

with a woman of the taverns.....well, we could not do the work required of us, the hard work of men.....and then the famine shriveled the crops, and diseased the sheep and the cow, and we had nothing to eat, nothing at all......."

.....Maria felt the fingers of the sun reach deeply inside him. He heard the wind breathe through the dry grass and sumacs. He heard the soft drone of insects, and the whir of the leaping grasshoppers, even as they were miniature herds and flocks. He heard the girl's words.....the music of her babble, lovely as a singing brook......

"....The winters are the hardest. The rivers freeze, and it is difficult to catch the fish. At first the men killed rabbits and deer, and sometimes fine partridges, but when they thinned, or had fled into the deeper parts of the forest, we killed and roasted the dogs.....the old ones, and the ones with only three kegs first. The berries were not good this year, and the few that were, the blackbirds and grackles ate, as they were starving too.....sometimes we boil twigs and bark for our food.....sometimes we find roots of turnips and parsnips and the like.....sometimes we make gruels with grass and snails..... the snails being tasty when they're boiled....."

......He felt the sun drinking the river of the earth.....O how small and insignificant he was, a husk or hull, a buzzing insect or whispering blade.....and still the girl babbled on, like a little bird in a bush, full of worry and song...a little bird, yes, a little bird, filling her moment with fret and happy song.....unconcerned with the immensity of things.....and yet part of them, giving an exquisite meaning, a flowering to this immensity, and to this moment the sun was drinking......

"......I was married once, but I did not love him....and if the truth be told, I think I hated him in my heart. A drinking man, a cursing man, a philandering man with every creature who wore a skirt and a fancy for the hay.....no matter how fat or ugly.....and me left for him to lay with only when he could not find something other......he went a-whalin', and like all sailors a-whorin' I suppose.....I've not seen him for more than two years now, and I'm not sorry.....you see he beat me more than he loved me, sir, until his love became a kind of habit, a thing expected and endured....a kind of chore if you will, and more than even a chore, a punishment........"

......Oh, to be alive....to drink the good sun, to live one's little moment, to be gentle and tender.....oh sing little brook, little bird, little angel..... your song more meaningful than the sermons of Saints......

".....I am sometimes very afraid, sir. If the truth be known, afraid of

starving.....afraid of my bones being picked by birds or animals.....afraid of perishing I suppose......."

......be not afraid, little bird. Be brave, for life is brief.....sing and weep your heart to the sun.....for the sun listens, even though death is deaf to its song.......

".....Sometimes men come from the village to ask for mama.....She leaves with them into the woods, many times with a small flower tucked behind her ear......I think I know why she goes with them, and why she tucks a flower behind her ear......you see there is still a prettiness about her, and we have nothing.....you see we need to eat.....you see we might not live through the winter......and well, serving a man's needs in return for bread is not such a bad thing, is it sir?.....To make a little sin to stay alive, that is not so very terrible, is it sir?........"

......Sing, little bird.....the earth and sun are kind, but they will not save you.....you are alone, and the world is an endless forest, one full of wolves, and men with sharp knives in their hearts.....sing, weep, live my little bird!......

".....I am afraid of losing all of my prettiness.....that even if I tuck a flower behind my ear......I am afraid of being picked apart by crows and foxes.....I am afraid, greatly afraid of dying sir......."

Maria rose on his side, and without a word brought his cheek to the girl's thin knees; with closed eyes resting it there as it was a pillow. At the same time he reached below her long ragged skirt and caressed her thin calf with his large hand.

This was the language he needed to speak; the unspoken language, the first and truest language; the language in which Earth's creatures sang their needs and dreams. He needed this girl's closeness, perhaps more than she needed his. In this language he could cry out and sing; he could speak the poetry of his soul. His caresses would say: *"You are my mother, and I am your child. All I wish to do is to love you, and be loved in return! Yes, let us touch, for in that touch, my sweet mother, we will be safe from Death."*

When his cheek came to her knees, the girl's babble had stopped; the brook flowing from her heart freezing with the touch of his beard, and his hair that now fell like a sheaf of wheat upon her lap. In this little nook, in this last hour of golden warmth, *Time* had frozen, and here lingered for one last moment in this timeless, wordless intimacy; a last nectar in a last summer blossom; the last sweetness in the heart before it too would freeze.

Maria felt the girl lightly, hesitantly touch his hair, and then begin to more deeply run through it with her fingers, as it was a luxuriant piece of wool given her to comb and card. At her touch he lifted the skirt of her smock, and gave each of her bony knees, small as wizened apples, a gentle kiss. Continuing to caress her calf, as he would the back of a purring cat, he laid his head upon her lap; more deeply and comfortably into her sweetness.

......*yes, this was the only language he wished to speak, the only language that would not lie, that he could trust.....the only language that was tender, sweet and true. With this language he could sing. With this language he could feel and know.....with this language he could die........*

"Sir, kind sir, could you.....I mean I think you are a good man, and a kind man....I can see it in your eyes, and I heard it when you sang your song....I know that the famine has made me thin and pale, and ringed my eyes with dark circles......I know it has robbed me of my prettiness.....and I know you are still very strong and handsome, but you see, I think we are both wandering and homeless.....and well, such a life becomes very unsure, unsure and lonely......."

......*the only language that contained a meaning.....the only language he could rely upon, depend upon, embrace....the poetry of his soul, with which he could commune with the earth and sun.....O sing, sweet bird, sing to my soul the song in your heart!.......*

".....In our own way I think we are both starving. I think, sir, in our own way we are both running from death. You see, I may not be alive come spring, with the winter and the famine and all...you see, I think I am failing, good sir.....something deep in my heart, withering away, something that I do not think will come again......"

.....*yes, life was very great, but the moment in its greatness was very small and brief.....yes, fleeing death, was not each moment fleeing death?.....sing, little bird, even when death surrounds us.....even when we know we shall soon perish, and our little dreams will be pecked by birds and scattered by the wind......*

"....And well, it is sweet here.....and you see I sometimes have a pain, like a sharp knife in my chest, and sometimes a coughing of blood in the night.....and well, to be cared for a little......my husband a rough, cruel, cold man, with his drink and tavern whores and all....and well, to know love a little, before the winter and the wolves, and maybe even death.....

yes to be loved a little, like the sun loves these little red flowers you picked for me......"

......his mother with her bright skirt, blouse and bandanna, lying in the grass and calling him to her arms......the song of the wind and clouds, her laughter and her kisses.....and the song she would always sing to him......

.....'Bells in the breeze,
Make ring the forest trees,
Bangles on the flowers,
Make sing the little hours.....
Life's a gypsy gone a-gypsying,
A gypsy gone a-gypsying'.......

".....Handsome sir, could you find it in your heart to pretend, as in a story.....well, I mean, to pretend I was your sweetheart maybe?.....I do not ask for bread, like my mother does.....I've done that but once, for an older man.....and he with his need and the drink in him......just the once I lifted my skirt for an onion and a handful of radishes, a little thing done quickly, and we so very hungry.....O good, kind, handsome sir, what I am trying to say, could you find it in your heart to.......?"

He brought his lips to hers....brushed them with the thick brush of his beard.....wetted their lost, desiccated sweetness with the tip of his tongue..... asked them to open and give of the tender pulp he was sure still lived, sweet and succulent, protected inside their husks.......

.....and slowly their dryness opened to small white teeth and a small pink tongue, a shy little worm still warm and moist....afraid to peek out from its secret den to a world of want and need, and a thing called 'death'.......

.....he felt the thin sticks of her arms fumble and reach around him..... squeeze him with their frailty.....cling to him as for food, as for the sun, as for life itself......

.....Softly, tenderly, wordlessly he asked for her depths, and she gave of them, yielded what had been starved from her heart, what had slept and waited, resigned itself to dying.....what she had never known, and not known, never given. He murmured in her ear:

"Oh my little flower, my sweet little flower."

.....He felt her purr.....no, not purr, something softer, gentler......a faint tremor that shivered a fever through her body, tearfully pleading to be petted, touched, fed....to live even as it was in the iron grips of its dying......

......the female animal waking, wishing to be cherished, to love and be loved, even midst such rags and dishevelment in which it had been cast

away....life's womb thawing, throbbing, yearning to be filled.......

As it was a scarf of silk, he slipped her dirty smock over her head. Closing her eyes she lay back on his coat, made shy not with her nakedness, but from the reverence with which it was being adored....spreading her bony legs, as she was a beautiful butterfly sunning on a flower. He held her filthy feet in his hands, and kissed them as they were jewels on the hand of a queen.....

.....a gypsy gone a-gypsying,

yes, a gypsy gone a-gypsying.......

.....As his kisses were a breeze, her body a vine of roses, he began to visit and blissfully play among each part of her.....her body more famished for kisses than for bread. How valiantly the shriveling traces of her maiden gifts still clung to her body, and how sweet it was to kiss these last vestiges, these last roses here in the warm kind sun.....as if with kisses he and she were dying together, becoming skeletons together in this soft bloom of grass. How sweet it was to forget hunger, dangers, death.....the uncertainties and treacheries stretching all about them. How sweet it was to touch and be warm.....how sweet it was to be alive......

......the wind whispering 'death! death!', through the dead grass and the bare boughs, herding the last flocks of bees, grasshoppers and butterflies into a last moment of golden warmth.....this last little cove of the year's goodness.....their innocence, about to be slaughtered by the frost.....death! death!....O when the sun would set, and the frost would come....death! death!.....

..... "Sing little flower, my little bird, sing......

Let us go a-gypsying together......."

.....death tearing the flesh from her limbs.....and yet through her thin hips, thighs and shriveling breasts her loveliness still wanting to bloom.... .these last autumn roses still thirsting for the summer sun.......

.......the wind through the dead grass and the dead leaves and the dead promises of green glad dreams.....a laughter that whispered.....'death! death'.....'I have not forgotten you, no, I have not forgotten you!'...'Play my little rabbits, play in your little nest, but know that I have not forgotten you......!'

".....Sing my little bird, my little thrush bird, sing!......"

......the dead grass, bare trees, ruined stalks in the muddy fields..... all around the winter and wolves, stalking nearer this warm plash of sun, this first and last moment.....this smile, song, beating heart.....this depth deeper than any sea, sweetness sweeter than any honey, this exploration into

the mystery of things.......

.....her body stirring with its want to sing, to feel and know and live a last moment midst the dead grass, the shriveled bonnets of summer flowers, the bare bleak trees..... starvation, winter, wolves....the wind's laughter.....'death! death!......I have not forgotten you!......I will never forget you!'.......

.....he saw her lips tremble, as to at last speak out the secret she had kept in her heart.....the secret she had not given a husband, a pitiless sun, a God that had starved and cheated, traitorously killed her.....the secret that she had never given, and that she would not give again......the secret to love and be loved.......

.....a-gypsying, yes, a-gypsying.......

.....her thin pelvis thrusting, her thin legs squeezing....the whites of her eyes flashing with the welling might of her ecstasy.....smiting starvation and the loveless dishonesty of life with the lightning of her pleasure.....her mouth at his ear, pleading and weeping the heart of every barren field and every hollow stare:..... "Love me! Love me! Love me!".......

.....he slid his hand over the bones of her starving body, searched, found and held its mighty castle.....eliciting a gasp, and then a quiver from the deepest part of her.......

.....he felt her hand come to his, not to rebuke it, but to hold it tightly, as with gratitude.....this warm, tender little place, soft and hidden, like a nest.......

* * *

IN this way; with a glance or smile, a caress upon a cheek, or a feathery stroke on the nape of a neck, Maria kept flesh tacked upon his ribs, and was saved from starvation. As winter came on with its first frosts and snows, and the last dogs and cats were roasted, Maria was invited to the tents and cauldrons of these makeshift camps; not by his appeals, but on behalf of the recipients of his flatteries and kisses.

For days and weeks he would live with these bands; hunt and thieve with them; break into shops, barns, and wine cellars with them. For days and weeks he would play fiddles by their fires. He would drink wine, trade amorous glances, and in secret places kiss mouths that hungered as much for love as for bread.

......strange days, unearthly days, when the sun glared, and the moon

leered.....when rains did not nourish, but pelted and stabbed, chilling the rags of flesh with fever......night and sleep no longer a safe retreat, but a place where fears shivered and hungers growled.....autumn no longer a maid with a basket of plums and poppies, but a hideous witch that flung curses and rottenness.......

In these camps he heard many terrible stories about the famines and their horrors. Whether true, of partly true, or born from distract and fearful minds, minds made hysterical with starvation, none doubted their possibility, even their probability of truth.

.....churchyard walls scaled in the middle of the nights by men with lanterns, spades and shovels......coffins unearthed, skulls cracked opened, and the jelly of the brains scraped out, as from the shells of large nuts..... the brains of friend or foe, of maid, drunkard or churchman, eaten for their life-sustaining nourishment.......

......crowds of the starving gathered around gibbets, not to cheer or mourn, rather, when the sentence was completed, and the criminal dangled, twitching with death before them.....rushing with knives past the outnumbered priests, monks and constables.....in their eyes the victim no more now than a beef hung in a butcher's stall.......

And for the doubters of these stories, there were scenes in the fields and village streets that lent credibility to, and even paled such ghastly storytelling; scenes that Maria, now among a band of the starving, saw with his own eyes.

.....groups of men, women and children fighting off the crows, and then each other from the bloated carcass of a sheep, goat or horse they found in the fields.......

.....men, barefoot and bare-chested, so filthy and disheveled they seemed as they had crawled from their graves, walking and stumbling, crazed with deliriums, speaking, laughing, cursing crazily at the wind.......

......mothers wandering with dead babes bundled in their arms..... babes they had not been able to give suck from their milkless breasts.....preferring to have them shrivel in their arms than forsake them to scratched out graves in rocks and weeds.....others, lying moribund or dead, their babes still alive, vainly trying to suck their dead dry breasts......

......husbands and wives found in each other's arms, choosing to die in love's embrace......

.....some slumped listlessly beneath bushes and small trees, or in doorways, hoarsely lisping, no longer able to stand, to lift their hands to

beg.....*no longer sane enough to know or reason, resigned to the inevitable.....slaves of death, whose sole purpose was to quit this world, and the devils gnawing inside them....*

.....children that would never have the chance to be children, that had been cheated of their youth by the barbarity of an uncaring world and the uncaring God that made it.....protruding spines and ribs, hanging jaws, eyes hollow and bloodshot, filled with sickly rheums.....vacant with want, idiocy, the wandering ghosts of dreams.....children that like old men were withered, bent, crippled, becoming bald, toothless, crusted with sores..... children that were too weak to sing, too disfigured to play, too hopeless to crawl........

.....in the village streets, the beggars and pickpockets, those that doubled as cutthroats.....those that would slit throats for a crust of bread.....those that picked through corpses on streets, or left at churchyard gates by those too poor for a plot or a sexton....little more than dogs, scavenging as much for crumbs as for watches and snuffboxes.....stripping shirts off dead backs and shoes off dead feet.....leaving the dead to rot naked in the muddy fields......marketers that stood before a caged chicken or rabbit with clubs and knives.......

......crowds of urchins surrounding passers-by with cups and bowls, urchins made dangerous, murderous with their hunger.....young girls begging in the streets, and when they were refused, falling to their knees, and shamelessly offering to use their mouths in exchange for bread.......

.....the processions bearing reliquaries of dead Saints......their bones, beads, sandals, skulls and hearts....those in white robes, disrobing, and with nail-studded flogs flogging their naked backs.....atoning for their sins, and asking for mercy for the terrible judgment they were receiving.....

.....the wretched bands and gangs in the country-side.....some meek and listless, timid as sheep, as if waiting to be pardoned by Providence.....others wild and purposeful, full of serious menace...//some that were ever hunting for sheep, dogs, vermin.....eggs in bird nests.....others that were foraging for roots and berries, crickets and worms beneath logs and stones....../

.....some tame and harmless by day, but by night plunderers and looters.....breaking into barns, stables, granaries, shops of all kinds.....often good and well-mannered men that had become savage for the sake of wives and children, or for the barbarous cry of their own bellies........

......bands like Maria found his self consorting with.....eating their thin gruels, making love to their spindly women.....breaking down doors

and looting whatever lay behind them…….

But something happened one night that made Maria grow wary, even afraid; something that made him leave these camps and gangs. Something happened that once more sent him wandering and fending for himself, alone.

He had heard of a tavern in a hilltop village, one that had maintained a small clientele, and had not been boarded up against the famine. Early on a cold, gray and blustery day he undertook the climb to this village with a crust of bread and a hopeful heart. The climb was steeper than he had anticipated, the wind colder and more biting near the hill's crest; and what was more, when he arrived he found the tavern shuttered and locked, and the keeper nowhere to be found.

Discouraged, he waited through much of the afternoon, speaking only with an old servant, who, unlocking the tavern, had come to sweep it.

"I've no idea, no idea at all where he is, sir. He's a sot, and a sleeper with sluts, and they the lowest of their slut kind. Sometimes he's in bed until after noon, sometimes until the following day. Sometimes he does not open the little tavern at all for a week. I sometimes don't know why he keeps it open at all, only for his own bibbing and slutting I suppose.

I'm very sorry you've hiked the hill, sir, and the wind so bitterly unkind. But if I may, sir, I don't think he'd hire you to play upon your fiddle, not for ribbons would he. He's a blithering sot I say, and to boot a bloody skinflint miser, and whatever jingle he might have in his pocket he throws on the sheets of his sluts like a baker throws crumbs to pigeons."

It was late afternoon, and the wind continued cold and un-abating, taunting with a gritty spit of snow. Maria was in no mood to ask for shelter. If what the old servant had told him was true, the keeper was a depraved and surly sort, and might not appear again for days; and when he did, would more than likely pack him off with a scowl. He would return to his camp where he had a bed, and in the morning, a few spoons of thin porridge.

But Maria once more miscalculated the hill's steep flank, and his descent down it, as well as the late season and the early, thickly clouded night it brought. Midway down the hill the dusk came, and by the time he had reached the hill's foot, night had captured him. The camp was still a good walk away, and Maria was not sure he could find it in the pitchy dark; and even if he did, he might be mistaken for a thief, or even worse, a village constable emerging with a warrant from the dark woods.

He decided instead to seek out shelter in a derelict byre he had passed many times, one that was not far from the camp to which at daybreak he would return. Finding the door shorn of its bolt, he slid inside it, and curling up in his coat and a pile of musty hay, he fell gratefully, but coldly asleep.

His climb up and back down the steep hill had tired him greatly, and consequently his sleep was deep and profound; too profound to be waked by a band of unfriendly men that slipped through the unlocked door a short while later. With a sharp kick to his ribs, Maria woke, a torch blinding his sight of all but a filthy crescent of six or seven pairs of terribly worn, rag-bandaged boots near his face.

"*Wake up, gypsy man!*"

Maria sprang to his feet, only to find himself surrounded by a band of uncouth men, several of which he recognized from the very camp that had lately taken him in; men whom he had broken into a shop with only a few nights before. Gone were their stony and listless stares. They were keenly alive, alive as men are alive only in war, drunkenness, and the height of passion. Their raggedness bristled with ill-intent; their dull stares, now fed with dark fires of brutality. With the torchlight enunciating their hard and haggard features, they seemed not men at all, but wild dogs baring their fangs.

"*Search his coat pockets. Fleece him, as I am sure he has fleeced many in the camp. And his bag, search that old bag that he always carries with him.*"

Maria had allowed them to search the pockets of his coat, but when one of them picked up his satchel upon which he had pillowed his head, he lunged at the man, and with a sharp blow from his fist sent him sprawling. Wresting the satchel away from the felled man, and then clinging to it tightly in his arms, he glared at the ugly stares surrounding him, as if this pouch of weather-worn leather contained the meaning of his soul; of his life itself.

"*No. There is nothing for thieves here. I have no money or jewels, or treasures of any kind as you suppose I have. All gypsies do not steal, as all men who are friends in the sun are not thieves in the night.*"

The man who held the torch, a rough, and particularly unkempt man that Maria had recognized at once, retorted:

"*But I know a gypsy who has stolen many treasures, the treasures of wenches' groans that is, groans they would not give others, not for rubies would they. Give us your satchel, pretty gypsy man."*

"No. I will not."

"I said give it here, pretty, wenching gypsy man."

"Go to hell."

The fight was over very quickly. Two men lunged at him from one side, and with his feet and fists he easily beat them back. But as he did a cudgel struck him wickedly in the ribs, and then another across his shoulders, and yet another on the back of his head. Maria fell to the hay unconscious.

But it was only for a moment that his senses fled. Awakening, he lay there, with his eyes closed, listening to the foul men pick through and mock the contents in his satchel.

"Ah, the wenches give their gypsy lover flowers."

"And a scarf, yes, while we're starving, some wench has given him a scarf."

"And look, a slipper."

"And a barrette."

"A tress of hair."

"Snippets from smocks and skirts."

"Why, any wench that looks at him lifts up her skirt for him."

"Not only lifts it, but gives him a piece of it when he's done with them."

"With a wink he makes harlots of virgins. He's a bedeviller he is, and the wenches he bedevils, fools for being so easily bedeviled."

"I think he wore something about his neck. It might be of some value, some amulet or charm to work his whoring I suppose. Let us see."

Maria felt the men's rough hands upon him, as they were the talons of carrion birds about to pick his bones.

"It is only a small wooden crucifix......"

"Take it. We'll find some fool to pawn it off on......"

At once all flashed before Maria's mind: the cellar, the hour for his hanging, his friend giving him a priestly disguise, risking his life that he might flee and live.....*and the crucifix, the little crucifix he had taken from his neck and placed about his.*

Maria sprang to his feet, seizing the cudgel from the startled man standing nearest him. With a fury the thieves had neither expected nor bargained for, and finding they were no match for the waked wrath of a madman, they fled; all except two who lay hurt and groaning, and begging not to be broken more.

On his hands and knees, blindly, Brother Maria gathered the scattered treasures that had been spilled from his satchel. Looping its strap over his shoulder, he stole away into the darkness, his ribs and back aching, and his head throbbing with a great pain.

* * *

Late Autumn, 1347
Winter, early Spring, 1348

IT was not that he had not looked for employment; some way to keep a smatter of flesh upon his bones. He had asked many keepers of inns and taverns, at least those who had not boarded up their doors against the looters, and a clientele of tipplers to whom they could no longer lend credit. He had even climbed to the small villages in the hills, asking only for wine and bread in exchange for fiddle songs. But it was no good. For the first time he was confronted with a lady he could not cajole with words or seduce with smiles. He was trying to humor the lady of *starvation*, but staring at him with hollow eyes and ghost-pale cheeks, she had flouted him time and time again.

On a cold day when flakes of snow had begun to fleck his beard and hair, and drift over the sodden leaves on the forest floors, he had spoken with an innkeeper at a small tavern in a hilltop village. Maria had tried to pull the man's heartstring, even telling him he had once been a monk, and showing him his crucifix as a proof, but he had been answered in much of the same way, if only a little friendlier than by all of the others.

"*No, no, I am sorry.....you see the ruined harvest, the coming winter.....I must think of my family. You seem like a fine, strong young man. I like you, and my wife and daughters like you.....ha! my dog likes you.... and when the sun shines again, and the grapes and olives are once more sweet and plentiful, I am sure many would come to hear you play and sing, yes, right here in my tavern, and in the little arbor where in the summer I bring tables.....yes, to hear you sing your beautiful gypsy songs beneath the stars! But now, no, I am sorry, son. You must be on your way.....but be careful. Those who are not bad men become the worst in these days.....and the wolves are hungry too, they cannot tell a man from a rabbit! Good luck, young man, and may you walk with the Saints!*"

Maria had kindly thanked the man, and told him that he understood his plight, and then walked away. But after a short way the short, corpulent keeper ran after him, without a coat on his back or a hat on his bald head.

"*Gypsy man, please! It breaks my heart to turn you away like this, in the gray and the cold and the snow. And Gino…..my name is Gino….. some call me 'Gino the Fat', and others call me 'Gino the Bald'…..neither one, 'the Fat' or 'the Bald' has ever turned a begging man with an empty stomach from his door…...I hope I do not insult you by calling you a begging man…….*

…..and your name is Maria, is it not?…..like the Mother of God….. when my wife heard your name, and that I had turned you away, I got her wicked tongue…..you see she is a religious woman, and always counting her beads and praying aloud to the Saints…..ha! as if their dead ears could hear her every word….well, what I am trying to say, young man…..oh, it is so cold!…..come back to the tavern for bread and cheese…..and tonight you may sleep in a little garden shed in the arbor if you like…..there's a bit of hay there, and the wind won't bite off your toes there…..come! before 'Gino the Fat' freezes the balls off 'Gino the Bald'….and good lord, it could not be worse, without either bread to eat or balls to play with, ha ha!…...come along now, young man, come along…..."

Gratefully, Maria returned to the tavern, and sat at a table near the fire. Kindly, even subserviently, the good man and his wife set before him a mug of strong spicy wine, and a plate of bread, dried olives and cheese. When he had finished, the keeper's wife came to take the empty plate and mug away. Bending low over the table, the woman stopped, and with her long salt and pepper hair hanging down like a curtain, deftly unbuttoned the top button of her blouse, exposing the cleft between her full breasts, in which a crucifix dangled, one that was similar to his own. Without lifting her eyes to him, she softly said:

"*You may kiss my cross, tonight if you like, good sir, perhaps as you would let me kiss yours.*"

Maria did not reply. Quickly the woman buttoned her blouse again, gathered his plate and mug into her arms, whispering as she did:

"*I will make a bed for you in the garden shed behind the tavern. I will bring you a meal before you sleep. Perhaps you will be hungry then, and before you eat, perhaps we may say prayers together.*"

For the next several hours Maria restrung and tuned a lute that the keeper had found for him. To the fascinated delight of his two young daughters, his fingers made it come alive, and when it did, he sang several songs for them. When night fell he thanked the keeper, and retired to the shed. There he found a bed prepared in a soft mound of hay, replete with a pillow and several warm blankets. Gratefully, Maria lay down upon it, listening to the wind that was rattling through the loosely timbered walls, and in its gusting arms bearing pounding fists of sleet and snow.

What a mystery was love, and with what a mysterious language it sang the song of its needs. Words were only a cloak that disguised its yearning, a yearning as naked and lonely as this wind.

How did love plead its need, its longing, its vulnerability? How did it whisper to the heart? Was it a cry of the blood; a growl of the bowels? Was it a faint, delicious perfume, like some flowers breathe to the night?.....or a certain lilt, purr or tremor in the voice, like the song of mating birds? Was it a thunder, a different, but no less mighty kind of thunder that thundered silently through the loins and the womb.....threatening the soul, striking it dumb and irrelevant, helpless as a doll, its eyes and smile unable to make defense against such an unworldly storm?

Maria was startled from his muse at the sound of the opening of the shed's door, sitting up in his bed to see the keeper's wife enter. She was cradling a basket of food in one arm, and with her other hand she held a candle, shielding it from the wind with her shawl that she held outstretched about her like a wing. She did not speak, nor so much as once look at him. Setting the candle on the floor, she removed her shawl, and without the least hesitation lifted her simple smock dress over her head, making her strong, thick, but not unshapely body naked; all but the small crucifix that dangled between her large breasts.

She unpinned her graying hair, and knelt down beside him. She held up the crucifix in her hand, and kissing it, held it out to him to do the same.

"Please, you must kiss it, as I will kiss yours. In that way we will not go to hell."

Maria kissed the crucifix, as she did his, and only then did she lift her eyes to him. They were deep and smiling, and swimming with unabashed desire. Sliding beneath him, she wrapped her strong arms and legs about his body. She kissed his lips, and whispered in his ear:

"Do not worry. He will not come. I told him that I wanted to say prayers with someone who was once a holy brother in an abbey. Come, beautiful

one, we have kissed each other's crosses, our naughtiness will be forgiven."

She was a wonderful lover, but she was not an expert one. She gave herself fully and completely, but with a child's artless simplicity. Her love was raw, not suave; unschooled in the cleverness of lovers' games. Her passion was sweet and simple, all but chaste. It was obvious to Maria that she had not received caresses and pleasures in return for those she had been ready to give.

But there was something that she had in common with other women he had lain with during the famines. When in the height of ecstasy, when she was in the bliss and crisis of her final pleasure, she held him as to break him, as to kill him with her final joy. In these embraces love became more than tenderness, more than a pleasure game of affection. It assumed the drama and brutality of a storm. There was desperation in these embraces, desperation to extract life's essence; a kind of mad greed to save its moment, a last wish to care and be cared for midst death's environing grip. Like a wild vine, these embraces clung to him as to strangle him, as they had found the last flower of pleasure they might ever know.

When their love was over, the woman whispered in his ear:

"You are sweet, and you are very strong; and you are very practiced, like a soldier who has loved many. I have never been loved by a sweet strong man before, only by my husband. He is a good man, but a very simple and silly man. He is not beautiful like you. He has a big stomach and a bald head. He is a bad lover. I do not want you to leave in the morning. I want you to stay. I want you to kiss my crucifix, as I want to kiss yours. I want you to sometimes lie down with me."

"But your husband, he has told me that......."

"Leave my husband to me. As I said he is a silly man, and a bad lover, but he is a man, and being a man, he is always wishing for a groan in his bed, a groan that I know how to give in many, even in naughty ways.....but only after he has kissed my crucifix.

I have friends in the village. I will find you a room. You will not need to wander through the snow and cold, and be afraid of the wolves and the blackguards. You will play your gypsy music by our tavern fire. You will be safe, and I will sometimes come to you, and after we kiss the crucifix, we will play games and be happy."

The woman stood, and as she slipped into her clothes she spoke to Maria with a kind of Sybil wisdom.

"*You are very tender, Brother Maria. I like you very much. But in your beautiful eyes I see a deep sadness, as if your eyes know all they look upon will fade away; as they know each joy will wilt like an autumn flower. But I must go now. Here, kiss the cross of Jesus again. He will forgive our little sins in such cruel times when death knocks at our door and peeks in our windows.*"

With this the woman slipped from the shed into the howling night, and was gone.

But Maria could not sleep. He lay on his bed listening to the many voices of the wind, as they were the many voices of death laughing and mocking the frailty of this little garden shed, and with it the little games he had played beneath its shelter, and the little dreams that lived behind the brittle sticks of his ribs.

His spirit was heavy; not only with this adultery committed with the good man's wife, but with many other doubts and sorrows. It was not long ago when, as a monk he had kissed a crucifix before saying his prayers, not before he lustfully fornicated; when he lifted his heart to God, rather than give it to lascivious games with a woman. It was not long ago when he regarded love as a divine spark in the cruel, fickle seasons of the world, one that gave his shambling life a purpose and meaning, and not a casual pleasure. It was not long ago he regarded the loving of a woman as a salvation from life's storms, a pardon from death itself, rather than an exploitation, a whoring for bread and shelter.

Unable to sleep, Maria rose, and from the shed's door he looked out into the night. The storm had glazed all with a thin icy snow, but now all that was left was the wind, its breath still furious, but its arms emptied of snow. High above, the rags of clouds were being shredded away from their thick tent. Breaking away, they were scudding across the dark sky, silky and white, like the wind-blown down of giant thistles.

The moon was in its last quarter, and from time to time it shone bright and gypsum white through the disintegrating clouds, and when it did, Maria was gripped with an urge to run into the cold forest; to forget all the sorrows and confusion his heart had gathered. He had an urge to run naked into the forest, to howl at this beautiful moon, and to find a she-wolf with which to share his howls.

He lay back down on his bed, and burrowed warmly beneath its blankets. As sleep crept near him, tears slowly trickled through his beard, but he did not know why. And when at last sleep had seized, claimed, and spread its shroud over him, the eye of the moon continued to burn brightly in the clearing sky; laughing, like a beautiful gypsy woman through his dreams.

* * *

HENRIETTA, the tavern keeper's wife, proved good to her word. Not only did she work her cunning upon her husband, until he was agreeable to having a vagrant musician play music in his tavern, but she had procured a sleeping room in a house not far away. The house was owned by a friend of hers, a frail, purblind spinster lady who was glad to have the company and the protection of a male lodger. All had happened quickly and easily, the result of kissing a crucifix and a few amorous embraces in a garden's shed. Maria was welcomed into the small tavern family, and guaranteed a safe warm room for the winter.

Instruments were soon found and loaned from several villagers: a lute, an accordion, a flute and a fiddle, even a *zampoigna*, with which Maria at once began to nimbly and magically play. With the gypsy music he coaxed from these various instruments, he sang, and sometimes danced, captivating his sparse audiences with the spectacle that had come to visit their hilltop village. And when the winter storms came, or at any other time when his strong arms were needed, Maria was ready for any odd job asked of him. Even his living conditions were pleasant. The room was well furnished and well lighted, and the old spinster lady was kind, but never intrusive or meddling.

The one thing that bothered Maria was the adultery that he was committing with his benefactor's wife. Still, Henrietta was very clever, and he did not think their liaisons were suspected. Once a week, on market morning, when the old spinster hobbled away with her sack and stick, she would come to him under the pretense of bringing him a basket of bread. Answering her tap on his door, she would enter, set the basket down, and immediately undress. She would lay down upon his bed, naked, all but for the necklace with the small crucifix that fell between her breasts. Without a word she would hold it out to him, solemnly, and as it was a ritual, he would kiss it, as she would kiss his. Her face would soften, and her arms would open with invitation and favors.

"It is a little sin we commit. We will not go to hell. God will forgive us."

As on that first night, she would give herself completely; clasping him with her strong arms and legs as she wanted to crush him, to kill him, and killing him take, and not receive what he was giving her. Still, with each of their succeeding intimacies her passions seemed to increase the more, until at the last, in the gasp of her final pleasure, she would kiss the crucifix, as if asking God permission to finish, and once receiving that permission, scream out strange and incoherent things, things that seemed uncharacteristic of her even tempered nature.

"Kill me you bastard! Kill your little whore! Kill me! Murder me! Make me hate you, Giacomo!"

After their lovemaking she would say nothing of the things she had said in her passion. She would only bring her crucifix to his lips for him to kiss; and as he did, she would kiss it with him, as they were completing the ritual they had performed together; as they were asking for a mutual forgiveness for what they had just flagrantly committed.

"He will forgive us. He has sent His Angels to watch over our naked bodies as we play and defile them, and He will forgive us."

She would then rise, dress, and with only a few prosaic pleasantries, return to the tavern. Only a few times did they engage in anything resembling a meaningful conversation.

"Thank you, Brother Maria. Thank you for being a very good lover, and a very sweet man. I like you very much. Do you like me?"

"Yes Henrietta, I like you too. You are very sweet."

"But you do not love me Maria; I can see it in your eyes. And I understand, and accept that you do not love me. There is another woman in your heart. I can feel her. When you give yourself to me, you are giving yourself to her. You are very kind and sweet to me, but she is your lover, not me. She owns your heart, as very likely you own hers."

"You are very sensitive; and very wise, Henrietta."

"You are a wanderer, and a dreamer of dreams. Such men love many, but in reality love only one, and that one is a face he may never find, and a breast upon which he may never sleep. It makes me happy to be the lover you give your dreams; the lover you are looking for, but may never know.

I must go now. I have much to do at the tavern. I will come again next week on market day. Gino is busy then. Next market day the Angels will watch us play again, but they will not blame us, because we will kiss our crucifixes before and after we sin."

On another occasion they spoke, again as she was about to leave. It was a strange conversation, one that in the end gave Maria great relief, but with that relief, a premonition of concern.

"Another woman is in your heart, Maria, both of us know that. But do you know that I love another man, and, if I may make a confession, two men that are in my heart?"

"Two men, Henrietta?"

"Yes, Maria, two men. You see I love Gino very much. He is a fool, but he is sweet and good. But Gino, through no fault of his own is short, fat and bald, and is not a good lover. He has a big heart, but a small cock. He tickles me with his love, but he does not punish me with it.

When I was a young girl I had a handsome lover. He was a strong man, like you, and almost as old as my father. One day he made love to me against my will. I hated him for doing that to me, and when he raped me a second time, I hated him even more. The more he raped me, the more I hated him. But in a strange way I grew to love him. I grew to fear what he did to me, and that fear grew into a need; a need into love.

That is when I began to kiss my crucifix, and when he was raping me, even when he was drunk, I made him kiss it too. I held him tightly, as I hold you tightly, and when I did I screamed out my hatred, my hatred that I now think was love. He is dead now, and I miss him very much. I miss what he did to me in the stable and beneath the hedges in the sheep-walks. When you are inside me, you are this man, this man whom I loved and hated as no other."

As she was about to open the door to leave, she stopped and spoke again.

"I will come no more on the market days, Brother Maria. I will not ask you to love me again. I have ears and I have eyes. I know other women give you kisses, and let you hold their breasts in the doorways when the tavern closes. Jesus knows our secret, Maria, but I could not bear it if Gino knew it. I would hang myself if he learned another was doing what he cannot. I have chosen the very rafter, the big one in the tavern's parlor, where I would prove my love."

She opened the door and began to leave, only to stop, reenter his room, and close the door again. There she stood, speaking softly; not to Maria, but to the door itself.

"You see I think love and hate are the same thing, Maria, a creature that forever wears two masks. But when it takes off its mask, it is no creature at all. It is a ghost; a ghost none has seen, but all are forever trying to hold

or to murder. Thank you for letting me be your ghost, Brother Maria. I look forward to hearing your music in the tavern tonight."

In this strange mad way, and with this strange confession, the love-making with Henrietta ended. In the tavern she was always pleasant and polite, even cheerful with him, but never again did she knock on his door on market day. Never more did she ask him to kiss her crucifix.

Still, Maria did not begin other affairs with other women, even when they invited him to dark places in the streets, kissing his hands, and then thrusting them inside their thick coats, offering their warm bodies to him; whispering in his ear that they knew places where they would do things that would make him very happy.

A strange need to be alone overtook him. It mastered him as no woman could master him with sly and artful seductions. This strange need laid claim to him; possessed him; made him its slave; its hopeless lover. Suddenly the games he played with women, these games he played so easily and expertly, lost their charm and savor. They now seemed more rehearsed than heartfelt; like the tricks he had once taught the bears to perform in the streets. More than these frivolous games that pleased, but never satisfied, his soul was aching to slough its skin; to bud forth another flower; to sing another song.

But what was this flower? What was this song?

He asked Henrietta how he might obtain a quill, ink, charcoal and a modest supply of parchment sheets. Soon his request was known throughout the small village, and soon the villagers, eager to show their appreciation for their eccentric musician, furnished an abundance of the things for which he had asked. One by one Maria began to fill these sheets with the dreams and voices, long imprisoned, long aching to be released from his soul.

Slowly, shyly, this great urge, the urge of flowers wishing to bloom from the dark roots of pain in his heart, began to show their strange, lovely, sometimes wicked faces before him.

Hour after hour, and day after day as the cold, snow and famine gripped the desolate hills and forests about him, Maria sat at his table sketching images that had touched him most deeply since his departure from the abbey, many years ago. It was a great unburdening, the sketching of these cherished possessions he had collected, collected and preserved in the secret chest of his soul.

.....the face of the shepherdess who had first lured him away from his

vows and his life of prayer, she who beneath the great old tree taught him to be a man.....oh, what had been her name? How could it be that he had not asked her name?.....Would he see her again?......Or was she only a pretty bird, the first of a great flock of pretty birds that had flown through his arms, a treasure of the wind, but never to be his again?.......

.....He sketched ragged children weeping in the streets, crones leaning on sticks, drunkards at their cards and dice.....maidens, gentle as nibbling deer in the vineyards.....lusty harvest men wielding sickles, shirtless in the frothing wheat.....a singing thrush, a fox, a splendid horse....the hungry, on their hands and knees in the fields, digging like rooting pigs for snails and worms......whores giving pleasure to sailors on the quays.......

.....And once he had started, there seemed to be no end.....fields and forests, hills and valleys, flowers and storms clouds.....the Spring, Summer and Autumn that cloaked the hills with their green, gold, and brightly colored liveries......the drunken, the starving, the thieving.....the simple, sly, cunning.....the brutal, craven, stupid.....men to whose throats he had held knives, left drubbed from his fists.....lovers impassioned faces yielding, giving him the secrets in their wombs........

.....yes, the women he had loved, those he could not remember, those he would not love again.....their embraces becoming one embrace that for an instant had held him, stilled him, blessed him.....made him forget his pains and needs.....their faces becoming one face, one face contorting, grimacing, becoming unlovely when it yielded its beautiful secret in passion's fever.... like a man with a knife in his heart, a woman in her final throes of travail, a criminal swinging from a noose, twisting to his end.....life's secret identical with love's secret, love's secret identical with death's secret........

Beside some of these sketches he wrote lines or verses of poetry, poetry that he had scribbled on little scraps, saved in the catch-all clutter in his satchel, but many more times, retrieved from pieces of his memory. When he wrote these lines, like epigrams beside the sketches, he was surprised to see how different they were from each other; ranging from the reverent to the profane; from the shy and wistful, to the shameless and overtly depraved, even wicked.

Which, if any, were true? Who was this Brother Maria who professed his love in both pure and shameful ways? Whose tracks had been those that had followed him in the forests and the snows?

......I do not want to only know your lips,
Though petal soft, and coral pink are they,

But to deeply, more sweetly stay, taste, explore,
With a more lasting, lingering kiss,
To find your palace of deliciousness,
That hive where woman's sweetest sweets are stored,
To burrow in love's den,
play winter long in wicked bliss.......
Or.....
......Your fingertips, like budding violets,
Your toes, like pinking buds of roses,
Oh, when thus peeps such sweet beginnings,
A beauty that hints, but not discloses,
Who may guess the lovely secrets, that,
Their treasure hunter finding,
Riots wildly in their garden's depths?
Tonight, young maid, when moonlight glows,
Let me be the first to find,
Let me be the first to know......
Or......
......I want to know what lends you wings,
That root that tapped, beget your flower,
That jewel, the nerve of Woman's tenderness.......
O let your body wrap me like a shroud,
Beneath that shroud, your nails tear at my hair.....
Toes, heels, teeth, digging to my bones!
O murderess of my love's despair,
Scream in my ear, 'my love is yours alone!'
A whisper, whose thunder, every star may hear......

Upon the largest sheet he drew sketches of women's naked bodies posed in erotic and orgasmic postures.....erected breasts, arched backs and necks, thrusting bellies and buttocks.....thighs that were lifted and widely spread.....vulvas, staring like the quiet eyes of owls, or the fierce eyes of wolves....faces in the throes of their sexual ecstasies, grimacing as they were being murdered in the moment of their uttermost pleasure.......

In one of the top corners of these many sheets he sketched a man's face, one that was half-concealed with a raised cowl of a monk.....its demeanor austere, stern and pure, looking upon this orgy of images with a stony equanimity.....with neither disdain nor rebuke.....with a kind of wise acceptance.......

On the opposite corner he sketched a woman, a beautiful young woman with deep dark eyes and long lustrous hair......her face as he always remembered it.....with a smile that accepted all with a secret joy, a higher joy that could participate, but not be bound by lesser things......

Yes, these were the voices of his soul, they that had guided and mentored him.....one of rigidity, discipline, and spiritual austerity.....the other of sensual play and abandon.....one who lived and loved in abnegation of his senses, considering them something lesser, and a great danger.....the other who delighted in all things sensual, giving them permission to take wing. These were they who dwelt deepest in his heart; that together had given his being its ragged sojourn.

Upon the top center of this sheet he drew another figure; a muscular, uncouth man with a beard and long flowing hair. This figure lacked any hint of civility or moral rectitude, rather a complete negation and absence, even a savage ignorance of such things. But it was not without its own kind of beauty. The figure was disheveled, almost barbaric, as if hardened by the elements, but at the same time softly honed by them; as he was born of them, belonged to them; as he was part of them. Surprised at what he had drawn, Maria found himself thinking the figure of this man was most like the bears that he and his mother danced with in the streets; sweet and docile, and yet wild; guardians of a sleeping strength none could defend against when waked. He smiled, and drew an earring that dangled from the bear's ear, one in the shape of crescent moon and star.

Below this man that others knew as 'Brother Maria', this half-man, half-bear sketch of himself, he simply wrote:

"The bear that broke from its cage."

He sat before the last blank sheet. Time and time again he had brought a piece of charcoal to it, only to time and time lay it back down again. He rose and looked out his window at the small village; the bare trees, and the gray bleakness of the late winter day that spread over chimneys and gables. Why could he not sketch what was most dear and lovely in his heart? Why could he not sketch those dark eyes, that shy sweet smile, that kindness that had come to invade, haunt and command him?

He had loved many women, but had he ever been loved in return? He was not sure. Was there an aloneness inside him, a natural aloneness, his father's aloneness, one that was wild and shy of being tamed; one that could not be reached or touched; one that could not be loved; a ghost forever wandering, eternally banished? Or was it that no man or woman could be truly reached, touched or loved, that all men were itinerants, and love was the bread, like the altar's wafer they nibbled on their way.?

Many women had surrendered in his arms, but had he ever surrendered in theirs? After lovemaking had he not often laid awake, feeling the emptiness of the night that was one with the emptiness of his soul? Did he not sometimes feel as he was a stranger to the one who clasped him with her arms? Did he not sometimes feel ashamed when he thought of the intoxicated heights he had reached only moments before, heights that once attained and enacted, were quickly rushed upon with a lonely dark despair, sometimes even a loathing of both himself and the one whose favors he had enjoyed? He thought of Henrietta, and the half-mad, half-wise things she had said about being forgiven when she kissed her crucifix, endlessly repeating this debate in her heart like a cuckoo bird its song. Were love and worship poetic names given to rage and sin.....the heart a cuckoo bird repeating its lonely call forever?

He had written her many letters, and with them many poems, but he had sent only a few, and in drunken bouts and fits burned the others. He had sent them with the most reliable couriers he could find, and they had professed they had delivered them to the young lady with a limp in the Siena bake house. But there had never come a reply to these letters. How could there have been? She had seen firsthand what kind of man he was, even after she and her father had so tenderly nursed his wounds and brought him back to health and strength. She had seen with her own eyes his profligacy. She had heard the women that had clung to him when he returned late from the taverns, drunkenly giggling and propositioning him in the square below. When he was gone for days at a time, she knew where and how he had spent them. When he stumbled up the stairs she could smell the reek of lust, and she could hear the lies in his lame excuses. And yes, she had seen him bloodied with the blood of other men, those he had brutishly throttled..... and another, yes, that other man he had killed.

Still, when he had softly sung by the fire, she had stepped from the shadows like a gentle deer. She knew he caroused; she knew he was an inveterate womanizer; she knew he had murdered; but still she had stepped from the shadows with the delicate grace of a deer, not with love, but with wonder; not with shyness alone, but with nobility; not to listen to a man's music, but to a man's soul.

He had written a poem for her today, but holding it to his fire's flames, his hand had frozen in a war of nerves. Pitting a fool's dreams against the *wisdom of priests and sages, he chose the fool's side, and laid it back on the table; as it was a sacrifice too dear to sacrifice. After drinking much wine, and a walk through the snowy streets, he returned to his room with a fixed resolve, one that crumpled it up and threw it into the fire's red embers.....only with cat-like quickness to kneel down and deftly pluck it out again....prompted by a will greater than his judgment.....one that arbitrated a compromise with his foolishness, converting the poem to prose....prose that was enveloped in a letter.*

.....There is music in your beauty, a kind of poetry that speaks with eloquence through every part of you; that rhymes your feet with your eyes, your fingertips with your smile; your heart with every chore you undertake, making each chore a gift. It is as though the light of your soul is uncontainable, insuppressible, that it is not content to remain only in your soul, but it must exhale its sweetness from the sill where it flowers, sharing it with all that the sun kisses. You are made of sunlight, a sunlight that makes every part of you sing and flower in the festivals of day and night, festivals whose feasts are tables spread with kindness, your kindness. You, Sister of Light, look upon the world, and like a candle, bless its darkness with your flame.

And your hip? It is not a disfigurement in the eyes of the Angels, why should it be in mine? For I, with they, look not on it as a broken wing, but as a much mightier one, one that like an eagle's, lifts you to heights that others may not visit. You have not fallen from your nest, but soared above it, lifted with the nobility that beats its wings within your breast. It is this noble spirit that allows you to fly above what so clips the wings of others. It is your spirit, my darling, that lifts you above the iron chains that weigh men's feet to the stones of this world. It is your noble spirit that I honor. It is your noble spirit that I love.......

It was several weeks later when the courier, with whom he had entrusted his letter, returned from Siena with a reply, the only reply he had ever received from her.

"To the sender: Sir, the one to whom you address your letters and poems does not exist. She is a ghost who dwells in your dreams, or in the fumes of many mugs of wine, or again, in a kind of twilight of jollity that joins both worlds of excessive dreams and excessive drink. Please send no more to this ghost, this ghost that dwells only in your mind, and not in any little bake house of this world. The shutters of its window are closed, as is its heart."

A week later he received another letter, one sent in her father's hand.

"Brother Maria: I of course read all of your letters and poems to my daughter, for she cannot read as well as I; (a little thing I picked up while dressing wounds of those poor bloody bastards fighting that bloodthirsty Bishop's bloody war). I also am the scribe that aided her reply to you, a reply whose blind fury of sentiments could only be attributed to a theatrical tantrum of tragic heroic love.

I feel quite sure that you understand, Maria, those woman winds and storms of passion, and I am quite sure you have come to respect and navigate about them, and in the end, with a sinking poop and drooping sails, be utterly defeated by them. I also feel quite sure that you understand the spirit that lives in my daughter's being, an extraordinary spirit indeed, one that is as gentle as a flower, but is capable of mustering the terrible winds and fires of dragons.

Gypsy man, Brother Maria.....son, (may I call you son?)..... in the great mysteries that God spreads all about us in His nights and days, do you understand the mystery that is His hardest nut to crack; that sweet and bitter nut of a woman's heart? If you think you do, you are a bigger fool than even I. And do you know why it is so uncrackable, Maria my son? Presuming to be life's queen, a woman is only a little girl forever falling from a make-believe throne.

To whit: After I read your letter to my daughter, her eyes were swollen for days, as they had been stung by wasps. Frankly, I never saw them prettier! And again, another 'to whit'; I think my daughter is in love with you, son; and I think she could give you a lovely, gypsy brood of sots, louts and rois-terers, and if all else fails, perhaps a useless, blithering Saint, or a paunchy, bloodthirsty king.

P.S. A strange sickness is afoot. Is killing Florentines like our Sienese never dreamed of killing the cocky bastards. Ha! Doing our bloody murder-work for us! Rumor has it that it is in the country about us, and will be rapping its knuckles on our gates any day now. Even at my crotchety age, and with my penchant for plum wine and doting on widows' plump asses, I fear I may be called upon, as death has a way, like a good hunting dog sniffing a grouse, of sniffing doctors out.

I beg of you, my son, to remember the driveling of an old drinking companion. Though a blasphemer, a lecher and a blusterer, his words were as earnest as a Saint's prayer when the subject was his daughter. Some are calling this thing worse than Saint Anthony's Fire, worse than the God damned famines, a plague of some murderous sort that our loving God is murderously, lovingly casting upon His children, and, well, the thought of leaving this accursed world is not half so bad as the thought of leaving my darling alone during the Reaper's heyday.

Yours; and whether her heart, and herobstreperous, harebrained reason admits it or not......Katrinika's.......

....

....

CHAPTER TWO

THE GATES OF HELL

Part I
'Isabella'

Spring: 1348

SPRING arrived, bright and warm, its ample rains and abundant sunshine promising an end to the famine's scourge. The oxen were hitched and yoked, the ploughboys readied with hats, togs and boots, and at the urging of the mighty beasts, the teeth of the ploughs began to once more bite through the mellowing soils; soils at last free of winter snows and autumn muddiness. The disenfranchised began to be called back home, and once more be employed. Boards were taken away from shop doors and windows, their floors swept and their shutters thrown open, admitting fresh air and sunlight; announcing that their owners were not dead. The dangerous bands of robbers began to disband; the camps of the starving to decamp and diffuse; the sick and the discouraged, to dream of living again.

Good men that had gone rogue, and had been driven to malfeasance by starving bellies, once more became respectable, quitting their marauding for the seed sack and the plough. Women were seen digging in their gardens, planting bulbs and erecting stakes, and exchanging tattered shirts for fresh ones on the sticks of scarecrows. Primly potted flowers were placed on window-ledges, dabbing the drab streets gay. Rose-vines budded, and once more began their green odysseys up their trellises to the sun.

The grapes and olives blossomed, and wildflowers bloomed where drifts of snow had melted. Shepherd boys began to play upon their flutes; women to sing at wells; old men to talk of youth and lechery. The barks of dogs rang more clearly; the songs of birds, more sweetly. Once more maidens unbound their tresses, and began to comb them in windows, playing the *coquette*, soliciting songs and whistles from the young men that fell into their spells.

Brother Maria also felt the freshness of the new season, and the hope that it brought with its sunny and singing waves. The sunshine pierced the darkness of his thoughts, freeing them from the dungeon where the winter through they had been imprisoned. The sketches and verses he had dawdled with for long gray days in his room, now seemed exercises in wasteful idleness; trivial and unimportant, like fallen leaves that had been usurped by new green ones. His vivid memories were just that: *memories; and what were memories, however painful or sweetly poignant, but ghosts in the parade of the living?*

And his musings of death, and its mastery over life's vain dream? Death would come when it would come, despite the pleas and prayers of men's defenses and fears. Life was meant to be lived, not brooded upon. He was a 'tzigan', a gypsy. He had his mother's heart. He held Eternity in his fists. It flowed and sang through the rivers of his blood.

With the genial weather, and the prosperity it promised, a new enthusiasm woke in Maria. His fingers danced on the lute's and fiddle's strings with new eagerness and vivacity; his voice became more resonant; a new skip and spring sprang in the steps of his gypsy dances, even as he remembered dancing in the village squares when he was a boy.

And in accord with this new enthusiasm, his audiences began to grow, congesting and cramming the small tavern to its gills, until, on the first warm nights, he performed outside in the arbor; candles at his feet, and a vault of candles above his head. The villagers, young and old, knowing of the resident gypsy, and wanting to cast off the dolor of the famine with a night of gay music, at twilight stepped from their huts and houses, and made their way to the tavern.

"Why not go listen to the gypsy sing tonight at the Bear Cub Tavern? Gino the Bald does not charge, although I think Gino the Fat would like to. They say he is a real gypsy, one with a silver earring and a bright scarf wrapped about his head. They say he plays many instruments, and sings beautiful gypsy songs that he once sang about fires in gypsy camps. They

say he even waves batons of fire when he dances, sometimes with flowers between his teeth."

"They say he was raised in a gypsy caravan. When his mother died he fell into Christian hands, and became a monk. That is why his name is Maria. Both Gino the Bald and Gino the Fat say he is very polite and honest, and does not steal.….."

"….. only the women's hearts, for they say his melodies may swoon a Tartar."

"Whether he is a true gypsy, or a defrocked monk, or both, he is a magician with any instrument placed in his hands!"

"And with any woman's heart, young or old that his blue eyes flash upon."

It was at this time of renewal and rejuvenation that Brother Maria was visited by two strange dreams, dreams that seemed incongruous with his popularity, and the spirit that was revivifying the villagers, and the country-side all about him.

Both dreams were unnaturally strange, and seemed imbued with allegorical significance, but a significance he could not construe; as they were more portents than dreams. Both of these dreams involved his sleeping room, and the one window that looked to the street below. Both of these dreams seemed sown with bits and pieces of memory.

The first dream……

It was a snowy night, and he was writing at his table. He heard his name ring out: "Brother Maria! Brother Maria! O handsome gypsy of the Bear Cub Tavern! Come play with us! Please, come and play with us!"

And with this he heard snowballs pelted against his shutters from the street below. Smiling, he opened the shutters to the cold night air, and the moon that shone brightly, making a sparkling counterpane of the roofs and chimneys, and shimmering like glistening marble the street in which a number of girls were playing in the snow.

Strangely, the girls were not clothed for the bitter cold. They were naked; all but for large furry boots and mittens, boots and mittens that seemed the large paws of beasts. They also wore hooded vests, furry vests that did not cover their bare breasts, but whose hoods concealed their faces. They were playing; some wrestling in the snow, ending in postures that seemed lewd, even profane. Some were kissing, not upon their cheeks, but like lovers, long and lingering upon their mouths. One of the girls had knelt in the snow, and was burying her hooded face between another girl's naked legs, eliciting a giggle of delight from the one so kissed.

When they noticed that his shutters had opened, they removed their hoods and lifted up their faces to him, faces that did not fit the slender nakedness of their young bodies......faces that had grotesque snouts, bloody teeth, and eyes that swam with savagery......faces that were not the pretty faces of young girls at all, but wild and savage, like boars and wolves of the forest.

"Come, handsome gypsy from your cage! Come play with us in the snowy woods! Come! It is too dangerous in the village. Come! Be an animal like we have become animals! It is too dangerous to be a man. Come to the forest where it is safe, and play with us the games the animals play!"

Several nights later he was visited by a second dream, one that was laden with terrible memories......memories fraught with warning.

This time he was not called to his window by snowballs cast at its shutters, but by a scratching, as by a twig that a wind was scraping against them. He had opened the shutters, only to find the window not open to the cold night, but as if walled by a latticework of bars; as the window of a prison, or the grille of a confessional. Before it was one veiled in the veil of a nun; the twig that he had heard scrape against the shutter, no twig at all, but a bony finger that this figure had reached through the bars.

The holy sister whispered strange words to him, words that no holy sister would say.

"You must free me from this prison. I have money, much money......you need not worry about money. You must only protect me, love me as you like, as you love your tavern whores, only you must protect me....yes, I will be your whore and we will be very happy together; I, your whore, and you, the user of your whore......for I have much money......you must only love me, love me as your whore and we will go away and be very happy........"

Mesmerized by her strange whispers, he had watched as her veiled face had pressed close to the grille, and then bringing her hands to her throat, she had suddenly rent her robe, exposing her voluptuous breasts. Pressing them against the grille, she whispered:

"They are pretty, are they not? And you would like to give them your kisses, would you not, gypsy boy? But first, my lips, you may and must kiss my lips, and then I, and they are yours."

Made dumb with what was being offered him, he pressed his lips to the grille, even where she pressed her veiled face.

"Oh, but this veil, this veil, you need to kiss your naughty little whore,

537

your whore without her holy veil."

And with this she tore the veil from her face, revealing a face decayed and skeletal, caked with clay and worms.....as it had lain long in a grave.

For several days afterwards he had thought of these vivid dreams, trying to decipher messages from their strange morbidities. But with the warmth and flowering of spring, they were washed away, and he gradually forgot them.

Once more his blood began to thaw and hatch awake its needs, needs that were seeds he had thought had frozen dead, but had only lain dormant beneath the snows that had fallen on his heart. Once more his eye dwelt upon, and received special delight in the shapeliness of breasts and waists; slender arms, dainty knees and taut hams. Once more he was roused by teasing titters, sly smiles, and storms full of lightning flashing in deep dark eyes. Once more he was challenged to hunt and play.

.....and again all of their smiles became one smile, their eyes, one pair of eyes....one Woman who was as much a mother as a maiden.....as much a seductress as Madonna.....moonlight in her hair.....the perfume of blossoms in her sighs......

"Come Maria! She is a cripple, and I am not. She cannot play the games I know how to play. Come, you will forget her in my arms. I will do things she cannot. Come Maria, come play, play like the beasts of the forests play!"

* * *

HER name was Isabella; a young, very pretty and vivacious girl, one that had caught his eye, as he had hers as they passed in a street; she, surrounded by a little flock of children, children obedient and responsive to her directives, lending the impression they were her young brothers and sisters. Maria had given her a broad smile, and she, caught off her guard by both his effrontery and his handsomeness, crimsoned, and with a brief shy smile, and a spark that flashed alive in her dark eyes, continued on her way.

He saw her again the following week, this time with only two of the smaller children clinging to her hands and skirt. She did not see him, and this gave him a moment to study and admire this one that had snared his eye, waking his loins from their winter sleep.

She was a peasant girl, but one that was not abjectly poor, rather as Maria supposed, one whose father was probably a member of the independent peasantry, the yeomen that had broken away, or had been dismissed by their masters; one that had not been driven to the fields and the forests by the bared fangs of the famine. Her hair was long, glossy, and trailing, and was adorned by a small pink ribbon tied in a bow about a single plaited tress, giving its raven luxuriance a simple decoration, like a candle.

There was a voluptuousness about her; not showy or gamesome, but quiet and true; one that modesty could not hide, only encourage.

Maria felt his eye grow keen and steady.....his blood to quicken, his heart to hunger as he studied her.....a prey not to seize, but to invite with the song of courtship.......

.....the slender tapering waist, firm round breasts, the full haunches, buttocks, thighs.....the silver ring of her laughter, that like a bird sang to the hills and valleys, and to what slept deep in man's creature....'Oh, I am a pretty-feathered, sweet-throated bird, but I have no one to sing to. Oh, the summer moons and blossoms are brief, very brief.....oh, how I wish to sing to another.....to love, love, love!.....I was made to love....to sing and love, to love and be loved!......."

Maria jogged after her, and in a few strides addressed her, startling her vivacity into silent demureness.

"Good day, signorina! Please, may I have just a word? You see I saw you last week....perhaps you remember, because I think you saw me too. Well, I've come to know most faces in the village, but I do not think I know yours, and, well, I thought I might introduce myself. My name is Brother Maria.....a different name I know, but you see I was once a monk in an abbey, many years ago.....and as for 'Maria'.....I think because my hair was gold, and my mother thought I was very beautiful, like a girl......."

The girl was made shy by his bluntness, and kept her eyes downcast; the children, even more shy, peeking from behind her hips and the curtain of her skirt.

"Signorina, might I ask you your name?"

But the girl, unused to such forwardness, especially by one whose hair, eyes and dress were so different from any man she had ever seen, made no reply.

"Most ladies have names, ha! at least those I have known. I only thought that if I would hap to see you again, I might halloo you with your name."

But the girl would not be cajoled, and as speech had been taken from her mouth, would neither answer nor lift her eyes to him.

"*Her name is Isabella!*"

The little girl had dared to peek from behind her older sister's hip and blurt out her name, only to bury her face with laughter back into the skirt from which she had peeped, receiving a playful slap for her audacity. Maria smiled, and knelt down to the sheepish little child.

"*Is Isabella your big sister?*"

To which the child peeked out again and gave an enthusiastic nod of affirmation.

"*Could you tell your sister, Isabella, something for me?*"

Again the enthusiastic nod, peeking bright-eyed from behind the lovely thigh and hip that were hiding her.

"*Would you tell her that Brother Maria plays lutes, fiddles and bagpipes, and that he sings songs in a tavern called the Bear Cub Tavern? Would you invite her to come listen to me some time? I would like your sister to hear me sing and play.*"

The child nodded, but although her older sister's fingers played with her hair, she did not lift her eyes or speak to him.

"*Could you tell your sister, Isabella, something else for me? Could you tell her that Brother Maria thinks she is very pretty, and when I see her it is like the full moon rising with a band of angels into the night sky?*"

Maria did not see her again for several weeks, until the spring had warmed and deepened. One night when he was singing in the arbor, he had thought he had seen her face in a shadow. Looking again, the face had disappeared. When the night grew to a close he looked for her up and down the streets, but he saw no trace of her; as the face had been a pretty phantom. Yet he was sure that it had been her. When he closed his eyes to sleep, he saw her face as he had seen it in the arbor, glowing young and radiant, her eyes, swimming with sweetness, fixed upon him.

But several nights later, when he again glimpsed her face appear and disappear in the smoky shadows he made an excuse to abruptly halt his playing, and stole out the tavern in search of her. He saw her running away, and easily caught up with her.

"*Isabella! Isabella! Please wait, pretty one, I want to speak a few words with you!*"

Out of breath, and surrendering to his chase, she looked in a defensive, half frightened way at him.

"Oh, it is you. Yes, I think I, why yes, you are the man who spoke to me in the street, a musician, a gypsy musician if I am not mistaken."

"Yes, lovely one, a musician, a musician whose lute has been singing your beauty since the hour I first saw you."

"I, I must return.....you see we have friends in the village we are visiting, and I only walked out for a breath of the spring air......"

"Then stay for another breath, and we shall share its sweetness together."

"Please, I must go. You speak very nicely, uh, Brother Maria is it not?......"

"My name is the name you wish it to be. Pronounced by your lips, you would make sweet the names of the bad Angels."

"I....I must go. I should not have gone to the tavern, yes, I went to the tavern, it was silly of me, silly and wrong......you see I have never been to a tavern before. If my father knew he would be angry.....but our friends said there was a man who sang gypsy songs there, songs that he brought from the mountains, songs that touched the heart deeply....and well, you had invited me."

"And did my songs touch your heart, for they were played and sung for you, sweet Isabella. And if they did not, though they gained the applause of heaven, I have failed."

"You say sweet things, sir, flatteries I am sure. Yes, they were sweet, yes, very sweet, almost like lullabies.....but I am saying stupid things.....how could they be for me?....but, really, that is a very nice thing to say, Maria, or is it Brother Maria?.....oh, I really must be gone!"

"I want to hold you, Isabella!"

"Hold me!"

"Yes, I would like to hold the lovely Isabella in my arms."

"But I could not let you do such a thing....and why......"

"There is no 'why', only this great 'wish' in my heart. It is not for the bee to know 'why' it is drawn to the lily, but only for it to obey the reason it is a bee."

"You do speak sweetly.....a poet, yes, a poet......but I must go......"

"Besides, it is written in the stars. I am a gypsy, and you must know that gypsies read many things in crystal balls, and what are the heavens but a giant crystal ball that spell out many things with the letters of the stars. Look, I will show you!"

He pointed earnestly to the starry sky, at which the ingenuous girl lifted her eyes in concert with his. Bringing his face close to hers, he pointed with his finger, and slowly and sweetly spoke in her ear:

"*There, see. it is written: Brother Maria must hold the beautiful Isabella. It is a thing that is meant to be.*"

Spellbound with his words, only to suddenly realize she was being toyed with, the girl broke into a small laughter and shrank away.

"*You are sly, a kind of wizard with words, Maria.....I must say it is a different name, a beautiful name for a man......but, well, I do not know you.*"

"*That is why I want to hold you; that you may know me a little, and I may know you a little.*"

"*But......*"

"*One cannot say everything with words. One must touch and taste the world as well, as sunlight kisses its flowers.....do you not agree?*"

"*Yes, when you put it that way; there are things that cannot.....*"

"*I like you very much, and I think you like me. I want to know you a little more, to touch and taste you, to know the beautiful flower of your heart.*"

"*How can you say that I like you, when.....?*"

"*Do you not like me?*"

"*No.....I do not know.....it is all very strange.....you seem a very nice man, a very handsome man with a beautiful voice.....your songs stirred my heart, very deeply...but, well, I do not know you.....yet I feel in some way I know you very well.......*"

"*Oh lovely Isabella, at night when I close my eyes, your beautiful face is before me, welcoming me to the garden of my dreams....like the moon, it gives lamp to the darkness of my soul. Have you ever thought of me when you have closed your eyes? And if you have, do you not like me a little, Isabella?*"

"*Yes, perhaps a little....but no, how can you ask me such brash things?*"

"*Because you came to hear me sing, tonight and other nights, yes, I saw your face, your lovely face glowing like a white flower in the shadows..... because you ran from me through the streets like a doe of the forests, like a shooting star, like a beautiful ghost.*"

"*You speak strange words.....lovely words, yes, strange and lovely words......but I cannot stay longer, I must go back now to the house where I am staying.*"

"*Come, only for a moment, let me hold you, here, in this dark place where no one but the stars may see us, and they, sworn to silence for eternity!*"

She paused; equivocating; and in that pause he believed her beautiful dark eyes more than her words, and more than her eyes, the tremor in her voice, a kind of signal meant only for love's ear; a sweetness breathed from her soul, rich with the spring song of her sex.

And then she was in his arms, in the darkness, receiving and timidly giving back his kisses, and as she did he could feel desire making trespass on her heart, tempting and threatening, assaulting the fastness of her innocence for the first time. He could feel her many fears trying to restrain her, defending her against the enemy that her heart was telling her was no enemy at all. He could feel her curiosity, stronger and more demanding than any fear, mastering her defenses, begging her surrender.

Lost in this first, abundant sweetness, she pressed into him with her breasts and thighs, their secrets for the first time found, and found, guilelessly given.....her heart breaking into its first blossom, a blossom that murmured into his ear like a little child:

"I love you, Brother Maria, I love you very much!"

With these words he let his hand fall over the pillows of her loveliness until it found and held her most tender place. She started with a little gasp, but he continued to tenderly hold what had been first found.

"O my little angel, I know a place not far from here, a stable with soft dry hay.....we could be so very happy there!"

But at this she broke away from him.

"No, I cannot! You are a sweet man, and I like to give you kisses, because I like you very much, yes, very much.....yes, I think I might love you, yes, I think I love you Brother Maria.....but I cannot give you that.....not now, I am not ready to give you that now. Oh I must go. They will worry, and I must go back to them before they look for me."

She broke abruptly from his arms and stepped into the starlit street, only to return to the shadows where he remained.

"Will you come visit me, Brother Maria? You need only ask for the Molierri farm.....it is only a half day's ride away, and the roads are safe there. Will you? I think my papa would like you very much.....you see my mama died, and I only have a papa.....and my little brothers and sisters..... you are all they talk about, and they are always teasing me about the gypsy man who told me I was very pretty. There are places I can take you to, secret places where we can kiss and say sweet things to each other.....oh, but I really must go......will you come see me Brother Maria? I will say prayers on my pillow, so that the Angels will tug at your cuffs and bring you to your Isabella......"

*Again she stepped into the starlit street, but again returned to the
shadows where he continued to stand. This time she began to unbutton
her blouse, not hurriedly, as had been her words and steps, but calmly, and
purposely, as with a great, ceremonious decision made by her soul. Exposing
one of her breasts, this precious jewel of her young womanhood, she looked
into his eyes and whispered:*

"You may kiss it if you like, Brother Maria."

*At which Maria bent down, and as he was kissing the ring of a queen,
gently complied.*

*Buttoning back her blouse, she stretched up on her toes and kissed
Maria's mouth, and then whispered in his ear:*

*"I would like to give you many such presents, darling, but for now I may
give you only my heart. Come visit me, Brother Maria, and until you do,
know that the heart beating in your breast is Isabella's."*

* * *

Several weeks passed before Maria borrowed a horse and set out to
ride to this new young love. He had been asked to help with chores
at the tavern, as well as with friends of its kind keepers, and he could
not refuse, especially after the great kindnesses lent him through the
winter. In addition, a snap of cold weather came from the north, gray
clouds bearing chill and bluster; pregnant with the fears of the famine's
dreadful return.

Still, anticipating his departure, Maria was filled with a new
happiness, the old happiness, the only happiness; *the love of a woman
in his heart.*

Gone were the malaises of nostalgic regrets, and a dark forest of
memories sketched with charcoal, and the scribbling of words, like
epitaphs on the stones of graves. Gone was this cold season in his heart
when pretty eyes and smiles neither reached nor roused him. Gone was
love's vanity and silliness, making way for the music of love's eternal
song; giving a meaning to all that he did, and all that he was.

This lovely young peasant girl had swept away all such dark children
of his despair. She was a warm fresh breeze, one that breathed through his
days and nights with sweet songs and perfumes, fluttering with a tender
lovely breath the curtains of his slumbers, and splashing moonlight into
the rooms of his dreams. Once more love let fall its sweet dews upon

him, waking his dormancy, begging his loins and heart to bloom the seeds he had thought cold and dead. A warm spring wind now breathed through him, a wind named '*Isabella*', and though the world was filled with fear, war and hunger, and the rumors of a strange disease brought by sailors, he, Brother Maria, was alive, singing with a peasant girl's love.

Once more love invigorated him, pricked awake his senses and languid dreams, but this time its beauty was a darker beauty, one that, however much he tried to dispel or ignore it, bore a frown in its radiant smile. Many seasons and years had passed since he had left the abbey, and in that time he had come to understand that love was also a kind of war, and the blissful victories it offered came with much trepidation and danger, and often with irremediable sacrifice and cost.

Once more he was a soldier, a mercenary heeding love's call, one that was bearing scars in his heart. He knew that as deeply as love had rewarded him, so had its sword deeply wounded him; that its armor had not made him a brother of the Angels, only a tried combatant. Like soldiers, staring into their fire the night before a battle, he knew that for its cause he could bleed and die at dawn.

......the parting from warm arms and naked breasts into early mornings, bleak and gray and cold, the world's wilderness stretching before him...... from passionate lovers who in the end preferred warm hearths, houses and gruff husbands to his embraces and the poems he whispered in their ears..... waking stiff and rusty in barns and stables, damp fields, riverbanks, groggy, hungry, lonely,.....unsure of his next meal, where he was going, who he was......

......the painful refrains of tearful partings..... "I love you, Maria, but I know that I cannot have you for a husband, because only pretty songs and pretty dreams will own your heart."..... "You are a magician with your hands, words and kisses Maria, but does the magician ever reveal his soul?"..... "Your eyes are beautiful, but they are also sad, O so sad, a sadness deeper than any sadness I have ever seen."..... "One day you will go back to the forests, the gypsies and the wolves, and I will spend my life climbing to the top of a high hill, looking for your return, a return I know will never come......."

There was something dark; something treacherous, even fatal in love's games. He had learned that love was not a songbird he could keep in the cage of his heart, or a bright fish he could catch in his ardor. Love's pretty bird could indeed sing, but after some time it would fly away. Love's glittering fish could indeed be caught, but as he slept it would swim through the net of stars.

In love's first spice-laden breezes was sown the dark seed of its doom. Though sworn with all the vows and protestations of Heaven, it was not to be relied upon; not to be trusted. Though sweeter than any honey, it could quickly spoil to gall. Though brimming with a sea of promises, it often was as hollow and fitful as the wind. *And yet it was a honey, a delicious honey.....and yet it was a voyage, the only voyage......*

At last the weather turned bright and sunny, with a waxing moon and a wind from the south, and on the third day after its change Maria rode into the country-side, his heart burning for this newfound sweetheart whose kisses he could still taste, and whose young body he could still feel fitting so perfectly into his. He borrowed a horse, a beautiful mare from the tavern keeper, and refusing a saddle, he rode bareback into the new glow of day, but not before Gino the Fat railed at him good-naturedly.

"*Well, take good care of her Maria, ride her hard and gentle, ha! Bareback! Both the mare and the one you will take to the hay! Love her, whoever she is, like Gino the Fat would like to, and Gino the Bald dreams of, like neither of the poor devils will ever love one of Eve's daughters again! If you return before night falls, shame on you! And if we do not see the gypsy fiddler again, we will know his fiddlestick got the best of him!*"

He rode into the infant day, glowing, like a new-forged sword; brandishing his expectant love, as he would help light the earth and sky. He felt the horse grow warm beneath him, until he too caught fire, his blood warming and pounding one with the horse's heart, as beast and man had melded into one flame, as beast and man were lovers in the youth of the world.

And as he rode and the sun rose, the spring welcomed him with its glories. All was a part of his heart's song: the flowers and birds, the swift clear brooks and the forests' fresh green fires. All were refrains of the same theme; of the new season, the new day; the new love that this human rider was bringing into it; each refrain shouting, as his heart was a bugle: "*Love is the meaning of all! Love is life's reason that Man has found in his heart, that even death cannot take away!*"

The ride promised to be a happy one, especially after winter's confinement, as well as a long one, at least a six hour ride to his sweetheart's farm. But as he rode into the morning, its golden happiness seemed to curiously fade and cloud.

For the first hour or two, those he saw in the fields, those who had risen early to move stones, mend fences, and ready their oxen, as well as those who were seated on rattling carts on the same small roads he was riding over, were bright and jovial, greeting him with halloos and blessings of the Saints. But as he reached midway in his journey, these smiles and salutations seemed to lessen, and as it were, to cloud. Those he saw in the fields did not wave their hats and cheerfully call out to him. They seemed instead to crouch and slink away, only to study him with distrustful eyes. Even the children, playing outside their houses, were rushed inside at the sound of his horse's hoofs; and the place where the road forked, the half of its fork blocked by wagons, and grim, unfriendly looking men who were armed with clubs and sickles......

And when he shouted out: "*Is this the road to the Molieri farm?*", he received only the slightest, most curt and cautious nods; nods without friendliness; nods with scowls and wrinkled brows; nods that could not hide the fists at the men's sides.

It was as he was riding into a land under a spell, and the closer he neared Isabella's farm, the deeper, more gripping and more menacing that spell became. Though the sun brightly shone, it could not dispel a gloom that seemed to hang over all, and though the breezes softly combed and tickled the new leaves of the trees, they did not sweep away the heavy silence that had settled among them. As he neared the farm he saw no one at all; not in the fields, not on the roads, not near the farmsteads. It was as though the country-side was forsaken of the living; as though only the deserted husks, bones and memories of the living remained; as though he had entered a kingdom of ghosts. The spell was more than a spell; it was a pall, one that had draped a cloak over the lantern of the sun.

He had imagined himself galloping his horse into the farmyard, but instead, he dismounted, and on foot slowly led his horse tenuously up the lane. He had imagined her raucous little brothers and sisters first seeing him, shouting and running to greet the gypsy man with long blonde hair and a silver earring dangling from his ear. But there were no children; there were no shouts; there were no dogs with wagging tails; there was no greeting at all. Even the song and chatter of the birds in the bushes rang hollow, muted of happiness, as they were afraid to sing in such a sad and heavy silence.

There were other signs; signs of life being discarded, of its being abruptly halted midst its vigor and industry: a plough standing unmanned in a field, still fastened to its harness; a spade and shovel standing in a garden, and in that garden a rooting pig; a wagon full of rotting hay; a cow loudly mooing, as if begging to be milked; goats in the flower patches; chickens broken from their pens, some of which were casually pecking their way in and out from the open door of the small house.

And near the house the crows in the trees, and some roosting on the peak and sharp pitch of the roof.....some fallen into a black flock on the ground, a flock that, when his approach scared them away, not into the blue sky, but into the overhanging trees, revealed a carcass they had been feasting on.....a human, half-eaten carcass, naked of all but the remnants of a ragged shirt......a little boy's carcass.....its eyes pecked from its head, and the viscera from its ribs.....all of its soft and naked places....the nose and ears and lips, the neck, the breast, the genitals......

From depths reached only by horror, horror whose teeth had rent the very pith of him, Maria screamed forth a bloodcurdling scream:

"Isabella! Beautiful Isabella!"

But it was a scream that was answered only by the bedlam of the crows, their caws and wings lifting from their roosts to hover in a dark corona above.....their echoes echoing endlessly, hideously, as into empty halls that had been vacated by the living.

Approaching the house, Maria did something he had not done for many years. A short distance before the door, left widely ajar, gaping, as if staring like the eye of an evil spider over its web, he fell to his knees and made the Sign of the Cross, his lips whispering to a God he had long forsaken.

"No, dear God, make it not true, make it not true."

Slowly, and without a knock, he entered to darkness, darkness and a dirt floor scratched and pecked at by chickens, chickens that had been lent a strange license to do so.....and a scurrying, squeaking herd of rats that, thick as ants on an anthill, seemed to have made it their home. But after only a few steps, he retreated outside again, the darkness too dark for him to see, and the malodorous stench too pungent for him to breathe.

With a grim determination, a determination that was a sentence, as one that had been doomed to descend the steps of hell, he once more entered the open door, his shirt covering his nose and mouth. He flung open the shutters, shutters shut by hands that would never open them again; vainly attempting to make leave what had invited itself to enter and inhabit.

Room by room he let in the bright spring sunshine through the windows, only to illumine a grisly charnel house of death; death inflicted not by famine, but by something even more uncompromising, more unmerciful.

The corpses were recognized only by their clothes, for what disease had not blackened and bloated, and death had gruesomely disfigured, the rats had eaten, having feasted on those feasts spread before them......on ears, noses, lips and eyes.

Only the father's face had partially survived, for the rats could not reach where it hung, broken-necked in its noose above his dead children, their half-naked, half-eaten corpses strewn on the floor and beds beneath him. He had probably been the last to perish, preserved by the perversity of fate to watch each of his children agonize and die, corrupted by a contagion against which his strength and his love were impotent to defend. His tongue was black, and prodigiously swollen, spilling from his mouth like the head of a dead snake. But most peculiar, death's assassin had left his eyes open, though bulging from their sockets, as if even in death he was sentenced to stare upon the morbid corruption of all that he had held dear. Yet for all this, Maria thought this strangled man had shown a kind of nobility at his end; unwilling to let death dictate, and separate him from what he had most loved.

And Isabella?

When Maria had flung open the shutters, disrupting and scattering death's feasters, the sunlight rushed in, the sunlight anxious to wrap her in its golden arms. Like a queen, she lay in a bed with three of the dead children, two of them in her arms, as if they had sought her out in the tribulation of their dying, even as they had sought her out in the brief joy of their living. Her pretty face, as well as her dainty feet and hands had been greatly eaten away, but Maria knew that it was her by the ribbon that was still bound in her hair, as fresh, pink and prim as when he had first seen it adorn her beauty in the village street.

As in a spell, a spell whose web death's spider had woven, Maria stood in a kind of enchantment before her. He had the strange impulse to lie down beside her, to have the rats swarm over him too; to share her corruption. He wanted to take her in his arms, kiss her, and whisper tenderly in her ear.

.....“I am here, Isabella, as I promised I would be, the gypsy fellow you heard sing in the Bear Cub Tavern....the gypsy fellow who told you that you were beautiful, like the moon is beautiful.....I have come to look into your

dark eyes, and to ask if I might taste the honey of your kisses......"

......For the past two weeks he had done little else than think of her, waking in the nights with infatuated dreams of her......imagining the kisses and caresses she would give, and the fruits he would taste in the pleasure garden of her arms......blissful dreams being dreamed even as the tender fruits of her body were rotting in this bed, the loot and plundered booty of death.......

He did not know whether to feel ashamed, or guilty, or degenerately foolish when he thought of the fantasies he had enacted with her, the endless games he had played in his dreams with her in blossoming orchards and soft spring grasses......imagining her little moans and purrs......her first passionate embraces......while all the while she lay here, a putrefying corpse.

He could not quit the room where she lay. He could not leave her. He was held spellbound, strangely enamored, death's spell a kind of consoling madness to know that he was bound in the same web in which she was bound......his dreams, ambitions, pleasures, snared by the same threads of the same web woven hour by hour, day by day and year by year by the same spider......some prank that had cleverly, inescapably snared both of them like gnats......a lovely maid and a golden-haired gypsy, together.......

Gripped by a fascination beyond his reason, he remained standing before her, this queen upon death's throne, to give reverence, pay a strange tribute.... to worship death's augustness by breathing its foulness into his lungs, its fumes, like wine fumes dizzying and inebriating his brain..... letting its horrors parade into his heart, and to feel that parade set to ruin its pride and petulance. Yes, he needed these moments to commune in death's cathedral, to stand in adoration before its sacred mystery......the gruesome throne before which all men must prostrate.

He looked at the half-eaten body of the girl, and the children she had held at her last in her arms......now fodder for the herds of vermin, and he imagined the eye of death's spider, dilated with its evil omniscience, laughing at him......laughing at all the sweet things he had wished to tell her, and the moments of ecstasy he had wished to share with her......the spider, bloated with its poison, gloating over its lovely prize......the pretty face it had nibbled until it was no longer a face......hissing at him... "You too are in my web!".......

But it was not too late to cheat this spider of its feast. No; Isabella and her brothers and sisters, all of life was too sweet, too innocent to perish so grossly. He would deny death its last epicurean pleasure. He would spoil its feast, and not let it lick such lovely bones. He would laugh back at this eye that with an evil mirth was mocking him.

There was a small door near this bed of death, a small door that opened to a garden enclosed by a breast-high stone wall. The garden was unplanted, but its earth was newly turned and furrowed; several spades and shovels stuck upright, standing ghostly in its midst. Near the wall were a number of blossoming fruit trees; apple and fig and plum. Maria went to these trees, and gently, methodically began to break off large twigs of their beautiful flowers. Gathering armful after armful, he returned time and again to lay them beside and upon the corpses. As he did he spoke to them with words that defied death's madness.

"Isabella, you must tell the little ones when they wake that the gypsy man will play the fiddle and bagpipes for them. Tell them they will sit on his knee and he will teach them to play gypsy tunes that his gypsy mama once taught him in the mountains of his childhood; mountains called 'the Carpathians'.

You must tell them not to be afraid of the large black birds in the trees and on the roof. Tell them they are Angels wearing black frocks, like priests, and soon their screams will change to beautiful hymns.

And you must tell them that you are wearing a terrible mask only to frighten and play with them; and that soon you will remove your terrible mask, and their older sister will be gayer and prettier than ever before.

I met your papa outside, Isabella. He was chopping wood. I like him very much, and I think he likes me very much. There is goodness in his eyes and sincerity in his heart, things that I see in your eyes and feel in your heart. I told him that I liked his dark-eyed daughter, and that I thought she was very pretty. He smiled, and his eyes filled with little tears, like drops of morning dew on flower petals, for I could tell he was very proud of you Isabella, yes, very proud. Yes, darling, I like your papa very much.

I will stay with you, sweetheart. When you wake we will steal away to some secret place, where I will hold you in my arms. I will pick flowers for your hair, and place some pretty buds between your toes, yes, I will make a queen's crown of your little toes. And you, my angel, you will teach Brother Maria to love, for I am not sure he ever learned to love, and in return I will teach you to read the words in the stars, words that sparkle brightly, and say forever: 'Brother Maria will love the beautiful Isabella for eternity'.

And thank you sweetheart for your present, your braid of hair, and the pink ribbon tied about it. Your gypsy lover will carry it near his heart, in a satchel, for as long as he lives."

Maria knelt in the brook. He had stripped nearly naked, having cast his clothes into the open door of the house, to be burned in the flames that were now sending black billows with the hysterical crows above the trees.

But the clear water of the brook could not take the stench of death from his nose and lungs. The brook could nor purge the scenes of horror in his brain. He would ride back in nakedness. He would enter the village under the cloak of night. He would tell no one of these things he had seen, and how he had tried, in vain, to burn the spider of death in the very web it had woven.

. . . .

. . . .

CHAPTER THREE

THE GATES OF HELL

Part II
The Countess Agatha

Late Summer and Early Autumn, 1348

BROTHER Maria did not speak of the things he had seen that day, or the thing he had done to destroy their vestiges. However, there was a man, a drinker and a frequenter of the *Bear Cub* who had seen him ride back into the village that night, nearly naked, and he had quickly told others, trying to make a great jest of it. Soon Maria was assailed by a gang of jokesters, men whose good, well meaning natures received his moody taciturnity in return.

"*I thought it was a simple peasant girl had won your heart, Maria, and not a hell-cat!*"

"*The things I have heard about you, Maria, are all wrong. You are not the ravisher, but the ravished!*"

"*My question is this: did she wear her skirt or your pants after her throw in the hay?*"

"*And was it you or she who did the throwing?*"

"*Did our fiddler leave her moaning, snarling or laughing after his fiddling?*"

Even Gino tried to tickle Maria's sullenness, to a great roar in the tavern.

"*At least the belladonna left the mare's bridle!*"

But one night one of the jests probed too deeply. It was told by the man who had seen Maria's return, he who had reveled in the acclaim he had acquired from his accidental, late night espial. He was terribly, blithering drunk, and he had persisted in nettling Maria for an hour, trying to pique and provoke him.

"I'll bet the lass never knew such a mounting and butting by such a rutting bull before! I'll bet you left her dizzy and moaning in the straw! I'll bet your love killed the poor thing......"

Maria sprang at the man, and as to strangle him held him by his collar, pressing him against a wall.

"The only one that Brother Maria will kill is you, if I hear one more word of your drunken claptrap!"

It had been an uncharacteristic, if not an unnecessary show of violence by the gentle gypsy musician, but one that did not go unheeded. All gibes and jokes about the event came to an abrupt end, and with the same abruptness the gypsy returned to his sweet and melancholic musicianship. Only Henrietta detected a change in Brother Maria, one that, like a mist, from time to time cast dark moods over him; as of something that had deeply touched and troubled his soul.

But there was something else, something strange and unforeseen that had come to concern Maria, as well as to concern, even trouble all others in the village.

What Maria had formerly regarded as bits and pieces of rumor, was now heard with a more attentive ear. He listened closely, avidly when people spoke of ships infected with a pestilence arriving in the ports; bloated corpses of sailors floating ashore, and those of the living, drunk with fevers, staggering down gangplanks with death upon their backs. He heard of some ships, manned only by the sick and the dying, and others called *ghost ships*, only by the dead that were not allowed to port at all, kept from the shores by thousands of burning arrows that lit up the night sky. He heard of those falling dead in the fields, the streets; upon church steps and before holy altars.

He heard of men who watched the stars, men called astrologers, who had seen comets with flaming tails trail across the heavens, some that seemed to singe the rooftops; expostulating on *Saturn* and *Mars*, and other signs of the stars and seasons. He heard of men who had received visions of burning *Angels*, rains and hails of blood, tempest-tossed coffins, ghostly howls, shrieks and moans about churchyards, all portending some calamitous event. He heard that the disease turned its victims mad, raving and frothing, that it swelled and crippled the body, set to burning fevers the mind, and in days, or even hours, choked dead the blood. He had seen several peddlers in the street, men with dark hats and dark velvet coats, men who with wild eyes and gesticulating arms collected little crowds about them; selling cordials and amulets, even dead toads. He had seen old women letting loose white rats in wooden boxes fashioned into intricate mazes, predicting terrors to come.

Maria remembered how his mother and other gypsy women set up little tables in the backs of their wagons, and in the candlelight read the palms of villagers who brought them garden fruits, and even chickens and rabbits to pay for their predictions. She had said this was reading 'fortunes', and that the human palm was as vast as the heavens if one knew how to read it; that Man was the child of Heaven, and Life had given him the planets and stars in his hands to hold, and to help navigate his way through his days. He remembered that once she had read his own palm, and when she did a cloud came over her face. She had said he would become a wanderer, one who passed through the seasons as both their friend and their stranger......one whose fists would fight against their storms, even as his heart would love them.

He thought of his discussion with Giovanni, and the reports from the monks that had told of a terrible contagion arriving in the south, and was crawling northward. And now this: a similar pestilence, pushing southward from the north; like two giant waves, swelling and crushing all in their paths. He imagined they were two horrid monsters; one male, and the other female, staggering towards each other, smelling and lusting for each other's evil, seething to spew their poisons. He thought of his abbey days, and the beast that Saint John had seen. He thought of Isabella, and the spiders and vermin that he had cheated of their dinner.......

Still, spring gaily marched into early summer, even as such things as *famine* and *sickness* had never been, and *health* and *plenty* had always abounded for this people and their fields. There were only rumors of a few corpses being found here or there, and they strangely mutilated with a strange corruption. But these reports came from a good distance away, and seemed not to touch upon their lives, or hazard their hilltop village in any way.

But gradually these rumors waxed into more than rumors. Those who found themselves in the path of this distemper's ugly rage attempted to flee it. Those with means: merchants and guildsmen, gentry and royalty, and indeed, any with a cart and horse, and even many on foot fled the contagion, seeking the hilltop villages where the air was believed to be more pure, and the winds able to whisk the foul miasmas of disease away.

Stories reached their streets, and at night found their hearths, and the ears of those who sat about them; trickling into the tavern where Maria continued to sing his gypsy tunes before a fire on the cool nights, and beneath the stars on the warm ones. These stories told of roads being clogged by refugees fleeing a tide of death-dealing contagion: coaches and carts and horsemen, beggars on crutches and the sick on litters, the weak who fell to their knees, only to be left behind by the strong; of families whose backs were bent beneath the sum of their life's belongings; of wailing children, cursing coachmen, moaning invalids; of drivers mercilessly whipping their drays, and drovers goading their oxen; of robbers and looters whose practiced hands seized bags and slashed ropes of bundles; those who preached, those who hawked, those who had frozen numb or mad with the fear of their own mortality; the congested streams of human fear slowly fleeing, climbing into the hills to save their lives.

Though still distant, this exodus was not entirely unfelt in their tiny village, the dark rumor gaining credibility with the arrival of the count and countess to their castle, situated like an eagle's eyrie on top of the steep hill that rose directly above their streets. Normally used as a retreat in the late summer to escape the baking heat of the valleys, the Count Ferdinando, and his Countess Agatha arrived early, their arrival seen more as an escape than a retreat; a sign that the fantastic stories about the sickness were not to be taken lightly, as the weather had not yet turned hot.

But rather than an occasion of dread, it was one of great excitement to the village and the surrounding country-side. The count's coach and entourage of courtiers, emblazoned horsemen, and caparisoned steeds made its way on the road that cut through the heart of their village, before starting its steep rocky climb to the castle.

The coach was brightly painted, varnished and gilded, and the horses that pulled it, magnificent and proudly stepping; the guards, stern and stately uniformed. The villagers lined the way with beaming faces, shouting the blessings of their Saints, and throwing flowers before the hoofs and giant wheels that bore their royal guests. In one of the coach's windows was seen the count, his chubby, ruddy face returning this show of rustic welcome; waving and throwing kisses of his appreciation. But the countess was not seen, only guessed at, sitting in the soft leather upholstery of the coach's box. Although the villagers pined to have a glimpse of the count's young bride, the curtain was pulled across the window where she sat, and no glimpse was given or offered.

It was a fortnight later when Maria first saw in plain view the countess. He had heard of her great, all but unmatchable beauty, but a beauty that was aloof; marred with a marble coldness and *hauteur*. Although the villagers loved and warmly received the count, a reception that he warmly returned, they had not the same feelings concerning the cold-blooded young countess.

With escorts, the countess descended from the castle to the village in the mid-mornings, when Maria was still in bed, sleeping away his carousals and late night performances at the tavern. Besides, he was not interested in royalty. He did not care much for them. They and their habits and fineries had nothing to do with him; nothing to do with the hills and forests, and a vagrant's lonely ways and dreams.

But this morning as he looked from a garret's small window upon the sun-scoured street below, his eye fixed on a young, beautiful woman stepping from her gilded coach; a beautiful woman dressed in scarlet velvet, lily-white gloves, and a matching white scarf that wrapped her face like a nun's wimple, its tails laying like drifts of snow upon her shoulders. His eye fixed upon the countess, and despite his antipathy for such royalty, a deep part of him was quickened; and quickened, unexpectedly challenged.

He stood before the half-open shutters, partly dressed; waiting for the countess's reemergence from the shop she had entered. The garret in which he stood was not his own. It was rented by the one in the bed near where he stood, heavily asleep with the opium they had smoked together. Her name was *Larissa*, a woman ten years his senior, who was always eager to share her companionship after the closing of the *Bear Cub*. It was rumored she was a whore, one used and paid for by drunkards and cheating husbands, a rumor whose veracity Maria suspected was on occasion true, although she had never asked, or even hinted at payments for the company she offered him.

Since the terrible event of Isabella's death, he had chosen not to accept any of the young pretty ones that had invited him to their pillows. The experience of his visit to Isabella's farm, its tender, pent-up expectancy dashed apart by a house of corpses had harrowed his soul. He wanted nothing to do with beauty's bewitching spell, and the dangers it seemed to attract.

Was it that he had come to believe that in love's every tender smile, and in every innocent kiss it offered, there was something disingenuous, something murderously sly, dark, evil; as if even flights of the most intoxicating passions were illusions, and behind the mask of their sweetness laughed a ghoul, ready to gnash apart the foolish prey of the heart?

Abstaining from the prettiest, he had taken instead several that were not pretty, that were hard and coarse, the jaded booty of drunkards and ruffians. He had found himself preferring their unkemptness and their indelicacy. With them he had not needed to spend words of flattery and seduction. He had no need to woo them. He had not asked to unbutton their blouses, lift their skirts, or to ask to explore their secret places. If they had briefly struggled, he had not heeded that struggle, and had either walked away, or continued to enjoy what he wished to enjoy. For the first time he had not asked permission to be gratified. For the first time he had not whispered poetry in their ears. For the first time he had not kissed his lovers when love's embrace had been completed.

Maria looked at the sleeping woman, steeped in the oblivion of her opium sleep; naked, and only partially covered by the ragged blanket. The morning light poured through the cracked shutters, and fell upon one haunch and buttock, her stomach and her breasts; enlightening in sharp relief how age, dissipation and promiscuity had polluted her once youthful loveliness.

The haunch and buttock had lost their slender firmness, and were now bovine and flaccid, all but beefy. Her stomach was bloated, and hung in a superfluous slab, while her breasts fell like un-milked udders down her side. Robbed of her paint and jewels, and the animation that drink and opium lent her disguise, her face appeared gray and tired, and cracked with spider webs of wrinkles.....her chin beginning to double, and her missing teeth showing as she wheezed through her mouth, as it was a fish's gill. In the morning light he could see the hair between her legs had lost its tender mossy-ness, and had become coarse and oily, like a brackish growth of weeds.

.....for an instant Maria thought of his youth, and the life in the abbey he had forsaken....the pristine courtyard and arcades, the gleaming altars and chapel, the roses and the swallows.....for an instant he filled with nausea, the nausea of regret to think he had forsaken such purity for such a

fetid nest, and its cavern into which he had spewed his holy dreams.......

Maria's attention was called to the sunny street below, as the countess reemerged from the shop, surrounded by a gaggle of those wishing to behold her royalty. She stopped before her coach, removed her veil, and turned to her adorers, giving Maria, with the aid of the summer sunshine, an unadulterated view of her regal, superior beauty.

And it was this diamond-like superiority, its many facets sparkling in the morning sun that smote Maria's heart with a hundred reflections of its perfectness. He had never seen such a divine creature before; such a perfectly beautiful woman; her beauty carved from a purer marble of purer flesh; a beauty that suffused each part of her, like the crimson that suffuses the rose's every petal.

.....her profile, carved by a more expert hand.....the noble brow, nose, chiseled chin.....etching eternity itself, as they were too perfect to ever fade away.....each part of her, tapering and fitting.....shoulders, haunches, thighs, taut as a bowstring, and yet as fluted as a swallow's wing.....each part as strong as it was delicate, at once as goddess-like as warrior-like, as ready to wield a broadsword as it was to purr warmly against one's cheek........

.....and her hair, lovely and lush and golden, even as his hair was golden.....and her eyes, blue as heaven's azure, even as his were blue..... as she was a twin....as she was a sister.....as she was an equal, matched in competition before him.......

She was a lioness, yes, but no ordinary lioness. She was made only for a lion that lorded over other lions; for one that was worthy of her regality. Embodied in such a creature was a will that could not be cozened or seduced; a pride that could never be broken, only surrendered; her beauty, so sure of its own miracle, it bristled with brazenness.

.....to unclothe such a creature would be to unclothe an Angel.....to love such a creature, to know the secrets of Heaven.......

.....a creature bred to rule and command.....a mare with the spirit of a mountain stallion, one whose only rider had been the wind.....a cameo raised like a throne from the dirty straws of this world.....a star making clods of a queen's jewels.......

.....one could only kneel before such beauty; one could only be subservient to it; for only in serving it could one come to own it.......

Just at this moment the coach door was opened by one of the brightly uniformed footmen, and the count himself emerged to the applause of all. Beaming ruddily, he went to the countess, and taking her hand, kissed it, and then escorted her ceremoniously back into the coach.

At once many things were told, shown in sharp relief in the bright summer sun.

The count was many years her senior, so much that, if they were not count and countess, they could be easily mistaken for a father and his daughter. The count was thick and paunchy, his short squat stature a full head less than his youthful wife. His hair was thin, and his beard and moustache grizzled, while her hair was luxuriant, and sparkled like harvest wheat. His face was so ruddy it seemed on the verge of purpling, as it had become permanently flushed with wine; her complexion was luminous and fair, almost translucent, like sunlight falling through almond blossoms.

As the coach lurched away, Maria turned from the window, and went to a small stand upon which was a basin of water. Above the basin was hung a small mirror on the wall. Leaning down to the basin, he drenched his face with generous scoops of water, and then peered at the reflection in the mirror.

He had aged; yes, he had aged, perhaps more than his actual years. There were tiny crow's feet that had crept out about his eyes, especially when he was tired, or in the mornings, after late bouts of drinking or lovemaking. Gray flecked his beard, like flakes of dirty snow. Several of the tavern girls had teased him about finding gray strands in his golden hair, and had begged to snip them out as little keepsakes and prizes.

And his heart? Yes, sometimes something autumnal.....a tiredness, a vague feeling of having had enough, and a want for rest and sleep had settled there too. Had drinking and wandering aged him prematurely? How long had it been since he had left the abbey and Giovanni? And the rat-eaten corpse of Isabella....it had entered his heart like a knife.....perhaps its sharp blade had helped age him also.....killed something vital inside him......

Still, he was not an old man. Youthful vigor still flowed through his blood, and young women still flashed their smiles, bared their knees, laughed their titillating laughter and waited in the shadows for him. But this thing with Isabella.....her rat-eaten face, the bloated, putrefying corpses, and the haunting image of her father hanging broken-necked above her, his eyes still open, staring frozen at the horrors that death inflicts on life's honest toils and simple goodness.......

Once more Maria bent down and splashed water on his face, but this time when he looked in the mirror his eyes brightened, and a small smile crept from out his beard. With his wet fingers he combed back his unshorn hair, and with his fingers brushed his moustache and beard. Leaning close to the mirror, he looked into the blue eyes under whose spell so many had fallen, the spell that only he knew was cast by someone other than Brother Maria; a man whom he had long hunted, and in his hunting had become. He knew he was looking upon the father he had never known. Yes, this was he, the man who had once loved his mother; the man whose seed had flowered into this face that was looking at him in the mirror.

Quietly he dressed and began to leave, but as he reached the door he stopped, and looked back upon the naked woman sleeping on the bed. Had his love for her been a blind whoring, or was her slovenliness also possessed of a kind of beauty and sweetness, one that had danced like a moonlit butterfly in the wine fumes and the dark flames of his dark desires, that in the midnight hours he had given his heart to?

Maria bent down and gently kissed her exposed buttock; and then covering both it and her haunch with the blanket, as with a coverlet of silk, he quietly left the room.

Tomorrow he would climb the steep hill; the one on which the castle stood.

* * *

THE following morning Maria climbed the hill to the castle, un-barbered and un-groomed. He wanted first to know more about this sleek golden queen before he initiated any kind of courtship. He wanted to learn more about her character, her habits, and the schedules that she kept, so that he would know what tactics to employ, what strategy to use in the conquest of such a royal prey.

There was a spring in his step and a smile in his heart as he climbed up the steep road. He picked a bright red haw, and held its bittersweet twig between his teeth. He hummed some little melodies, and like a small boy imitated the calls and songs of birds he heard in the thickets about him.

His heart was light, and his steps full of bite and vigor. Gone was the gloom and melancholy that had invaded his heart. Gone were the grotesque images of death; those he had set aflame, and now only remained in a dark corner of his mind.

But what had happened to him in such a short while? What had lifted this cloud from his soul, replacing images of rotting corpses, a terrible spider and its web with morning sunlight, flowers, and the sweet caroling of birds?

He knew very well what it was. The moment he had looked upon this celestial creature he had felt as one called to battle; challenged to taste the fig of her beautiful mouth, and swim victoriously between her golden thighs; to melt the cold haughtiness in her heart, and make yield her woman secrets in his arms. Oh, to unclothe such a creature would be to unclothe an Angel!

Yes, that was the reason he felt so renewed. That was the reason that the youthful prime of his manhood had returned, scoffing at, and driving the gray and drear of age from his blood, making him feel foolish that he had succumbed to such notions and fears.

Yes, that was it; this lovely ambition of caressing the rich garments from her loveliness, of encircling her slender waist with his arms, of smelling and tasting her nectars.....to harvest her breasts, feeling them swell and prick alive in his hands.....to know her woman's most secret bloom, that surely must rhyme golden with her tresses.....yes, that was what had filled him with youth, as if baptizing him with new reason and purpose as he climbed to the castle's walls on this bright morning.

He smiled at these thoughts, that like happy trumpets blared free of the snares of guilt and conscience, from the stale robes hung in death's closet..... as if he had been newly confessed.....Oh, was love not a kind of confession?.....oh, let his kisses up and down this lady's arms be his penance!...... oh, little thrush bird, how sweetly you sing! Shall we sing a duet?.....and the salvation of his soul?.....oh, he would let his soul melt into this beautiful woman's body, and find his salvation there!

Now as the castle's turrets appeared above the trees,, and his senses were piqued and poised, never more eager for a new adventure, how meaningless and monotonous, like games played by a prisoner in his cell, the playing of his fiddle, the drinking of wine and the throwing of dice.....the frolics with tavern tarts....how predictable and uneventful, as his life had been a nag hobbling to the market of old age!.....But now this mission, this crusade to win this beautiful woman's heart! His life was not worth the living, if not to win its royal treasures!

Upon reaching the castle he found a small group of people milling about its gates; castle guards and keepers, as well as peasants gathered to chance see and pay tribute to the royal couple. Asking and insinuating, Maria learned bits and pieces about the beautiful countess from they who daily waited upon, and paid regular tribute to her. Most of the things told to him were more scandalous than flattering, and yet in Maria's ear, they were intriguing beyond all measure.

He learned that the countess seldom spoke to any, save to give an order. There was a strident coldness about her, an icy chill, one that amounted to an arrogant aloofness; that made her flower-giving votaries feel as they were chattel. Yes, she was possessed of an incredible beauty; blue eyes, a flood of long golden hair, and a slender, porcelain delicate figure, but she wore this great beauty like a knight wears his armor into battle, impervious to his foe's spears and swords.

Maria learned salacious rumors about her; how, less than half the count's age, she must have acquired her countess-ship.

"*She's young and pretty she is, and has the old count wrapped about her little finger.*"

"*Yes, and we all know what part of the old count she's got her little finger around.*"

"*She's got him by the balls all right; got a leash on his cock, and pulls the kind old man around like a silly little dog.*"

"*The count is a goodhearted man, but his brains are in his balls, and he's given them to her; she's the keeper of the jewels.*"

"*Which she stuffs in the cleft of her bosom, while showing her busty diamonds to the world.*"

"*I cannot imagine the count laying his great belly upon her, like a great toad on a daisy.*"

"*I do not think he does. My horse says that she rides him, and not him, her.*"

"*My horse says she neither mounts nor is mounted, but finds other clever ways to spur the count on his rides.*"

"*My horse says that once the crown was on her head, the count begged for any crumb would come his way.*"

"*…..they say there are whores about the castle, whores that perform the marital rites that are absent from their marriage bed…….*"

Maria learned her name was Agatha, and that she came from the castle each morning for a ride in the country-side. With anticipation he waited, until suddenly the castle trumpets sounded, and the gates were ceremoniously opened…..*and yes, there she was…..in a riding suit of wine-red velvet, replete with cap, boots, silk scarf and whip…..icy, aloof, imperious, with slight nods and quivering nostrils commanding all about her.*

Feeling like a common pauper, Maria stepped to the rear of the crowd that now rushed forth to greet and pay homage to their countess, and there studied her, not in adoration as the others did, but with another kind of worship, another kind of need.

......Oh, to unfasten, button by button that velvet suit, to tenderly squeeze the two peaches that hung woman ripe beneath it.....to free the silky luxuriance hidden beneath that cap, caress the small white feet nestled inside those boots.....oh, to melt that cold heart, humble that regal haughtiness.....disarm her of that whip with kisses, and make such a creature sigh its secret desire in his ear!.......

For the next week Maria repeated what he had done on that first day. He climbed the hill in the early mornings, waited for the clarions to blow and the castle gates to open, and when the countess appeared on her beautiful sorrel, not sidesaddle, but as a man upon a charger, he would slip unnoticed to the rear of her greeters; observing this goddess in one of her smart riding suits, as she was a huntress off to the hunt.

In the interims Maria was not idle. He had tailored for himself a splendid new wardrobe; including a light blue blouse, a canary yellow scarf, and a new coat of forest green. He repaired his boots, and polished their leather agate smooth. In addition he cut and trimmed both his beard and his hair, making sure to pluck out the gray hairs that had insolently invaded his goldenness. He also did something he had never done before. As to assure himself of his handsomeness, and to measure that handsomeness with the great beauty he saw issue from the castle gates each morning, he inspected his reflection closely in a mirror.

.....Yes, he was still young, strong and handsome. Yes, he was this golden lioness's golden counterpart and equal. Yes, he was one to conquer such a special creature, and make her surrender in his arms. Yes, he had willed age's first assault away; cowed it back into shadows that the sun could not reach.......

One morning, groomed and polished, and ready to make his hike up the hill, he needed to make an errand to the Bear Cub. As he was about to leave he saw Henrietta. She was at the well in the inn-yard, and when he walked past her she spoke to him, even though she did not lift her eyes as she continued to draw and fill her buckets.

"*Be careful, Maria. The count is a good man, but beneath that big heart and big belly is a jealous eye. He knows he is a bitch's minion. He knows he is neither worthy nor capable of her bed. If he has the least hint of someone stealing his moan, the pudgy old devil would cut that someone's balls off, stew him in brine, and then hang him for the kites."*

Maria climbed the hill, Henrietta's words ringing in his heart, and for a short while polluting his happiness. But as the hilltop turrets appeared before him, even as he sported his new suit of clothes, and held a beautiful red rose in his hands, these caustic words faded away, overwhelmed by his blissful mission. This time when the trumpets sounded and the gates opened, he did not slink back to the rear of the crowd, but instead muscled boldly to its fore. And when the countess passed by on her sorrel, he did not kneel as did the others, but only bowed, and then boldly walked forth, offering her his rose.

But she did not receive the rose; she did not seem to notice him at all. Only her nostrils seemed to slightly quiver, and her lips, to slightly press and purse with disdain, as she gave a sharp whip to her horse and coldly rode on.

For the next week Maria did the same: the climb to the castle; the wait and anticipation with the others at the gates; the bold offering of a rose to the countess when she passed with her servants. But to no avail. He did not once receive a nod from that cold angelic face; not once a look from those eyes of hard blue crystal. As she was a statue, and not a woman mounted on a horse, she rode on, leaving her gypsy devotee standing, rose in hand, where she had passed.

But one day as she passed, and again disdained the rose he offered, Maria made bold to take hold of her horse's bridle, and there deftly fasten his rose. Briefly holding the horse, he looked into her startled face; startled that a lowly one would dare do such a thing.

"Royal countess, O beautiful lady, I give thee a rose, the rose of my heart."

Her footmen rushed forth to constrain the harasser, but in that instant when she had looked at him, Maria saw the fury of a storm in her eyes, one whose lightning was shot like a fork of venom at his heart. At once she raised her whip as to strike him, but at the last whipped the butt of her horse and galloped away. Maria thought he had never seen such loveliness in a woman before.

On the following two days, when she rode forth he made no attempt to give her a rose, but instead stood inconspicuously buried in the rear of her admirers. On the third day when she and her retinue issued forth, Maria's heart leapt with what he thought might be interpreted as a first sign of hope. At the very place where he had offered his roses, she halted her horse, and straightening her cap and fitting her gloves, she slightly turned her head and gave the crowd a glance, before a sharp slap from her whip commenced her ride.

This was a sign he had waited for. The next day he brought another rose, and when her servants seized him as he once more placed it in her horse's bridle, she was quick to speak, with a voice as shrill and commanding as her beauty seemed soft and delicate.

"No, stay back! Let him be!"

At which they retreated, leaving the mounted countess and the gypsy standing at her side. Without once looking at him, and again fitting her riding gloves snugly on her hands, she whispered coldly, callously:

"I will ride a little ahead. Come, follow me. I wish to have a word with you."

Imperiously motioning with her whip for her grooms to stay behind, she rode ahead several hundred paces, and there waited for Maria to walk to her. As he did he remembered Henrietta's warning at the well:

"Be careful, Maria. The count is a good man, but beneath his big heart and big belly is a jealous eye."

But seeing the countess, as beautiful as a flower seated on the horse in the tree's shade, he was ready for anything. He would fight armies for such a woman. If she wished to whip him, he would endure her lashes, and say he had been punished by an angel. He would receive her reprimands like blessings. They would only make him want to taste her mouth and drink her breasts the more.

When Maria reached her, he received neither a reprimand nor a longed for glance from her beautiful eyes. Looking not at Maria, but only directly before her, she whispered, even as she was speaking to her horse:

"The count is something other than his affable seeming. He is a jealous old man, and his jealousy knows no bounds. He is also bloody, and capable of the greatest wickedness; tortures that cut tongues from mouths, pluck eyes from heads, and tied to the tails of horses, dismember, piece by piece men's bodies.

The count is an old man withering in drink and whores, and I am a young healthy woman. Anyone can see that. I know what my subjects say about me, and they have not entirely missed the mark. I have earned my crown with duties performed in an old man's bed.....performed, but never volunteered."

Here she paused, her slender hands once more fidgeting with her riding gloves. Still, she did not bring her eyes to him as she began to speak again, her gaze buried in her fur-trimmed gloves.

"You were very brave, even audacious to offer me roses, and that in plain sight of the peasants and my grooms. Such an act could cost you your life. I like that; I like that very much. I like men who would dare their life to praise my beauty. I like that so much I feel obliged now to punish you."

Maria started:

"My lady?"

"All eyes are upon us. They cannot hear us, but they can see us. They expect me to punish you for your insolence, and for several reasons I do not wish to disappoint them."

"As you like, my lady, punish me. The lash of your whip would be like the kiss of an Angel's wing."

With this the countess turned her eyes to him. They were no longer hard and cold, but liquid and soft, their blueness shimmering with tears of tenderness. Tearing a glove from her hand, she leaned down, and with it slapped his face with several quick sharp slaps, while all the while looking tenderly into his eyes.

"Now turn around; I would not whip the face of such a handsome man."

Maria returned her gentle stare.

"Yes, whip me my lady, whip me until I scream. Punish me with the feathers of your sweetness."

Turning around, Maria received the sharp lashes of her riding whip, and as he did her whispers fell on those same shoulders like a rain of petals.

"Do you know where the ruins of the deserted nunnery are? Good. I will ride there this afternoon, perhaps two hours after midday. I will be alone. Come to me, alone, and tell no one that you are doing so."

And with this she gave his shoulders each a final, very sharp lash with her whip.

"Now go, beautiful gypsy man, the Countess Agatha will salve your wounds later."

* * *

MARIA knew these ruins of which the countess spoke. He had walked to them several times. They were upon a different hill than the one upon which the castle stood. Yes, that would be very nice. They could be alone there. This solitary place told him that the countess did not fear him; that she trusted him. It told him he had pleased this heavenly creature with blue eyes, golden hair, and velvet-rich riding suits.

And yes, she had slapped him with her glove, and whipped him with her whip…..acts that disguised her tenderness…..and did she not say she would salve him?…….

In the interim that led to this appointed hour of their meeting, he did not want to see or speak with anyone, least of all Henrietta, who with a lover's omniscience he knew was privy to the roving, hungry eye of his heart. Therefore when he returned to the village he avoided the tavern, and went instead to a bake house where, with a poem and several caresses on a sweetheart's cheek he begged a sausage, a little bread, cheese and wine. Returning to his room, he packed them in his satchel, and then left the village on a path that meandered lazily to the deserted nunnery.

He wanted to rid his mind of all its hideous webs and grotesque memories. He wanted only this sunny moment, and its expulsion of *death* from the castle of its sparkling treasures. He cared not if he died tomorrow. He cared only for this moment, and this beautiful woman who filled each part of it; she whose slaps and lashes had fallen on him like a gentle rain on a dusty garden; whose iron stare had become soft when it had looked at him. He wanted only to dream of the honey in her mouth, and the riches beneath her riding suits.

It was early; he heard noon's toll in the village below. Halfway to the old Roman nunnery, he found a pleasant place to rest and repast; a large stone in the shade of trees, one that he could recline upon. Lying down on the cool stone, he found himself musing on the great turns of his recent fortunes.

It was not long ago when death, not life had cast its net upon him. He had stumbled into one of its galleries, a gallery that its artists had decorated with their gruesome handiwork. He had seen it; touched it; breathed it. He had tried to burn it, only to have the horrid ghouls escape the flames, and haunt his dreams.

But now, so quickly, a fresh breeze had swept death's ghastly art away. This beautiful woman, this golden lioness of beauty and smoldering sen-suality had invited him to a rendezvous! With only a few words, a certain tone of her voice, a certain softening of her eyes, a certain scent exhaled from the flower of her female essence, all had changed. Gone was the stale and hopeless march of tomorrows; of endless drinking, gambling, and whoring with tavern girls. This fresh new breeze had baptized him anew. There was only today, this hour, this moment, and a burning desire to taste this beautiful woman's mouth.

But why was life this way? Why was it so inconstant; a seemingly endless succession of sorrow and joy, of pain and rapture; a funeral march with children tumbling and laughing in its wake? A wedding feast with death's ghouls glowering in its windows?

Life was a riddle, one that none, even the wisest had ever solved. But why was it never solved; its mystery never known? Was it because Man was part of that riddle; that he was the riddle itself, and the more he tried to solve it, the more he knotted and tangled the riddle's strings? Was Man's heart an endless maze, and the more he explored it, the deeper and lonelier he was lost?

What was this mystery Man was ever so zealous of obtaining? Why climbing to the top of a hill was there ever the desire to climb another hill? Why reaping a plentiful harvest was there ever the hope of reaping a richer one? Why after loving a lovely woman, was there always the promise of a woman with silkier arms and a sweeter wine in her kisses?

Was there never a time when life's mystery was found and known, as when one was deep inside a lover, deliriously thrilled and quivering, melted drunk and blind with ecstasy? Was there never a time when one's pleasure quenched one's pain, when one stood still midst all yesterdays and tomorrows, when life screamed in its climactic surrender: 'Yes, you have found me! Yes, I am yours forever!'

He knew he was not a responsible man, and would never be; that at heart he was a dreamy boy who was a truant to the harsh realities of the world. He knew his mother had given him a gypsy's heart, and he would always be a vagrant who wandered through the seasons, and not one who labored, built walls, or combated in them. Women, and the brief flame enkindled in love's games was all that mattered to him; this alone gave his life meaning. These games had replaced the sacraments before holy altars. Love's moment was his one reason and reward; its brief blind flame at once fed and quieted the great monsters that growled inside him. He could cling to this moment as it was a salvation from Life's violent storms; from death itself. When he loved a woman, he sipped the nectar from Life's flower; drank from its sacred springs. He stilled the wings of time, and tasted Eternity.

Still, why upon leaving his lovers did he often feel a deep sadness? Why did he feel forsaken and more alone; once more an outcast in the world? Why did such a flame of ecstasy leave in its wake the gnawing tooth of guilt, as in loving he had committed a sin, one that had prided itself in thinking it could escape the jowls of death? Why in the cup of every happiness were there bitter dregs of anguish? Why did the prettiest smile and the sweetest kisses leave their adorer stung with a sting of rankling pain?

But these were questions and ponderings for wiser men, for scholars and theologians to answer; for keen minds like his friend, Father Giovanni to explain. He was not a scholar. His soul could only brood and dream. It wanted only to be filled with sweet tastes and perfumes, to stroll in gardens of fruits and flowers.....like the garden this beautiful woman was now offering him......

Maria came from his reverie. He looked at the sun, Yes; it had inched across its zenith, but not by much. It was still early. He would climb to the ruins and wait for her. Yes, he would climb into the ancient nunnery's bell-tower, and from there watch her approach on her horse. Yes, that would be very beautiful, to see this queen of a woman riding alone, bringing her treasures to his arms.

....

....

CHAPTER FOUR

THE GATES OF HELL

Part III
Kisses of Death

NEARING the ruins Maria grew excited when he saw that the countess had been the first to arrive. Her horse was grazing in the bloomy grasses before the skeleton of stones, her whip and velvet cap hung upon its saddle horn. But looking about, the countess was nowhere to be seen. With a quickened heart, he called out:

"Countess! Beautiful lady! Rose of my heart!"

His call received no reply. Maria smiled. Ah, yes, he had almost forgotten. Although she was a countess, and he only a fiddle-player of the taverns, in a deeper world, the primal world of courtship, he was her pursuer. Without her crown, throne, castle, she was but a timid doe, and he her hunter. Eagerly Maria entered this stony forest of long deserted halls, arcades and courtyards; this forest into which this beautiful doe had fled, hiding from the arrows of his affections.

But he did not see her, as he had hoped at once to see her. Stopping after a short way, he called out again:

"My lady, beautiful lady! I bring thee a rose, the rose of my heart!"

Again there was no answer. Smiling, and quickening with eagerness, Maria went on, hoping to glimpse this slender golden doe dart before him, or to find her trembling in some ivied nook, wounded with an arrow he had loosed from his heart.

"My lady! O little doe, where are you? Come to my arms O beautiful one!"

Maria smiled. His calls receiving no replies, he imagined he was only a voice of the wind, a bodiless spirit, a ghost that had been wandering through the maze of this nunnery for centuries; yearning for another ghost, a beautiful ghost, one dressed by turns in riding suits of wine red, dark green and sky blue.

"*My lady! O sweet lady of my heart......*"

And there she was, sweet and fresh, like a new-made Angel, leaning against the ivied wall; the rich cloud of her golden hair falling over her bosom; a red rose held to her lips, and kissing it with puckering, pouting little kisses. She stood there as she had been standing there for centuries, waiting for the one who had hunted her, who needed her; waiting like a ghost that had forsaken its vows, its grave, to wrap her devoted lover in her slender arms; *waiting for him.*

"*Yes, you have found me, your frightened little doe; your holy nun of the nunnery.*"

Smiling brightly, Maria approached her.

"*Nuns take vows.....*"

"*As do brothers, Brother Maria.*"

"*Yes; vows dashed to pieces at the feet of such beauty as I now look upon.*"

"*But surely you would not dare make trespass on such modesty?*"

"*Only with invitation, and then with the devotion of the Saints; to honor and adore it, and in no way disturb or molest it.*"

"*And yet this nun is married. I am afraid, good sir, the treasure of my modesty has been given.*"

"*I do not think it has been given, for I do not think any man has won the treasure of your heart, the treasure I seek on bended knee, and would give my own heart to win.*"

"*You speak brazenly; remember, I am a countess.....*"

"*I know or remember nothing when I am near you, other than this: you are the most beautiful woman I have ever seen.*"

"*I see my whip did not tame you.*"

"*But you are wrong. It tamed my soul into submission, even until it howled with a pleasure it could not contain.*"

At this, to hide her flush, and the sparkle that came into her eyes, the countess turned and sauntered a few steps away.

"*You speak cleverly, gypsy man; or shall I call you Maria, Brother Maria?*"

"*Call me thief, brigand, scoundrel, I do not care, for uttered by your lips, each breath is perfumed with blessedness.*"

The countess gently, but condescendingly smiled.

"*I have made inquiries. I have found out that you are a gypsy, as well as a defrocked monk; that you play gypsy tunes in a tavern, the 'Bear Cub Tavern' I believe it is called. Is a gypsy who plays a fiddle in a smoky tavern worthy of a countess? Is a defrocked monk worthy of a Bride of Christ, albeit that bride is married? What is it that you do, and what is it exactly that you want of your countess, Brother Maria?*"

"*I am yours, and being yours, I am whatever you wish me to be, beautiful lady. If you wish me to be your clown, I will tumble before you, nibble at your toes and tickle your nose until you laugh like a little child. If you wish me to be your protector, I will be a soldier, and stand with a bared sword against valleys filled with infidels. If you wish me to sing, I will transform myself to a nightingale, and in the tree outside your window I will sweeten your dreams with my song.*"

Overcome by this poetry of passion, with which she, a royal countess, had never been addressed, she turned away again, and softly spoke.

"*You must be careful how you speak to me, Brother Maria.*"

"*Careful?! How can the river be careful rushing to the sea? It sings as it crashes down mountains, seeking its mother's arms!*"

"*I am a countess, and though as you have guessed I have compromised my heart by marrying a much older, less handsome and less passionate man, I will not be the mistress of any wandering, fiddle-playing gypsy. I will not be a tinker's whore, no matter how blue his eyes and golden his curls.*"

"*Then like the nuns that once lived in this nunnery, you will grow old and die, not with age and holiness, but with age and pride; the fruits and honeys of your body withering, wasting away in that sun beneath which their loveliness so proudly flowered.*"

Moved, and still with her back to him, the countess paused, as if her breath had been cut in twain. When finally she spoke, she spoke with a voice shorn of condescension and mockery, but now one tender and trembling, like a child's.

"*Again I ask, Brother Maria, what is it that you want of your countess?*"

"*I want my countess to be my student, and I, her teacher.*"

With this the countess turned sharply to him, her face full of question.

"*Student? Teacher? What are you talking about? What is there that you,*" *a gypsy playing a fiddle in a smoky, squalid little tavern could teach me, a countess living in a castle?"*

"Something that I think you have never learned before."

"And what is that? Fiddle playing?"

"Yes, something very like the beautiful melodies that the virtuoso brings from his fiddle."

"What do you mean? What are you saying?"

"I want to wake the beautiful melodies sleeping in your heart. I want to teach you how to love, my lady, how to love."

With this the countess loosed a sardonic laugh, and with a sneer turned to him.

"You are insolent! I should have you beaten! If I had my whip....."

"It is fastened to your horse's saddle. I saw it when I entered the ruins. If you would like, I will fetch it, and falling at your feet, receive your punishment, even until I bleed.

You asked what I wanted of my countess. I but answered honestly. I want to teach her lessons that I do not think she has learned before."

"Lessons? What kind of lessons? If I am such a little child of love, how would you teach me, mister fiddle man, to play my first notes?"

"The gypsy would like to teach his countess how to kiss."

"Teach me to kiss! You? A tavern fiddler, the wearer of a bandanna and earring, like one wandering in a carnival!

"Yes, even such a one. I would like to teach those precious children on your lips, eager but afraid, to give the song of your heart."

"You are insolent, and have become brash and brave by having your way with the tavern sluts!"

"If I may, my lady; these tavern sluts may know how to love more than kings and queens know how to love."

"I am leaving. It was wrong of me to come. It is late, and my grooms will come looking for me. I only thought that we could talk a little, and that......."

"And that you could feel a man burn with desire for you, his body wanting and needing to press against yours.....a young and strong, and not an old and weak man's body, one that would make your blood wake from winter into spring.....that would make your breasts swell, and the deepest, coldest part of you thaw, stir, and feel alive."

As she had quit all words with him, she made for the portal, but just as she was to pass through it she stopped, and without turning back to him, whispered softly:

"*You think, gypsy man, that I have never learned to kiss?*"

"*I do; but I think you could be the best of students.*"

"*Why? May I ask you why you think I would be such a good student?*"

"*Your lips are exquisite; full and lush, like the heart of a rose, a rose waiting only for morning to fully bloom......and I am sure no fig has ever held such sweetness as your mouth contains, a sweetness I do not think, even as I would wage my lute and fiddle at your feet, that you have ever let another taste, and tasting, savor.*"

Too proud to answer, or even look at him, she stood frozen, helpless in her royal silence, a silence she was too proud to break. Maria laid his hands gently on her shoulders, and with surrender, not rebuke she answered his touch. Leaning her gently against the ivies, he brushed the golden vines of her hair away, fully exposing the golden flower of her face, and then gently nibbled her brow, cheeks and chin with kisses, before bringing his lips to hers. Feather soft, he brushed them, then tenderly pressed them, as they were the petals of a flower; and then lifting away, paused briefly, before returning to brush and press them again; this time more earnestly, fitting them more exactly; asking permission to taste them more deeply.

Yes, they were sweet lips; round, full and sensual, but as he had guessed, they were not practiced lips. Although they did not reject his, they were stiff and waxen, ignorant of affection, and did not know how to return what had been so sweetly proffered them. But they were not the lips of a corpse, rather a sleeper, a beautiful, voluptuous sleeper, one with warm dreams flowing through its veins; one that had been asleep forever; one that desperately wanted to be wakened.

"*I must go now, Maria; may I call you Maria? It is late, and the count will send out a hunting party to look for me.*"

"*No, it is not late. Time's wings have hummed still, and are blessing us with eternity.*"

"*But, Brother Maria, well, do you think.....what I am trying to say..... do you think I am a good student?*"

"*I think you are the loveliest and ablest of students.*"

"*You see, this kind of thing.....these kisses.....the count and I do not.....*"

"*You need only to practice.....and have a wish in your heart to learn.*"

"*But I must not be late.....and perhaps another time, yes, Mister Maria, perhaps another time.......*"

Maria felt her shy shame at not knowing how to expertly kiss. Again he brought his mouth to hers, and tenderly brushed and pressed her lips with his, and then patiently waited to be answered. Slowly these stiff lips, these lips of a countess that had never known such a simple pleasure warmed and moistened; became pliant. Slowly the sleeper began to waken; her lips parting, yielding luscious fruits she had never known she owned, but that her heart had long wished to give.

As a young shepherd girl once taught a curious monk, so now a gypsy imparted the mystery to a countess. Slowly and patiently he taught the ageless secrets of how to kiss, even as his eager pupil grasped those secrets, and eagerly asked for others.

With the wisdom gained from untold lovers, most whose names and faces he had long forgotten, and now were only ghosts he had once played with in doorways, alleys, meadow flowers and stable-lofts, as well as the beds of other men's wives; with the wisdom he had gained from these loving ghosts he began to instruct his pupil how to give and accept the blissful sweetness of a kiss: the occult of how to seize and let go; how to linger, and by lingering ask for more; how to tease, tempt, tickle and steal, but always how to return what had been stolen; and then politely ask to play and steal again.

And yet the wise teacher knew his teaching was only a waking of his pupil. He was only asking a flower to yield its own miracle. Gently and lovingly he asked the petals of this sleeping flower to open; and as they did, he found the pearls of small white teeth, and the delicious candy of a curious tongue; as well as something deeper, sweeter, where all kisses begin.

These cold lips that had thrilled with a first warmth, now began to burn, to fever.....they that were husks of pride and scorn now began to soften.....they that had jealously hoarded their honey for so long, now gave it freely.....and giving it, thirsted to be replenished, that they could give the more......

.....The sleeper a warm-blooded woman that no longer wanted to only dream.....not an iron-willed countess with a whip and scowl.....but a child whose secret wish was to love and be loved.......

Maria felt her sighs begin to well from deeper depths. He felt her stir, press into him with a need to be filled, a thirst to drink and be drunk. He brought his hands to her breasts, and as they were doves, gently sleeked them until he felt them gently coo; prick awake and be freed of their cage.

But with this the lesson ended. Taking his hands in hers, she kissed and removed them from her breasts, and then laid her head upon his shoulder. Clinging submissively to his strength, she whispered:

"I must go; truly I must go. This is the time of day the count begins his drinking, and he will become angry if I am not back from my ride. He will send men to look for me."

"When may I give my student more lessons?"

She lifted her face from his shoulder and looked into his eyes. She was flushed, perspiring and mussed; her face as vulnerable in her waked passion as a child in its bedtime fears. The coldness in her eyes had gone, and had left tears where the ice of their sternness had melted.

"Oh, I do not know, I do not know. Perhaps this is the only time.....you do not know how dangerous.....and the count is irritable, restless to leave the castle.....but I must leave at once....not with you, I must never be seen with you!.....for you have no idea how jealous....oh darling, thank you for being so sweet with me, and so clever to look into my heart and know I have seldom....no, that is not true.....that I have never loved or been loved before......."

O Maria, my darling Maria, I am very fond of you....perhaps, yes, perhaps, oh, it sounds so foolish....perhaps I even love you.....yes, I think I may love you a little my golden-haired, tavern gypsy boy!......"

With this she broke from his arms, began to compose and walk briskly away, only to stop and run back to him. This time there was a storm of wildness in her eyes, a need and a hunger that had torn the disguise of a countess from her face.

"What am I saying? You are my 'maestro', and I wish to learn in no other arms! I will tell the count of your music. He will ask you to perform for him in the castle. I will send word to the tavern where you play your gypsy songs. Leave the rest to me, yes, I will arrange all! There are still many lessons that I wish to learn! Oh, 'maestro', you are so sweet! You have wakened my heart!"

With this she placed her hands about his face, and rather than passively wait for his mouth to come to hers, she seized his lips with her own; giving him a kiss that was burning with the flames of her heart.

* * *

TWO days later a courier brought an invitation from the count's castle to the *Bear Cub Tavern*. It was addressed: '*Brother Maria, Gypsy Performer*', but it was entrusted to the innkeeper, and when Maria entered the tavern in the afternoon, Gino, beside himself with excitement, placed it ceremoniously in his hands.

"*Maria! Maria! The count wants you to play and sing for him tonight in his castle! I do not know how he heard of you, but the good-hearted rascal did, and the courier told me all's plain in the missive for any who can read a jot, and I know, Maria, you were one of those clever monks who learned to read!*

And if the count's heard about the gypsy singer at the 'Bear Cub Tavern', then by the Saints, he's probably heard about the innkeepers of the 'Bear Cub Tavern'; 'Gino the Bald and Gino the Fat'! An honor! A great honor gypsy boy! Henrietta is not so happy about the thing, a little down in the jowls for some reason, but you know how women are Maria; sour as curdled milk, moody as the moon, sly as a grimalkin when they want to be. I'll send you with two bottles of my best wine; one from the Bald, one from the Fat! Ha! By the looks of his paunch and the ruddiness of his cheeks, the count's a bibber, and knows a good bottle of wine when he swallows one!"

That afternoon Maria bathed, combed, and tuned his fiddle. As the sun was setting he walked up the hill to the castle. A knock on a door next to the gates resulted in the immediate opening of its peephole, the appearance of a guard's congenial face, and the door being unlocked and opened for him.

He was led to a hall lighted with a blazing brazier and a great number of candles. On the walls were hung beautiful tapestries, and from the rafters were hung trophies of bygone hunts: the antlers of stags, the pelts of wolves and wildcats, the colorful feathers of game birds. Before him the count and countess sat on sumptuous chairs; the countess in a light blue, ermine-trimmed gown, the count in a royal-red robe. About the hall was an audience of several dozen, from knights and courtiers, to the least of the castle's scullions.

The count was courteous, but tired. After politely accepting the wine Maria had brought him, he slumped in his chair, his head leaning like a child's on the countess's shoulder, and then sleepily asked Maria to begin.

But all changed when Brother Maria the gypsy began to play and sing. The dull hall, asleep for years, began to throb and sing; the hearth and candles seemingly to brighten and dance. The count lifted his head from the countess's shoulder, like a child from his pillow, and with the gay and poignant melodies of the gypsy songs, waked from his stupor. Commending the gypsy's talent, he began to freely drink.

Never had Maria's fiddle sung so sweetly, so passionately; never had his voice rung so richly and sonorously, reaching such heights, plumbing such depths, exploring such caves of sentimental sweetness. Never had he played for such a royal, appreciative audience; but more, never had he played for such a beautiful woman, whose passion he had stirred, and wanted nothing more than to fully enkindle. Directly before this blue-gowned angel, he did not play his fiddle, he ravished it; making its strings surrender exquisite moments of sweetness it had never surrendered before; as his fiddle was not a fiddle at all, but the golden body of a woman that was yielding the ecstasy of her soul to his loving hands.

Still, the countess seemed less moved than the enthusiastic others. Dressed in her beautiful blue gown, she sat icily in her chair, in sharp contrast to the count's adolescent joy and drunkenness. Her eyes seldom turned and lifted to the performer, and smiles did not break across her face; as they had not been given permission to do so. When loud applause broke from the others at the end of a song, she only gave a slight nod of her approval. When the increasingly inebriated count childishly kissed her bare shoulder, it was as if that shoulder was a drift of snow.

When Maria had finished his music, he was given a guard to usher him away. Passing through a corridor, they were intercepted by a dwarfish, middle aged woman, one who insisted upon having a few words with the guard; after which she assumed the leadership of showing Maria from the castle. By the light of her candle, Maria saw that a great scar was furrowed from the corner of her mouth all the way to her jaw, a scar that in the candlelight lent the impression of a malicious sneer, one that no smile could melt away.

But the woman did not usher Maria from the castle. She instead made an abrupt turn at a juncture of hallways, and led him without a word through smaller, darker passageways, before at last stopping before a small, nondescript door. Turning to Maria for the first time, she spoke in a hushed tone:

"I am Elisabetta, the Countess Agatha's chambermaid. Please, through this door, Maria sir. The countess is waiting for you."

Without a word Maria opened the door, and inching and feeling his way through a dark closet or vestibule, found another door, one that he opened to the candlelit opulence of his dreams.

Maria entered a vaulted, ornately decorated room, softly aglow with candles burning in silver candelabra, and in angel gilded sconces on the walls. A great feast was spread on a table, with a chair placed at each of the table's ends. The countess had changed into a loosely falling, lemon-colored nightgown, one whose cuffs and collar were trimmed with white fur, its silken folds draping to the floor. Perfumed, and with unbound hair, her breasts partly showing, as if anxious for their escape, she welcomed Maria with a warm lingering kiss, and flames of desire dancing in her eyes.

"*Oh my darling, you are here, and we shall be alone! The count is drunk, and after playing with his whores, he will sleep deeply. He will not come to me tonight. You have my word, your naughty student's word. My chambermaid will stand watch, and alert us of any danger. Oh, I am yours, all yours my gypsy minstrel, my darling Maria!*

But first let us eat.....you see I have ordered many dishes for my darling: venison and trout....teal, pheasant, pigeon and lark....and here are tarts and scones.....here salads with rosemary flowers and violet buds.....and wine, we must have wine.....anything for my darling gypsy who plays and sings so sweetly, but not nearly so sweetly as he kisses!"

He wrapped her in his arms, as she was a sheaf of wheat he was gathering to his breast. Gently he caressed her nightgown from her shoulders; smelled the honey of her woman sweetness; tasted her with nibbling kisses; brushed his soft beard over her golden nakedness. Softly he whispered in her ear:

"*I want no wine but the wine of your kisses, and I want to partake of no feast other than the feast of your loveliness. Oh, you have but heard the melodies that these hands bring from a gypsy's fiddle, but you do not know the melodies they shall bring from the golden harp of your body! Come, love, let us sing with the Angels!*"

It did not take long for Maria to realize he had found an apt-most student, a creature that was made to love; one who eagerly exulted in the appetites of the flesh. He had learned and long known that different women gave themselves in different ways: stiffly and awkwardly, timidly and fearfully, lustily and greedily; brusquely, patiently, passively. But rare was the lover who felt, answered and urged the needs of the one in her arms; who participated in and wanted to share his every need; who was not afraid or aloof, but who wished to burn, combat and surrender with the other's heart; to be her lover's match and twin; one who wished to make of love a festival, that festival a conflagration of passion.

It did not matter if she was unpracticed, a novice of many games and adventures. It did not matter if her only lover had been an old man with a paunch and gray beard, who came to her blind and stammering with drink; who, mindless of giving pleasure, was only capable of his own selfish groans. She was that rare creature with the innate capacity to warmly and sincerely love; an artist who painted love with caresses, a poetess whispering love with tender moans and sighs. Nature had lavished her with gifts; fashioned her as time and practice never could. Nature, not a dusty, wandering gypsy had been her *maestro*.

Nor was her beauty an illusion made of paint, perfume and ornament. It was as genuine as a lily. Beneath her gown were treasures that baffled illusion itself; that outshone adornment and exceeded wish and dream; a creature of marble slenderness and feline sleekness, whose fruits, from her lips to her toes hung in perfect ripeness for the child of desire to worship and enjoy.

And as the castle, the village, and the surrounding fields slept, the lovers were awake in the secret garden they had found. Like nectar-drunken bees, they drank to drunkenness, and were oblivious of all; of the world, and all of its dangers and uncertainties....free of its rumors of age, sorrow, war, death. They had found what nourished them more than bread, replenished them more than sleep or sunlight,......delighted them more than any dream they had ever dreamed.......

They had found paradise in the great wilderness of the world, a garden whose lovely fruits were plucked with reverent hands. Nor did there seem an end to these fruits, nor the hunger that hungered for them. Shortly before dawn, when Maria was about to leave, his lover beckoned to him again, to be kissed, filled, harvested again, and it was a loveliness he could not resist, no, not if the sun would snare him in its net of beams, and the price he must pay was death itself.

......and in the culmination of that last embrace, as in his arms her passion sent its swells of storm in answer to the lightning shooting through his bowels.....in this exquisitely perfect moment, when pleasure grew numb of the pleasure that was killing it, becoming a higher sweetness, Maria felt that all of the rapture that could flow through a man was now flowing like a river through him........

In the wake of that immeasurable joy, as he lay complete and happy at her side, she whispered in his ear:

"Oh Maria, my darling Maria, I want to have your child, yes, I want to have your child; a golden child with your eyes and your strength and your heart!

I am yours my darling, completely yours. I have money, much money. We will go away, and we will be very happy.

You must come back to me soon, for I will not be able to live long without my gypsy's love. I will send word. Do not worry; I will take care of everything. Yes, we will be very happy. But now you must go. Elisabetta will show you the way. The dawn is near, and the castle will be stirring. Kiss me once more, sweetheart, my 'maestro'....oh, gypsy man, I give my heart, the heart of your Countess Agatha to your keeping!"

* * *

MARIA heard nothing more from the countess for several days, but this did not concern him. He knew that she loved him, and that, cautious of the perils presented by the count and the traffic of visitors to the castle, she was carefully arranging the hour when he could once more come to her arms. He did not doubt her heart, for it had been set aflame with passion.

He found his self lightheaded; dizzied with blissful memories of their night of love, and dreams of many more such nights that that night promised.

.....*images swam through his mind, delicious and shameless and enchanting.....like flocks of beautiful birds, or schools of beautiful fish.......intoxicating both his waking and sleeping with the perfumes and moonlit shadows of desire and love.......*

.....*caresses, kisses, moans of gratification.....the skirmishes of love's battles.....their inceptions, broils, truces and consummations.....their modesties and wickedness.....the dares and invitations.....the kindling, fueling and quenching of love's flame.....like two sporting dolphins.......like mating lions.....like a gentle doe fleeing a leopard, and then that leopard fleeing the gentle doe.....over and over, through endless forest paths.......*

Through the flood of these images of love's abandon, Maria remembered the countess's words; some of which pleased, and others which troubled him.

"*I want to have your child, a golden child with your eyes and your strength and your heart.*"

Yes, this was sweet, and pleased him very much; another poet to wander the hills and forests, to sing of clouds and flowers, and to taste the kisses of pretty peasant maidens in the orchards and tall grasses.

But that other thing that she had said……..

"*We will go away. I have much money. We will go away and be very happy…..*"

…..he needed to wander, to hunger, to know life's pangs and perils….he needed to climb the precipices of death before he could be happy…..the heart that his mother had given him, and the barbarity of his father……without these things he would not know how to live, to love…..without these things he would not know how to die……

…..and there was more, something he did not wish to think about, but something that haunted, and as if tried to poison his blissful thoughts……

…..He had heard these words before: 'I have much money. We will go away and be very happy……' Had the abbess not told him the same? Was he a thing to be purchased, a possession, a pretty doll to be cradled in pretty arms?……

And yet time and again in the weeks ahead, these doubts and fears were dispelled by the delirious lovemaking offered him by this goddess. Never had he been so enraptured, so rewarded, so satisfied; a delirious satisfaction that seemed to have no end, as night after night he answered the invitations given him to the castle.

The hot and dusty hours now became a fantastic dream, one filled with delicious memories, and even more, delicious anticipations. Maria did not walk or tiredly trudge through the days; he had been given love's wings to fly through them. Each morning he parted day's curtains to a new dream, a new dream with ever new pleasures and adventures waiting for him: creating a happy delirium from which he did not want to ever wake.

…..pleasures and adventures with invitations delivered to the 'Bear Cub Tavern' by the count's royal courier…..his singing and drinking at the tavern, and after, his stealing away and up the hill to the castle's walls…..the soft little knock at the door…..its unbolting, and then being led silently away by the chambermaid, the great scar on her face grinning like the teeth of a shark in the candle's light…..even as she swam through the dark ways to his golden lover……

.....and then the opening of the little door, the darkness of the vestibule.... and the door that opened to the raptures of his dreams......

But one night marked itself like no other, and interrupted these blissful excursions into paradise. Leaving the tavern and walking towards the small road that climbed to the castle, Maria was stopped by a hand that sharply grabbed his coat in the darkness; a faceless and bodiless hand, one with a stern voice, a woman's voice. Pulling him into the doorway, at once Maria recognized Henrietta.

"It is a dangerous game you're playing, Maria. Sooner or later the count....."

"What is wrong, Henrietta? The count has requested me to play for him tonight, as he has on other nights. He likes my gypsy music when he is drunk. See, tonight I take my lute."

"Tut! You know as well as I, Maria, that the only instrument you will play tonight is between your legs, and that to exact the melody of a countess's moans..

Please Maria, the count is nothing more than a childish old drunk, but he commands others that are not. If it is pretty smiles and pretty pieces that you want, I can help you. I know widows, pretty and young,.....and girls, used and unused, girls who are cheap, who would be glad to throw up their skirts and do your pleasure."

"Henrietta, please, I do not know what you are talking about. I must not keep the count waiting."

But as Maria began to leave, a second hand joined the first to passionately waylay him, and a voice with a cry to match that passion.

"Maria, please, Gino may know. He may have found out about us. He is rough and rude with me, unlike my sweet Gino.....he does not kiss the crucifix before, or when he finishes......"

"But how could he know?"

"I do not know.....but perhaps, yes, perhaps when I brought my crucifix to his lips, perhaps, yes, you see I was tired.....I think I asked Brother Maria, and not Gino to kiss it. His face darkened and became ugly. It was not Gino, neither 'The Fat' nor 'The Bald', but another Gino. He said his wife was a gypsy's whore. He looked into my eyes, and when he did, he knew.

O Maria, Gino is not Gino, and if he finds out for sure, I swear.....I told you the thing I would do......."

But lust, under the guise of love held Maria thrall, and brusquely shaking free of Henrietta he walked away; Henrietta's frenzy of strange words and fears being quickly replaced by visions of a voluptuous angel.

But it was not Henrietta's passionate warning alone that imbued the night with an otherworldly strangeness. Walking through the end of the village a great scream and wail broke from a house in the darkness, so piercing it stopped Maria's brisk steps, and with them his heart, as it had risen through a fissure of hell. It was joined by a choir of more wails and piteous weeping, the like Maria had not heard before, even in churchyards.

Stranger still, as he ascended the hill to the castle, he heard other moans and cries from another dwelling; more muffled and less shrill, but with the same heartrending passion.

But there was more. Reaching the castle, and knocking upon the secret door, he was greeted by yet another surprise and irregularity. Elisabetta was greatly, uncharacteristically agitated. In the circle of her candle's light, the scar that scored her face appeared to have deepened, so that it seemed the tusk of a wild boar.

"The countess is unable to see you tonight, Brother Maria sir."

"But what do you mean, Elisabetta? The Countess Agatha sent me a missive in the morning……"

"Something has happened, sir…..something has…..the countess, you see, the countess is not well……"

"Not well? Do you mean she has taken ill?"

"No, not ill…..well, perhaps, yes that is it, she has taken ill…..yes, that is it Brother Maria sir, she has had a faint, a dizziness….."

"What is it, Elisabetta? What is wrong? Why are you shaking, and why do your eyes stare from your head? What has happened to the Countess Agatha?"

"She is not herself tonight, that is all I can say…..all through the afternoon as well, master Maria, that is all I know, and all I can say…… she cursed me, whipped me, as I was a dog she did, but shortly after she took me in her arms and gave me a great many kisses, as she never has before."

"Has the count….."

"No, she has locked him out of her bedchamber. He is drunk and raving, and gone a-fiddling with sailor girls……says he'll breed sons from an oyster girl or a tart on a wharf if he cannot from his own wife….."

Maria grabbed the much smaller woman's collar, pinned her to the wall, and brought the candle to within inches of her face. In the candle's light her face seemed shrunken, full of snout and tiny teeth, like the face of a weasel.

"*Damn it woman, tell me! What has happened? What is wrong with the Countess Agatha?*"

"*I do not know, master, and that's the truth of the thing. She seems as though she has drunk too much wine. Sometimes she is very cross and full of curses, and at other times very silly and giddy, and talking nonsense to the air.....sometimes she seems greatly fevered, and the next moment as collected as a nun with her beads......*"

"*I must see her.*"

"*No master Maria, the countess is not in her right mind.....*"

"*Take me to her Elisabetta!*"

"*I'll not do it*"

"*Damn it, give me the key to the door Elisabetta!*"

Maria held her by her collar, even as he would choke her, even as he would shake the key free from whatever pocket it was hiding in. In an act of loyalty she attempted to resist his strength, in the candle's light her weasel face pinching into something feral, lending the obscene illusion that not only her mouth, but her scar was about to bite his neck with a row of razor teeth.

Her small body housed a hidden might, and struggling, she managed to hold the candle inches from the scar, starkly revealing how the wound must have nearly sliced her face in half.

"*No, you mustn't....look at me, Maria.....please, you must be careful.... you see I was once pretty, when I was a child.....and the count had his sport with me.....and then finding another man on top of me.....with a burning knife had done this to me.....so none other would want to lay with me!*"

Still, Maria easily overpowered the woman, and thrusting his hand into her coat's pockets, fleeced until he found the key. Letting loose her throat, he strode to the castle door, determined to proceed without a candle through the tunnel-like passages he had come to know so well, the vain pleas of the dwarfish chambermaid ringing a few paces behind him.

"*She's not in her right mind, Maria......a kind of madness.....a kind of distraction.....a kind of fever, and not my mistress at all!.......*"

But when Maria had opened the secret door, crept through the dark closet, and then opened the inner door to the countess's chamber, he found his lover as he had found her on their previous liaisons. Although the candles were not as many or as bright, and she had painted her face more lavishly, she was gowned, jeweled, and perfumed as on other nights, her golden hair adorned with a lovely net of pearls. With bright eyes and a bright smile she fell into his arms and welcomed him with a tender, lingering kiss.

"Oh my love, I am so happy you have come! You have no idea how I worry that you will not, that each time you leave my arms will be the last time I will see you, and that I will be left to pine for you through eternity.....and what would eternity be without you, but a cold dark prison without my gypsy's love?

Come; tonight we must dine a little, just a little, before we feast in love's garden."

Maria was confused. She was sweet and warm, and her eyes clear as *Venetian* crystal; and if she was drunk and giddy, it was only with the love that her heart was bearing him. Why had the chambermaid said those things, and with such tenacity, almost ferocity? The countess was not gripped by fever or illness, and certainly not by madness. But as they ate their pheasant, drank their wine, and dreamed in the eternity of each other's blue eyes, the conversation seemed to adopt erratic turns, touching unusual bounds it had not touched on before.

"Yes, it is true my darling, true and silly. I sometimes fret that I may never see you again; that I may never look into your blue eyes, or be embraced by your strong arms again! And then, la, I think how foolish I am, and that in only a few hours you will appear, like a magician from my door, and you will be mine for another night.....oh the night, the accursed night, why is it so short Maria? It is as dark as death, why can it not be as long?

And do not worry that you have no money. I have money, much money, and we will be happy together, whether in a hut or a castle, whether in silk or sackcloth, la! And do not worry about the count.....I will take care of the fusty bastard......did I tell you he knocked upon my door tonight?.....softly, with his fingertips, and not his knuckles, the knock of lechery.....his bowels afire, and caterwauling about his love for me. I did not open the door. I told him to fetch his whores, and if not his whores, his hounds, and he would be far happier than he ever would be again with me.....for never again would his countess be his barn loft strumpet......

......O I know I ramble, la la la la, la, but it is just that your little nun.....you remember the old nunnery and the lessons you gave me there?..... it is just that your little nun, your little nun that is your little pantry whore loves you so, so much that I felt flushed and dizzied today, even as I would faint and fall, and a certain pain gripped my chest, here, a pain in my heart

for you, my gypsy sweetheart....and it would be so easy to poison his wine, or slit his throat, then stuff the fat pig in a wine cask and send him down the river...O, and as he floated away how we would celebrate in naughtiness together.......

But come! I am not my gypsy's tweeting canary, I am his wickedly passionate lover! Come, give me your hand, let us to bed.....let us teach the Angels a thing or two about Heaven's business!......."

She had prepared a storm of rapture even more passionate than the others; giving him supple caresses and daring, shameless favors she had not given him before. Over and over she breathed into his ear:

"I want to please you, my love. I want to make you happy as you make me happy. Tell me, oh tell me darling what you would like me to do! Your royal countess wants to learn what the tavern wenches give you.....what they do with their hands and mouths.....your countess wants to be your little stable whore!"

But there was another difference. From time to time she screamed out incoherently, as in fever, not love; and at other times she broke into laughter.

"Hurry, finish.....I cannot breathe with your guts upon me!.....Elisabetta, bring me the hemlock, you know where I have hidden it.....or stand in the shadows and stab the bastard as he grunts and groans.....or if you've not the nerve, hire one of his sailor sluts, I will see that she is paid with jewels.......

.....oh, but what am I saying?.....darling, forgive me.....for a moment I thought......my head is throbbing, and my breast is paining.....see what your love does to me?.....it makes my body shiver and my mind swim with crazy thoughts.....forgive my silliness.....Only love me! Love me! Come play with me and love me! Kill your little countess with your gypsy love, as I will kill an old count and his disgusting lechery with my cunning.....I have money, much money.....we will be very happy......"

Maria lay awake, as the countess slept in his arms. She was exhausted from the orgy she had prepared and given him, but her sleep was fitful, and not peaceful. It was broken by moans, laughter, and sometimes blasphemies, and a strange gurgle in her throat, and her calling out of names and places that he did not recognize.

What was wrong with her? Was it drunkenness? Madness? Passion? Was she in earnest about killing the count? And what was that odd smell, that smell that her heavy perfume had disguised, and for a good while succeeded in smothering, but now seemed to be asserting its unpleasantness, even its foulness? Oh, but she was lovely, and she had given him her loveliness tonight as never before, even as she felt she never would again.

He heard a distant cock crowing somewhere deep in the night's last darkness. He must go while the night was still his friend. But not before he kissed her awake, and in the ritual of farewell, given her a last passionate embrace.

He began to kiss her body.....even as he had learned the kisses she liked best, those that made her purr and sigh, wake and rouse with desire.....first on her feet, then up the slender, marble smooth lengths of her legs.....and yet these kisses did not elicit purrs of satisfaction from her as they were wont to do, but instead sharp cries of irritation, an irritation she had never shown before.....and more strangely, her calling out the count's name..... "Ferdinando, no, you are drunk, and you know I do not like that! Your beard is an old man's beard, a stinking goat's beard.....I will not let you have what you are after.""

Thinking she must be dreaming, Maria then kissed the soft place of one of her groins, at which she sighed and dreamily tittered..... "Yes, oh yes, I know what you are after"..... but treating the other with the same caress, she screamed out with great pain, as he had stabbed her with a knife.....and stranger still, she did not wake with the scream.....the scream trailing into inarticulate moans and murmurs of pain, and the mysterious gurgling in her throat.......

Maria rose from the bed, and brought back a candle from the room where they had dined. As the countess continued to moan and murmur, and sometimes incoherently blurt out in her restless sleep, he brought the candle near her naked body.

He saw at once that her beautiful hair was clinging to the sweat that had broken out on her brow, neck and back, indeed all of her body....that she had indeed broken into fever......and that little spasms of shivering were now passing over and through that fever, resulting in her uneven breaths, gibberish, and a sleep that was no longer sleep, but a delirium. He brought the candle to the intimate place where his kiss had elicited such a violent scream, and saw several lumpish swellings, surrounded by bluish rings.... grotesquely staining this soft place of her most secret, ivory beauty.

Gently he urged her from her side to her back, and then brought the candle to her breasts, and at once he saw that the pillow of her feminine loveliness was riddled hideously with strawberry sized tumors, sprouting like bruise-blue mushrooms from her delicate whiteness......then bringing the candle to her face, he illumined swollen, blackening lips, and dark rings about her eyes that were breaking through the thick paint of her desperate disguise.

In the light of the candle, before his very eyes, Maria saw his beautiful lover quickly decaying into a ghoul.

Quickly Maria dressed, and went to Elisabetta, slumped and sleeping in a chair in the dark vestibule. He knelt down and violently shook and slapped her awake.

"Listen to me, Elisabetta, and do not cry out. The countess is ill. She is dying. She will probably not wake again. Fetch a doctor, and wake the count, no matter how drunk he was last night, or how many the whores in his bed.

You were right, Elisabetta, and I was wrong. I should not have come. I have loved an Angel, but one that has become a corpse in my arms. I will not come again."

Harried, Maria fled out the castle and down the hill, but midway to the village he saw someone climbing the road towards him. Afraid of being recognized, he stepped behind a tree and let the short, stout, swiftly walking figure pass without being seen.

Reaching the village he went directly to his room, packed his few things in his satchel, and prepared to leave. Below the stairs his landlady stood in her nightgown, with long ropes of gray hair falling from beneath her nightcap. She was leaning on her stick like one blind, and trying her best to scream, but her screams were tiny and feeble, like the squawking of a dying bird.

"Gino was here, Maria, but he said he was no longer 'Gino the Bald' or 'Gino the Fat'. His name was now 'Gino the Murderer'! He has a knife, Maria! 'Gino the Murderer' has a knife and he is climbing the hill to kill you!"

Leaving the village as day was breaking, Maria did not go to the 'Bear Cub'. Someone else would cut her free. Some horror was afoot, and his heart had seen, and now owned too much of it. He knew the very rafter from which Henrietta would be hanging.

. . . .

. . . .

CHAPTER FIVE

THE THEATRE OF THE DEAD

Part I

Late 1348, thru 1350

THERE is no theatre like the theatre of the dead; no awe and wonder, as in the audience of the living. Held captive by what all dreams come to know, and what all flesh must come to be, all who live are intrigued with a drama whose final scene was written on the first page of the world; a covenant, etched as in stone, upon the fragility of all men's hearts.

Like a band of actors, its giddy players rush upon a stage whose flambeau is the moon, and whose footlights are the stars, their troop enacting the one dark end of all bright beginnings: poisoning the king upon his throne, cor-rupting beauty to a ghoul, stabbing the poet in love's garden; breaking the staffs of prophets, the scythes of the simple, the hopes of the devout; making fools of wise men, and weeping clowns of princes.

All are enchanted by what they behold; only to realize, squinting and palsied at the curtains' close, that they who hooted, cursed and cheered, were they themselves the ones they watched perish before their spellbound eyes; that spectator and performer were one.

THERE is no carnival like the carnival of the dead; no freaks or tricks, like those that cozen the children of the living.

Its lions break from their cages, and with bloody maws and razor claws maul at will, as they were kittens playing with balls of thread. Its puppet shows make the Child in Man laugh, only to make that same Child weep in the infirmity and madness of its age; the painted figures that bobbed and danced on strings, made to dandle by the fingers of mountebanks and lechers.

The monsters behind its curtain are but devils in the dungeon of the soul, baiting with crumbs of sugar the maid of Curiosity; the elfish magician pulling surprises from his sleeves, a cutthroat holding his greatest surprise between the fangs of his heart; the sorceress who peers into a crystal, telling the credulous that they are stardust, when the moon sets and the wagons creak away, is but a seller of buttons and a picker of rags.

THERE is no music like the music of the dead; that hymn that shook heaven's rafters with laughter and lark song, in the end but groans and harrowing screams on kite-infested battlefields. On the heels of the merry organ grinder comes a funeral train full of wails and shrieks, its wheels dirtied by the vomit of drunkards, the dung of drays, and the peanut shells of monkeys; beneath its veils of wailing mourners, smile the painted faces of harlots.

The nightingales that sang in the midnight forest were but jackals in the bloody throat of darkness; the lovesick minstrel in love's ivied shadows, an assassin bought with a tankard of ale; the harps of Angels at the sick man's ear, no more than screaming ravens hungry for their feast.

THERE are no paintings like the paintings of the dead; no one to study and marvel at them like those who stroll through the dream of the living.

Their galleries are but a charnel house; their Venus's, hags; their Madonna, a vixen; their mightiest heroes, forgotten fables peeling with decay, like a leper's scabs.

The portraitures frescoed on their walls are not of Man reaching to the balcony of the Angels, but rather the orgy of death, portraying those celestial creatures fallen from the height of men's dreams; their wings, draggled, balding, broken; their nimbuses, shattered like glass; their divinity violated by men's barbarity.

THERE is no God like the God of the dead; spitting on rites, defecating on altars, tearing to confetti the sacraments of that tale dearest to the living.

He sends his messengers through every pretty street, squalid alley and nettled path, and behind them, his collectors and his carts. To those who flee into dens of dissoluteness, or resort to cathedrals of sanctity, to those who bravely bare swords, or hide in crevices with charms and cordials, He sends worms and vermin to eat through daub and timber, rains down toads that mash the harvest wheat, sluices forth serpents that slink beneath pillow and cradle-hood.

He tramples Belief as a horse tramples a viper with its hoofs; decapitates the heads of Saints, and parades them on the tips of His swords. He laughs in the face of that General who takes his massive army afield, and regarding the promise of his salvation no more than flatulence, blows a kiss through the righteous ranks of his righteous sheep, killing man, beast and dream as they were flies; making a slaughter of the salvo of Man's effeminate myth.

THERE is no revelation like the revelation of the dead, a testament inked in blood and sung by worms to the credulity of the living: the falsity of Love; the vanity of Hope; the hypocrisy of Truth.

There are no walls that will stay the ghosts of death's reconnaissance. Death peers into all windows, and with a leer of lust, itches as much before the nunnery as the brothel. Eavesdropping on all moments, it is the uninvited guest at the celebration of all dreams.

There are no horrors like the horrors of the dead, loosed like a sea of wolves into the streets of those, who, like flowers, lift their faces to a flattering sun.

* * *

Madness

AFTER he had fled the village that fateful night, Maria hid from the light of day, and the dangers he was afraid might be pursuing him. For more than a week he was strictly nocturnal, subsisting on the few crusts he had brought in his satchel, ears of milky corn in the fields, and the nuts and fruits that were now beginning to ripen in the first days of autumn. He approached no farmhouse, and spoke to no person. He begged no bread, asked no shelter, drank from no well.

He was riddled with fears, both in his daily hiding, and in his nightly roving, fears with apparitions fashioned from those fears: a posse of villagers, headed by an insanely crazed innkeeper, vowing vengeance for he who had fornicated with his wife, his wife he had found hanging from a rafter; and a posse of soldiers, headed by a count, who, upon finding his beautiful young countess dead, hideously blotched and carbuncled, eaten alive with disease, may have learned of the one who had played a fiddle for his ear, only to caper in his bed.

.....and there were other apparitions that haunted him, haunted him and would not let him go.....apparitions that began to appear to him, talk

to him, craze him.......

.....a peasant girl with a pink ribbon in her hair, whose lovely dark eyes hatched maggots, through whose ribs crawled rats, and over her body crews of spiders were weaving her shroud.....a small boy picked to the bone by a flock of crows.....one who had given him pleasures that had crowned his manhood, only to discover in a candle's light that the arms that had enfolded him had not been an angel's wings, but the arms of a ghoul......a wise mistress of a tavern hanging dead from a noose, her stare shouting: "Beneath the count's big belly and big heart....." a chambermaid with a hideous scar, that scar still sneering in the bucket into which its head had been lopped..... and a stare that stared through all these stares......of a dead man lying in the snow, speaking to his soul:....."I know what you do not".......

What was happening to him? What was happening to the villages, the country-side; everywhere he went and every place he looked? What blight had fallen like cold poisonous dew on the sleeping world? All gazes were furtive and wary; all bloods, cold or full of spleen. Madness seemed to have broken down the walls of sanity, and free of all reason, was now having its barbarous way. Goodness sickened and reeled, and retching openly, was not ashamed; and though the sun shone brightly, its golden beams were full of dark shadows.

He had continued his aimless way at night, even after he had begun to feel confident he was out of danger's reach; as he had become a creature who had learned to distrust the sun, and all that the sun shone upon. The night was his friend, his helpmeet, his mother, and gave to him dreams that the day would not. In darkness he could think and see things that the sun kept from his knowing. At night the stars were the cage that let his spirit take flight; in the day, those same wings were cramped, imprisoned in the world of men.

The weather had turned cool, its winds breathing through the hills and forests, chiding summer away, and whispering a myth called 'winter' to its children. The moon was in its third quarter, limning the scudding clouds, their profusions of crashing waves piling into feathery banks and wooly cliffs, forcing the moon higher, that its eye might look down upon the dark ways where its silver tears were dripping.

These first breaths of autumn were invigorating, and helped to sweep away the memories of the things he was fleeing. Their breezes tumbled like happy clowns through the fields and orchards, and yet in the caravans that lagged somewhere behind them, voices of ghosts hung in the air; moaning soldiers, wailing widows, crying orphans. Yes, autumn was splashing the dust from his boots and his face, but behind its sweetness was a cold, ruthless, inexorable monster, one with growling bowels full of sharp knives and bloody teeth.

Why was it always this way? Why did life's callous coldness always tear him away from life's gentle warmth? Why did the tender hand that guided him always turn cruel, tearing him away from the cheer of the sedentary to the hardships of the banished, expelling him from the nests of love and friendship, ransacking his comforts? Why did life give him exciting pleasures, only to deprive him of those pleasures, making their re-attainment just out of reach, like a king's crown sparkling beneath the swift clear current of a stream? Why had whatever fate that ruled over him dictated that he be a brooder and dreamer, one passing through seasons whose pageantries he was ever a stranger to? Why was he a recruit that for some reason did not fall into step with life's army; rather a malingerer, a rebel too swift or too lagging, out of step in its march?

Still, as he journeyed through the nights, he became more and more comfortable in his aloneness; the aloneness that he had always feared and fled; the aloneness that he had festooned with many songs, many dreams, many lovers, but in the end were only decorative, tinsels hung in the destitution of his soul.

He began to feel his smallness, his briefness, his insignificance. Yes, the night and the stars were very great, and he was very small; a rag of flesh stitched to a few bones; a few dreams housed in a little brain; dreams that stared like a sleepy child from the windows of his eyes into a mysterious vastness that the child knew it would never comprehend. Once more he knew that life would forget him; that the one who was called 'Brother Maria', would die. And it was this certainty that quickened and exhilarated him; that filled him with song and hunger; a mad poetry of passion, an anguish that was the secret of the lonely flights of both his pain and his ecstasy.

There was a strange rapture in this aloneness, as it was first and foremost, and in the end the way he was meant to be, perhaps the way all men were meant to be: mother-less, father-less, child-less, lover-less; perhaps even God-less. It was the loneliness of the wind that moaned through husk and reed; of the tree whose roots clung to a high cliff; of a ghost that cried out to the deaf ears of the living. It was a sentence whose harshness was its sweetness; a bondage whose chains were its freedom; an endless exile whose doom was a wish to ever return.

There was only one loneliness that could match, equal, mirror this lone-liness; that answered and sang back to him, that was as untamed, original and forlorn; that spoke the same language of eternal longing. It was in the desire he saw in women's eyes, and heard cry in women's wombs.

Again and again he saw it in their eyes when they stood from their toils in the grape yards, or when they drew water from a well, or brought cows from the fields; when they danced in his arms, or sat at his feet when he played the fiddle; even as they nursed, even as they prayed. In all of their eyes he saw one like himself, an itinerant, a sojourner lost and aching, one who called out to him as he passed.

"Yes, I am lonely too, sweet stranger! I have always been lonely, because I have always been waiting for love! Come, golden traveler, come sing and sleep in my arms! Give me the seed of your loins and the dreams in your heart. Let us together steal this little sweetness, this little moment from the Reaper's scythe, from the cold uncaring yesterdays and the cold uncaring tomorrows."

And yet, try though he may, he could not fill their loneliness, as they could not fill his. Like two winter-meeting winds, they passed through each other's arms, sowing no summer flowers, and continuing on with the same howls in their hearts.

There was something dark and dreadful about love; something dishonest; something fatal. Love inebriated and dizzied, woke, crowned and chris-tened; thrilled the flesh as it exalted the spirit; made one feel as though one was more than dust, bone and veins of salty blood. But in the height of its ecstasy, was there not always a shadow, as of an assassin, watching it midst its playful romp?

Still, was it so wrong, that one should want to steal a trinket of life's immensity? Why, standing midst a sea of flowers, was it wrong to pluck one or two of those flowers? How could God, who owned the treasury of Earth and Heaven, mind a child's tiny theft? How could He who had so much, slap the hand of one who wanted so little? Why was He who created the wicked murderer in Man, jealous of that murderer's petty thieveries? What did God care of Man's naughtiness?

Each time he fell in love, was he not merely trying to halt the accursed pounding on Time's anvil, hush the tolling of Time's bell; forget the dull march of its boots as it trudged past his door? For a brief moment was this blind, silly, wicked lovely gratification that men called love not creating a truce in life's incessant battles? Was he not, like a bee, trying to sip a drop of nectar in life's garden? Was it wrong, in love's brief spell, to steal a moment of Time, and in the theft of that moment, close one's eyes, and dream a stolen dream of paradise?

His heart was the root that kept him clinging to life's cruel and lovely mystery; its beating was his sail, sword and drum, and though the voices that spoke in it were not wise, full of misgivings, greed and trespass, it was the trumpet of his being. Although it was blind and willful, less loyal than rebellious, it was the compass given him in a sea of stars.

Was it not the same for all men; the knight as well as the pauper? Did not all hearts dream beneath the moon, give counsel, kindle passion; goad on the nerves and muscles of their brute masters? Was not this little thing pounding in men's breasts the arbiter of good and evil, pain and pleasure, life and death? Or was the heart of the wolf so very different from the heart of the rabbit? Did the eyes of the stars fill with tears of care, or stare on with their icy, eternal stupor? In the end, did the mother who looked upon the world weep or laugh, or stare in wooden numbness on her crippled child?

After several weeks, these long nocturnal walks and meditations came to an end, forced as he was into the daylight by the angry shouts of his empty stomach. He had long exhausted his bread, and the grapes, ears of corn and orchard apples were no longer sufficient to appease the pleas of his ribs for warm milk and roasted meat.

But as Maria once more stepped into the light of the sun, it was as though he was stepping into a darkness darker than the night he was leaving; as he was not entering the vibrant song of the sunny earth, rather a lower, darker realm, one that, albeit glowing with bright sunlight, was filled with shadows of menace and dread.

Although the days were warm and bright, it was as though a killing frost lay upon the land, one that did not freeze flowers and butterflies, but smiles and laughter; man's spirit itself. Its strangeness was a kind of dark enchantment, one that greeted Maria with sights he had never seen before, sights that frightened, bewildered and appalled him, yet at the same time fascinated him with their dark beauty, so that, as if hypnotized, he could not run from the arms that were gathering him into their embrace.

The autumn was prodigal, and this only enhanced the strange spell under which all seemed to be darkly dreaming. Everywhere the season was boasting its abundance, decorating vines, boughs and stalks with its jewelries. And yet, in some great, secret irony of things, there was barrenness in this abundance, for it was a plenty that was wasting away, crying out to be garnered by hands whose ears did not heed their cries. Trees, fields and gardens cried out like a woman in travail, begging to be harvested of their beautiful burdens.

"Please, take the fruits I have born for thee, the fruits that I have ripened through sun, rain and storm for thee! Come, take the children I have made in my womb! Do not let them fall unharvested. Do not let them wither and die at your feet!"

But the stewards to whom this mother cried did not come, and seldom did Maria see anyone in the fruit-heavy orchards or the golden-bearded fields.

As he entered this strange forsakenness, he saw only a few people, and those few, fearful and shy, and sometimes fleeing from his presence. One of the few he stumbled upon was a poor wretch who did not run away; one who was so slovenly, filthy and crazed, she seemed half dead, and not entirely alive.

She was knelt in the corner of a much neglected garden, the garden only a little way from a poor hut made of crude planks and a caked mud of plaster. A spade lay at her side, but as she appeared too frail to wield it, she was instead digging through the dry stony soil with a large knife. Whether she was too weak, exhausted, or too mad to care, she did not stand; nor did she lift her head at Maria's approach, or even when he stood looking down upon her.

Maria saw at once what she was doing. He saw the small bundle near where she knelt, wrapped in a meal sack that was twisted into knots at both ends. He saw the other graves, those in which he assumed she had played the heroic gravedigger for her family; their cracking, sun-baked mounds adorned with scrawny bunches of wilted flowers. On these mounds were ill-propped crosses made of sticks, as a child would make for a favorite dog or cat, and from the arms of these crosses hung clutters of gauds, bleached ribbons, and little dolls of rag and straw; as well as tresses of the woman's hair, that in the craziness of her grief Maria saw she had haphazardly cut or torn from her head.

The graves were very shallow, probably no deeper than her enfeebled body and her misery-blasted wits could dig, so shallow that Maria saw here and there bits of sack, blanket, sleeve and boot, even arms and legs that the teeth of the rain and sun were determined to gradually exhume; as if even death could not hide what life had done to them, and they were now to suffer life's final indignity; one that would be inflicted by crows, dogs, or rooting pigs.

Maria knelt by the woman's side, and gently spoke to her:

"*Here signora, here, let me help you.*"

But at this the woman convulsed, lifted up her head and violently turned to him, revealing a hollow-eyed, ghoulish face hideously blackened and disfigured, death having scrawled its grim signature over it. Her blouse was unbuttoned, plainly exposing her boil-infested breasts, as they were rotten gourds left clinging to their vine. Like one crawled full of vengeance from a grave, she lifted up and made a feeble, ineffectual swipe with her knife, like a blind man stabbing at darkness. Falling on her face, and then raising up as to make another feeble stab, she began to cackle, then to speak in a whisper full of a hoarseness whose bitterness had shed the last traces of its humanity; a voice that was spoken even as death's hands were strangling the throat from which it was being rasped.

"*Death! Death! Nothing but disease! Nothing but devils! Nothing but death! No life! No God! Nothing but death! Run! Hide! Nothing but death!*"

He had left the woman to her madness, and the death that was devouring her. But he did not forget her. As she was a prophetess, prophesying those things he would see in the weeks and months to come, she visited his dreams with her ruined face, and her knife raised like a warrior's sword, stabbing weakly and blindly, as she wished him to share in the unfairness of her fate. He thought this woman embodied a kind of beauty, a kind of glory in the rage of her final madness. He imagined that the grave he had left her to dig was her own grave, and that with the bundle of the dead child in her arms, she would heroically, defiantly lie down in the hollow place she gouged out with her knife and nails; and with no one to cast shovels of dirt upon her, wait for her own end, and the weather and animals that would eat her.

The country-side lacked any sign of husbandry; the paths overtaken, and some completely shut by an unchecked harvest of weeds, their ways having not been trodden by foot, hoof or wheel for a long while. Fences were broken, and left unrepaired; grapes hung in wizened clusters on green vines; rotting apples, cherries, and mulberries carpeted the orchard floors. There were no sounds of swishing scythes, hammered anvils, or axes being ground on whetstones; no whistles or flutes of shepherd boys; no creaks of cart wheels, or the jangling harness-work of horses.

All seemed to have died beneath a suffocating blanket of silence, one that magnified the buzzing of flies, the humming of bees, and the hops of grasshoppers through the dry grasses; a silence which birds were afraid to disturb with their piping notes. It was a silence that held a kind of victory in its suspended breath, a giddiness of dark laughter in a dark parade of triumph, one whose pounding drums was heard by none but the ear of the heart.

Cows, goats, sheep and pigs had broken from their bounds, and with no one to call and shepherd them back, wandered here and there in their strange, new, nomadic freedom. Milking one of these goats, Maria warmly filled his stomach as it had not been filled for many days, and with that full stomach reflected upon the dark dream into which he had entered.

Yes, a great pestilence was moving through the land. Although the sun shone brightly, and earth's womb was teeming with abundance, death walked in that sunlight and through that abundance, laughing and killing like a merry infidel, shooting its bloody arrows into those, who, naked of armor, were defenseless against their venomous barbs. Death, not life was the Reaper that had come afield, and all fell to their knees, withered and died in the dark glory of its passing shadow.

Yes, death was paying men a visit, and with that visit making small and vain all that they lived for: vineyards, horses, jewels, castles, love.....yes, even love, this hallowed temple in the heart, before whose altar men fought and groveled, sailed seas, swore oaths, knelt and prayed.....for whose trophy they would become drunk, silly, barbarously bloody, for whose bauble they would die.....Yes, love too was being crushed like a blade of grass beneath the bruising hoofs of this merrymaker from hell.....this intruder that had no qualms in leaning over enamored lovers, and slitting their tender throats as they were pigs.

He had stepped into a dark dream, a great sticky web he could not wrest free of. But was that unjust? No; it was not more or less than what was frightening, and bringing its bloody ax to the doors of all of those about him. It was the same tap that Isabella and Agatha had heard upon their panes; the same fire that had raged through their bloods. He would accept it, nay, he would embrace it. If heaven wished to rain death, he would lift his face like a dusty flower. If God decided to slay him, he would stand before His scythe, gritting his teeth at the one who had made such a mockery of mercy. No, he would not run. No, he would not play death's game. Fright would only fuel the madness that he could feel, even now, toying with his nerves and trying to insinuate itself into his heart.

Early one morning, Maria made his first approach to the living. But nearing a small farmhouse he was met with a gruff shout and a pack of the shouter's snarling protectors. Calling off his dogs, a man stood in the doorway with a threatening club, and with a few blunt malicious words told him in no uncertain way he wanted no beggars or vagrants, and if he would stay about, he would kill him, and then feed him to his pigs.

This episode was repeated at other doors that same day, and when he happed on a small hamlet, scowling men emerged with cudgels and large hammers, some throwing stones that landed at his feet. This was repeated before two other hamlets on following days. They had no gates, but before them stood, like packs of ferocious dogs, knots of sullen men, haggard women, and spindly children, all with looks of fear, sickness, and a kind of insanity in their eyes. All held sticks, stones or knives in their hands, and shouted for him to stay away or they would kill him. The gates of a larger village were shut, and upon those gates were nailed corpses, corpses being eaten to skeletons by feasting crows. Near this grisly scene were smeared large, scarlet crosses, and the words: *"Holy Mother of God, Forgive and Protect Us!"*

What was he to do? His flesh was shrinking from his bones, and he was starving, hungry for things that the abundance in the fields did not provide for him, and his fear prevented him from stealing. The nights were becoming cool, and without food or shelter he knew he could not easily survive the winter; or if he did, survive it only as a beast or a madman.

If he lived away from the living, there were three foes, other than the contagion itself, with which he must contend, each presenting him with a mortal danger.

The wolves had smelled a prey that no longer was protected by barns and fences . Lured by the aroma of such a feast, they had come from the hills and the forests, and finding no one to obstruct their coming they now roamed and killed at will. Again and again Maria came upon carcasses of goats, sheep and pigs, and even mutilated cows and horses, the work not of the knives of hungry men, but the teeth of hungry beasts.

The second foe was another kind of beast, a human beast; mangy, lawless men that he did not trust, and that he kept his distance from; men that perhaps disease and death had driven from wives and children, or perhaps from debts, or from jails where death, having sentenced all, like a drunken jailor had freed them from their chains. Gathering into bands, they wandered through the country-side, robbing and looting, and making bestial sport of women; death having made them fearless of any recrimination, as well as any salvation for their souls. These wild bands, unchecked by authority, and fed and remunerated with the plenty they freely looted, only proliferated and gave savage license to the wild dangers afoot.

But there was another foe, a more formidable foe that was beginning to stalk him, haunting his steps through the shaggy meadows and autumn forests; one that was following him into his dreams. It was a foe that he knew he would not be able to hide from, outrun or out-fight, that would become only more dangerous as the days went by; as death's grip grew tighter, and its pall, darker.

He knew that *loneliness* was a cage, one whose captive beast died whining at the tormentor grinning outside its bars. But his was a different kind of loneliness, one whose bars were the beams of the sun and moon. He was not afraid of dying, and if the contagion smote him, he did not care if there was no one to bury him. He did not care if his sextons were the beaks of birds and the teeth of animals; his shroud, rotten leaves and cold snows. He had long since made his peace with God, a peace acquired with the sacraments of wine and kisses; a peace that refused any pious surrender to the myth of an all-merciful kindness.

Still, as the days passed, the weather cooled, and death bolted the doors of his escape, Maria became lonely in a way he had not been lonely before.

As he was once more a small child, he became lonely for his mother. But it was not the flamboyant, dark-haired and bright-eyed gypsy mother of his childhood for whom he longed, rather the mother he had seen smile *through* the smiles of maidens when they had yearned for him; when they had given their love to him. It was for this mother his heart ached and cried out, the mother that smiled through every maiden. It was for this mother, as cruel in her illusoriness as she was sweet in her seduction, in whose arms he wished to fall, be embraced, and die.

He dreamed of loving, and being loved in this mother's arms, and in the aftermath of love's storm, whispering into her ear; a lover that did not speak, but only listened, and listening, gave brief pardon to his fears; she, the God-less God that he worshipped in a God-less world; that smiled her pretty smile in a world of death. Yes, in his madness he reached our for his mother's arms; lost himself in her love; confided to his mother the dreams in his heart.

"Oh my love, my love, we must remain sweet to each other, and in that way Death shall not touch us. It shall pass us by as we hide in love's flowers. Or if Death finds us, we shall decay and die together.....return to the wind and the seasons together, having gathered the sun and moon in our embraces."

In the long weeks of his wandering, he had seen few women, most of which were old and hardened. There had been wariness and fright in their eyes, and they had fled his unexpected, uncouth presence. And yet he dreamed of these old women about his fires, even though they were thin, twisted and knotted with age. He had dreamed of their haggard faces, and lying upon their withered bodies; of kissing their shriveled breasts, and being wrapped in their bony legs and arms. He dreamed of playing lewd games with them; tickling them wickedly with his passion; making them moan and scream out in the height of their pleasures.

He dreamed of how, when passion began to move its storm through their stiff unlovely bodies, they whispered in their crisis, even as the fear of death was the deepest secret of their love:

"Love me! Love me! Give me your life! O darling boy, I do not want to die! I want to live! Yes, O yes, give me your life my sweetheart, and let me live!"

In his roaming Maria had come upon huts and cottages, many of which were deserted by the living; some having fled death's rumor, others, having been slain in the defense of its bold attack. After hallooing loudly before their doors, and then approaching with caution, he would determine if they were inhabited by the living, the dying or the dead. In those in which he received no response, he would enter and freely pilfer; a living thief robbing death's spoils.

Horror had gripped him, and gripping him, benumbed him. Horror permitted his thieveries, as well as shielded his eyes midst his thieving, as in some last attempt of mercy, protecting him from being blasted brutish dumb. Entering deserted rooms that displayed death's grisly machinations, he would walk numbly past those who had sat bravely propped at their last, or dangled by ropes in doorways, like convicts left to rot on their gibbets. He stepped numbly over those that lay decomposing at his feet, their blackened flesh rushed upon and scurried over by troops of gorging vermin.

At one such cottage he fetched wine from its cellar, and then chunks of bread and cheese that he had found protected in a cupboard. He went outside to eat, only to find before the very place where he sat, several corpses, sprawled and half buried in the tall grass before him. Desensitized by death's carnage, he did not turn away, but proceeded to eat his meal, his eyes riveted, and strangely fascinated, even infatuated with death's handiwork that was so vividly shown, as in proud display before him.

They had not been long dead. Perhaps only this morning this maid and her younger brother had escaped, burning and frothing with fever, made mad with death's tokens clinging like leeches to their bodies. Disease had blackened, bloated and disfigured them, but rats had not yet arrived to scavenge them. Only death's scouts, the blowflies, had located them in the grass, half naked where they lay, and now, unmolested, buzzed about, alighting and crawling upon the carnage left in their dark master's wake.

Both were slack-jawed, their mouths wide open; as were their eyes that stared glassy stares, like fish on a fishmonger's table. Grown brave from their inertness, Maria watched as the flies landed upon, and then set to explore the places of their nakedness; some stepping into the cleft between the boy's buttocks, others alighting on the jellies of the girl's unblinking eyes, while still others were beguiled into the caves of their tongue-swollen mouths.

The girl had been slight, and probably, without the distemper's ghastly blains and boils, possessed of prettiness. Maria found himself staring at one of her slender, well formed, uncorrupted legs, death having left her skirt lifted immodestly to her thigh. Mesmerized with her young beauty, and with fate's cold abandon of its murder, Maria knelt beside her, and lifted the skirt all the way to her ham. Here she was still fresh with a rosy loveliness that probably no boy had ever known. Seized with an urge to do the unthinkable, the unnatural, with none but death, and a cold compassionless God to watch his sin, Maria unbuckled, only to stop with a last plea of his sanity.

Still, in a capitulation to his reason, and a compromise to his madness, he was compelled to lean down and kiss her naked haunch. It had become stiff, with a cold clamminess, like a midnight dew upon it, and u was beginning to exude a pungency that he was now familiar with; the sickly sweet perfume of death. Knelt at her side, he looked into her eyes, and then into the boy's eyes, as their vacancy had made them twins. He had seen this stare before, this stare filled with the same strange vapidity; empty of all human faith, hope, and entreaty. Maria thought that if any trace of human emotion was left in these eyes, it was a heroic surrender, a surrender that was a victory that had conquered all vanities; a kind of last, innocent laughter in the face of death's blood-thirsty sword; an ineffable gladness to be rid of that nuisance men call life; from buzzing flies, to the untold wars and labors that would trouble it to its grave. In their stares was laughter, laughter that was laughing at the world they were leaving; but also at him, at Brother Maria, and all the gallant dreams he had so foolishly dreamed.

Maria bent close to the dead girl's ear, and as she was a sleeper wrapped in sleep, whispered:

"*What do your beautiful eyes see my love? And what is your pretty mouth trying to say? What song, O my sweet little bird, are you trying to sing?*"

He brought his face to her quickly decomposing one, and then his mouth to her mouth that death had frozen open. Softly, tenderly, he fitted his lips to hers. For many days he was haunted with this kiss; with her lips that felt like no lips at all, but like the rind of a fruit, one that had long dried in the sun.

He was wandering midst the dead and the dying, and those, even more unfortunate, that had gone mad and distract with their fears of the dead and the dying. He had been caught in a web, and the enchant-ment that some dark spider of evil had cast queenly upon it; a web that now claimed him too as its prize, like a midge or a gnat. Death blocked his every path, laughed in every frightened eye, played its fiddle through the streets of his dreams.

He had entered a dark and lower realm, one in which the sun shone, but did not cheer or heal; a realm from which there was no road of escape. Gradually he realized that he was part of this realm, that he had become one of its citizens, and those who looked upon him, either with fear or maliciousness, looked at him as he had come to look at them; as one with death's curse written upon him also. He gradually realized that he too was a member of death's dark brotherhood; that he too was now a ghost wandering among ghosts.

How small and petty now seemed those things he had counted most dear, when seen against the awful majesty of death, and yet how he now missed and longed for them as never before.....the lute and fiddle, the dice board and wineskin, the senseless childish games of love played in dark doorways and in summer grasses.....yes, they were foolish, vain, petty.....but their pettiness had been treasures held for a moment in a splash of sunlight, free of death's shadow.

Madness had invaded him, filled him with Death's horrid rituals and dark poetry.....carcasses he had stumbled on, hastily buried, rooted and gnashed apart by wild pigs and dogs, crawled over by rats, scarce recogniz-able as men at all.....the angry scowls and knives, and the stones cast at him from village gates......the rapacious bands, the fields un-harvested, rotting thanklessly, even as they beckoned with gold and ruby-ripened abundances in their arms.......

.....the dreams he dreamed at his fires, making wicked love to withered crones.....mounting them like a boar mounts a boar, or like a hawk smothers a songbird.....making its wings beat helplessly beneath it.....inseminating even as he killed.....lusting with death itself.....as he was no longer Brother Maria, but a lesser, wilder, more inhuman thing.......

Yes, death had gripped him, and that grip had unbridled madness.....a madness that cackled in madness.....a fool to think he could wrest free from such a monstrous hag.....an idiot to beg the madness of its mercy......

It was no longer a matter of staying alive, for with the autumn plenty about him, and the herds and flocks no longer tended, and the cellars, pantries and cupboards left with victuals by their dead tenants......he could live like a king.....albeit a mad, lonely and loveless king.......

.....or if death's sickle slew him, that would be another thing, yes, another, perhaps much sweeter thing.....to be cropped and be no more.......

* * *

Need

AS his needs and fears spawned these strange thoughts and wicked desires, as if wishing to be in cadence with the orgy of death all about him, one day Maria met a young girl collecting hips in a basket. Absorbed in her task, and softly humming, she did not hear his approach.

"*Good morning, signorina.*"

Startled, she looked up at him, her eyes full of surprise, but not the terror he had met in others.

"*Ah, pretty one, I see you are collecting hips left by the summer roses. Perhaps to crush for a broth? Or for a medicine?*"

At these words she did not flee; and this Maria interpreted as a permission to flatter her more."

"*But the rose whereupon I stumbled this golden morning has not shed its petals. Heaven has bloomed in the face I look upon. You are very pretty, 'signorina'. Has no one ever told you so? With death all around, has no man ever told you that you are as pretty as a rose?*"

The girl did not speak, but gripped with distrust of his strange words, recoiled, and began to slowly step away.

"*Please, do not go away. You see, I have been alone for many days, alone and wandering, like a ghost in death's mists.....yes, this death that is all about us, weaving its web like a giant spider. I only wished to tell you that you are very lovely, sweetheart, yes, lovely, and to ask of you one little favor.......*"

These words arrested the girl's flight. She lifted her eyes to him, their distrust changed to curiosity, a curiosity that asked what that favor might be.

"*I wanted to ask you, pretty one, if I might taste the honey the golden bees have made in your mouth, for I am sure they have sipped ten thousand flowers to make such sweetness. You see I hunger for such honey, like a man long in a desert thirsts for water. That is the favor I wanted to ask of you, if you might let my lips taste that little hive where stores such sweetness. With so much suffering and dying all about us, I wanted to ask you for a kiss.*"

With this, fright seized the girl, and she hurried away, disappearing in the trees. He did not shout or run after her. Realizing his words must have seemed very strange, especially from such an unkempt, wild-looking stranger, and sorry, if not ashamed that he had spoken them, he turned and walked away.

But after crossing part of the meadow, a voice cried out to him. It was the girl. She had returned to the place where she had been collecting hips. Meekness, not fright was in her voice, and a wan little smile was breaking in sunny fits upon her face.

"*Sir, please, I was only a little frightened, that is why I ran. You see, with the sickness and all we have come to be afraid of travelers; afraid they might be toting death upon their backs. Well, you seem to have health and strength, and not death upon yours.....the blue sky is in your eyes. If you would like to come back, sir, I think I could give you the little favor you asked."*

The smile that Maria gave her was from his loins, not his lips; his need now far greater than politeness or courtship. Immediately, with hurried steps he walked back through the waist-high flowers of the un-grazed meadow, his eyes gleaming. The girl, feeling his approaching need, and knowing she was about to make a sacrifice to that need, tried to primp and tidy as best she could, wiping her cheeks with her sleeves, tucking loose strands of hair behind her ears, and despite herself, moistening her dry lips with the tip of her tongue.

Made nervous with her boldness, she became flustered as the stranger approached.

"It was just that you asked so nicely, sir, and with such pretty words..... calling my dish clout face a rose of the morning, or something like that..... and that thing you said about death being all around us.....and well, a kiss is a little thing, a sweet thing, a thing of life, not death.....a thing a maid is born to give, and a man born to ask and take....like a cow's milk I suppose......"

Mid stride, Maria wrapped her in his arms, and brought his mouth to hers; not tenderly or gently, but hungrily, as she was a lover he had lost at the beginning of the world. Surprised and frightened at his passion, the girl struggled, but vainly, and only briefly, like a little bird caught in a fowler's net.

"Please, kind sir....."

"O rose of the morning, I am hungry for your honey, the sweetness of your nectar!"

His words, his strength, the kisses of his need raining on her neck, face and eyes, things that her provincial upbringing had never felt before.....the girl yielded to him her mouth to taste and explore, as it had never been explored before.....yielded, and in yielding answered his passion with both greed and surrender.

And as she did Maria seized her breasts, one in each hand, at which the girl did not struggle, or make an attempt to fight off his attack, but instead whispered tenderly in his ear:

"A moment, sir, you may see and hold them as you like, although they're not as nice as ones other maids have hidden away....small as pippins they are...."

Parting from his arms, she quickly lowered her blouse and jostled free her breasts, and then lifted up her eyes to him, as for his approval.

They were as small as onions, a disproportionate smallness that did not match her buxomness. Womanhood had not yet come to swell and rescue them, and they were left to cling to the boy-like breast of her youth, like late fruits struggling to catch the rest of her body's maturation.

Enclosing them in his large hands, he tenderly squeezed their nipples between his fingers, as he was squeezing juice from berries; and then like a blind, newborn puppy, brought his mouth to them and greedily sucked. This elicited a moan of pleasure, as wells as consent from the girl, at which his hands slid down to her haunches, and gathering her smock's skirt, his fists filled with her thick hams. As a shepherd with a sheep, in one swift motion he lifted and trussed the girl in his arms, then laid her on the ground. Lifting her skirt up to her waist, and propping her naked legs upon his shoulders, he prepared for his satisfaction.

But before he knew that happiness the helpless girl stopped him; stopped him without struggle, fear or pleading. She spoke softly, with a voice free of fright, and when Maria lifted his eyes to her eyes, they were without fear or defiance, only a gentle concern.

"Please sir, I know you are with need.....and if you want I will give you your pleasure without a struggle.....give you the happiness a maid gives, and a man takes. You are a very handsome man, and I would be proud to give you what you wish.....but, well, you see I am very young, and with death in the fields and forests, surrounding us like an army, I know I may not live long.....perhaps not another plough or harvest time. As the old ones say, youth comes a-dallying but once, and the moments of its tenderness are few, and if I might ask, sir.....well, if I might ask that this be one of those moments.....a moment without roughness, and only a little tenderness, if it would not be too much to ask."

With this the girl freed herself from Maria's embrace, stood, and in an instant stepped naked from her smock. Laying back down on the grass and flowers, she smiled.

"There, that is better. Now you can do the same. And then come back atop me, like you were. You mustn't be ashamed. I will give you what you want, because it is what I want too, and not against my will at all. Only be tender sir, if you would.....I ask only a moment of a little tenderness."

Maria did as she asked, and after their sweetness together, remained upon her, looking into the girl's face.

She was homely, not pretty; her nose large and crooked, and one of her eyes slightly crossed with the other. On one of her jaws, and part of one lip was a pronounced scar, as they and her broken nose had come from the same kick of an animal's hoof; things that time would never mend or take away. She was big-boned, and an overall ungainliness was about her, a boorishness that would certainly never blossom into a sensual shapeliness of womanly allure and seduction. Without knowing a maiden's beauty, soon she would wake to a tired, unlovely prison of chores and motherhood.

And yet when hearing her gentle words, and looking into the plain simple sincerity of her face, even as he had prepared to violate her with his lust, Maria thought this must be what it is like to be looked upon by an Angel.

He kissed her cheeks, and then her cracked and husk-dry lips. He kissed her not with desire, but with gratitude, and then whispered in her ear with the tenderness of a prayer.

"You are not a rose, but an Angel. You are very, very beautiful."

And with this he laid his head gently upon her breast, her stomach, hips and legs stretching like the loveliness of a rolling meadow before his tears.

Her nakedness was not tawny, as were her sun-browned arms, neck and face, but a pearly white, like the inside of a shell. She was a rough, thick, bovine girl, but her secret places were exquisitely soft and pliant; the tuft blooming between her legs, a silky down, like the crown of a bird. She smelled heavily of sweat and soil, and late summer weeds, and her kisses tasted of fish and onions, but somehow these smells and tastes were made sweet with the simple way she had offered her love; as it was a flower, a child of the earth itself. Gratefully stilled of his passion, he wanted only to dream forever on the pillow of her breast.

The girl did not move, startled as she was to find this wild, older man lying upon her; both of them stunned, as from a mutual fall, at this rash act that had resulted in this unlooked for peace. She could feel his tears well, rise and spill in gentle sobs upon her belly; the soothing rest she offered him; the acceptance she was giving his madness. She could feel his gratitude, a gratitude that allowed her to trust this strange man and his madness, even when his hand culled tiny flowers in the grass where they lay, and with them began to make a coronet in and about her maidenhair.

At last she began to speak; words that reflected her youth, but with a maternal kindness that belied that youth, as if the earth and the flowers were speaking; gently singing, and sending their consolations through her.

"*I do not want you to think you did what you did against me, sir, or that I was afraid of having my treasure stolen for the first time, for it's been given away three or four times before.....the first time more than a year ago by the river, when I was fifteen summers, and that a full summer more than some I know, some who gave boys what they came a-mooing and mooning for.....and after, whatever and whenever a boy had the look upon him and the itch to have a throw......."*

......death's spider was weaving its web, as it had woven its web about beautiful Isabella and her family, the Countess Agatha in her castle, the mistress of the Bear Cub Tavern.....it was weaving its web about the mad old woman digging graves in her garden, and the peasant girl covered with blowflies....its web like a shroud, slowly covering the fields and forests, the sun and stars.....he could feel it spinning its thread about his heart....... yes, spinning its threads about his heart, snaring the prize of a man's dreams, his dreams........

"*It is one boy only I've tumbled with, and other than him, by the Savior, good sir, you're the only other who has had his pleasure with me. He's a peddler sort, and comes by every now and then with his combs and pots, and sometimes ribbons and lambskin caps, and once with a sparrow bird in a cage, a dab of red feather, like a spot of blood on its breast.....red as they say is a ruby jewel......."*

.....he remembered the abbey.....the bell, the swallows and roses..... the smell of incense, ash and tallow, and the gentle anthems the brotherhood lifted to a God they did not see, but faithfully believed in.....this web was strangling these things also.....the great iron bell, the arches and the courtyard.....binding like mummies the brothers as they prayed and lifted their beautiful voices.....wrapping their beards and gentle smiles with its threads.....muffling their voices, bandaging shut their eyes.....choking their prayers with dust.....oh was life so very unimportant, something to be peddled on a road, like spoons or ribbons.....to know for a moment, only to forget?.......

"*He's not at all handsome and husky like you are sir, and he speaks but little, and instead of sweet words like the ones you speak, his are full of curses of the Saints and the Mother of God. But I don't mind. 'The Death' took father, and my brothers ran off after that, and when the peddler boy comes, my mother knows why he has come, and hopes maybe if he likes what I give him he will one day stay. We have a tumble or two in the fields, but after a short while he saunters away.....and even if he takes others beneath the hedges, well, he says that he likes what I give him best of all, and if it be a lie, it's all one to me.....and one day when he makes his way with his sack and his itch back down the road, and I be not with the sickness, or be a skeleton of bones in a garden grave, back of the potatoes where there is a nice sunny place, near the wall where we buried father.....I am sure me and the peddler boy will marry......."*

.....and what of Giovanni?.....would his learning and his holiness save him from being bound in this spider's threads?.....or was he also snared, with the thieves, the paupers and the murderers?.......did this spider not spin its web about sanctity, or were even Saints bound and eaten beneath its shroud?.......

"And do not think age has a thing to do with it, kind sir. All men have the flame in their loins, ploughboys and graybeards alike, and the need to have it taken away. I know a girl who swears she's never been pizzled, and many there are who call her a little nun and the like, but I think their little nun's her father's whore. I think he snatched her jewel before she knew she had one.....and she no longer knows the difference between a lad's love and a father's chore."

......and would the spider's threads wrap about the green shutters and the red flowers in the flowerboxes.... her soft smile, and her eyes that had looked like no other eyes into his soul?......oh, sweet Katrinika, would he never stand beneath her window again, and receive warm bread from her hands, bread that had been consecrated by her tender heart?....would death's spider bind and strangle her sweetness too?.....

"It is not a shameful thing for a grown man to cry. It tells of a full heart. You may cry on my belly all you wish, sir; it feels sweet, like dew on my bare feet in the morning. And you may sleep a little if you like. Mother and the dogs will not hunt me till the sun is low and the shadows come......."

.....oh how very sweet and lovely.....oh to die here, to have his miserable, wasted life end in such sweetness.......

"And thank you for the flowers about my privities. A man's never done such a sweet thing for me.....like the crown of a queen it is. I will save each one of them.......the peddler boy I tumble with is not half so sweet......he calls my privities his cock trap, sometimes Eve's tail, and sometimes hell's secret,* *and all sorts of silly and vulgar names like that.....but he's never decorated it nicely with flowers like you have, sir, like it was a little queen........"*

......perhaps death was not a bad thing, a dark thing, a thing to be feared.....but a sweet thing, a merciful thing, a thing to be lost in, like the naked body of a woman.......

"Have your cry, and a little sleep, and if the grim old man with his scythe does not crop us like wheat, when you pass again, whether I'm the wife of a peddler boy with sparrows, or a fat spinster with a hoop and a squint, I would be proud to tumble with you, or just lay like this with your handsomeness, sir.....not like a man buys a whore woman in a city, mind you, but like two lambs in the grass and sun......."

* * *

Resolution

HE lay on his belly in the crisp dry leaves, looking at the scene below him.

The road was not a good one. It was roughly hewn, and crumbling with years of disrepair; pitted with great ruts that, when filled with mud or snow, made it impassable; only in weather fair and dry, like today, permitting the wheels of wagons and coaches to gingerly pass over it. But it was the only road that connected the larger village with the smaller one atop the hill, where the air was freer of the oppressive, late autumn heat. Desperately desiring that air, even as it was life itself, the road was clogged with a great traffic: carts, horses and mules laden with crates and bags, men on foot, with chests, tents of sailcloth, and children on their backs; lumbering ox-carts loaded with cluttered hills of furniture, and fathomless miscellanies of provisions and possessions.

Watching this human river trickle up the steep hill, in stark contrast with this fine autumn day, grim meditations were inspired in the one looking down upon its stream, that, like a dark blood, was staining the day's goldenness.

.....this then the dark king, the dark king with his chariots, generals and armies, and his consorts of fear and pain that comes to claim all of life's beauties and idolatries.....his entourage that did not know they were his entourage......this his dark pageantry, that with such dark, ragged pomp parades victoriously through all valleys, over all mountains.....topples all

thrones and smothers all cradles......poisoning every well, peering in every
window, laughing at every prayer.......

......Was the plague and its horrid spoils simply enacting the rites exacted
from all men, the rites performed in death's eternal chambers?.....as if hell
had regurgitated, spilled the guts of its horrors in the light of the sun that the
living could see with their own eyes, shudder with their own souls at what
awaited the journey of their own days? Was the death that had spread all
about them not the same drama enacted in every pauper's grave, in every
prince's tomb?.........

......Was the handiwork of Death, and the dark miracles it worked in
the grave not being revealed to all who plowed, prayed, and waged battle
above the palace of its dark bowels?.....its revelation, the truth the Angels
do not tell? Death had raised its grisly head; its clayey hair full of bones and
skulls, its mouth crammed with broken spines of love and crushed wings of
hope. The secret of the ages was being plainly told to all: the breaking apart
and crumbling.....the decay and disintegration of the god of Man, like a
wind-fallen fruit, bored by worms and picked by birds....dunging the earth
with hair, teeth, brains, viscera......the mansion of the heart plundered by
armies of slugs and nettles.......

Beside him lay a satchel, its weather beaten leather camouflaged,
as if melting, decaying back into the brown leaves of the forest floor.
It was not his original satchel, the one that a servant girl with deep
dark eyes and a yellow bandanna had once given him. He had made
another, exactly the same as the first that he had left in the city where
he had narrowly eluded death. He had escaped with his life, but he had
forgotten his satchel, the thing that had been indispensable to him in
his wandering; not only his prized, but his sole possession.

In the days after his escape he had mourned the loss of the bag
he had carried so long and far, and was filled with the mementoes of
so many dreams. Yes, deep in the forest, and in the dark of night had
he not mourned its loss: a grown man, a brawler, drinker and hunter
mourning the loss of a leather bag and the whatnot it contained; the
little remembrances left by lovers whose names and faces he could not
recall; as well as the childlike rhymes he had scribbled of flowers, moons
and clouds? Had he not even entertained the thought to enter the city
again, a convict with a bounty on his head, only to retrieve it from the
lover with whom he was sure he had left it; counting it more precious
than his life itself? That is when he made the satchel that lay in the dry

leaves beside him, using meticulous care to make it exactly like the first. And had he not quickly, shamelessly replenished it, using his blue eyes, his fiddle and sweet words to fill it with other silly little gifts, and other childlike dreams? And had this not consoled him, helping to fill the missing part of his soul? When his heart ached, and he was alone, did he not sometimes use the satchel for his pillow?

From this vantage and this distance, the stream of those fleeing the walls and gates of the village seemed almost not to move at all, as they were a procession of turtles painstakingly picking their way up the sunny rocks of the hillside. But Maria knew that this was a deception, and was not true. He knew there was the ferocity of lions in the slow struggle of these turtles. He knew it was not true because he had been a part of such crawling turtles of fear and dread. And though he had deserted them before they reached their destinations, he knew that what he now saw slowly creep up the hill was full of an incredible tumult; the tumult caused by life's flight to escape the ravenous jaws that had opened for them.

.....the creaking wagons heaped with furniture and keepsakes, and those stacked with cages of pigs, rabbits, chickens, guineas, and trailing behind them cows, swine and goats....the rattling harness-work, the cracking whips and rearing, hysterically neighing horses.....the squalling of babes, the groans of the halt, the aged and the weary.....the curses of they who were punishing their over-laden drays, mindlessly butting their way into the congestion of the inching throngs.....

......tradesmen with as much of their shops as they could shoulder on their backs, others with as much of their homes, still others with nothing more than the rags on their limbs.....the tools and whatnot of their trades hanging from them like fantastic peddlers of the road.....saddlers, cabinet-makers and joiners, cobblers and chandlers, rope-makers, soap-makers and ribbon-weavers.....hat and glove-makers, brewers, butchers, coopers and milliners.....all those who made their livelihood from the commonweal of the village, disgorging from that village and forsaking that livelihood that had sustained them.......

.....laden mules, wheelbarrows, goats, dogs.....cruelly heaped, chest-bearing servants.....priests swinging smoking censers....those on crutches, those on litters, those in mothers' arms and on fathers' backs.....those who stumbled, limped or dragged.....those who fell by the wayside, left to languish and cry out like blind men to those whose hearts had turned stony,

mastered by their fears.......

.....those who begged, and those who hawked.....trinkets, pills, powders, herbs, amulets, exorcisms, charms of Saints.....gauds and painted cards of quackery.....as even in the face of death their god spoke to them in jingling pockets.....young boys whose practiced, magician-quick hands grabbed bags and purses, tore rings from fingers and bracelets from wrists, and whose quick feet gave them wings to disappear with impunity into the sweating waves of men and horses......their thieveries made trivial and irrelevant, forgiven by the desperation of those who feared their flesh was about to be taken forever from their souls.......

And in the eyes of them all.....the sickly, the ruddy, the blusterous, the royal, the wretched......in the eyes of all was the same stare, the same stare that was the same fear, the same fear that was the same desperation to flee the ferocious monster that heaven or hell, or a collaboration of both had thought it time to un-kennel upon them.....making the mightiest, weak, the richest, poor, the proudest, groveling.....making starved dogs of those who had roared like lions from castles and pulpits.....stripping them bare of their houses, trades, belongings, until naked in their fear they became brothers in their fear.....and like frightened sheep they chivvied up the hill together.....sheep that were slaves chained to their doom.....goaded by the goad of a shepherd that some called 'sickness', others, 'plague', others, 'God's judgment'.....different names that they called out in their panic and distress, but all agreed were different names for one and the same 'Mortality'.......

Maria turned on his back and looked through the bare boughs at the blue sky and white clouds above them. Despite the grim scene on the road below, the autumn sun was warm and sweet, as if unconcerned; and with the confused piles of white clouds tumbling playfully about it; oblivious of men's world, and this little thing called death.

.....The astrologers and soothsayers had spoken true. They had seen death in eclipses, the conjunctions of the planets.....and comets, like the tongues of dragons blazing through the frozen fields of the stars.

And with those who read the stars, old women who were visited by the portents of evil dreams.....milk turned to blood.....serpents slinking from cisterns, grape tubs, icons of the Virgin.....those who had heard wails and shrieks in the dark night........

Yes, they had been correct. Those that had become comfortable at their hearths were now fugitives of the roads, little more than wretched beggars begging to a God they had never believed in.....begging the one they had

ignored, scoffed, cursed, begging Him to show mercy and spare their lives.....
fear making hypocrites of the least and the greatest.......

But was their flight, although knitted into this concentrated stream, so
very different than the flight, the incessant, perpetual flight of all things?

As he had walked through the forest today he had seen many butter-
flies fluttering about late-blooming flowers. They were drunk with their
carousals, their heavy wings fluttering leadenly, reluctantly away, only to
return again and again to imbibe still more deeply.....as if incapable of
leaving such sweetness.....as if wanting to extract the last smile of autumn,
the last drop of its honey.....like an infatuated youth, unable to forsake the
kisses hung in perfect ripeness on his lover's lips.....preferring such pleasure
to breath or sleep.....as if afraid love's spell would not come again.....afraid
Time might never again suspend its wings, and from its trove of surprises,
give such a delectable treasure again.......

.....And yet he had seen butterflies that had gathered into colorful flocks,
lifting with sun-gilt wings above the trees.....as if drawn by some sweetness
sweeter than any flower.....flocks that were gathering and lifting, giving
themselves to cloud and breeze.....breezes whose gusts and swirling eddies
were warm playgrounds, playgrounds soon to be cold graveyards for their
angelic kind......their bright bits of wings, like a confetti of farewell......

.......All things were leaving: the flowers, bees and birds, the squirrels and
the rabbits, the trout in the streams and the clouds in the sky.....the sun their
shepherd, shepherding all things windward, winter-ward, death-ward.....
yes, all things were leaving, bidding farewell, joining the endless caravan,
the blindly trekking dream of things.....drawn by some ineffable sweetness,
some inexorable certainty.....to fall into death's voluptuous arms, each tiny
heart, each little warmth at last embraced, possessed, quenched.......

.....He too must leave; cease his play in the summer fields. He too must
join these flocks of farewell. He had become tired, exhausted of reasons and
melodies.....of lips and breasts and thighs.....there was nothing left but
to leave, because there was no nectar sweet enough to keep him. He had
wandered long and far, and he had come to know the secret in the hearts
of all wanderers.....the faltering and the forgetting, the freezing of all
bloods....the perishing of those children men call 'dreams'......he too must
obey this tolling bell, this promise of night and chill....this frost that stuns
to stillness every flower......//

.....man, not a sedentary creature, but a nomadic one, not a prince, but
a fugitive, not a lover, but a hunter.....not one who inherits, but one who

is disinherited.....the tent of the stars his only shelter.....his homelessness his only home.......

.....Yes, he must leave like the butterflies were leaving.....leave the hills and forests, the sun and moon, all that he vainly tried to keep in his satchel.....those things he could not keep in his embraces, or capture in rhyme and song in the cage of his heart.....things that he must leave behind, forsake, forget.....as age must forsake youth, death must forsake life.....as night must forever murder all that was made warm and tender, promised immortality by the sun........

.....and as he joined the butterflies, the falling leaves and wilting flowers, all that is shepherded by the sun, maidens lifted their faces from their garden toils.....ran from vineyards, stepped from orchards.....with wistful cries cried out to him as he passed them by:

....."Do not leave O golden Wanderer of the green summers! Stay with us, O poet of pretty words! Stay and play in our arms, for we have many games yet to play, many secrets yet to tell!".....*

.....a farewell, not a greeting, a defeat, not a conquest.....a forest that held a mystery for all adventurers, a dream for all dreamers of the days and nights.....a dream that once entered, becomes a memory full of confusions, heartaches, remorse.....that ever longs for a lovelier forest, one whose green arms hold another, deeper, more imponderable mystery.....another infatuation, another amorous dream........

.....some of the maidens with golden leaves in their hair, some with sprigs of red berries, some with the evening star.....some showing slender arms, throats, thighs.....some stepping naked from the skirts fallen to their feet.......

....."Do not leave us, O golden Wanderer.....come kiss our lips and drink our breasts.....come, Wanderer, fill our arms, bellies and hearts with your need.....stay, golden Wanderer, for in the summer garden of our pleasures, there are still many games to play......."*

.....leaving the sharp ferment of orchard fruits, the sweet decay of sodden leaves, the languorous sighs, poignant pangs of lovers.....all sounds, echoes, whispers.....moonlight, honeyed flowers, the choirs of waking birds.......

.....some with rosebuds in their hair.....some with red hips, others with drifts of snow.....waving farewell to the one passing them by on a river of butterflies, red and golden leaves.......

.....these angels of the seasons' dream.....their sad dark eyes no longer beckoning to the vagrant who once made love to them.....this boy who had

been drunk with the blue breeze of never ending youth.....their eyes now brightening, as for other wanderers.....other love-drunken lovers whose golden words tickled their hearts.......others with fists of wildflowers, quivers of arrows, eyes eager and hearts lonely to lay between their thighs with the world's first fresh hunger........

.....forgetting the one who had played a fiddle beneath their window..... the ghost who kissed their feet and lips.....left poems and roses on their pillows.......

.....in death's arms forgetting the dream of the sun and the seasons..... in death's arms forgetting a thing that fools and dreamers had named 'love'.......

.....these maidens taking the hands of new wanderers stepped from the forest....wanderers as starved as they were young and strong....taking their poets to fields of tall green wheat, their warriors to meadows of pretty flowers......to give each their breasts and their hearts.....to drown them in the arms of the seasons' dream......in a moment called eternity.......

* * *

Maria woke in the dry bed of leaves where he had dozed; waking to the same bare boughs through which the sun was shining. As if obedient to that sun, and the dream it was shepherding, he rose, slung his satchel over his shoulder, and began to walk down through the few larch trees to the road. Yes, he would join them; yes, he would join their fear and their flight from the great monster of death. They would not raise their fists and shout hateful words at him; they would not throw stones or shoot arrows at him. That had been only the preamble of their fears. Thoroughly harrowed, they would now numbly welcome him to their accursed tribe, as they would recognize that he was one who had also looked upon the gruesome dalliances of their enemy; one whose dreams had also been befouled, his nerves twisted and his reason curdled by the same dark foe. They would silently, numbly accept him in their flight. They would understand that he too was a thrall of the same king.

Still, after several hours, Maria stopped, as he was incapable of climbing the rest of the way up the hill. He stopped as he had stopped the other times when he had joined the cavalcades fleeing the hot, poisonous airs that were hatching and feeding the terrible contagion.

He was not certain why he could not complete these flights. He

619

only knew that each time he tried, he was gripped by something deeper and more passionate than his reason had reason to tell him; something as blind as an infatuation with a beautiful woman. And like such an infatuation, he could only be obedient to its allure. He broke from those about him, deserting the army of their fear.

And yet he did not walk back through the larch trees and into the forest. Instead, he began to walk against the slow current of those who believed they were making a great exodus from death. He began to walk away, for he did not want the cool, disease-free airs upon a hilltop. He did not want to heed crones or wizards, or pray for forgiveness from a punitive, death-dealing God. There were no flights from death; only a surrender. He did not walk away to live, but into the cruel face of this God of curses, to die.

Yes, that was it. As he became infatuated with a beautiful woman, he was now infatuated with death. He wanted to see the dark rooms of its gluttony; where it played its filthy cards, rolled its greasy dice, drank tankards of ale and shamelessly whored in a corner of fetid straw. He wanted to find the dark alleys where it played its fiddle, sending its sad sweet melodies, like poisoned arrows into the dreaming hearts of all.

He had turned his back on friends, lovers, the God of his pious, happy youth....oh, how many years had it been since he had deserted the abbey for the arms of a shepherd girl?.....twenty, no, perhaps more than twenty years......he was no longer a young man, and he could not continue to live and wander through the summers and winters, eating berries, dreaming romantic dreams, loving women who would fade nameless and faceless into the years.....women he embraced, only to discard or be discarded from....it was time to turn his back on life....to fall into other arms, truer arms..... arms whose embrace would continue to hold him.......

......and this wound.....this secret, sacred wound that he would let only the tender fingers of women, and no harsh God see or salve.....this wound that would not heal, that he did not want to heal, that would bleed him to his end.....this wound that he had told no one about, that had come from the swipe of the bear's claws and a mother's smile.....this wound had begun to ache again in his side, to wake him in the night.....its ache singing to him of autumn and farewell....as his mother was singing in the wound, bidding his return to her breast.....as it was the hour to be suckled, as it was the hour to sleep.......

Like a fish swimming up a stiff current, he would climb back to the diseased village, enter the hungry jowls of its wide-open gates. As the ca-thedrals tolled their sullen bells, and were joined by the raucous choruses of crows, he would turn from the pretty faces smiling at him in meadows and from shop windows, from the pretty bodies laying down in beds of straw…… preferring another lover, he would instead fall into the arms of this mistress more beautiful than them all….this mother-mistress that was smiling, and baring her breasts for him.

. . . .

. . . .

CHAPTER SIX

THE SATCHEL

Part I

The Abbey; early Spring; Circa 1352

AT the completion of *Compline*, Brothers Antonio and Anselm assisted him from his prayer stall. They aided him down the few stairs of the choir, even as several other brothers lighted his careful steps with candles. The brothers had held his arms as he knelt before the great Crucifix, and then accompanied him out the dusky chapel into the last glimmer of twilight.

Tonight he did not want to walk back to his cell through the Night Stair, as had come to be his custom after the final office of the day. Bidding his escorts leave him, he had chosen to cross the open courtyard alone and unaided; a kind of maiden voyage after the cold months and the disabling injury that had hampered him. Free of the crutches he had relied upon through the winter months, he could now manage, albeit slowly and carefully, with a cane alone.

He breathed deeply the fresh, still frosty air. He was not a young man, and he thanked God that he could still mend. His knee seemed to be strengthening, and could now support much of his weight; his steps gaining confidence with each passing day. He had no doubt that once fully healed, his limp would be negligible, or not at all. And his hip... *the Saints and the Madonna had heard his prayers, as well as the prayers of the brotherhood entire!*....its sallow blue bruise had disappeared, and it was now free of pain, even when he slept. It seemed to be only waiting for

622

the smaller part to catch up and match its larger part's recovered strength.

There had seemed to be a divine irony at work in the thing. He who had survived the *great famines*, when the country-side had withered, and the *Great Mortality*, when so many had perished in the flames of the pestilence; that he who had survived these wrathful admonishments of God had stepped upon a sliver of ice one snowy evening, and with the whimsy of fate had had his legs taken out from under him. Unable to stand, or even to crawl, he had .lain unnoticed until *Vigils*, at which time he was found half conscious, half frozen, and half covered with snow. The brothers had joined their hands together, creating a litter with their arms, and then gingerly navigated him to the infirmary. With hands soft and tender as partridge wings, they had passed over him again and again, gently pressing his hip, and up and down the length of his leg. Although they could not be certain, they had been hopeful; with the mercy of the Holy Mother, no bone had been broken.

As the days passed their hopes and prognosis prove thankfully correct. His hip and knee had been only bruised; bruises with which time, rest and prayer would allow their abbot to heal, and hobble back into his old self.

But time and rest exacted a price, and a session was held at once in the Chapter House, a session in which the brothers voted that the sub-abbot, Father Sebastiano, would temporarily assume their injured abbot's duties, at least until he was no longer bedridden. Still, once out of bed the resumption of his former duties would be a gradual one. During his convalescence his afternoons would be left free for him to rest, exercise and heal in the spring sun.

And this is exactly what he, Father Giovanni, had done for the past few weeks. With the strengthening of his leg, and the resulting freedom from his crutches, he had taken many long walks about the abbey's grounds. He had watched the bare twigs break into buds of leaf and blossom. He had smelled the rich new pungencies breathed from the waking soil. He had felt the golden fingers of the sun reach through the thick wool of his robe, searching until they found the wounds in his hip and knee; and finding them, giving them their healing kiss.

He had even ventured from out the gates, and with the patient help of one of the brothers, he had descended the hill to the fields below; the fields now being freshly turned by the brothers; their oxen, like gleaming white gods deigning to be yoked to men's ploughs, kneading soft the rocky dough of the soil yet again.

Father Giovanni paused in the middle of the courtyard near the well, breathing the perfumes of the fresh spring air. Above him appeared the first sprinkling of stars, adorning the naked breast of night as with pearls. He was very thankful to the God who had made these stars. He was very grateful for the healing of his hip and knee, as well as the revelation that had been recently given him, helping to heal a long forgotten wound in his heart. Pausing with gratitude for these things, he reflected.

Several days ago, something remarkable had happened; something that he could not rid from his mind. As he had watched the brothers and their oxen break the soil, the brother who had accompanied him pointed to the forest, where another brother had stepped from the tree s at the field's edge.

This good-natured brother had returned his abbot's smile, and then excitedly began to trot towards him. He was holding up his robe, like a kitchen maid holds her apron when it is filled with eggs or apples, comically exposing his thin, bandied legs waddling like a turkey beneath him. With a flushed face, and brightly animated eyes he reached Father Giovanni, and midst his panting breaths exclaimed, while proudly displaying the treasure he had found:

"Look, Abbot Father! Look at what I've found! Mushrooms! The large, chestnut ones that poke up their heads each spring! They've just sprouted, perhaps only last night.....you know how they do! I had no bag or basket, so I used my robe to gather a good bunch of 'em. There are many, many more, thick as mayflies, plentiful as June blackberries, if you know where to look that is.....I went to gather simples for Father Gregorio, but stumbled on these instead! I'm sure he won't mind! We've the summer through to hunt John's wort, Goat Weed and the like, but such lovely mushrooms, only a few days.....brief as an April snow....as a sparkle in youth's eye!"

He had commended the brother on the harvest he had collected, agreeing that he had found the mushrooms that were the tastiest of the entire year.

"And are they there, just inside the forest, Brother Vittorio?"

The simple brother, forfeiting humble decorum to the exuberance resulting from his great discovery, blurted his words as he gasped for his breaths.

"Oh no, Father Giovanni, no; they are much deeper, much deeper in the forest!"

"Yes?"

"Yes, much deeper, father. Do you remember the great tree where we found our brother's habit hanging like a dead man, many years ago? You must remember, the brother who sang and danced, the blue-eyed gypsy brother, the one the brothers nicknamed 'Brother of Gold'."

"Of course, I remember him......"

"The squirrels ran up and down his legs and over his arms.....ha! would have built their nests and hid their nuts, slept the winter through in his cowl if he would have let them.....the one that spoke a different language, and sang it to the birds......."

"Yes, I remember him very well. His name was Brother Maria, and the language he spoke was a language he learned when he was a boy; a language brought from another land. It was called 'Romani'."

"Yes, yes, Brother Maria, that was the brother! Danced before the Holy Mother, played tricks with knives, tumbled like a circus man.....the brother that some felt deserted the brotherhood, others, that he was captured by thieves.....others that he had passed through the bowels of wolves."

"And near that tree you found these mushrooms?"

"Yes I did, Abbot Giovanni, about that very tree, the one upon which the golden brother's habit hung, and the blanket was found in its fork......"

"Blanket? I do not remember a blanket being found."

"Yes, father, a blanket. I found it with these very hands."

"What did you do with the blanket, Brother Vittorio?"

"Why, I do not remember. It was many years ago, and the blanket was damp and musty when I found it. Perhaps we cast it.....no, now I remember.....I think, no, I am very sure I left it in the stable."

"The stable? Is it still there, brother?"

"Why, I think it is, Father Giovanni. I think the brothers still use it for lambing and calving.....a filthy rag of a thing for the stable stalls, and nothing more than a rag now."

"Do you think you could look for this blanket, Brother Vittorio? And if you find it, could you come and tell me? Could you show it to me?"

The next day Brother Vittorio had sought him out after morning prayers. The good, deferential, eager to please monk was very excited.

"I have found the blanket, father, even as you asked me to do! It is greatly worn, and a sight of hair, burrs and filthiness, but it is the blanket, the very blanket I found in the great tree, the very one, as I am a man, and that man a monk it is."

Several hours later, he had gone to the stable with the brother. The blanket was incredibly worn; so worn it was almost no longer a blanket at all. He had asked the brother to take it from the stable and spread it out in the sun, where he had proceeded to inspect the threadbare, straw infested piece of wool more closely.

It was as he had suspected. It did not belong to the abbey. It had no cross of heavy brown thread sown into its gray wool. Seen plainly in the bright sun, it had instead the brocaded patterns of two sheep; one in each of two corners, and between it a shepherd's crook. It was torn and filthy with the years, but touching it he felt the weave of its wool was not coarse, like a horse blanket, but must have once been carded fine and soft.

"*Brother Vittorio, will you collect the tasty mushrooms in the forest this afternoon?*"

"*Yes, father, why yes I will. Ha! But this time I will take a basket with me, so that I do not need to use my habit like a maid's apron.*"

"*Could you take me with you? I would like to know where they grow.*"

"*But your leg, father.....*"

"*My leg is much stronger now. I will take a crutch, and of course, I will have your strong shoulder if I need it.....*"

The brother beamed brightly, to think his Father Superior would take an interest in the special treasure he had found.

"*It would be a great pleasure for me to show you where they grow, Father Superior. They bring a flavor to the soups and the stews, do they not?*"

"*Yes brother, they do. And Brother Vittorio, could you see to it that this blanket is cleaned, at least as best it can be, and no longer used with the animals in the stable?*"

"*Of course, of course Abbot Father, that I will. I'll pick it clean of straw and burrs with these very hands, ha! Like picking nits from a brother's scalp I will. I'll clean the old ragged thing as best I can for 'ee.*"

That afternoon he had slowly limped across the newly tilled field and into the forest behind the path-finding brother; exchanging his cane for one of the stout crutches he had used in the initial days of his convalescence. The woods were still bare of greenery, and for all of his boorish simplicity, the brother knew them well; threading his way deep into the naked trees on the soft dead grass made into paths by the deer, and the other unseen citizens of the night. Babbling about how delicious the mushrooms made their stale soups, and from time to time excitedly kneeling, and here and there finding and picking one as it was a precious jewel, he had needed to be encouraged and constantly reminded of the large tree and the treasure trove he had found near it.

"*Yes, yes holy father, worry not, we are very near the large tree now, the tree upon which the brother's habit hung like a dead man, where the mushrooms are sprouting about its old roots! I know these woods like the back of my hand…like I know my missal and prayer beads I do…ah, here it is! Yes, see, here's the old tree….and here's the little darlings just crying to be picked!*"

Immediately the brother knelt, and began to crawl about on his hands and knees, avariciously gleaning the new crop of mushrooms that had sprouted overnight. This had left the abbot alone to muse upon the scene before him, the scene he had no doubt had been a place of rendezvous where his former friend had once played with a shepherd girl on a shepherd's blanket.

…..he imagined the habit again hung high in the tree, how it had seemed animated by the ghost of the wind, as if in farewell to the fleshly brother that had inhabited it……and the tree's fork where the shepherdess had cleverly hidden the blanket, and then must have spread and laid down on it with the net of her young charms…..and these great old boughs, through which the stars must have rained their beams upon their illicit escapade……

…..of course; this grassy place deep in the forest would offer a perfect place for lovers to meet and play…..un-guessed by the brotherhood, and unknown by a jealous drunkard of a husband…..a kind of asylum, a kind of lair where they could whisper dreams and play forbidden games together….. wrestling in the blind eagerness of their desires, imagining a great meaning in the secrecy of their sin…..the place where his friend, if indeed such a defrocked one had been a friend, had once been stolen away from him…..

……he had not thought of him for a long while, for many years…… through the famines and 'the mortality'……his memories fading into the foolishness of his younger years, when God had not yet filled the needs of his loneliness with the duties of his abbacy…….

……and when he had thought of him, he had questioned their unlikely friendship…..at times becoming embarrassed, even ashamed to admit to himself that he had become fond of such an apostate……one who had forsaken prayers for kisses, his eternal salvation for the brief pleasures in women's beds…..and that thing in the dungeon, that thing he had done,

that still weighed and bit deeply into his soul........

But his muse was suddenly interrupted by the mushroom hunting brother crying out to him.

"Father! Abbot Father, come, I have found something, something you must see!"

He remembered smiling at the simple brother's cupidity as he limped upon his crutch towards him.

"You are quite the hunter, Brother Vittorio, you have found a real treasure trove this time........"

But the simple brother had turned a concerned, and not an excited face to him, even as he continued on his hands and knees brushing away the sodden leaves, and tearing away the entangled mesh of roots and dead grass from before him, .

"No, Abbot Father, it is not the mushrooms I have found, but something else.....something very different! Look! See the stones.....and the mound, melted down greatly, but still a mound.....as it is a grave, Father Superior, as it is a grave!"

The stones he had found were smooth, light-colored stones, and the more of them the brother unearthed, it could be seen that they had been carefully placed in the form of a cross. And indeed, as the brother continued to dig and tear away the years of roots and mulch of leaves that had enveloped them, there could be distinctly seen, though all but sunken completely into the soil's dark eternity, a mound stretching away from the stones; a mound whose width and length at once suggested, if not shouted that it was a grave.

.....his heart had winced as with a sword thrust through it.....a different kind of sword, one that cut more sharply, deeply, through flesh and bone to the spirit's quick.....a blade of flowers, not steel.....a sword forged by human love, not God's love....a love that God might even forbid and despise.....but one that kings would give their kingdoms to own.......

He had no doubt whose bones were in this simple grave. He remembered her, and that cold drizzly day when she had climbed the muddy hill, knocked on the gates, and had bravely spoken with him. He remembered unwrapping the scarf she had so heroically bound about her bruised and beaten face, the severely cut lip, and the broken tooth.....he remembered her swollen belly, and the pride of a queen that had lifted her face from it to him....the valor of her love shining through her brokenness and her hapless plight.

.....a monk with whom she had played one night, here beneath this tree and stars.....a young monk who had broken his vows for her.....whose name she had not known, whom she had only briefly embraced, and had never seen again....in whose lapis blue eyes she had been enchanted.....in whose arms her wretchedness for a moment had been forgotten, and in that moment, taken wings...to this monk she had given her heart, and he had no doubt, her bones.......

Continuing across the courtyard, Father Giovanni had entered the cloister, where he had found two of the brothers waiting with gentle arms to guide him through the sparsely lit corridors. Upon arriving at the door of his cell he had smiled, and in observation of *the Great Silence*, he had thanked them by pressing his fingers to his lips, and then with a kiss on his fingertips, gesturing to their breasts. Wagging his forefinger back and forth, he told them he would need no further assistance.

Upon entering his cell he had prayed, removed his habit, and blew out his candle; then laid down upon his bed. But his thoughts were busy, and did not wish to partake of the pleasure that had been offered his tired body.

He had scarce thought of him for many years. He had been given the abbacy, and with it, its endless responsibilities, duties and concerns. There had been the intervening years of the famines; the years of rain, starvation, and looting vandals; and after the famines, the Great Mortality..... breaching their holy walls, killing three out of four of the brothers, leaving maimed, demented and simpleminded many of the survivors.

He remembered the last times he had seen Brother Maria: in the count's dungeon; as he was about to be hanged for being caught midst an amorous intrigue with a Bride of Christ, perhaps even with an abbess; and then so surprisingly again at the inn. That morning when he had seen Maria disappear in the blizzard, like a wild animal back into a forest, it was as he had disappeared into life's mystery forever, the great unfathomable mystery full of the incertitude of life's snares and dangers, and the one unanimous certitude of its death. Burdened with the rigors of his office, he had forgotten his heathen, child-hearted friend; he for whom he had once risked his robe, and with it his soul to save.

But finding the blanket, and the grave that certainly kept the bones of the young shepherdess......the large old tree, and the memory of the habit

629

dangling in the tree's crown.....these things had made him vividly recall the lost friend of his younger days......

.....no, there was more...there was something that these things had stirred awake, like a live ember beneath cold ashes.....something that had haunted him like a stalking ghost, that whether he had thought of it or not, had not left him through the years......something that had continued to dwell and live inside him.....that would not let him go.......

.....the satchel.....yes, the satchel.......

.....the satchel that the brother had given to him that morning, shortly after Brother Maria had disappeared into the snow and forest.....the satchel that he had refused to discard or inspect, that he had kept, no, that he had coveted, as it was a treasure waiting to be discovered, but never to be revealed....that he was ever eager to explore, but whose exploration he strictly denied......that something inside him forbade him from knowing, and at the same time gnawed with sharp teeth, tempting him to know.......

Since the discovery near the tree, he could not stop thinking about it; in his walks and at his meals, as he recited the litanies and intoned the psalms.....as he lay awake, like now, in the silent hours of the night, as if its weather chewed leather was alive, and a whisper came from inside it.....a whisper that was the pleading of his own heart.....a part of him that his prayers and austerities had never touched....like the music of a violin whose violinist could not be seen......the satchel spoke to him, sang to him, haunted him.......

But why? Why had he kept it at all?

At first he had explained it away by trying to convince his self that he would see Maria again; that their paths would again cross in the divine warp and woof of things. But as the years passed, he knew that that was very unlikely. He was growing old. His days were numbered, and he would certainly make no more journeys away from the abbey. And Maria? It was very likely that he had fallen prey to the pestilence, and if not the pestilence, to any other of a thousand dangers and treacheries that lay in wait for such a homeless vagabondage as was his existence. He had become very wild, rolling the dice of fate, and taunting death each time he stepped into the arenas of wine, brawl and women. And if by some miracle he was still alive, what cause would bring him back to the abbey that he had deserted in his youth?

He had also told himself that the satchel was not his, and being not his, he had no right to know its contents. Although he was sure it held no monies, it surely held valuables of some sort, if only the meanest kind for the one who had carried it. By opening and inspecting the satchel, he would be no better than a common thief, like those that had broken into the abbey during the great sickness, and had stolen the holy vessels from the sacristy, and had even rifled the sacred ornaments from beneath the shrouds of their dead. Would he, too, not be guilty of a larceny, of stealing things, however insignificant, however valueless?

Then why had he kept it over the years? And though he had not let his fingers touch it, and seldom his eyes to dwell upon it, what was its great attachment that, however he tried to deny or explain it away, bound him as with chains? As a monk, was he not to renounce all attachments, to stand before God naked of all possessions? And was the satchel not a possession, one that he held very dear; one that he refused to relinquish, one he had hidden from his brothers, and had even taken special care to hide from the raiding vandals?

Had he not heard of dead monks who had been found with gems and bejeweled crosses sewn into their robes, and in consequence of such covetousness and venality, were denied a burial place with their brothers? Was he not like a dog that had buried its bones; a miser whose dreams were filled with the riches buried in his cellar? Was his keeping of the satchel not a veritable thievery? Was it not a sin, a sin that he knew was a sin, but a sin he would not confess? Did it threaten the salvation of his soul?

Why in his heart did he wish to know what the satchel contained, even while his heart disdained and denied that wish? What was he afraid that he would find? Was it something that would be at odds, or pose a challenge to his faith, his lifelong faith that was nothing other than a preparation to leave this world?

Over and over he thought of it, and pictured it clearly in his mind. It invaded his prayers, its bag of weathered ox-hide hung in his cabinet in the vestry, silently taunting, as if smiling at him each time he donned his stole, and prepared to dispense the Eucharist.

Over and over he had resolved to burn or bury it. He would not see the friend of his youth again, his friend who had died long ago, who had squandered away his soul in profligacy. He was a monk, a monk who was the abbot of a brotherhood. The satchel was a vain and worldly attachment. To look in it would be wrong. It would be a sin. It would break his vows, even as Maria had broken his vows when he had lain with the shepherd girl in the forest.......

.....*then why had he risen from his bed and dressed, and with his cane limped from his cell through the Night Stair?.....and why, reaching the sanctuary, why had he lighted a candle and entered the vestry, and entering it, opened the cabinet where he kept his stole?.....Why, when he knew God's eyes were surely watching.....why had he lifted the weathered pouch from where it hung?*

......*What temptation of love or evil had made him remove it, and removing it press it to his breast, as to insure himself it was real, and not a dream.....and then to return back through the Night Stair, through the silence and the sleeping brothers.....to enter his cell, sit down at his desk, and in his candle's light, proceed to unknot the time crusted knots.....then to open the stiff hard jaws of its long neglected leather?*

.....*what made him reach his hand into the dark of the pouch, and despite the screams of his conscience, compel him to look at the hidden, perhaps most precious treasures of another man's soul?........*

.....*ribbons, yes, there were ribbons, a bound bunch of many ribbons..... yellow, red, pink.....silk and velvet ribbons, long and short, soiled and clean ribbons.....all bound together, like a bunch of radishes or garlic to economize the pouch's space.....ribbons that had certainly adorned not one, or two, or three, but many flowing flows of tresses....ribbons that had been loosened by many hands.....unbinding, and letting fall the last reservation of feminine modesty.......*

......*jewels, yes, there were jewels.....earrings, barrettes, bracelets, necklaces.....wrapped and bound tightly together in a piece of calf's leather.....a few that contained precious stones, but most mere trinkets, gauds hawked or sold in travelling carnivals to the peasantry.....hammered by tinsmiths, or stitched together by roadside weavers.....but each no doubt with a meaning and a memory.....as they were pieces of their givers' hearts.......*

......*in another packet; locks and tresses of hair, still lustrous, still as silky as the wings of swallows.....some short and some long, some no more than dainty curls.....and yet all as dark as the raven's wing, as night and the earth, as the mystery of life itself......*

.....*and a packet of a great many flower petals, like a sashay, dried and brittle, but still alive with faded colors....petals of many different kinds of flowers......that had captured the intermingling of their perfumes, like a beehive captures and keeps the honey gathered in many meadows.......*

.....*and this small bag filled with pieces of cloth.....snippets of smocks, aprons, gowns, shifts....remembrances of clothing that lovers had shed, and from which they had stepped........*

.....and this larger, heavier object, this object wrapped and bound, as if swaddled in doeskin.....a kind of portfolio, and in it a confusion.....a confusion that seemed the making of a living thing, as it was a fetus, a fetus with a beating heart, struggling to come alive in a woman's womb.....a collection of parchment sheets......sheets upon which were words and drawings..... phrases, fragments of thoughts and rhymes.....some scribbled, some illegible, some boldly and neatly lettered......covering and decorating each page, as boys carve profanities on fence posts.....a graffiti of the soul that was somehow its testament.....a kind of hymn, not to an unseen God, but to a God of sunlight, storm, stones and flowers.....prayers of thirst and hunger, pain and need....a thanksgiving, but one not to God and Heaven, rather to the abundance of the Earth....a hymn of despair, loneliness, and the mystery of the passing wings of the days and nights.......

At first sight, the thoughts and pages seemed random, chaotic, disjointed, but examining them more closely there seemed thematic orders that pieced their disjointedness together. There were tiny drawings near many of them, drawings that symbolized the adjacent words; the first page a kind of frontispiece.....upon one side a sketched flute, and on the other side, a cross and a monk's cowl.

He began to read; the words catching something dry, something empty, something dead in his heart, and catching that deadness, quickly leaping into flames.

'She is more than a young girl who shepherds her sheep in the hills and meadows. In her smile are both spring and autumn, and when she tumbles free her hair, its dark river is full of stars and roses.

In her dark eyes is a dark forest, a forest filled with sweet smells, sweet melodies, and strange sweet creatures. I am afraid to enter that forest; I am afraid I will become lost, and never find my way out of it again. I am afraid my soul will be swallowed by some dark evil, some evil full of unimaginable pleasures. I am afraid I will become lost, and lost, I will never want to leave this enchanted forest called 'Woman'.'

Written in bold letters, directly beneath this passage, was the fragment of a poem, one that was entitled with a half-legible title, as it had been a hasty afterthought: 'THE CALL OF THE FLUTE'.

.....SOUL of my soul, and flower of my flesh,
With whom I wake to sunlit, starlit glories,

God's Hand, but now, lifting us from Earth's nest,
Granting us visions revelatory.
It was a dream, Sweetheart, that marred our sleep,
We from long banishment have been recalled,
There was no serpent with beguiling speech,
We did not pluck the fruit; we did not fall.......

Father Giovanni was startled from the strange, if not profane enchantment of the words by a feather-soft knock on his door, a knock followed by the great bell brazenly breaking the silence that, like the wings of a mother bird had settled over the abbey. A brother's voice whispered from behind the door:

"Abbot Father, do you need assistance walking to Vigils? I saw the light beneath your door, and I......"

"Thank you, brother. No, I am fine. My hip and knee are much better. I will walk to prayers alone; thank you, brother."

Carefully the abbot bound the manuscript back in the piece of doeskin, and with the lovers' keepsakes, placed it back into the satchel, after which he knelt to the floor, and pushed it deeply beneath his bed. Taking his cane in his hand, he blew out the candle, and left his cell for his midnight prayers.

But though he had whispered the words since he was a young man, his prayers were filled with the strange, and even wicked things he had found, superseding and bullying their familiarity; among which was the last he had read, directly below the poem's lines.

.....What is this great abomination I am committing as I walk through the abbey? Each time I lift my eyes to a statue or a painting of the 'Madonna', I have unholy desires in my heart. I want to bring my mouth to the Holy Virgin's mouth, and to make naked her breasts and hips. I want her naked body to enfold my naked soul.......I want to burn and die in the mystery of her arms......

.....does an angel urge me on, or a demon?.....Is this a sin of my soul, or its lonely worship?.......

He was afraid of what he had found, for never had he seen sin painted so boldly, so shamelessly; words painted with the hot ink of a young man's lustful blood. Never had he seen words so depraved. Never had he seen wrong desires painted in such a tender, loving way.

CHAPTER SEVEN

THE THEATRE OF THE DEAD

Part II

THE air was smoky with dusk when Maria reached the village gates. As he was about to enter them he looked back at the train of fugitives climbing the hill, their candles and lanterns now lighted like a religious procession. Above them the sun was setting, its chariot returning from day's battle; the first stars struggling to bloom in the violet fields outside the vermilion of its daylong slaughter.

For a last brief moment he thought of rejoining them. But when he did he thought of the cruel savage God to which they were taking their hopes and prayers. He smiled at the irony of it all: at the cat and mouse game of a God whose scourge had driven them away, only to welcome them with a smile, one grinning through a blood-red sun. No, he had spent his hopes and prayers. Bereft of these crutches, he was left only with a curiosity; one that was blind, dark, and final. He turned and entered the village.

He would remember passing through the unguarded gates as he was stepping down steps into a nether realm. Night was indeed settling, but there was a darker, heavier night possessing the village's streets. In a few places the people had built bonfires with heaps of fence posts, doors and discarded furniture, and in their flames they had thrown boots, saddles and harness-work, as well as pitch, brimstone and salt peter, creating fumes of acrid pungency with which they were attempting to purge the corruption from the air. But these fires proved incompetent to dispel the suffocating pall; indeed, they seemed to augment the spectral gloom. In the delirium of his fatigue, they seemed to Maria forges of hell.

The streets were full of rubbish, and overgrown with a promiscuity of weeds and nettles, deserted of all but indistinct forms of wandering pigs and master-less dogs, and occasional passers who scurried by in the shadows, more like ghosts than men. Most of the shops were boarded shut, and no lamp or candle shone inside those that were not, as they had been rifled by a barbarous enemy. There was only one small street that was illumed with torches, that was filled with chatter, raillery and music, a street where a few who had not fled the village, and were either smugly or stupidly brave, drank and roistered, uncaring if death rollicked among them or not. Passing the mouth of this street Maria was accosted by several young prostitutes. Gaudy and perfumed, and sloppily drunk, they held his arm, and like geese hissed their brazen offers in his face.

"*Still healthy my love? Then come play with me, above the tavern there. It won't take long, and I promise you will be pleased!*"

"*I've not a spot or a boil on me sir; you may examine my parts before you have your pleasure. The ones who are afraid, the ones praying with their beads day and night, and all those that are fleeing are the only ones who are dying, not the ones with play left in their bones, and not afraid to live their days as life should be lived.*"

"*Do not walk on sir. It's hard times for poor girls. If you like you may have the two of us for the price of one, a bargain come your way, lucky sir, the plague having cheated us of a clientele, and we, braving the contagion to do the gents a favor with a moment of mirth.*"

"*Who knows but this be the last chance for you to have your tickle and your groan? Who knows if tomorrow the rough men might not toss you on their cart, and clippety-clop you to the pits?*"

"*And our bodies still fresh as roses of May for any to enjoy!*"

Unspeaking, Maria walked on. No, he did not want to drink, or play silly games with a woman. He was very tired, as tired as he could not remember being tired. He only wanted the pleasure that sleep could give him; the pleasure not of enjoying, but of forgetting. But where? His first instinct was to seek out the village stables, but he quickly dismissed that thought, knowing that with the sickness lawlessness would be more rampantly, dangerously afoot. He had passed several shoddy inns, but they were dark and boarded shut, having no customers to sleep on their beds, and perhaps no keepers to rent them if they had.

He tried to ask the few shadowy forms that passed him by, but they gave no response to his question, rushing past him and disappearing in the gathering night. But at last one of these shadows stopped, and from a distance shouted back to him.

"I think the Angel Inn is open for business sir. I passed it just now, and there was a candle in it burning. Turn at the second street, and a hundred paces will bring you to its door. The keeper's a decent man, and keeps a clean and rabble free house, and not yet with the sickness, at least that's what I've heard. God bless you sir! May God have mercy on your soul, and on the souls of us all!"

Following the good man's directions, Maria quickly found the inn. But standing before its door, and the sign painted with a worldly, flirtatious angel upon it, Maria was not sure that it was open. Indeed there was a candle burning, as the man had said there was, but it was small and weak, and buried deeply inside the inn's gloom. But with a soft shove of the door, the door was easily persuaded open, and with it the tinkling of a bell overhead that announced his entrance. Maria found himself in a small reception room, one whose appearance was made to seem smaller by the paltry poorness of the light cast by the single candle.

"What is it that you want?"

Spoken hoarsely from the shadows, the voice was disembodied, but in no way sinister. To the contrary, there was something indefinably friendly about it, something that made its gruffness seem pretended and incapable of concealing its benign nature; as it was a ghost long confined to its nook of darkness, a ghost that was not inhospitable, but rather longing for a visit from the living.

"This is the Angel Inn, is it not?"

"Yes, it is the Angel Inn; yes, the Angel Inn."

"And you rent rooms......."

"Do you have any spots or boils upon you?"

"Sir?"

"Any lumps about your throat, beneath your arms, about your belly or privates? Purple pimples......

"If you are asking....."

"A dizziness, a crick in the neck or a hitch in the hip, or any kind of shivering or fever? Visions of things that are not there? Angels, devils, ghosts? Bluntly: is death and any of its signs upon you man? For if the black devil clings to your back like it clings to the backs of half the village, 'the Angel'

has no room for you at all, and you and the devil monkey can leave and do your dying in the streets midst the weeds, pigs and corpses."

"I am not sick, but I am very tired. You see I have walked many days in the fields and forests, and I have had many dreams. I need to sleep; I need, you see, please, only to sleep."

"I want none of the buriers and their rough lot tramping with their muddy boots, and the filth and stink of the churchyards upon their clothes, with their curses and their tavern songs going up and down the 'Angel's' stairs, fetching corpses to throw in their carts. If a man walks up these stairs a live man, I expect him to walk back down them a live man. The Angel Inn is a clean inn, clean and respectable, has been since I was a boy....I don't want vulgar, blaspheming brutes lugging death's booty from its clean pretty arms. The Angel's to sleep in, not to die in."

"I am sound, but again, very, very tired. I need only a bed to sleep in."

This brought the ghost shyly shuffling and peeping from the shadows, and with it a softening of the pretended gruffness it had assumed. Stepping into the penumbra of candlelight was a tall, but somehow mousy man; floury pale, thinly haired and thinly limbed, but without the least hint of mean-spiritedness attached to his person. Lowering the scarf he had wrapped about his mouth and nose, he revealed a simple affability that, like his voice, was impossible to mask and conceal.

"Would you, sir, be so kind as to bring your hands to the candle, and there hold them for a moment, so I can see if the tremble or the frenzy is upon them?"

As the man asked, Maria held his hands near the small sputtering candle.

"And now, if you would, kind sir, if it would not be too imposing, would you bring your face near the candle, so I can make sure death has not written its warrant upon it?"

At which Maria bent to the candle, and anticipating what the man was about to ask, turned his face so that he could examine both sides of it. This relieved and relaxed the man very much, a relaxation that emboldened him to shuffle another small, timid step into the candle's light.

"Thank you, thank you very much, kind sir. You see with the tolling of the bell, the roofs black with crows, and the dead-carts and the hearses creaking and clopping past the Angel's door, and the folk dropping in the streets and being thrown onto carts like cordwood.....what was a live man with a beating heart and a talking mouth ten minutes ago, in the shake

*of a sheep's tail becoming a heap for dogs to sniff and beggars to pick......
The beggars did not accost you? The damned rascals! They ape the dying,
and beg for mercy in coppers, and if you do not show pity to their sores, the
sores that they cleverly draw with charcoal on their bodies, they press a knife
to your throat......but you see we've become a village of the dead, a regular
'Golgotha', all but the tipplers, the whores and the crows......I would go
up the hill with the others, but you see 'the Angel' is mine, and I want to
die in her arms.....but yes, yes, of course I've a room....no travelers, no
pilgrims, ha! no drubbed husbands or cuckolds left to drub or cuckold more
I guess.......all leaving or dying, and none coming....of course, why of course
I've a room for you to take your rest my good kind sir....."*

Maria removed his payment from his pocket, and reached out to
give it to the timid, thoroughly fright-blasted man. But at this the man
instinctively brought his scarf back to his face, and recoiled, as if to
retreat once more to his native shadows.

*"No sir, I'll not touch it at all, for fear the mortality is on it! You seem a
good and right man, and God protecting you with a sound health, but if you
would sir, would you drop your coins in the bowl of vinegar by the candle?
The midwives say it's the thing to do."*

Maria complied, at which the man stepped back into the light,
lowering his scarf and venturing a wan, but gentle smile.

*"Thank you, thank you kind sir. You see it's a kind of precaution, one of
many the midwives and the Merlin-men suggest, along with the garlic, rue
and the dead toads that they say will keep the breath of death from a man's
lungs.....see, I wear one about my neck, dried and shriveled.....sucks the
poison from the blood, or so they say.....and I would none of the garlic or
the arsenic, no, not for me.....I've not a spot or a boil, the toad does the trick
for me.....the women hold scented hankies and flowers to their noses....but
no, a toad for me, sucks the poison fine......."*

At this the curious, diffident man gave Maria the key to his room;
not with his hand, but cleverly attached and dangling from the end of
a broom handle.

*".....up the stairs, past the second landing to the third, the second
floor's locked up until the rat catchers come.....at the third landing, the
highest one.....where the rats seldom come.....the second door on the right, ha!
starboard as the sailors say. A bed clean and warm, and a basin and pitcher of
good clean water.....here, let me light a candle for you sir.....the stairs are steep
and many, and they and the hall are dark, dark as the grave they are......."*

Maria began to climb the stairs, and only then did he realize how weak his tiredness had made him. His boots seemed unnaturally heavy, as they were caked with clay, and his satchel, as it was filled with stones. Each stair demanded a great effort from his legs, even as he gripped the railing with his free hand to help hoist him. Remaining at the foot of the stairs, and fishing out the coins from the bowl of vinegar with a pair of tweezers, the man chirped on, as if the long confined ghost had waxed loquacious in the company of the living.

...... *"No, no, the death is not upon you, sir, not to these eyes it's not.....at least the death that will tumble you in the churchyard pits......you're a wonder of wooliness and a sight of savage shagginess, but without the boils, the knock-knees or the trembles.....no, the ogrish bastard's not got you by the gills yet......*

.....but when you leaned near the candle, ugh, this vinegar! If I may be so bold my good sir.....many kinds of death in the world, that's what I think.......a death of sickness, a death of hopelessness, a death of sorrow.....maybe even, if I might say sir, a death of loneliness upon a face like yours.....but listen to me, rattling like an old fishwife....a good night's sleep will do you good....and if the good Lord be not too angry with men and their chicanery of sin, he will light the lamp of the sun tomorrow, and wake us from our beds to see it.....but whether those that see it are lucky men, or unlucky wretches, well, that's quite another thing, is it not?...."

.....he had paused on the first landing, as to summon more strength.....he wanted to sleep, only to sleep......to forget, only to forget.....and that thing about his mother.....something about wanting to return to his mother......he could not remember.....he did not care to remember.....he wanted only to sleep and forget.......

..... "Only one other guest in 'the Angel' sir, and she an angel fallen, fallen and hobbling.....Eleonor, the one all call 'Peg'.....Peg for the peg leg she buckles to her hip......hair red as a rooster's comb, red as she paints her lips and cheeks, red as the crosses painted on death's doors.....out-cheat any card man, out-drink any tinker.....a nice lady, pays her rent, been here a year come Annunciation, without a spot or boil.....a good, honest, one-legged, fire-headed whore is Peg......anyone's guess if the leg is on or off when she does her business.....her other leg is fine, shapely as a brood mare's, silky as a queen's glove.....ha! makes up for the missing other, or so her gent-folk say......"

.....oh, to sleep, to sleep and forget.....to be carried back down these

stairs by strong rough hands.....tumbled like a sleeping child into death's dark arms......to sleep, and never wake again.......

...... "Her customers come up the back stairs, not these, silent as mice they are.....shame hushing the best of men.....Sir? Are you well? You seem to be having trouble.....your back pressed against the wall and all..... 'the Angel's' stairs are steep, steep as a cliff, are they not?.....but as I was saying, Peg's visitors won't be bothering you......that's not to say you won't hear an occasional moan or giggle come from the room at the end.....the kind that men and women make when they have their play.....and the other sounds.....the bell and the cart, the moans and the shrieks......well, death has its giddiness too....its own kind of music one might say.....one that one learns to live with eventually....to roll over and sleep on one's other side with, as my dead wife used to say.....God bless the good woman's soul, her spirit still dogging and nagging me, though she be rotting in a pit with a thousand others...... "

He reached the landing.....the chirping ghost gabbing on somewhere below him..... "Biscuits, beer and eggs at dawn sir, a bit of dried fish if you wish.....no bacon since the plague took the butcher, though Lord knows there's pigs a-plenty, they with the rats ruling the streets like princes.... 'the Angel' treats her clients as guests, not vagabonds.....ha! a Christian Angel, and not a heathen one my Angel is.....treats all as they were members of the living, ha! the living on their merry little jaunt to the grave, as all of us be.....goodnight sir, the Lord have mercy, and may He give us health and rest, and the faith to deal with what's befallen man's poor creature...... "

.....Here he stopped, as to regain his breath. He looked down the stairwell at the keeper. He had remained in the candle's light. He could see him lift a bottle to his mouth, even as he continued to mumble, not to his guest, but to himself, or as a ghost to a crony ghost.....drunk as much from fear as drink......

"The night is the worst time, when the light goes away.....when the darkness and the silence come, like they will stay forever.....as if each night is a new eternity, the wrong side of eternity that is, the side no man wants to be on.....when the crows stop their noise, and that accursed bell stops its tolling, driving the living deaf and daft with death's proclamation..... like a man becoming hoarse from his cough, and losing his voice to say more words......then can be heard more clearly the unfortunate ones, the poor damned devils.....you know what I mean.....the terrible music...... the shrieks and the cries, and the laughter that is only lamentation in

disguise.....from those gone giddy mad maybe from knowing they are about to leave the horrors of this life.......”

Maria entered the small sleeping room, and set the candle on the table. He removed his satchel and his coat, letting both fall to the floor at his feet. He sat on the bed, and with a great effort removed his boots, and then leaning to the candle, cupped its flame with his hand, only to stop before blowing ii out.

There was something the man had said, or that he thought he had said when he was climbing the stairs.....something that had stung him deeply.

.......many kinds of death in the world.....a death of sickness, a death of hopelessness, a death of sorrow...a death of loneliness like I see upon a face like yours.......

Maria stood and went to the pitcher and basin, above which was a small mirror. But he did not look into the mirror. He did not have the strength; no, that was not true; he did not have the courage to look into the mirror. He stood with bowed head before it, as he was afraid to see the death the man had said he had seen on his face in the candle's light.

He had stood before a mirror like this not long ago.....in a small room like this one, a garret above a street.....yes, now he remembered.....the morning when he had first seen the beautiful countess step from her gilded coach.....the morning after he had smoked opium and drunk much wine, and fled to the older woman's bed to forget pretty Isabella.....to forget the hideous corpse she had become, and his burning of that corpse, his burning of pretty Isabella..... the older woman sleeping not far from where he stood, even as he had looked out a window and became enthralled with the countess's young fresh beauty....forgetting Isabella, corpses, death.....the thing he had done.......

It was then he had looked in the mirror, and alarmed at the gray and untrimmed shagginess that had looked back at him, he had resolved to groom and make the image young and handsome again. And with its handsomeness he had won the beautiful countess's kisses and embraces. But the countess had died.....as had Isabella and her family.....Henrietta, the mad old woman in her garden.....the young girl and her brother with the blowflies in the grass....those decomposing or hanging from nooses in the farmhouses....those fallen in heaps, rotting in the fields and on the village streets, picked by scavengers, eaten by birds and dogs....all had died....as were dying the flowers, the butterflies, the hills and forests....as the entire world was dying.....as he too, the golden-haired gypsy, the one who was called 'Brother Maria' was dying.......

Slowly, as it was a final, joint effort of flesh and spirit, he lifted his face to the mirror.

It was a face he was not prepared to look upon, as one is not prepared to look upon a face exhumed from a grave. And yet, though he could scarce recognize the image that once wore a tonsure and was full of humble piety, that was once young, golden and handsome in the morning of life.....a face that women called 'darling', one as beautiful as their own.....albeit now horribly transfigured.....now ashen, mangy and uncouth.....it was an entirely true face, one that exactly matched the weariness that had come to lodge and be entrenched in his heart; a face that he felt strangely comfortable with; a face that he liked.

......Death? Was this death? Yes, of course it was death. Life was shedding its mask, the mask it had worn in its masquerade, the masquerade of the illusory and the unreal......the illusions of summer and winter, anguish and joy.....life was returning from its battlefield, removing its helmet and bloody sword, as well as its ribbons and precious jewels......

.....and yes, as the man had seen, this death was one with the loneliness that stared from its sunken eyes.....a loneliness that had forsaken all companions and all lovers.....that had turned its back on the company of men, and the altars of God.....a loneliness that had not been rejected, but had deserted, preferring to wander lost in the wilderness of its dreams.....a wolf hunted by the most heartless of hunters.....a loneliness against which it could not defend, from which it could no longer hide or outrun.....or in any way charm or fight with fangs or fists.......

.....the stare of a man stabbed and bleeding in the snow.....of a blow-fly-covered maid in the grass, an innkeeper's wife hanging from a noose, a pretty one with a ribbon in her hair, being woven about by the webs of spiders......the stare, the same stare of ten thousand others staring, decaying, breaking apart in streets and fields.....beneath garden fences and bushes.......

Maria weakly smiled, a smile that was full of tears, tears that had turned to dust, and choked with dust, would not fall through his beard. No, he would not barber his beard and hair. No, he would not don that mask again, only to be pretty, and win the arms of women. Like the ghostly keeper that had spoken to him from the shadows, he would no longer stay in those shadows, pretending to be something he was not.

Maria leaned to the mirror, and kissed the lips of this tired and lonely man, this tired, pathetic man he had companioned for so many days and nights; this stranger he had sung and become drunk with, argued with, told strange and profane stories to….this stranger that had watched him steal, commit adulteries, cheat and lie and kill.

Maria struggled to the bed, blew out the candle, and midst his welling sobs that were at last dredged from the tender childhood of his heart, laid his head back upon the pillow.

But he did not sleep, or if he did it was for a black, incalculable lapse; whether for a moment or for hours, he did not know. He only knew he lay awake in the night, as on a bier of darkness, awake to voices, terrible voices; perhaps the voices that the man had called *death's music*. Or had he only dreamed their doleful moans and shrill shrieks, the moans and shrieks that were perhaps the cries of his own heart?

The night was quiet, very quiet, as the man had said, the bell no longer tolling…..but no, not quiet…..there, again, a low, keening moan, unlike any moan he had ever heard…..as the one who was moaning was spent of his allotted sorrow, and was scraping the dry shell of his heart with the dull claws of his last need, desperately wanting, begging for more…..as the moan wished to voice something beyond sorrow, beyond human endurance…..a deeper kind of sorrow that had broken its victim, and breaking him made him less than alive, less than human…..a beast of the wild slowly dying with the arrow it could not dislodge……as death was slowly twisting and strangling its last moments….savoring it, as a snake swallows a rat, with a dark exaltation……

…..and now a shriek, a shrill inhuman shriek, one whose raw pain chilled the blood…..that seemed to mock laughter, as it was its idiotic twin…..a shriek that slowly, exquisitely rose in crescendo to a high-pitched squeal, as it wished to break the bounds of its own agony, only to plummet into guttural sobs of tears…..as death was a kind of hilarity of abandon, a false abandon that was a prison filled with an eternity of false promises…..of a higher or lower door…..the eternal illusion of escape…….as death was life's mother, and in its travail was forever giving birth to dying children…….

…..and now another moan, another cry and wild raving vented from another dark place of dying…..as if their unspeakable pain and sorrow were speaking, answering, befriending each other at the last, seeking each other's sympathy in the cold kingdom of the night, in the mutual predicament of their last tortures…..the moans, starved raw and stupid, stripped of human

care, as they were passing through a monster's bowels.....as they were not being moaned, but retched....the shrieks, full of babble and silliness.....the sobbing a raving laughter......as madness was the final language, perhaps the truest language, that Man was doomed to speak.......

.....And as they answered each other, they built into a swell, like the billow of a great wave, or the gathering of stillness into the birth of a wind.....until all joined, melded, culminated in a tumult, like birds before a storm.....a tumult of delirious, cacophonous woe.....a choir that was singing an exultant requiem of the dying.....voicing the final madness of the soul before the verdict that cannot be repealed.......

.....and now another sound.....not a lamentation or a cry of pain, but something without feeling, without a human heart.....something dull, staid, sullen, and yet more piercing than a wail, shriek or moan......something that lent a refrain to death's dark concert.....punctuating its darkness, like stars define the night.....something fraught with a stately, immeasurable dread, an inexorable certainty.....as it was the laughter singing in death's heart.......

.....a bell, yes, the slow ringing of a bell....not a cathedral bell, but one held and rung by a man.....the timbre of its slow dull ring, a ring that did not ring, but thudded with a leaden coldness, a dread that deafened like a hundred cathedral bells......or like a chorus of weeping Angels.......

.....and behind its dull ringing, the slow creaking of wheels.....a slow creaking of the start and stopping of a cart's wheels....now closer, as they were passing in the street below.....as they were passing through his room, as they were passing through his soul.....the plodding of a horse's hoofs on cobbles.....and now an obscene cry, as of the ferryman of hell, joining the wails of the dying....."Dead-cart! Bring out your dead! If you've not the strength, ten coppers and we'll do the job, wrapped or not! Dead-cart! Dead-cart! Bring out your dead!"

.....and as it was an answer from the living to the dead, a loud guffaw of laughter and a shrill giggle erupting from a room in the inn...... "Both legs tonight, my cherry sweet, the peg on my Peg tonight, right alongside her live beautiful one!"......and then a loud shrill giggle, piercing the darkness of both night and death.....as life was gasping for breath through the throat of this degenerate woman and the man who had purchased her.....only to be followed on its heels by the bell, the creaking cart and plodding hoofs, and the rough voice of death's ferryman....."Dead-cart! Dead-cart! We won't pass again until the morrow's night! Dead-cart! Bring out your dead!"

Maria closed his eyes, and when he did the wails and raving of the dying, the whore's laughter and the bell, the cart and the collectors became indistinguishable with the madness of the anguished voices in his own heart. Yes, he was mad, and his heart was madly singing.....as it was strapped to a rack and being picked apart by kites. Yes, his heart was singing the dark jubilation of its humiliation and degeneracy, its wails a lullaby lulling him asleep with pain and loneliness....sung by a mother whose arms would always gather him, would always love him.....a mother whose arms were death.......

" .....You have wasted your life, my child; yes, you have wasted your life.....you have been a lost and foolish lover of dreams, and you have wasted your life.....you are mine now, now that you have lived what you have wasted.....

* * *

The sleep that at last came upon Maria was filled with a strange dream.

He dreamed of the shepherdess who had tended her flock beneath the abbey; she who had played her flute so sweetly, and who had initiated him into the rites of love so many years ago. In the dream he was once more a young callow monk, one who was being teased by the trills of her flute, and the sly invitation in her eyes. He followed her into a forest, eager to know the wonderful thing she promised to give him.

But she had run laughing from the forest into a village street, and running past its huts and shops, she had stopped abruptly before a door. He had lifted his eyes to where she was pointing, only to see the sign of '*The Angel Inn*' above him. But the painting on the sign was not the same flirtatious angel he had seen when he had entered the inn. Its caprice had changed to a tawdry lewdness; its face painted garishly, and its robe lifted to its waist, revealing one wooden leg, and a black mass of pubic hair, from which protruded a man's phallus in the shape of a spitting serpent. Before it, knelt on its knees like an obsequious servant, or a begging beggar, the artist had painted a skeleton of bones.

He woke from this strange dream to dawn's first light. Most of the wails had ceased; the last lingering few more like the tired, hoarse, nightlong caterwauling of cats, or the croaks of toads at summer's close. The cries of agony were now replaced by the recommencement of the slow dull knells of a cathedral bell, and great dark flocks of crows that were waking with the hideous joy of their renewed hunger on the roofs overhead.

Un-rested, but eager to depart, Maria rose and readied, and then left his room and descended the stairs. The candle by the bowl of vinegar was burnt out, but with the help of the first vague light of day, he saw the timorous, fear-harrowed ghost of the keeper, sleeping fully clothed in his place of penance, cradled and curled in a small couch, only a few steps from where the candle had ceased to burn.

Unbolting and opening the door, the little bell above it jingled, at which Maria was called to a movement in the dim light, only a few paces from where he stood. It was the backside of a woman; a large, slovenly woman hunched over a table, with feathers, like a molting bird threaded crazily in her hair. When she slowly turned to him, Maria did not see a woman's face, but a clown's; her cheeks and lips excessively rouged, and her soul-less eyes ringed with dark blue circles. Beside her plate of biscuit and cheese laid her leg, its wooden length decorated, all the way from its thigh to its peg foot with graffiti of flowers, *Cupid* hearts and arrows, and a pornography of both men's and women's naked parts. With her mouth crammed with biscuit, and the poor vestiges of a seductive smile, she spoke to him.

"*If you're still whole tonight, love, and still free of the spots and the lumps, and you've an itch to play, come see Peg at the end of the hall.*"

With this she tapped the leg with her knuckles, and smiled a smile full of biscuit and depravity.

"*With or without.....as good as you'll find in these days of death..... you'll forget about the carts and the pits, Peg will see to that.*"

Stepping from the inn, Maria felt he was stepping into a dark dream, one that offered no hope of waking. The air was warm, and promised to be bright and sunny, but an oppressive, suffocating desolation lay upon the street into which he had stepped, one filled with filth, a slowly tolling bell, and the furious cackling of flocking crows. But more than these assaults to the eye and ear was the one waged on the olfactory. The air was filled with a sharp, piercing stench, one that the burning pitch and sulfur could not conceal; the stench all flesh saves, like a secret perfume, to exude from its final corruption and decay.

He saw at once what darkness had prohibited him from seeing in full last night. A jungle of unchecked weeds and nettles had invaded the village; some waist-high, even breast-high, blooming and seeding from ruts and gutters, while others had shut paths and alleys altogether; still others, taking root in thatches of roofs, and about chimneys that had long stood smokeless and cold. Rubbish was all about, rubbish and dung, but Maria was quick to notice that the offal consisted of scraps, not heaps; that it had been thoroughly picked through and rifled, as if nothing of the least value was left to be salvaged. The gardens and small orchard plots had not been tended, and had quickly become half wild and mangy; summer's opulence rotting on the ground where unpicked it had fallen.

Most of the shops were shuttered and boarded up, but there were some whose doors stood wide open, or had been torn away, granting a view to the gutted emptiness left by their looters. Upon some of the doors and shutters were painted bright red crosses, and on their boards, words in matching scarlet, as if daubed with blood; words that were the desperate pleas of their authors' souls. These words pierced Maria's heart like a sword.

.....*Madonna, Hear Our Prayers!......Gesu Cristo, Save Us!......Lord God, Have Mercy On Thy Children!.....*

The streets were desolate and silent, as if in preparation for a barbarous conqueror, or an angry Savior. There were no signs of the carts and horses he had heard in the night, the grim, funereal business of loading the corpses taking place only under the tent of darkness. The only traffic in the shop streets were devil-eyed crows, jackal-lean dogs and rooting pigs. Bereft of their dead owners, the dogs were skittish, as if they too had become fugitives of death, and had begun to seek others to stray and run with; others that would grow into packs, returning to their feral origins. Here and there a squatting beggar picked through bits of rubbish, or an uncollected corpse. A lost few, their wits blasted with the idiotism of fear or fever, walked aimlessly, or stood stonily still; staring vacantly, or babbling to the air.

He passed the mouth of the street where the prostitutes had accosted him with their invitations last night, the street of taverns, opium and gambling houses, the only street that had seemed vital and alive midst death's invasion. Illumined by the sun, it too now seemed dead, as the roisterers he had seen had not been men, but ghosts, ghosts that only issued from their graves to drink, whore and debauch in night's arena.

Walking down this street Maria saw one of the girls who had tried to provoke him last night. She was sitting on a bench, ravenously eating a large piece of bread. Absorbed in her gorging, she was oblivious of his presence, even when he stopped directly before her. In the light of day he saw how young, thin and frowsy she was, and when she finally lifted her face to him, he saw at once that her dull eyes and muzzy mind held no recollection of their former encounter.

A sallow, crapulous man stepped from an open door a few paces away, and without looking once at Maria, spoke sharply to her.

"*Show the man, Carlotta. Show the man your wares. It is early, but he may have a need, and you must earn the bread you're stuffing like a pig in your mouth.*"

This order did not greatly disturb the girl, but with a shrug, only slowly moved her jadedness. With a piece of bread half stuffed and hanging from her mouth, she tiredly stood, turned to the wall, and brusquely lifted her skirt up to her waist, displaying her undernourished legs and scrawny hams, pathetically decorated with a frayed garter, and the tattoos of two ill-drawn roses. After a few seconds, and a jaundiced: "*Enough darling?*", she sat back down, and without a word, or even lifting up her eyes to him, continued to hungrily eat her piece of bread.

Leaving the main thoroughfare, Maria began to ascend a smaller street that branched into rutty lanes lined with huts of wattle and rough plaster, and some of only loosely piled stones fitted and filled with mud, rags and moss. Here he was greeted with even more woeful scenes, ones that were full of the distress of the living, the anguish of the dying, and the corruption of both.

The last wave of those who were frantically evacuating the village were loading carts, horses, and their own backs with the possessions they were taking in their desperate, life-or-death flight. Most of the men's faces were wrapped with scarves, or hidden with uplifted collars and large-brimmed hats; while many of the women wore veils, or held little bunches of flowers, balsams or aromatics to their noses; attempting to prevent from breathing the pestilence, and the general rancidity in the air.

These narrow ways were filled with pounding hammers, the clamor of crows, and the constant, ubiquitous tolling of the damnably dreadful bell, but despite this pandemonium of doom, a great sullenness undermined their busyness. The children, sensing the grave spirit that had seized their parents, stood frightened and saucer-eyed, frozen with the strangeness of the things happening before their young eyes. Even the squalling of babes was muffled in their mothers' arms, as if innocence itself was discouraged, afraid it might incite death's monster to a deadlier rage.

Some of these ways were incredibly narrow, so narrow that they disallowed the passage of carts, and they stank foully with rank garbage, urine, and uncollected dung steaming in the hot sun; as well as the sharp, even more penetrating putrefaction of death and sickness that their narrowness had trapped, and would not let go.

In some of these streets Maria noticed conspicuous bundles covered with horse blankets, curtains, or pieces of sailcloth, some merely with meal sacks, or a loose scattering of straw; corpses that the collectors had failed to reach in their nightly rounds. Vermin scurried over and about them, even as crows alighted and waddled upon them, stabbing them with the shiny black daggers of their beaks. Maria watched dogs pull arms and legs from beneath these makeshift shrouds. Even more horrid, several corpses laid uncovered, and as if unnoticed, open-eyed and open-jawed, one in a muddy gutter, and another sprawled across a doorway. Maria could see that they had been stripped naked of their shoes and much of their clothing; the hair cropped from the woman's bald scalp, probably to sell to a wig maker. Disfigured, bloated and blackened with disease, and swarmed by clouds of flies, they were quickly quitting their human likeness.

Other corpses were watched over, guarded by the living, even as they were chained to them; fathers, mothers, children or spouses, unwilling to abandon their loved ones to scavengers, whether those scavengers be men, dogs or vermin. As in a kind of vigil, the last vigil, they waited for the collectors to climb the narrow ways and find them. There was a kind of tenacity in their eyes, a fierce loyalty, a willingness, if needs, to wither and die in the streets holding them in their arms; sharing death as they had shared life; full willing to be tossed with their precious bundles on a cart; to be eaten by birds and dogs; corrupt in oneness with those they had loved.

Unintentionally, Maria's steps were leading him to the cathedral and its bell; its imbecilic tolls of remorseless repetitions announcing the remorseless redundancy of the dead; the narrow ways wrinkling into a major way, one that was filled with weeping and wailing mourners; as all those remaining in the village had joined into one unanimous funeral train. All were wrapped in scarves or draped in veils, muffled like black mummies, or like the dead that had been brought from their graves by such an unearthly sorrow. All were ascending and descending from the stone wall surrounding the cathedral's churchyard, those ascending bearing religious relics and fistfuls of flowers, leaving them in brightly colored drifts outside the yard's high drab stones.

......*And the closer he came near the cathedral, the louder and more deafening became the bell.....its knells chasing all thoughts and all feelings from his heart and mind.....as there had never been, and would never be anything but this tolling of life's doom....becoming one with its doom, its tolling, this madly cruel, eternally repetitive, idiotic laughter of a God who swatted the gnats of men's dreams........*

......*Clang! Clang! Clang! Clang!.....this tolling a summons, a summons commanding the dead who dreamed they were the living.....they with death upon their shoulders and in their hearts.....clang, clang, clang....its knells swelling, erupting from the earth's bowels.....louder, more deafening true than fear or sorrow....death louder than any fear or sorrow, pain or pleasure.......*

......*Clang! Clang! Clang! Clang!.....reverberating through his bones, his teeth, his soul, lifting, enrapturing, purging his soul of all guilt and regret, the silly games of love and worship.....no longer a bell of death, but a gentle rain of life...one that greened the fields and brought flowers from the forest floors.....CLANG, CLANG, CLANG, CLANG,.....yes, like a gentle rain, one that made him want to lift his face, and like a child catch its drops in his mouth.....even as death had come to feed the worms in the clay of all flesh.....as its corruption was life's salvation.....the salvation of its meaningless idiocy.......*

Returning to the *Angel Inn*, Maria found himself once more standing before the valiant ghost of its timorous keeper. Creeping from his den of shadows, with a nightcap perched lamely on his head, and a wooly rug slung blanket-wise about his shoulders, he began to speak:

"*Oh, why it is you good sir.....and, uh, not a spot or a.......?*"

Without a word more, Maria stopped his inquisitor's anxiety, holding out his hands, and then his face to be examined by his fright-demented host. This pleased the man greatly, and when Maria placed his payment in the bowl of vinegar, he informed him that he wished to stay another night, that he liked his '*Golgotha*' very much, and if possible he would like a lunch to take with him as he walked through its pleasant streets.

Wasting no time with his readied gloves and tweezers, the keeper answered him as he fished for the coins in the vinegar.

"Why of course, of course my man; bread, cheese, some pickled olives, a bit of lamb's meat, still on the bone....never a more tender one on my spit... and a flask of wine, I mustn't become all addled and forget the wine.....why yes, I'll gather a bit of food for you sir.....my Angel's a commodious angel.... she takes care of those that come to nestle beneath her wings.....always has, always will....

.....Uh, but you say you like the village, sir? Yes, a nice little village, that is before death knocked on its doors and spat in its wells. Be careful, sir, I would not wish the boils, lumps or blotches upon you. There are those walking about who have been made lunatic with fires of fever.....frothing at the mouth and breathing death's fumes in faces of any they pass.....as for a want of company in their wretchedness I suppose. I beg you not to companion such ones, sir, not bring death back to 'the Angel' sir. I beg you as a Christian man, one who's missed no more confessions in his days than he has teeth left in his head.....I beg you heartily and humbly sir/.....beg you from my cockles I do."

A short while later Maria climbed a footpath that led to the hilltop of the village. As if completely unconcerned with the cries of misery, and the litter that fear and death had strewn in the streets, the sun shone with a gay autumn brightness, making the shadows crisp and inky dark, and the killing tide of the contagion, but a rumor drowned by its flood of golden goodness; a rumor far too cruel to be true.

Attaining the top of the hill, Maria found a shady place to sit near the ancient remnants of a crumbling wall. From here he could see the adjacent, brother hill, crested with the higher village, the one to which such a stream was fleeing with heaped carts, laden beasts and bent backs; all goaded like goats, by the goad-herd of their fright.

The choice was still before him. Or was it? No, there was no choice. He knew that he would not join those he could see climbing the road to the higher village. He knew he would stay here, where the ferocity of the pestilence was breathing its fumes into the lungs of all.....where Death rode on its pale horse through the streets in the terrible majesty of its victory.

But why? Was it because there was something that had died in his heart, that its candle was spent, and he had nothing more to live for; that he no longer believed life's promises and idols, its tender whispers and embraces? Was it because of the misery, the utter bankruptcy in his heart, and his realization that death was only playing with him, waiting for him like yet another lover, like the many lovers that had waited for him in the dark doorways and alleys when the taverns closed?

How silly it was to think one could conquer death; that one could flee from it, climb a hill and hide from it; beg, pray, or slip free of its stranglehold. Death was not a thief interested in velvets, jewels, or cherry-wood fiddles. It could not be bartered with, flattered or bribed. Death was a thief unconcerned with wealth or beauty, only the owners of such things. It smiled with a dagger up its sleeve, wooed with poison in its wine, seduced with words soaked in brine. Death looked in all windows; snickered at all treasures; mocked all altars. It played its fiddle over cradles; coiled beneath silkiest pillows. It picked the locks of slumber, and like an assassin stole into the bedchambers of dreams. Quiet as a saint, and as silver-tongued as a rake, it invited itself into every sanctuary.

Or was it more; more than this readiness, this readiness in his heart that had had enough; that was prepared to quit and be no more? He knew very well it was more. He knew it was a strange eagerness, a dark fascination; a morbid, but piquant curiosity that compelled him. Like a beautiful woman, death held him in its spell. Ruled by its allure, he wanted only to make naked its voluptuous secrets; to be wrapped in its arms, and with a burning heart give all to its seduction.

He could not quit thinking of death. He fell asleep and woke to its grotesqueries painted all about him. Sleep or drunkenness could not drown its fiddle song. Its arms entwined about him when he loved, and the more he loved the tighter it held him......its seduction and strangling arms bearing a strange beauty that charmed and enchanted his soul, and enchanting it, commanded it into more and more surrender; a queen, between whose silky thighs he was exhausting himself; a queen most beautiful, and at the same time most cold, most evil; most exacting of his manhood.

What happened to all those fallen in the streets and fields, all those that had fallen into death's arms; those that were heaped on carts and spilled in pits? Many would be eaten by dogs, vermin, crows; yes, that was sure. Left undiscovered, ignored, or discarded by the living, many would simply decompose in the sun and rain; be buried by winter snows; in spring, manure the weeds and flowers. The hair, the teeth, the jelly of the eyes, all would pass one way or another through death's gut, then be defecated by death's gluttony, a gluttony that had been disguised with sweet words and kisses.

And what of Man's heart, the mansion of his dreams? Would it also be eaten by dogs or rot in weeds? Would there be a trace left where death had claimed its kill? Would flesh become a ghost, a ghost in the wind that only spoke to the keen ears of hounds? Was there anything left; a scent, a shadow, a memory of what had ridden horses, wielded swords, kissed the lips of women? Would there be left anything of Brother Maria and his dreams: a smile, a sigh, a sparkle in an eye?

He needed to taste, touch and smell death's enigma; to feel the kisses of this mistress flay open his ribs, be haunted by her dark laughter, drink the foul sweetness of her perfumes. He wanted to hear the music that death's sickle made as it sang through the streets and fields, as it harvested all prayers and hopes.....the music of life's impermanence, the shrieks and mad laughter of life as it was eaten by death's sharp teeth....to join the wails of its giddiness....the song of its cruelty.......

What more had he to do with the living? He was aging, perhaps more than his years. Soon women would not find him fit to be their sweetheart, and women were the only thing that had given his wandering a semblance of meaning. He could not continue to walk through the hills and forests, through the summers and winters like one banished from a tribe. Was he to grow ragged and decrepit playing fiddles in lowly taverns, before tavern wenches who gave their breasts and kisses to younger, lustier men?

Could he fall on his knees and beg to be taken back by a brotherhood he had deserted in his youth? No, that would never do. That would make him a hypocrite both to himself and God. And his dreams? They would grow old too. Like songbirds they would fly away, or grow mute and die.....that he could not bear, that he could not endure.....no, no, it would be best to end with this final fascination, this march of defeat into hell. A rebel to both Man and God, there was nothing left for him but to grow mad and join the army of the dying; to give his squandered life back to the wild dogs and crows.

All life was cyclical; seed, flower and fruit; the spring followed by the summer, the harvest by winter snows. It was the same with a man's heart; Brother Maria's heart. The seeds in his heart had flowered lovely dreams..... poems and songs and the loving of women's beautiful bodies.....but these dreams withered as quickly as they flowered. The harvest was always brief; insufficient; vain: a stalk of fruited wheat toppled by the swishing lightning of a sickle's sword.

The harvest of his friend, Father Giovanni, would be his salvation. Day after day he planted the holy seeds of prayer, penance and duty, seeds that he *believed would one day bear the flower of salvation for his soul. It would be a harvest that had been hard earned, that he had given himself wholly to; that he had believed in; that he had deserved.*

But what would be the harvest of Brother Maria's soul? He had no money, no possessions; no belief. Salvation was a thing he did not think about; indeed, he had grown doubtful of its existence; disdainful of the cost it exacted if it did. If there was a God, he was sure He would not accept one who so flaunted His dictates. Discipline was a thing he had long forgotten; and ambition was a thing he shirked, or treated with repugnance. He gave himself only to playing melodies on fiddles, scribbling silly rhymes, loving women's naked bodies, but even this enthusiasm was followed by spates of idleness, moody disillusionment, and a need, like a young boy to amble off, sulk and dream. The only treasures he had to show for the many years since he had fled the abbey were the keepsakes given to him by lovers, lovers whose names and faces he could not remember: ribbons, shells, flowers, tresses of hair.....pieces of undergarments....the mementos of lovemaking in fields and barns, things he could not pawn at a pawn shop; things no beggar would want. Were these, then, like the nest of a packrat, the harvest of his soul?

Death had come as it had ever, and would ever come: as the proud dark king of eternity. There was only one difference. It ceremonial rites were now being performed openly before the sun's eye; not with hidden, but with brazen pomp. Its mystery was now paraded before the eyes of those who most feared it, and not secreted away in the cult of graves and tombs. He too would laugh through the hollow eyes of a skull, as all skulls laugh with hollow eyes at the silly carnival of men's dreams. Brother Maria would also quit this carnival of heartaches; laugh from the eyes of a skull propped on a post, upturned by a plough, kicked by a boot or hoof beneath a bush; receive the stones of children.

No, he would not join those climbing the higher hill. He had been rebellious in his life, but he would be obedient in his leaving.

But how would he stay alive? The peasants would not glean the fields, and there would be no teams to hire him, and even if there were, the winter was near. All but the most miserable taverns were boarded up, and these few would gather only the ugliest and most scurrilous clientele. He might seduce a rich widow, make her sigh and moan, play between her shriveling legs in exchange for meat and bread......yet, even this.....was he still handsome enough, pretty enough for a widow's bed? Did he still have the prettiness and boyish charm to play the whore?

Only this was certain: he would turn his back on the living and run like a child into death's mothering arms. He had come to trust death more than he trusted life. Death was a more honest, truer lover. Life had cheated him; betrayed its promises; given him sweetness after sweetness that had turned bitter as ashes. Death made no pretense of being something that it was not. It would not break its vow. It would either consume him, or permit him a walk through its bowels for a short while.

Dusk, like a fisher, had cast out its silent net, capturing him midst his contemplations. The sun had set in the west, even as the moon was rising in the east.

Death was like this moon; this lovely, cruel, blood trickling moon.

It rose on the world's edge, like a maid scorned by countless suitors. With spite she reached down and plucked flowers from the valleys and mountains, only to tear their petals apart, like an impudent child tears off the wings off butterflies, murdering their miracle, and then dropping their pieces into the abyss of darkness. The star that had sparkled in her hair was a spider, and her smile was as icy as the north wind. Her beauty had turned to a scowl of hatred; and the milk in her heart had curdled to an oath of vengeance.

Night was falling. He must return to the inn. Tonight he would again listen to the music of the dead; the music that was the music of his own heart.

. . . .

. . . .

CHAPTER EIGHT

THE SATCHEL

Part II

The Abbey; Spring thru Autumn 1352

.......BACK of the wine house, in the little garden, near the statues of the kissing angels! There, my darling, I will wait for you after the tavern closes. There, I promise, I will be yours. There, in the company of the marble angels, it is there we may be naughty.......

.......Do not worry about my husband. He is a lazy pig and a drunkard. I am not afraid of him. And even if he beats me, what is his anger and his blows compared to the honey of your kisses? Only tell me when and where, and I will dare an army of such husbands to sing in your arms!.......

.......I know a little barn not far away, full of fresh soft hay. It is in a field where no one goes. I will show it to you if you like.......

.......Night after night I watch your hands dance upon the lute's strings. I am jealous of that lute, and the beautiful melodies you make it sing. Come to me, tonight, in the darkness of the abbey wall, where the ivy falls with a river of leaves and blossoms. My body is a lute. It also longs to sing!.......

.......Did you like where I hid the grapes and cherries last time? You are a devil, Maria the gypsy, the sweetest devil I have ever known. You know there are jewels where I have hidden those fruits, jewels that are yours! Yes, they are yours my darling. And yet....it is so much fun to have you hunt for them each time anew! Come, tonight! The grapes are ripe, they and the sweet red cherries!.......

He knew that for each of these little notes of proposition and invitation, there surely had been many others. He knew that despite any and all risks, even infidelity, that countless others had solicited his embraces in countless other, illiterate ways. As he had combed through the satchel's contents, he had gathered that most of Maria's admirers were rustic and unlettered. They did not know how to write. There were verses of poems he had scribbled, verses that he had probably sung or recited to such pastoral lovers.

.....free the black tresses from you bright red scarf,
and bind your skirt above your milky thighs,
make dance the gypsy sparkling in your eyes,
and crush the ripened vintage in my heart.......

From the great wilderness of this reckless manuscript, he deduced that most had communicated their desires in other ways; other ways that only a woman's instincts would know how to use in love's adventures.

But as there were invitations, so here and there were the flatteries that had surely prompted them.

.....All women are both a thief and an angel. Oh, thievish Angel, you have taken and blessed my heart!......

......I do not want to kiss your lips, I want to bruise them. I do not want to melt your heart, I want to eat it. I do not want to tickle you with my embraces, I want to smother you with their wings!.......

......Your teeth are like the milk of the corn, your skin, like the honey made by spring's bees; your feet, dainty as meadow daisies.....your lips, a rosebud, waiting only their hour to blossom into kisses.......

.....Your body is like a violin, and when my hands touch its loveliness, it yields a melody that swoons the night.....stilling its winds and wolves to silent envy........

......I will come to you any way I can. Let fall your hair from your window, and I will climb its vines full of jasmines, nightingales and stars.....I will climb it to the soft nest of your arms.......

......I will tame you, as you were a wild beast of the forest; not with whips, but little by little, as with sips of wine. I will make you tame, silly, mine. I will make you drunk and helpless with the wine of my love.......

.....Your kisses are like a gentle rain upon my body. They wake a thousand sleeping buds, a thousand aches and longings, until my soul exhales its flower into the night.....breathing its fragrance into the eternity of your arms.......

And the poetry, always the poetry, their random lines hastily, almost illegibly left here, there and everywhere on the pages, as they were the honeyed flowers on these madly rioting vines of words.

.....outside your window I stood drunk last night;
wounded, bleeding in your garden's dark,
dying with Love's dagger in my heart,
watching the ritual of your maiden might.......

There had been many: tavern girls, harvest maids, shepherd and shop girls.....

.....angel of oatcakes, biscuits, leaven and flour,
with a red kerchief bound about your hair.....
.....O forest bird, child of the Earth Mother,
With copper bangles in your hair.....
.....young shepherdess, what spell is in your kisses,
stilling Time, while your sheep nibble the grasses?....../

There were even lines addressed to widows in mourning.

.....the days of your long mourning are long gone,
your lips, too long un-kissed behind that veil,
your ripeness too ripe to wither in the sun,
deep in your heart, still sings the nightingale.......

Even for Brides of Christ......

.....I beg but one brief moment, holy sister,
now, when your sister brides are in the garden,
or Choir, or Chapter.....one moment to whisper
my spirit's passion pleading for love's pardon.......

Their names appeared in the pages like the fruit of a prodigally fruited tree: in verses and titles of poems, in sketches and musings, in invitations to clandestine and adulterous trysts; in passionate, even lurid love letters. And with these names were the pet names these lovers had attached to him, and in return, the pet names he had attached to them.

.....Your Angeletta, Celia, Leonetta.....'My Treasure', 'My Heart', 'My Golden Bird'.......Your Contessina, Lisabetta, Junipera......'My Little Nightingale', 'Thief of my Heart'......Your Angelucia, Beatrista, Giulia.....'My Blue-eyed Lion', 'My Angel Fiddler'......

One in particular, he addressed as, 'Little Pigeon'.

.....at night I dream of where my darling sleeps;
near what gargoyle, or crouching lion rests,
and what it would be, for her pink feet,
like fingertips to shyly walk upon my breast.

flutter from your nest, O Little Pigeon, come!
For you my heart is broken, into ten thousand crumbs......

More than seductive invitations and erotic innuendo, there were other notes of those who had given themselves to him, and having given themselves, wanted only to give themselves again. The reader noted that there was seldom envy, jealousy or bitterness in these notes, only a pining; a pining that brooded on despair; a sweet thrill of despair that drowned such things that are wont to envenom the hearts of abandoned lovers.

Neither was there pride or conquest attached to the responses made to these pining lovers. They did not seem to be regarded by their gypsy sweetheart as trophies. The one who kept these little notes, and bore them through the summers and winters had regarded them as gifts; secret, perhaps even sacred gifts that lent a meaning, probably the only meaning that had been given to his aimless, shameless, often precarious existence. Devoid of the least pecuniary value, they were the immeasurable treasure of this shiftless wanderer's heart.

.......I wake in the night, but alas, you are not in my arms my darling! O, how I long for those sweet things you are giving another: the music in your whispers, the wine in your kisses, the tender wings of your caresses!.......

....And when I long for you I stir. The very thought of your love makes my breasts ripen, like buds of roses pricked before the warm spring sun.......

.......Do you know what you mean to me? Your love has melted the icy brooks of my blood with spring; I, who have never known such warmth before, even in my marriage bed. Please come to me, or tell me where I should come to you my darling. You alone can thaw the winter in my blood and make it sing!.......

.......When I think of you in the arms of younger, prettier lovers, I quiver through and through, even as your hands were on my body, not theirs. I surrender to the tender ghost of your love, and fall into a pleasure garden of dreams......dreaming until the deepest part of me wells into a sigh, and in that sigh, love's sigh.....I complete the passion meant for only you.......

.......Take me with you, my Gypsy. I will leave my husband, my gardens, my jewels and gowns, the very roof beneath which I sleep! Though I would live in a castle, I would starve without your kisses. Though I would be a queen, without your blue eyes and golden laughter I would be a pauper of the roads. Take me with you, Maria, even as your servant, even as your

whore; a whore whose heart is a virgin avowing the purest kind of love for you.......

As the bell began to ring, clanging its concussions through each part of the abbey, he wrapped the portfolio in the soft piece of doeskin, and slid it gently into the weathered satchel. Kneeling, he shoved it deeply beneath his bed; and then once more standing, gripped his cane, and left his cell for his prayers.

This had been his routine for weeks and months: painstakingly reading and examining the writings in the afternoons, the afternoons that his injury had freed from the duties of his abbacy. He read sometimes in the garden, sometimes in the scriptorium, sometimes in the seclusion of his cell, careful to always be alone. Although he knew that God was watching his sin, he nevertheless became emboldened with the secrets he was discovering,; sometimes walking through the corridors, across the courtyard, past the the statues of the saints with the satchel strapped over his shoulder; the lurid intrigues of a reprobate hanging at his side.

He also knew that as God was watching his sin, He was also hearing the lies he devised to disguise that sin.

"Good afternoon, Abbot Father. How is your knee? Better? And that manuscript that you found? Ha, that manuscript you carry around like Moses carried the tablets down from the mountain?"

"My knee is much better, and the manuscript is coming along just fine. Thank you, good brother. Thank you very much for asking."

"What language, father, if I may ask? Latin? French? Hebrew?"

"Brother?"

"What language is the manuscript written in, Abbot Giovanni?"

"Ah, in the mother tongue, brother, the mother tongue of love."

"The work of a famous Saint, holy father?"

"Not a Saint, brother, but perhaps, well, perhaps a sort of mystic"

"This pouch seems very worn and weathered, Abbot Father. If you wish, I could ask the shoemaker in the village to make another for you. They say he is a veritable tailor when it comes to leather. And as you know, Brother Egrigio is a carpenter. He could make a beautiful box for it. Only this morning I saw a piece of rosewood in his shop; a very fine piece indeed."

But Father Giovanni deflected such questions, and declined such offers from his innocent brothers. He demurred with a dishonesty that in his heart was nothing less than spiritual perjury, an unequivocal sin in the eyes of God. And yet, as he had once done in a count's dungeon, he found himself being duplicitous on behalf of this womanizing degenerate he had once called his friend in his youthful days.

"*Thank you, brother. I would like to keep it in the same satchel as it was given to me. Call your abbot 'sentimental' if you like, but I fancy the manuscript has a certain mystery, a kind of sacredness about it, and I would not want to disturb it from the feathers of its original nest.*"

Against the honor of his conscience, he had even continued to use his cane when he knew full well he could walk free of it, at times favoring, even exaggerating the slight limp that lingered in his step. This prolonged the illusion of his injury's nagging hurt, hence leaving time free to explore the satchel's great abundance.

But why? Why was he, an old monk and the abbot of a brotherhood, so fascinated with the things he found in this mystic's scribbling; the best of which were flowery and frivolous; the worst, lascivious and debauched?

He knew that it was not lechery that had gripped his old age. Although *Woman* had been a brief threat and danger in his adolescence, he had long since conquered that mountain, the mountain that many ecclesiastics and ascetics stumble upon, and find it difficult, or impossible to climb. Sex no longer posed a temptation to him. It had long since ceased being a sparkling-eyed serpent on the path to salvation. The sensuous allure of the fair sex was but a vague memory, a stale perfume that no longer piqued his senses. It no longer breathed its song into the tent of his dreams.

No, it was not lechery. Such desires hatched in young warm blood, not blood that was turning cold with age. But if not lechery, then how could he explain the chains with which the things in the satchel so bound him? How could he account for the curiosity and fascination that had taken hold; nay, that had come to possess him?

Patiently he read each phrase, line, word and rhyme no matter how random, trivial or profane. When he finished the thought or passage he had been reading, he began to read the same again, studying each cluttered sheet as if indeed it was a rare manuscript that held a mystic significance. As the weeks and months passed, their clutter began to gradually take on a form, a body, as they were the journal of a man's soul; a man's soul that in some odd way was not so much unlike *his own soul*. Page after page, word by word he combed through their wilderness with an eager hunger, as it was a forest he had ever wished, but had been too afraid to enter; a forest full of terrible beasts, poisonous flowers, and beautiful wonders.

Slowly, like the head, shoulders and torso emerging from the sculptor's stone, the one who had so colorfully and shamelessly littered these pages, emerged as a living spirit from their carnality. Slowly the author of these dawdling dreams gathered form, and stepped from their mists, and when he did it was with a strange, almost godly might. As the abbot read through the pages, the winebibber transformed into a kind of passionate soldier; the adulterer into a kind of mendicant; the shiftless wanderer into a kind of earnest pilgrim. Slowly the callow monk he had counseled many years ago, the monk who had become an idler lolling in sties of profligacy; the monk he had regarded as a child, yes, a child, had developed into a strong, and in some inscrutable way, magnificent man.

He who was the recipient of such idolatry from the fair sex at first seemed surprisingly, intensely lonely; but reading more, the abbot felt it was not loneliness alone; rather an impervious *aloneness* possessed of a rugged, season-tested identity. He was a nomad whose existence was a tent through which the wind blew and the rain fell. Although befriended by all men, he remained a stranger of their friendliness. Although loved by all women, there seemed a part of him that remained unloved. A practitioner of wickedness, there seemed a part of him that was unsoiled; a part that seemed almost heroic, that had retained the innocence of a child.

What seemed on first sight as a confused jumble of partly legible ideas observations, and poetic flights, upon patient reading gradually obtained distinct threads that wove their confusion into the intricate patterns of a fabric, a very beautiful fabric. Certain themes appeared, like refrains, appearing again and again, sewing and binding all of the fragments together.

Over and over these refrains spoke of the dream of life, its transitory, unreliable nature, and the futility it presented Man as he journeyed through it.

.........*Life is autumnal; a continual farewell to the brief hour and flurry of youth. It is a departure, a departure at twilight that ever pines to return to life's golden morning. One passes through forests, and says goodbye to the pretty birds and flowers. One crosses over brooks, and says goodbye to the fish in its silver pools. One passes sunny gardens, and says goodbye to the bright smiles and dark eyes of maidens digging in the brown soil.....and yet*

663

all wish this passer-by to return, to stay and sip the nectar of their golden sweetness......

> *.....and as softly, silently I depart*
> *into the wilderness of the years,*
> *when Winter's in your hair,*
> *Autumn's in your dreams,*
> *that ghost that kept your memories in his heart.......*

.....Green summer turns to golden autumn, autumn to winter's blizzards. One's step begins to slow, lag, limp; one's sight to blur. Cold and sleepy, the bag becomes heavy on the wanderer's back, and he seeks out a shelter where he may break bread, drink from a cool well, and rest his head.....and when he begins to grow numb and drowse, a child's laughter breaks from his heart.../as if he suddenly knows all of his ambitions and struggles had been a game, a game all men are born to play, but none to master.....to wander in, but never to find an end to the child's first wishes.......

.....Man is very small, a creature that finds itself lost in a vast, snowy forest, a forest whose frozenness stretches to the rims of the world.....its unending silence pierced only by the cries of crows and the howls of wolves. Small, yes, very small.....a bit of flesh stitched to a few bones, a few dreams housed in a little brain, a heart ticking behind a few sticks of ribs. And yet that heart is convinced it is a mighty thing; that it is a king, and it lords over the forest.....that its warmth will not turn cold, and its candle will never sputter.....that the dreams called 'wisdom', were not a fool's delusion......

Fascinated with beauty, there were passages concerned with the creation of art.

.......We grieve to see the flowers fade, the leaves fall, the dearest dreams in our hearts crumble apart and die. We grieve because we know we are a part of life, and in being a part of life we are not exempt from that law that all things are born to obey; that caught in Time's web, we will wither and waste away; that we too shall soon be given to the jaws of a dumb dark grave and a jackal laughing wind.......

.......What is art but an altar erected by the artist in his heart, an altar with idols of flowers, pretty birds, and silver moons? The artist erects his own temple, one that demands he quit the faith to a God all others worship. He turns his back on the promises of Heaven, that he may worship miracles of flesh and blood.....miracles of paint, marble, ink, strings of a lute...... miracles he brings from the dust with his own hands.........

.....The heart of the artist is full of howling winds and snarling beasts, terrible monsters that break from hell's chains into the sunny fields of this world. It is only after these monsters fall into his hands that they become wondrous lovely, their savagery changing to marble gods, colors of the rainbow, the warbling tongues of Angels.......

,,,,,remove your ribbons, then your tortoise shell
barrette, tumbling free a cataract
of raven glory sparkling down
the ivory valley of your back! Your gown
slipped from your slender shoulders to your feet,
unveiling what only angels or madmen paint.......

.......Good poems and good songs open their arms to all of life. They gather both its storms and sunlight; its widowhood, and its first coltish play in spring flowers. Only then may their melody pierce the heart with truth; that truth which is the oneness of pain and joy, the eternal marriage of love and mourning.....the smile that trembles like moonlight on the life-mother's lips as she watches the caravan of the seasons pass by.......

He was a lover of women, but he was as much a disciple as a master of their mystery. He did not regard his lovers as hussies, slatterns or whores, even when they invited him as such; but as something sweeter, dearer; nearer the beating heart of life. He had seemed to love them with the same love he had stolen from the God he had once worshipped.

.......The language of 'Woman' is a different language, a deeper and more primitive language; a language of the forest, and the creatures that live and die in the forest. It is a language of glances and gestures, blushes, smiles, scents; quickening breaths and dilating nostrils; a language of erecting breasts and stirring wombs.......

Its songs and cries come from the heart of the first forest. Leaving words behind, it steps in shyness from that forest, teasing its hunter with the want to be hunted.....the perfume of its desire filling the night, saying: "Come, O Hunter, lay down your weapons! I am ready to be slain in your arms!".......

.......In her surrender, the mistress is like the soft clay in the potter's hands. She wants to be treated tenderly and patiently, but with strength and confidence. Only then is she willing to be pliant. Only then is she willing to be shaped into the beauty that has long slept inside her. Only then will the clay yield its many treasures in the potter's hands.......

.......Two of the greatest mysteries in life are the night, full of the dark forests, wild creatures, and the stars......and death, forever crouched with

hunger for what beats behind men's ribs. But greater than these mysteries is the mystery of 'Woman'. She is deeper than the night.....and her sweetness is more shyly sly, and far more sweetly cruel than death.......

And then there were his many lovers: some that he wanted only to adore from afar; to paint and gild with words; others he had serenaded with a lute or fiddle, or with the golden poetry of his heart; some that stirred and teased him, that called him to the hunt; some that had fled his advances, that had rebuffed him, only to repent, and swoon into his arms; many that he had passionately embraced, and had been lost in those embraces.....the portfolio in the satchel strewn with the gods of love's immortal arena.....*infatuation, seduction, passion, apology, poignant farewell*.....an arena that, even in the cruelest defeat, he accepted with a kind of worship.

.....Unconscious of her own beauty, she quickens all hearts about her into light and song, as their drowsy spirits were wakened, like thirsty flowers lifting their faces to the rain. Though it is the deep of winter, the very birds begin to herald spring's return. Morning is her sister; summer her castle; the stars, candles that light her every step across the footbridge of this dark world......

.......Her modesty invites a kinder, sunnier presence, one with which her every gesture lilts with Heaven; her every movement, dances with a different partner of Grace.......

.......Stepping into her circle, Time becomes enchanted, dreaming the timeless dream that dreams in poppy-blooming meadows, on the rosy brows of babes.....that blesses exhausted lovers with peace. Stepping into her circle, Time becomes enamored, and swoons into Eternity.......

.....Her body is a garden filled with sunlight and flowers. Oh, how I would like to sip such beautiful flowers,- the flowers of her knees, toes, fingertips, her brown throat and coral lips. Oh, how I would like to taste their honey before their summer fades.....to melt into the golden sunlight that kisses each leaf and petal of her garden........

.....There are serpents in her hair, storms in her eyes, and knives gnashing in her heart. She comes to me like a mad tiger from the forest, and I am afraid that her love will murder me. Oh, but her mouth, her sweet little mouth! It is a honeycomb that melts in mine, one that holds the sustenance of the Angels!.......

.......Her beauty is of the earth; a beauty of the peasant, not the queen; for she owns the brown earth that every gilded slipper has paid homage to.

She is not haunted with a 'soul'; no, her body has banished such a pagan superstition from its keeping. Her hips, breasts and lovely slender neck 'are' her soul, a soul that dreams not of salvation, only a need to sing, and singing to surrender and be drunk, saved one more time in love's arms.......

There were sketches of disenchantment and disillusionment, things that seemed to wage cynical battles with his love for love, women and art.

.......Then was this all there was to love's mystery, the tumult of its hymn, its secret little flower?.....this clutching, this gasp, this little cry in the night? Was this all, this brief lightning of pleasure passing through the bowels?....this stab of a knife that killed with secret joy?.....this little quiver, like the ghost fleeing the body...leaving it still, as with death, in its murderer's arms?

.....softly, silently, early I will leave,
banished from your arms, I will softly go,
that you will never know
how their embraces made my heart to bleed.......

.....There is a great nobility in these street girls, they who sell buttons and flowers, oysters and scones, and with these things the treasures of their bodies. They touch the heart of life because they 'want', and to fill the hunger of that 'want' they wage their flesh, even at the expense of losing their very souls. In the dark hunger of these girls' eyes, life choirs its salvation.......

Not so with the feathered and the jeweled, the rich and the painted. In their attempts to become lovely, they strangle their loveliness. They gore their beauty with the claws of their pride, their artifice rendering them haughty and soul-less. Their blood is as cold as the north wind.....as it was the blood of ghosts. Their arms are drifts of snow, their hearts, frozen brooks.....their lips, giving kisses of the dead.......

.....it is neither scriptures nor saintliness that curb men's sinning, for they who think so are full of timidity and cowardice, and a fear to go a-soldiering with their hearts. It is better to sin in an attempt to live, than to shrink into lifeless shadows; a hermit afraid of the sun's eye, cursing thieves and harlots in a cave. To live, one must be willing to die.....to know a single joy, to bare one's soul.....to taste the burning lips of love, to bury a dagger into one's own heart......

.....then tell me, holy sister, it is not true,
when counting beads, or praying in your cell,
that you do not think of our rendezvous.......

In these many pages, Maria mentioned again and again a certain young woman who bore a pronounced limp. He had thought her beauty was a special beauty, as if her handicap had lent her a vulnerability that freed her soul to more fully flower its charms. Like a painter, he had studied her beauty; and with a quill and ink, not a brush, he had painted her.

……*There was a music in her beauty, a poetry, an unseen breeze that played through the leaves and blossoms, the forest of what she was; a light that illumined each part of her, like sunlight on a flower after rain; that gave all rhyme, melody, meaning…..that sang of something sweeter, higher, truer; her toes no less than her lips, her knees no less than her arms, her calves and thighs no less than her ears and eyes…..as each part of her rhymed, like the bells of the meadow goats with the church bells on the hills…..as her parts were not separate, but a family, her every part melting into the harmony that gives reason to the seasons…..a melody to the birth and death of things.*

Nor does her limp impede the grace of her creature. It rather gives it buoyancy, like that which the wind lends the swallow. It is no crutch, but a wing; a wing that is not broken and dragging, but with the feathers of an Angel, bears the weights and worries, the very chains of this world as they were strings and straws. She does not limp. Borne by grace, she glides through the storm of this world like a swan glides over a still pond……that swan a queen that does not know she is a queen……

For Katrinika
YOUR
Lonely loveliness a violin
With sweet sad melodies sleeping in its strings;
Come, darling, to my arms, and, like the wind
Of the south that wakes the forests in the spring,
Let my hands caress awake your heart;
Beneath arcades, on esplanades, your head
Upon my shoulder, we shall serenade
The twelve moons sailing through the stars.
We shall extol love's mystery and meaning;
Its aches and joys, its defeats and crusades,
Its lovely longing and cruel seeming-
Those hoofs of storm that richest roses made.
Your face upon my breast, gentle as moonlight,
A violin that sweetly sings, love's melody to the night.

* * *

HE had left the brothers as they busily mowed down the golden wheat in swishing swaths before them. Once out of sight in the trees, he had no longer used his cane. With the satchel hanging at his side, he had walked briskly on the circuitous path until he reached the grassy little place he had visited on that day in early spring, the day when Brother Vittorio had made the discovery at the foot of the old tree.

He was not sure why it had seemed so important to him to be near the tree. Perhaps it was because the spring and summer had passed, and like waves, autumn was now threshing its reds, browns and fiery yellows free of the fields and hills. Winter was not far behind, and it would soon be impossible for him to leave the abbey's gates, and make his way through the snow-drifted forest. The winter of age was also approaching. Life was brief, and full of uncertainties. The abbot knew it was entirely possible that he would never make this walk to the old tree again.

But upon arriving at the tree, he knew why he had come. It was because of the satchel, and the catch-all abundance he had found inside it: the keepsakes of lovers, and the careless and haphazard things the friend of his youth had once written in poems and ragged flights of his fancy. He had read and re-read each word, no matter how foolish or profane, and what he had read had crushed his heart, crushed it to dust, and made it sing.

Yet he was not sure why he had pressed his face against the tree's trunk, or why the rough bark felt soft to his cheek, as it was the soft folds of a pillow. He did not know why something broke inside him, and in this solitary place, why he had given that *something* permission to pour in scalding trickles from his eyes.

But why had he brought the satchel?

He had imagined climbing the tree like a squirrel, and hanging it from a limb in the tree's crown, near where Maria had once hung his habit. He had imagined falling on his knees, and like a dog burying it in the grave with the shepherdess's bones. He had imagined leaving it in the tree's fork where the brother had found the incriminating blanket. But upon arrival at the tree, he knew he would do none of these things. He knew that he would keep the satchel. He knew he was not ready, and perhaps would never be ready to part with it. He knew that he needed to keep it near him, perhaps even to die with it. He knew that he would fiercely guard it, as a rich man guards his riches; that his soul would not renounce it.

His fear of the satchel had been well founded, but his fear had not warned him he would be shaken to his roots in such an unlikely way. Its scraps of poignant sweetness had pierced his heart; pierced and slashed it to ribbons like a sharp knife. He had never held in his hands such a collection of 'love'; such a simple, palpable, prolific collection of purest 'love'.

.....and as softly, silently I depart,
into the wilderness of the years.......

Yes, it was love; it could be called nothing else.....that mysteriously divine, illusive thing he had sought and believed in all his life; that he had endeavored to cultivate day after day, and year after year in his prayers, studies and devotions. But the love he had endeavored to embrace was entirely different than the love he had found in the satchel. It had been a love of God, a God he had never seen, and had never spoken to; who's Silence he had accepted and opened his heart to with a life of unquestioning faith. It had not been a love of flesh and bone; of want, pain and privation; a love of the earth itself, one that burned with the kisses of hardship, joy and death upon its lips.

.....when Winter's in your hair,
Autumn's in your dreams,
that ghost that kept your memory in his heart.......

What he had found in the satchel was a different kind of love, but it was still 'love'; yes, unmistakably, 'love'. If one closed one's eyes and bit into an apple, one would know he had bitten into an apple. If one smelled a certain heady fragrance in the spring night, one would know the mimosas had bloomed. Though much of what he found in the satchel was degenerate and irreverent, it felt and tasted, and exhaled that mystic, albeit certain quality men call 'love'

.....that ghost shall softly return,
to softly whisper in your ear:
'I loved you as no other; I held you most, most dear'.......

This pouch of weathered leather contained a journal, a journal of a fornicator, drunkard and shiftless dreamer, of one who had wandered and stumbled through the dark and sinful world. The many keepsakes of his many lovers.....the ribbons, tresses, snippets of undergarments, though they had been given by ignorant peasant girls, tavern wenches, or other men's wives, attested a sincerity that he was sure they had never offered another, even a husband......perhaps a sincerity they had never offered God.......

And this portfolio? Were its words a picture of a soul that had turned its back on God, a God whose face was everywhere? Did they portray a soul fallen, or one that in its own way was trying to stand, and standing, kneel and surrender to the certainty to which all men must surrender?

Maria had left the safe confines of the abbey, guided by the dark drives of his blood and the intoxication of his senses. He had discarded both his faith and reason, only to replace them with the blindness of his passions; intent on feeding his desires, rather than starving them. He had performed shameless, if not wicked acts with women, acts that the Angels surely could not condone. He had become a drinker of wine, an adulterer, a wielder of knives and his own two fists. He had stolen. He had whored. He had been imprisoned. By his own admission he had killed, and probably more than one man.

And yet had there not been a kind of courage, a strange, noble kind of courage in the degeneracy of his former friend's life, his life that had probably ended with a ruffian's knife or in a wolf's jaws; whose ribs and skull were now probably lying somewhere beneath the rotting leaves of a forest? Had his life not been honest, and un-pretended? Had it not been a reckless, but somehow honorable crusade; a blind, stumbling, reasonless crusade in which he had abandoned himself to the cruelties, dangers and hardships of the world, rather than trying to escape that world by reciting prayers behind high stone walls? Was it nobler to confront sin, or to hide from sin's temptations; more manly to accept sin's consequences, or to live in constant fear of them?

.....when Winter's in your hair,

Autumn's in your dreams.......

The ribbons, flowers and tresses, the love letters......these were not from caprices in barns, in alleys or on riverbanks.

.....that ghost that kept your memory in his heart.......

These were tears wept and bled from hearts that had been quickened by one who had touched them; with love seldom known in cathedrals.

.....'I love you as no other; I held you most, most dear'.......

Oh, did the child not know the world by playfully stumbling and reck-lessly romping through it? Was it not braver to walk through the perilous world burning with one's own truth, rather than continually seeking shelter from its angry beasts and winds? Was it not, in the end, perhaps more innocent?

He heard the tolls of the abbey's bell, calling the brothers from their toils. And when he did, like a small child wrapping its arms about its mother's hips, the abbot spread wide his arms, and tightly embraced the girth of the old tree; as he did not want to leave it; as he wished to die with it. He did not want to go to his prayers. He did not want to leave this moment, this tenderness; this lovely gentle tree that once had understood and protected his friend; that had faithfully kept his living memories in its veins. He wanted only to stay here; to cling to what had reached its roots deep into the earth, and lifted its brave, gallant branches into the sky; its burnished leaves fluttering in the wind; as with song.

. . . .

. . . .

CHAPTER NINE

THE THEATRE OF THE DEAD

Part III

MAN had stubbornly insisted that his God was a merciful God. But as to scoff at and sweep aside this age-old tale, his God had sent a merciless, uncompromising scourge; one that slew without warning, without remorse, without discrimination. His Silence had at last spoken, and when it did it did not whisper with love, but howled with rage. Without reason or compassion, this God punished His children with a rod that crawled over their naked needs like a sea of scorpions. He commanded His Angels to assemble their armies, and let loose arrows of burning fire into men's hearts.

Like a dark river, Death breached life's festive walls; broke through its flowering vines. It gushed through each field and street, polluted altars, marriage beds and cradles alike. Its contagion seeped beneath all doors; breathed in all faces; blew out each candle. Like a drunkard, Death laughed in all dreams. Like an adder, Death rose where it had coiled, and with dilated eyes, hissed its answer to men's every hope and prayer.

* * *

* * * * *

POSSESSED with its dark enchantment, abandoned and drowned in the parade of its dark rapture.....those of the living, a pilgrimage through hell; an aimless, senseless ghost wandering through fields and villages.....through a world forsaken by the sun.....looking with eyes of the living at scenes that had heretofore been reserved only for the dead........

.....Those that lived; those that saw; like a child before magicians and jugglers, charmed by death's circus, mesmerized by the wonders of hell......a lost child of a ghost marveling at the dying and the damned.....and in that marveling, joining.....and joining, becoming mad with the carnival, the carnival that was a theatre of the dying and the damned.......

* * *

DEATH had made him break his vows as they were straws, making him not only a coward, but a hypocrite in his cowardice. Rather than surrendering to the pestilence, he had begged, thieved and groveled to stay alive in it. He had no money, no food, no shelter. He became a frequenter of the dark dens of the depraved; those that erected stages for the most degenerate audiences, making shameless displays of whoredom, sodomy and bestiality.

He had sung and danced, played fiddles in the streets. He had given himself to withered, love-starved widows in exchange for a warm bed and a piece of bread. He had let himself be taken into the arms of these withered lovers; their embraces smothering him with jewels and perfumes and dying needs, tearing at his hair and digging into his back as they wished to extract his strength and health.....as they wished to be sown by the fire that was still alive in him; as their salvation was one with the quivering of their wombs.

In the passing weeks and months, he too became lawless, shameless, and giddy with madness, as he had become a silly clown in death's circus. He too abandoned the decency and the sanity of the living, joining the debauch of others, who, gripped by the blind needs of self-preservation, had rid themselves of the petty strictures of reason, the trinket of conscience, and the glittering idolatry of worship.

He too stripped boots and coats from corpses when the cold came upon him. He too picked the pockets of the dead, and with these pickings he too drank, gambled and roistered in taverns; jeering, toasting and mocking the dead-carts when they passed the tavern doors. And when the bakers and butchers died, and the garden vines and orchards froze, and he could not find a widow's bed in which he could earn his meals, he looted with the camaraderie of fellow looters; men he did not know, but was bound to by the bond of desperation.

It was on one of these occasions that this licentious merriment changed, granting him even closer, firsthand scenes of the rituals of death that were being performed all about him; permitting him not only to be a spectator, but a participant in the sacrificial rites of its spectacle.

One night he watched as a band of three or four men broke down a bake house door, using a great plank as a battering ram. He had watched as the men had entered with lanterns, and then raced away with loaves of bread in their arms. Quick to exploit the opportunity before him, Maria rushed in the broken door, and stuffed his pockets with several large biscuits. But his theft had not been quick enough. Leaving the shop he was greeted by a group of men armed with scowls and ugly clubs; a group of men consisting of the shop's owner, a constable, and a number of husky fellows the constable had deputized to help keep order in the lawless streets. Caught red-handed, and with no chance to fight free of such odds, Maria surrendered to his arrest.

They had bound his wrists, but did not imprison him. They had instead informed him that as a criminal, he must serve on a team of the collectors and buriers that were soliciting corpses each night in the streets. The band of deputies was in fact the same team he was to join. He was told in no uncertain way that if he shirked or fled from this duty, these men were given license to kill him, and to throw him on the cart with the victims they were collecting; a thing that, with one look at these rough men, Maria did not doubt.

But to Maria's great surprise, as soon as the constable and the shop's owner departed, the men showed him an enthusiastic, rowdy kind of welcome, even a congratulations for his thievery. Although night had newly fallen, their first duty led them to a small inn, one that was called the '*Sickle and Plough*'; an actual sickle and plough mounted on one of its walls, like trophies of the hunt. With wine, coarse laughter and hearty claps on his back, this strange tribe welcomed him to his penal consignment. Albeit relieved that he was not in chains, it did not take long for Maria to discover what kind of uncouth company he had fallen among.

They were not men of the village, not even of the surrounding country-side; rather, they were ones that had been recruited from remote places in the hills, for very few, or none at all could be found to volunteer for the grim business with which they were to be entrusted. The monks that had not died were squirreled away behind monastic walls, and with the pretense of praying for the abatement of God's judgment, swore off such a hazardous service. Most of the priests had either died or fled, and as the fury of the distemper raged on, most of those that were still living refused even to mumble prayers over the pits in which the dead were spilled; many fleeing like rabbits from the death they had so boldly assayed to meet head on. The sextons were few, and those that were still living were in charge of keeping the fires fueled about the pits, as well as directing the teams of the diggers, carters and buriers. Indeed, with the fever and abandon with which death was raging, the living feared they soon would be outnumbered by the dead, and were not confident they would be sufficient to bury them.

But these men from the hills were either brave or foolhardy enough, and in any case hard enough to do what the dying and the frightened would not, and with the goodly remuneration offered them, they had departed from their wives and children, and eagerly shouldered the ghastly labor.

Their hardness and uncouthness fit them for their employment, a most necessary and vital one. Without anyone to collect, transport and bury the dead, the village would become an open, vermin infested grave, a veritable charnel house of stench and corpses. Thus in doing what no other was willing, able, or too frightened to do, these gross men acquired a stature they had never known before. The citizens became dependent on their brutishness, and these men soon realized they were the only ones to rescue their desperate plight. This need bloated their self-esteem, and lent them a kind of swagger in their unsavory chores. They could speak as they pleased, drink as they pleased, carouse and whore as they pleased. In the realm of the dead and the dying, they were its princes.

Drinking with them at the inn, Maria quickly learned that their team was not only from the same place in the hills, but all but one of the five were brothers. They had worked in a quarry since they were boys, and they were burly strong. The burliest, as well as most gregarious, was a beast of a man named '*Bruno*'. He was their undisputed leader, and he spoke a cheery gallows humor to Maria as they drank, and the others huddled in a card

"*Welcome, welcome my golden-haired prisoner! Welcome mate to our little crew! We always drink a flagon or two before our nightly rounds, do we not bro's? Here, drink up, you've no need to be down in the jowls, man.....*"

676

it beats chains and the pissy straw in a jail, or maybe even the scurvy hull of a ship. You'll come to not mind it, no, not a bit......after all, a dead man is a dead man, like a dead sheep is a dead sheep....we stack fifteen or sixteen in our cart.....that is if they're wrapped and bound.....as many as twenty if there are babes or urchins.....we'll have you singing sailor chanteys before long......its not a bad life, not a bad life at all.......

.....Alfredo my brother, the shaggy one there.....his tongue tied to the roof of his mouth since birth.....rings the bell, ha! announcing us to the corpses and their bringers.....and Mauro there, another brother....we call him 'Mauro the lame-brained'.... he leads the horse.....while the rest of us do the collecting, the toting, the heaving and heaping......we've got smithy tongs, shepherd crooks, poles and boat hooks......all kinds of things to help us drag, pitch and spill em'.....a corpse is a heavy and unwieldy thing you know. But you've got a good pair of shoulders on you blond man......you'll be with us, fit right in.....you'll be fine."

The master of the inn brought a great pot of stew, and sat it in the middle of the table. The mistress followed with a stack of bowls, spoons and ladles. Both were diffident and wore pinched faces, waiting on the men with silent deference. But their deference was stilted and slavish, and not warm and accommodating, more of bondage than polite servility, and even a fear of the ones they were bound to serve.....more like heeling hounds, than the rightful masters of their inn.

Bruno slid a bowl to the table's edge, and looking at the keeper's wife, a slight, middle-aged woman full of fret and worry in her face, nodded authoritatively at the bowl, at which the woman darted forward and began to ladle if full of stew. He spoke to her in a brazen, shameless way as she did, only half under his breath, so that all, including her husband, could hear his insolence.

"Not tumbled in the grave yet, my pretty? Come to my bed when I come from my rounds. I'll give you another kind of tumble, one that will make you glad to be alive."

With this the disgusting man reached quickly down, lifted up the woman's skirt, and with his large filthy hand grabbed, held and squeezed the woman's nakedness. This elicited a shriek from her, and a great laugh from the brothers eating about the fire, but nothing from the constrained and defenseless husband who, afraid of these vulgar brutes that had come to rule his inn each night, could but wrap his arm about his humiliated wife and walk away.

677

Regaling in the attention he now commanded, Bruno continued to speak to Maria, even as he gorged himself with stew. wine and bread.

.....*"I'll tickle the wench, don't think I won't.....with or without her wish, I'll tickle her and make her squeal I will.....now, where was I? Ah yes......*

Many of the corpses have valuables upon them....watches, lockets, brooches, snuffboxes...in their pockets, or tucked in secret places....and some of the lassies have gorgeous manes of hair they no longer need.....fetch handsome lots from the wig makers you know.....We make it a practice to cut open some of the shrouds, fleece 'em before we spill 'em.....especially the shrouds of the clerics, they've usually a prize of some sort.....rings, jeweled crosses, once a chalice, the rascals as much thieves dead as they were thieves alive.....and the widows.....the ones wrapped tidily and nicely we always inspect.....three out of four times we find the old hags bogged with jewels..... jewels we could not bear to see buried, and never sparkle in the sun.......

.....all in all, this thing will make a poor man a rich man soon enough, blond man, yes, a rich man this pesky death will. No, no, things have not turned out bad at all for you, blondy, not bad at all.....a reward and not a punishment....wine, meat, merriment and riches in exchange for the pilfering of a few measly biscuits......."

Sopping his bread in his bowl of stew, and grossly filling his mouth at once with bread, stew and wine, he suddenly fixed a keen sober stare upon Maria midst his gluttony.

.....*"You'll do fine....be a good member of our crew, Maria is it?.....a woman's name.....a woman's name with a man's shoulders, ha!.....well, you'll be a good lugger and toter of corpses I'm sure.....a good life it is..... drink, meat, and hussies on the knee.....but I must tell you, Maria my man, if you've got a notion to run, the bro's and I will hunt you down and slit your throat like the windpipe of a pig we will, and that without a cart ride back to the pits.......*

Now eat a little bread and stew. Build up your strength. We need to take several loads to the churchyard tonight......maybe even to the pits outside the gates. A great many died today, I can tell by the moans and wails of the women.....and the stink, ha! I can tell by the smell in the street.....and the piles I saw mid-afternoon.....we'll heap the cart a couple of times tonight, by Jove we will.....heap it high as hay with two or three good loads of 'em tonight we will."

Bruno sent two of his brothers to ready the cart and horse. A short while after, he pushed his plate and bowl aside, swigged a long swig of wine, and with a kind of grotesque magnanimity stood, belched and scratched, and announced to Maria and the others it was time to begin their rounds.

"*Come, it's time to take the cart to market lads. Oh don't look so glum Maria my man. You'll become used to it, won't he brothers? You'll be glad you snitched those biscuits. A merry little jaunt, really, with wine and song.....and plenty of pickings for a working man's pockets......a pretty night with the stars brightly shining.*"

As they reached the door, Bruno stopped and turned, and with savagery replacing flippancy in his eye, once more stared an iron stare at Maria.

"*And remember, Maria my man, if there's any trickery beneath that blond mane and beard of yours, you're a heap for the pits, with my own hands you are.*

Now, come on, ha!, let's go a-maying."

Thus with this sordid tribe, Maria began his penal duties, slowly walking through the streets with these collectors and scavengers of the dead. Torches were lit, the mute began to ring the bell, and as the cart began to funereally creak away behind the plodding horse, Bruno grinned detestably, swigged from his wine flask, and with the hubris of a confident general, nudged Maria in the ribs.

"*Like this, blond man, like this.*"

With a great bellowing voice, the loathsome devil rent the silent darkness, as he was cleaving it with a sword of blood:

"*Dead-cart! Dead-cart! Bring out your dead! We'll not pass again until tomorrow night, or the night after! Dead-cart! Dead-cart! Bring out your dead! Wrapped or unwrapped, bring out your dead!*"

And to this gruesome incantation the darkness responded, speaking with distressed cries, waved lanterns and the beating of pans. Muffled and weeping forms crept from houses and alleys, fences, bushes and trees, bearing their cumbersome loads to the street's edge. Wrapped in sheets and other bedclothes, or in old rugs or curtains, some in meal sacks, and often nothing at all, the collectors went to work, kneeling and wrestling death's unwieldy bundles expertly into their strong arms, and then bearing them to the dead-cart.

In some places corpses had been piled in grotesque piles near the street fires, like cordwood, one on top of the other, as they were scarecrows that had been gathered from summer's fields, and had never been living flesh at all. This lessened their labors, and delighted the brothers greatly. Sometimes they stumbled on stray corpses that lay sprawled where they had fallen, and these they sometimes roughly kicked to make sure they were felled by death, and not merely by drink or fever. Mindless of the sobs, wails and prayers of those that accompanied these bundles to their wretched hearse, the gross men tossed them roughly onto the cart's boards, or with great swings atop the top layer made by the other corpses, and wordlessly, unsympathetically and unconcernedly, with a kind of cavalier *bravado* plodded on.

Maria quickly saw that they had learned to minister cunning tricks in their trade. When they plodded down streets where the wealthier villagers lived, they sometimes pretended not to hear the cries of those left with the dead upon their hands. They continued on, baiting the distressed, until the distressed often ran after them, sometimes in desperation throwing coins or jewels at their feet, begging them to return and remove death's foulness from their keeping.

Increasingly drunk as the night wore on, and without inhibition in the kingship he had assumed, from time to time Bruno danced with a woman's corpse in his arms, much to the delight of his brothers. Sometimes he grabbed a shroud-wrapped babe from the cart, and with a great roar of godless laughter held it high over his head, swirling it about like a chieftain brandishing his sword, booming out with the audacity of his profane soul; his drunkenness commensurate with his despicability.

"Dead-cart! Dead-cart! Bring out your dead! We'll not pass again until tomorrow night, a tomorrow that might never come! Extra if we wrap them, or need to bring them down stairs, up from cellars or out of thick thickets or muddy gardens! Bring out your dead, ha! while there are still carters to cart 'em! Bring out your dead! We'll load 'em, cart 'em, spill 'em."

Many were the dead that were not brought by the living to their cart, that dying alone, or in the care of the old, the feeble and those who were themselves dying, were still in beds, cellars, sheds and hedges, rotting where they had expired.

.....husbands and wives, embracing in the final embrace of death..... babes still sucking at their dead mother's tumor-ridden breasts.....whole families in one bed, choosing to quit this world together.....some still bound by ropes to ceiling beams, some by belts, harness straps and chains to bedposts,

the distemper having made frothing monsters of them......some partially, or completely naked, their shoes and clothes, stuffs for pawning....stripped by their soul-less nurses and other sleek, opportunistic thieves.......

......some that had greeted the Reaper with fists and clenched teeth, even as they had readied to fight this unbeatable foe.....many that had met him slack-jawed and open-eyed with horror.....those who held in their hands rosaries and crucifixes....those who held at the last dolls, wigs, bolts of silk, boxes of coins, jewels, perfumeries......those who had met Death with pride, those with terror, those with submission, or even a strange smile of gratitude.......

.....some that were hanging bloated, blue-lipped and broken-necked from nooses.....some that had managed to stagger or crawl from their imprisonments, found beneath hedges, decaying beneath houses, in creeks, or in corners of muddy gardens.....some dismembered, or half eaten by dogs and vermin, some that were now only bones and pieces.....some who bore the sure signs of being strangled, or smothered by wet cloths of avaricious nurses grown impatient with waiting for their patients to die....some that life had not yet released....that moaning and struggling with last breaths were nevertheless accounted dead by their brute collectors.....tossed on the heap of corpses.....and would breathe their last on the way to their grave, or in their grave itself.......

.....those whose proud lives were to be interred in family crypts and vaults.....the princely, the queenly, the knightly.....those meant to be ornately dressed, laid on gilded biers, paraded in the pomp of solemn funerals in honor and mournful celebration....not carried, but roughly dragged down steep stairs, or dredged from sodden orchards.....their royalty pitched like dung on a cart.......

And as the night continued to offer its grim offerings, this vile bunch seemed livelier, even merrier midst their dismal chore. The brothers continued to openly drink, even before the mourners of the dead, stowing their demijohns midst the cart's corpses only when it was necessary to load another corpse. Most despicably, as they warmed to their task they began to sing tavern songs, like sailors singing chanteys, even midst those who were weeping and wailing their losses, and praying all about them; midst those who walked by the cart's side, accompanying their loved ones to their inhuman burials.

And yet, more detestable than even their open drunkenness, obscenities and unconscionable carousing, were the times they halted the cart in dark, fore-planned places. Here the soul-less devils would stop their drinking, their voices would hush, and they would go to tearing open shrouds, searching for jewels and relics, snipping off hanks of hair, and stripping the dead of shirts, belts, shoes, anything they could trade, use or pawn; the very shrouds in which they were bound. Aghast, Maria watched as they tore open winding sheets in which they knew young women were wrapped, and shamelessly denuding them, passed their goatish hands over their secret places; even bending down and kissing their bared buttocks, like hellhounds licking dead *Angels*.

"Ah, here's a pretty one, at least she was yesterday I'm sure!"

"And this one.....her face blackened and rotting, but her body not too bad yet.....a nice body she has, all but this swelling about her privities......"

"What a shame to throw this one in the pits.....oh, what a groan she must have given a fellow......."

"An' lookee' ee' here, a Sister of Chastity we have.....well, her cross I'll have with a snap.....it'll pawn on a rainy day.....but the other treasure's that she's kept through the years, well, I'm a religious man, and I'll leave that for her God and the worms......"

When the cart was piled full with its grim load, they brought it to the great mass graves in the churchyard. The timber-yards were long since exhausted of boards for the coffin-makers, and the places allotted for gravesites were far too small for such a glut of death, so great trenches, long and deep had been carved both near the churches, and some others in the fields outside the village gates. Although there had been those who had buried their dead in gardens or cellars, or even beneath the planks of their floors, eventually the terrible putrefaction of the corpses demanded mandates from the village leaders to bury the dead in mass graves.

Entering the churchyard was a trespass into hell: the air a terrible admixture of death's corruption, reeking dung, and the strong fumes of pitch and brimstone excited by the fires burning about the gaping mouths of the trenches. Here the collectors brought their harvests; here they up-turned their carts, and with poles, crooks and tongs, spilled their loads into the pits, many of the corpses without shrouds; many of them partly or completely naked.

Like catches fishermen spill from their nets, the corpses were spilled open-eyed and open-mouthed into these gruesome maws.....the priest with the drunkard, the harlot with the virgin, the duke with the pauper......mortal enemies at last embracing in the immortal embrace of death......those who but hours and days ago boasted of their riches, who drank and cursed, knelt in earnest prayer......now staring dumb and glassy-eyed at the world they had left, and with a few shovels of dirt, would be blackened forever.......

......*about the rims of these great trenches their loved ones wailing and sobbing, tearing open their shirts, crazily tearing their hair, beating their breasts......some wrapped in blankets or rugs, leaping into the mouths of the pits......in the insanity of their grief preferring to be buried alive than to wait the approaching hour of their own burial........*

......*and when the pits brimmed full, teams of muffled buriers stepped forth, like hooded henchmen......solemn and dumb, as they knew the hangman was only one step from the hanged, the burier one step from the buried......sprinkling quicklime, and shoveling dirt over the corpses to tame death's reek......beating back the dogs and scavengers......the bravest of the priests, their faces hidden deep inside great hoods, raising enormous crucifixes and screaming midst the smoke and stink, warning that from this gash in the earth Man's soul sank to perdition or took wing to Heaven......that it was whipped by devils, or serenaded by Angels........*

......*and as the wrath of the distemper raged, it seemed that the living would be too few to bury the great numbers of the dead, that the nights were now too short to perform death's labors......that death's orgy that had hitherto been held exclusively in darkness was to be unabashedly performed before the eye of the sun. The cathedral bells, grown croaking hoarse in the ears and minds of all, were ordered to stop their knells......only to make more poignant, when they did, the hideous choirs of the dying.......*

......*night after night, as in a dream that would not end, Maria continued his rounds with the collectors......joining their fellowship...... sharing their demijohns of wine, their profanity, their churlish, callous godless coarseness......falling into lockstep and becoming one with death's jocund and plodding cadence, its perverse romance......loading the cart as the peasant pitches dung......with tavern braggarts and drunkards he had known......with women whose kisses he had tasted, skirts he had lifted, gifts of lovemaking he had received......mocking the dead, pilfering the dead, numbly dragging, toting, heaving and tossing the dead......even as life had been a lie......even as the sun had burnt its wick........*

* * *

AND yet this seemingly interminable march of madness that Maria had fallen into step with was to end as abruptly as it had begun.

One early evening before Maria started his rounds, he entered a small church; one that had been looted and much defaced by the wild and the lawless, leaving but a shell of its sacred beauty. Its entrance was left wide open, the doors having been torn off; their precious slabs probably used for coffins. Lighted only by a few small poor candles, the church had nevertheless remained open with a show of religious welcome.

Maria saw at once it had been almost completely cannibalized; the benches and altars torn away, more than likely to fuel the bonfires that burned in the streets. Its air was pervaded by smells of sodden straw, urine and dung, as if it had been used as a cote for sheep or a stable for horses. The sacristy had long since been looted; the polished altars and vessels, ravished. Only a few of the frescoes had survived, but even these were obscenely defiled; great beards drawn on the faces of Mary; goat horns on the heads of Christ; abnormally large genitalia dangling from the loins of the children angels.

A woman's giggle broke from the shadows, and in the next moment a girl, followed by an older, rough-looking man walked past him and out the door. The sacred place had not only been used as a stable, but a makeshift brothel; its shadows affording places where harlots served their customers' wishes.

Maria did not want to leave, but he was not certain why. He felt a kinship with this gutted sanctuary, and in this kinship a remorse for something that had been lost, something that had been wasted or stolen, some sacred part of him that was no more. He was looking for some vestige that had survived, both in the stone shell of this church, and in the empty shell of his soul.

He walked to a little heap of flat stones, a candle burning on top of them, where the main altar had been torn away. On these stones were several small crosses, amounting to no more than pieces of thread that bound tiny sticks and twists of straw. About these childish crosses were sprinkled petals of flowers; some wilting, some husk-dry and long faded. God had forsaken Man; razing his place of worship, and sending death into his streets; but Man refused to forsake God. Like a dumb brute Man had continued to worship the One who was raining death upon His children. Like a beaten dog, Man still knelt at the feet of the

One who had mercilessly beaten it.

Maria knelt. Instinctively he made the Sign of the Cross, then kissing his fingertips he touched the cruciform pieces of stick and straw. He closed his eyes, and from a deep, forgotten place in his heart the words welled up and whispered from his lips.

......*Pater noster, qui es in caelis,*

......*Sanctificetur nomen tuum.......*

But the rest of the prayer, the prayer that he had recited ten thousand times in his youth stopped upon his lips, and would not be completed. Again he whispered:

......*Pater noster, qui es in caelis,*

......*Sanctirficetur........*

Again the words stopped, but this time Maria knew why. Knelt in the shame, disgrace and pollution of his soul, he did not feel worthy to ask forgiveness from a God he no longer believed in, that he resented....a God he had learned to loathe.

He had long lost his sympathy with a God who could harbor such brutality, and so cruelly punish His children; who slew innocence itself. He no longer believed in this God who, in a reason-less tantrum punished His child beyond the bounds of bone and flesh to be punished, leaving his brothers to toss him on a plodding cart. No, he could not pray to such a father. No, he did not want to ask the blessing from such a God.

And yet he felt a great need to unburden his heart; to break, to cry, to sob forth the anguish of his soul before these childish crosses of sticks and straw...to weep for the death he saw littered everywhere.....and the cold stars and a cold sun that had not intervened, but permitted death have its drunken way.

Only a few paces away Maria saw a large drawing chalked upon a wall. Not seeing it clearly in the dim light, and curious of what it might be, he brought a candle to inspect it more closely. He saw at once a strange and primitive caricature; a dance of skeletons; the dance of death that he himself had become a part of.

Yes, this, this was what had kept him here. This was what he had been looking for; not the faith he had lost, but a confirmation of the barbarity he was now part of. Drawn by a coarse hand, perhaps a drunk and looting hand, the artist had masterfully cartooned a profound wisdom he had never guessed he was in possession of; starkly depicting the truth behind the dreams of ornate altars and beautifully painted frescoes.

......an orgy of death where the skeletons of men danced and played flutes, drums and fiddles.....where skeletons fornicated with skeletons, and the skeletons of midwives brought the skeletons of babes from the skeletons of mothers......where laughing skeletons, tickled by death, were piled on carts, still playing their lutes and fiddles.....carts pulled by skeleton horses, pecked by skeleton crows and eaten by skeleton dogs.....skeletons burying skeletons in graves prepared for skeletons.....prayed over by skeleton priests.....picked and fleeced by skeleton rats.......

.....yes, the artist had drawn it very well.....life was no more than death burying death.....for a short while singing, drinking and fornicating, imagining it was enjoying a thing called life.....only one day to be tossed on a cart, and then tumbled in a dark throat filled with worms and bones..... to be what it had always been.....a dung and not a flower.......

Maria was startled from his absorption by a touch on his arm. He turned to see the girl he had seen leaving the church a few moments before.

"Excuse me sir. I do not wish to disturb you, but if you are looking for something, I mean something other than what prayers may give you, I can perhaps be of some help."

Maria did not answer.

"I mean, there's a nice place over there, a nice clean place in the shadows of the alcove where no one could see.....where the priests slip on and off their stoles, the priests that are no more I mean, that are dead, or have fled their parish.....you could bring the candle there...inspect me before you have your enjoyment if you like......but I swear, there's not a spot upon me sir, not a least boil or pimple.....clean of death, like a polished pot I am......."

As she was an Angel made manifest from the darkness, Maria did not speak.

"I don't ask much, and it wouldn't take long.....after all, a little pleasure midst so much death......and none knowing if the tomorrow......."

With a boldly sly suggestion, the girl brushed her hand over Maria's coat pocket, and then from his pocket reached down to his groins, finding, and then holding his manhood with a suave, swallow-soft touch of her profession. She lifted her eyes to him, and smiled the smile of her harlotry.

Maria answered her provocation by taking her small homely face in his hands; tenderly, as he was holding a fallen bird. It was a gesture the girl liked, at once interpreting it as an acceptance of her offer, and she smiled as he pressed into her, pressing her face against the drawing of skeletons on the wall.

Like a magician, Maria brought a florin from his pocket, and the girl at once brightened, and greedily tried to grab it, as it was a baited hook hung before a hungry fish. But instead of giving it to her, Maria quickly reached down, crumpled up her skirt, and as she had done to him, held her private place. With his hand firmly holding the treasure of her trade, he pressed the coin into its tenderness, even as to buy it. He brought his face close to hers, her smile turned from a frown of incomprehension, to one of fright.

"Please do not hurt me sir."

But it was not the girl's face he was seeing. It was not a face at all. It was a face of the living that was joining the hollow-eyed skulls of the dead. Bringing his lips to her lips, even as she was one among the orgy of those on the wall behind her, he whispered:

"No, be not afraid. Love is only a shudder, and no more. Life is only a forgetting, and no more."

And with this Maria held the fistful of her skirt more tightly, pressed the florin into the gate of her secret more firmly.....tightly and firmly, but tenderly, masterfully, coaxingly.....as it was purchasing its secret, and the performance of that secret.

Still frightened and frozen in his strong grip, the girl weakly asked:

"If it is a thing you wish to watch, sir.....there in the shadows I can perform it, and without any pretending.....or perhaps here.....there is no one about.....if that is the sum of your needs and wishes....yes, here is fine, I will pleasure myself.....but do not hurt me......do not kill me sir.....it is a house of prayer, and maybe full of watching angels......."

"Kill you? Love kills us all.....makes bones of us, and dust from our bones, and with a little puff blows us away. Oh, pretty one, a florin, a whole florin to see love make you yield, surrender your soul, and flower life in the dance upon this wall....."

"A whole florin....."

".....Yes, a whole florin, 'this' florin I hold in my hand.....do you not feel it speaking to you, pleading to you, needing you?......."

"Only to pleasure myself......"

"......Yes, for a whole florin.....to give yourself to the hand that holds it.....the florin, and not I shall be your lover......."

She did not understand the words of his madness, but she understood the florin and the hand that was now doing gently pleasing, coaxing things to her. Pinned against the wall, she could not escape. She could only yield, do the little thing he was asking, the thing she knew best how to do.....become blind to her fears.....give herself to the gold piece pressing into her, and the strong hand that was asking her body to bring forth its little flower, its little spasm of song.....for an instant shudder free of the misery of its bondage..... of death itself.......

Maria felt her body begin to stir, and with it her arms to relax, exchanging her fear with trust, and then with need.....he felt the first pulse of a thrust from that little mound he held.....and he was grateful that she was not pretending.....that something in his life was honest, true and unpretending.......

"Like this sir? Like this? Only this for a florin, a whole florin? And it will be an easy thing to do, sir.....your hand more gentle than the hands of other men......."

"Yes, for gold, for all the riches in the world, this little quiver men call love........"

And as his hand helped to bring forth the first fires of her pleasure..... her face began to tighten and wince.....as if the pleasure she was feeling was a kind of pain.....the travail of birth, the anguish of death.....her young comely features beginning to fade, and fading distort, so that her prettiness disappeared into a kind of horridness, a horridness that now scowled, and scowling laughed at its former sweetness.....as the others, the countless others he had held in his arms had with scowls laughed at the love they had promised........"

.....and from the contorted features of that face, and the throes of pain it was sustaining for the sake of its pleasure, a weak whisper, as from one dying....

"Like this sir?.....does this please you?.....for the florin in your hand.....?"

"Yes, yes, for the florin in my hand.....I want to see you die in your love, as all of us must die in our love.....to join the skeletons that are waiting for us all.....only a shudder.....a little cry.....a forgetting........"

She disregarded his madness.....felt only the florin.....and with it the magical things his hand was doing.....and the fever, this small brief fever of this simple happiness she had felt flush through her countless times before, that was the toil and duty of her trade to feel.....earned bread and meat, sustained her.....her face now unrecognizable from the face he had seen run from the shadows, from the face that had propositioned him.....from any face at all.....its features contorted, grimacing to something other, something lesser.....deteriorating in its approaching ecstasy, like the faces he threw on the dead cart, found in gardens and under bushes.....only a cheap mask, a carnival mask that masked a skull.....a skull like the skulls drawn upon the wall behind them, whose eyes stared and laughed upon this ridiculous thing men called 'love'......

.....her quickening and readying, her brief fever about to break......no, she was not pretending.....no, this was real.....yes, very real....perhaps the only reality, the only truth in death's circus.......

".....the florin, for the florin sir.....please, you will give me....."

.....from the sticks of her body a faint tremor,.......a tremor struggling, laboring to become a shudder, the shudder a flame, the flame a mysterious, unseen jetty of joy.....a letting go, a surrender, a weak, pitifully weak little cry.....a dying in the clasp of a stranger's arms, a stranger whose name was both 'love' and 'death'.....erupting into a peculiar thrill, a little spasm that weakly and briefly flowered in his hand.....gratifying some dream of the heart, while being blind to the edicts of the soul.....this shudder, this quiver, this laughter of a ghost freed from the prison of its body.....giving life its pathetic meaning before fleeing to the skeleton buriers, midwives, carters scrawled on a wall.....they who welcomed it to their dance in eternity........

Maria loosened his hold on the girl, and as he did she spoke, her voice now coarse and cold, free of any grip of passion.

"*The florin, sir.....you promised the florin.....and I didn't pretend at all, not one little bit, not like the other girls.*"

Maria let fall the florin to the floor, and turning away, he heard her drop to her knees to pick it up, and picking it up at once bite it. He walked away; through the shell of the church, out into the desolated streets. It was time to collect the dead.

* * *

HE walked away from the church. It was nearly time for his nightly rounds. He knew he need not return to the inn; the boorish brutes would never hunt and find him. They would probably not even look for him. Still, it was something he felt he must do. He was under death's enchantment, as well as its commission, enslaved by its spell, as well as its duty.

But approaching the *Sickle and Plough*, he did not see the horse and the cart with its lighted lanterns, nor the lamebrain and the mute readied with his bell. He heard no bluster or cavil, no swells of coarse laughter from the team of brothers, only something low and guttural, something akin to weeping.....dark and heavy weeping, like a chorus of softly bawling bears. Something was different. Something had changed. Something had broken the spell in the den of their depravity.

Maria entered the inn to find a bloody scene. In his accustomed chair at the table, Bruno sat slumped in a great drench of blood; a knife's hilt protruding like a fin from his heart. His mouth was hung open, still crammed with food, like a glutting ox at its slaughter; as open too were his unblinking eyes in a stare of fixed amazement; as if amazed that death could find him too.

On the floor not far away, two of the brothers lay, bloodily hacked, one with his head partly severed from his bullish neck. Near them lay the murder weapon, the scythe that had hung on the wall, now soaked in the fresh red slaughter of the deed it had reaped. Within an arm's reach laid the murderer, the timid innkeeper sprawled in a bloody mess, no doubt from his retaliation of one too many offenses made against his wife.

As it was the assassination of a king, about Bruno the imbecilic mute and lame-brain wailed and moaned, like children orphaned deep in a cold forest.

Maria asked no questions. He turned and walked briskly into the night.

* * *
* * * * *

MARIA woke, and for an instant he did not remember where he was.

He woke with the old ache aching in his side, the ache that nothing, not even wine or women had ever healed.....this wound made by the swipe of the bear's claws.....the wound that ever tried to speak to him, to soothe, console, and woo him.....that like a lullaby sweetly sang to him in the dull pangs of its hurt.....that held in the cradle of its pain the memories of his mother's sweetness.....

.....*a dream, a strange dream; one in which he was a small boy dancing at night in a village square, making configurations with lighted candles as they were batons. There were people all about him, bright-eyed Hungarian people with bright coats, scarves and tasseled hats, men and women that were laughing and clapping, and tossing coins, flowers and candies at his feet. The gypsy men were playing fiddles, accordions, and cobzas, and the bears in the cages were standing on their haunches, as they too were laughing and clapping spectators. They had thrust their paws through the bars of the cages, but their paws were not paws, rather the smooth and slender hands of fine women, with jeweled bracelets dangling from their wrists. Their faces were not the faces of bears, but the gentle faces of monks with shaven, tonsured heads.....and all were shouting with the crowd of the others: "Dance, Ohai, dance!"*

But the recollection of the dream, still lingering on the shore of sleep, was interrupted by the sleeper next to him; a moan, and then a giggle, a giggle that was still a prisoner of sleep and drunkenness:

"Come sweetheart....stay by my side.....love me again."

And with this, even as she slept, she lent him an invitation with her arms and legs, like the spreading wings of a bird, inviting him to her nest that he might be safe from the great ills of the world; from age and death, and a pitiless God who offered neither answer nor shelter to the child He had orphaned in a wilderness, the widlerness He had with deceptive contrivances had conceived.

And then another sigh and giggle, another pleading from sleep's prisoner; as if it was not a woman, but a *need*, a tireless *need* that knew no rest; a tireless *mother need* that was speaking through sleep and death and darkness.

"Do not leave me sweetheart. Please, do not leave me. I need you. Stay by my side. We will sleep a little, and then play again."

Slowly he woke, and with his waking bits and pieces came back to him. There had been many in the street, drinking and dancing about a fire, masked and costumed like animals.....boars, foxes, wolves.....some with tails, some with horns and manes, some with fangs and large phalluses..... they who no longer cared about the plague, no longer were afraid of dying..... who laughed at the ogre of death.....who were tired of running and hiding from the inevitable.....those who only wanted to be freed of their fears, to live even in the face of death.......

He had played a fiddle, and when he did a long forgotten music sang through all parts of him.....one that had lived through the fields and forests of death and starvation.....through the nights of lugging and loading, and spilling cartloads of corpses in pits.......

He felt once more young and strong, and with the fiddle dancing in his arms and the wine in his blood, he looked through the fire into eyes dancing brighter than wine, music, or the fire's flames......he a shaggily-maned lion; she, a sly lynx......her eyes sparkling with invitation, her womb crying out to be filled.......

......and as he was tethered to her pointed ears, tufted tail, the slyness of her feline smile, she had led him away to this barn and the soft hay in its loft. As wordless as beasts, they had played like the beasts of their disguises......cuffed and wrestled like lion and lynx......mounted and moaned like animals, mastered and were mastered like animals......as the scream of the lynx and the growl of the lion were the roles that life had given them in death's dance....the cries of the prey as it surrendered......its pain one with its ecstasy......these games of lovely wickedness offering a pleasure that for a fleeting moment would extinguish death from the world......this world of beasts and their beastly gratification, life's first and last, single salvation......

There came a sigh, giggle and murmur from the sleeper at his side, as if confirming the beastly play he was remembering......as if all that she knew in sleep or waking were these carefree, childish adventures......this simple, thoughtless, compulsive urge to love and be loved......to flower, only to again be sown......to scream out, that again she might purr. Again, from the deeps of sleep she murmured, her words slurred into a garble of drunkenness:

"Sweetheart, do not go away; come back to my arms; love me."

Did she remember his name? He could not remember hers, even as he was not sure he could remember her face. He could only remember a lynx whose snarl was a smile in the firelight. Seeing her in the sun, and without wine in his blood, would he recognize her? Would she recognize him? Would she be pretty to his eye, or he, handsome to hers? Would they pass each other like shadows; like thieves of the night; thieves intent on new treasures; tired of the old ones that were not worth robbing again? In truth, had they given themselves more to beasts than to lovers in the darkness?

Who was this 'sweetheart' she was calling out to in her sleep, this ghost that she was begging to love her? Was it like the ghost he was always wishing to hold and to love....a ghost in the darkness......faceless, bodiless, nameless, and in the end, loveless? Was love not a blind need, a blind need making blind and silly promises, in the end those promises tumbled from a cart into a dark trench, abandoning the dreams of the soul to stare through eyes stupidly cold, shorn of all reason......of all vows of paradise?.......

Maria brought a kiss to her cheek, this lynx's cheek, and then softly whispered in her ear, a whisper that sent a thrill of pleasure through her body, even as she slept:

"I am here, love, and I will not go away. You are the most beautiful woman in the world, and I will love you forever."

He laid his head upon her breast, and listened to the brave, blind, undaunted beating of her heart.

The night was silent; its stillness, voluptuous with the velour of its infinity. He heard the owls and the crickets, and in the distance, like lonely Angels, the howls of wolves. He heard the horse rustle in its stall beneath them, as it was dreaming in its sleep, the beast at peace with the animal acts enacted above it. He smelled the sweet smells of manure, harness-work, oats and straw, and the smells of the woman with whom he was laying. He saw the starlight that had fallen through some missing board or thatch, enkindling the hay with a soft silver fire.

He listened to the beating heart of his lover, and it seemed the heartbeat of the never sleeping night. How lovely were her breaths, her perfumes, her softness, and how lovely had been the gifts she had given him.....her secret sighs and caresses, her secret tufts and down, her tender skirmishes and final raptures and surrenders.....this delicate flower that would soon wilt and die, be forgotten in this silence full of owls and crickets, wolves and stars..... this flower that had bloomed its miracle in his arms.

How could 'death', this thing full of fear, panic and pain ever intrude upon such loveliness?.....the dead-carts, the burial pits, the weeping and raving.....dogs starved on their chains, crows pecking out eyes and hearts of children.....dead mothers with babes sucking their milk-less breasts..... this great pageant, this tableau of anguish that seemed a malignant dream dreamed only by men......but this never sleeping, ever respiring, tender singing of night's loveliness seemed incapable of perturbation.....un-concerned with men's dreams and men's dying.....as they were part of its care.....part of its song, its smile.......

And as he lay listening to this nameless, faceless lover's heart, this heart that beat as it was the mother of the night, the ache in his side spoke to him with a deep and tender poignancy. It spoke of something that had happened to him several days ago, making its secret hurt ache the more, and yet so exquisitely sweet, it cried out to be felt again.

He had seen a young ragged girl walking alone down a squalid way, past a slew of corpses, and those fleecing the corpses' pockets, stripping them of their shoes and clothing, and cutting off the women's tresses with knives. The girl was walking away from him, but he saw at once that she was hampered with a pronounced limp, one that made her seem as she was constantly about to gallopaway. And when he had seen her, all of the misery in his heart seemed to break from his heart, and in a fit of madness he ran after her. Catching and taking her by the arm, he knelt before her, blocking her way and raining kisses on her little hands.

"Katrinika! Katrinika! Is it you? Forgive me, O my angel, forgive me!"

Frightened, the girl had broken away, and as hurriedly as her limp would allow, fled from him with loping strides. But seeing Katrinika's face, and no other's wrapped in the ragged yellow scarf, he had run after her. Arresting her again, he spoke to the spirit that misery and death had conjured in his mind.

"Katrinika, do you not know me? Yes, I have grown shaggy and savage, perhaps no longer handsome.....you see I have seen much sorrow, much death, much wicked destruction by God, a God who sent his Angels howling like bloody wolves......please, darling, beneath this beard and long hair is Maria.....you must remember Brother Maria.....and I need to tell you how much I love you, how much I have always loved you.....that you give reason to madness.....that you give reason to death!"

But the frightened girl had broken from his craziness again, this time running into her mother's gathering arms not far away, even as her father approached the maniac who had accosted his young daughter, a stout board lifted above his head.

Gripped by the delusion in his mind, the delusion that was now much stronger than the reality of death all around him, he had continued to call out to the girl, even as she burrowed in her mother's arms:

"Katrinika! It is me, Maria! You must remember Brother Maria!"

But this time his delusion was answered by a solid hit to his head, and then another to his back, and when these blows had only staggered, but failed to topple him, there came another great blow of the board to his side, hitting square the wound he had concealed since his boyhood.

He had cried out, and crumpled to his knees, the man standing over him with the board, his scowling, anger-ruddy face shouting down heated words.

"Go away! Leave my daughter alone! Her name is not Katrinika, a name I have never heard before, a name not of our language! You are mad! You are with the fever, and you have gone mad and raving! If you stay I will kill you, even as I would kill a mad dog! Do you hear me? If you do not leave my daughter alone, I will kill you with this very board, and leave you for the crows and the pickers!"

He felt the wound that the man's board had at last found, the wound in his side, the wound in his heart.....the wound that told him he was old, that he had had enough, that he no longer had the strength, or a reason to fight, wander, dream...the wound that was the deepest wound, the cruelest wound...the wound of loneliness crying to be filled, to be healed by the only one whose care he would let touch it.

He felt this hurt beyond all hurt, and he wept with gladness; even as he felt sleep and the night begin to once more gather him into its arms.

Tomorrow, at dawn, he would leave. He would search among the dead and the living. He would search until he found the one who could heal this great wound in his side; even if she had been tossed on a cart, even if her eyes had been pecked out by crows or she had been eaten to the bone by dogs. He would find the one that had made this wound, and making it, owned a part of him.....this wound that was deeper than any bear could make.....

. . . .

. . . .

CHAPTER TEN

THE BEAR-TAMER,
AND
THE BLOOD OF A MOTHER'S HEART

HE no longer knew where he was; or always what direction his steps were taking him. The days were full of mist and low thick cloud, and in the declivities between the steep hills, especially now, when it lowered like the eye of a sleepy lion on the winter horizon, the sun would disappear, and lend no helpful torch for his tiredness to follow.

Nor did he ask the few people he saw, for grown fearful of *the sickness*, they wanted no nearness, and in particular, no parlance with a stranger. Some ran from the sight of him; others shouted harsh words; others threatened with clubs and dogs leashed at their sides. Still others approached him like a herd of wild animals, halting his steps with ugly scowls, and stones cocked and ready to hurl.

He soon grew as afraid of others, as others were of him, for he knew all had grown mad and murderous in their distress. Sharing a mutual dread, the dread of *the Great Mortality*, he soon learned the unspoken law of the fearful; *to evade and be evaded.* The only ones who spoke to him were of a rough, brigandish sort, and more than once when approached by their brutish vulgarity, and addressed with their roguish slang, he pushed them away, drew his knife, and prepared to defend himself; only to have the scoundrels, friendly a moment before, scowl, curse, turn heels and run away in the true colors of their thievish designs.

He was not familiar with the way he had chosen; picking at it like a goat among rocks; somehow surefooted in his forlornness. He did not know the names of the hamlets and villages he passed, but even if he had, most were tightly closed against any show of welcome or charity, or the least communication with the world outside them. Many of their gates were shut, and smeared with giant scarlet crosses, their walls painted with matching scarlet letters, as the brush that had brushed them had been dipped in the same palette of blood: '*Lord Have Mercy*', '*Lord Protect Us*', '*Lord Forgive Our Sins*'. They were guarded by bands of men either before or upon these walls; gaunt, fierce-eyed men armed with swords, longbows and stones. A step too near brought a rain of rocks and arrows at his feet, as well as savage shouts in his ears;

"*Plague here! Death here! Pass on! No strangers! No pilgrims or beggars! We are armed, and we will kill any who attempt to enter! Plague! Death! Do not come near! Do not try us! We have arrows, and packs of dogs! Pass on!*"

But more than this fear and barbarous hostility exhibited by the people, after a week of his travel Maria began to grow weak; not from hunger, for the dead had left many cellars, as well as abundantly fruited fields and orchards to freely plunder, but from a fever that now burned through his body. His mouth grew dry, and he began to dizzy and stumble. His thoughts began to blur, and to form strange pictures and stories in his mind. He began to see reptilian-headed, snake-like creatures slither across his paths, and satyr-like men with horns and tails crouched behind trees; strange animals and strange men he at once believed and disbelieved were real. Chill invaded and shivered through his blood, and would not leave even when he was inches from a blazing fire. His throat began to sorely swell; and there were pains throughout his body; angry, illusive pains, as his body was a cage that caged a rabid animal, one that was continually seeking a new place from which to bite free.

He thought of one of the rogues whose attack he had beaten away..... his disfigured, jaundiced, cadaverous features, the rabidity in his eyes..... his tongue that his swollen lips were not able to contain, poking its dark tip from his mouth, as it was a giant slug crawling from his bowels.....and how the man had scratched and bit at him, more like an animal than a man..... his teeth succeeding in inflicting a wound upon his neck, as he was trying to take a hungry bite from an apple.

He had heard of such ones gripped by 'the sickness', they that grew mad and desperate with death in their blood......how in the lunatic hours of their dying they grew jealous of ones who were whole and healthy, and wanted to zealously share the terrible fate that had befallen them......wildly biting and scratching at others, sometimes violating maidens......as if craving company in their horrible departure from this world.

.....Yes, the curse, the sickness, the 'mortalita grande' was upon him. He had not been able to hide, elude or outrun it, not in the deep forests.....not in fumes of wine or in the arms of women.....not in the strings of his fiddle or in the green hills of his dreams and poems. Yes, death's sharp sickle had found him out.....its bony fingers clutched his heart.....and as he deliriously walked on he heard this accursed harvester hissing and laughing in his ears:

"Did you think I had forgotten you, oh blue-eyed gypsy? Did you think one who played lutes and fiddles and balalaikas, who played in hay mounds with women, and dreamed the flowery dreams of poets was too special to die? O how foolish! O how vain! You are mine, oh lover of wine, song and women, as all men, from beggars to kings are mine!.....no different than those you heaped on a cart and tumbled in a pit......no different than dogs.....Come here, fool! Come die in my arms you silly, bumptious, ridiculous fool!"

At night, when he shivered with chill and burned with fever, he inspected his body in the light of his fires, inspections that found no fateful blotches, pimples, carbuncles or swellings. If he was indeed in the clutches of the plague, it was only its harbingers that held him, those that breathed delirium and hallucinations into his mind until their morbid general would arrive. For as no fire burned hot enough to free him of the cold that now had taken possession of his body, none burned bright enough to purge the strange visions that had taken possession of his mind.

Curled close about these fires, he no longer knew if he was awake or dreaming. He no longer knew if the feral eyes, sharp fangs and hungry growls of wolves were encroaching upon the circle of his fire's light, or like phantoms they were creeping closer, making a murderous trespass on the forest of his dreams.....nor did he know if the great owl-like birds that swooped near him with knife-like talons were real.....whether or not he had somehow become a mouse or a rabbit, and was now their prey.

.....and the women.....those that he had passed in sun-lit fields and gardens, on rain-dripping verandahs or twilit loggias.....those he had seen at tavern dances, at wedding feasts and funerals.....milkmaids, tavern wenches, marketers....holy sisters knelt at their prayers, slatterns in the

streets, widows mourning at graves.....now naked and jeweled.....now the proud mistresses of giant wolves, riding them like horses, their nakedness trimmed in fur boots and mittens.....beckoning him to ride with them to their dens.....to lay with them.....to become beasts with them.......

.....those that he had met on his journey, that had run from him, that had thrown stones at him, that had tried to rob and murder him.....now mobbed together, encircling his fire with raised clubs and stones, and twisted scowling faces.....all chanting in unison: 'Plague here! Death here! We will kill any who attempts to enter here!'.......

The wound where the sick man's teeth had bitten his neck reddened and swelled. Fever ensued, and trapped in its flames, he was no longer sure if it was night or day. He no longer knew or cared where he was going, or why; or had the sense or will to know. His steps were no longer firm, and he was now prone to dizzy stumbles and hard falls. Many times he saw trunks of trees that he was sure he had seen not long before, as death was playing a game with him, leading him in circles, as children at play at 'blind man's buff', or as he was a dog whose tail men had tied with a skillet, and was now whirling crazily to its death.

He became drunk with fever, and the more it inflamed him with its fire, the more it freed him of inhibitions, until life and death blurred and united; became one kingdom; a graveyard disguised as a circus. He began to call out to those he had once known, and now stepping from his memory like ghosts, appeared with stark vividness to his eyes.

..... "Did you like what you saw through the knothole in the board, you lecherous old goat?! Did you like seeing me tickle your wife, and make her moan as you, your one leg, and your sack of guts never could?"

..... "Where is your salvation now, Giovanni? Where are your Saints and Angels? Did your sacraments turn out to be a fruitless beggary? Read books until your eyes turn to stones, kneel with prayers before your altar dolls until your knees wear to bones......death has us by the throat and the crotch, 'amicus meus'..... even you, yes you, Abbot Giovanni!......"

..... "You! Ha! So it is you, a harlot hiding behind a veil! You are no Sister of Charity, rather a tart pining to be plucked and plowed in the hay! Yes, it is me! The one you tried to dangle from the gallows.....the one you wanted to watch the birds peck to a skeleton of bones! Lift your veil, and with it your robe! I have come to lie between your shriveled legs, and murder the hypocrite of your virginity!"

..... "Ah, so it is you, and you and you.....those that I left in pools of

blood, for the daisies to bloom through your ribs and skulls. Forgive me brothers.....yes, we are brothers now.....brothers in death as we were killers in life! Bear me no grudge, for life was as much a carnival of dreams as death is a feast with the chambermaids of worms!"

...... "Katrinika, please, come to the window with the red flowers in the green boxes! I want to take you into the forest, deep into the snowy forest in a sleigh like I rode in when I was a little boy.....a 'troica' they called it, yes, a 'troica'......a sled pulled by horses, horses we will feed with red apples, you and I, apples we have saved from the autumn harvest....and the horses will jingle with little bells we shall braid in their manes...oh, remove you kerchief, and let your dark tresses fall with their stars and roses!....oh, come to the forest with me my darling......there we will live and be happy, happy with the bears and elves!...... "

Dusk and night had fallen, but he did not care. He built no fire. He only wanted to stumble forth; only to burn with fever until, like a firefly, he was extinguished by the darkness. He no longer knew what was real. He no longer knew the difference between the darkness of day and the darkness of night, for the phantoms in his mind were as vivid in one as they were in the other. He only wanted to stumble, to blindly stumble forth until he blindly, helplessly, thankfully fell; fell in the cold dark arms of a mother who eats all dreams, and with them makes them anew, flowering them through teeth and bones.

He had seen lights through the trees, and he had heard voices, happy singing voices.....but he knew it was only an illusion that death was teasing him with.....the circus that was a graveyard.....an illusion like love and women had been illusions.....like the forests and the hills, the silver moons and dark rivers.....like all of life had been an illusion....where nothing could be trusted, nothing believed....not a glance or a word or a prayer....... nothing embraced, nothing held long enough to impart a tender secret to the lost child of the heart........

......he had imagined seeing through the trees an encampment with fires, and wagons overarched with canvases.....with brightly dressed, brown-skinned, shouting and singing people......even as he remembered when he was a boy......the horses, mules and wagons.....the forges, anvils, looms.... the bright cloths and the kettles.....the bearded, high-booted men draped in wolf-skin coats, some with fur caps, others with bright bandannas wrapped about their heads.....busy with hammers or lazing with lutes.....and the black-haired women with bright bracelets and necklaces, and bright tasseled

shawls......as they were not women at all, but fantastic, brightly-feathered birds.......

......yes, an illusion, perhaps the last illusion......as if God and the Devil were standing arm in arm at all men's end, laughing and taking long draws from the same hookah.....congratulating each other for the little trick they had played.....the beautiful idols of faith and love they had neatly placed with bouquets on altars....the smiles and charms of maidens in windows and gardens.....the forests, hills and clouds they had brightly painted in children's dreams.......

He called into the darkness, into this graveyard's circus, and the marionettes Death was so happily, cruelly dancing before his eyes.....a horse neighed, a dog barked, a bear bawled.....the hammer stopped its hammering, the lute its song, the dancer its castanets..... the beautiful bird halted its dance of mating, of love's eternal mating about the fire......

......in the tongue of his heart, the tongue of the 'tzigans', he called out for his mother: "Mamica! Mamica!".....and knew no more.

* * *

* * * * *

HE was not sure he was awake. He was not sure he was alive. He only knew he was washed over, caressed and permeated by waves of a long forgotten friendliness; a friendliness that filled him; that embraced and cradled him.

......the soft bed of sheepskins.....the lovely, aromatic fumes of herbs, sweet and tart.....above him, a forest with mystical shapes of shadows cast by a small oil lamp on the table.....the fox, martin and rabbit pelts, the copper kettles, the long bright scarves and the knotted kerchiefs, falling like ropes of parti-colored ladders....the glittering strands of beads, like vines, fruited with amulets and medallions hanging down the ribs of the wagon's walls.......the curtain of beads that were sometimes parted by large brown hands, brown hands that were attached to kind, brown-eyed, anciently earthen-browned faces......

......and there was the soft murmur of a chant, yes, a chant in the tongue of his heart, the tongue of his boyhood.....of Moldavia, the Dobrudja, and the Carpathians.....a woman's chant.....like the beautiful mother-woman he had dreamed he had seen dancing about the fire.....the bright scarf and skirt, and the copper bangles dangling from her ears.....the woman who

now turned to him, knelt, and brought a bowl to him, and then a spoon to his lips, saying......"Drink, Ohai, drink......drink and dream the dream that is binding your soul with chains......I will not leave you.....I will walk with you.....speak to my ears.....show your trouble to my eyes..... remember, Ohai, remember, and though it is painful, tell me this story that has troubled you for so long, this secret story in your soul....."

And as the potion trickled into, and melted away the dark shadows in his mind.....and at the request of the sorceress's tender words, he began to speak the thing he had never spoken before.....but whether he narrated it in words, or only in thoughts and pictures to the one that was at his side, he did not know.....

.....he spoke in the tongue of his heart, the tongue of the 'tzigans'...... and when he did the words flowed from his depths like a mountain brook.... .a brook that flowed in a twilight of dreams......

"The weather had begun to warm, and the snows to melt. We had moved from the valley to the foothills of the tall mountains to graze our flocks and herds. I remember the day when he rode to our camp, and spoke with Dimitru, the leader of our tribe."

"Who, Ohai? Who was it rode to your camp?"

"His name was Jorga. He was well dressed, with the hilt of a Turkish knife, one carved with crescent moons, that he had fitted in the red sash wrapped about his snow-white shirt.....the glistening handle of a whip protruded from one of his knee-high boots. His hair and beard were glossy and wavy black, and his moustache was waxed as for a great purpose that he carried proudly in his person. The horse he rode was a strong, splendid stallion, and as black as night. Its saddle was polished and studded with copper, and made of the finest kneaded leather.

All day he was alone with our leader, Dimitru.....but for what reason the stranger had come none in our caravan knew. Late in the day he emerged from Dimitru's tent, mounted his black horse, and rode away; but when he did, Dimitru did not divulge the meaning of the stranger's visit.

There was debate, even the wagering of bets as to the reason of his coming. Some ventured it had to do with arms, or the rights to summer graze-lands; others thought it might be the trade of wine, wheat or furs, or the bartering of sheep and goats. Some guessed it involved a secret plan for the stealing of horses. But it was not the place of any to ask Dimitru; only for Dimitru to tell. The mystery of the stranger's visit was sealed in his heart, and told to no other, and gradually the days and nights removed it from our minds. The stranger was no longer talked about. He was forgotten."

"Did this Jorga, the man on the black horse return?"

"Yes, Jorga returned. After the moon had twice grown full, and the spring had bloomed the tender grasses on the hills, the man returned to our encampment, this time with a number of servants, and a wagon with cages........"

"Cages, Ohai?"

"Yes, two cages; each one with a bear inside it. You see Jorga was a bear-tamer, a very famous bear-tamer. He knew the bears' haunts and habits, and the dens where they wintered. He caught and caged them, baiting them with dead horses, with goat-kids or bleating lambs bound on stakes. But more often, in the spring when they stumbled sleepily from their dens, he wrestled and threw nets about them, capturing the strongest ones to train with a prod and a whip through the summer. In the autumn he would sell them to the gypsies to take to the inn-yards, the village streets and the fairs. The gypsies performed tricks with them, clever and amusing tricks, many of which Jorga had expertly taught them. In this way the gypsies earned money, in return for the bears' performances."

"Then Dimitru bought the bears from Jorga? That was the mystery?"

"No. That was not the mystery. Dimitru did not buy Jorga's bears. Jorga gave them as a payment; the bears and the beautiful black horse with the copper studded saddle."

"But what did Jorga buy with the bears and the black horse?"

"My mother. Jorga bought my mother with the bears, the black horse and the beautiful saddle. You see my mother, Fanutza, was unmarried. The golden-haired man of the mountains, he who had stolen her from our tribe when she was a girl, and with whom she had made me, had left her when he returned her to her people. But no one in our tribe would marry my mother. Though they were kind to her, and though my mother was very beautiful, they said she had been corrupted by one who was not their kind, and to marry and lie with her would bring corruption into their own blood. It would defile the children she would give them.

But Jorga was different, and this did not matter to him. He bought my mother, my mother and her blonde, blue-eyed son who was only part 'tzigan', and not a thoroughbred 'tzigan'. The next day my mother and I left with Jorga, the bear-tamer, to live in his hut halfway up the side of a distant mountain."

"Did your mother like Jorga, the bear-tamer?"

"She neither liked, nor disliked him. Once at the inn she had glanced at him, and they had danced an 'hora', and it is said the glance of a beautiful woman may make armies kneel; and so the bear-tamer was smitten, and knelt at my mother's feet, the sparkle in her eye infatuating him with her great beauty.

But there was only one man for whom my mother fully gave her heart, for whom the rose of her smile bloomed all of its petals, and that was the man who had stolen her when she was young; the man who fathered me; the man who had tamed and won her with his love. My mother was obedient to her people. She wanted to be good to me, because she said she saw my father in my eyes and in my ways. The bear-tamer promised her many things. He promised to take care of me as his own son. He promised to visit our people when they came from the plains and the valleys to graze each summer."

"Jorga the bear-tamer lived alone?"

"Yes, on the mountainside, alone."

"And was he wealthy?"

"No. I think the things with which he had bought my mother had been stolen.....the black horse, the beautiful saddle, his Turkish knife with the crescent moons.....I came to believe all had been stolen in one way or another. It is true he had a great reputation as a bear-tamer, but I think no greater than his reputations as a thief and a wine-sot. He had lied to Dimitru. His possessions were scant; his hut, poor and decrepit."

"But was Jorga a gypsy, like you and your mother were gypsies?"

"He was a full-blooded 'tzigan', but he had broken from his people, for what reason I never knew. He was courteous to both the peasants and the gypsies, and they were friendly and courteous to him; but I think a little fearful as well. When he drank much wine he cursed them behind their backs, and called them 'oafs', 'pigs' and 'sluts', and many other names that showed the great disdain and hatred he honestly held for them."

"Was he good to you, Ohai?"

"I was a young boy, only eight or nine years old. I liked him, but I cannot say I loved him. I feared and respected him, but I cannot say I honored him. He was good to me, but a goodness that did not own a genuine kindness.

Jorga taught me to speak to the bears and the horses, both with the soft words of a lover, and a whip full of cracking thunder. He taught me how to look into their eyes, and to speak to their hearts; to not be afraid of them, for with fear they could not be mastered. When the last snows came, before the bears migrated up the mountains to hunt for berries, and for young goats and fish in the cold brooks, Jorga showed me dens in the vales where the bears slept. He showed me how to smoke them from their dens when they were still asleep, and when they drawled drunkenly forth, how to wrestle them into submission.....how to place iron rings through their noses.....how to tether them, and lead them by dangling fresh-killed rabbits to our cages."

"But you were very young, Ohai, and wrestling bears is very dangerous, even if they are still dazed with their winter's sleep. Where was Jorga?"

"Jorga looked on, drinking.....he was always drinking.....he looked on with indifference, but there were times I thought his eyes broke from that indifference and gleamed with a kind of pleasure, even hopefulness as he watched me wrestle with the bears. And when I had succeeded in caging them, his praise seemed stiff and wooden, and slowly offered, as he was not proud, but inwardly disappointed in my success, and my opponent's failure."

"And your mother? Was Jorga good to your mother?"

"He was good to my mother, but a goodness that did not make her laugh and sing. Several times I found her crying, and once I found her washing raw lash marks on her haunches. She said that I must not tell, but that Jorga had whipped her with his bear-whip. She said some men, like Jorga, became violent when they were drunk, but when drink was not in their blood they were kind, and forgot the violent fit that had seized them.

And when I asked if my father had ever beaten her, she said 'no', that she had been much crueler to him, than he to her.

Once, as I stood outside the hut, I heard Jorga, full of drink and rage cursing my mother. He was very wild, and said strange wild things. He said it was not his fault she did not have more children. He said he gave her sons, but she strangled them in her womb. He said she killed them because she hated him, that she loved her golden-haired son more than she loved him. He said that he thought her pretty son was her lover, and when he was in the village, or on a hunt, she took her darling to the high grasses, and there gave him her woman pleasures.

And one other time, one other time I remember very well, when after hunting bears Jorga had taken me to a small village. He went to a tavern to drink wine, and as he drank he became loud and boastful with his words, I stood outside the tavern, and listened to things he said, terrible things that I will never forget."

"I whipped my first wife, Erica, very much. She was a wild creature, like a she-bear guarding her whelps. When I entered the marriage bed it was like entering a wolf's den! Ha! I was afraid her kisses would sink sharp

teeth into my throat, or that her nails would scratch out my eyes like a cat. I whipped her, but her wildness was too wild for my whip, and she only became the wilder, even when I whipped her naked butt and breasts, and made them run with blood. So I began to whip her like she was not a woman, but as I was whipping a bear. The neighbor men came to my door, gathered about, and listened to my whip and her screams.....screams that scared the crows from their nests.....you see when she howled her soul was in her howls, and the men became enchanted with the great beauty of her wildness being tamed. In her screams was a wonderful music, and when she cried for mercy it was mercy itself.....little by little I tamed the hate and murder from her, like I tame the wildest of my bears......I tamed her until the hatred in her heart became sweet as honey.......

.....but she was like some bears that cannot be tamed.....she would be sweet and tenderly play, only to become wild again.....and one day, after her wildness had returned, and I had whipped her very hard, harder than I have ever whipped a horse or a bear.....ha! the she-wolf screamed no more!......."

.....After a pause, the gentle voice resumed her questions......

"And the fairs and inns Ohai, did Jorga take you and the bears to them?"

"When the snow melted each spring we went to the inns, the villages and festivals with our bears. My mother would adorn herself with bright scarves, shawls and jewelry, even brass bells for her ankles, and topazes for her toes. She would darken the lids of her eyes, and paint her lips with carmine. She would dance in the streets or in the yards of the taverns and the inns, and as she did the bears performed the tricks that Jorga and I had taught them; rolling and balancing on barrels; juggling pins and balls, walking through fires, dancing in our arms.

Sometimes we would dress them in skirts and bonnets, and we had dolls that they would cradle and coddle in their arms as they walked on their hinds. Sometimes the children would give their own dolls for the bears to hold as they waddled about. Once when I gave our oldest bear, Katinka, one of the children's dolls, a doll with a velvet jacket her mother had made for it, Katinka suddenly erupted into a fit of wildness. He tore the doll's head off, and with his claws and teeth tore its body to pieces before the shrieking child and her mother. There was nothing left of the doll but a few sticks, and a little straw and flour that had stuffed it. Katinka had eaten it. I struck Katinka with my whip, but there was fear in my heart, and I was not its master. I could not control its fit of savagery."

"*And Jorga? Where was Jorga, your father, the bear-tamer?*"

"*He was not there, as he was seldom there with my mother and I. He would become drunk, and dice and play cards in the taverns. But when Katinka tore apart the child's doll, and there were shrieks lifted about the bear's wild tantrum, he ran out from the tavern, stupid with wine. Yet when he comprehended what his oldest, most favorite bear had done to the child's doll, he broke into great guffaws of laughter before the horrified child and her mother. That is when my last respect for Jorga t turned to bitter disgust. That is when I began to detest him. That is when, even as a young boy, I began to want to kill him.*"

"*Kill him, Ohai? The man who was married......?*"

"*.....the man who bought my mother with things he had thieved, only to treat her like a beast with his whip!*"

"*Go on, Ohai; speak more.*"

"*One day, months later, when the hills were colored with autumn, and the first snow had fallen, I climbed back from the village to Jorga's hut..... and found the thing I have never told another I found.*"

"*What was it that you found, Ohai?*"

"*The terrible thing.....the terrible, unspeakable thing.*"

"*What terrible thing, Ohai? Tell me the terrible, unspeakable thing. It will be our secret. I will tell no other.*"

"*Jorga had chained Katinka to a large tree. He was bawling loudly. The snow about the tree was not white. It was red, red with blood and gore, as a wild animal had entered the circle of Katinka's chain. He was crazy with its murder; crazy with the gluttony of death. Its muzzle dripped with blood, and its maws were filled with gore and hair, as were its claws and the draggled breast of its fur. Its eyes sparkled as I had not seen them sparkle before.....as they were full of diabolical laughter, as it had eaten another child's doll, but this time one of flesh and blood.*"

"*Katinka had killed a deer Ohai......*"

"*No, not a deer. You see I think Jorga had given Katinka many bowls of wine, and it had made him wild and drunk, drunk with death and killing. Some bears, like some men, thirst for wine as they thirst for blood. They know only one trick, and that is to kill. There is wildness in their hearts that will not go away, as dishonesty will not go away from a thief's heart. Some bears are killers. It is not their fault. They are not meant for hoops, barrels and little children's dolls. They have a great pain, perhaps a great loneliness*" *inside them. Katinka was a killer. He thirsted for blood because he wanted to be free in the forests. Such creatures must kill to be free. They cannot be other than what they are. For such a creature, to kill is to live. They must kill or be killed.....that is their reason they roam the forest. That is the reason they are alive. And when I went near it......"*

"What happened when you went near it?"

"It was drunk with wine, blood and murder....."

"And then?"

"And then it swiftly turned, and its claws tore open my side, as it wanted my heart."

"And then you killed the bear, Ohai?"

"No, I did not kill the bear. I did not kill it because I did not hate it. Although I was only a boy, and its sharp claws had torn open my side, my fury had made me its master. I looked Katinka in the eyes, as he looked me in the eyes, and both knew I was his master. Yes, I goaded it with my prod and whip to its cage. I was its master because there was no fear in my heart.....only rage, like Katinka's rage.....I was now the bear's brother.....I wanted only to kill.....to kill and to kill and to kill.....but not my brother of the forest.....I understood my brother of the forest, but I did not hate him......"

"And then?"

"And then I went back to the tree, and the bloody gore strewn on the snow."

"But why did you go back to the tree, Ohai?"

"To collect the pieces of my mother.....the pieces that the bear had torn apart with its claws and teeth, as my mother had been a child's doll of straw and sticks......I collected her arms and legs, hands and feet, scarves and jewels and slippers.....and the head, the beautiful head of Fanutza, my mother......"

"But how did such a thing happen, Ohai?"

"The accursed devil had chained both Katinka and my mother to the large tree. It had not been enough for him to whip my mother with his whip. For his anger and amusement, Jorga had bound a chain about my mother's waist, and then to the tree with the wild bear that could not be tamed, that once tasting blood on its tongue.....would never be sated of blood and death again.

I collected all of my mother's pieces. I took them to a secret place on the mountain and buried them. But I could not bear to bury her heart. I could not let it be eaten by worms. So I ate my mother's heart. I ate my mother's heart so that my mother's love would always flow through my blood. I ate her heart, and it was the honey of every flower, and the secret of every wind."

"Did you go back, Ohai? After you buried your mother, did you return to the bear-tamer's hut?"

"I returned the next morning, after I had laid upon my mother's grave, cursing the stars, the million eyes of God that had stared coldly and numbly upon the butchery......the eyes of a God that had watched, but had not lifted a hand in my mother's defense.

Yes, I returned; soaked with blood, as my brother Katinka was soaked with blood. I was no longer a boy, a gypsy, or a bear-tamer's son. I was no longer a man. I was a bear like Katinka, a bear that could not be tamed, that was crazy with rage.....that thirsted for blood like Jorga thirsted for wine....like Katinka thirsted for the blood of dolls. I understood Katinka. I understood why it had killed my mother. I understood it had a hurt like a thorn in its heart, a thorn it could not be rid of. I understood that to kill was its effort to pluck out that thorn....that such a savage pleasure was the only way to briefly forget such a terrible pain.

I found Jorga in the barn, asleep in the arms of a peasant woman. I stood over them, looking down upon their naked bodies with my whip and prod and rage.....and when the woman woke to the murder in my eyes, the eyes that had found her in her shamelessness, she shrieked, and grabbed for her skirt to cover her. But I would not let her have her skirt. I would not let her be clothed. I would not give her the dignity of hiding what I knew she was. I drove her off with my prod, naked and screaming, like a beast into the cold fields.

Jorga was very drunk, and lolled about like the bears we smoked from their dens. His blood was still sloshed with wine, and he was weak and slow from spending his lust. He tried to cajole me, to sugar my anger....he promised to give me money.....but I would not be tamed. I 'could' not be tamed. And when he saw that his words could not weaken me, he became angry and tried to strike out at me. But I would not let him. I prodded him with my sharp prod, a prod made to pierce through the thick furs of bears. He cursed and cried out, and said many wild things, but I was deaf to his curses and pleas for mercy, for my mother's heart and Katinka's rage were now both inside me. I had become his master because I no longer feared him.

And when he reached for his clothes I would not let him have them. I prodded him sharply, until he screamed out and bled. I made him cover his

*nakedness with the skirt his whore had left behind, and then I ordered the wretched creature from the barn, and made him crawl on his hands and knees, on his very belly, prodding him before me to Katinka's iron cage......
and when he would not enter the cage as I told him to do, I whipped him until he bled, cried and begged me to stop. But I was deaf to his tears and his words. I was deaf and blind to all but the beastly drunkard who had amused himself by mutilating my mother as he guzzled and whored.*

I locked Jorga the bear-tamer in the cage with Katinka, with the bear that could not be tamed. I gave Katinka this doll dressed in a pretty woman's skirt to play with and maul, to tear off its head.....I gave him to the bear whose maws were always thirsty for death. Before Jorga's eyes I mangled the lock's key by pounding it on an anvil with a hammer, so that the cage could not be opened. I turned, and walked away, from the hut upon the mountainside.....the screams of Jorga, as he was being torn apart like a straw doll, joining Katinka's exultant roars."

"And after? What did you do after that, Ohai?"

"I knew his screams would be heard in the village. I knew both peasants and 'tzigans' would come, and that when they found their bear-tamer dismembered and eaten in the bear cage, they would hunt for me. I knew I must leave my people. I ran, like the man-bear I had become. I lived in the forests. I ate bark, grubs and berries. I crossed the frozen Danube into Hungary. I begged in village streets until the religious people took pity on me. They cared for me, and were good to me. I sailed with them to this land, to a port named Brindisi. They taught me their language. They taught me to pray. They named me 'Maria', because of my hair, golden like a woman's hair, and because of their Christian faith. I became a monk, and worshipped their God.....a God I no longer believe in."

* * *

Two weeks later Maria prepared to leave the camp of the friendly wanderers; the camp of his people. It was not *the contagion* that had seized him. The sorceress had told him it was another sickness, one that afflicted his soul as much as his body. She told him that his soul contained a wilderness of dreams as vast as the earth and sky, and that he had become lost in its storms. It had left him weak, but his heart had greatly healed with the kindnesses the *tzigans* had shown him. He grew restless. At night as he stared into the fires he saw a window with green shutters and red flowers, and from that window, dark eyes that sparkled with flocks of stars.

Before he departed, the elders invited him into their tent.

"We are sorry that you are leaving, Ohai. We like you. You are one of us, a 'tzigan'. You must come back to us. It is not good that you wander alone. You must wander with other wanderers. If you need a woman, we have daughters that you could marry. They have pretty faces, light steps, and strong wide hips that could give you strong children. There is no woman like a 'tzigan'. She is life's mother, lover, daughter. The sun and moon are not in the sky. This is a dream other men dream. They are in such a woman's soul.

You are not like other men. You are a 'tzigan'. You cannot be tamed like others are tamed. You cannot live beneath a roof, or be yoked to a plough like an ox. The souls of others are but ghosts. They live in shadows, as sunlight was full of dangers. But you are like us. Your soul is a thing of flesh and blood, and because of that you do not fear and shun the world, but rather befriend it. Your soul is a bird, a sweet-throated bird, and though it perches above jackals, it sings its song. What other men call 'sin', we do not call 'sin'. What they call 'want' and 'need', we call 'pleasure' and 'duty'. What they call 'death', we call 'honor'.

Our kind must wander through youth and years. You must wander also, Ohai, because you know that not to wander is to be winnowed from life like chaff on a threshing-floor. You take your directions from the wind and stars. You know you are a child of the seasons; that you are meant to hurt, bleed, love in the sun and snow; that in the end you are meant to die in the arms of storms.

You are a good man, Ohai. You are a true 'tzigan' Your father looks through your eyes, and your mother's blood runs laughing and singing through your veins. Come back to us, Ohai. Wander with us. Come live and die with us."

Maria kissed their kind brown faces, and then silently left their tent, their words having pierced his heart to the quick:

"There is no woman like a 'tzigan'. She is life's mother, lover, daughter. The sun and moon are not in the sky. This is only a dream dreamed by other men. They are in such a woman's soul."

. . . .

. . . .

CHAPTER ELEVEN

THE MISTRESS OF 'DEATH'

Early Spring: 1351

THE winter had come late, but had stretched long and heavy with a deep burial of snow. The largest drifts had yet to melt in the hills and in the ravines where the sun had not yet bent its gaze. Here and there frozen white beards still hung on the boughs of the tall pines. As if unsure if they had miscalculated the season, the first birds were still hesitant to break into song; the tiny black beads of their eyes peering with distrust at the half frozen world to which they had returned.

But finally and surely, *damsel spring* was beginning to lift her head from her frozen sleep; to shake the dead leaves from her hair, and lift her face to the new light that kissed her eyes and breasts. The brooks had broken free of their icy chains, and like laughing children were racing breakneck down the slopes . Here and there were flowers, shivering in their naked littleness, flowers that had dared to peep from the cold soil to adore a warm, benign goldenness called '*the sun*'.

As if a thing named '*death*' had been unimportant, too slight and irrelevant to concern the scheme of things, spring began to wake in the hills and forests, and to smile its smile through all miseries left littered in this mythical creature's wake; flowering, laughing and singing through the bones and cruel memories made by its ghastly *dream*.

And yet, though spring was waking free of this dream that men had dreamed, it had yet to fully break through the gloom in the hearts that had dreamed it. Only slowly, and with great mistrust, were men waking to the sun and the happy flowers again; to the sounds and sights about them: the creaking wheels of carts, spades digging in gardens; red flowers newly planted in clay pots, a maiden's dimpled smile. Only slowly, groggily, painfully were they waking from this terrible dream; this scourge dealt by their God, and the rod with which He had chosen to so unmercifully wield it.

Malice seemed to linger in the loveliest things. Though never were skies so blue as those which arched cloudlessly overhead, nevertheless those blue skies seemed gray and leaden, and full of frowning possibilities. Though the brooks warbled, their singing seemed as much dirge as hymn; and there was something tentative, almost menacing in the trills of hedgerow birds. The first flowers seemed offerings left by widows at husbands' graves, and though the last snowdrifts were as white as sailors' sails, they seemed inseminated with dark seeds.

Thus was the illusion that *death* had left in its path; the memory of dread that would long linger; of the enamored *killer* who with maniacal abandon had bludgeoned an entire people as they lazily toiled, loved, dreamed.

The villages that Maria passed by or through seemed not of the living, but the dead; as they were either sinking and being devoured by the spongy earth, or were being exhumed from its rocky entrails; as they were the relics of a forgotten civilization, or the sarcophagi of a remembered one; a land of tombs, peopled by a citizenry of ghosts that, dazed and only half-sensible, peopled it.

Though the cobbles and chimneys glistened in the sun, all seemed filthy and contaminated, as though no rain, snow or sunlight could ever polish them clean again. Though cocks crowed, horses neighed and babes bawled, their voices seemed muffled and choked, as death was not yet ready to let innocence have its voice. When a peal of laughter broke, it was quickly hushed, as with the closing of a dungeon's door. When a bell in a cathedral rang, it knelled a memory of doom, not hope into the hearer's ear. The trees and shrubberies seemed stunted, as their roots had sucked poisons. The very dogs seemed to restrain their barks and growls, as if they were now owned by a master that threatened to not merely kick them with a boot, but strangle them with their chain.

Death had proven as much an enchanter as a reaper. After its sickle had mown down its harvest, it had left a spell in its wake, one that winds could not sweep away, sunlight dispel, or prayers lift from the broken shells of broken hearts. Those it had spared, it had left cursed, leaving many only half alive; with squints and blotches, limps and crooked spines; with grotesqueries of flesh, blasted wits, harrowed souls.

It had wounded their spirits, and often, completely broken them. Many of the bravest were now timid, even mousy; many of the God-fearing, drunkards; many of the learned, little more than idiots driveling in chimney corners. Braggarts had become skittish, and the friendly, pinched and wearing strange scowls. Many who had owned pretty faces now hid their ruined ones in shawls and large hoods; former princesses now creeping like rats through the nighttime streets. *Death* had breathed it's horrors into the temples of men's souls, and rifling them, left their parishioners frail and fearful; more ghosts than men.

As Maria neared the village he could see its stone walls and tightly piled dwellings climbing up the hill. Here and there he could glimpse the cathedral, its cupolas burnished as by lackey angels in the morning sun. It rose queen-like above the roof-tops that, as they were its subjects dressed in patches and homespun rags, clambered to touch her royal gown. And yet, in his eyes, the great cathedral did not crown the village. He cared only for another place of worship; a dilapidating, two storey house whose bright green shutters opened to a window, and a dark-eyed angel that lowered fresh warm biscuits in a basket on a pole; a basket in which he had placed his heart.

.....*Was she alive? Death was cruel, but it could not be so cruel that it would pluck this modest little flower with a kerchief and a limp. What did this monster want with such a tiny flower?........*

As he walked through the forest, here and there catching glimpses of the village he had known so well, his steps grew at once both more hesitant and more eager; both light with hope and heavy with dread. When the sun was behind a cloud, the village seemed dark and foreboding, and when it again shone from that cloud it sparkled resplendently, as it had been chiseled from gems of crystal. At times he imagined bounding up the hill, and upon entering its gates, venting the thunder stored in his heart; *"Katrinika! Katrinika! Forgive me! Love is a strange beast, one that one tames only when one knows he is not its master!"* At other times he became faint of heart, and thought he wanted only to peek from dark shadows at the window that opened to the banished wanderers of his dreams.

The latter, more than the former ruled him.

Yes, he was afraid; afraid as he had never been afraid before; but not of his own farewell to the sun, rather of hers; this one little flower he so wanted to hold and cherish midst death's victory parade through this world. Or if death had frightened him at all, he had been afraid that he would perish before he saw those green shutters and red flowers, and those dark eyes again; that alone and forlorn, a deserter from God, God would send His jackals to encircle him, waiting for him to flag and stumble, to fall to his knees and be picked to the bone before he stood beneath that window again. He was afraid that madness was the end of his pride. He was afraid love had passed through his heart as it was a sieve; like all other things, even as his youth with the butterflies of his dreams had passed through it; like the seasons through the forest; like the night forever falls through the net of stars.

The road up the hillside was rife with the scars of death's invasion. It was in great disrepair; full of stones and deep pocks that the living, overwhelmed with the dead and the dying had neither the numbers, nor the care, nor the will to tend to. Here and there were clusters of roosted crows that blackened the tops of naked trees, their diabolical eyes upon him, as if waiting for a return of the plenitude upon which their generation had gorged. The road was also deceptively steep, its climb taking longer than he had anticipated, and by the time Maria reached the village wall, dusk was beginning to fall, and the wound in his side, the wound made by the claws of a crazed bear, and deeper, by the moon- bright smile in a bake house window, had begun to ache and bleed.

The gates were left open, as if in the aftermath of a barbarous raid; as if the village now knew beyond all doubt its walls were no proof against death's army; or as if having been conquered, there was left nothing more to sack. Neither walls nor prayers had served as a protection. Death had laughed at the marble saints and gold-leafed angels. It had sent its legions of noxious, death-dealing fumes to march through stones and holiness. Once inside the village its soldiers had whored, feasted and killed to their heart's content. They could wreak no more misery and desolation than what they had left in every street, on every doorstep, and in every broken spirit. The attack had been a successful one; slaying with invisible swords, and strangling with invisible hands. Its victory had been complete.

There were guards at the gates, but they seemed scarce to notice him. Shaggy, ragged and indolent, they sat withdrawn, huddled about spindly fires, playing card games, and roasting bits of meat on sticks, not bothering to stand; casting only numb disinterested gazes at the straggler, as they had been emasculated with defeat. There were several beggars that came to greet him, but even they seemed tentative, like beaten dogs, having lost the boldness of their trade; as what they had survived paled the pangs of starvation; their begging as cowed as it had formerly been audacious.

The streets that slithered like serpents through the tightly bound, highly piled houses, and up the hill of the village were largely empty. What little twilight found the bottom of these serpentine gorges seemed a filthy snow, as if the sunlight gilding the western clouds changed to ashes as it fluttered into such human devastation and misery. All was quiet. All was sepulchral. All was left cold, stunted, and stale with defeat and decay.

Death seemed to have not only pillaged, but to have taken possession of the houses he passed. Many were dark and unlighted, no doubt having lost the tenants that had tenanted them. Many had their windows and doors heavily boarded, or bound with thick chains. Even the lamps and candles in those now being lighted seemed cold and feeble, not warm and convivial, as the cheer of light itself was disheartened, even forbidden, and like the eyes of hungry cats watched from the darkness where they crouched with a dark menace.

In the dusky light these houses acquired something of the preternatural. All seemed abandoned, even those in which candles burned; abandoned by the living, only to be repossessed by ghosts of the living. Death smiled through their windows, as they were the hollow sockets of skulls; skulls that were laughing at the insignificance and impermanence of all that passed them by.

Many were the scarlet crosses he saw painted on doors and walls, and the large scarlet letters that accompanied them: '*God Have Mercy!*' *Heaven Save Us!*' *Forgive Our Sins!*' These crosses and these letters seemed to burn as with sulfur in the dismal dark through which he passed, as they were kindled not by their bright paint, but by their dreadful significance; a graffiti written by an unseen hand that was as much an admonishment in the day, as a prayer in the night.

He saw few people, and received even fewer nods and greetings from these few. Their forms were shadowy in the half-light, and wanted nothing of friendliness or conversation, as they no longer cared for anything but their own tomorrows. They scurried like vermin along the walls, and then behind objects, or waited in doorways and alcoves until he passed; most of them hiding their faces beneath hoods, hats, uplifted collars and shawls; some making a brusque *Sign of the Cross* as they cast their eyes to the ground; some staring at him from souls that had been starved and tortured with untold misery; left widowed of their humanity. Many of their forms seemed misshaped and twisted; their gaits, skewed and dragging; their stares, meek and demented, as they were criminals loosed from their prisons; criminals who had had red-hot irons pressed to their brains, and whose deformed bodies had been long cramped in cells too small to stand aright.

As he continued to climb into the higher reaches of the village, he passed through unlighted tunnels of stone, tunnels that opened into small squares that he remembered well, with fountains in their centers, and arcades about their edges. One of these squares was a notorious haunt of prostitutes; prostitutes young and old, and of many pedigrees. They would stand in the shadows of the crumbling arcades, dolled in their various costumes, advertising their endowments, and boasting their proficiencies to the men who came to appraise and purchase them. But when Maria entered this square he saw no display or promenade of these promiscuous merchants. Only when he had passed through the square and was about to leave it, did a form step from the shadows. As it was too afraid to approach him, the faceless form stopped a few paces away, speaking to him not with a voice bold and solicitous, but with one weak and pleading; shorn of all catty seduction.

"*Sir, if you are looking for a lady....well, I am one you might have if you wish......and most of the pretty ones either carted to the pits, or greatly marred or crippled from the sickness.....no longer fit for their former business. I'm not the prettiest in a candle's light, and a little older than many, but in the dark of the arcade you'd never know.....my hands are like feathers, and if you wish, my mouth is deep and moist, like a ripe plum it is, one with a playful tongue....and I'm not a tattler like some of the other girls.....that's why the monks and priests come to me....I'd serve your need, sir, if you have a need, and I would serve it nicely, happily and cheaply, and never telling a wife or sweetheart of your visit.......*"

Maria felt for the few coppers in the corner of one of his coat's pockets. Approaching the girl's vague form, that form recoiled, at which Maria stopped, and spoke tenderly.

"Here, take this."

Maria held out his hand. Slowly the form came forth, and fearing some trickery, with darting quickness grabbed the coins, like a fish gobbling the angler's bait, and once more retreated.

"And what favor sir?"

"None."

"I am not a beggar girl. I earn my bread honestly. Tell me the thing you wish, sir, on my knees, or fours, or otherwise, and I will do the thing you wish."

"No favor, no favor at all."

"Sir?"

"Pray for the bear that mauled a bear tamer in a cage. We are all wild animals, wild animals in cages. Like Katinka, we all hunger; we all hurt."

This was followed by an interminable silence, one that was finally broken by the girl's meek voice of gratitude.

"You are a kind man, sir, a very kind man, even if there is drink in your blood and makes you say strange things. Why would you give this to me, when you cannot see me, and in no way would have me.....and the boils of the sickness leaving a bulge on my neck and a squint in my eye?"

"Because you are alive, sweetheart, because you are alive."

With this Maria turned and continued his climb to the upper village. The narrow ways, steps and streets, the houses, shops and little squares were deserted as had been its nether part, but as he neared the bake house there was a certain welcome, a certain fragrance of friendliness that greeted him. Yes, death had trodden upon these stones; looked in these windows, broke down these doors and with its assailants violated the frail child of *life*, but it had not killed the sweetness, *her sweetness* that lingered in the fountains and porticoes; that had touched the winged lions and spitting serpents carved in the arches and cornice-works; taming and blessing the pagan malevolence of the gargoyles themselves with her simple goodness.

The dark eyes of this angel had looked upon these things.....the limp of her step, like the melody of a forest bird, had echoed on these stones. The smell of the bread she baked had filled these airs. Her sweetness had painted the arch of the night with stars!

And then he was there, standing in the square, the *Piazza Lucia*, as his soul had never left it; as only a silly, thoughtless, childish part of him had wandered away from its meaning, perhaps the only true meaning he had ever known. Here the roots of his spirit stretched deep and happy, roots that wrapped and interwove about the stones of this moldering house; clinging to them as they were their only nourishment. Here, and only here did his heart lift up its branches. Here and only here did his heart flower its roses among the stars.

Not far away the silhouette of the majestic cathedral rose into the heavens, but it was this house, pale and lonely that had the only altar he wished to kneel before; the only shelter that protected him from the wolves and savagery of the world; the only window in which an angel appeared to give him the bread of salvation.

The moon had not yet arisen, and only the first stars had peeked wet and silver from the darkness. The bake house, though visible, was still veiled in shadows. As in a trance, Maria walked across the square, only to stop a few paces before it, a cold terror shooting forks of cold fire through his heart.

The shutters of the window in which his dark-eyed angel appeared, the window that had filled his dreams for so long, through so much hardship and anguish, through death itself were shut; and not only shut, but with boards nailed across them!.....as was the front, seldom used door, and all of the other windows.....all, all shuttered tight and boarded over!.......

He ran to the rear of the house, where death had kept its sharpest spear to thrust through his heart, a spear in the shape of a blood-red cross. This door, and the entrance he had used so often was also emphatically boarded shut with large solid boards. Above it, and painted in large scarlet letters, letters that detestably and damnably gouged, like a devil's teeth upon his heart, was written: "The Lord Have Mercy!".

His heart broke, but its tears froze, and refused to pour from its break. In fierce defiance it rebelled against what his eyes were telling him.

.......It could not be true.....no, it could not be true! God, life, Angels, the great powers that turned the wheels of birth and death could not be so heartless and vengeful.....no, the very stars could not be so delinquent in their watch over her!.......

Once more he ran to the front of the house, and lifted his eyes to the window that had been his altar for so long, his soul trying to conjure the beautiful face and its red kerchief from the boards that his eyes and their profane testimony were trying to convince him had been nailed across it. But although his soul gallantly tried, his eyes, like impish devils won that battle of wills, over and over again.

.......It could not be true!.....he would not let it be true!.....he was Brother Maria.....he had once been a monk, a Brother in Christ who had prayed and fasted and counted the beads of a rosary......he had once befriended a brother named Brother Giovanni, a brother who was very wise.....a monk who became a good, wise, holy abbot, perhaps a Saint.... no, it could not be true.....Father Giovanni would tell him it was not true.....he was a wise and learned man.....he had read many books about the church fathers and the Saints.....Giovanni would not let it be true... the very Angels would come to his aid....they would not let such a thing be true!.......

He began to run in mad circles about the house, like a calf that had lost its mother cow, or like a man whose wits had been lost from his keeping. Over and over he circled, looking for a lamp or candle burning in its cold darkness; some crevice of the living that had not been boarded shut by death's fastidious workmanship. Over and over he ran into the square to look up at the chimney, only to see a smokeless, deserted relic, like the stub of a burnt out candle, frozen in obsoleteness against a mockery of cold stars.

Only gradually did his eyes and brain win the argument, and convince his heart that what they were telling him was true: that he was looking upon a skeleton picked clean, picked clean and damned by death's gluttony.

He pressed his cheek against a board nailed across the entrance he had entered so many times before.....that had opened to the steps that climbed to the smells of baking bread.....to simple meals prepared for him after his foolish philandering and carousals...and the fire before which he played his lute......the fire and the music to which she would step, like a shy doe stepping from a dark forest into a meadow of moonlight.

He kissed the painted cross, even as its redness was the blood of the Savior he had deserted in his youth, a Savior he no longer believed in, but was now willing to fall at His feet if He would only hear his prayer...."Please, not Katrinika, O dear God, not my sweet Katrinika".......

And pressing his cheek to the board, and opening his arms wide as to gather a lingering trace of her warmth, he felt the hurt he had felt when the bear's claws had tore open his side.....the hurt that was more a theft than a wound.....a wound not made by a bear's claws, but by the hand of

*a deceitful, sinister God that had only made men believe He was kind......
that had plucked the heart from his side, only to replace it with an empty
promise.......a promise that was a dream, a dream that was an illusion of
what is good, sweet and real.....a throbbing ache that laughed with howls
of meaninglessness........*

*......no, he would not cry......to spite this evil God, this God who had
shown no mercy.....this God who had sent crows and dogs and vermin to
eat His children and their dreams.....no! to honor this child, this innocent
baker of bread, this beautiful woman that in some way had touched his heart
as no other had touched it...he would give this godless God his madness, but
not his tears.....*

Gradually the board became rough to his cheek; gradually it became
cold, losing the warmth that he had willed into its hardness. Gradually
the night became silent, all but the beating of his heart and the throbbing
of his temples. Once more he was alone, as all men are alone, orphaned
into a world where death smiled in every smile, and winked in every
gaze; that traduced and trampled every promise.

He wandered away, not knowing where to sleep; not having the
means to purchase a place if he did. Although he had walked these ways
hundreds of times before, he no longer knew where he was. Nor did
he know *who* he was; nor did he care. And yet some of the archways,
the climbing ivies and crumbling chimneys knew him. They vaguely
remembered a blue-eyed gypsy who had played a fiddle, drunkenly
cursed and brawled, and was led by giggling tavern maids to secret beds
of feather or hay.

*.....Had this been Brother Maria? Or had Brother Maria been a dream?
What had been this Brother Maria's substance, his pith, the flesh and bones
that had crushed twigs beneath his feet, had been kissed by the rain and
sun; had dreamed pretty dreams? Had this Brother Maria seen horses in
meadows, walked through winter's cold and summer's heat.....played games
with women's soft bodies?.....Had this Brother Maria watched a dark Reaper
called 'death' mow down the beautiful flowers of this world.....a God that
men worship, that rained scorpions and serpents upon His children?......
Had this Brother Maria received warm biscuits in a basket, and a gaze
from two dark eyes in a window?.....Had this Brother Maria once dreamed
a dream midst death, a dream called 'love'?........*

Yes, some of the porticoes, fountains and winding streets through
which he walked remembered this Brother Maria, but only vaguely, as

a gust of wind that had once whispered past them. Yet others remembered him more dearly, as a lost son, and not a ghostly wind. Such was
the street he found himself walking on, and the tavern whose owner
was bolting shut its door to the lateness of the night. Yes, there was
something less vague and more familiar about this wine house where he
had once played a fiddle, slept in its loft, and had diced and brawled.
But more than these things there was something about the woman
who was bolting shut the door. Yes, though age had made thicker her
shoulders, legs and hips, she was one he had once known, once spoken
sweetly to, once held in his arms.

As a ghost desperately wanting to be other than a ghost, that wanted
to reach its hand from the webs and mists of death, Maria spoke to the
woman, surprising and alarming her.

"Marianna, Marianna, it is you, is it not Marianna?"

The woman turned, and without the least recognition of him,
winced with fear and began to walk briskly away.

*"Leave me alone. You are drunk. If you do not leave me alone I will
scream out. My husband will come! He is a big man, and will throttle you!"*

*"Please, please, I am sure I remember you. You are Marianna. You
served the master and mistress keeper, here, in the Sickle Moon Tavern. I
am Maria. You must remember me....Maria the gypsy, the one who once
played a fiddle, sang and danced for his room and board. Please, you must
remember me. We were sweet to each other. We laughed and danced together.
We slept in each other's arms........"*

At this the woman stopped her brisk steps and turned to the man
dogging her at her side. She looked at his unkemptness, but more closely
at the part of his weathered face that his grizzled beard and tangles
of long hair did not conceal. All seemed to belie his words; his rags
and leathered, care-scarred face, the disappearance of the wheaten gold
from his hair; and yet the earring, and the blue eyes that shone midst
the distress and chaos of his dishevelment, sparkling like stones of lapis
lazuli, pleaded the truth of his words.

*Yes, she had once looked into those beautiful eyes. Yes, she had once
wrapped this man in her arms. Yes, she had once given her love to him, as
he to her.*

The woman's face, also greatly hardened by the torments exacted
by the years, softened, and with compassion at once fearful and kind,
whispered:

"Maria? Is it you, Maria?" .....at which Maria, grateful to be recognized and remembered, crumpled halfway to his knees, bent his gaze, choked with tears and shame, and nodded.

Alarmed at his raggedness, his emaciation, and perhaps even his derangement, the good woman unlocked the door, and with an arm about his shoulders, helped her former lover into the tavern. There she lighted the fire anew, and proceeded to prepare a meal of warm bread and milk. Placing it on the table before him, she attempted a conversation.

"I am glad to see you again, Maria."

To which Maria faintly smiled and nodded, but offered no reply.

"I did not think I would ever see you again. I did not think you would ever return."

"The man had killed my mother.....I locked the man in the bear's cage....the bear tore the man apart....he drank his blood.....he danced with his head in his paws, as it was a child's doll......."

"What man, Maria? And what bear?"

But it was as though he did not hear her.

......*"and the pain in my side, yes, it sometimes hurts very much, a sweet hurt, a kind hurt.....you see Katinka swiped open my side with his claws..... but when Katinka saw that I did not die, and I had no fear of dying, I became his master.....but love is much stronger than Katinka......its pain is deeper, sweeter.....it claws out the heart with its tender fingers......no man may be its master.....all must die from its wound.....like flowers die in the sun that blessed them......."*

Making no sense of his replies, and fearing he had lost his mind, Marianna left to prepare his former sleeping room in the loft above the tavern. Returning, she found that he had eaten only a bite of the bread, and was staring absently into the fire.

"Maria, there is no one in the loft you once slept in. We have had no roomers since the beginning of the plague. I want you to sleep there tonight, and for as many nights as you wish. I am the 'Sickle Moon's' owner now; an inn as well as a tavern now. The sickness claimed the keepers and their children.....and many others....I am sure you know about the great sickness....yes, I can see that you have seen much death and great horrors..... oh Maria, my sweet Maria, it pains me to see you so!"

Feebly Maria answered; vainly trying to summon a manly strength that was no longer there, that had been spent by the toll exacted by the sorrows of his wandering, and finally ended by the dagger that had been thrust through his heart at the boarded up bake house door. The result was a faint mumbling, not to Marianna, but to the ghosts that seemed to have baffled his soul into a final surrender.

"*I have no money. I have no fiddle. I have no reason to live, because I have no more dreams in my heart. To live a man needs dreams, and a mother to give them to.*"

"*You will feel better, dear, after you rest. We will find you a fiddle. You will make it sing like you once made your old one sing. I will see that you are taken care of. I am married now.....a smithy.....a good man. He and I will take care of you, Maria. You will be well and strong again.*"

He offered no resistance to his former lover's invitation, only disconnected and incoherent words as she helped him to stand, and to walk up the stairs, step by step to the room she had prepared for him.

"......*yes, much death and much horror.....death everywhere.....horror everywhere......dogs starved on their chains, men's bodies rotting in fields, on streets, under bushes......pretty smiles and pretty bodies tossed from carts into the throats of worms.....bloated, blackened, rat-eaten bodies......never to be told they are beautiful again.....never more to be cherished.....never to be loved again........*

...but you see it was not so bad, no, not so bad, because there was a window midst the horror, a window in which she appeared in the golden mornings.....the angel with dark eyes and a red kerchief.....she blessed death with her smile......she fed death with warm biscuits......she was a flower that bloomed midst death, and made its bones sing and dance.......

.......all men need such a window.....a melody of a flute, a trinket to dangle about one's neck......for death is a mighty foe, much mightier than the clay doll of men's God.....death has woven a dream called 'life'...a dream that is a shroud.....a shroud that death dances over with its bloody feet.......

.....still, death is not such a bad fellow, he plays his fiddle outside all windows.....he is a maestro, and I have listened to and learned his melodies.....I will play them for you, Katrinika, one day when I am well I will play them for you......I will put them in the basket to pay for my biscuits......we will play them together, and fill the night with the songs of death......the next time I see Father Giovanni I will tell him my heart is full of death's sweetness.....that I have fallen in love with the mistress of death...he will understand......my friend Giovanni understands everything, everything......."

He was in bed for three days, delusional, and wrestling with fever. Deeply concerned, Marianna cared for him; keeping him warm, swabbing him and feeding him spoons of warm gruel in his brief fits of consciousness. Her husband was against the idea of taking in and caring for a shiftless wanderer who had vagabonded through the contagion, especially one who had struggled to their door, starved and sick. But Marianna convinced him there were no boils or blotches on his body, and he was free of any and all of the disease's tokens.

On the fourth morning, Marianna was greatly surprised to find Maria out of bed, fully dressed, and sitting in a chair, bathed in the bright sunlight that was pouring through the window. And when he looked at her, she saw that the mad dreams of the fever had left the blue crystals of his eyes. They sparkled with their old clarity, and with their sparkle was spread a gentle smile over his face. But it was his mind that Marianna was not fully sure of.

"*Thank you my dear. Thank you, Marianna for taking care of me. You are very sweet and kind. If I may rest here only a day or two more, I think I will be strong enough to leave. I will travel. You see I 'must' travel; I must always travel. There is nothing more than to wander and dream through the seasons, to love a little, sing to the moon, and then to die.*"

But the convalescent had this good woman's protestations, warm care and iron will to keep him from his travels. She loved him more deeply and possessively as his nurse than she had loved him as his lover. She would not let him leave, and the patient only halfheartedly objected, before acquiescing like an obedient child.

But it was not Marianna's insistence alone that had worked his capitulation. Although he was half ashamed of it, after so much aloneness he enjoyed the care and friendliness being provided him. Yet even more, there was a great sadness and tiredness now in his heart, one that, like a deeply embedded thorn, he was afraid could not be removed. Besides: *where was he to go? What was he to do? What dream was there left to dream, now that the beautiful bird of love had flown away? Was he, Brother Maria, becoming old?*

Marianna's husband, Alberto, grew to like their penurious roomer. Learning that his guest was a *virtuoso* with the fiddle, one morning he presented Maria with just that, as he ate his breakfast at a table in the tavern.

"*Look what I have found for you, Maria old chap! It was my father's.*

Well, death and his dark-hooded crew carted the lazy old codger away one night, but he was good enough to leave his fiddle behind. I do not play, and never wish to learn......a rooster can crow and a cat screech sweeter than ever I could make a tune. Marianna tells me it could not fall into more able and loving hands. After death has tromped through our streets, a fiddle could do the heart a great kindness......give it back its pluck, one might even say its rightful wings."

It was a beautiful fiddle, and like a beautiful woman there promised to be wonderful melodies asleep in its beauty. Maria tightened and tuned its slack strings, and once or twice danced the horse-hair bow over them, only to lower it from his shoulder, and set it down again. He was afraid something had died inside him, and he was afraid to try to wake it, lest it could not be waked. He was not sure he could make another beautiful woman sing. He was not sure he had dreams to give her heart; make her sing melodies from the depths of her soul.

Maria had fallen into good hands. They were kind people; in love, and big-hearted and generous with their love to others. A new suit of clothes was found for him, and Marianna barbered his hair and beard, as well as cooked good meals for him. They asked nothing in return.

But Marianna privately worried about him. She had not only known, but had loved another Maria, a garrulous, devil-may-care Maria, a Maria that had not seen, and lived through unspeakable horrors, some of the greatest horrors hell had ever loosed in the world of men. This Maria seemed quiet and tame, as if death's visage had not only blasted his senses, but had broken his spirit. Although occasionally the old smile flashed, the old laugh welled with a hint of its former thunder, and the blue eyes boyishly danced and sparkled, Marianna was not convinced that Maria was entirely well.

Several times when she had asked Maria to unload bags of flour from a cart, she had seen him wince, and even let go an involuntary groan when he had bent to lift a sack. She had seen him grimace when he stood up from where he sat; and once as he climbed the stairs she had seen him stop, hold his side, and grip the railing for support, something she had never seen him do before.

But there was more; something that was less tangible, but to her woman's sense, more telling. Despite the bravery of his good-natured appearance, Marianna was convinced that there was not only a secret pain in his body, but in his spirit as well; a pain that gave him a hurt that did not break into words.

He played the fiddle her husband had given him very little, protesting that his fingers had become thick and stiff with age, and that the years of the plague and wandering had robbed his memory of the gypsy songs he knew in his youth. There were only a few rare exceptions. Once, after breakfast, he went to his room, fetched the fiddle, and sitting on the top step proceeded to play a happy little song of gratitude. Another time, begged by some children, children whose parents remembered the gypsy fiddler of the *Sickle Moon Tavern*, he delighted them with a little *pizzicato* riff, only to end his concert with the excuse of tiredness, and an errand he had forgotten about.

Great then was Marianna's surprise when a neighbor told her that she had heard violin music in the middle of the night, music that came from the small gable atop the tavern. Even more of a surprise, there were those who heard violin music in the little square below the tavern, music they had said was very sad and soulful; music that haunted their sleep with sweetness; that sounded at once like the mourning and the serenading of a ghost. Marianna listened in amazement as still others told her they had seen this fiddler once leave the village gates after these interludes, only to play the same melancholic melodies among the deserted trenches, now overgrown with nettles, where cartload after cartload of the dead had been buried during the height of the distemper's rage.

Curious at this mystery, especially when Maria seemed so disinterested in the fiddle, Marianna lay awake for several nights, listening. She and her husband lived only several doors from the tavern, and they would surely hear a fiddle being played in night's stillness. But lying awake, she heard nothing but sounds of the tranquil night.

Yet on the third night she woke to music; although at first she thought she had been dreaming. But as she began to fall back to sleep she heard it again, and this time, though faint, it was unmistakable. Rising from her bed, and opening the window to the cool spring air, the fiddle's sweetness entered the room like a blossom-laden breeze.

She woke her husband, and he too came to the window to hear the music that their enigmatic tenant was playing. Smiling, and promising his wife not to mention the thing to Maria the next day, he went back to sleep, jokingly telling Marianna that it was probably a gypsy's way of baying the moon.

But Marianna did not go back to sleep. She was touched very deeply by the music coming from the small garret; a music very different, and unlike any she had heard Maria play before. A deep part of her, a *woman* part of her was entranced, made tender with the forlornness and need in its song. Yes, as her husband had wryly said, it was like a baying of the moon; an exquisitely tender moaning by the animal in a man's heart; as it was trying to be purged from its cage......a purge that was a worshiping of a moon that not only shone in the night sky, but burned through its animal blood.

Suddenly the music stopped, and the night, as if listening with its silent ear, applauded with an ovation of deeper silence, as if its heart had been pierced by the poignancy of this human passion. Remembering what some had said about the violin music in a square only a short way down the hill, Marianna opened the door, just in time to see Maria step from the tavern's alley, his fiddle beneath his arm. Captured by the intrigue of the thing, she quickly wrapped herself with a coat, and careful not to wake her husband, Marianna followed this one she was no longer sure she knew in the light of the sun.

What she saw was a great mystery; a greater one she had never seen.

Maria stood in the middle of the little square, the one that was called *La Piazza Lucia*. He stood directly before the deserted bake house, one of the countless victims of the plague. He began to play his fiddle, and indeed it was like a mourning ghost, one that was serenading a sister ghost behind the boarded up doors and windows that had imprisoned it.

Never had Marianna heard a melody of such sadness, a sadness that was imbued with such rich sweetness.....as the fiddle's strings were the strings of the heart, all men's hearts.....the tones rising not from one soul, but from all souls, from all pain, all need, all desperation to love and be loved......a nostalgia, a remorse, a timeless melancholy for what autumn takes from the spring flowers.....what age takes from the flight of youth......what death takes from the brief, struggling bloom of life.......

......Her heart swooned. She wanted to take this loneliness into her arms, to embrace and be embraced by it; melt and surrender to it, die in its loveliness......as it was a sweetness death had never found or violated.......

It was more than a melody he was playing before the derelict house. It was a lover with caressing hands, tender kisses and passionate eyes. It was a lover who had walked through a world of horror and anguish, through a hell of the dying.......a lover wrapped in love's dream, a dream he was bringing back, like a soldier to his Beloved......a dream that he had preserved....that death had not killed.

Its melody filled the sleepy little square, lifted to the stars and told their gallery of a man's emptiness, and his eternal need to fill that emptiness......a smitten lover singing beneath a balcony, begging for his mistress, the beautiful mistress of death to remove her veil, and step forth from her palace......

Returning to her house, Marianna was even more perplexed than when she had first heard of Maria's nocturnal serenades. She remembered the night of the brawl outside the tavern, and the great knife wound in Maria's side. She remembered the old man who protested to be a doctor, and who insisted Maria be taken to the bake house where he lived with his crippled daughter. Maria had stayed in the old house until he healed, and then one day departed into the woods, and was not heard of again.

And then returning after many years, tired, delusional and sick, professing that he no longer could play the fiddle, but in secret playing melodies with far more exquisite beauty than ever he had played before......serenading a deteriorating, boarded up house whose tenants the plague had claimed. Was Maria's soul lost and wandering in dreams? Had he become deranged from horrors that had been too great for his eyes or his soul, perhaps any man's eyes or soul to behold? There were only two people who had lived in the bake house: the old man, a hopeless drunkard, and his lame daughter who baked bread for pennies. Who was he playing to? When many women in the village would be his paramour, why was he playing love songs to the boarded up bake house, and not beneath their windows?

Several days later Marianna tenderly probed and explored the mystery. There were no customers, and Maria sat alone, lost in thought at a table. Health had returned in his eyes and in a new bloom of ruddiness on his face. As it was a battle it had not finished fighting, even the blond hairs of youth seemed to wage a retaliation against the gray ones of age, and shone victorious in the sunlight. But there seemed a cloud settled on his heart that his returning health had not lifted. Marianna sat down on the bench opposite him, and began a delicate surgery of words.

"How are you feeling, Maria?"

"Much better, Marianna. Thank you. You and your husband have been

very kind to me."

"You know I was very frightened, especially when half the village passed the Sickle Moon's door, piled on dead-carts.....the very monks and priests deserting their duties to save their skins. I sometimes still hear the crier crying out for the dead....the horse, the cart's wheels, the knell of the death bell.....waking in the night and feeling my hands and face to make sure I was among the living.....I will probably hear them in my tomb. You had a great fever, Maria, and we thought we might have to cart our fiddler to the trenches with the others."

At this Maria faintly smiled, and even more faintly shrugged; as the thought of death amused him. Marianna continued.

"You said many things in your fever, most of which I did not understand, nonsensical things born in the flames of sickness.....death's dance, life's dream, the prison of the flesh.....the web of a spider, wolves copulating with Angels.....your mother calling to you in the faces of whores.....and many other hysterical things. Over and over you spoke the name, 'Giovanni', Father Giovanni it was. You said he would understand; that he alone understood your heart."

At the mention of the name, *'Giovanni'*, Maria started, and his eyes, despite his numbness, watered.

"You must love and respect this man very much, Maria, to have him live so strongly in your heart. Who is Father Giovanni? Who is, or was this man?"

Pausing, Maria spoke softly, but succinctly; deliberately.

"I think you remember that I once told you I was a religious brother when I was young; a Brother of Christ in a Franciscan Abbey. It may seem amusing to you, you who have seen me drink and brawl, and in the arms of many women; but I assure you, it is true. Giovanni was a friend of mine in the abbey, a brother whose wisdom and goodness made him an abbot. He never knew it, because I do not think he ever thought I was much more than a child, but he was a great inspiration to me, and perhaps the dearest friend I ever had."

Encouraged that he spoke to her, and in a coherent, confiding manner, Marianna pressed nearer the wound.

"Well, your fever was not the first time we thought we might lose you, my dear. There are those that survived the sickness who still talk about the fight you waged against those brutes in the alley.....that night when you sustained your injury.....I think it was the stab of a knife to your side, was

it not? There were four of them, four against one, I remember. You were a wild man. Ha! Daniel in a lion's den full of very unfriendly lions."

Maria was slow to answer, and then only strangely.

"I wrestled bears, not lions. When they were smoked from their dens, drunk with berries, or their winter sleep, I wrestled them. I was a boy. A bear tamer taught me how to wrestle them, and in return, I taught the bear tamer about a bear's wrath."

Not understanding, she could not reply to his strange answer, But unfazed and undeterred, Marianna continued.

"The plague took all but one of them I think, the brutes I mean. I saw two tossed on a dead-cart with my own eyes. There's still one about, I think the one who stabbed you. He survived the plague, but it left him with a crooked neck and spine.....and a muttering dimwit to boot. A queer man now; little more than an idiot now. The plague left its mark on many; made a race of cretins; humpbacks, clubfoots, babblers, creatures mangled in mind and body."

Maria stared directly ahead, dumb of any response. Marianna was undaunted.

"I was there that night. I saw the gypsy who made beautiful music become a Daniel fighting a den of lions, or rather, a den of bears in the alley. I saw you, my sweet Maria lying in blood. I went to you, but I did not know what to do. And then the old man, the old man who always became drunk with plum wine.....the old man who claimed he was a doctor in the wars ordered that you be taken to where he lived......to the house in the little piazza, the Piazza Lucia, to the house where they baked bread and biscuits I believe......"

At this Maria seemed to quicken, as if the throbbing nerve could feel the approach of the surgeon's knife. Carefully, and without a show of notice, Marianna proceeded.

"Yes, I remember. The old man took you into the bake house. He dressed your wound, and gave you a bed. And as you healed, I, and many other women who loved you discovered where you were. We stood beneath the bake house window, the window with green shutters and pretty red flowers in the flowerboxes, and ordered fresh biscuits from the ovens. And when the girl lowered them to us with a pole and basket from the window, we placed bouquets, and love notes, and other little gifts for you in the basket with our payments. Yes, yes, I remember that very well. Your wound was serious, and you lived in the bake house with the old doctor and his crippled daughter

for weeks, perhaps months."

Marianna could tell that Maria listened attentively to her words, but still did not speak. Thinking he was in no mood to converse, she made to stand from her chair.

"Well, I have things to do, and soon Alberto will......"

"A moment more, please, Marianna, could you please stay only a moment more?"

Stirred from his stupor, Maria placed his hand on Marianna's arm, and she sat back down in the chair. This time she did not speak, but only looked at Maria, and patiently waited for his words; words that when they came, came soft and measured, and with an uncharacteristic hesitancy.

"Yes; they were very kind to me. I think the old man saved my life. We became good friends. We drank wine together. He told me stories of the famines and the wars. He told me that his first wife died in the famines, and his second wife, the wife that gave him his daughter, ran off with a band of wanderers. I think these things broke his heart. I think that is why he drank much wine, and I think that is why he so adored his daughter.....the bake girl that lowered the bread basket from the window with the green shutters and the red flowers."

Here his words stopped, and only after a pause, one in which he seemed to have made a great decision, he said:

"Marianna, what became of them, the old doctor and his daughter? The house is forsaken; dark and boarded up......"

"The plague, Maria, the accursed plague took them, like it took half the village. The smell of death was great in the streets......folks walked about with scarves and sleeves, with garlic, sprigs of juniper and bunches of flowers pressed to their mouths and noses.....you know, not to take the contagion into their lungs.....and many used to gather in the Piazza Lucia, the little piazza with the bake house, for the smell of fresh bread was a great relief to the smell of disease and decay.....a kind of fragrance in a garden of death. But one day the shutters of the window did not open, and the smell of fresh bread did not fill the Piazza Lucia. The flowers in the flowerboxes wilted, and several days later men boarded the old house up, and painted the red crosses and letters of death upon it."

Maria did not speak; only stared fixedly ahead. Seeing that he had no more to say, Marianna began to leave, saying as she did: *"A pitiful thing, a most pitiful thing, would try the faith of a saint it would."* But again, as her leaving was the only thing that could stir his tongue, Maria spoke.

"*The men who boarded up the house, Marianna, the men who painted the blood-red crosses and letters.....are they still alive?*"

"*Some, yes, some. One of them comes to the tavern each night. He and a crew of others painted a slew of them....up and down the streets.....into every little alley.......nary a nook or hiding place that death's curse did not ferret out and find.*"

"*Could you introduce me to this man, Marianna?*"

"*Why of course, Maria, I will introduce you to him tonight.*"

This had ended the conversation, and Marianna thought it wise not to soon initiate another with her much altered ex-lover; not to probe too closely the mysterious thorn that had lodged, and still was not ready to be pulled from his heart. She thought it best not to mention other things he had blurted midst the fires of his fever, and the names that he moaned, like refrains midst them: *Sacu, Ohai, Katinka, Mamica* and *Katrinika*...especially *Katrinika*, a name that often repeated, had caused her to smile, knowing that this unusual name must be one of the many women that had loved and been loved by this irascible adventurer and wanderer.

Days and weeks passed. Perplexed with the enigma, many times Marianna rose in the mid of night to sit by the window, drinking the blossom rich air, made sweeter and richer with the music that drifted on its breezes; the violin music that welled from a troubled, probably broken heart; pouring into the night its magnificent sorrow. Several nights, when the moon was bright, she even followed this mysterious, nocturnal fiddler to the small *piazza*, where, as before, he proceeded to poignantly play before the boarded up house, even as he was serenading a ghost; even as he was serenading *death*.

Piqued with the curious strangeness of the thing, Marianna once asked her husband:

"*Alberto, did you know the folks who lived in the bake house in the Piazza Lucia?*"

"*Still thinking about that deserted bake house, eh; and our midnight fiddler that plays to its ghosts? The sickness left many a sane man crazy, Marianna; those it did not kill, it robbed of their wits; blew them away like an autumn wind blows leaves from the trees.....left many laughing, others crying when there is no one about.....some continually itching and biting like a dog its fleas.....some wandering like drunk men, calling out names of dead sweethearts, ha! sometimes sweethearts that were not their wives...... some are still found now and then, their skeletons hanging from trees, or beneath bushes with knives between their ribs......only yesterday I heard of a man who was found stark naked, singing a silly, bawdy tune to the Virgin, while digging a grave, his own grave it seems....yes, I knew them a little, the drunkard and his lame-hipped daughter..."*

"Do you remember their names?"

"Which reminds me.....the constables told me some rascal boys painted over the plague words on a wall of that bake house.....used the same red paint.....crossed out some of the letters, added others, the damned little rogues, the varlets! I'm not a reading man, but those that are say the words read: 'Mother of Moons and Flowers, Have Mercy'. Hang 'em by their heels, that's what they should do to them, hang 'em by their heels, and while they're a-hangiin' flog their bare asses raw.....And another crazy thing, someone planted bright red flowers in those boxes by the window where each morning the bake girl used to lower the bread.....No, no my dear, I don't think I ever knew the names of the drunkard and his daughter......a pretty little thing really.....saw her once without her bandanna.....lovely hair, beautiful dark eyes, could haunt a sailor's dreams, if she had not been born gimpy.....too bad she had that limp, like a pretty little bird with a broken wing.....no, wife, I cannot say I ever knew their names......"

Later that night Marianna sat near the window, listening to the music lift from the small garret to the audience of mountains, forests and stars. As she did her husband woke.

"Marianna, come back to bed. My feet are cold. I need you to warm them. Leave our crazy gypsy fiddler to bay the moon, ha! serenade the harem of ghosts he once loved in the flesh.......

Ah, that is better, your body is like n little oven my love.....

...a strange thing, the plague must have taken half my wits with the other lamebrains in Siena. I remembered the crippled girl's name today as I was at the forge .....mending senore Matteo's bloody ploughshare again......it's like a thing been cursed.....the crippled girl's name, but not her father's..... the girl who lowered bread from the bake house window, remember?..... the one you asked about.....the one that the plague sent on a cart to the pits with that old guzzler of her father.....it was 'Katrinika'.....a strange name, a sweet name.....I remember the old sot driveling it in his wine......ah, you are so warm, my wife, and your Alberto's feet are so cold......"

CHAPTER TWELVE

THE CANDLE IN THE WINDOW

Part I

Early Spring, Thru late Summer; 1352

MARIA woke early. He sat at his table, idly sketching, but like a mug of stale wine, his dawdling could not excite him. He played a few strains on his fiddle, but the melodies seemed false and hollow, as if the sun did not exact the same *pathos* as the moon and stars inspired from its strings. The morning was breaking exultingly, fresh and cool through his open shutters, and neither words nor melodies could match the golden net it was casting on his heart.

He found Marianna alone in the kitchen, and told her he planned a hike in the hills today.

"*Could you find it in your heart, Marianna, to prepare a biscuit, and a bite of cheese and fish for me? Could you scrape a barrel for me my Heart? And I'm sure a flask of wine would bring a kiss to that rose I see blooming on your cheek; that is if there's no smithy husband hunkering about.*"

Busy with her chore in hand, Marianna did not look at him, but like an empress nodded, and then silently touched her cheek with the tip of her finger, to which Maria leaned and gave her his part of the bargain. Still without proffering a look, she said:

"*What a rascal and a devil you are, Maria.*"

And then turning to him squarely, and giving him a penetrating stare with the mildness of her deep brown eyes, a mildness that was impossible to escape from its capture:

"But I think in some ways a sad rascal and a sad devil. Do you love women so that you may break their hearts, or do they love you in an effort to break yours? Or do you love them as rainclouds love the flowers, and they, as flowers love the rainclouds? Is there no one for whom your heart not only breaks, but gives its sweetness Maria?"

To this Maria looked away, unable to answer the probe of her investigating stare. Seeing that he either did not want to answer, or was confounded of one, Marianna turned again to her chores, and said:

"Yes, of course I will bundle up some victuals for you, 'caro'; I would bundle up the stars for you if I could."

A short while later Maria walked through desolated streets lined with boarded up shops, huts and houses. As the snows and rains could not wash them away, many had scarlet crosses still smeared upon their doors, and with these crosses, heartrending words, as if dipped in the same blood-red pain that had painted them: *'Lord Have Mercy', 'Protect Our Children', 'The Valley of Death, Fear No Evil'*. Most of the few people he saw were scavengers, and there were a few with numb blasted stares standing in doorways, death having left them alive, but imbecilic and spectral. Only here and there passed a passer-by; some with a squint or limp, others stooped or twisted, never to be right in mind or body again; shorn of the least salutation or pleasantry by the horrors that had branded them, and were still fresh upon them.

Reaching the end of the village, Maria stopped. Somewhere, (although behind which door he could not tell), a woman was moaning, her moans a yawning drawl of pain that seemed long dry of sobs and tears, as it was the slow croak of a dying bird; its hoarseness surrendering its broken song to death's proud victor. Instinctually, not reverently, Maria made the *Sign of the Cross*, and walked on. Although the plague's rage had passed, and showed no sign of returning, Maria wanted to be free of all of the vestiges and reminders of its horrors. He wanted to breathe an air that had not been corrupted by death's foulnesses, and in which no echo of its wails still lingered.

A short ways from the village Maria broke from the small road, and climbed through an orchard of olive trees that, like crippled old men clung twisted and gnarled to a rocky hillside. Finding a shepherd's path, he began to climb up a second, taller hill that, like a kind father looked down upon the sad streets below.

The day was golden with sunlight. The larch, beech and chestnut were budding, and the first flocks of flowers were donning their spring bonnets of purple, pink and cock's-comb red on sunny banks and in tiny hollows. Fed by the last secret pockets of melting snow, brooks were rushing, carving their haphazard ways with fresh clean joy; and warbling birds were invading the woods with armies of merriment. Like a love-smitten youth, all was drunk and singing.

Maria breathed deeply the fresh clean air, his blood warming and rousing, pulsing alive through the dark sleep in his veins. Like one starving, he ate greedily of the delicious feast the earth was offering him. There was no death on these slopes and in these thickets; no dead-carts or death knells; no corpses, no scavenging ghouls. Nature was singing with triumphant innocence, an innocence that had slept inviolate beneath the winter snow, and the horrors that had visited men.

Was this God? Was this His sword, His trumpet, His redemption? If it was, Maria thought this God aloof and uncaring, indifferent to the sufferings He had loosed on men. How dare this God be laughing and singing in these hills, unconcerned with the dead-carts, buriers, orphaned children and wailing widows at His feet! This God was an unfair God, a smugly selfish God; one that doled His love only to His pampered Saints and darling Angels.

Or was it something sweeter, gentler; something that harbored no grudge, no retaliation; something that sprang like crocuses in the bloody footsteps of God's terrible slaughter; that endeavored to repair what *Man's* God had recklessly ruined? Instead of insipid love from tired, sun-leeched priests, from stale sermons and the dull drone of hackneyed prayers, perhaps it was another army, another kind of army, one volunteering to vanquish *Man's* God and His murder-minded soldiery; one that sprang from the bloodbath of this God's punishment, waving banners of a *mother's* love; a love of children blades, buds and blossoms, of the earth itself; the pretty flowers chastising the bloody Angels, and teaching them to sing.

After several hours, Maria attained the hill's summit, breathing heavily from the steep climb. Choosing a place where the sun shone pleasantly, he lay down on a new bloom of grass, and with the grateful joy of his fatigue, closed his eyes. Like a flower opening its petals, he spread wide his arms, as much to drink as be drunk; to be rained upon, and be melted by the sun's kindness.

And when he did, his face softened, smiling a smile that was one with his tears.

He believed in this sun. He believed in the goodness and abundance of its simple light; a light that gently rained on rotten leaves, despairing faces and deserted graves, bringing bright-faced flowers from ribs and skulls; that would not forsake *man* even when *man* had forsaken himself; these golden kisses an unconditional forgiveness, granting a reprieve, a second chance of new bloom and verdure to the winter forests, and new dreams to the broken heart of the human child who wandered through them.

This is why he had felt such a need to climb the hill.....to be closer, closer that he might be crucified by this sun, exorcised of the terrible memories of what he had seen, driving them like evil spirits from where they had come to lodge.....from the darkness where they piled their morbid riches in his heart.....rat-eaten faces, disease-eaten faces, sorrow-eaten faces.....the eaten eyes of the dead asking the same question that they asked when they had been filled, lighted with living candles: 'Why? Dear God, why?'

.....these sunbeams like gently hammered nails, these nails, like golden fingers reaching through his ribs, tenderly incising his heart, kissing the tortured child of his soul.....hammering, raining, bleeding through his flesh back to his mother, the only mother, the mother who reverenced death as much as she nourished life....the mother who did not distinguish between flowers and bones.....whose smile melted the line that foolish men had drawn between good and evil, reason and madness, life and death.....the ever fertile, all-loving mother, the Earth-mother.......

.....yes, the sun was crucifying him, and as it did a thousand pains woke and ran laughing and weeping from the graves of his wounds...... the sun doing what a cold stony God and His tired troops of priests had not......thawing him, healing him, blessing his hurts and aches.....his guilt and shame and broken dreams......the breaking of his holy vows, and his desertion from the abbey.....his aimless, shiftless wandering, his laziness and dissipation, his impiety, his whoring......the squandering of his youth..... the senseless, willful and utter ruin of his life.......

.....crucifying, exorcising, forgetting all that he had known, all that he had cherished, melting away, dissolving in the warm rain of these sunbeams.....becoming a dream too dreamlike to embrace, a mystery too large to know.....a dream and a mystery of endless hours and seasons, of which he was only a trembling leaf......a grain, a breath, a moment in some eternity that had forgotten, and perhaps had never known one called 'Brother Maria'.....

Maria came from his doze as the sun was nearing its zenith overhead. He reached into the bag of things Marianna had prepared for him, found a large biscuit, and bit lustily into it; and then uncorking the flask, joined it with a generous swig of wine. Commingling the bread with the wine, and thus allowing the bread to sop its juice, he held the delicious mouthful in his mouth, tasting it, savoring it, before gently swallowing it. *Was this not also, in some strange way beyond his knowing the flesh and blood of a savior, a sacrament, one that he was receiving from the presiding priest of the sun?*

He knew he should return, that he had promised Marianna and Alberto to perform some chores; but the first warm sun of the spring, his meditations, and the thing he felt in his blood and soul, this thing he was prepared to do, that he was committed to do, that he *must* do….. Propping himself up on one elbow, he looked out upon the vastness that the hilltop commanded.

For as far as the nerves of his eyes could see he could see forests, fields and hills, reaching to the hem of heaven, where a fleet of white clouds were sailing the blue sea of the sky. Here and there he could see a small flock or herd, and stone fences, like vulture-picked spines of ancient monsters that contained them. Still barren in the aftermath of the pestilence, he could see unplowed fields, and weed-infested orchards and vineyards. Here and there were wisps of smoke, struggling frail and sickly from small simple huts.

He had walked over these hills and through these forests, and he had encountered many struggles and adventures as he had. He had scythed wheat, pressed grapes, picked orchard fruits. He had become a thief, gambler, drunkard, played a fiddle at weddings and funerals, brawled with knives and fists. He had loved many women, some behind their husbands' backs. He had heaped corpses on carts, only to spill them in pits. Like a wild animal of these forests, he had shed other men's blood; yes, he had killed.

How small, like a mote of dust the creature of *Man*, and how precarious his existence, whether he be a *Caesar* or a peasant beneath the torch of the sun and the tent of the stars. How small and insignificant was *Man* in the magnificent arena into which he walked. How small was the one named *Brother Maria*; how very small; how very brief.

And everything in this immensity was a mystery. Each hill and vale, each field and barn, each gentle eye of a horse, song of a bird, smile of a shepherdess; all were irresistible invitations to other, deeper, more mysterious mysteries that promised to be discovered. But these mysteries were never found, never solved, for one was beckoned and seduced by yet other mysteries with yet other, and endless other promises of hills, songs, tender smiles and pillowing breasts.

Still the greatest mystery was this creature, tiny as an ant or a beetle, that tilled these fields and hunted these forests; that was born to briefly explore the unsolved riddles he found at every step of his way; this sojourner wandering through the wilderness between dust and star, and this other wilderness, even more vast and inscrutable, even more wildly dangerous: the wilderness in his own heart.

Once more Maria leaned back, closed his eyes, feeling his smallness; a husk or a leaf, a seed fallen from a seedpod, one that would disappear, melt and be lost in the immensity of the hillside. He felt the priest of the sun anoint his eyelids, an anointing that warmed and goldenly smiled through all parts of him. Oh, how kind was this sun, its kiss tenderly exorcising *Man's* demons, encouraging and evangelizing them to Angels; and how small; how very small and brief the moment to know and feel its golden miracle.

......but then there was death, a thing far more cruel, and mindless of the sun, corrupting its kindness.....death, always, forever death.....this dark wing that blotted the sun, ate it like jaws of locusts.....impaling men on its horrors, closing their eyes to the dream they had dreamed, only to open them again, hollow and empty, buried forever in their graves......

His hour was gone; the grains of his dreams, spent. He had lost her; like a beautiful bird that had flown through his arms, he had lost her. Brother Maria must prepare to leave, and in these hills and forests, perish and be no more. This sorceress had played him for a fool again. This dark-eyed angel, 'love', would no longer come to a window with green shutters and red flowers in its flowerboxes.

* * *

RETURNING from his hike in the hills, and climbing the narrow, spider web of streets back to the *Sickle Moon*, Maria heard someone call out his name.

"Sir, please, might I have a word, just a word? Good sir, Maria is it not? Brother Maria?.....to say it fully and rightly....Master Maria, I am sure it is."

Maria turned to see a young man, only twenty or so paces behind him. He was shyly, but brightly smiling, and climbing the street as to catch him. Reaching Maria, his excited words were full of breathiness, as much from his excitement as his exertion.

"*It is you, is it not? Maria, the man who fiddled at the Sickle Moon…… the one who was once stabbed by a knife in a brawl…..a brawl in which you broke three or four of the jakes' heads…..and you were brought to the bake house for the old doctor to bandage and heal?…..whew, the climb!……yes, it is you, of course it is you…..there's no one else has blue eyes like yours, Mister Maria…..and the dangling earring…..yes, I'd bet my boots and cap on it, my horse if I had one!*"

The one who had hailed him was not much more than a boy, albeit a boy that was fledging the gangly limbs of early manhood. He was tall and stick-thin, his wrists and ankles having long outgrown the coat and trousers meant for the boy he was forsaking, poking from their cuffs like necks of turtles from their shells. His hair was dark and long, a shaggy stranger to scissors and comb, and his face was thin and bony, as starvation was a sick brother he carried on his back. But the ragged skeleton of his person was animated, made kindly by his bright dark eyes that shone with exuberant sincerity. Still, it was a face Maria could not recall.

"*Do I know you, young man? You do not look familiar to me.*"

"*You knew me once, Master Maria, but that was years ago, before you went away, before the plague ate half the village and spat 'em out in the churchyards and the trenches…..and well, I've grown…..'A boy grows faster than weeds or wheat', as the saying goes.*"

There was an immediate likability about his young face; his smile full of the eternity of youth; its sunny, felicitous daydream not yet found out by the cold winds of manhood's cares. Still, Maria could not summon recognition of the boy, and excusing his self politely, began to climb on.

"*Forgive me, but I do not remember you, and I am a little tired now. Stop at the Sickle Moon some time, and we will have a talk.*"

But the boy refused to be dismissed, and tagged enthusiastically at his side.

"*But you must remember me, master Maria, you gave me lessons on your lute and fiddle. On the morning you left the village you gave me a copper to buy a biscuit from the lady in the bake house, the kind of biscuit I liked best, the biscuits with the custard. You gave me a note to place in the basket the bake lady lowered on a pole from the window."*

At these words Maria stopped, turned, and peered more closely at the excited boy dogging his heels. The boy's exuberance was fanned even brighter when he did.

"Yes, master Maria, I am Salvatore!.....the boy who lived with his mother and sisters a stone's throw from the bake house door!"

Slowly it came back to him; the features of the gaunt stripling he had once been very fond of, and with those features, the early morning of his departure, full of snow and cold, and the pain of heartbreak and forlornness. The lines of Maria's care-carved face relaxed, and from its grizzly-ness flowered a gentle smile; a flower whose blue eyes sparkled with tears.

"Why yes, now I remember, Salvatore, yes Salvatore! How you have grown my friend! Why, another moon or two and you'll be a man!"

"You have changed too, Mister Maria, if I may say the thing. But when I heard there was a fiddler fiddling in the middle of the night, one that some called a phantom fiddler playing in the Piazza Lucia where I once lived..... and then when I heard the fiddle music with my own ears.....well, as I know it is a rooster when a rooster crows, and it is a dog when a dog barks, I knew it was the gypsy fiddler I once knew, the one who played at the Sickle Moon. No one could ever make a fiddle sing so sweetly, like an Angel perched on a man's shoulder, as you, Mister Maria."

The boy's sweetness was disarming. Maria smiled, tousled the boy's hair, and gave him a warm hug; his heart grateful for his kind words.

"You are very kind, Salvatore, and I am very glad you remembered me. I remember your mother......."

"The plague took mum and my sisters, as drink and the devil took the scoundrel that laid on mum to make me.....ha! skaddled before he knew me. I'm on my own now. I work for a cobbler and leather man: oakum, pitch, neat's-oil's my life now......play the fiddle some too, when I've the time and my fingers are not gummed with pitch or sore from the awls. I tell all who like my tunes that a blue-eyed gypsy taught me. There are still some who remember you, Mister Maria, some that were not thrown on the dead-carts, ladies mostly, they who remember you and your gypsy fiddle and dances."

Maria smiled warmly and approvingly.

"I remember now; you were a very good student. I am sure you play very well.

And that morning when I left, Salvatore, that snowy morning when I gave you a......"

"I gave it to the bake house lady right off, Mister Maria, by the Saints I did.....and the note you gave me too, probably before you were out the gates and into the wilds."

"And did the bake house lady say anything when you did?"

"Not a word, master. It was the end of the thing, when she retrieved the basket back into the pretty window. Only once when I saw her in the streets.....before the streets were full of wails and the great smell of corpses..... phew! the tanneries and dye-houses were nothing to the stink of the dead, Maria sir......like wagons of rotting fish the smell was, so terrible they said the living monks would not bury the dead monks in the crypts below their prayers, as was their custom.....but in pits with the sinfulest of jakes, jakes that could not tell a prayer from a belch.....molls and drinkers, ha! monk and murderer together I suppose......why, a king could not have bought his way out from those pits, not with his crown, throne and horse.....the best and the most pious tossed together with the worst and the most villainous..... death making a family of the lot of 'em......."

"And when you saw her in the streets, Salvatore, the pretty bake house lady, did she speak with you?"

"Only a few words, master. She asked me if I knew where Brother Maria had gone, and I told her what you told me.....that you had gone into the hills and forests to sing with the bears and wolves. Her words were few, but they told a great story, they and her soft dark eyes, because it was then I knew the beautiful lady loved you, Mister Maria, and that she had given her heart to you, a very sweet and tender heart, as sure as sure can be."

The words were like a knife to Maria's heart. They cut him to the quick, and he looked away. Struggling, he said softly:

"And, Salvatore, when the contagion came, do you remember the collectors collecting the doctor and his daughter, the bake house lady, upon one of their carts?"

"That I do, master Maria, for it was not a week after they threw my poor mama and a sister on one, threw them as they were sacks of flour upon the other corpses heaped in their cart.....and they wrapped as best as I could wrap them, with coats, shirts, bags......and the pickers, thick as crows on a dead sheep, picking at the corpses' necks and ears, their fingers scurrying through the pockets of the dead, like mice at the end of the reaper's row..... and my other sister gripped by the rage and rave of the thing, with the

*swellings and fever, and talking to ghosts in the air....and the streets full of
madness, as the end of the world had come....."*

*.....he did not know why he wanted to know, why he had this blind
compulsion to know.....why he must hear the finality of the words, like the
doom of a death knell in his heart.....why he must hear the words that he
knew would kill him yet again.....that would reverberate through his soul
as long as he had a soul.......*

"And that is when.....the doctor and the beautiful bake house lady....."

*"Yes Mister Maria, that is when they threw the old doctor on another
pile of corpses in a cart one night, shortly after the hooded men took my dead
mother away.....the doctor was a good man, a drinker, but a jolly one, a
very good man with always a crust or a little piece of cheese in his pocket
for me.....I saw the dark-hooded fellows pitch him, pitch him like a pitch
of dung they did.....wrapped and bound like a mummy at the street's edge,
and cart him off behind a wretched nag and a hooded priest swinging a
smoking censer.....the fleecers grabbing at the dead each step of the way.....
like dogs they were......and the bake house lady, with others, weeping and
limping at the cart's side...no doubt to the pits and the brimstone fires
outside the village.......a great sorrow it was for me to see it, the beautiful
bake house lady clinging to the bundle of the dead doctor, and batting the
scavengers away........"*

*"And the bake house lady, the beautiful bake house lady......you saw
them throw her on a dead-cart some time after that?"*

At this Salvatore's animated face became blank, and his chirpy
tongue stopped dumb. He gave Maria a puzzled look.

*"And how long after that.....the bake house lady, Salvatore.....how
long after.....did you see the collectors throw the beautiful bake house lady
on a dead-cart?"*

*"But that they never did, Mister Maria. I thought you knew. The
plague did not take the beautiful bake house lady with the limp. She was
not thrown on a dead-cart and carted to the pits. She is alive, by the Cross
and the Crown, alive as you and me, master Maria!"*

Maria heard the words, but he could not comprehend the words.
His tired heart, his resolution to leave and wander, and perish in his
wandering; he could sustain no such mistake, even in jest. He grabbed
the boy by his collar, and lifting him clean off his feet, pinned him
roughly against the stone wall.

"Boy, I do not like your jest! I liked the lady.....I, I loved the bake house

lady very much! You must tell me….I need to know.....it means everything to me to know…….did you see when they threw her on the dead-cart or not? Was it like you said they threw your mother on the cart, like a sack of flour, or a pitch of dung? For if they did, and I will find out their names..... collectors, pickers, the very priests I'll hang by their balls and send their souls to the fires of hell!'

But the face that Maria had pinned against the wall showed no artifice. His eyes were clear with the boyish soul that shone innocently through them.

"But Mister Maria, it is a thing as honest as I honestly know how to tell; the sickness did not take her. The bake house lady is alive. I thought that is why you play your fiddle so sweetly in the Piazza Lucia each night, a kind of serenade to her…..Katrinika I think the name of the kind sweet lady is."

Maria looked at the innocent face he held pinned against the wall. Slowly the words began to assume a strange meaning, melting his anger to incredulity: *'the sickness did not take her…..the beautiful bake house lady with the limp is alive, alive as you and me'……..*

Maria lowered the boy to the ground, but with his hands on his shoulders, kept him pressed to the wall.

"But the boarded up doors and windows, Salvatore…..no lamps or candles…..no smell of meat or bread, no smoke from the chimney….."

"A strange queer thing, and that is no lie…..but sorrow makes the wisest mad, so they say. She comes from the house at night, though I know not how….does her errands when the cats and owls are about…..then back in again. Lights no lamp or candle; lights no oven and bakes no bread….. as she is content to live in dark and cold……like a proud queen with a broken heart, prepared to die in her defeated castle…..a broken heart, the beautiful bake house lady has I think, a broken heart from the day they threw her father on a cart of corpses…..or maybe from the day you went away, Mister Maria."

Slowly the words sank into his deadness, like a pounding rain into parched dust. Like one waked from the grave, his lips struggled to remember the forgotten speech of the living.

"She is alive?......Katrinika….alive?.....No, yes, it cannot be….."

"She loves you dearly, Master Maria, as I know you love her. But she's willing to die with her love, alone, like a queen in her cold dark castle, for what pity and for what reason I do not know."

Loosening his grip on the boy's shoulders, Maria gently held his face between his two hands. The boy had been left an orphan in the world, as he had once been an orphan. In some way they were brothers; this boy the stronger of the two. His eyes burned with a special brightness, as he was a flower that had survived a killing frost. Gently Maria brought his bearded lips to first one of his cheeks, and then to the other, and then bringing his face to his breast, let fall the warm gush of his tears:

"*She is alive.....Katrinika is alive.....oh dear God, she is alive!......*"

* * *

When Maria returned to the *Sickle Moon*, he went directly to Alberto and Marianna, and asked them if he might take his meal alone in his room.

"*Why of course, of course, the wife will be happy to fix a plate of bread and meat for our fiddler man, and a bowl of soup with beans.....have we any left, my dear?*"

"*You are well, are you not Maria?*"

"*Of course he's well, Marianna. Can you not see the flush in his face and the bluer blue in his eyes? Why, one can see the devil's secrets in eyes as blue as those. Ha! Nowhere to hide the devil's deviltry in such eyes! The hill's a good steep climb, is it not, Maria? Did you good, the spring air and the jaunt up its steep side, did it not?*"

Indeed, Maria did look much more robust, much more *alive* to Marianna also. His eyes sparkled, and he seemed to have regained not only some of his old vigor, but his jocundity as well. But for all of this change, she could not help but think it was a mask worn over a heart that had been violently weeping.

"*And you haven't given other thoughts to your leaving, have you? We want you to stay. The garret's yours, Maria. Ha, I'll make a sign and hang it over the door; 'The Fiddler's Cave' it will say. We're a family, and the little fellow growing in Marianna's tummy will be making his grand entrance soon. I want him to be as much a fiddler like you, as a smithy like me. And the customers are slowly returning. The plague killed better than half of Siena, but has whetted double the other half's thirst, making up for those who have drunk their last. We could use fiddle music to make them laugh and sing.....wake the lust in their loins and the thirst in their throats don't you know.*"

Maria smiled brightly and laughed. Uncharacteristically, he warmly embraced both of them, knelt and petted the cats, and then climbed the steps to his room.

But there was more to this epiphany he had brought from the hilltop, this change that had changed his melancholy into intoxication. As the afternoon waxed, there came sudden moments filled with passionate fiddle music from his room, music that was unlike any of the brief little flourishes he had played to thank his hosts or amuse begging children. The music was poignantly impassioned, ranging from deepest explorations of sadness, to lilting flights of exultation.

The melodies struck deeply, halting all talk and lifting all faces. Marianna's hands stopped their stirring of a spoon in the bowl, the strains reaching deep inside her until, despite being with child, her body quickened, pricked and moistened with the emanations of her sex. Alberto's rough face softened; as a newborn child had been laid in his arms; and he stepped an involuntary step towards the stairs, as his soul had heard an ethereal music. The three men at the table near the hearth froze, crinkled their faces, mindless of the cards they held unprotected from the others' eyes. The two young girls came from a back room, and hugged Marianna's hips as for assurance.

"*Is it Maria, mama? It is so very, very sad. It frightens me.*"

"*No Adrianna, it is very sad, but also very beautiful.*"

"*What kind of music is it, mama?*"

"*It is the music of a man's soul, 'cara mia', the music of a man's soul.*"

Broken from the spell, Alberto turned and winked at his wife:

"*The sun and a climb, does wonders for a man's health, wife. Doeswonders to rouse what sleeps in a man's blood.......*"

But Marianna thought there was more. The music sought out and found depths in her heart where men cannot go; depths that were the sovereign dominion of *Woman*. Never had she heard Maria play such rich melodies full of such *pathos*, not when he had played at weddings or at funerals; not even in the midnight concerts he performed before the derelict bake house. And later when she knocked on his door, and he had opened it to receive his meal, she saw that his table was cluttered with papers, as in a hectic fever of revived passion his soul was divided equally between ink and quill, and the music it was bringing from his fiddle's strings.

That night as she listened at her window, her intuition became certitude. Although his playing in the summer nights had been impassioned, it now reached new heights of stormy rapture and new depths of abject torment; deeper hells and higher heavens of the human heart. Its passion seemed not to cast a spell, but to break all spells, the spells of all dull yesterdays and vague tomorrows, leaving one alone, stunned and trembling, listening to the mystery of one's own heart.

There was another difference in this session. He sang intermittently; lifting his beautiful voice sweetly and boldly into the crisp night air. As in competition to see which of the two could draw most deeply from his soul, he would first play long, yawning strains from his fiddle, and then, as in an attempt to match these strains, he would sing words with a matching poignancy. Marianna remembered his cluttered desk when she had taken him his meal, and knew he was singing words he had newly composed. She also knew that his heart had been touched very deeply; as nothing other than a *woman* may touch a man's heart.

She could not hear all of the words, but those she could, complemented and accentuated the melodies lifting from above the tavern to the attentive stars.

.....Your eyes are in the deep dark river,
And when I bend to kiss them,
I drown in love's illusion,
Swimming like a fish into your arms.......

There were a few lyrics that hinted at the mystery of the story that Maria's strange behaviors had told in inexplicable pieces since his return.

.....O Lady fair, unbind the kerchief
from your hair,
The seven stars sparkle there,
where, in raven glory,
Is told this pilgrim's story, there,
The journey of my heart has been ensnared......

As her husband slept, Marianna listened at the window to this sublime, adventure into the mystery of love's soul; this deeper reach into love's bowels, and its higher one into its dreams. A short while later, as the cathedral was tolling its midnight toll, the passionate ghost stole from the *Sickle Moon*, fiddle in hand; carried at once like a bouquet to an altar, and a saber to war.

The temptation was too great to withstand. Marianna quickly wrapped a shawl about her shoulders, and followed to the *Piazza Lucia*, where again Maria stood before the bake house, and commenced to serenade its boarded up doors and windows.

Like the roar of a wounded lion, the pain in his heart filled the night, a pain loosed from his breast like a flock of swallows. It was as he summed the tears and wails of funerals, and commingled them with the joy and songs of weddings; together telling *the mystery of the human heart.*

A thing unusual about this passionate display of passion: although his fiddle and voice rent the night, they did not disturb it. Here and there Marianna could see sleepers that had awakened from their beds, not to rail at the audacity of this midnight concert, but to be entranced by it. Spellbound, those that stood like statues at doors and on balconies woke to a dream sweeter than any their sleep could give them.

" ......*Oh sweet bird of the night,*
With feathers sparkling bright,
Fly, sweetheart, together with me,
Into the deepest forest trees!
For your ears I have bangles gold,
For your throat, painted shells,
For your ankles, copper bells......
O come to the forests and vales,
We, like brother and sister nightingales,
Shall sing till night and time grow old,
Love's but a warbling brook of song
Sung to the stars, life's secret song to tell!......."

But his melodies and lyrics did not always profess longing and courtship. As this was only a small part of love, he played and sang up and down love's clavier of notes and moods; from the crisis of love's agony to the crisis of its joy; from the courtship beneath love's window, to its grieving at love's grave. Alternating these sentiments, and weaving them into one outpouring of his heart, he stood, played and sang to the bleak stones, boards and rioting ivies before him; even as his fiddle was the magic lamp of a genii; one that contained wailing ghosts, howling wolves, and wounded Angels.

.....*I am dying! The knife of your smile*
Thrust deep into my heart!
O bury its sweetness to the hilt,
That like a rose plucked to adorn,

My song may on your bosom wilt,
If love be not a blossom,
Let it then be the sharpest thorn,
Come to your window,
O sweetest, meekest lover,
Open the shutters of your heart,
If not for me, then for another,
And like a murder in the dark,
Whose swiftest dagger stabs and kills,
Upon your smile, this heart will be impaled.

When, after several hours he had finished his enigmatic courtship, there came the most peculiar thing of all. He removed his worn and tattered coat, the coat he had long wandered in, and proceeded to wrap his fiddle in it; but curiously, not before he tenderly bound it in a yellow cloth, like the bandannas the maids wear in the harvest fields. He placed the bundle on a crate directly beneath the boarded up window, the same window from which bread was once lowered on a pole and basket. Leaving it there, unguarded, only then did he return to his room above the tavern; an inscrutable practice this lovelorn ghost began to repeat every night.

And there his fiddle, wrapped in his bright but much worn coat stayed on the crate through the daytimes. Oddly, if anyone came near to inspect it, or in any way molest it, there came shouts of defense at once from those who lived about the piazza.

"No, do not touch it! It is the gypsy fiddler's coat. It is wrapped about his fiddle! He comes each night to play it before the old bake house. Mad or not, his melodies fill the night, and give us dreams sweeter than those in our sleep. Do not touch it. He will come, the fiddle-playing ghost, to play his sweet madness again.....tonight!"

And so he did return, night after night, pouring out his heart before the deserted edifice smeared with the red crosses of death. The consensus was that he was a victim of the plague, like the plague had made victims of so many others; that it had left him mad, a harmless kind of madness, like the simplemindedness of an ill-gotten child. Soft, sad, sweet, like songs played by a mourning angel, all who lived about the *piazza* anticipated his arrival each night, waking and smiling on their pillows, or silently appearing in nightshirts and gowns; like spirits, conjured from the graves of their sleep; afraid to applaud, lest they disturb the deathless spell.

After these nightly concerts Maria slept late into the day. When he awoke he was quiet, even withdrawn, but his eyes were alive, as with burning coals. Although others now knew of his nightly serenades, none dared ask, or in any way allude to them, as if they were afraid to break the trance that each night gripped him. In addition, one sensed something at work inside him that, like a distant thunder was felt, not heard; as though something else was quickening and swelling; some storm of fury in the depths where brewed such a dark and profound beauty.

On some of the days Salvatore visited the tavern, ragged and dirty, after his day's work with the cobbler. He brought with him his fiddle, and Maria gave him lessons on how to make its strings sing in oneness with the strings of its player's heart; until man and instrument sang in harmony and were one.

"You must love your instrument, Salvatore; you must love it as it was a beautiful woman. You must caress it, like your hands tenderly caress the hills and valleys of her body. You must wake her lovely secrets. You must make her deeply sigh. You must make her want to tell her beautiful mystery."

"But Mister Maria, I have never loved a woman. I am afraid to touch one."

This reply gave Maria pause. He liked the boy's innocent and honest reply. He remembered when he was a boy, when he had looked upon *woman* as a sacred, untouchable thing, a goddess to be adored, not seduced and greedily explored. How many hills and valleys of women's bodies had his hands caressed and adventured over? From how many mouths, like deep wells, and how many wombs, like rich hives had he partaken of love's pleasures? He remembered the shepherdess, and the moment he had first brought the hands of a monk to her woman glory; how it had set his blood afire. He remembered the beautiful melodies her body had yielded, stilling the night and fluttering his heart into a new and wonderful tumult.

Maria smiled at the scraggly, wide-eyed boy, but it was not age smiling at youth in his smile; rather a tired comrade smiling at a fresh one. At that moment the boy seemed every bit his equal, perhaps even his superior; one more wise than he; one that would carry on the quest in which he had failed.

..... Who was closer to life's pulse; dearer to life's Mother? Was he wiser,

after loving hundreds of women, than this boy who had loved none?.......

"Then when you take your fiddle into your hands, Salvatore, you must imagine you are sleeking a beautiful dove, so that it purrs and coos....so that it trusts you, like a pet bird its keeper."

Salvatore brightened.

"That I can, and that I will, master Maria. I'll imagine it is a dove, and I sleeking its soft feathers to make it sweetly coo."

Maria found Salvatore an apt student with a good ear and nimble fingers. He was impressed with the things he had remembered from the brief lessons he had given him years before. After they would play, they would sometimes sit together and talk, as the boy had become Maria's *confidante*, even his dearest friend. And as his friend, Salvatore was sensitive about speaking of Maria's midnight serenades, his fiddle left daylong on the crate, and the great gash in his heart that he knew inspired his beautiful melodies. But after some time, one day Salvatore dared to break this delicate, unspoken sensitivity.

"You know, Mister Maria, there are tunnel-ways below the village, tunnels where our people may escape the Florentines, and other heathen armies that might climb the village walls....they say they were carved out in days before the Caesars, by the Etruscans I suppose. I think, master, that she uses one of these old tunnels. Peeps her head out like a weasel somewhere in the lower part of the village, buys her bread and needs, and then weasels her way back to the bake house. I think that's her trick, Mister Maria..... the trick of a beautiful queen in her defeated deserted castle, to go on living with a great hurt in her heart."

Maria looked away, and was silent.

"She's there, master, she's there. By the Cross, it was surely no lie I told you. She hears your music, and your heart that is in it, I'd bet my fiddle on it."

Maria offered no response. This encouraged his adoring pupil.

"I've smelled meat roasting, I am sure of it, although the chimney is cold and bone dry......and I am sure I saw a candle......."

At this, quick as the flint's spark, Maria turned to him, his eyes burning and riveting.

"A candle!"

"Yes master, a candle. I sometimes see one burning through a crack in a board of one of the boarded up windows.....not the window where the beautiful lady with the red kerchief lowered the bread on a pole, but another

window.......and when the moon is dark, and I stand just in the right......."

"*Always the same window?*"

"*Yes master, the same window and the same cracked board......*"

"*You are sure, Salvatore? You are absolutely sure?*"

"*By the graves of dead men's mothers, I am!*"

"*Will you show me this board and this window Salvatore?*"

"*With gladness, Mister Maria, with gladness I'll show it to you this very night when the dark falls and the stars rise.*"

But when evening came, it came not only with darkness, but with rain and wind, and crouch and crane though they might, neither could catch a glimpse of the candle that Salvatore avowed he had seen. Undeterred by either the harsh weather or his great disappointment, his great hope dashed, but his great love rekindled, Maria resumed his serenade. Like a draggled cat, he stood before the wet bleak boards of the house, bleeding forth his heart.

"*......I will not place you in a cage,*
O dark-eyed doe, O spangled bird,
I will not sprinkle crumbs of words,
Nor bind with strings your little legs.....
Love is no sly dark capture,
But an uncaged rapture,
The song it sings, only with unbound wings......"

The next night shone soft and clear. The new moon hung glimmering in the east, like an earring of pearl; the stars sparkling like dewy clover in the meadows of the night. Insisting to Salvatore that he must go alone to the bake house, Maria once more found his self looking up at the shuttered window, and the cracked board nailed across it.

And there it was! Like a fallen star, the candle's flame, clearly seen through the cracked and splintered board!......its spark lighting all that had become dark and dead inside him, all that had gathered, like dry dead leaves in his heart, its spark setting him ablaze, as it was setting heaven's candles ablaze, its fire shouting: "She is alive, dear God, Katrinika is alive!"

.....this glint of light making this skeleton of boards and stones a living thing.....animating it, giving it a beating heart! Like a giant waking from an ancient swoon, this spark its opened eye, an eye that had forgotten the sling that had felled it, the tiredness of death that had benumbed it.....its blood now enkindled, thrilled with warmth, the warmth of a woman.....a very beautiful, nay, the most beautiful woman!.......

He could not contain his passion. He must go to her! But the window was very high, and there were no footholds of any kind whereby he could climb to it. There was a trellis, yes, a trellis! But it was meant only for the delicate hands of vines, not the heavy feet of men. Crazed with desperation, he cried out:

"Katrinika! Katrinika! My sweet Katrinika! It is Maria! I see your candle in the window, through the crack in the board, I see it! Come to the window my love, like you once did with your gentle dark eyes and your hair bound in a red kerchief......as you did when I called out for the biscuits your dear hands baked..... when like the morning star you appeared! O my love, death has spared both of us! We are both alive! Please Katrinika, sweet angel, I must see you again!"

But his passionate pleas fell on the night's deaf ears, and were rebuked with silence. Only once did the light that stared like a gentle eye through the cracked board blink; as a moth had flitted across the candle's flame; and if not a moth, a body, *her body*!

Yes, she was alive!

"O darling, if I could, I would become a bird that would fly to your window's ledge, and there sing to the bright moon of your face.....or a vine of roses that would climb up this trellis, bringing roses to your hands! Oh Katrinika, it is Maria! I want to tell you many things! I want to tell you how foolish I have been! I want to take you in my arms, and tell you how you have saved me from death!"

But in response to this overture of passion came a disappearance of the candle's flame from the shutter's crack, leaving but blackness; a blackness blacker, deeper, and more unresponsive than darkness; leaving the one who had seen it, unsure if he had seen it at all.

"Please darling.....do not take away your candle.....bring to the window your kerchief and your baskets of bread, your little smiles and your dark eyes wherein dwells the beginning and the end of this world.....the sweetness that is my meaning, life's meaning.....Katrinika! Katrinika! Do not be a ghost! You must not be a ghost! I have wandered too long through a world of graves and corpses for you to be a ghost! Live, Katrinika! You must live! You must not be a ghost!"

Those who had risen from their beds and stepped onto their balconies to know the cause of the disturbance, at once saw that the man circling the deserted bake house, screaming out and beating his fists against its boards, was the fiddler who had delighted them with such sweet concerts.

"*Katrinika! Katrinika! It is me, Maria! I have come back to your arms my love!*"

Those who had been enchanted the summer through with his concerts were now convinced that madness was the muse that had inspired such sweet and soul-stirring melodies.

"*The poor man has gone wild. He has been touched by the distemper, a touch that has not gone away. He will never own a right mind again.*"

"*His wits are no longer his. He speaks to ones who are no longer alive.*"

"*There are many like him; those that speak to the air and wander among the streets and graves, made simple and silly by the plague's curse......*"

"*He calls out a woman's name, 'Katrinika', over and over again, but only the old sot, half mad himself since the wars.....and his crippled daughter lived in the bread house.*"

"*Katrinika was the cripple's name; the girl who always lowered bread from the window with a pole and basket.*"

"*A sweet girl.....shy and simple, but a sweet girl was the bake girl with a limp. A sad thing, a very sad thing that she was carted with her father to the pits.*"

"*My husband went for the constables.....they will be here shortly......*"

"*I am not sure a dead-cart took the crippled bread girl.....I am not sure that the sickness alighted on her at all.*"

"*He is a drunk man.....*"

"*......perhaps, but I think more mad than drunk from 'the Mortality'.....*"

"*.....The Lord God protect us all......*"

"*.....I will never miss devotions again.....*"

"*More mad than drunk I say, mad as a frothing dog he is.....needs a chain and muzzle, or to be driven clean from the village for such a ruckus. I've a notion to break the mad creature's fiddle over my knee if he leaves it again.*"

"*But see, the men have reached him, wrestling and pinning him to the wall.*"

Indeed a group of four or five men, some in their nightshirts and caps had reached Maria, pinning his shoulders to the bake house wall. But they found this raucous one neither drunk nor difficult to constrain. He was weeping, but so strangely the men did not know if his tears came from happiness or sorrow. He did not try to resist or break free from their restraining arms. He seemed rather to welcome them, crazily mumbling midst his sobs:

"*She is alive! She is alive! My angel is alive! She will heal the great gash the bear made in my side.....I saw her candle, the candle in the window!*"

The men, seeing that his faculties had fled with madness or grief, not drink, and was perhaps one of the many lingering, demented victims of the sickness, tried to console him; some even circling and inspecting the dark, solidly boarded up house to give mettle to their words.

"*There is no one living in the house, sir. The sickness took them away. See how the doors and windows are boarded shut, and the large scarlet crosses, as they painted on all of the houses in which the plague breathed its fumes. All who once lived here live here no more. They are dead, the Lord God have mercy on their souls.*"

Without a struggle, Maria wept in their arms, and tried to convince them, as well as his self of what he had seen.

"*But I saw the candle, her candle in the window. Perhaps she is coming down the stairs, even now.....the stairs I climbed so many times to the milk and biscuits she left on the table for me.....you see the bear clawed my side.....the bear and Katrinika, the bake girl, the angel in the window..... but I threw the bear-tamer in the cage, and the bear tore him apart......and I ate my mother's heart, and it was sweet as the sweetest honeycomb......as it was a sacrifice I was giving the wind and sun.....and I ran into darkness and death.....and I saw my mother smiling through her eyes, her dark eyes smiling from the window with the green boxes and the red flowers.......*"

The men, compassionate with his grief and the great sorrow left in his blasted wits, spoke gently to him.

"*There are no candles, sir, and no windows in which one could see a candle burn in this house. It is a death house. It is deserted and condemned. And there is no lady; and if there was, no door she could open, no window from which she could lower baskets of bread.*"

"*Death visited the house, sir, and the priests sprinkled holy water upon it, and then came men that boarded its doors and windows, and others that painted the red crosses and red letters upon it. These things I saw with my own eyes.*"

"*The plague has left all of us with great hurts and sorrows, great hurts and sorrows heavier than death itself.*"

"*But the candle, I saw a candle.......*"

"*The death and its fevers have left much mischief behind, tricked the mind into seeing what is not there......*"

"*Many see dead loved ones that others do not see, ghosts that haunt the soul.....their stuff made of dream and sorrow, not the flesh of men...."*

Shortly thereafter the constable, flanked by several deputies arrived. They recognized at once the good-natured gypsy who had played a fiddle at the *Sickle Moon*, and compassionating with his delusional state, they escorted him back to his lodging above the tavern. Seeing that he was lost in dreams, but causing no real dangerous disturbance, they did not arrest him. Maria offered no resistance, only now and then muttering midst the shivering of his tears:

"She is alive.....Katrinika is alive, the queen in her cold castle.....oh, the candle in the window, there was a candle in the window....."

Afterwards the posse went to the home of Alberto and Marianna. Knocking on their door and waking them in the late hour, they explained the sad and enigmatic thing they had been called to.

"He is like a dog waiting for his dead master to come home. He pounds against the boards nailed across the doors and windows of the deserted bake house, and calls out for the dead crippled girl.....I think her name was Katrinika.....a simple common girl, one with a lovely, but unusual name, as from another land......the girl who baked bread in the ovens each morning."

This was followed by one of the deputies.

"It is a true thing Umberto says. I was a collector. Most of the corpses were wrapped in rugs or blankets, but I am sure the girl with the limp was one I threw upon the cart, as was her father the old doctor."

This was followed by another deputy's interjection.

"It is a sad thing that so many lost their minds in the plague. It is a sad thing, but also a very strange thing with the fiddler man.....a very strong and robust man calling out to the ghost of one who limped and was full of shyness.....and he with the reputation of enjoying the favors of any 'belladonna' that winked at him, or he at them."

The days after the dramatic incident found Maria much changed. The vivacity that had awakened in him, once more moodily retracted to his former taciturnity. He was rarely seen, and when seen, he rarely spoke, even to Marianna. He did not eat in the tavern, but alone in his room. Many opined about his retreat; among them, Alberto.

"The poor fellow has been shamed, humiliated by the spectacle he has made of himself, and that before many whose eyes saw and whose tongues wag. Either that, or the plague has caged his mind in dreams. After all, wife, we do not know the horrors that Maria has seen, and perhaps the horrors

he has committed. Something has blasted his wits....made him speak to the air....pound his fists like a madman against boards....serenade the ghosts of poor cripple girls.......his wits, wife, his wits.....perhaps little more than porridge now, as poor as porridge and no more."

Still, Marianna was not certain that some secret grief had not left Maria so altered. Occasionally he spoke to Salvatore, alone in his room, and once, climbing the stairs with the pretense of cleaning them, Marianna listened as best she could.

"But you are sure, completely sure you saw her in the piazza below?"

"It was her, Mister Maria, true as wheat it was."

"But did you see her face, her pretty face? It shines like a moon peeking from a cloud."

"Her face was hidden by a hood and a scarf wrapped about it, master..... to protect her from the sights and fumes of death, for when I saw her, or was very sure I saw her, death was in its fiercest rage."

"Was there a limp in her step?"

"That there was, Mister Maria, that there was.....but then again, the sickness did many terrible things.....many of those it did not kill, it left crippled and mangled.....there were, and still are many who limp and drag......."

"And the candle, Salvatore, the candle in the window? Are you sure you saw a candle?"

"I was sure until you asked me if I was sure, Mister Maria. But, well, when I heard tell you had returned, and remembering the note you had asked me to give the lady in her biscuit basket.....and, well, it was but a flicker I saw through the crack in the board....."

"Are you perfectly sure you saw the candle, Salvatore?"

"And I knowing such a thing would so greatly please you, and I wanting nothing more than to play a fiddle like your gypsy self one day......and the stars bright as diamonds on the cold nights, the belt and sword of the Soldier Stars hanging on the peak of the bake house.....as they were candles themselves.....like the little candles that the folk carry to the churches on the holy nights........"

"How many times did you see the candle Salvatore?"

".....but you see, Mister Maria, I so wanted the feet of folks to dance to my fiddle like you made them dance......I thought I saw it.....I wanted to see it...but whether I saw it a hundred nights, or only once, or not at all is now a confusion to me.....a kind of muddle made a muddle by my love for you, master......"

Although Maria displayed no more midnight tantrums about the boarded up house in the *Piazza Lucia*, he continued to frequent it. Love had sown *hope* into his heart, but it had also sown *doubt*. For long hours he stood beneath the same window. He imagined it was the closed eyelid of a dead angel; one that had only flickered briefly open, but distraught with the dismal tale of this world, had closed again.

Had he seen a candle, or had 'love', with all its mischief enkindled it in his imagination? Like a kitten with a ball of string, was love playing with his heart, cuffing it back and forth with its soft paws, entangling it into knots that never could be disentangled? Salvatore had spoken true. The stars kissed the rooftop thatches near the window.....Could it have been the sparkle of a star, and not the spark of a candle that had caught the corner of his eye? Salvatore wanted to please him, and he knew that the bake girl owned a piece of his heart.

And there were those who attested they had seen the bundled up corpses of both the bake girl and her father cast on dead-carts with the thousands of others; and with these, those that had boarded up the house, and painted the red letters and crosses on its doors during death's visitation. And the tunnels that were reputed to spread like a spider's web beneath the city?.....This at least was true, for the ancients had been workers in stone, and many of the villages and cities had had their bowels carved out for protection from their enemies, as well as the storage of their oil and wine.....But were they still passable, or caved and crumbled impossibly shut? And if they were, how could one find his way through their deserted, subterranean maze?

Again and again he circled the old walls, now resigned to boards and strangling ivy; always ending where he had begun: the window with the cracked board nailed across it. He remembered this window. It was one of the windows in the room where he had been bedridden, where he had convalesced in the care of the old doctor. He remembered when the shutters were thrown open, and the sun shone brightly through them.....the terra-cotta roofs of the village, and the sun buttering them, like loaves of bread tumbling tawny-gold to the lower part of the village.....the emerald sea of meadows and forests stretching to the blue sky beyond. He remembered the clouds, the bell-towers, the swooping swallows.....and Katrinika, unconscious of being looked upon, standing before the splendid vista, as she was the maiden mother of it all.

.....Had he seen a candle, or had he not? And had he been a fool, or had he not been a fool with his desertion from the abbey, his wandering, his

life, foolishly believing his soul's salvation lived in women's eyes and smiles and kisses?.......

Confused and disconsolate, Maria no longer sang in his midnight visits to the bake house painted with death's crosses. In his nightly *concertos* he would only offer a heartbreaking, soul-piercing melody from his fiddle, one that his listeners condoned, attributing it to his pathetic lunacy; even as it stirred their hearts with remembrances of their own losses, their own lunacy as they had watched death parade through their village.

Only once did Maria cry out to the boards and stone-work of the old edifice, not with song, rather with a poetry of pain alone; with words whose nakedness pierced the hearts that heard them even more deeply than had the passionate melodies of his fiddle; words that froze the hearts of all that heard; that stilled the night to a deeper stillness.

"*.....Oh, if you are a ghost,*
I will tear out my heart,
And plant it in your breast,
That you may know
Again the earth and all its charms......
Or, if you wish,
I will stab it with a knife,
Quitting this world of the sun,
Content to be a ghost
Longing through death for your arms......"

. . . .

. . . .

CHAPTER THIRTEEN

THE CANDLE IN THE WINDOW

Part II

AS summer began to close, these strange nocturnal performances came to an end. The candle did not re-appear; neither in a boarded up window, nor in the stars that kissed a rooftop; nor in the wistful love of a lover's imagination. There was no Katrinika; or if there was, there was only a ghost of a Katrinika that did not want to show itself; as Salvatore had said, a queen who wanted to be left alone in the cold castle of her sorrows.

During the day Maria was regarded as one who had been permanently touched by *the sickness*, much like the one that had once stabbed him in an alley. Passing Maria by with his twisted jowl and strange smile, Maria wondered if in truth he had begun to mirror this fellow's idiotism; if he too had become a queer plaything, a kind of mongrel in the hands of madness. He became distrustful of glances and greetings, even consolations he received from others. It was time to leave; to wander, to dream a few last dreams. It was time to grow old and mad, perhaps become giddy with both. It was time to die.

One evening Maria retired very early to his room. Having told no one of his determined plans, he wrote a letter of heartfelt gratitude to his benefactors, and left it on his neatly ordered bed. He packed his fiddle, along with his few belongings in his satchel, and when the cathedral bell tolled its twelve somber tolls he left, even as the ghost he felt he was, with the firm resolution of never returning.

There was only one last thing he must do; one last thing that would take him to the *Piazza Lucia*, and the skeleton of boards painted with red crosses. But it was not to play his fiddle with the deepest melodies of his heart, nor was it to circle its deserted castle over and over, looking for the spark of a queen's candle through a cracked board, all the while imagining a sweet face whose dark eyes, like a warm rain had once melted the cold places in his soul.

Tonight he went directly to the house's rear entrance, the entrance he had used so many times before; the entrance painted with a blood-red cross and the terrible letters that he had painted over with his own words; the entrance boarded against life's intruder, as if death's handiwork was too horrid for men's eyes to see. Maria set his satchel on the ground, removed the crowbar he had stolen from Alberto's forge, and wedging its iron tooth beneath the foremost of the thick rough boards, began to pry away death's ribs.

And as one by one the nails began to be uprooted, and the boards surrendered to the iron tooth of his insanity, Maria remained calm; calm and lucid; as madness had fully embraced, and become indistinguishable with his reason. Locked in each other's arms, they had forfeited their differences, becoming the best of friends; becoming one.

He wanted to know.....no, he 'must' know. But what must he know? He must know if he saw a candle, yes, a candle in a window......if there was a biscuit and warm milk waiting for him.....and a sweet smile and dark eyes.....or if they had been cast with thousands of nameless, faceless others by an uncaring God into the cold uncaring earth......if a bake girl with a red kerchief, a red kerchief that matched the red geraniums in summer flowerboxes, and the blood-red crosses smeared on countless doors....if such a one had been a ghost, or an angel that had led him through death........

.....but more, he must know if his love was an apparition or a thing of flesh.....a creature with burning loins, prayerful hands and a bleeding heart.....if love was a substance, or only an indulgence.....a wine or a perfume......if his heart owned a meaning, or was only a silly show on a stage.....a skirted bear dancing in a street for bits of fish and the hoots of drunkards.......

.....still more.....as the nails were extracted, and the boards fell to the ground.....he must know if the clouds, hills and forests were 'real'....or only a dream in which man is born to wander, and wandering, die without waking from that dream....He must know if pretty words and pretty melodies had painted over madness, not only with red crosses, but with a

red kerchief and red flowers.....and if it had.....if death had strangled this sweet child of the heart, tossed it on a cart, shoveled it over with dirt, burned it with brimstone......if death had played this trick, this trick called 'love' on him, sending a shy doe from a forest of shadows.....if this same cruel trickster would permit him to step upon a stool, hang in its web, and be the brother of all fools.......

With a great lunge of his body and hit of his shoulder the hinges rattled, and with a second lunge and hit, they rattled more, but still held, still unwilling to admit life's intruder. Encouraged at their weakness, the third and hardest hit of his shoulder broke the jams, and the door surrendered. Without a candle, only that one in his heart, Maria began to climb the dark flight of steep stairs he had climbed so many times before.

.....let him be arrested as a vandal or a madman, but he must know..... he must drink these memories one more time.....these voices and fragrances, these dreams that lingered between the dead and the living like the trail of a perfume...

.....the creaks and loose boards he knew so well, kissing his feet like the cheeks of flowers......smelling the smells of bread, meat, plum wine.....no, those were memories, only memories.....but now a candle's smoke, as if newly snuffed.....not a memory, this, but a thing not mistaken, not disguised with the wiles of delusion, the dreams of the mind......a candle's smoke the tracks of a ghost that is not a ghost.....and then more piquant, more poignant, the intangible, salty smell of the living.....the acrid sweet perfumes of its flower that its flower cannot conceal.....the secretions of life, of its very heart....the perfume of flesh, a perfume called 'woman'.......

Attaining the top of the stairs, he whispered into the darkness:

"Katrinika! My love, Katrinika!"

But the darkness and the silence refused to relinquish any secret they might be harboring.

.....like a proud queen with a broken heart, prepared to die in her cold, defeated castle.......

Maria began to explore, one by one the rooms he knew so well; navigating through the darkness unaided by a candle, a sprinkle of starlight.....and yet exploring each room as he was holding a lamp.

"Katrinika, dear one, I am sure you are here. I saw your candle, and I can feel the beating of your heart. Yes, I can feel it beating because it is one with my heart, as it has always been one with my heart. Darling, be not

afraid, it is Maria. I have returned to take care of you. I have returned to take you away, and to give you happiness after so much sorrow."

But his words, as if spoken in a crypt, received no reply.

"Be not afraid my love. If the plague has hurt you, I will take care of you, as you once cared for me. Death has wounded me also. It has left me mad and lonely, mad and lonely and longing for only you. Please, I need you. I need you to tell me if I am a man, or a ghost wandering in a dream… if life is real, or only a dream that has woven all in its web…..if there is a flower that flowers a preciousness from the bones and skulls of this world."

He moved from room to room, both upstairs and downstairs, as he was a ghost native to their darkness…..and yet not a true darkness, for this darkness possessed a faint light, a light so faint it was not light at all but a lesser quality of darkness; one that called upon something the eye could not reach, that its organ was denied; something that was man's before he was a creature of the plow and the winepress; when his sight was as much of his soul as his eyes, guiding him, like no stars could guide him through the night.

…..Was this love? Yes, yes, this was that ancient hunt, that ancient need that men, emerging from the forests called 'love'…..that called and guided them, spoke to their loneliness…..that was blind, but could see in its blindness…..even in darkness….even in death……..

…..there, seeping from beneath the door…..the kitchen door where the ovens had been, where the bread had been once baked…..a faint light, like a frost or a dew…..but why was there light? He had heard of vagrants occupying houses of the dead…..scavengers that preyed like rats upon their properties, making camps where death had visited……..the scurrilous and dispossessed, like dogs gone feral, who had ceased owning a reverence for either the dead or the living…….

Maria opened the door, and stepped into the large open room. It was indeed lighted, but only faintly; by one tallow candle burning in the middle of an otherwise bare table. The two ovens were cold, and gave the feeling they had long stood so. Their mouths stared at him like the eyes of skulls.

The room was as he had remembered it: neat and clean, with a great order spread upon it. It had no signs of being ransacked; of being a thief's den or villain's hideaway; but neither did it have a sign of the living, other than its cleanliness and the lone candle. Only the silence that filled it seemed heavy with threat, as from something trapped, something brooding; like the silence that gathers and sulks, silently fomenting its poisons before a storm.

Tenderly Maria whispered into that strange silence.

"Katrinika, it is Maria. I know that you are alive, sweetheart, and that has made me happy, yes my love, very happy."

They were words that elicited no response, and yet standing near the table and the candle he felt the silence listening, and listening, quicken. After a long moment, he whispered again.

"Sweetheart, Katrinika, I have not forgotten you, but you see I was afraid that you had forgotten me.....even that you hated me.....but I so want to see you, to talk with you, even if just for......."

And then the scream and the lunge of the attacker, and the knife raised in the uplifted hand.....and the wrist that Maria held frozen above his head until, weakened midst the deadly poise of its strength, it fell on the stones of the floor.....and after several bounces at his feet, like a flailing fish, lay cold and still of its murderous intent......

Loosed and recoiling a step from his grip, the attacker looked at Maria with wild dark eyes, eyes that burned through long disheveled hair with the savage hurt and loneliness of one who has been abandoned by the living, an abandonment that had filled it with a starvation of want and need;; as a prisoner in a lightless dungeon.....*a queen in a cold dark castle.....*

"Katrinika!"

But the one he had once known as Katrinika had grown deaf to the tone of tenderness, perhaps even to her name. Exhilarated with her fury, a fury fed by untold horrors, she lunged at him again, not with a knife, but with her fists, flailing them upon his chest, all the while screaming:

"I hate you! I hate you! I want to kill you! I want you dead like my father is dead, like all the others they threw on carts and carted to the trenches are dead! I want you to be picked apart by birds and dogs like they were picked apart by birds and dogs! I want to throw you in a hole of corpses with my own hands!"

Like breakers crashing on rocks, she pounded on his chest with swell after swell of her fury, a fury dredged from the darkest deeps of sorrow, from the dark bed of death itself, until her fists, unable to hold such inhuman wrath, could pound no more. She stood away; panting, flushed and deranged, the wildness in her heart glaring wildly from her eyes, as if pausing for a next attack. In that pause, Maria attempted to speak to her.

"I know you have been greatly hurt, darling, and I am part of that hurt. But now I want to take you away, and live in a forest, a quiet forest full of songs and flowers.....to watch the moon and the seasons pass through our souls, together......oh, after so much death, let us share a little happiness together!"

Maria stepped towards her, offering to take her into his arms. But her madness was too wildly proud to be coddled or consoled. Quickly she bent down, and with cat-quickness reached for the knife, but not before Maria's boot was upon it, at which she shrieked, as by one who had been denied the key that could free his soul from hell.

She recoiled, shaking as with seizure, her hair disheveled and her eyes unnaturally wild, in fits turning to white pearls as they rolled up in her head. Without a place to go, or a weapon with which to kill, without the faculties to restrain the monster of her passion she began to crazily whirl in circles, tearing at her hair and beating her breast, venting moans that were part shriek and part howl, as her spirit was no longer her own; as it had become a dying animal's; as it was a creature now made forfeit to both life and death.

Amazed, Maria watched her whirl in place, her sound leg the pivot around which her crippled one dragged and loped. But he did not try to interfere with her craziness. It seemed a thing not to be disturbed, its madness a kind of sacred ritual; one being performed for the dead as well as the living; not to invoke, but to rebel against a God that had dealt such unspeakable horrors upon His children. Through her both the dead and the living were crying: *"Why?! Why?! Why?! O bloody, murderous God, why?!"*

Only when finally she ceased to whirl, and stood helpless with dizziness and utter exhaustion before him, did Maria take her in his arms. But even then she did not want to succumb to his kindness, as if only her body, not her soul was defeated. With her face buried in his chest, she spoke as through clenched teeth, teeth that wanted to eat through his ribs and gnash apart his heart.

".....the moans and the wails.....the carts and the hooded collectors..... the thieves and the pickers and the crows.....and the bell that would not stop clanging.....night and day.....in our sleep and dreams.....as it was the heart of death beating in our own breasts......"

".....yes, but now the bell has stopped, and the darkness has passed.....

the sun shines, and we may live again......."

".....as it was the end of the world.....as the world had become a place only to die, and not to live......"

".....it has passed, it has passed.....the flowers are once more blooming in the meadows and the forests......"

".....and I had sent you away into death......"

"......no, something in my heart, something I could not live with sent me away......."

"I hate you! I hate you! O, I so hate you! And I hate myself for so loving you!"

To which Maria softly replied, running his fingers through the sweaty tangles of her hair.

"And Brother Maria hates Brother Maria for not knowing that he loved you the first time he saw you; and ever since, ever since."

And there they stood, in an embrace that was meant to kill as much as it was meant to love....as much a fire as a gentle rain......loneliness, fear and abandon slowly falling away, and in their place sending roots of a first tenderness into the other's heart......madness becoming sane, wildness becoming tame.....untold pain and untold anguish softening, sweetening to a renewal......these tender roots reaching, taking hold.....gripping, suckering, intertwining.....an embrace interminable, timeless......whether a moment or an hour, working its ageless miracle.......

....and at last the whispers that were not afraid of that miracle, but embraced it.......

"But the others, the many others with light feet, shapely hips and pretty faces, that give you their kisses, and their lovely bodies to play with......"

"But none has my heart, because you have had it always, always."

"But beauty has countless faces behind its veil, and there will always be another....."

Maria knelt down, picked up the knife at their feet, and then standing, wrapped her fingers tightly about its hilt.

"But only one has parted the veil that has hung over my heart. If you do not believe me, then take my heart. Cut it out, and cast to the dogs. I have no use of it, if it cannot sing for you."

Casting the knife away, she pressed her face deeply into his breast, like a child intent on finding a deeper place in its pillow. Full of sobs, the sweetness of her words pierced his heart as could no sword.

"How could I, when you have stabbed my heart with a knife of flowers?"

Maria then spoke to her as he had always wanted to speak to her, with the language of his youth, the language of his soul; the language his mother had given him; the language he was sure she knew too.

"*I have wandered through heaven and hell to find you.*"

.......Am ratacit prim rai si iad sa te gasesc.......

And she answered, even as he knew she would, with the same beautiful music of her heart.

"*Come my love, fill my arms. I have waited since the beginning. It is our destiny to be one. I love you dearly, forever.*

.......Saj aves; mangraves, O trajo amaro. Khetanes si sinado.

Zorales Tut kamav......."

......two new brooks, at last melting racing free.....singing the same music, the same poetry of their souls.......

"*How did you know?*"

"*Your father told me. He told me that your mother was beautiful, dark-eyed and dark-haired, glittering from her ears to her toes with paint and jewels.....that she was a lover of song and dance.....that she had once traveled with a wandering tribe of kettle-makers, star readers and bear tamers. And there was the 'cobza', the beautiful 'cobza'.....it sang like no other in my arms.....and your eyes, the dark wells of your eyes that spoke the deepest poetry of my heart.....the deepest poetry of my beginning.*"

Katrinika lifted her face, and taking his bearded cheeks tenderly between her hands, stood on her toes, and as with the gift of her soul brought her lips to his; a simple kiss that paled the tawdriness of passion; one that she had saved, like the hive saves its golden honey the winter through; honey made from a thousand summer flowers.

She pressed her face again into his chest, and as Maria stroked her long hair, whispered:

"*If I own your heart, you must allow me to share it. It would be selfish to keep its songs and courage for myself. They are too sweet to covet. I want to give its dreams to other dreamers and wanderers.*"

"*Yes, we shall have children. We shall give them both of our hearts, and they shall journey beneath the moon and sun, and sing of the dreams of men.*

But we must first go to our people. Tomorrow I will leave. But I will return before the dark of the moon."

"*And I?*"

"*Prepare to leave. We will go to our people, the 'zganes'. I know where they are encamped, many hills and rivers from here. They are our brothers and sisters. They will welcome us. They are our home. They are our destiny."*

"And tonight?"

"It will be our wedding night. I will make a fire, as before, when you stepped into the firelight like a doe from the forest, and I was mastered by your beauty and your sweetness; when my heart became yours forever."

"I will wash and comb. I will dress with necklaces and earrings, and a bright skirt and scarf. I will come to you by the fire, not as a doe of the forest, but as a 'tzigan', a 'tzigan' that is your bride."

"Yes; and we will dance before the window, with your mama's and papa's ghosts before the window."

"And you must play and sing for our wedding.....I have kept the beautiful 'cobza'.....my mother will sing through the beautiful 'cobza'.

"Yes; she will sing of the forests and the hills, and the season of our love."

* * *

MARIA did not leave on the following day; or the next. He found it impossible to leave the arms for which he had voyaged through death. Never had he so loved, for never had he been so loved.

It was on the third day, before dawn, that he walked through the streets and out the lugubrious gates; like doors blasted from their hinges by incensed giants. He told Katrinika that he had preparations to make for their journey, and that he would be gone for a week, perhaps more. Katrinika did not ask questions. She knew he would return to her. She trusted him; her *blood* trusted him; not only as the man who had made her a woman, but as the lost brother of her kind.

The preparations that Maria needed to make amounted to the beggaries and thieveries he could successfully make. He had no money, and what little Katrinika had would be needed in other ways. He needed to beg and steal their provisions.

He walked away from the village on the main road, and after a half day's walk, he changed to a much smaller one that broke crookedly from off it. He knew this road, and by early afternoon he reached a farm he also knew. Tumbledown and in shambles, it was a familiar scene that Maria knew all too well. Standing before the sagging, weed choked house, a thin wisp of smoke struggling from its chimney, he shouted out:

"Halloo! Halloo from a friend! God bless this house and all who live

beneath its roof! Does one named Dorothea live here? I am Maria, Brother Maria, the gypsy man who once played his fiddle at the 'Sickle Moon Tavern'. May the Virgin and the Saints bless all who live under this roof.....I wish only a piece of bread, and perhaps a few words with an old friend."

The degeneration of the house was familiar, and so was the silence that responded to his salutation; a silence full of wariness and distrust, born of untold fear, suffering and morbidity. After a long stillness, one in which no dog barked or chicken clucked, he shouted out again.

"May the Virgin and the Saints bless this house, and all the good souls who live in it! I once knew a lady, years ago, a lady named Dorothea who lived......."

Maria's words were stopped short by the opening of the door, and the emergence of an old woman; gray, cruelly bent and shuffling. Propped upon a stick cane, she stood upon the stoop as one who could only vaguely hear and see, or who was daft with age; as one who had risen from the grave. After a pause, she whispered faintly:

"Dorothea, yes, there was a Dorothea who once lived here."

Seeing that the old woman posed no threat, and that she was probably no longer in possession of her faculties, Maria approached her in a friendly way.

"You say that she once lived here, grandmother? Perhaps the plague.....I am sorry, it was terrible, yes, like the world had come to an end, and that end was the mouth of hell.....perhaps you are her mother, eh, and death robbed you of your beautiful daughter, the daughter I once knew and danced with.....made her heels skip beneath the pelts, ploughs and casks in the tavern rafters......"

The old woman, unable to straighten her severely hooped spine, worked either a bitter sneer, or the crescent of a droll smile upon one half of her mouth, probably the only half that was still alive, and shot a shy, but sharp, sidelong glance, like the eye of a pike at Maria.

"Maria, Brother Maria....."

"Yes, my name is Maria, like the Mother of our Savior, yes dear grandmother, 'Maria'..... and I once knew your beautiful daughter, Dorothea, before the great death came."

The old woman, slow to reply, lifted one eye to Maria, its keen, hawk-like stare holding him fixedly.

"I am Dorothea. I am the beautiful one whose heels you made skip about the barrels, on the oyster shell floor of the Sickle Moon Tavern."

Maria looked more closely at the old, horribly disfigured figure standing before him. Yes, incredibly, it was true; she was the woman he had once played many erotic games of adulterous love with, her vivacity and voluptuousness broken and twisted now to a pathetic decrepitude.

Seeing that his astonishment had frozen his tongue, she once more offered her half dead smile to Maria, and said:

"You see one night I heard a fiddle play a sweet melody beneath my window. I thought it was the gypsy of the 'Sickle Moon Tavern' who had come to make love to me. But it was another gypsy. It was a gypsy called 'death'. It was 'death' who wandered to my door and seduced me with the tune of his fiddle. It was 'death' that I held tight in my arms. It was 'death', masquerading as 'love', that made passionate love to me; whose embraces did this to me.

Come inside, Maria. I am very glad to see you. I am alone now, and as you can see I can no longer play; but we shall talk, yes, we shall have a nice talk."

She had been made a widow by *the sickness*. Although she had been stricken, she had survived, and her mind was left lucid enough to tell of it. With a mouth part dead, and one eye that was frozen open in a blind glassy stare, and the other that squinted keenly, as if compensating for the loss of its blind twin, she told her story to Maria.

"Two of the children were the first to swell and fever, and the most painful to watch die. It was brief. The blotches and the tumors came upon them, and they began to smell terribly, so that it was difficult to be near them.....but my husband and I told them they would be well again. We lied to them. We knew the tokens were death's warrant, and they were riddled by them.....being eaten alive by them.....their midsections, throats, armpits, and though we lanced and bled them.....applied pastes and poultices..... no, it was too late. Writhing and retching together in the same bed, on the third day the tumors began to swell monstrously, to choke and strangle them, and though they begged for water in their burning fevers, their tongues had swollen so that they could not swallow a drop. They were brave. They told us they would wait for us at Heaven's gates, that they would not enter without us. We wrapped them in blankets, and my husband buried them, digging graves for them in the garden.

The eldest son, made crazy with fear, ran off, and has never returned. I do not know if the sickness caught and strangled him, if beneath some bush he died, and he was found by the carters or the birds.....or somewhere in some corner of the world he is still alive. Each day I pray for him.....one-eyed and one-handed as I am.....ha, my one eye not closing even for sleep.....I count my beads there in the corner, before the oil lamp and the icon...but I am sure I pray for bones, or maybe a ghost.....at best a criminal, for he was always mean-spirited, the devil in his heart, like his mother I suppose.......

We were left alone, my husband and I. And though we thought we had escaped the contagion's rage, our spirits were broken with the loss of our children....left barren in our age. But one day as my husband worked in the fields he suddenly fell to his knees and violently retched. He left his plough standing in the middle of the field.....I think it is still there.....and struggled into the house, with death flaming through his blood and shooting from his eyes. Shortly both of us were stricken, and helplessly, in two beds, we watched each other turn to monsters of boils, blotches and swellings.... unable to minister, or even console the other's dying.

My husband was made crazy by the fever's fire. He spoke to ones I could not see.....he no longer knew who or what I was, sometimes shrieking out that I was a devil come to take him to hell. The distemper owned him, and I became afraid of him. One day he ran from the house, naked, screaming that he would finish plowing the field. But the plough did not move in the field. Weeks later, after the sickness had left me the mangled thing you now look upon, I found my husband hanging from a rafter in the barn.....a good man, a good man I did not deserve, nor love properly, for as you know, Maria, I gave myself to other men behind his good, hardworking back."

Maria listened attentively to each word of her story. When she had finished, she cast the squint of her one eye at him, and with a slyness that the plague had not killed, asked:

"And Maria, my sweet Maria, what of you? As you can see, I can no longer play games with you in a hayloft, but 'the great death' did not find the soft place in my heart I still have for you. Tell me why the gypsy fiddler has come to my door after these many years."

Maria told her his story briefly, but without touching on his wandering through the plague's horrors. Her soul had drunk death's fumes and seen death's grisly handiwork. She, and he, had looked death in its cold unpitying eye. He merely said:

"Death and dying were everywhere; in the forests, in the villages, in the cities. It was terrible. As the sun had been eaten by locusts, the earth no longer seemed the earth, but a darker, lower realm......as if hell was purging, regurgitating its horrors into the world of the sun."

Briefly he told her about his return to Siena, Marianna, and the *Sickle Moon*. He told her of Salvatore, and his midnight serenades before the boarded up bake house. He told her of Katrinika, and his wish to join his wandering people with her. He told her of his penury and his needs for the journey. He told her he loved Katrinika very much, as he had loved no other.

At this Dorothea's one eye softened, and welled with a tear, a tear that Maria wanted to drink, as in its drop was a rain that would make flower every flower in a garden. With that tear the terribly mangled woman managed a compassionate reply from her half dead mouth.

"I remember that girl. I bought loaves from her. She was very sweet, and I think very pretty, although she seemed to take pains to disguise her prettiness. I think she was a virgin, a virgin that her father jealously guarded for the right man, or shall I say for the right 'gypsy'? I am very happy for her, as I am very happy for you, Maria. Death comes one day, bearing his sickle, as smug as he is grim. But when he does, my dear, you must laugh at the bloody old bastard. Let him eat out his heart with jealousy for the treasure you hold in your arms, and that he will never own.

Of course I will help you with the things you need: food, blankets and the rest. But not with the horses. I have no horses. When my husband died the wolves came, and frightened them into the fields. They killed and ate them, and the goats, sheep and chickens as well. Thieves ransacked the barn of all tools, saddles and harness-work. I cannot help you with horses, saddles or bridles. You must steal them. I am sure that will be easy for you. I remember you talking to horses at the inn, speaking to them tenderly, even as you spoke to your lovers; even as you once spoke to me.

You may stable your stolen horses in my barn. And of course I will prepare provisions; presents for you and your gypsy bride."

* * *

Maria was good to his word. Two weeks later he returned to Siena under the cover of darkness, just as the new moon was appearing. Warbling like a night bird below a window, the window where now he saw the spark of a candle in the crack of the board, Katrinika silently opened the door. After love's embraces, she asked him:

"Will we leave tomorrow? I have packed my few things.....among them the jewelry and amulets that my mother gave me when I was small. I will

take nothing more. You are my treasure. I have waited for you forever, and now that I have you, all that I held dear is of no use to me.....this bake house on a hill is now a mound of straw, a mansion for memories and ghosts to moan and wander in. I can feel my father's smile, and hear his whisper in my heart: "Yes Katrinika, yes my daughter, be the 'zgane' your mother was; be what cries in your blood!"

Maria smiled, and spoke gently.

"We will not leave tomorrow. We will leave the following day, early, after the new moon sets; when the roads and forests are cloaked in darkness..... then we will go to our horses, and the things I have gathered for our journey. In the meantime, there is something I must do, something very important before we join our people."

Maria left early the next morning, careful to walk through the smaller streets that snaked through the village. After a few questions asked of shopkeepers, he arrived before a cobbler's shop, hollowed like a cave from the stone upon which the village had first been hewn. There he saw Salvatore, mussed, sleepy, filthy, at work on a stool. Maria approached the master cobbler, an old man bent over a table littered with boots, oakum, and scraps of leather.

"Good morning, good sir. Might I have a word with your apprentice?"

The old cobbler looked at him with myopic eyes created by a lifetime of tailoring and eyeleting, and with an acerbic frown and shrug of his slumped shoulders, and without so much as standing or turning on his stool, gave his indifferent permission.

At the sound of Maria's voice Salvatore had spun on his stool, brightening from his drudgery, at which Maria bowed, and addressed him formally.

"Signore Salvatore, cobbler apprentice, may I, if you please, have a word?"

Beaming, Salvatore followed Maria across the street, where they sat down on a low stone fence beneath a tree whose long dry leaves rustled like castanets in a brisk autumn wind. Salvatore was exuberant to see him.

"She was there, was she not, the beautiful bake house lady? I knew you were not playing your fiddle music for a ghost! I knew that I saw the candle in the window, and I knew that you had found her. I saw the boards torn from the door, even if you tried to replace them.....I've a keen eye, a thief's eye.....and I heard no more of your croons that made the heart bleed with sad tears!"

"*Yes, I found her, the bake house lady, the beautiful ghost; the queen full of hurt, in her cold dark castle. I have come to thank you, Salvatore, and to tell you that we are leaving Siena.*"

"*I am very happy for you, Mister Maria, in my cockles I am.*"

Maria looked at the fledging young man, staring with innocent adulation before him; his youth believing in one who had long since drank, diced, whored and murdered his innocence away. Beneath his filthiness and shagginess, Maria saw a gallantry that begged to be groomed and encouraged; but was resigned to live a life of stifling chores.

"*Then you are leaving soon, Mister Maria?*"

"*Yes, when the moon sets, a little after midnight, tonight.*"

"*With the bread lady, the beautiful ghost you found?*"

"*Yes, with the beautiful ghost I have found.*"

Maria stood, and with his back turned to Salvatore, and his eyes burning, said softly:

"*And you as well, Salvatore, if you would like; and you as well.*"

Salvatore laughed good-naturedly.

"*That I am not and cannot, Mister Maria. I will be here, in the cave with the old growler, pitching and gluing the boots of the shepherd jakes, even as he hocks and curses, and pulls his flask of drink from the tall boot that hangs on a hook near him always.*"

Maria turned and knelt down before the youth, and the earnestness of prayer was in his eyes and heart.

"*But do you not want to play the fiddle like a gypsy once fiddled at the 'Sickle Moon Tavern', Salvatore? Do you not want to celebrate the sad and happy seasons that pass through the sieves of men's hearts, their wicked storms and nights of starry sweetness? Do you not want to make the soft feet of beautiful maidens dance......make warble the brooks of their throats? Do you not want to glimpse the eternal mystery in their dark eyes and flashing smiles?*"

His soul filled with amazement, and not sure he understood Maria's flourish of words, the dumbstruck boy looked at Maria quizzically, innocently; empty of a response to the magnanimity cloaked in these words.

"*Do you know how to ride a horse, Salvatore?*"

"*A little, Mister Maria. Before the sickness came I stabled and foddered at the inn for beans and bread. I like them. I'm not afraid of their creature at all.*"

"Tonight, shortly after midnight, at the bake house door, be there with your boots, shirt and fiddle. Come with me, Salvatore, not as my servant or my son, but as my brother."

. . . .

. . . .

CHAPTER FOURTEEN

LAST RITES

The Abbey: Circa 1360

THE AUTUMN had been warm and golden; lingering as it would stay, as this once it would not be swept and bullied away by snow and cold. Likewise, the summer had brought alternating gifts of rain and sun, gifts that had pampered the fields, orchards and gardens into rich abundance. Many of the trees still clung jealously to their leaves, as if their pride was unwilling to relinquish their liveries of citron-gold, cinnamon-brown and florid red, glistening like the robes of kings and queens in the sun. Want, famine and sickness, the very ogres of death were but memories now, memories that youth could not remember, and that age only saw in the mists of its dreams. New life had lifted up its head of darling curls, and lazily yawning, its eager eyes made toys of the bones that had been left everywhere as it had napped.

Even in the Franciscan Abbey on the hill, there were few relics left by the sad dark years. True; famine, sickness and death had taken turns knocking at its gates, and not being answered had barbarously scaled its walls. Once inside, these foes had performed their dark deeds of starvation and murder as ruthlessly as they had performed them everywhere in the land. The monks' prayers and austerities, and the idols on its altars had not been sufficient to allay their perniciousness. But there was now left little to commemorate or document these savage attacks; attacks that slowly, but surely faded into myths too horrible to be real, too ghastly to be recollected.

Oh, there were vestiges seen here and there, and commented upon by the younger monks: elderly members of the brotherhood that limped or were prodigiously hunched, or whose awkwardly cocked heads and twisted spines would never straighten again; some that were stutterers, some that queerly squinted, some that were left excessively crabbed or ignorantly daft. And from time to time there were relics found by peasants in the fields; skeletons that were unearthed by ploughs, nooses still dangling from tree boughs, skulls that boys sat on stones or posts, as targets for their rock-throwing.

But by and by, death had had its merry day, and leaving the horrid memories of its merrymaking in its wake, had gone away; leaving memories too dreadful to be real for the old, and tales too fantastic to be real for the young.

The new monks attributed these things simply to that marching army called *time*. Yes, many monks had died, but they had been replaced by new monks, and life at the abbey had continued as always, with the ringing of its bell, with slapping sandals and gently droning prayers; as if death and its bands of horror had never breached its holy walls; or if it had, it had been defeated, and would never come again.

Despite the sieges of death, the years had brought few changes to the abbey on the hill: to its walks, gardens and altars. Its pillars, arches, cornices and architraves had remained remarkably the same, the years finding their sculpted flowers, angels and apocalyptic beasts stubbornly difficult to erode. So too the statues of the Saints; staring with the same imperturbable stares, and freely giving their stony benedictions, despite the bloodthirsty predators that had brushed by their marble robes. When an orchard tree rotted away, a new one was planted in its place. When roses grew barren of blossoms, a new generation was lovingly planted. The doves in the dovecote begat new hatchlings; the swallows in the bell-tower came and went exactly as had their forebears; playing on the summer breezes, and chidden away by frosty autumn. The great bell continued to call the monks to prayer, and these hooded soldiers continued to obey its brazen clanging, as in a kind of sacred slavery to their unseen God. Sunlight fell and dreamed timelessly in the courtyard; with the same allotted doses, and at the same allotted hours, making the same golden trespass on the shadows of the arcades; as if the stones of the abbey were a kind of sundial that measured the endless passing of *Time*.

But this is not to say that some of the older monks had not retained vivid memories of *the sickness*; for indeed they had; memories they could not rid from their minds: not in their prayers; not in their dreams.

They remembered brothers keeling over as they were knelt in prayer, or dementedly screaming out their secret sins, or finding their brothers decomposing in the fields, where, in the idiocy of their fevers they had fallen. They remembered their sacred *Silence* infected and incited into purgatorial wails and moans; and the foul smells that their incense could not smother or dismiss. They remembered the black flocks of crows roosting on their walls and roofs, some daring to alight even on their marble saints and marble Madonna; and the carking of their hungry, insane choirs that their clanging bell could not chase away; that they could not escape, even in their prayers.

They remembered their brothers' ruddy, good-natured faces turning to blotched and blackened, blue-lipped cadavers; their bodies swollen with stinking tumors; some the size of apples, some the size of gourds. They remembered the wrapping and burying of their holy, often scarce recognizable brothers, burials that were first in the crypt below their sanctuary, but whose awful fumes of putrefaction had seeped into their robes, lungs and prayers, chalking their tongues and throats with the exhalations of death, necessitating the burial of their dead Comrades in Christ outside their walls; the pallbearers bearing them on planks, their faces hooded and wrapped in thick scarves. They were buried hastily in a makeshift graveyard, the cold iron bell their only requiem, in graves only deep enough to keep their venerable bones from being unearthed by the wild dogs; beneath crosses that quickly became roosts for the feathered feasters that death had invited.

Some of the survivors were still haunted by dreams of these terrible things, but seldom was it talked about, and when it was, only briefly; referred to as 'The Mortality', or 'The Devil's Blight', or 'God's Terrible Voice'.

Still fewer of the monks were old enough to remember the great famines that had preceded *the sickness*; famines that had been deadly in their own right. Those that had seen both the plague and the famines said the plague was the more merciful of the two, for it killed quickly, at times almost instantly, its victims stung dead by the flaming arrows of the wrathful angels; while famine prolonged death's escape, torturing its victims as in stocks or on racks, with the insanity that hunger's slow sharp fangs bring to body and soul.

Among the few older monks that remembered both of these terrible visitations was the former abbot, Father Giovanni. The memories of both the famines and the plague lived on in his mind. But with the shadows brought by age they were gradually ebbing away; chiefly with that shadow that promises to eclipse all things of this world; that approaching shadow that cloaks all to forgetfulness at life's end.

Father Giovanni was no longer *Abbot* Giovanni. He had relinquished his leadership of the brotherhood voluntarily, his decision made in the light of two things that had happened to him.

One winter night he had fallen on a snowy walk, at an hour when the brotherhood had retired to their cells. He had been too injured to stand, or even to crawl, and not until the monks were called to their midnight prayers was he found, nearly frozen to death. With time his leg and hip had wondrously healed, but even when they had he was visited by bouts of dizziness, and even more disturbing, spells of forgetfulness. He found himself forgetting prayers he had recited since his youth, the hours for the offices, and even once a session with an important prelate in the Chapter House. Realizing what was happening to him, and the importance of his position, he had selflessly resigned his abbacy by citing his own infirmities; the most difficult thing he had ever done in his life.

Yet with a reverence unspoken, one given him by all of the brothers, young and old, he was in many ways still honored as their abbot, even by the newly instated abbot himself. He was one of the most elder, and unquestionably the most erudite of the brothers, and when there were questions of theology, or any disputes on monastic etiquette or morality, as well as sundry other issues of daily life, it was Father Giovanni who was looked to and first consulted. All knew that he had maintained his post, and with unswerving faith had shepherded the brotherhood during death's great siege. Like the lions and angels carved in the stone cornices and lintels, he was an integral part of the abbey, and all had come to love and revere the old father. There were even those among them who regarded Father Giovanni as a Saint; still others who regarded him as something other, even something more than a Saint; a warrior whose sword of holiness had been unsheathed in the face of death's invading army. If it had not been for his strength and leadership, even midst the rage of death, the abbey would have fallen prey to death's horrors; would no longer be a fortress of God. And even midst these great, sleepless, unspeakable battles, he had found it somewhere inside his soul to succor those outside the abbey walls with charities of food and care; things attested to by those who still walked up the steep hill to place offerings of gratitude at the abbey's gates.

One night after the brothers had finished the day's last prayers, when they had descended from their stalls, kissed the feet of their Savior, and were filing in silence from the sanctuary, Brother Otto approached Father Giovanni, and in their silent language, the language of signs told the old father that there was a new member of the brotherhood who had an urgent need to confess.

"*He wants you to be his confessor, Father Giovanni, you, and only you. He is in great need of a confession, for some sin weighs heavily on his heart. Could there be an exception made this once? Could you hear his confession before you go to your rest?*"

Father Giovanni looked about him, and then continuing the silent dialogue of signs, asked where this penitent was, to which the brother answered:

"*His heart is heavy, father. His sin has cast a great shame and self-reproach upon him. He has told me he will wait inside the confessional until you come to him, and if you do not come to him, there he will stay and pray the night through.*"

A gentle smile shone through Father Giovanni's dark eyes, and spread across the thinly fleshed bones of his face. The long thin fingers of his hands moved eloquently, more like wands than hands, with the signs with which he spoke as fluently as his Latin and Greek.

"*Tell our new brother that sleep is also a confessor. Sleep listens to and consoles a troubled heart. We must obey the regulations that our seraphic father, Holy Francesco has set down for us. I will be more than glad to hear this brother's confession tomorrow morning, after 'Lauds'. Goodnight, Brother Otto, and I pray you sleep with God in your heart.*"

And with this Father Giovanni turned, and still lightly crutched by a cane, walked across the courtyard, and on to his cell.

Once inside his cell he genuflected before the idol of *the Virgin*, crossed himself, and snuffed out his candle. In the darkness he removed his habit, but not the hair-shirt that he had secretly worn for many years. He lay down on the boards of his straw-less, pillow-less bed, pulled the blanket up to his chin; but did not at once fall asleep.

He was strangely, almost giddily at peace, and in the darkness his thin worn face glowed with pleasure. The weather had been fair, and had delayed its amorous leave. The harvest had been plentiful in their fields, orchards and garden-plots; and the bees had had a wilderness of flowers from which to sip their bonnets for the soon to be snowbound hives. The brothers would have ample food through the winter, and perhaps enough wheat, millet, prunes and apples to give the beggars that would surely climb the hill to their gates. Drinking the rich showers of late sunlight, there was yet another crop of roses blooming in the courtyard. Even some of the swallows had tarried about the bell-tower, as if reluctant to leave the arches through which they had careened and played the summer through. God was a good and generous, not a hurtful father. He cared for His children. After the chastisements He had justly delivered, He was now smiling, like the sun emerging from angry clouds,

But there was something more that kept the old father awake, something that was trying to speak to him, to make its voice heard.....that was trying to unveil the veils of memory and time, and step from the mists of his soul.......

.....something that tried to hold and claim him even as he drifted into sleep.....that strove to articulate, to become sweet, meaningful......that resonated with something that had once happened to him in his younger days.....

......something about the brother who had spoken to him in sign language after 'Evensong'.....yes, something familiar about the brother who had curiously spoken to him, asking permission for another brother's con-fession....a new brother, an unseen brother, one that he had not been told about.....a brother waiting in the confessional for him........

".....he wants you to be his confessor, Father Giovanni, you, and only you......."

......had he not once confessed a brother after 'Evensong', when the brotherhood was sleeping, even though the Rule strictly forbade it?.....a note.....he remembered a note.....the curious look in the brother's eye, as he knew more than he was saying.....as his kind abbot, Abbot Augustine once looked at him.....as there was something peculiar and special about the brother waiting for him in the confessional.......

.....Maria! Brother Maria! It could only be Maria! He had returned, wanting to confess, perhaps with some great need, perhaps wanting not only to confess, but to personally confide in him after all these years!.......

Within moments Father Giovanni was walking as briskly as he

could down the solemn corridor, a much weathered satchel hanging at his side. Once more he was ignoring obedience to the Rule, as he had done that night so many years ago, when he had found the note in his cell and had secretly gone to the love-drunken monk who had deserted their Order for the arms of a shepherd girl.

"…..*some sin weighs heavily on his heart…….could there be an exception made this once?…….*

Once more he was doing something forbidden; once more he was leaving his cell and trespassing on the *Great Silence* for the sake of this profligate who for some reason beyond his knowing owned a piece, nay, was an immeasurable treasure in his heart.

And as he walked out into the splashes of the courtyard's cool autumn breezes, his normally sedate and neatly-ordered mind fevered, and swam with memories of that last time he had spoken with Maria in the confessional, so many years ago…..of how the young golden boy had pressed his face to the grille, and then his lips, kissing it with a fervency that had touched him as no prayer or ritual had ever touched him……and how each time he had looked upon his empty prayer stall his heart had contracted with pain…..how he had secretly despaired, grieving like a grieving lover when his habit was discovered high in the old tree…..the great, perhaps unpardonable sin he had committed on his behalf that morning when he was about to hang, exchanging his holy robe for a prisoner's rags…….and the last time he had seen him during the blizzard at the inn…..a thousand sins upon his shoulders, sins of brawls, women, murder….and yet a boy's irascible innocence sparkling in his sky-blue eyes…….

…..oh, many years had passed, and there were so many things he must tell his friend, things that only he and his heathen gypsy heart could understand…..he must confess to Maria, as much as Maria to him…..yes, confess! He must confess that he had given a great meaning to his life….that he had ever remembered and prayed for him through the years…..that he was filled with a great joy that he was still alive…that The Mortality had not claimed him…….

…..he must speak the words, yes, the words he had never spoken before, not to Maria, or any other…..he must tell him; yes, he would tell him…….

Entering the sanctuary, Father Giovanni did not dip his fingers in the font, nor did he make the Sign of the Cross, but absently leaned his cane against the wall, as if discarding it, as it it was now only an encumbrance to his joy…..

"......*he will wait inside the confessional until you come.......*"

He walked through the dusky nave with brisk light steps, even as he was about to break into a run; his heart beating quickly, like a battle drum, as it had not beaten since he was a boy......*as that moment in the schoolyard when the pale pretty girl......*beating as it would break through his ribs.....as it was about to lift him with wings.

"......*inside the confessional until you come.......*"

....*Was this not a kind of lovers' rendezvous?......a secret adventure of the heart?.....a stealing away to arms beneath a forest tree.....too late to repay the kiss given on a children's playground? Was it a sin to seek another person's warmth and closeness, to give one's heart to another?......*

"......*and if you do not come, he will stay.......*"

Was there a time when flesh grew too tired, the mind too weak to love?......Was he, Father Giovanni, too tired and weak to love?.....Had he, Father Giovanni, ever loved?.......

.....Insignificant now the Rule, the Great Silence, the abbey and the God that watched over it, the God he had prayed to since he was a boy......all now were chaff, chaff winnowed away by the fluttering of his heart.....all now was a cold world of meaningless candles and chants, lifeless frescoes and dead idols.....for this once the things of this world through which he was walking were not important.....for this once he must be like other men,.....this once know this secret joy, this forbidden ecstasy that they had known, but he had not.......

Reaching the confessional, he pulled back its curtain and placed his candle on the shelf, and without a word of benediction pressed his cheek against the grille; and there kept it, as if clinging with gratitude for his friend's return. Soft as the voice of a lover on a midnight pillow, he whispered through his tears:

"*Oh Maria, Maria, how glad I am that you have returned! You have no idea how I have missed you! Oh my dear friend, you are a singing bird in the night of my soul! You have taught me how to love, Maria; yes, to love!*"

But to the passionate unburdening of his heart, there came no response. Slowly the old father pulled his cheek away from the grille, and holding the candle near it, saw that the other half of the confessional was empty; that he had confessed the depths of his heart to an empty box; to the lonely child of his own heart. There was no Brother Maria, and there was no other brother waiting to be confessed. He had only confessed his loneliness to a ghost that had left long ago.

Father Giovanni walked back through the nave, without genuflecting before the great Crucifix. He did not want to be blessed. He did not want to ask God for forgiveness; no, not this time. This time he did not want to be forgiven. Unashamed of his fervor, he wanted to keep his sin, yes, like a child wants to covet his treasure. He was glad to be painted scarlet with his silly fault; to be made a fool, Love's fool; a fool as countless others had been a fool. He did not care if every martyr, saint and angel in the frescoes he passed looked upon him as such; regarded him as such; jeered at him as such.

Nor did he take the cane he had left by the door. As he walked across the courtyard his steps felt lighter, stronger, and in some inscrutable way, humbler.

* * *

ONLY Father Sebastiano came to know of this incident. He was Father Giovanni's confessor, and Father Giovanni had confessed it fully to him. Father Sebastiano was the senior-most citizen of the brotherhood, and he was one of the few brothers who remembered the young, gypsy-blooded brother with blue eyes and a golden tonsure, he who had been such a favorite, and caused such a controversy with his defection.

In the course of their advanced years, both of the old fathers had seen many things. They had seen brothers grow fond of other brothers; most of these friendships capricious and harmless, only a few becoming dangerous, brooking on violations of nature. But the confession Father Giovanni had made to his confessor was very different. Although it had greatly surprised Father Sebastiano, he had inwardly smiled when his friend, the former abbot had divulged this secret he had lived with for so long. He smiled at the saintly innocence with which he had loved this colorful friend of his younger days; how his heart had been touched, and even partly stolen by this rascal monk who had deserted the brothers for a reckless life of profligacy. Still, it puzzled and somewhat troubled him to think that the faith of such a reverend cleric, one who was so highly regarded, even reverenced by all, should be challenged in his old age by this fondness developed so long ago.

"Brother Otto had asked me to hear the confession of our new brother, but I had refused, citing the Rule of our seraphic father. But when it occurred to me that it might be Brother Maria who was waiting in the confessional, I went at once to the sanctuary, unmindful of the Rule that only moments

before I had so rigorously upheld.

You see I was seized with a kind of sweet anticipation, a kind of rapture to see the friend of my youth. When I entered the chapel I did not kneel or genuflect. I did not bless myself from the font. It was as I had forgotten about the God I have worshipped since I was a boy. It was as I had entered a mud hut. I wanted only to be near this one who had shed his habit and dashed his vows. At that moment, the moment of anticipated reunion, his friendship was more important to me than the Rule of Francesco; more important to my heart than God.

And even more, yes, perhaps more serious, I did not feel like a fool or a sinner. I felt a great thrill, as I had been baptized anew. Even now I do not feel as I am confessing my sin to you, reverend father, but as I am singing its praise."

Several weeks later another thing happened, a more serious thing that gripped the entire brotherhood with great concern and grief. Whether due to his frailty, or an apoplectic fit, Father Giovanni had once more fallen; this time in the garden where he daily enjoyed his morning walks. When he was found lying on the frosty ground, his eyes were open and awake, but his mind was dreaming; and his speech, incoherent and rambling. In an attempt to catch his fall, he had fallen upon a stone bench, breaking a number of his brittle ribs, and a great bruise on his face testified that he had hit his head as well. He was unable to walk, and only with the most ginger care was he placed upon a litter, on which he was conveyed to the infirmary.

The brothers were distraught for the saintly kind, learned old father. They were instructed to pray for him; intoning extra *Paters* and *Aves* at the close of each of their offices. The injury was serious, and the father, very old, and it was tacitly understood that it was doubtful that he would recover. His frail, thin body seemed to be holding onto life by a merest thread.

He was confined to his bed in the infirmary, and visited and watched over by only a few of the old brothers; those few that had sailed the storms of the years together with him. But however serious was the breakage of his bones, it was his mind that concerned the covey of his cronies more than anything else. Father Antonio, the abbey's infirmarian, he who was nearest to his patient, whispered in private to the others:

"I am not sure his bones will heal. Like broken branches of a tree, the branches can but wither when deprived of the trunk's sap. I am not sure his

bones still flow with living marrow. I am not sure that they are fed with sufficient life to be ever whole again.

But it is his mind that worries me most, that wonderful mind of his......."

"What of his mind, Antonio?"

"At times it is lucid, and he is the old Giovanni. We share a mug of wine together. We reminisce and laugh. But at other times, when he is racked with fever, he lapses into deliriums, and he speaks of strange, even unholy things; things I do not understand; things that seem very queer, even unworthy of his saintly soul; things that seem heretical to our faith.....things that seem in some way to be the words of another.....calling out that the great sins in his heart, those he has never and will never confess, are the true treasures of his life.......

And there are still other times when I enter the room, and his eyes are clear, and his voice full of vital goodness, and there is a gentle smile like the light of a lamp spread over his face.....times when he is speaking tenderly, as with ones the eye cannot see; as with ghosts at his bedside.....He raises his hand and blesses them, yes, blesses the ghosts, one by one as he whispers their names.....the names of former brothers who have died, who were once a part of our brotherhood.....many that the famines and the sickness claimed.......

And there is one more thing, one very peculiar thing. When he was brought to the infirmary I asked him if there was anything he needed. He whispered in my ear that he would like his missal and his beads, but also to bring him a leather bag that was beneath his bed in his cell.....even in his great pain he had requested this thing of me. I could not help but question the rightness of his mind, but I did as he bid me, and was not a little surprised when I found the very thing he had asked for, even as he said, beneath his bed. You must remember the bag he carried about a number of years ago, after his first fall....a bag that contained some rare manuscript, or some such thing.....Well, he had me hang this same bag on a chair near where he is resting. It is very old and worn, as it had been beaten by many years of sun and rain, filled with things I know not what. It is very peculiar, especially to hide it beneath his bed, and though it is difficult for me to say, I believe it may suggest an infirm mind."

It was apparent to his caretakers that Father Giovanni was failing, and not rest, nourishment, or the remedies of herbs would keep him in this world. He was very frail, and grievously broken, a brokenness of a frailty that would never be repaired. His sleep became even more feverish with delirious carnivals of dreams and delusions; his hours of lucidity, fewer. Several times Father Antonio knelt at his side to receive his last confession, and Father Sebastiano prepared to minister *Extreme Unction*. But each time with a wan smile, and a wag of his forefinger, the bedridden whispered:

"Not yet; not yet. Neither God nor the Devil can have my bones yet."

Father Giovanni's soul seemed to have entered a twilight between this world and the next, and like a bandit raiding back and forth between the gates of two villages, visited both. In that twilight he no longer was sure what was real or what was not real. His dreams were very lucid, at times much *more* lucid than the dim world he woke to in the candle-lighted infirmary. Once, after a long, fever-troubled sleep, one in which the old fathers were afraid they were about to lose him, he woke immersed in an unusually vivid, reality colored dream, one that seemed more vital than his waking. The struggles of his body had passed, and his soul was filled with calm and peace. He was not sure if he was awake or asleep; the kingdoms of this world and the next having met at their crossroads; declaring a kind of truce in these last hours of his life.

He woke to softly burning candles, and the sweet smells of herbs, alone with Father Antonio. Father Antonio was standing over the table, his apothecary vials and tools spread out before him. Yes, there was the simple crucifix on the wall, and the statue of the blue-robed, dolorous Mary in the niche. The night was cool, and Father Antonio stood with his raised cowl drooped baggily over his head.

But Father Antonio had changed in his dream. Those were not his old hunched shoulders, and that was certainly not his shrunken, dwarfish height. No, this was not Father Antonio, nor was it any other brother in the brotherhood. And yet he knew those broad shoulders, and that tall straight spine. They were familiar; unmistakably familiar. And there were boots, not a monk's sandals peeking from beneath his robe. No, this was not Father Antonio. There was both a smile and tears in his voice when he faintly whispered:

"Maria!"

At once the figure turned from the table, and taking his hand in his, was knelt at his side.

Yes, it was the face, the tender boy's face he had once known.....although its peach-soft cheeks now rioted with a grizzled beard, and the stubble of his tonsure had bloomed into a grey jungle of shoulder-length tresses......and though there were wrinkles about the eyes, a scar upon his brow, and an earring dangling from his ear......midst all of this the same blue eyes, and the same sparkle of the soul that shone like two stars through those eyes.......

"But I do not understand. How did you enter the abbey, Maria? And the habit....how? where?......."

"I knocked upon the gates like any other beggar would. I asked for Father Sebastiano, because I knew the old rascal was never beyond a bribe, and if not a bribe, a threat. I plucked a button off my coat with my knife, told the old fool it was a gold ducat, and as the stars and the devil would have it, the rest was easy!"

......and then the grin and the sparkle in those eyes......the grin and the sparkle he remembered when he was teaching the old monks to dance and sing in the courtyard......that had brought a grin and sparkle to his own......

"I still know how to climb trees and walls, and how to salve an itching palm, good father......and I have not forgot my way around the abbey....the pillars and arches have not moved much, not even for Mister Mortality they haven't....and this habit....the old skinflint Sebastiano probably stripped a dead monk in the crypt for it.....but not to fear, I'll give it back to the poor fellow when I'm done with it, wouldn't want him to catch cold in the sleep of death, now would we?.....a beggar, but no thief am I......neither am I an angel, and could not fly over walls, not for the moon could I.....but to see an old friend, a very dear friend, well now, that's another thing.......

I am very glad to see you again, Father Giovanni. I am very, very glad."

It was the same Maria, the same devil-may-care, boyish heart.....the same whimsy and tenderness that had spoken so deeply to him when he was young, that he had never had a defense, nor ever wanted a defense to defend against. The same lyrical innocence still sparkled in his eyes.....danced with irreverent, half-pagan, irascible joy in his heart.

"Are you well enough to share a mug of wine with an old friend, even if that old friend is a defrocked reprobate, one who would have swung from the gallows if......well, I think you know the story. Father Antonio left a flagon of warm wine, seasoned with cloves and cinnamon I believe. He said that was the wine his patient likes best. Ah, and just the thing, two empty mugs waiting to be filled."

"Yes, yes, I think I am well enough.....if you could just help prop my

bones up a little.....you see I had a fall, Maria, and they tell me I hit my head.....but I can scarce believe you are here, as if I was dreaming....a wonderful dream to see you here.....yes, that is good, thank you.....you see I am not strong....they tell me that I will heal, but I know better...I know I am about to do that silly little thing all of us must do, I know I have grown tired and useless in this world, and well, dead limbs need to be lopped off, and I'm ready to be pruned....and yes, warm wine with cloves and cinnamon, that is my favorite.....and whether I am awake or dreaming, I do not care.....it is so good to see you Maria!......."

Maria had bent down, and gingerly scooped up the sheaf of the frail brittle bones in his strong arms. He sat him up in his bed, cushioning and comforting him with pillows.

Pouring two half mugs of wine, Maria sat back down; very close to his friend, so that the bedridden would not be unduly taxed when he spoke..... the bearded, shaggy, bear-like man with broad and husky shoulders next to the enfeebled old father with the last few hairs of a tonsure clinging stubbornly to his all but bald head.....the one wild and roughened from a life of aimless wandering and profligacy, near the one who had been whittled to bones by a life of prayer and holy duty.....the one who had turned his back on God, the other who had ever knelt before Him. Still, it was the lion that would remain the disciple of the lamb; the hale that would submit to the weak; the prodigal whose eyes would burn with tears before the emaciated ascetic.

As they sipped their wine, they spoke as old friends speak of this or that, as they had been parted for days, and not years: about monks that had passed from the brotherhood; about the grapes, olives and wheat harvests; the dovecote; the goldfish pond; the roses in the garden. But as they continued, and their conversation deepened, some of Father Giovanni's words shouted with trenchant truths to Maria's soul, engraving his heart as a chisel engraves stone. Such were his last words, the last words of that last discussion that Maria would never forget; that he would treasure more than gold.

"You may think it strange, Maria, but I do not think we are so very different; no, not so very different after all; for beneath a holy habit and a dusty coat, beneath a long mane of hair and a sparse tonsure, first and foremost we are men. And what are all men but the dust of the earth, the blood of the grape, and a spark of the sun? We are the sons of the Earth before we are the recruits of Heaven; our nostrils breathing the flowers before they breathe the incense of the altar.....children that count their beads and

shoot their arrows, intent on embracing those treasures they have promised their own hearts, and yet and always, in the end, how phantom-like those treasures remain.

After all, we are all the progeny of Adam; a little dust that bears a little flower, only to wither and die. And this all men have in common, Maria; that in the end 'Brother Death' humbles the pride of all crowns, all dreams. After a thousand battles all who have toiled, fought and dreamed beneath the sun are foiled by the very dreams they dreamed; all in the end, the king with the pauper, lay down their weapons and know they are beaten soldiers."

"I have wasted my life, Giovanni. I have thought many times that I should have stayed in the cloister; near you; near the brothers; that I should have given my life to prayer and the sacraments. But there is something wild, even mad, like an imprisoned child in my heart....and this child would murder Angels to be free. I do not see our likeness, Giovanni, no, not at all. You have hallowed your life, but I have gambled mine away in drunkenness, sentimental tunes on fiddle strings......silly games with women......."

"But what is a sacrament, Maria? A sacrament is not only bread and wine, as our Savior has given us. These are only symbols that symbolize the sacrifice, the giving back of a heart that was once planted like a seed in one's breast. And there is never a sin so great that it is not forgiven by a compassionate God. It is forgiven before it is committed, and thus no sin at all; only the stumble of a child as it runs to strong arms."

"But the Mortality, Giovanni, the Great Mortality? Your God stood by and watched as His Innocent children were tossed on dead-carts, spilled in pits, were eaten by crows and dogs......babes in their mothers' arms, husbands and wives embracing......maidens fresh as summer roses......blighted and blackened, their faces gnawed off by rats, ugh! What of these terrible things, these horrors of hell that your God loosed upon His children?"

At this Father Giovanni made a small wafture of his hand, as it had been a thing of no consequence. This surprised Maria, for he knew that The Mortality had ravaged the abbey, as well as the surrounding country-side, and that the abbot had earned the respect of all, as a saint earns respect for working selflessly and tirelessly through its rage.

"Death will come when it will come, Maria; and there is no guarantee that it will be kind and pretty, even for the pious and prayerful. You see me here in this bed, a bed from which I will never leave again, only as a heap of an old man's bones. But am I so very different than those that were thrown on carts and spilled into pits? I do not think I am. Are not the hungry

791

mouths of worms waiting for all of us?

You see I think the Great Mortality was a 'Great Harvest', a 'Great Harvest' of souls: one might say a winnowing of wheat from the chaff on the threshing-floor of men's souls......a thing as much of life as death.....you see this is the miracle of belief.....belief that in the end there are loving arms that are waiting for all of us.....for me, a father's arms.....for you, perhaps a mother's."

At this his whispers became faint, as there was a struggle for him to make them; as he was beginning to dream; and his words seemed to dizzy and lose sense, the sense and meaning that had been the prize and pride of his life.

".....and yes, the tree that you hung your habit in, like a corpse hung from a gallows..... I visited it often.....Brother Vittorio, or was it Brother Gregorio.....well, he found the grave beneath it.....the young girl loves you even in death, Maria.....I sometimes still hear her playing her flute, calling you to her arms in the forest......and the note beneath my door......yes, the note.....yet he knew, he knew.....he was in the shadows all the time...... but is that what you asked me?......I forget......not always pretty or kind, but I do not think it is ever cruel.....I am very tired......forgive me, please, I must rest, close my eyes and rest a little.....do not go away Maria....or are you Brother Antonio?......do not be a dream, no, not now, not now......."

His eyes closed, and he swooned into a doze. Maria carefully took the mug of wine from his hand, and placed it on the table, and as he did his hand involuntarily moved, crawled like a crab on the bed towards Maria. Maria held it, kissed it, and looked at the face of his dearest friend; the man he felt nobler and braver than any man he had ever known. The face was illumined with a smile, a smile like morning light falling in an eastern window. Maria laid his face upon the hand, closed his eyes, and knew this moment would be the perfect moment to die; the perfect time to know no more.

Waking moments later, the dying priest spoke again, even as he had not slept at all.

"I have kept your satchel; yes, your satchel, Maria."

Maria lifted his face to see Giovanni's eyes open, clear of the daze that had clouded them. He had momentarily dozed, but now seemed renewed, like the flame of a candle rediscovering its wick; as this man knew only how to lend light, using his last breaths, even as he had used the countless ones before them to give light to the world about him; the world he was leaving.

"*Yes, my satchel, I see it here. When I remembered it, after my escape, I was far away in the forest, running and hiding.....I was too afraid to enter the city again. It contained nothing important; trifles only; nothing more. I recognized it immediately, but I was very surprised to see it here, hung on this chair near your bed. How did you.......*"

"*A lady gave it to one of the brothers, and he gave it to me, at the Howling Wolf Inn where we talked that snowy night. But you had disappeared into the forest and the blizzard.*

So I kept it for you; kept it and secreted it away for you.....even hiding it from the vandals that ransacked the abbey. For a long time I did not look inside it. But it spoke to me, even in my prayers it spoke to me; pleaded to me with a great temptation to open it.....and well, frankly Maria, the temptation won out, a temptation I justified by believing I would not see you again. Finally one day I looked inside it; at the trove of things that I presume many friends, many women friends had given you....ribbons, earrings, tresses of hair.....and with these gifts, many poems and thoughts you had written......."

"*They are but toys and trifles, Giovanni, gifts of tavern wenches, some from unfaithful wives, some from harlots.....and the poems, the dreams of a lonely and aimless man.....dreams of an idler and loafer that never found his foothold in this world, and never truly looked for one.....I am ashamed.....ashamed and perhaps glad you saw how I kept such buttons and bows, such a frowsy rubble in the den of my heart....like a dog's its bones.....glad because they are a kind of confession of my soul......yes, the satchel, a kind of confession.....a confession that somehow found your hands, Giovanni.*"

"*I think you are very wrong, Maria. They are a treasure of holiness, in a sense as holy as the bread and wine I consecrate at the altar of Christ; a treasure, yes, a treasure, as if this old satchel you carried for so many years was a nest that was being feathered by a mother-bird.....feathered with bits and pieces of love by a very kind, beautiful mother-bird whose wings were watching over you.*"

"*Please Giovanni, if you only knew.....*"

"*They are the bread and wine of your soul, Maria. You have touched many; you have given of 'your' heart; you have loved, Maria, and I believe, nay, I am sure you have been loved in return. Do you know how rare, and more than rare, what a miracle it is to love and be truly loved, Maria?..... to be cherished for a moment in this world..... held dear, even by a glance or smile?.....You have partaken of God's miracle......you have known its pains, its yearnings and regrets, the joy that its knife brings when it stabs the pith of the heart....yes, you have tasted this great thing that moves the wheel of the stars, even as holy priests stand woodenly before the altars of a God they have never seen or heard."*

After a silence, a suspended silence, one in which neither men knew what to say, Maria spoke again.

"I have spoken with Brothers Sebastiano and Antonio, and they have told me the things that you did, even as the dogs of death were at the brothers' heels and throats.....how you were their pillar.....how you greeted hell with the candle of your faith. No Giovanni, you are mistaken. I have done things that would make angels blush.....but you, Giovanni, but you......."

"Oh Maria, my dear gypsy lad, my dear, blue-eyed, eternal child, Maria, I think it is you who are mistaken, mistaken because you have thought the blush on these angels' cheeks was of shame or scorn, while all the while it was the blush of compassion, even a proud approval."

"Giovanni, no....."

"Please.....the hour is late, and the candle is short. I must say these things......you must let me say these things, confess these things, for only to you, my beautiful friend, not to my confessor, not to God may I speak them.

Again and again I read in your poems a theme, a theme you called 'the dream of the seasons', and how man becomes lost in this dream of sun and storm, a dream composed of foolish ambitions, selfish schemes, and yes, the appetites and pretty snares of the flesh. It may surprise you, Maria, but I too believe in this 'dream of the seasons', this unsubstantial illusion of good and evil, truth and lies, pleasure and pain. We differ only in the different ways we attempt to explore, navigate, and find our way through this dream; different ways to lift its veils, to worship its hidden mysteries.....veils of which there is always one more to be lifted.....mysteries that perhaps are not intended to be discovered."

Hearing the quaver in his voice, and the last heroic passion and lucidity his weak heart wished to share with him, Maria lay his head gently against his friend's side; as his rugged body craved the protective lea of his wasting one; a frightened chick seeking the hen's brooding wing. And finding the safety of that wing, he closed his eyes, and let the dying man's words, like the whispers of a reed fill him with music, as if that reed held the harps of a thousand Angels."

.....it was the Father Giovanni he first remembered in these whispers,

that had always been, and would always be a part of him.....the quiet priest that always had taken time to speak to him about his little cares, his boyish dreams.....the words in these whispers welling from his soul, as they had always welled from his soul.....feeding him, gathering the wings of a great wind about him.......

"I think you have been much more honest, much more honest and brave than I with life Maria, this 'dream of the seasons' our God has presented before us. I have lived my life behind stone walls, hiding behind altars and rituals that I have pretended kept the world's evils at bay. And yet the wasps of sin may fly over walls. They are borne on the wind, and may sting the monk's heart as easily as the infidel's. And as we both know, and as we both have seen, walls form no protection against death and sickness; like a knife through warm butter, their armies break down gates, scale walls, march like libertines through prayers."

Again he struggled, a struggle that pitted his will against his deteriorated body, his last breaths against that eternity eager to clasp him to its bosom.

"Please Giovanni, you must not try to speak."

"No, no, you must let me finish. You see my next nap might be my final one."

.....And then the flame licking once more from the ashes, the heroism, like the warrior takes into the battle's heart.....the smile that broke the back of death, and with that smile, its words.......

"You, my dear, dear Maria, have journeyed through the forest of this dream, the 'dream of the seasons', the dream that contains one's inevitable end. In this forest you have hunted and been hunted. You have become lost; you have hungered; you have become distraught. You have taken your soul into its dangers, as soldiers take their swords into battle; your armor not of iron, but of a kind of sympathy, a sympathy that is a respect, a respect that is a kind of bravery; a bravery that can only be called 'love'.

Yes 'love' Maria, 'love'.

And with that love you have made a mistress of death. You have lifted her crepe veil and stolen the kiss all men are afraid of, tasted honey in its venom, knowing that she too is shy, even afraid of this strange human thing called 'love'. Unafraid, you have become infatuated with the mystery she promises to tell, but will never yield. You have courted 'death', the mistress beneath whose balcony all suitors are afraid to sing, for you know that behind her veil, she is also beautiful.

You have sung your heart to many, even those in an abbey on a hill. And yes, you have won an old priest's heart, for I must tell you now, now when there shall never be another time to tell it, that I love you, as I have always loved you my dear Maria."

Thence came a pause, a silent pause that Maria neither could nor wanted to interrupt. Words had reached their end, and when they did they brought forth their exquisite flower. It had been said. It had been given; simply given and simply received; as a sip of wine, a bite of bread. Faintly, even more tenderly, Father Giovanni continued.

"You see I think I have lived a stale life, while you have lived a very rich one; tasting, and not abstaining from the fruits of life's garden. Yes, I am certain you have taken wrong, foolish, errant paths; paths that pricked you with countless thorns, stung you with serpents that coiled beneath pretty flowers. But you see........"

His head leaning against Father Giovanni's side, Maria felt the grimace of pain suddenly stab sharply, rip like a savage fang through the frail body it had seized, the body whose soul the Angels were waiting for. Seeing his struggle with the pain's sharpness, Maria laid him gently back down on the bed, and full of worry, asked:

"Do you need Father Antonio? He is near; outside the door, shall I fetch him?"

But Father Giovanni managed to wag the bone of his finger, and smiled through this last skirmish with the inevitable.....his words as faint as the whisper of a reed.

"No, no; a few words more, before I must say Amen.

As I was about to say, before death's hungry teeth so rudely interrupted me.....it is true we are born to surely die, but we must attempt to live, even when we know we cannot......a lesson in the vanity of things really......a universal defeat against a tyrant men call God.....a tyranny championed only by a tender heart."

The father winced and grimaced again, but with closed eyes continued to whisper; whispers so soft Maria placed his ear inches from his mouth, as he was imparting a secret, one whose sacredness would not be given to another, and never again.

"I do not think God's Eyes are the stars. These are the eyes of His Angels. Nor do I think He smiles through the flowers, for they are a carpet the earth casts before Man's feet. God's Eyes and God's Smile are our Souls, Maria. He weeps when we weep. He sings when we sing. God is a lost child; a lost child that we must take into our keeping; that we must give our love."

Father Giovanni opened his eyes, and looked into Maria's eyes. In his stare was a well, one that was bottomless with kindness; a kindness pure as the spring rains that replenished it.

"It was not I who saved your life in the dungeon that day, but you, Maria, who saved mine. I must say that I would do it a hundred times over, and risk my soul going to hell each time I did. You have given me the chance to love, Maria."

At this he lifted his habit's sleeve, in which was held his skeletal arm.

"In Nomine Patris, et Felii, et Spiritus Sanctus,
bless O Lord this son of the earth and sun, he who has gathered
the lost children of wicked and lovely dreams in his heart. Amen."

Maria kissed Giovanni's hand, pressed it to his cheek, and as he did the old father whispered:

"Now, my dear friend, now it is your turn to bless me."

Maria was not sure he heard the faint voice rightly.

"What is it that you say, Giovanni?"

"I ask you to bless me Maria."

"But Giovanni, it is not for me to bless you. I am most assuredly not a priest, and I have lost my belief in God a long time ago."

"But I am sure that He, the little child in your heart, still believes in you, Maria. Please, friend, give me your blessing; the blessing of your faith in the fields and flowers, of the birth and death of things.....of the Earth, Maria, of the Earth."

Maria stood, lifted and closed his eyes, and spread open his arms, as he was making a crucifix of his body.

"Earth Mother, sing this man's heart with the children of your flowers forever."

Maria bent over his dying friend, and pressed his bearded lips to the brow whose starved flesh, thin as the rind of a fruit, had left little more than a shell. Taken by surprise, the pale, half dead face flushed, enkindled as it had been warmed through and through with wine, the roots of its nerves tingling one last time awake, startled and humbled with this gift, blushing like a shy maiden.

"I am very glad, glad and grateful that we have had this moment, Maria. Now there is nothing left for me but the soft feet of rain upon my bones....and then, as Brother Death would have us do, the forgetting of those bones.

Now , please, if you would ask Father Sebastiano to come, I have some last little things to get off my chest; this or that to sweep from the cellar of my soul."

Maria stood and turned to go, but reaching the door, he stopped, and then convulsively spun and threw himself at the foot of the bed. Lifting the blanket, he clasped the naked, bird-like bones of the feet beneath it..... clasped and kissed them with hot tears, more passionately than he had ever kissed a lover........

* * *

STEPPING from the infirmary, he met Father Antonio, duteously waiting just outside the door. Upon Maria's leaving the infirmary, the old father at once made for the door to return to his beloved patient. But Maria held his arm.

"A moment, Father Antonio, only a moment."

Maria held the old father's face between his hands. It was the same face that had once cheerfully sent a young monk on an errand, an errand to look for watercress in a forest; that had once bandaged a lesion on his arm, and after had given him a tour, plant by plant, and name by name in the abbey's herb garden. The years had left little more than a skull; whittled its cheerful ruddiness to bones, bones that were thinly covered, like the skin of a drum by the last scraps of his flesh. The face was full of fret and fear, and it trembled in Maria's hands, even as its teeth were chattering with cold. Maria felt as he was holding a rare and beautiful flower.

"You must promise me, Father Antonio, you must promise that you will tell Father Giovanni the words that I am about to tell you."

As the old father was a child about to cry, he was frozen of a reply.

"It is important, very important that he hears these words before it is too late. You must promise me, Father Antonio, you must promise me!"

"Yes Brother Maria, yes my son, as Jesus Christ is my Savior, I will tell him the words you wish me to say."

"You must tell the abbot that God has heard his prayers; that He has heard them, and he has answered them.

You must tell him that the younger sister he never knew will be taken care of; that Brother Maria will take care of her; that he will guard her with his very life. You must tell him that her children, our children, Giovanna and Giovanni, will ever revere the memory of an abbot of an abbey on a hill."

HE refused to be escorted back to the gates. He did not want to be escorted and politely ushered from the walls he had once broken free of. He wanted to escape, as he had escaped when he was a young monk. But after returning the habit to the brother, and then bidding him farewell in the courtyard, he did not at once climb the wall and flee the home of his young days; the home that had given him so much. He wanted to stay for a while longer, to savor the shelter of a silence, and a friendship he knew he would never know again. He walked from the courtyard into the gardens, and from the gardens, into the orchard.

It had frosted heavily. The roses were frozen mid-bloom, their beautiful faces stunned still in the cold grip that had gripped their maiden blushes. The trees had shed their leaves, and with them their last pears and apples. When spring came, and they once more bloomed and fruited, they would not recall the ghost that had walked by their barrenness, tarrying with his reflections. There would be other, younger monks, monks of flesh and blood to delight with their fruits and flowers; but no Brother Maria.

"*Brother Maria, please, wait.....it is Sebastiano.....please, a moment please.......*"

Brother Maria turned to see the dark form of a monk approaching him, a lantern bobbing at his waddling side. When he reached him, the old father was out of breath, his words interspersed with his heavy pants.

"*Brother Maria.....oh by the Virgin and Her Angels.....I was so afraid, so afraid you had shinnied over the wall....left us!.....the reverend father said you had forgotten this.....said this bag was yours.....and that you must take it with you!*"

Not wanting to refuse either Giovanni's tender thoughtfulness, nor Father Sebastiano's great exertion that delivered it, Maria received the satchel and slipped its strap over his shoulder.

"*How is he, Father Sebastiano?*"

"*I fear he is slipping.....slipping from our hands into eternity, Brother Maria.*"

Choking with tears, the old father could not say more. He worked a little smile through his pain-racked face, a face that the plague had left pocked, crooked on his shoulders, and with a drooping bloodshot eye. He lifted his hand with the lantern, and blessed Maria.

"*May God bless you, Brother Maria. May He bless you wherever He takes you, and whatever He bids your soul do, my son. I know Father Giovanni owned a special fondness in his heart for you. But I must return, return to him.....you see Maria, if.....I could not bear......."*

"I understand, Father Sebastiano."

And with this the old father abruptly turned and hobbled briskly away, only after a score of paces to stop, set down his lantern, and run waddling back to him. Like a child he threw himself weeping into Maria's arms, burbling out words that were one with his tears.

"There's never been a better abbot, a better and a more saintly.....or more properly, a better, more fearless man, one to make Francesco himself proud. He was our pillar, Maria, our rod and our sword.....against the vandals, the famines.....the Mortality itself.....he saved us Maria, he saved us.....lion strong, lamb gentle.....his heart a well of charities.....and he little more than bones with his prayers and austerities......he saved us because God is in his heart, Maria.....and when he leaves, O dear God when he leaves, Maria.....what will I do?.....How will I live?.....How will I even pray?"

After Brother Sebastiano had returned to the dying father, Maria returned to the chapel, and the memories of his youth that it so faithfully had preserved. He was sure the statues, idols and frescoes were different than the season-fickle flowers and leaf-shedding trees. They would remember him; yes, they would never forget this ghost that had wandered past them in his youth, fresh and neatly groomed; only to come one last time to visit them in his age, worn and shaggy. Their gazes, benedictions and winged flights had remained, suspended, unchanged, even as they had been when he had walked beneath them as a young novice; Saints, Angels and martyrs frozen in the eternity of paint and stone, smiling at this ghost who had grown old and tired with the years of men. They alone would hold his memory in their stares and smiles and tears. They alone would know the secrets in his heart that had made him desert them.

They would remember this human ghost pass once more before their beatific eyes; a worn and dusty, very contrite ghost, one that walked through the dusky light cast by the small oil lamps; who knelt before the altar of the Virgin, and whispered a prayer to the one whose name had once been given to him; a prayer not for his own soul, but for another's.

"Holy Mother, as a winebibber becomes drunk with wine, I have become

drunk with my sins. I have loved unchastely and excessively; I have diced and gambled; I have become lazy and slept when others toiled in the hot sun. And I have shed blood, nay, I have murdered, Mother......yes, I have killed my brothers. But I do not ask for forgiveness, for I would not want cowardice or hypocrisy be heaped on the sins I lay at your feet. I pray instead that you bless one that has loved me like no other. Wrap your arms, like a tender vine around him; hold him to your heart; give him a mother's love."

Maria walked from the chapel out into the cold, moon-less night. He returned to the naked orchard again, and like a young renegade monk many years before, climbed into the fork of a tree, and then up a limb from which he leaped, gripped the ledge of the high stone wall, and pulled himself up until he sat atop it.

But he did not immediately leap to the ground below. There he sat, like a bird perching after its flight; as he remembered pausing when he had stolen from the abbey so many years ago.

He looked back at the walks and arches, pillars and porticoes, at once sleeping and awake in the starlight; the statues of the Saints standing like sentinels in its midst. This nest of stones had once been his home, and perhaps, like a swallow that comes and goes with the seasons, it still was. But who was this swallow that came with the wind and left with the wind? Who was this one who had played a fiddle, caroused, and loved many women? Who was this one named *Brother Maria*?

Like a tender woman, the starlit abbey only offered a silent smile, one that seemed to own the secret of this answer. It remained with outstretched arms; a *Madonna's* arms through which the wings of men's hearts had come and gone; arms in which *death* had been laid like an orphaned child.

When he had stolen away as a young man, enamored with the embraces of a shepherd girl, he had sat upon this very place on this very wall, and said farewell to the dream of his youth. Was he not now saying farewell to the dream of his age? Were they not somehow the same dream; two tiny threads interwoven into a cloth, a cloth whose patterns were the stars and seasons??

Somewhere in the midst of these stone pillars and arches lay his dying friend, a friend who had perhaps parted the curtain of this dream as best a man could.

".....veils of which there is always one more to be lifted.....mysteries that perhaps are not meant to be discovered......"

.....*What a flame had burned in this man's heart, a heart that had always listened to his, but had not once mentioned, and had overcome a father that had given him away.....a father crazy with drink, sorrow, and the scenes of war and famine.....that spoke and danced with the ghost of a mother who had been eaten alive by swine or dogs, or by the knives and teeth of starving men......*

From the forest he heard the screech of an owl. Salvatore, or his gypsy sweetheart was calling him. Smiling, he remembered a young shepherd girl whose flute, like a bird of the forest had once called him to her kisses.

Maria turned his back to the abbey, and leaped to the ground. He must find Salvatore and his horse where they waited for him in the forest. He must return to Katrinika, his children and their camp. He wrapped his arms tightly, very tightly about his breast as he walked briskly down the hill. He must not look back, lest sorrow turn him to a pillar of salt.

* * *

There were two peculiar things that happened later that night, the night when the saintly old father died in the Franciscan Abbey on the hill.

Many in the village and the country-side woke in their beds, or stepped to tavern doors, or with fur hats and wolf-skin coats came from their huts and tents into the cold night to hear a strange music; a music that stilled the blood of beasts in the same way it stilled the blood of men; as it had stilled the heart of the night itself.

It was the music of a fiddle; a fiddle playing a melancholy, dirge-like melody, like the wail of a widow at her husband's grave....a melody of mourning followed over and over again by strains of delirious, pizzicato rapture, like a man's heart, full of drunken giddiness on his wedding night; a storm of pain followed by a choir of singing flowers.

And then in the silence that followed, the trills of a flute.....a flute like the shepherds play in the fields.....even like the flute that was once given to the abbot of an abbey on a hill.....and saved by that abbot through the years.......

The music came from deep in the abbey forest; and strangely, as from high in a tree.

The second peculiar thing of that sad night was discovered by the monks who rose shortly after midnight to recite their prayers. Filing into the chapel they found a large pouch upon the altar of the Virgin. The pouch was leather, and it was very old, weathered and wrinkled; as it was an apple fallen from the tree that had ripened it.

. . . .

. . . .

CHAPTER FIFTEEN

THE TREE

In the forest outside the Abbey, Circa: 1380

"MARIO! Here! I think I may have found it! Mario, yoo-hoo! Over here! Your little sister has found what the great scholar and priest-to-be could not find! It is large and old, like the father of the forest! Come Mario, I think this might be the tree, the very one you are looking for!"

Yes, this was probably the tree. For one thing, it was a beech tree; she could tell by its glossy leaves, and the hard little nuts forming on its tender stems. It was large and very old, so old it seemed to have grown tired of growing, and was now at last surrendering to the sky it had so vigorously tried to touch for so many years. And the low wide fork, just as Mario had described it; a perfect foothold from which one could hoist oneself into an exploration of its vast branches.....and the grassy place about it, spread like an apron about its gnarled trunk, one with freckles of flowers upon it.

Yes, she was sure this was the tree Mario had described to her, the one he so wanted to find, but for some reason would not tell her why......something about a story his father had once told him.....about Mario's grandmother when she was a young girl, when she was a shepherdess in the fields below the abbey.....a story about her and a monk from that abbey.....and a grave, something about a grave......oh, but she did not care if he did not want to tell her the complete story.....what was important to her was that she had found the tree, and this would make Mario very happy.

With a smile of satisfaction the young girl looked up into the tree's canopy of softly lisping leaves; but only briefly, for her discovery seemed empty and unimportant without her friend's acknowledgment. The tree did not seem at all special to her. True, it was a little larger than the other trees, and it was old and knotty, and in places a bit broken, a battle-worn survivor of countless storms and seasons. But the tree was only important to her because she had found it, and she would be the beneficiary of her friend's smile, and his laughing approval because she had.

It was a small thing, this expedition to find this tree, but it was also a very important thing to her. It would be one of the last times she would see her friend for a long while, if ever again. Tomorrow he would ask the Father Abbot of the abbey for permission to become a postulant, and with time, take holy vows. Mario would become a monk. He would dedicate his life to silence, study and prayer. She would no longer be able to talk and laugh with the friend she had known since her childhood. She would miss him, this friend that had watched her be baptized at the baptistery, and who had held her high in his hands so that she could kiss the wounded feet of the carved Jesus each *Pasqua*; he who had held her in his arms when she had run to him with the joys and travails of her young years.

Although Mario was only eight years older than she, each year was many years when one was a child. Her parents were good friends of Mario's parents, at least before Mario's father had disappeared. Both lived on the same street in the village. They attended the feast-days and the Saints' days together. They ate polenta and shepherd's pie, drank wine and laughed about the harvest presses together. She had no brothers, and her one sister, sickly from her birth, had returned to Heaven in her infancy. Feeling forsaken, she had often toddled to Mario with red eyes, skinned shins, or little bouquets of flowers held in her chubby fists. Mario would sit her on his knee and listen to her stories. With a tender voice, and a gentle smile in his sky-blue eyes, he would say consoling things to her.

"*Now, it's not so bad. Heaven seems only to be raining a little from your eyes. Let's dry those tears, and let the sun kiss your cheeks again.*" or, "*Let's go to the garden. Let's see those tiny birds pecking from those speckled eggs!*" or, "*No sweetheart, it was not the bogeyman who was peeking in your window, it was me, your uncle Mario, peeking at his favorite little princess.*" or, "*Oh, what a lovely bouquet of flowers! You must have climbed the highest mountain to find such beautiful flowers for me!*"

Mario had taken the place not only of a brother, but at times, a second father. When her own father had journeyed to the city, or had left on boar or wolf hunts, she was left alone with her mother. In times of hurt, loneliness, or a secret rapture, when she was in need of empathetic ears and paternal arms, she had sought out Mario. To him she had confided her secrets and wonderful discoveries. In his strong tender arms she had laughed and cried; she had been dandled and thrown high in the air, only to fall back into the soft net of his arms. Mario had listened to her. He had cared for her. Mario understood her as no other had ever understood her.

She looked through the trees at the gentle slope up which Mario's strong lithe body was bounding. As he passed through the dapples of bright sunlight she could see the reddish brown in his straw-gold hair, the secret beautiful veins exposed only by the sun's scouring eye. His hair seemed to burn, as it was aflame with the zeal and purity of his soul; as its goldenness was the tongues of his wonderful fire. Mario was very pious. He would be a very good monk, and then of course a priest; a very wonderful priest; perhaps one day even a Saint who would speak wise words; who would pray and fast long in a cave or a cell, and who would perhaps perform miracles.

Seeing Felicia, Mario paused in his climb, beamed and waved broadly to her, and she in turn waved back and shouted:

"Here, Mario! I think this is the tree you told me about! I told you I would find it! Women always find things before men do, even men who know how to read books and speak Greek and Latin!"

To which Mario let forth an abundant, free, never to be slighted laughter. He called back to her:

"Yes, Felicia, you are a smart little hound, and you find things before I do! A moment more! I think this is the place where Antonio and I found the skulls of dead monks when we were boys. I remember setting them on posts, and throwing rocks at them!"

But then she did something she had not done before, something that she did not entirely understand; as if it was done in slyness by another pair of hands, without the permission of her own. She unpinned her hair, and quickly shook it free, allowing it to tumble in its full dark redundancy upon her breast and shoulders; its glossy secret falling to the small of her back. Yes, Mario would like that; he would like its ringlets, like ripples of a dark silky river spilling over her.

She heard Mario's approach, as he called out to her:

"So my little child has found the tree? Well, we shall see, we shall see!"

Quickly culling a few flowers from the grasses, she placed them in the tree's fork, only then, after a pause of indecision, to remove them; then, after another pause, placing them back again. Seized at the last by a kind of panic, of which her thoughts had forfeited all reins of judgment, she undid her blouse's pretty bow, and let the strings hang loosely, as she had forgotten to tie them, their pink ribbons mingling with her dark tresses.

Mario entered, panting and laughing. But upon seeing the tree he at once sobered, as he had entered a church. Without a word he began a reverent survey of the tree's trunk, it's graciously wide and lofty branches, and the grasses that surrounded it. Without turning to Felicia he whispered, as to himself:

"Yes, yes my little sister, I think this is it! My father showed it to me when I was very young......a few years before he went away."

And with that Mario went to the tree, and wrapping his arms about a low bough, swung one foot up to the tree's fork, only to stop when he saw the bunch of blue and golden flowers. He laughed, and for the first time turned to Felicia with a broad warm smile.

"Thank you, my sweet little sister. Ha! Just like the ones you used to bring me from your mother's garden! Remember?"

With this Mario swung his feet once more into the tree's low fork, stuffed the flowers into the front of his shirt, and began to climb upward through the secret paths and leafy grottoes of the old tree.

Felicia was very pleased. Mario seemed to be certain this was the tree he had set out to find, the tree that she had found for him. And the flowers; yes, she was glad she had left them in the tree. Mario liked them, and he rewarded her with his bright smile, one that washed over her like lovely warm waves.

Still, there were things that had not pleased her. Mario had said nothing about her long, unpinned hair......and he had called her his 'little sister', as he had always called her his 'little sister'. But she had found the tree for him, all by herself, and because of that, and the unbinding of her dark thick tresses, as well as the blouse she had left untied about her neck, she no longer wanted to be called only his 'little sister'. She wished he would call her another name. She was no longer a little child, and she wished he would use another, less childish name of endearment.

Felicia watched as Mario agilely climbed up into the tree; first on one of its broad arms, and then changing course, leaping to others. It seemed altogether easy and natural for him, as he was a panther loosed from its cage into its native habitat. Mario was lithe and strong, and his feet seemed firm and sure wherever he placed them. His boots thumped to the ground, as he quickly found that they were an encumbrance, making his climb with bare feet even more sleek and cat-like. Without a word Felicia gathered the boots and called to him as he disappeared high in the tree.

"You are sure this is the tree you wanted to find?"

At which Felicia, without seeing Mario, heard Mario's laughter and response; as it was not Mario, but the tree that was answering her.

"I am sure of it!"

"But why are you so sure of it?"

"I don't know; perhaps because it is in such a deep and secret part of the forest, where no one could find it. Perhaps it is because I remember it from the time my father showed it to me."

"I found it Mario."

"Yes, you did Felicia. You are a little angel."

She liked that name. It was sweeter, dearer. She liked Mario calling her a 'little angel'.

"Mario, why won't you tell me why the tree is so important to you? Why won't you tell me the story behind the tree?"

"You are very young, my 'little sister'. I do not think you would understand, nor should you. Some day when you are older I will explain it to you."

Again he called her 'little sister', as she was still the little girl that had cried, pouted and buried her face with hurt and shame in his arms. Suddenly, with a rebellion she had never known lived inside her, she shouted back at him:

"I am no longer a little girl, Mario. I am nearly thirteen years old. I no longer want to be called 'little sister', because I am older now."

To this Mario, as he was the invisible spirit of the old tree laughed and answered:

"What do you want to be called then?"

"I do not know Mario."

"Little angel?"

'That is nice, Mario......"

"Or what about 'sweetheart', 'my little sweetheart'?"

At this Felicia beamed, and shouted to Mario as he continued to explore the wilderness of the tree's high branches.

"Yes, Mario, I like that name very much! I want you to call me 'sweetheart' even when you are wearing a monk's hood and robe!"

Although Felicia could no longer see Mario in the tree's foliage, she heard his lovely loud laughter, and it was as if the giant tree, and not a man was laughing; as if that joy had been drawn by roots deep in the earth, from the secret well of life itself, and it was bubbling like a fountain to the clouds and sky. It was music, a beautiful music; sweeter than the mandolin the man played in the street at nightfall, and that the fiddlers played while she and the other girls danced in the grape tubs at harvest..... 'sweetheart', 'sweetheart': yes, a beautiful music that made her heart flutter, as it had wings.

Mario had worked his way into the crown of the tree. As he had reached the edge of a cliff, he could climb no higher; the limbs tapering to a thinness that would not support his weight. Here he stopped, in the utmost of his climb, in the softly swaying, whispering dome of this green cathedral from where he could see the tops of the other trees, and the hills and meadows beyond; all of which, like the nest of an eagle, the tree's great height afforded him.

This height to which he had climbed, and the vista it had lent him, inspired a moment of thought.

How immense life was, an immensity filled with endless clouds, hills and forests; and each leaf and clod, each bleat of a sheep, eye of a horse and leap of a hare in that immensity a mystery unto itself. And how small was a man, like a little bird in a tree, even as he was now perched on this bough, a little bird that gave its song to life's unending wonder, only to be drowned and forgotten in that unending wonder.

He remembered when he was very young, lying in bed awake one night when his parents were sure he was asleep. He remembered his father weeping in the kitchen, weeping and apologizing to his mother for things he had done. He had never heard his father cry, and he had never heard him speak of his own father, the father he had never known. He had lain awake in his bed, frozen with terror, but a terror fraught with curiosity, listening as to a story from a book about this man who was said to have been a monk in an abbey, the same abbey he could see from this tree; the very abbey he would soon enter for the rest of his life. His father had been drinking much wine, and he spoke in a way he had never heard him speak before.

"*Forgive me Francesca, it will not happen again. Perhaps it was the wine fumes.....or my father's ghost speaking through my blood.....I don't know.....I saw her, I kissed her, and before I knew it my hands were holding her breasts and lifting up her skirt.....a slut of a thing, the throw of widowers and rough shepherd men, and no more.....it will not happen again, I promise sweetheart.....never again.......*

.....it was my father's blood I tell you, that skirt-chaser in a monk's robe who played with the young shepherd girl beneath the big tree, the shepherd girl that was my mother.....and then the rascal hanging his habit crazily atop that very tree before leaving to go a-begging and a-whoring, and some say fiddling for the rest of his days......leaving my poor mother with me swelling with his blond hair, his blue eyes and wicked heart inside her. For some reason she was heartbroken for this monk who had plucked her.....and rather than live and be beaten by the drunkard she called her husband, the poor woman hung herself, and had a neighbor bury her beneath that very tree in the forest.....buried in the same place where that damned monk, that damned monk who was my father plucked her.....in the same place where she made me....her bones somewhere below it to this very day......

......that's where my blond hair and blue eyes come from, you know that, Francesca, and those of little Mario.....the itch of that philandering goat of a renegade monk is in my blood....it's because of him I have a wandering eye and hands hungry for what's under women's skirts.....it's not my fault, not my fault at all.....and it's more than prayers to the Virgin on the feast days, or bending my back to a plough a summer of Sundays would rid its fiddle-song from my heart......"

It had always been a mystery why this man he had never known, this reprobate monk who had been his grandfather, and for whom he had been named had reputedly hung his habit high in this tree; perhaps upon this very limb upon which he now stood. This is why he had so wanted to find this tree, and climb to this high place in it, for from this vantage he thought he might better understand this enigmatic person who had ever wandered in the mists of his past.

From here the abbey seemed a child's toy set on the green shelf of the green hill. Perhaps this toy had been too small for the child of this monk's wayward heart. Perhaps he wanted other toys; other things than beads and candles to play with. Like one who longs to sail on sailing ships, one who smells the spray of the sea in his dreams, perhaps this monk, this *Brother Maria* had been born to be a mariner in life, and not an ascetic. Perhaps he had seen clouds on the horizon, like those he was now looking at, imagining they were the rigging of ships bound for exciting, uncharted seas beyond.

Mario climbed down a notch of the tree, and sitting on a sturdy bough, he leaned against the tree's trunk. Below him he could hear Felicia's soft and lilting voice. How happy was this silly child, this flower of the sunlight; this fallen star, this sweetly cooing dove.

"Do you like the tree I found for you Mario? I like it very much. It is peaceful here. I feel as no one could find us here. And I like the flowers in the grasses.....the yellow and blue ones....do you like the bouquet I picked for you Mario?.....I picked it just for you."

For some reason she began to sing an old cradle song, its words drifting upwards through the tree's leafy branches. And as she did he closed his eyes, feeling the soft, maternal sway of the tree, and the soughing of the wind through its sibilant leaves.....as the breezes were waves of a sea, as they had sung their song through this tree forever......as the dreams of men, with the dreams of the seasons were forever passing through its gently rustling leaves.......

.....He knew this cradle song she was singing. He knew it very well. It was called, 'Capra Capretta'.....about a little goat. He remembered singing it to her when she was a little child.......

....."Goat, O little goat,
Grazing in the grass,
Do you want a lick of salt
From the bowl of my hands?....."

"I will miss you Mario, I will miss you very much."

Keeping his eyes closed, he smiled at her childish words, and it was as the tree was smiling lovingly through him when he answered her.

"And I will miss you, Felicia. I will miss you very much also."

......something forever breathing, whispering, exquisitely and forever caring.....something singing through the dream of the fields and forests and clouds....as he was a child being sung to, dandled by the hands of the breezes.....

....."La la la la la, la la la la la,
The children are in the meadow,
The mother is in the spring......"

"Will you hear the confession of my sins when you are a priest Mario?"

"I will if you want me to, but I think you are too sweet to ever sin Felicia."

.....as men press their ears to the earth to hear the hoofs of their prey, the breezes held the whir of passing wings.....the brutalities of storms, the bloom of flowers.....things that had been, things to come.......the tender song and death of things.......

"I will sin just so I may confess it to you Mario."

"You must not do that sweetheart."

"But I will! I will invent sins to confess to you. Andrea Cabalerri told me she imagined sins because she wanted to whisper them into the ear of a young priest that she thought was very handsome. At her confession she told the handsome priest that she had naughty dreams, naughty dreams of kissing him on his lips.....la la la la la, la la la la la......"

Mario opened his eyes, and looked through the tree at the girl on the ground beneath him. He settled upon a lower branch, from which he could see her more clearly. From here he could observe and study her as she lay on her back in the grass, happily singing and prattling, playing with the flowers she had collected. She reminded him of a bird happily splashing its dusty wings in a gentle rain.

She was very young, and yet not so young that she could be still called a child. She had changed greatly from the times when she cried, cuddled, and slept in his arms. Like the bud of a flower, she had blossomed before his eyes, but without his eyes telling his mind of the miracle of her apotheosis.

In truth she had entered that timeless, suspended moment between childhood and womanhood; neither one nor the other, but wielding the charms of both. It was that exact moment when she was entering the prom-enades of the world from the enchanted garden of youth; opening its wicket, but there halting, between her piqued curiosity and the vague premonitions of regret. There life enthroned her; held her in its palms, like a fledgling bird before it flies forever away; frozen, as in a frieze of forever-ness; a cameo lifted from the tragic darkness of things. She was poised in that moment artists call 'eternity'; poised to exchange her smock and basket of flowers for a gown and jewels; still fresh from her dreams among fountains and sweet-throated birds, and not yet afraid of crouching beasts that growled with menace; beasts that wanted to harm her.

Entranced, Mario lowered himself to a still lower branch, and from there studied her as he had never studied her before; as with a new pair of eyes in his head; as with a new spirit in his breast, even as she continued to sing and idly babble.

"…..The sun is in the mountain,
The mountain is in the grass….."

"And you will take your vows, the three vows all of the monks take?….. Obedience, Poverty, and Chastity……."

"Yes, sweetheart, I will."

"And they will shave your head. They will cut your lovely golden curls, like the curls your father had. I want those curls Mario! I want to keep them forever. Do you think the monk that cuts them off will save them for me? I will put them under my pillow, and each night they will give me dreams of you."

Recumbent in the grass, she had doubled up her knees so that her skirt slid to the mid of her thighs. Oh, how supple, and how lily-lovely were those calves and thighs! How like opals sparkled the precious gems of her knees! And her feet, buried in the grass, their little heels and toes, treasures waiting to be found! Oh, how very beautiful was this child of the earth, rain and sunlight, this flower no boot had stopped before, no rough hand had yet reached to plunder. Had a young shepherd girl once been so lovely in a monk's eyes; even as Felicia was to his as she lay in the grass, perhaps upon that shepherd girl's very bones?

"…..Goat, little goat,
That grazes in the grass…..

"La la la, la la la…..la la la, la la la…..and you will forget all about this day, this tree, your sweetheart Felicia and the pretty flowers she picked for you…..you will pray and pray and pray, and you will forget these things as they had never been…….."

…..her hair, unbound as he had never seen it unbound before…..and the little curls that kissed her brow, trimming it like lace, and crawling down her neck like amorous snails! Oh how dark and lustrous were those tresses, like a forest full of night's secrets….full of perfume and songs, full of stars……

"Will you remember me in your prayers, Mario my love? You do not mind me calling you 'my love', do you Mario, my 'Capra Capretta'?"

…..and her blouse, left untied, as if the buds behind it seemed to be swelling free of their concealment, swelling with the milk of the leaf and the blade, desperately, violently needing to peek forth, to know warmth and light…..and the little bouquet of flowers she had placed between her legs, *as if they had bloomed from the deepest part of her....as her womb was thawing, first stirring with the hunger of its emptiness, its blind need.....exhaling the fertility of that need.......*

"I will miss you Mario. I will miss you very much. I will dream of many sins, so I may confess them to you when you are a priest. I like you very much, Mario. I have always liked you. I like your golden hair, your blue eyes, and your gentle words. I like you so much I think I love you Mario, yes, I think I love you."

.....how beautiful she was, how beautiful and how mighty.....yes, mighty! As she could command the winds and thunder, the hearts of armies/....as she was a flower summing the hills and valleys.....the Earth itself.......

"You think I am still a little girl Mario, but I am not. I have dreamed many dreams of you. I will confess the secrets of my heart to you when you are a priest. I want you to have my heart, Mario; yes, I want to give you my heart."

.....and the smile that shone upon her face, not of youth's brief, soon wilting moment, but of something deeper, ineffably sweeter.....something imperishable, inexhaustible....at once hiding in shyness in the shadowed corners of her mouth and eyes......glowing queenly, imperially.....waiting only to be crowned.....waiting to step forth, to rule and bless.......

"I want to give my heart to you Mario. I want to give you my heart because I love you Mario."

......a smile innocent of its glory, that had never looked over the pool of its own reflection.....like a lark deaf to its song.....like an angel shy of its resplendency.....a smile whose mystique asked, and asking demanded to be kissed, and in exchange offering a nourishment of sweetness.......

"The children are in the meadow,
Their mother is in the spring....."

.....a smile that was a mystery, more mysterious than the hills, forests and clouds....as they were her children.....as she was the mother of them all.......

His tranquil vision was interrupted by the dull, distant tolling of a bell, the abbey's bell calling the monks to their afternoon prayers. Again Mario scampered up into the heights of the tree, from where he could see many monks leaving their toils in the fields, and filing into the abbey's gates. Soon he would be one of these monks; one whose life was dedicated to serving and giving humble thanks to an all-merciful God.

He began to quickly descend back down through the tree, for, hearing the bell and seeing the file of monks, he would join them in their devotions. Yes, he could do that. The Father Abbot had invited him to participate in their prayers. If he would hurry, he would have just enough time to reach the gates before they were closed.

Oh, how he loved the liturgies.....the rhythm of the hymns, the cadences and refrains.....the candles, and the incense that lifted on the wings of the psalms......the idols that beckoned to the mystery in their eyes and smiles.......the reverence and worship of something higher....something beyond this world, beyond flesh, blood, bones.....something divinely pure. Yes, his decision had been a good one. He would live a good and pure life, one of discipline, silence, and selfless devotion.......

Mario leaped to the ground, only then realizing he had shed his boots. He looked to Felicia. The boots stood neatly together near where she lay in the grass. He sat down beside her, and quickly began to bind them on.

With closed eyes Felicia softly spoke, the tears in her voice having sent two crystal drops, like emissaries of her woe trickling from her lashes down her cheeks.

"You must go to pray now Mario?"

"Yes, I will go to join the monks at their office."

"I do not like the bell, the monks and their prayers. They take you away from me. They will always take you away from me."

"I will pray for you, Felicia."

"I do not want you to pray for me. I want you to stay with me."

"But I will pray for your soul, sweetheart."

"I do not care about my soul. I only care about my heart, my heart that I want to give to you."

Mario stood, the last tolls of the abbey bell dying in his ears. He must hurry before the second bell rang, before the gates would close. But as he began to leave the girl began to sing again, although still lying with closed eyes in the grass. There were tears in her voice....and it struck Mario that there was something courageous, something undying and unbearably sweet in the heart that sang through them.

".....Capra Capretta,
Who grazes in the grass,
Would you like to lick
The salt in the bowl of my hand?....."

Mario stopped, and looked back at her; at her skirt lifted to her thighs, at the dark river of her hair flowing over her shoulders and breast, at the flowers she had nestled between her legs. She had not opened her eyes. She had not moved. She had not sat up to bid him a last goodbye....as if she had become the earth itself, and she knew there was no place that he could flee from the charms and sympathies of her love.......

".....your golden hair, your blue eyes, your gentle words....."

Mario knelt at her side. It was as moonlight lay on her eyelids, and a crystal fountain trickled from her eyes. Upon her new-ripening bosom there were hills and valleys, and in her hair sparkled the first stars of eve.

Like a priest kissing bread, he softly kissed each of her thin bare knees, and then the nest of flowers she had made. Sliding her skirt up to her waist, he lay down beside her.

. . . .

. . . .

WICKED RHYMES
FOR
A KIND MOTHER

POEMS BY
BROTHER MARIA

THE GRAPE HARVEST

MAIDEN
Of bandannas and gay colors,

Stepped from the wilds, quiet as a deer,

O forest bird, child of the *Earth Mother,*

With copper bangles dangling from your ears!

Free the black tresses from your bright red scarf,

And bind your skirt about your milky thighs,

Make dance the gypsy sparkling in your eyes,

And crush the ripened vintage in my heart!
Dance, harvest angel! Barefoot upon my breast!

Between your white teeth hold a reddest rose!

Make earth and heaven sing, as with castanets!

My dreams, like grapes, squeezed through your little toes!
O pretty feet, eyes, lips, dance on this heart of mine,
 Trample the dreams I bring you, into the richest wine!

TO THE WIDOW I SEE EACH MORNING LEAVE THE CATHEDRAL

THE
Days of your long mourning are long gone;

Your lips, too long un-kissed behind that veil,

Your ripeness, too ripe to wither from the sun,

Deep in your heart, still sings the nightingale.

Life, not *death,* lives for *love's* immortal being,

Bleak Winter, with its dolorous costume,

Cannot forbid the Spring's philandering;

When frozen, Nature readies a fresh bloom.
At moonrise, shed thy grieving widowhood,

No longer be the bride of death and fate,

No longer starve the angel of your blood,

Let fall your veil, your tresses, your gown of crepe.
Above the tavern, I will wait with candlelight;
There bring, what virgins bring, their wedding night.

THE SHE-WOLF
OF THE SICKLE MOON TAVERN

"HA!
She was whelped beneath an evil moon!"

"She is a she-wolf muskets may not tame!"

"Pretty, but no less than the Devil's dame!"

"Her nails like claws, a lion in her womb!""

"She brags the man that she will love must dare

To whip her till she screams!" "Snaps in two her will!"

"That she would only love one she would kill!"

"No rabbit trapper, but a hunter of bears!"
"No! You mistake her for another!

For, in dark alleys, when the tavern closes,

Her kisses are as sweet as summer roses!

Love is her iron master, her savage hunter,
To which surrenders she her woman charms;
No, not a she-wolf; but an Angel in my arms."

TELL ME IT IS NOT TRUE

(For the Abbess Giulia)

THEN
Tell me, holy sister, it is not true,

When counting beads, or praying in your stall,

That you do not think of our rendezvous,-

That, biting your lips in the confessional,

Our sin does not lift anthems in your heart,-

When, after midnight Vigils, you came, where,

My arms were waiting in the orchard's dark;

Tell me such sweetness sings not in your prayers!
My mouth upon your mouth, thirsting for its wine,-

One hand, sampling those peaches rounded ripe,

The other, venturing to dare a climb

Beneath your habit's skirt,- calves, knees, marble thighs,-
Until it reached, and reaching held that hallowed nest.....
Sister, in your prayers, did that hand beg to steal.....or bless?

WHEAT HARVEST:
HEART OF THE STORM

IT
Was meant to BE: long days of broiling toil,-

Glances, titters, blushes,- your pretty knee,-

All culminating in that wicked boil

That roiled bruise-blue above the alder trees......

You, racing through the ricks, a frightened doe,

I, lionish, to that decrepit barn!

A thunder! Mightier than men may know,

Commanding our steps to each other's arms!
Wordless, thoughtless, heartless to sin or shame,

Our needs made naked, blind to prayer or pardon,

A lightning, as to tear this world in twain,

Lashing through the mansion of love's garden!
And after, the sun breaking, beaming from a cloud,
The wheat still standing; bearded golden, solemn, proud.

LONE WOLF

I STUDY
Her; from shadows, where, beneath

These pelts and rafters, time after whirling time

She passes, dancing lightsome as a leaf

With partners new, heating my blood like wine......

Raven tresses, carmine lips, a slender waist

With silken sash, her radiant young face

A moon that parts the clouds with goddess grace,

Her mouth, a honeyed hive for gods to taste.......
Blue-veined her arms, her ears and ankles jeweled.....

Full her breasts, woman ripe her hams and thighs.....

Fawn-slender, virgin tender her delicate throat......

As with a bandit's mask, with cruel, feral eyes
I stir, from shadows step to seize, to slay.....
Only to blush, to stammer,- by her beauty made her prey.

AS YOUR FLOCK GRAZES

YOUR
Kiss, *Sweetheart*, is like a peony,

Wine-rich with Summer's first sweet nectar,

And I, a Winter-waked, carousing bee,

The first explorer of its lovely treasure!

A fountain of petals, lushly gushing sweet

Such moist and ruby, tender luscious fruits!

Each petal an invitation meek

To find more deeply, sweetly buried truths!
The longer, deeper, sweeter are his sips,

The more the winebibber craves his wine,

Whetting his thirst, as with a hunger blind,

His soul, 'my soul', seeking salvation in your lips!
Young Shepherdess, what spell is in your kisses,
That here Death's rumor passes, in these orchard grasses?

DRUNK IN
THE 'BEAR CUB'S' SHADOWS

SICK
Of the moon, and a fiddle's serenades,

Of tender, thankless niceties of *love*,

Now, when the wine wakes devils in my blood,

And my loins hunger for their savage play.....

Looking at your hips, and those milky breasts

Begging to have their bodice-strings untied,

The passing, brushing of your buxom thighs,

In whose lush vale I wish to sing and die.......
I want to give you all my wickedness!

To mingle oysters and onions in our kisses!

Without politeness or apology,

Shun love with lust, sharing deepest, beastly wishes!
Tonight I want to give the animal of my flesh:
Then sleep, my soul at peace, pillowed on your breast.

OUTSIDE YOUR WINDOW
I STOOD DRUNK LAST NIGHT

For Angelina

OUTSIDE
Your window I stood drunk last night;

Wounded, bleeding in your garden's dark,-

Dying, with *Love*'s dagger in my heart,-

Watching, the ritual of your maiden might

Remove your ribbons, then your tortoise shell

Barrette, tumbling free a cataract

Of raven sparkling glory down

The ivory valley of your back....your gown,
Slipped from your slender shoulders to your feet,

Unveiling what only maddest painters paint,

Lovelier than morning's rose, a masterpiece

That swooned the summer night into a faint;
I stood there; drunk, jilted, wretched with your lies,
Jealous of the heavens, doting with their million eyes.

MY ANGEL OF THE STABLES

(for Eleanora)

THEY
Slander; they who say you are a woman

Bred for the stable-yards and stable hay,

A hussy pleasing men with shameless play,

A child of wickedness, one beastly fallen.

They are but jealous tongues that scorn you so,

They of coaches, parrots, silks and ermine,

You are a *Lady*,- they, but shrewish vermin,

Whose lonely beds drift cold with midnight snow.
Your kisses are richer than their coffered gold,

Your palace, the tender sweetness in your arms,

You beggar royalty with your angel charms,

Granting poor flesh, the treasures of your soul.
It is they, not you, who are the prostitute:
They whore their soul; you share its burning truth.

SLEEPLESS

I CANNOT
Sleep at night; inebriated

With visions of your angel loveliness;

Writhing, dying, drunkenly infatuated,

Dreaming such blinding glory once undressed!

At last I rise; my violin, caress,

Sleeking my fingers softly, tenderly down

Its lacquered curves, imagining a gown

Slipped from a garden of voluptuousness.
Then, touching the strings, gently, adoringly,

Caressing your fairness in my arms,

Waking the 'Woman' from your childish charms,

Exploring, quickening, fevering love's mystery
Until that note is reached, held, heavenly rendered,-
That stills the heart of night, with exquisite surrender!

THE CONFESSION

For
The Novice Bernadette

I BEG
But one brief moment, holy sister,

Now, while your sister *Brides* are in the garden,

At *Chapter*, or in *Choir*.....one moment, to whisper

My spirit's passion, pleading for *love's pardon*.

Yes, now, while dozes the prioress,

Nodding with her beads and open missal,

Whilst bird and bee are busied with their nests,

One moment beg, stilled of time's rituals:
When the sun burns blind, the moon sleeps deep,

And the Child of this world dreams on yon sill,-

Now, Angel, lift your veil! Lean near the grille!

Bring your ear, your eyes, your lips so cherry sweet,
As I shall mine, and as the bud the flower unfolds,
Receive like light, bread, prayer, the confession of my soul.

TO A SEDUCTRESS

YOU
Need no ornaments, *sweetheart*, to seduce,

No jewels, or perfumes, or painted lips,

No naked knee or arm, no swaying hips.

No peacock charm to tell your *feminine truth*.

If is for others, their sly webs to weave,

To unman warriors in a tangled lair,-

You, with the *Pleiades* in your hair,

Need only your *God-given grace* to breathe.
You were not born to snare or to beguile:

Seduction is not provocation,

But an innocent invitation

Exhaled from the flower of your tender smile;
No purring, luring, to stir spendthrift 'desires',-
But modestly promising, treasures sweetly higher.

TO THE ANGEL
IN A BAKER'S WINDOW

ANGEL
Of oatcakes, biscuits, leaven and flour,

With a red kerchief binding up your hair,

A breeze from out the south perfumes the air,

Warming chill Autumn one last Summer hour.

Come from your ovens, kneading boards, joyless sighs,

Untie your apron from your pretty hips!

Your minstrel, I; you, my princess bride,

Joining the year's farewell of flowering bliss!
Drowned deep in amber wheat and blue cornflowers,

Let us enjoy that nectar given Youth,

Oblivious of the world, all sorrows dour,

Sharing our moment's golden gift of truth.
Ere Autumn's scythe, Winter's shroud,
before blood freezes,
Unbind your pretty kerchief, and taste what Nature pleases.

ON YOUR DISFIGUREMENT

YOU
Are not lame in the meadows of my eyes,

But winged, as with a breeze-borne buoyancy,

Your steps, a lovely lyrical poetry

Whose footfall is as modest as a bride's.

As rank weeds coronate the garden's rose,

Making their scarlet queen more royal,

Nettles adoring the celestial,-

So lesser things oft miracles disclose.
With imperfections Life declares Perfection,

Attracting the eye to its truest mirror,

To draw sight keener, truer, dearer,

Until the soul beholds divine reflections.
You are a swan, with one wing drooping down,
A flaw that is a jewel, a jewel that is your crown.

IN DEATH'S SHADOW

HERE;
Be not afraid; here we may hide;

Here in this loft of stable straw;

Here, this night, in my arms my tavern bride,

Safe from his hollow eyes, his ghoulish jaws;

Those lamentations, those heartrending wails

Are the heartfelt weeping at our nuptials;

Those dull tolls from the hill's cathedral,

The silver peals of our wedding bells......
The plodding hoofs, the slowly creaking cart,

A troop of clowns, and no corpse-heaped hearse,

Your fear, the fear that thrills each new bride's heart,-

This night, not the world's last, but our love's first.
Unbind your kerchief, your bodice strings untie,
Come, tender Flower, let the procession pass us by.

KISS OF DEATH

(upon finding Isabella)

ONLY
The mad, or the wretchedly depraved

Would shamelessly violate the dead,

Making a marital, or brothel's bed

With lovers made cadavers in their graves.

If mad they be, then mad am I, who find

Your beauty's petals falling from your bones,

Kneeling to embrace, and thus atone......

Love, like *death*, in the end made madly blind.
Such innocence was never meant to die,

But to bequeath its little, gay-frocked hour

Unto a thousand, thousand meadow flowers,

Cheating the avarice of the worm and blowfly.
Cold, bloated, blackened, what was once cherry sweet,
I kiss your lips left smiling, at a mad God's mad retreat.

AFTER 'THE SICKNESS'

Siena, 1350

AND
When I climbed the street, past the long rows

Of painted crosses; blood-red signatures

Of those told to lie with *Death*'s bedfellows,

Smeared on doors; where was their grim warrant served.....

Arriving where, with a red bandanna,

You, from that window, like morning light

Lowered loaves of bread, like an *Angel* doling *manna*......

But to be pitched, like dung, in life's dark night......
Then scarlet, world-ending words I scrawled as well!

A declaration on this temple's doors,

Nailing shut my soul with heavy boards,

Defying this killing God in league with bloody hell!
Softly, reverently, like an artist at his art,
I painted 'Katrinika lives!, the Angel of my heart'!

836

THE GHOST
IN THE CATHEDRAL

IN
This cathedral where no candle burns,

No kneeling pilgrim prays, no choir of nuns

Intones their midnight antiphons.....

Its vessels, stolen, its altars overturned

By godless mercenaries, lawless bands

That glutted *faith*'s riches to a shell,

Its rituals, unable to withstand

The wrath of God breathed from the bowels of hell......
I lift my turnip lantern to this wall,

Where some crude debauchee, a vulgar dance

Of skeletons, with lutes and fiddles scrawled

A merry bacchanalia of Death's romance:
Madness, charcoaling Truth with maestro care;
Saints, Angels, Saviors,- laughter in their hollow stares.

SOFTLY, SILENTLY

For Katrinika

SOFTLY,
Silently, early I will leave,

Banished from your arms, I will softly go,

That you will never know

How their embraces made my heart to bleed;

Taking its wound into the drifting snows,

Into the howling winds of wolfish sorrow,

Fading into the gray tomorrows,

The sweet smells of your body in my clothes.
But just as softly, silently I depart

Into the wilderness of the years,

When winter's in your hair,
Autumn in your dreams,-

The ghost that kept your memory in his heart
Shall return, haunt with whispers in your ear:
"I loved you as no other; I held you most, most dear".